I0738254

THE VIOLET CURSE

THE VIOLET CURSE

SENNA CROW

7Bloodfire Art & Story

Oklahoma

THE VIOLET CURSE

The main text of this book is set in Calibri Light.

Other fonts included in and on this book: Coquette, Aviano Royale, Aviano Wedge, AdornS Serif.

Published in the United States by 7Bloodfire Art & Story, an Imprint of 7Bloodfire, LLC, Oklahoma.

2021 7Bloodfire Art and Story Trade Paperback Edition

Copyright © 2021 by Cinthia McCracken
Illustrations © 2021 by Cinthia McCracken

Paperback ISBN 978-0-578-24455-6
Ebook ISBN 978-0-578-24457-0

First Edition: March 2021

9 8 7 6 5 4 3 2 1- E1 21

7BLOODFIRE.COM

BOOK DESIGN BY CINTHIA MCCRACKEN

This book is dedicated to my patient, goofy husband, who has been a rock in my life, (which I occasion to pick up, move, and berate in the name of love and sarcasm.) Thank you, honey. You've saved me from more than you will ever know.

This book is also for all the survivors in the world who have known hurt, sorrow, anger, and fear. You are not alone. Your voice matters. When you step toward happiness and surround yourself with those who love you, you will become the best version of yourself. The journey is often difficult, but take to heart that there are others like you, that we are all in this together. Love yourself, and others will follow. And you will begin to inspire many behind you who are waiting for the moment they, too, feel strong enough to take their own steps toward freedom and joy. I send you my prayers and love, and I wish you strength, inspiration, healing, and peace.

Faith and hope carry us far. Be determined, my friends.

TABLE OF CONTENTS

ARACANA
ALIANCE CITADEL
N
W
E
S
AELYNHOLD
LOVAEL
BALTHORA
STILLSET
TALLIL
EDANTINE
WICKER
HAGENHOLD
THE BELL
TOWER
ARDIMOND
TETROYA
ANARAT

THE REFORMATION
TULIAN
FIVE TOWER
FEILMEIN
TARVET
AEGIS PORT
The Flooded City
CYAN
DRY PORT
ACERAGE
OAKWALL
CRESSEN
SAVANAH
LIRIEN
The Haunted Road
ANISE
LAUREL
VIRIEN
WINHELM
CROW POST
Raven Trail
HALFWAY
ISOLD
Ender's Creek
OLD CROW TOWN
LAIREN
WIRESHON
ARGONIA
HARALT
LORENTON
BLACK TEMPLE
ORATH
SACRED WAKE
AVASK

PROLOGUE

A Dark Dream

"BRIGHT ONE . . ." *On the other side of the glass, the solemn shadows writhed.*

She always wanted to shy away, but her body would remain motionless, adrift in blue water. Lifeless.

"Shine, Bright One. Give unto us your Light . . ." The voices never seemed to stop, and the asomatous creatures swallowed up the world as they drifted nearer and nearer. Black tendrils, stretching outward and hissing with the aura of the creatures' hunger, would search for her. Like ink, the darkness would spill over the walls. Like fog, it would roll across the stones of the tombs. The shadowy beings never saw her through the cloak of death that she wore, but they always knew she was somewhere near. They always felt her. They didn't need eyes to know she was here.

Then there would be a lonely hand upon the glass, a hand branded with curling silver marks, and his eyes would be gazing down at her. Eyes which blazed the color of that awful, brilliant blue. And the creatures would stand behind him, reaching, reaching · · ·

After his scream, there would be only the water again. Nothing but the cursed water, which held her prisoner. Her soul would gutter, like a dying flame, and then it would wink out. And then his agony would stir her from the darkness again. And her heart would threaten to beat. And her soul would beg her to let it wake.

Nymeria woke from the dream, her breath raking through ragged inhalation, her body trembling and prickling with perspiration where the dark things had reached out to touch her. She drew her thin blanket tighter over her, and she curled closer to her little brother. Her fingers wrapped around the knife under their pillow. She watched the comforting sight of Jamie's chest rising and falling, and she moved her fingers to wipe away the tears that had begun to blur the bone-white trees that bowed low over them in the flickering firelight. She sniffled. "Jamie, they're back," she whispered. "The dark things that call out for me." Her brother's even breathing continued, undisturbed. As if he never sensed the danger of those terrible, relentless creatures. She moved closer to him, peering into the night with wide, round eyes. Desperately, she wished the creatures away.

The blackthorn crackled. The breeze moaned as it cut through the branches, and the silent cold spilled through them and sent the nocturnal fauna scurrying away. The darkness deepened. The faces, she saw first. The monstrous, eyeless faces. And as Jamie went on sleeping, unconcerned and unaware of the creatures whose forms spilled from the deepest recesses of darkness, they continued to call for her.

"Bright One · · ·"

CHAPTER ONE

Bright Night

JEANA PULLED HER COAT TIGHTER about herself as she clutched her two-year-old son. She was desperate to keep the stinging cold from him as she turned her back to the worst of the explosive gusts. Her face felt numb, burned where the keening wind raked icy spurs across her skin. She shut her eyes as the howling became a deafening roar, as particles of ice lashed, and bit, and scratched, and blinded her. She bowed her head and breathed against her precious bundle.

Below, a horde of Wolfshadow occultists waited for them to fall — she could sometimes still see their bonfires and their torches. Getting closer every hour were their most vicious and determined priest hunters, the Descendants of the Moon, who braved the climb after the three of them with picks made from the bones of the dead they'd eaten.

"Come on, Jeana!" her husband barked, and the vengeful north wind ripped his voice from him. She looked up as John knelt to give her his hand. Her every breath ached with cold.

The moisture that had beaded on John's forehead and gathered in his shaggy, bronze-colored beard had frozen, and chalky crystals clung to his wild, unkempt hair. His breath steamed the air white in the sagging lulls between the angry bursts of the blizzard. She reached out. Then she felt her feet slipping. Her heart did a somersault in her chest as panic gripped her. For a long moment, the world began to teeter and tilt upon its edge. Another strong gust slithered around her, and then it yanked.

John's grip was firm as he caught her wrist with his gloveless left hand — the rough skin across his palm had cracked and blistered during their relentless ascent.

Then mad laughter hacked its way up the cliffside as a wolfman's filthy, child-killing fingers clawed at her ankles. "Ahaha! Come here, angel! Come here! We will make it fly! Fly, fly! Let us have that boy to eat! Let us have that bright and blessed child!" Some of the wreckage about them crumbled and plummeted hundreds of feet down the cliffside as she struggled against him, and Jeana held her son, shielded him. John tried to draw his dagger to fight the man, but the wild-eyed, fur-cowled cannibal tumbled closer as the debris crashed around them. Blood seeped slowly from the open flesh where the ice cut John's hand again. His teeth snapped against a bark of pain, and the vibrations from the shifting wreckage crawled through the steel beams and made the rubble beneath them writhe. But the laughing madman slipped suddenly, and then he was gone. The wind rendered his screams mute. Yet the danger was no less with his absence, not for how the ground still trembled, slick with ice and burdened with the white atop it.

The mountain groaned as though to wake, to cast off the heavy blanket, to free itself of a burden both unwelcomed and unnatural. John drew Jeana to him and held her close, and he wrapped himself around her to protect her as chaos fell from above. He held her desperately as he helped her regain her feet and pulled her from the path of falling debris. The fleeting warmth of his breath cut through the cold for just a moment when he drew her closer to reassure her, and he pressed his lips against her forehead and said her name. He cupped her face as the dangerous quaking began to subside, and she saw the blood on his hand had already frozen. "Are you all right?" he rasped. She nodded against him, shivering, and she leaned into the kiss he placed upon the crown of her head. His glittering azure eyes flitted to their son, and when he was assured of Jamie's health, he tilted his head back to look upward intently.

Jeana's concern for her husband only grew. She felt the tremors that racked him as they traveled through his arms and into his hands. He was exhausted, and this climb had been especially difficult for him because he hadn't eaten well for days. Because he'd given his rations to her and to their son. They also hadn't had the time to tend his wounds properly. Even now, it was dangerous to stop for long, because more of the wreckage gave way every hour and because more wolfmen gained ground up the nearly vertical terrain.

John was exhausted, and the cold was getting to him. Even if he was too proud and too worried to voice his weariness, Jeana saw the strain.

John braced his feet as Jeana clasped his hands tighter, and he heaved with all his strength, lifting her from the icy stairway the wreckage had formed. Once she made it onto the ledge where he stood, at the very apex of the city — once her knees were scraping across the stone and crunching in the snow — John let his breath hiss through his teeth, and then he let her go. He staggered back, straightening, and Jeana scrambled away from the edge before daring to peer down again. They had about a half a day before other wolfmen made it up the cliff. Maybe longer, if that avalanche of stone and metal and ice had scattered the horrible men below.

"Those murderous *Wolfshadow swine*," John swore. He spat upon the snow as another string of vile cursing highlighted the cult's worship and child-murdering practices. "I can't believe the cowards sent the Descendants of the Moon after us." He stooped to loosen from the icy ground a jagged bit of stone, and he hurled it downward, into the storm, and more curses lashed from his tongue mightily. "Saura will hear of this wretched cult's attempts against us, Jeana."

Jeana shuddered as she dared to peer over the cliff. She couldn't see the ground anymore. The snow had washed it away. Clouds of snow. Rivers of it. It was like a white ocean stretching below them, its giant white waves tossing about them and rising tall above them.

The storm was monstrous in its intensity.

When at last Jeana's husband turned from the sea of white, so did she.

John's scrutinizing blue gaze searched about them, dark with uncertainty. From the billowing sheets of snow that fell about them as they sorted their way into the still-steaming wreckage of Five Tower, a limping old man with decrepit, oil-stained clothes and a balding, capless head came scuttling forward, directly for them. John's glare warned him, and the man paused with a cautious, frosted scowl.

As the old man watched them, they entered the protective bulwark of broken buildings, crumbling curtain walls, and high towers. At last, the storm's freezing fingers broke from around them, and the snow drifted more softly down upon them. The tempest beyond continued to scream through the spires above; it howled with warning from the cliffside, beyond the wall of wreckage.

The cold seemed to lessen as the world became still. The only furious movement remaining about them was the white breath of the pale, deathly ocean itself, where the storm washed over the cliffs behind the wall. In the middle of Five Tower, the dust and the smoke were still thick in the air from the explosion three nights before. Ash coated the snow — a blanket of gray and black still staining the white. The blizzard hadn't yet been able to erase the event that had rocked the wicked, now crippled, city. Jeana watched her husband's eyes scan the snow and the debris before she concluded that he could not see any bodies, either.

Jeana bent over double, coughing when the cloth wound around her face slipped. The smoke was too much to inhale after that spiteful, freezing wind. It was more than she could yet endure. She replaced the cloth quickly.

John simply grimaced, the skin around his eyes tightening as he gazed about, still searching. Cries came from the depths of the haze. Wounded people. Coughing. He hesitated as he took it all in, and then he moved forward.

Snow and ash crunched underfoot. Over what might have been glass.

Stop, she signed. *Stop!* But her husband did not see her hand flutter urgently. Jeana reached to tug at his torn sleeve. Her eyes slid across the clearing where the road used to be and fell upon the giant crater — the crater was as black as oil and still hissing with steam. Molten veins burned brightly along the edges. They shone red through the acrid smoke.

They were here, at the eye.

* * * * * * *

John started forward cautiously as a boy's cries rang out. His frozen fingers curled and uncurled over the bony hilt of his lengthy dagger. *"Momma!"* the boy cried. *"Someone help my mom! Help us! Please, someone help my mom and me!"*

"Hello!" shouted John. *"Where are you?"* The boy's continuing cries cut deep into John's heart.

"Help!" said the boy. *"Someone help us!"*

"Where are you?" But the boy's cries cut off, suddenly silent. *"Where are you?"* repeated John more loudly. There was no reply. He could smell scorched flesh, but he couldn't see very far through the gray veil. The faintest outlines of the two remaining skyscrapers towered over him, reaching high into the pale, blurry heavens. The soft tinkling of glass falling and breaking sounded occasionally over the dying howls of the wind. The storm seemed to be abating.

The streets also seemed deserted, and John did not know what to make of the devastation that slowly cascaded into view between the high drifts. Peeking through low banks, the grass and the trees that had taken root over the years were scorched, and, in places, the pavement was melted to what appeared to be black glass. Snow covered the rest, but he knew it was bad. Very bad.

This was where he and Jeana had seen the violet-colored explosion three nights ago, when they had been making their way over the tall hills to the west. The glass shattered in the explosion had looked like violet star fall, like purple diamonds raining down from the black ocean above. The blast had been so powerful that it had crippled the foundations of three of the five buildings in Five Tower. They had collapsed inward, one upon another.

Five Tower no longer had five imposing towers. There were only the broken fangs on the north side of the complex. There would be no shelter in them anymore, not with that dangerous teetering about them.

The biggest settlement for hundreds of miles — home to several thousand people . . . *in ruins*. But where were all the survivors?

John was overcome by the sight he beheld. Above him. Around him. He looked at his wife, and he signed for her to stay where she was as he motioned upward, at the deadly trap that loomed over them. The beams of one of the fallen towers groaned hundreds of feet above. His pulse quickened. Rubble began to fall from the sky.

The boy's cries raked through the veil of falling snow once more. *"Momma!"*

John couldn't see the child. Or the child's mother. But something else did draw him — and it wasn't the crater that made him start forward, with horror swelling dangerously within him.

* * * * * * *

"Stay here," John rasped, holding his shoddy, makeshift respirator to his face.

Jeana nodded, though she knew he wouldn't have seen her do so. She pulled her gun from the holster strapped to her left thigh and moved forward, and she put her back against a large concrete pillar so no stranger could slip behind her unnoticed as she blended into the bluish gray there. She watched. Her gaze flitted side to side, searching for movement that was not in sync with the falling snow. Occasionally, she looked up and searched the remaining towers' shadows for life. For threats.

Her husband moved with every confidence that she would guard his back. That she would kill any strangers who might try to ambush him in the middle of the ruined, ancient highway.

The old man scuttled across the street, his bad limp making him appear to hop and shuffle in a manner similar to the twisted, waddling gait of a hideous, tattered vulture. His head bobbed up and down much the same, but it always seemed to be tilted in their direction.

Their tiny son stirred against Jeana's breast. "Shhh." It was very nearly the extent of her ability to speak, and she repeated it as she rocked him, cupped his blanketed head, and pressed her lips against the cold material there. "Shhh . . ."

The gaunt old man had crawled back into his snowy tunnels, but she could see the bearded stranger peering out as John passed by him, jogging toward the crater. There was someone else in the dark hole with the old man, but Jeana could not discern whether the other person was old or young, or man or woman. It was just motion, a silhouette against a reflection.

"Don't touch it!" the old, buzzardly man screamed as he suddenly raced back outside. The old man gripped massive handfuls of his beard and wrung the peppery hair nervously, ready to dart away when John went to his knees at the center of the crater. "Don't touch it, lest its curse manifest, you fool! Get away from it!"

Jeana's attention snapped toward her husband's muted cry. "What in the hell . . . ?" John cried. "Jeana?!" He quickly dropped his pack and began shrugging off his black leather jacket, no longer mindful of the threadbare seams that needed repair, and not in the least worried about himself freezing. Jeana's heart skipped as anxiety filtered in. She shivered when her husband next barked urgently, "Jeana, come here at once!"

John glared at the old man with a disturbed gleam in his eyes. The look made Jeana more concerned.

Her husband was a strong man, a man with an enduring nerve and a strong sense of duty and compassion. He'd amputated tainted flesh from children to save them — he'd sung softly to them to soothe some of the agony afterward when his pack had been emptied of pain medication, and neither his hand nor his voice had ever wavered when he'd been presented with impossible situations. He'd always acted quickly. He'd tolerated the smells, the screams, the curses. He would help in the worst places when others would flinch away. Yet John seemed aghast at whatever he had found in that crater; there was hatred in his eyes when he looked at the haggard old man. "You would *abandon* — " He choked on the acrid smoke and then barked her name once more. "Jeana!"

Jeana's attention skimmed the broken high-rise, and she noticed for the first time the frightened faces now peering down at them. From every shadow and every corner, hundreds of people had begun to reveal themselves. They crept warily forward, one after another. But these survivors only watched. None made any attempt to move closer. In fact, many were armed. They looked afraid. Angered, even.

Across the street, from where the old haggard man had returned, something glinted faintly. A pile of purple rubble. The color was out of place. *Curse*, the haggard old man had said. It looked as though everything purple had been thrown there to be burned. There were canisters of various fuels — an expensive commodity not often wasted in such a way. Yet the canisters seemed to have been emptied and had been carelessly tossed to the side there as well. She could smell the putrid odors faintly through her scarf. Had that old man been hurrying to try to light it all on fire when they had appeared from the storm? What had they interrupted?

Slowly, Jeana began moving toward her husband, her unease growing . . . Her steps began to slow as the thing in the center of the crater began to take form through the smoke and the snow. It was small and broken, the thing beneath John's torn coat. She saw a . . . a hand. A tiny, pale hand. The delicate little fingers, which were covered in ash and soot and snow, curled almost imperceptibly.

Jeana stopped in her tracks as horror washed through her.

A little girl, she realized. A beautiful little girl with midnight hair lay there, and she was covered in so much ash. Her skin was utterly pale, and her little lips were tinged with blue. Jeana gasped, and tears suddenly rose to choke her. She blinked to clear her vision as she stared at the little girl, who had such wan, porcelainlike skin. This child was out in the cold, *alone*, and she was in the street, where she should have been found easily — and these people had done nothing for her. To a mother such as herself, the act of leaving any child to the cold was unforgivable. She felt a familiar ache in her belly. An emptiness. Sorrow such as none she'd ever felt but once, and it echoed the look upon John's face in that moment.

Now Jeana understood why her husband had been so taken aback. He must have already seen several of these people keeping their distance while the child lay there, abandoned to a cold and lonely death. Now she understood his murderous look. It was against everything he stood for, against his very identity, to leave a child to die alone.

Jeana's feet began to move, and then she was running. She clutched Jamie closer as she reached John, and she slid to the ground at his side. She grabbed his pack from him and urgently began rummaging through it as he picked up the little girl carefully. He checked gingerly to see if the child was injured in any way, but she did not appear to have any wounds. The little girl didn't have the appearance or the smell of a sick one, either.

Jeana wiped the cold tears from her eyes with the backs of her hands as they shook, and she turned the bag upside down to remove a thin shawl — it wouldn't be enough to warm the girl, she realized. It would not do. Instead, Jeana quickly began to remove her own coat. It was much warmer than John's.

The child didn't seem to be breathing when John lifted her, ever so gently, and brushed her dark hair back from her tiny face. Her head lolled as his fingers felt for a pulse. Jeana cupped the sweet girl's cheek, and she looked up and saw the crease in John's brow. "She looks relatively unharmed. I don't think she's gone just yet," he told her. "This ash may be the only reason she isn't dead yet. Some of it is still lukewarm." He pulled the child's tiny body against his to share his own warmth as Jeana handed him her own coat to wrap about them. The young one wasn't moving. "Put on my coat. It's too cold for you to be without it, Jeana."

Jeana shook her head with a grimace and wrapped John's coat over his shoulders as he shivered fiercely.

Get her warm first, she told him, her numb fingers forming the words as quickly as they could. *How strong is her pulse?*

She shrugged the tattered shawl over herself a moment later. The cold pierced it, as unyielding as the sharp, slender pugio she carried. The frigid wind seeped through the garment in waves, until it had gripped her ribs and she'd started shivering. She clutched Jamie closer to protect him from that merciless cold.

"My hands are too numb. I can't tell whether she has a pulse," John grimaced worriedly, flexing and shaking his hand to get the blood flowing freely again.

Jeana took his hand between both of hers and breathed on his fingers. She rubbed his frozen digits between her palms, praying it would heat them even a little. She doubted it did much at all, but it was better to try than to do nothing.

"Half her clothes have been burnt away," he said.

John withdrew his hand as Jeana nodded to a singed white garment which might have been a child's dress. Or a shroud. He disturbed it, took it in his fingers. To Jeana, it looked frighteningly like the shrouds used to cover the dead in Five Tower. Except it was white. And a white shroud in this city was the sign of the cursed, the shamed, the unwanted. John sucked in his breath.

His expression clouded with anger as he realized what it really was. "A shroud, Jeana," he told her. "Never mind that she wasn't given a proper dark color — this means these people *intended* for her to die here. They were going to leave her here to rot once she was dead. They weren't even going to bury her." He was very angry. "They left her out here on purpose."

She's not dead, is she? Jeana signed. *She doesn't seem to be breathing.*

John looked down at the girl, his fingers pressing against the artery in her neck once more. "She's alive," he said. "But her heartbeat feels very weak."

As though his words had breathed life into the child, the young one stirred. Her chest rose and fell with a feeble, wheezing cough, and her eyelids fluttered weakly. Tears welled in the young thing's lashes and glittered among the snowflakes, and then they began to freeze in thin trails upon her cheeks. "*Aaaaaaaaaaaaaaaaaiiiiiiiii . . .*" she wept, her voice splitting as her head lolled back. John brushed her frosted midnight hair from her pale, waxen face. The sound she'd uttered had been a long, cracking wail, and it was so filled with anguish that Jeana had to shut her eyes and turn her head away, to take a deep, faltering breath to keep that sound from breaking her into wretched, shivering pieces.

Anger flashed hot through Jeana's belly at that sound. Only monsters would leave a child to die in a blizzard.

We are not alone, Jeana signed discreetly, using her chin to motion to the buildings around them. The sound of sorrow scraped along her own throat as a sob lodged there. "Shhh . . ." she said to her son as he stirred restlessly against the cold. Another violent shiver stole through her own thin frame.

Some of the city's people had crept closer. Clutched in their hands, she could make out clubs and several twisted lengths of rebar, and splinters of wood driven through with nails and other objects. "Let it *die*," came the hacked, angry voice of some woman from among the crowd. Upon their faces, Jeana could see such ire written. Jeana gripped her gun and flipped the safety mechanism, and John slid his knife from its sheath once more. He put the knife across his knee, just in case.

"The woman has a gun," someone muttered. Jeana could hardly hear him.

"She can't shoot all of us," another said bitterly.

"What *happened* here?" John whispered as he studied the threatening mob and the wreckage about them. Jeana realized he, too, was unsure if these people would try to attack them.

"I told you to let it *die*," said the angered old man from before. "Let it die, I said. Let it die, after all it's done here." The elder scrabbled back when a tall, dark man clutching a thin, black staff brushed past him, moving him gently to the side so that he could exit the cave-like entrance of one of their snow tunnels.

"Move, Drego," said the tall man quietly to the old one.

Drego's long, filthy fingers shot out and wrapped around the other man's heavily padded wrist, over the stripe of red fox fur there. He clung to the man with both hands, shaking his head wildly. "Don't! Don't go near that child!" he squawked. "Don't do it, Taiir! Not after what it done to the others! Caol said to let it die after what it done!"

"I am not getting near tha child, Drego. Let me go. Easy, old man."

Drego's drooping, vulturelike chin wobbled as he stared up at Taiir, who carelessly swung the oiled staff up and over his shoulder. A long, silent moment passed between the two, and then the old man finally lowered his eyes and let go. Drego brushed away some of the sparkles that had begun to show at the corners of his wrinkled eyes, and he looked away to hide the rest. "It'll kill you if you get too close. I won't mourn you, Taiir. I won't! Your mamman, mayhap, but not *you*. I'll put a *violet* shroud on your dead body! Give you the color that it murdered half this city with! Every honorable man and woman will spit on your open grave to keep your dishonor raw." With that, the old man turned his back and disappeared into the dim snow tunnel for good.

* * * * * * *

Taiir shook his head, his grip tightening upon his black heartwood staff, his fingers finding and closing around the intricately carved wildcats across its center. He waded through the snow toward the strangers, and he stepped over the dead with practiced respect. The couple seemed to take notice of the bodies under the drifts for the first time as they held that accursed child like a fragile spring flower, worry pooling in both pairs of suspicious, glittering blue eyes. The woman stared at the dead longer. But her gaze was just as hard and wary as the man's.

Taiir saw the pack they'd shrugged off. He saw the gun and the wickedly lengthy gutting knife. The two expected a fight; they almost had the look of scavengers about them. But he wasn't sure whether they were that or worse. They could have been with the Descendants of the Moon but for the baby she held. "You came to scavenge, that right?" He swung the black staff in a loose arc and studied the shrapnel about them for a second. He then hefted the staff's thin trunk over his shoulder again, letting it rest. It was the smallest warning to them that if he so decided, all he had to do was signal his men.

The gun angled toward him slowly in the woman's left hand. She held her baby close with her other arm and flicked her wrist and fingers rapidly.

The scruffy, shivering man near her remained unmoved, except to turn his head to watch the furious motions she made and nod to her. He returned a few calm signs as well.

Taiir did not understand what they were saying to each other, but he could guess it was about him — and about what their next move should be. "I know you speak," he said to the man.

"I do," John said, placing his hand gently upon the boy's head and then the woman's cheek. Probably to let her know they would be all right. "I'm John Ivan, and this is my wife, Jeana. Our son, Jamie. I'm a certified field doctor, a marked servant of the Glass Chain."

Taiir started at that. He listened as John continued evenly.

"We didn't come to rob you. We've come to assess the situation and help. I work with the Enforcers on occasion, and they have offered their assistance should you require it. We were on our way to my new post. Supposed to make a stop to meet with an associate by the name of Amos Shipwright. But we saw the explosion three nights ago. Several of my other associates are coming as well, just a day or so behind. We were the first to leave the envoy. We have run out of food, however, and I would like to trade my services for it."

"Amos Shipwright," repeated Taiir. "He and his passers-through, come from tha dwelling of tha regency for Black Temple. Trained in Isold, I do believe."

"Yes. Isold."

"He is no longer welcome. None of you are welcome any longer."

"I am aware," said John. "We would not have trespassed, except that we thought to help. The situation seemed to us quite dire." John glanced upward as more glass fell from above. It did not fall silently but cracked loudly as it struck the oil-black ground that was the crater. Neither the field doctor nor his woman flinched. "And it seems we were correct."

Jeana set her gun down and placed her hand upon the little girl's cheek. The woman's mothering instincts were ferocious — the glare she gave Taiir, warning him not to approach them, made a small part of him recognize she was the bigger threat here, not her husband. She would kill anyone she perceived as a threat simply because the child had been left to die in the cold. John seemed to be more hopeful for a trade.

She signed something to John, and he nodded. "I know we need to move her out of the open," he said. She then pulled his pack closer and began rummaging through it again.

"If you are smart," Taiir said evenly, "you will leave her be. Tha child is dying, and good riddance, too, as far as everyone here is concerned."

John was angered by Taiir's warning. "Leave her to die? And just what would her parents say to that?"

Taiir replied coldly. "Parents? Not *here*, no. She has no family here. Unless they were blown up with tha rest of ours. She is not one of us, and we are not claiming her. No one here wants her to live, not after what she has done. Not just because of tha deaths, either. Tha strange ones who were brought here by that group of Enforcers, tha same sentence has been issued for them." It was difficult for Taiir not to spit the word *Enforcer* without any venom. He heard the angry sound that scraped through his raw throat just then, and he bit off the oath that rose before it was spoken aloud. "She is responsible for a lot, and in too short a time."

"Why was she left to the cold?" demanded John. The edge in his voice was growing sharper. "You're saying it wasn't some sort of sickness?"

"No. It is much worse than that."

Jeana's lips curled into a snarl, but she said nothing as she pulled from the pack a rather scratched, mottled old bottle whose label had faded long ago. She twisted at the waist, shielding it from Taiir, but he still saw it. His fingers gripped the handle of the staff tighter. She paid him little apparent attention as she hid it and then pulled out a scuffed black thermos and unscrewed the lid. Steam rose from the lukewarm contents as she poured the fluid into the lid. The woman moved closer to her husband to administer tenderly to the girl, and she eased the child's head up so that she could place whatever the concoction was in the girl's mouth. John took the steaming cup from her, and he placed it gingerly against the child's blue lips himself to keep it from spilling.

The girl began coughing, and that dark liquid seeped from her lips. Alderoot, Taiir realized when he smelled the familiar, acrid note on the cold wind. It was a rare commodity, a young species that seemed to have endless uses. It was good for blood flow and revitalization. Because of its warming effects, it was ideal for snowy climates such as the one he'd been born to.

The plant was rare to see even in his homeland. How surprised he was to smell the leaves *here*.

The child began to cry again, although her voice was but a broken sound. Still, she was not shivering. She should have been, Taiir knew. Especially with a good dose of alderoot. That child should have felt the cold or been dead already from the temperature.

"Shh," said John, wiping the girl's cheek clean. "It's all right, little one. We have you. You'll be warm soon, I promise. Drink as much as you can, it will help tremendously." Jeana picked up her gun and pointed it at Taiir when he stepped forward. John grabbed his knife instinctively at his wife's motion.

Taiir stopped when he was merely a meter from them. He knelt there, held out his hands in a gesture of peace. He looked over his shoulder cautiously, briefly, and then he looked down at the child. At the tiny creature who'd murdered so many.

John pulled long strands of frosty midnight hair from the girl's face.

Her eyelids fluttered open, and she looked straight into Taiir's eyes.

It felt as though she were staring at his bare soul. She didn't cringe at the anger she saw in him, either. She just looked at him with an expression as innocent as could be. Even though he, like every other soul in Five Tower, knew better than to trust such a face.

She continued to study him. She took in his plaited braids, noted the details upon the chain he wore about his throat, assessed the tension in his fingers as he gripped the black staff.

The child's curiosity gave way to confusion, as though she didn't know who he was or where they were. Her little brows drew together ever so slightly, and her gaze shifted briefly to the broken tower above before she returned her attention to him. She wasn't frightened. She wasn't in pain. She wasn't cold. She was simply *confused*. As though she'd awakened but still thought the world was a dream.

Jeana looked down . . . and when she noticed the color of the girl's eyes, she gasped. Her reaction was the same as Taiir's own had been when he'd first seen the accursed creature. The child's eyes were an intense green, as though light burned within them. The color was brighter than it should have been in the shade of John's shadow. It was as though her soul literally dwelled within her gaze and burned there as a bright, emerald fire.

"She is not a normal child," Taiir whispered to them apologetically. "You should know that. She cannot be."

"Isn't normal?" John said bitterly. But he did not see the color of her eyes. He did not know that she should have been dead for how long she'd been lying there, exposed to the blizzard. With nothing to eat or drink, and with nothing left to warm her but that accursed white shroud and the ash. "So you feel justified in leaving this girl out here to die. This shroud? I know what this color means in your city." John had clutched the burnt cloth as he'd said it. Now he threw it at Taiir, and it landed at his feet.

Taiir clenched his teeth.

"I've seen what superstitions do to the innocent," said John. "Because of those superstitions, otherwise good men stood by and did nothing when my wife was stabbed in the throat by a serial killer. He would have skinned her and gutted her, too, as he had her sisters and her brothers and her parents. The victim is always a witch, a demon — there is always *something* to justify it. And if you take one step closer, I *will* have to kill you. We may be here to help, but if you get closer, this won't end well for anyone. Us, or you, or this city. You understand that we work for Black Temple. You know our words and what they mean. We are here to deliver mercy, unless one among you does something to change that."

Taiir studied the child. He gripped his staff tightly when she blinked. He saw a predator in her. He knew she would get this family killed if he let them take her. But . . . then again, it would also mean she was no longer in Five Tower. He wouldn't have to watch the girl die a slow death anymore, gritting his teeth as he waited for the blizzard to claim her — as it should have days ago. The lord's order would no longer conflict with Taiir's late mother's words.

It's not her fault, Taiir, his mother had said. *Do not let them punish her for their sins. Send her away, my son! Send her away.*

Both his mother and his liege would be honored in the end if these people took her. But he couldn't let these determined fools do so blindly, not without warning them first.

"This is no superstition," said Taiir at last. "She has done something terrible. You do not understand. I do not know how long she has been here or where she came from, just that she caused this." He motioned to the ruined city about him. "*She is not normal.*" Those eerie eyes of hers; he could feel them boring into him, reading him. His grip upon the staff tightened again.

"My calling is to heal people," said John. "I am good at it. Whether your people want her or not, we are going to help her. Every life should flourish. Normal or *not*."

Taiir felt part of himself sigh with relief over their ignorance. They intended to help regardless. At least they didn't seem to be *child eaters*. Not even one among the cult of the wolf would be so fiercely determined or care much whether she lived. Every child eater he'd ever met had been a superstitious, paranoid, batty one — his warning would have sent them scurrying off in search of some other, *normal*, child. One that had no chance of passing a curse with the eating of it.

"She was not born of this city. She is not of our people," said Taiir after a moment of deliberation. "I concede that it means we have no real say in your decision to help her." The words gave him quiet relief. It felt right to say them.

The child shuddered weakly as her gaze passed from Taiir to John. Her small fingers curled around the gray fur collar of Jeana's coat as she seemed to wait for their decision. There was no hopeful look in her eyes, no dread. Just quiet observation.

"What's your name, little one?" John asked gently.

Her mouth opened, but none of them could hear the name she uttered. He leaned closer, turned his head to hear as she repeated. "*Nai . . . mierya,*" she whispered. Her voice was so fragile, so weak. It came hardly above a whisper. None of them realized what she was saying.

"What is your family name?"

"N . . ." Her eyelids drifted slowly downward. "No memory . . ." She lost consciousness. She did not open her eyes again when John gently prodded her to try to remain awake.

Taiir grimaced. "You need to take her from this city," he said quietly. "Do not tell a soul that I am tha one who gave you permission. My liege Caol has ordered that her death be slow and public. If he discovers I sent her with you, he will have you hunted and killed just to make sure she dies . . ." He frowned thoughtfully. "But he will not do it if he thinks she is already dead." Taiir's fingers tightened over the cold staff as he made the quick decision he knew might later get him killed. For now, it would buy them all some time and free them of such a sin. "Listen. I offer mercy. I will make sure tha watch at West Gate is lax. Take her when tha horns blast, marking shift change in tha morn. I will make sure Caol's loyalists are distracted. His nephew Timothy will be glad to encourage her disappearance, and he will be quiet about it. He did not agree with Caol's command and spoke loudest against it."

* * * * * * *

Jeana felt the tight grip of grief and anger loosen. At last, she nodded. She snapped her fingers so that John would look at her.

We'll take her with us in the morning, as he says, she said. *Tell them Mark will be here to help them tomorrow.*

"Are you sure you want to bring her?" John asked. "You don't want to try to find her family first?"

Taiir waited silently as Jeana shook her head.

Mark can help these people, she told her husband. *They do not want her here. We'll find her a home if she has no family to claim her.*

"Are you sure you want to risk it?"

Taiir spoke as though he had some idea what the conversation between them might be about. "If you are considering whether to keep her or to find a family for her, I would not trust anyone in or near this city. Most of tha families living just outside of Five Tower . . ." He looked up at the broken towers above, as though the city's name had become nearly unbearable to say aloud. "They bring in strange ones and trade them. Tha girls are treated tha worst before they are sold. Some are traded to tha Wolfshadow priests. As you know, some of tha girls are kept and bred, and their male offspring become a steady source of sacrifices for tha Descendants to consume."

Alarm flashed in Jeana's glittering blue eyes, and she looked down at the child her husband held before returning her gaze to Taiir. She nodded to show her appreciation in a way Taiir could understand. She began signing to her husband again, and Taiir waited patiently for them to come to some agreement.

She may as well become our daughter. Griggori stole our first, John, and I cannot have any more children. He took that from me.

John winced, but he kept listening.

I will not ever trust another soul with this little girl. She is precious, and she needs us. And everything in my heart tells me we need to take her with us. Perhaps this is destiny, an answer to my prayers. A chance to raise a second child, for Jamie to have a sibling he would otherwise never have had.

John nodded at last. "All right. Take out what medicine we have left so I can give it to him." He rose with little Nymeria cocooned protectively in his arms. He noticed how Taiir had risen and stepped away, his dark gaze following the girl suspiciously, as though she were diseased. John tossed a small bundle to the wary man. "This is all the extra help we can offer at the moment, in terms of medicine. You'll find several jars of potent antibiotics and various pain and fever-reducing remedies within. We haven't enough alderoot to share, the girl needs it. I'll take a look at your wounded if you'll give us about a week's worth of food and water so that we can get to my assigned post more quickly. We will then send the appropriate equipment your way. My associate Mark will be here tomorrow with more medicine since we've already gone through the rest of ours . . . It's all I can do for now."

"You won't be getting near anyone here with tha girl," Taiir said. "No one wants her. They will not want your ministrations after you have touched her, either. But I will have a few things delivered to tha gate for you. Consider it a trade. You are taking a curse from this city. Caol will be happier for it once his rage and his grief are gone. He would not want a single particle of dirt corrupted by her corpse."

"Then we will take her with us."

Taiir considered his words for a moment, and he looked up into the windows of the remaining two buildings before finally nodding. "Do not ever bring her back here. Ever. None here would mistake her for another, or another for her. I will not be able to stop tha people of this city from killing her. It would be wisest to take her as far from here as you can."

Jeana nudged John's wrist. *Ask him about the mountain of purple trash. Over there.*

"What is all of that?" John asked. He motioned to the pile of purple rubbish. A layer of white had already descended upon it like a shroud.

"Caol's orders. Everything purple is being purged from tha city." Taiir eyed the crater, and he placed his hand over a red vein in the concrete. It was hot to the touch. "Lay her close to this. It came from her, after all. She may be wanting some of it back."

CHAPTER TWO

KILLER

LUKAS KEPT LOOKING OVER HIS shoulder into the darkness, where he knew the creatures were waiting to make an appearance. His horse bungled noisily through the underbrush, and he reined her in. "Easy, Beastie," he whispered. Her entire frame quivered when he brushed his dirty fingers through her midnight mane.

She pulled against the reins and pranced sideways with a nervousness that set his teeth on edge, and the branches ensnared his pack and tore the strap. He caught it before it fell, cursing the volume of the blunder, and he tied it again, loosely, his hands moving with feverish urgency.

Again, he looked over his shoulder. He told himself nothing was there. Still, he heard the creatures . . . just beneath the creaking of the trees and the whispering of the quavering leaves. The sound the beings made rippled just below his threshold for sound. He knew he was imagining them, yet he also imagined the mere thought of them drew them to him.

Up the road, the wheels of an old horse-drawn carriage slushed through icy mud and sludge, and the pair of chestnuts sounded their distress.

Perhaps he'd gone mad, but he fancied they, too, sensed the tall, shadowy creatures.

Lukas slid from the saddle and clicked his tongue, and the stolen horse turned her head to stare at him with wide, unblinking eyes. The whites in them shone brightly in the waning moonlight as her black pupils rolled. She snorted and turned to dance away, and the night swallowed her. He was alone again. When the trees creaked with motion, a chill undulated along the ridges of his spine, and he pulled his hood low over his head to cover the filthy yellow hair that would flag him in the damp, rolling darkness.

His fingers clutched the carved bone handle of the chipped, rusted dagger belted to his side, and he crept toward the warm glow that illuminated the woods ahead. Insects of the winged variety were stirred to life by that light, and they fluttered toward it madly, seeking warmth, or light, or whatever it was that drew them toward the lanterns.

The laughter of an old woman slithered by as he pushed through the whispering foliage, and his aching, gangly frame bent double as he swiped at the spider webs he fumbled through. The forest was full of them. Every few paces, another faintly illuminated web of silver appeared too late to be avoided, and they entrapped him and wrapped about him. Several young arachnids crawled over broken webs and prickling flesh, and he cringed as he brushed them away.

He continued to creep after that ominously creaking carriage. For too long, it lingered far enough away that he could see only the yellow light among distant leaves. But he'd raced the carriage to a perfect ambush site where he knew the road curved just right, where the thick trunks of dead and dormant trees angled just so. He could hide there, then easily board the wagon as it rolled by. Even now, that flickering yellow glow grew brighter.

He couldn't see it in this darkness, but he knew the wagon was the correct one, that there was an insignia painted on the wooden slats that formed the wagon's rigid exterior. It was Black Temple's mark, a black quatrefoil, upon which lay the image of a scalpel dripping with blood. The inscription at the bottom always promised *Mercy and Wrath*.

He contemplated the two aged individuals inside the wagon, considered how to extract the information he needed from them.

Lukas drew his blade slowly as the mud sucked at his boots, and he crouched as the carriage approached. He glanced behind him again when he felt the night's unholy eyes upon him, but he kept himself hidden as the carriage neared. Then he leapt, his hand outstretched. But just as he grabbed the wagon's posterior railing and pulled himself against the back of the cabin, a pale, bony hand jutted out from a lightless, paneless window. Lukas's heart rose into his throat as he twisted sideways and forced his blade through the opening, just where the man's throat should have been. Just as that pale, bony hand gripped his sleeve to trap him. The hand shook severely at Lukas's assault as a blunted, gurgled cry of surprise touched his ears, too quiet to raise alarm.

What a waste, he thought. His blade had struck true, opening a yawning smile whose blood the bony hand now retracted to stanch desperately.

Again, Lukas's instinct had saved his own life and doomed another's in the same breath. He released the man's arm.

The old woman he'd heard earlier drew a breath to scream as Lukas flung open the door and entered the cabin, his cloak casting a blackness that stretched over her frail form. He saw the gray-blue color of her eyes clearly for a moment as the lantern hanging outside swung near her open window.

That moment was all he needed. She was dead before another sound left her throat, and her head fell back and hung out the window, bobbing with the motion of the wagon. The old man's horror was all but muted, like the small mew of a dying kitten. Lukas turned to his prey and pushed him into the corner of the seat, away from the dead wife. He held the chipped blade, its jagged point kissing the soft underside of the man's chin, just above the bleeding flesh the man clutched desperately. His forearm pressed the backs of the man's hands as he pinned him. "What did you receive from him?" he asked.

The grievous, haunted gaze of the old man still lingered on his dead wife. He could not seem to bring himself to look away from his beloved.

Lukas snarled. "Old man, I implore you to answer my questions before I cut off her head and let it fall into the mud behind this wagon, separate from her body and lost to the forest, to the worms and the scavengers. She is already dead. You are still of use to me."

The old man's lips quivered, but little sound came from him.

"Mr. Ivan," Lukas hissed impatiently.

The old man's body sagged, and the lantern light that swung back and forth caught the wetness in the crevices beneath his eyes. "Why have you done this . . . ? My wife — "

"Mr. Ivan, I am going to end your life, and whatever business you still have will remain forever unfinished. Be of use to me, or I will make your death more painful." Lukas dragged the man back to his feet, pinned him against the interior wall of the cabin. "What did you receive from him? And where has he gone? This mission is important to me. That means it is important to you, do you understand this?"

But the old man shut his eyes tightly against his grief, and the quiet sound that came from his lips gurgled with his blood. "Kill me however you will, I will not jeopardize the urgency of our news. I will not give away information that will keep us from saving the child."

"Child?" Lukas said, taken aback. "What in the *Maiden's Harem* are you talking about? I am not looking for a child, I am looking for the Defector. Rhael. Where has he gone, and what did he give to you and your wife to deliver? I know his messenger bore more than words. I cut from him precious little, but it was more than I needed to find you. You are to tell me everything I need to know."

The old man convulsed, and a tremor ran through his weakening hands. Red began to stream through his fingers urgently as he slumped further.

Lukas had cut too deeply.

"Answer me!" he spat quietly. "What did he give you?!"

"Th — " sputtered the old man, most sorrowfully. "Curses . . . which must be broken before they consume . . . . We must save . . . we mus · · · save — "

Lukas followed the old man's fearful gaze to first the cushions, then to the wall as he held the old man upright. "It's here, isn't it? What the messenger brought to you. Where was Rhael going?" He dug the blade in deeper and saw a fresh rivulet of liquid black glitter across the dull steel blade. Lukas searched the fading abysses of the old man's eyes, saw his own mad eyes reflected like empty sockets . . . saw tall, umbral beings behind him, reaching out at the taste of a murder reaching its conclusion.

The old man collapsed a moment later and convulsed only once, and his hand, covered in dark liquid ribbons, seemed to reach for his dead wife before it moved no more. Lukas flinched, aghast when he saw aphotic marks crawling across his own flesh as though a ghostly hand were penning the murder upon him. But the marks were gone in the next moment, just as he shook free to wipe them away in fervent madness.

Lukas took the ring from the man's bony finger and began rummaging through their clothes urgently. There was nothing else of interest on either person. He gritted his teeth and took a moment to gather himself, and the smell of blood began to mix potently with the musky, aromatic evergreen scent that hovered thickly in the back of his throat. Pine. He loved the smell of it. He didn't even mind the coppery scent of the couple's blood tainting it. Pine smelled of freedom, of home. It didn't smell like the cold, lightless cells beneath Five Tower. It didn't bring memories of the hair-raising screams in the dungeons, or of young Eiran's ire-tainted sneer always, *always* leering down at him as the wicked youth continued what experiments his father before him had turned his back upon.

Lukas's dagger ripped through the luggage when the cushions and the boxes forming the seats inside the cabin did not hold what he was looking for.

His teeth scraped at his lip, almost drawing blood. He did not have the time to search more thoroughly. But given the old man's surprise, he doubted it was hidden well. So where was the item, or *items*, in question?

Lukas paused when he felt the carriage slowing down, and he looked out the window to glimpse the driver and the heavily armored Enforcer. "I've gotta hit a tree, Davos. And save the rest of that brandy for me, will you?" said the driver. The reply was a halfhearted grunt, almost the sound a wild boar made as it sniffed about in the brush.

"Hand me the reins and just piss over the side of the wagon," Davos spat after a heavy swig. "We've got time to make. We've got precious cargo aboard. Have you forgotten Mr. and Mrs. Ivan's haste? The man said not to stop for any reason. They agreed to that homeless haggard's terms because of what he told them about the child. There is a damned good reason to hurry, carrying that heavy news."

"Oh, shove off," said the driver, "or I'll piss on you, Davos. I've not relieved my bladder in — "

"It's hardly been two hours. What are you? A swaddling of baby flesh, all wrapped up in a grown man's clothes? You're pissing on my job to protect these people and what they're carrying. And you're pissing me off with your constant getting in the way of that particular job. So hold it, or I'll just cut off your damned wiener and let you cry about that instead. You lose that, and you'll empty yourself of all the piss you keep holding back every time you *take* a piss, and then we won't have any more damned problems with your bladder."

The driver grunted. "Well, you're a sore one tonight. I'm stopping anyway, Davos. Just you go on and try to stop me."

Davos cursed in reply as the carriage continued to slow down.

The bodies of the old man and the old woman were wet with blood, and Lukas knew that if the lantern outside was lifted to the window, the red would be a blinding marker that the two inside were dead. Lukas jerked the old man down into the seat and then hauled the dead woman on top of him. He adjusted the old man's arms, and then he took the blanket on the opposite seat and covered the quickly — yet cautiously — posed corpses.

They looked as if they were sleeping but for one red smear upon the woman's cheek. He pulled her frazzled, pepper-colored hair forward to make it look as though it had fallen over her oval face. He closed her eyes in the same motion.

Lukas himself crouched, his knife drawn, the curtain pulled closed behind him.

There was a rapping on the door from above as the carriage rumbled to a rickety halt and the floorboards lurched beneath his feet one last time. "We are stopping for a moment for Taeryn," said Davos. "Give me the word, and I'll tie him up and let the horses drag him to keep him from stopping every other hour. Three days more at that pace, and we will set foot at Crow Post. I am sure John and Reid will like to see you sooner than expected. They will want to know what you've learned and of the one from whom you've learned it." To himself, he snorted, "Creepy bastard, that one. Never seen golden eyes, none like his."

Lukas drew on his recollection of the old couple's voices as he prepared himself to utilize his adept ability to imitate others' rising and falling intonations, pitches, tones, and accents. The old couple's voices were within his natural range and capability, which ensured the mimicry would be convincing. In Mr. Ivan's deceptively short-tempered drawl, he added a note of exhaustion. "Let us alone to sleep, Davos."

In Mrs. Ivan's singsong cadence, Lukas added, "The news can wait." To her dead husband, Lukas added one final touch. "Sweetling, draw the curtain, will you?" Lukas pulled the shade on that side of the carriage closed as well so that neither of the men outside could see him or the blood pooling on the floor inside, and so the crisp breeze would not carry the smell of their deaths out.

"All right. Sleep well," said the coach driver. "We'll wake you two when we've reached the outpost." Taeryn shifted overhead, and he chuckled. "So. That stranger made you uneasy, did he?" he asked Davos.

Davos didn't answer right away. "He did," he agreed at last.

"Why?"

"Will you hurry up and lose your piss already!"

The carriage rocked as the driver dismounted, and there was a wet shuffling of leaves and crunching of twigs. One set of footsteps, not two. Davos was still seated above.

"Looked a bit haggard, though, didn't he?" Taeryn asked from the brush. "As if he'd seen some terrible things. As if he was running from some terrible things." When Davos did not reply, Taeryn's footsteps continued away from them.

Lukas slowly, ever so slowly, eased the door behind him open as Davos muttered curses under his breath. One of these men had what Lukas was looking for. He knew it was so.

The air was chilled and damp upon Lukas's skin, as though some undead creature breathed down his back. He slithered out of the carriage like a lizard, using all four limbs adeptly and causing no sound. He crept over the roof as Davos took another swig from his canteen and then set it down at his side, and Lukas's sweating hands gripped the wooden slats tightly as he prepared himself to kill the man.

Davos stiffened in his seat as if some extra sense warned him of danger, and he drew his sword, even though Lukas was downwind and had never made a sound.

"Why would he be suddenly fine with Taeryn's behavior?" whispered Davos. The realization came off his tongue like a slithery hiss. He leaned to the side to call more loudly, his sword hand gripping the pommel tightly. "Mr. and Mrs. Ivan?"

Lukas cursed under his breath and prayed Davos wouldn't yet realize they were dead. That the Enforcer would believe they had already drifted off to sleep.

"*Taeryn.*"

Davos hissed, knowing Taeryn had not heard that half-whispered warning.

"T — "

Davos spun out of his seat, but he was too late. The man's dark, dark eyes swam with livid shock as Lukas thrust his blade down into his flesh, just above the collarbone where the armor did not protect him. The blade broke at the handle as its tip glanced off what felt like bone, likely the Enforcer's left scapula, and Davos sank against the carriage. A wintry, pained smile pulled at the corners of his mouth.

"What . . . awaits . . . you . . ." the man sputtered with great effort, as though to curse Lukas.

Lukas grabbed Davos's sword and pulled it stealthily on top of the carriage with him. He held the man up, clutching at his mail collar, and he searched through his raiment as Davos began to sag.

"Make yourself useful and stand *upright,*" Lukas demanded. "Where is it?"

Davos's sneer twisted the jagged scar that ran lengthwise from his chin to his pale left eye. The expression was curiously and bloodily humored, as though already, the man knew what was coming to Lukas for such dreadful trespass. "In the molten jaws of Hel herself." And then Davos was dead, and Lukas could hardly hold the man up any longer.

Davos didn't have anything, either. But he'd confirmed there was, most certainly, something they were protecting, something being delivered. Even if the Enforcer didn't give Lukas any clue where the Defector was going, that item had the slightest chance of bringing him back.

Lukas bit deeply into the flesh of his own tongue and then kicked the dead man off the carriage. The horses whinnied, startled by the sudden weight that fell upon their hindquarters. He cursed again and ducked. The carriage lurched forward, and he snatched the reins from the post and pulled on them gently.

"Davos?" Taeryn's voice carried back. The dead man's name slurred on his tongue just a bit.

"Hurry up," Lukas growled in Davos's ugly, impatient tone. "You're pissing away the night, already. I'm done waiting for you."

"Oh, choke on a bone, Davos," Taeryn snapped. "I'll be done when I'm done. You know I can't just be done at the snap of a finger. Prick."

Lukas grew impatient as he waited, and he also became more anxious. If Taeryn didn't have anything he was looking for, he was going to be vastly angrier.

He mulled over his options and then decided waiting put him at greater risk of being found. The coachman wasn't really much of a threat compared to the others anyway. He was the smallest man in the group, and he was also the clumsiest, as he often stumbled and dropped things in a drunken stupor. And having pursued these people from Hagenhold in search of the Defector, Lukas still thought Taeryn nothing more than a well-employed drunkard.

Lukas looked back at the carriage quietly, aware he would need to destroy it regardless of the results of his search. Make it look like a robbery. He chewed on his cheek nervously, also considering how close the other hunters likely were. There were so many of them that he would not be able to elude them forever. They would keep coming until they caught him and dragged him back to Five Tower — and he couldn't return empty-handed or his slim shot at freedom would evaporate.

If he had nothing to offer, Eiran would never deliver on his promise to free him of the tall wraithlike creatures, and Lukas was so desperate for that freedom that he was willing to kill for it. That slim glimmer of hope was enough for Lukas to shed blood and bare his teeth the way a savage animal would. It made him determined to outhunt the hunters. It made him willing to take bigger risks because he never wanted to see those creatures again.

He prayed Taeryn had whatever the Defector had given to the Ivans. *He had to have it.*

Otherwise, Lukas would have no choice but to retrace his steps to Edantine or Hagenhold.

Lukas then decided he'd had enough. He stepped onto the road and dropped the disguise on his voice, and he pulled back his hood, no longer worried that he would lose his quarry and be identified later. Filthy yellow hair fell over his eyes, curtaining the scratches and the blood-matted beard and making him easier to see in the dark. "Every person with you is dead," he said as he approached the brush. "I've come a long way, looking for the accursed traitor whose parcel you are carrying. I am willing to kill as many people as it takes to get to him and what he gave to you."

There was the clicking sound of a button being snapped apart as he spoke. The quiet hiss of something being slid out of a leather pocket. A gun cocked.

Lukas hadn't expected the man to have a gun. Those weapons were difficult to come by, and even coachmen were not often known to carry them.

"A cocky murderer, have we?" said Taeryn, sounding suddenly sober. His voice carried quite a bit more bite than before, and Lukas felt suddenly less sure of himself. "All three in my company, you wraith-robed robber? They're dead, are they? That's a mistake you'll be regretting sorely. Your blood will be spilled for theirs, know you that."

Lukas cursed his luck — for luck it surely was, even if it wasn't on the better side of it. The sword he'd taken from Davos was cold in his hand. It would not protect him from that gun.

He heard another twig snap from another part of the forest, but he had no time to contemplate it. He charged toward the shadow he knew was Taeryn's smaller form, and at the faintest notion of movement in the darkness about them, he ducked behind a massive oak that stood between them. Thorny vines raked across his bare feet, and branches caught at his hair as he leapt over fallen saplings, and leaves rustled to warn his quarry of his approach, and Lukas ducked and rolled when the faintest glint of silver fluttered across his vision.

The sword felt heavy in his hand, and his heartbeat raged against his skull as he slid from oak tree to hackberry tree, to another, smaller oak as he darted toward the man.

The gunshot was loud, and bark splintered over his shoulder, and then the burned chemical and metal smell of gunpowder and smoke clogged his throat . . .

Taeryn's gasping became the first raspy approach of a silence that lasted for the longest moment. Not a bird fluttered awake to flee. Not a breath of wind came to whisper which man would fall. The trees seemed to fold in on themselves with unease.

A drop of moisture splashed upon his brow from a leaf that swayed just above his head. It stung where it bled into the wound upon his jaw.

Again, the smell of blood invaded his nostrils and dragged his mind back to the hellish halls beneath Five Tower, to the screams and the deaths, and to the blinding light and the stirring shadows that birthed the dark creatures who haunted him still . . . To the end that would, perhaps, be waiting on him one day — if this day was not to be his last.

"Damn . . ." said Taeryn.

Lukas gripped the wrist of Taeryn's gun hand, and with a pained grunt, he pulled his sword free of the coachman's flesh. He also yanked Taeryn's weapon away and tossed it behind him so the smaller man could not wrestle it back.

"You're faster than I expected," rasped Taeryn as he sank to his knees. "You realize you'll have the worst kind of death when Reid and John find out what you've done?"

"Who are these men?" asked Lukas. "Who are Reid and John?"

"You're a lazy thief, not to know the names," sputtered Taeryn. "Should have done your job better. Who sent you, anyway? You must be someone's piss-poor puppet, to be after a vial of blood. Who's hired you?"

A vial of blood? Lukas's brow rose. What was special about this blood that these people were delivering? Had Rhael found something?

Lukas drew instead from Taeryn's breast pocket a vial containing a glowing shard of violet glass and a small scroll sealed with a silver feather. The violet shard, Lukas dropped with an apprehensive cry. Immediately after, he heard the whispering of those terrible dark creatures as the sound came again unbidden, and he looked about the two of them, into the darkness. His pulse thrummed. The rhythm of his heart beat deeply with his terror.

His skin grew clammy, and his hands shook immensely. He coerced a deep breath and stooped . . . He had to *force* himself to pick up that dreadful, glowing shard.

This vial was not the one Taeryn had just mentioned. It contained not blood but stone, and cursed stone at that.

Hastily, Lukas flung it far from them. He knelt to take cover in the brush when he swore he saw dark, ghostly forms chasing after it.

The note, he pocketed. "Where did you get that stone?" he snarled into Taeryn's ear. When the man did not reply, Lukas put the tip of Davos's sword to his throat. "*Where?*"

"Isn't my business to tell," said Taeryn. The man grunted, clutching his wound tighter when Lukas shoved him. He placed his boot on Taeryn's back and rested the sword's point against Taeryn's thin jerkin. The tip rested just over the ribs, slightly below the scapula. Lukas had but to lean on it, and the steel would go through cloth, muscle, and bone, and then Taeryn's left lung would be drawing in blood and he'd be spitting it soon after.

"Go on and do it, you bleating coward," said Taeryn defiantly, his mouth pressed into the leaves and the dirt. He spat out several curses as the blade slowly sank. As the cloth upon his back began to catch the distant firelight with its wetness. But Taeryn began to laugh despite how it must have hurt him to do so. "Every drop of blood will cost you once you're caught. This was a Black Temple wagon, you fool. No wise man attacks or steals from the Temple," said Taeryn. "*Blood, for the Bloodless, Shadows for the Living. Wrath and Mercy are One.* Have you never heard the words? *Mercy and Wrath* are painted upon every accursed thing belonging to the Temple! And for those who cannot read, the bleeding heart being cut apart by the scalpel painted upon it speaks for itself. They'll send out a warrant to the Enforcers to find you and arrest you. The wearyworn will want your blood, too, because the guild will withdraw its aid from this entire part of the map until you are caught or killed. Assassins will hunt you like a dog."

Taeryn's blood was seeping from his lips now. It had run straight down his chin like an arrow pointing into the earth. It had smeared across the side of his face when he'd tried to turn his head and had felt the sword twist fractionally. He tried not to let himself cough at all. Both of them knew the havoc a single cough would commit, what with the blade still biting his flesh.

Taeryn's next choked, haphazardly whispered promise of recourse caused the blade to advance. "The wearyworn — "

Lukas felt his lips draw tight across his teeth when he interrupted. "I don't care whether the common folk will want my blood. I've bigger problems than my popularity. Piss on the wearyworn. Where is the vial of blood you mentioned?" He held up the unopened letter. "The silver feather marker on this letter means this has much to do with the very man I am after. I saw a box given to the old man in the carriage. Did that hold the vial? *Where is that box?*"

"That box went to Reid, it isn't with us," Taeryn huffed. "Reid delivered it a week ago to his brother, when they left to Cyan ahead of us."

"Do not lie to me. What was given to the Ivans was instructed to remain with the Ivans. The man and woman in your escort were Mr. and Mrs. Ivan. The man wore the Black Temple signet."

"The people you killed here are not doctors, and that ring is no doctor's signet, it is an emissary's. The signets are similar but not the same. The Ivans you've murdered are Reid and John's parents, you worthless, *were-wishing* murder-thief," said Taeryn. "As I said, what you've done, killing them? Oh, what awaits you."

Lukas cursed malevolently. "*Whore's Mother, and Maiden of the Lost!*" he shouted. He saw red as his pulse beat furiously at his temple. "What else have you?" he grunted, and he tore through the rest of Taeryn's pockets, his hands pulling and ripping at the man's clothes to find anything else. He did not see that a second vial — this one containing a red substance — had toppled into the soil beneath Taeryn. "That courier may walk in eternal rot in his afterlife for this deception," said Lukas as he ceased his search and pressed the blade deeply against Taeryn's flesh once more. This time it rested against the artery along the foreside of the man's throat.

"Not as much as you for these deaths — "

Lukas slid the razor edge across the fragile skin of Taeryn's neck, effectively slicing short the man's gurgled warning. As Taeryn writhed upon the ground, clutching at his throat, Lukas retrieved the gun and then backtracked to the wagon and tossed Davos's too large weapon next to his body where it might look as though it had simply fallen from his hand. He grabbed the small bit of gold he'd found in the wagon from the mud where he'd tossed the satchel, took the lantern from its post, and then, with a snarl, he smashed the lantern against the wooden slats fencing in the driver's bench. Fire spread like liquid tongues and began to ooze into the crevices and drip inside and down the sides of the wagon. It did not take long for the dry timbers to blaze on their own, and blaze they did — and with a startling tenacity, too.

Lukas stepped back and shielded his eyes from the bright fury that he suspected would be paid unto him twofold one day. His mind raced as he put together a plan to track down the vial and to find the man who'd sent it. He needed to know where it was going, first. The missive remained rolled up in the confines of his deep pocket. He would be reading that soon. He prayed it held some hint of where to search next. He would figure out why the old man mentioned a child later, too. He would have dismissed the child as merely being some ill son or daughter of someone important, but in context with the vials of blood and stone, and with the Defector's seal . . . ?

Lukas wasn't sure he liked the way the clues were pulling him.

A shrill whistle sprang from the wintry darkness, and Lukas spun about, startled. Next, he heard several shouts from up the road and about the forest. Hurriedly, he drew his hood back over his head and darted into the trees to escape the horsemen charging toward the carriage at a full gallop. They were armed, and he knew he would be lucky if he seemed nothing more than a fleeting forest shadow, washed away by the flames. Still, he did not linger. They might not have seen him, but he knew it wouldn't be long before they began to track him. Mud as there was, they would know the tracks were fresh, and they would resolve to hunt him down like an animal. What he'd done to the old couple, they might gut and skin him like an animal, too.

He had a long trek ahead of him before he would return to his stolen horse, if the beast hadn't wandered far. But there was a river raging about two miles to the south. If the animal had failed to graze in the field, he might still gain a day or two against his pursuers with a brisk swim.

Perhaps he would make it to the river before they caught him.

CHAPTER THREE

Tracks

THE CHESTNUT HORSES BUCKED WILDLY as the heat from the burning carriage swept across the reins and licked at their flanks. The assembly took off behind them as Reid and his men pursued it. One of the wheels broke over a rocky patch, and the body of the wooden beast tilted as the wheel flew apart and pieces careered into the trees. The axle dragged behind the flaming vessel, forming a deep fissure that Robert knew might make their own horses falter.

Yet there were no screams from inside. No cries. Just flames, and the sloshing of mud water, and hoofbeats, and the distraught screeches of the horses. The men shouted wildly as they pursued the runaway carriage.

Robert was the one who saw the body upon the ground where the passenger-side wheels had pressed it deeply into the mud. He dismounted as the others chased the flaming carriage, and a sick dread began to pool low in his belly as his horse began to back away uneasily. His muscles corded with tension as he knelt by the body he recognized as Davos, the Enforcer that Black Temple had sent to them. The one who had said he would stay behind with Mr. and Mrs. Ivan. "Reid!" he called.

Reid looked over his shoulder as his dark horse cantered in a circle. "What is it, Robert?" Reid replied. His glowing, torchlit gaze flicked down, and his jaw ticked violently. Skeletal shadows rolled across his features as he shook his head angrily. "Is that Davos? Is he dead?" he demanded, and he held the torch aloft as he drove his horse closer and peered down at the dead man as Robert rolled him over. The face was covered in mud, but the features were unmistakable. His black hair was tied back at the nape of his neck, and his half-open, gray-green eyes were lifeless and dull. He had one missing canine beneath a wide-open harelip, and two snaggleteeth — one of which was broken at an angle, the other of which was malformed. It was certainly Davos, as few men were uglier.

"He's been murdered," said Robert. "A right worthless dagger still broken off in him. The blood is still hot."

Reid drew a breath and unholstered his gun with a curse. "We'll come back for him. Look for tracks and be quick about it! The killer can't have gone far. I want him alive. If there is more than one man, do not engage them. Radio me immediately if you find my parents and Taeryn are being held hostage."

His horse dipped her head as she eyed the corpse and pranced cautiously closer, her hooves rising high out of the mud and steam coming out her nostrils in mighty puffs. No doubt the intelligent animal could smell the blood. She had probably heard the wolves, too. But Reid jerked the reins and kicked his heels against the beast's sides. "Ha!" he hissed. "Move!"

Robert let Davos's body sink back into the mud, and he pressed his fingers to the dead man's eyelids to close them. He offered a quick prayer as he forced the handle of his own torch deeply into the muck so it could stand unaided. "I am sorry we were not here in time to prevent this tragedy, my friend." With his thumb, he drew a circle upon Davos's rigid brow to represent his life having come to its end. "Every circle begins anew," he said. "And so your death begins your next life." Then he followed that symbol with a vertical line from the forehead to the bridge of the nose, to offer guidance. "*Sojourne.*" *The Open Door.* "The brightest star, so that you might find your way."

Robert cursed when he heard another barking growl. The wolves were getting closer. They smelled the blood, surely.

Robert snatched his torch and began searching the mud for clues. Before him, among the darkest, drifting shadows in the brush, a pair of golden eyes blinked. The sound that came from the beast's belly was feral, and hungry, and unforgiving. Robert backed away, glancing desperately to either side of himself as the huge creature eyed the flames he held and continued to creep forward, into the light. The wolf was all black, and the gentle rain dripped from its fur in muddy, oily streams. Its upper lip quivered as Robert stepped away quietly, and its tongue lashed out as the scent of the fresh body beckoned to it. The wolf's ears pricked as it crept closer, and the lean animal slunk closer to the ground, its body quivering as it readied itself to spring upon him should he move suddenly. It did not attack him as he retreated slowly, but its eyes never left him or the torch in his hand.

Then two more pairs of gold and gray eyes flickered to life in the darkness, both to either side of the first. The growling became a constant warning, one rolling over another, and rolling over another. But they did not approach for the bright, flickering threat that Robert held between them and him. They did not like the fire. But they did not attack him as he backed away. Instead, they continued to lock eyes with him as they bowed their heads and began to rend the body of his dead comrade.

He fled from them, panic stricken yet grateful.

When the wolves were far behind him, it took his experienced eyes merely a moment before he saw more stirrings upon the ground. Even in his hurry, he saw clearly the prints left in the muddier patches, where even a blind novice would have been able to follow the tracks. There were several deep, bare prints that were already filling with the evening's drenching downpour, and he followed them quickly as the wolves and their meal fell behind.

Robert noticed from the hurried prints in the muck that Davos's killer hadn't even made an effort to be more cautious. Either the murderer hadn't planned on their unexpected arrival or the wolves had chased him off. The clues pointed to the former. The scene was too fresh to allow for anything else.

No shoes. The startling detail struck Robert as odd as his temple throbbed with fear and anger. He tried to concentrate on the tracks, but it was difficult to do so when he could still hear the bones in Davos's corpse crunching between teeth. When he could hear the sickening sound of flesh being torn. *No shoes* . . . It was dangerous and painful to navigate the forest barefoot at night, although it was quieter than certain footwear. The prints also came from a thin person — likely a man — judging from the size and depth of each impression. Maybe a younger man, due to the dexterous twisting and quick footwork the prints showed.

Robert was startled by deadfall which crashed noisily a mere few feet away. Nothing stood where the sound had occurred, and nothing else stirred there.

Below him, the prints indicated the murderer was not only barefoot but also traveling light. It meant it would be more difficult to catch the man.

He then thought of the weapon he'd pulled from Davos's corpse and considered details it may impart of its last wielder. The blade and its handle had no longer been in one piece but several. The blade had been badly cared for, as if to hint the killer was inexperienced and ill-prepared. An encounter gone wrong. Yet the strike had been one of precision. Only a well-practiced, knowing hand would have angled that blade right to have managed that kill. The man he was chasing was very dangerous, he concluded.

Robert's neck prickled as he prayed those wolves would not follow him, and he shrank from every unusual noise about him as he pondered what sort of man would have dared murder Davos and set fire to the coach.

A servant of one of the criminal lords who'd been taking slaves, possibly? Mr. and Mrs. Ivan were old, which would have been an unfavorable discovery for that line of work. And if that were the case, why attack a Black Temple wagon for slaves? It didn't make sense to try to attack such a prominent, dangerous target when many small villages and holds were relatively unprotected and offered easier prey.

Robert concluded that the killer had not attacked the wagon for slaves. The man had been after information, loot, or revenge, or he had been hired for another purpose. He hadn't been a wolfman, either, because it was highly implausible a wolfman would use a metal blade. And because it was rare for wolfmen to attack anyone from Black Temple.

Even the common folk — often called *the wearyworn* by Black Temple doctors and Enforcers — rebuked those who crossed Black Temple. Most of the wearyworn welcomed the Temple's agents, its doctors, its aid. To attack anyone from Black Temple was to reject the whole medical guild as well as all that it stood for. Without Black Temple's doctors, various diseases destroyed entire communities and cities without relief or relent . . . To oppose Black Temple was to condemn entire villages and posts and towns to death. And the coaches very rarely carried commodities or gold the way merchants did. Only coded information could have been valuable, and that would have been sealed in a small wooden box with a silver feather engraved upon it. Forcing the box open without having the proper knowledge on how to operate its tricky mechanisms would destroy the contents therein. It was a well-known fact the Temple did not hide in order to deter thefts.

Whatever this was, it was a desperate move, though Robert could not discern why, or by whom. There was nothing to be taken from this coach or these innocent people but for a small handful of gold. Not even their clothes were to be desired — and all of that was intentional. It was a deterrent, to prevent greedy thieves and desperate men alike from being tempted.

Robert put his questions out of his mind to focus entirely on catching the murderer.

The trail led deep into the trees.

He kept his knife handy in case any of the wolves were following him. In places, the bastard's clues altogether vanished. But Robert was no novice. He knew how to find the trail when it seemed to fade away. The general direction led toward a grazing field a couple of miles from his current location. Which meant the bastard had a horse waiting for him there, and he likely had friends there, too.

Robert cursed and whistled for his mare. Bane had followed behind him a good distance. She'd remained quiet, nervous the wolves were prowling. The mare's ears pricked at his call, and one more sharp, birdlike whistle had the sweet creature trotting nearer. She was still quite fidgety, and when his palm touched her neck, her flesh quivered beneath his hand.

Robert doused the torch and then grabbed the saddle's pommel and hoisted himself onto Bane's back. He pulled out a walkie and turned it on. He prayed the others weren't out of range. "Reid, can you hear me?" For a moment, there was nothing. He scanned the darkness cast from the trees leaning over him, and he watched for trails parting the long grasses in the fields beyond. He knew he might have to wait before one of the other men dispatched a walkie to Reid, so he remained alert as he waited. His mare shuddered. "Scout to Range Commander?"

"What have you found?" Reid asked from the other end. He sounded breathless, as though he was still riding hard. There was a brief moment when Robert could hear the other men in Reid's company shouting. They were still chasing down the carriage.

"I've got a solid lead, Commander. If you lot don't hurry my way, we won't catch him for days. He's heading back to the knoll. He's wasted no time getting there, either."

"He has a horse," Reid swore. "He knows where that wild graze is."

"Affirmative," Robert agreed. "He knows the area well. It isn't likely he found that spot by accident. You'd be mad to think there is a graze there, otherwise. Surrounded by too much rock and wild forest."

"We're about out of range, Robert. Just circle back and wait for us, and we'll follow you and catch this bastard."

"Reid . . . unless he has others waiting on him there, he's alone," Robert said regretfully. "There are no other prints." For a long moment, there was no reply. He knew that Reid had heard him. He knew that Reid understood what it might mean. "I'll keep looking for more prints if you want me to. Perhaps I missed them. The wolves got to Davos just after you left. Perhaps I didn't see anything else — "

"You never miss a thing," Reid sighed. "Wolves or no. Get back and see if you can find any trace of my parents, or of Taeryn. Be careful of the pack, though, I don't want to come back and find you dead or your horse lame."

Robert nodded, his mouth downturned. "All right. Going dark."

"Affirmative."

With that, Robert turned down his walkie and wheeled his mare about in a half circle. "Come, Bane." His tongue clicked, and the fine creature's ears pricked. A soft sound rumbled in her throat, and he scratched at her mane fondly. "Come on, girl. Back we go. You'll get some fine treats when we're back at camp, for all this fine work you've done."

* * * * * * *

Reid jumped from his horse and ran toward the carriage, where it lay crumpled in a ruined heap against the boulders. His heart was in his throat. Thomas was leaning into the door, his hand clutching at the frame to keep himself from falling in, where the fire flared hottest. His dark blue scarf was wrapped tightly about his nose and his mouth as he fought to break away the planks that had blocked the door in the wreckage. He couldn't grab on to the burning planks because they were far too hot to do so. He couldn't wedge his blade between them to pry them apart, either — he had already tried, and it had done no good.

"Commander, don't!" cried Baron Westfall as the man darted in front of him. Reid was wide-eyed and quaking when Baron took his shoulders to push him back.

"Let me go!" Reid barked as the other men stepped forward to prevent him from getting any closer to the flaming carriage. "My parents!" he shouted. "I have to know what he's done!"

Thomas shrank away as something combustible inside the carriage exploded. It wasn't a substantial explosion, but there was enough force in it to throw Thomas back. He fell into the mud when he lost his grip on the door, and he struggled to roll over, his chest heaving. But he made no move to get up and try to get into the carriage again. He pulled a couple of pieces of sizzling glass from his cheek. The lantern oil. That's what had exploded. The canisters of oil that usually remained beneath the seats with the spare lanterns.

Reid felt his own face twist with a savage expression when Thomas's shoulders bowed. Thomas pulled the scarf away and looked up at him, his eyes bleary, sorrowful, knowing.

"No . . ." Reid croaked. His throat had gone dry, and a dangerous tremor ran through him. He continued to shake his head as the truth struck the rest of them, and they let go of him for pity. His feet brought him nearer the fire, until Thomas rose and stood before him. Thomas held up his hands and pleaded with him.

"You don't want to see them," Thomas said. The smoke had transformed his voice into a hoarse, grating whisper. "Reid . . . I'm so sorry."

Reid looked at his friend, yet he didn't quite see him. His face blurred in and out of focus.

Reid's eyes stung as he tried to blink away the smoke and the ash. He pushed past his friend and bent over the carriage's frame, and he began to claw at the boards. The charred surface of the wood was blackened, and red embers glowed hot in the exposed crevices. Then he felt and heard the crack, and cinders sparked in his face as the planks broke entirely. The heat blistered his skin and singed his eyebrows and his hair. Another board, he grabbed. He could smell sizzling flesh.

"*Commander*," snapped Thomas.

He ignored Thomas and continued to pry at the burning timbers until the last one he held groaned and creaked but refused to break. Thomas hissed and then called to the men. "Help us, you dimwitted bastards. Before he loses the use of his hands."

Thomas wrapped his own hands and climbed onto the carriage, his scarf back in place. He gripped another part of the bench Reid was trying to pry free — and then Baron and Arnold and Raegan began to help, and Tim Aeron and Neathan Heinzrich joined them, too. Only Zacchary remained behind; he held the reins of the two freed chestnut horses, both of whom sported minor burns and scorched tail hair. The mare limped slightly and snorted in complaint, but Zacchary continued to calm her as he kept her from looking at the fire.

The bodies inside the carriage were burned badly. Neathan retched at the putrid smell of the still-sizzling flesh when they hauled the old couple from the wreckage. All the men stood silently as Reid knelt by his mother and his father, his burned hands hovering above first his father's corpse, then his mother's. His hands shook violently, but he couldn't bring himself to touch either of them. His breath came in harsh, grating wheezes. He opened his mouth, but nothing left his lips as he stared down at them and kept shaking his head in dejected, wrenching despair. His mother's neck had been broken, and his father's throat had been slit wide open.

"Reid, the killer is still within our reach. Robert has his tracks, but we are running out of time."

At the mention of the killer, the agony Reid felt became a plume of explosive hatred. Reid nodded silently and stood, his gaze never leaving his parents' blackened bodies. "My father's ring is missing," he said evenly, and he stared hard at the bony appendage where a strip of uncharred flesh shone in the firelight. Where his father had worn the ring remained a pale, wrinkled stripe. The sun had not darkened the skin there in many years because his father had never taken the ring off. Never once. That ring was gone because it had been stolen.

The orange and yellow glow of the flames sparked brightly, and he looked up at Thomas and Baron. "Bring my horse. We have a murderer to hunt."

"You can't kill him," Thomas warned. "This is Black Temple's coach — the regency will deal with him accordingly."

"I *know* what Black Temple's regency will do, Thomas," Reid snarled. "Until then, he is mine. I will not break the law. Much, anyway. This might have been Black Temple's coach, but those were *my parents*. If I were you, I would worry more about what my little brother does to him when he finds out what has happened to our mother and our father."

Baron shook his head. "It would be wiser to send the killer to the Temple before you tell John. That man has a perturbed temper waiting to explode. Too much like your father, he is. More people're like to die, getting in the way of stopping him. Friend or foe, or even you."

"Doesn't matter what John does with him," Reid spat. "Mount up and run this bastard down." When he turned from his parents' bodies, he saw Thomas exchange a fearful glance with Baron.

"I fear I might pity that killer for what the range commander will do to him," said Thomas, who then turned to the other men as Reid snatched up his horse's tethers with a hand that shook. "Best get after him before we can't stop him. Before he crosses a line that cannot be uncrossed. He's too good a leader to lose over a murderer."

"What about Taeryn?" Zacchary asked.

"Likely dead, too. We'll find him after we get this killer. Unless you want to volunteer to stay behind and search, and battle wolves for the carcass."

"If it's okay, I would like to try to find him. It would be a dishonor unto him not to try. If he is dead, someone should at least offer him the proper prayer. If he is alive, he may need help."

"Be my guest," said Thomas. "But remember protocol and keep the channel clear. And don't forget those damned wolves. Do *not* let your guard down. I don't want to come back and find another body."

Reid was the first to mount and the first to disappear into the night. He left his torch lying in the mud where he'd dropped it.

Chapter Four

Caught

THE RIVER HAD STOLEN THE GUN and nearly drowned Lukas, but at least it had also washed away the mud and the blood from the previous night. The sun was just beginning to crown when he saw the first signs of civilization, of smoke curling on the horizon. He gauged it was approximately twelve miles away. Crow Post, he was sure — if he hadn't his directions mixed up. It was another three days to Lairen after that, where he could disappear among the population. Then, at his earliest convenience, he could catch a horse back to Argonia, where he could again begin to track his quarry.

He was shivering uncontrollably when he let go of his bag, and his stomach and lungs emptied themselves of the frigid, fast-flowing water.

Lukas shrank from the shadows that seemed to swell from the darkness of the forest where its leading edge leaned menacingly forward, stretching over the water and toward him. He crawled over the littered sand to get away from the twisting roots and branches. As the darkness seemed to drift closer up the riverbank, his fingers brushed over a few slivers of weathered, broken glass and instinctively snatched them up, clasping the smooth, rounded shards as though they could become a weapon or protect him somehow.

It felt to him as though those familiar, unholy eyes were searching again. Even with the threat of morning brightness, Lukas could still sense those dark creatures. Surely, they knew he'd sinned. Surely, they felt the death that clung to him as the last vestiges of the night fell away.

But nothing happened. Nothing came from the darkness. The shadows twisted back among the maze of roots and the gnarled branches as the wind brushed them aside.

The glass slipped from his fingers as he dragged himself up the riverbank, and he braced his back against the bone-colored driftwood there. His head fell back as the shadows began to recede, as the sun's orange crown continued to swell.

Lukas dug the missive from his pocket and broke the seal. He read it as the darkness slowly obscured the writing less and less . . . and then his fist curled tightly around the note. Its contents swam in his head, its grim and lurid words echoing.

Lukas exhaled deeply. It was too much to keep sensing the dark creatures.

Then his gaze fell to the glass he'd dropped . . . He frowned. *Glass*. Of course, he'd chosen glass and not stone.

He looked at his wrists, then, wondering. When was the last time . . . ?

He was startled by the sudden realization — the Blood Light had not flared. "It's gone," he said, almost disbelieving the evidence before him. He did not comprehend how that could be when only nights ago, he'd struggled against its baneful effects. Sensing those *things* again should have caused the Blood Light to come alive.

His gaze lifted to the sky as though an answer might be found there. And though he found nothing in the coral and blue that fanned the heavens, he felt the first ray of freedom

rising over the dreary plain of his soul. It was the first tendril of hope in such a long time —
and yet it felt tarnished. Mottled and spat upon.

The dawn sky painted itself slowly with filigree the color of blood and amber, but the
beauty of it did nothing to warm the turmoil raging inside him. All that he'd done to be rid of
the curse. For all the cruel, misleading promises . . . The Blood Light couldn't be gone just like
that, or simply of its own accord.

Yet he felt only lingering traces of it within him.

That it was gone meant his many crimes had been in vain. And he'd done a great number
of terrible things, enslaved by his fear and his desperation to earn the freedom promised to
him.

Lukas bolstered his determination to get the target off his back. Unless he ended up
beneath the young torturer's hands again, Eiran would remain unaware that Lukas's chains
had at last deteriorated. And the breaking of the curse was Lukas's first step to gaining
leverage over Caol and Eiran. It had been his primary reason for searching for Rhael, even if
it had not been his only one.

But he was still not free to ride into the dawn without having to look over his shoulder.
Eiran's hunters would only find him and drag him back if he did. Eiran's obsession was ire
fueled and power starved, after all. And neither he nor his father would ever let Lukas go.
So Lukas could not let either of them realize that he was no longer in their grasp — and
therefore useless. If they discovered his curse had broken itself, Lukas knew he would either
be a dead man walking or be subjected to more of the horrors beneath Five Tower . . .

Hell, if he were honest with himself, he was a dead man already. His time was nearly up.
He had but a single week left before the sentence upon him was made into spectacle and a
competition for favor with the higher lords and ladies of Five Tower.

Lukas did not plan to return to Five Tower in any state where he would be forced to
kneel before Caol or his son again. More importantly, he would never freely offer them his
own head. He would back them into a corner, and keep them there, until they bargained for
their own.

With the chains off him at last, the only thing left to do was carry out his plot against
the men who'd imprisoned him. To find a way to force Eiran and his father to admit him as
an ally rather than as a slave. They would then discover how bitter betrayal truly tasted. And
the way it had sounded and felt for himself, they would suffer it all one long, raking scream at
a time. They would endure as many years of torture as he had. And when justice was finally
spent, he would kill them.

At least now Lukas had more to go on than he'd had last night. The threatening letter in
his hand had seen to that. He now had more knowledge about what Rhael had sent forward,
and now he also knew Rhael had been held prisoner somewhere. That did explain why Lukas
had lost the phantom's trail. But how long had the man been free from his confinement?
From Davos's and Taeryn's words, it couldn't have been long, and Rhael probably had other
pursuers hot on his trail. It still made no sense why he would have sent forward a messenger,
then escaped and raced to get the items and the letter into new hands — to ensure it
personally.

But Lukas had more to contemplate than Rhael's actions. Black Temple had something
of value to him. A child who could serve as the sort of leverage neither Eiran *nor* his father
would be able to resist. A girl who had been cursed by the same creatures as himself.

The rest of what was in the letter was far more frightening to consider.

Lukas glanced across the river again as he removed his heavy, cold, wet cloak. Still, he
could sense the dark things, hear the whispering flickers of their nearness. But he could see
only the flowering crab apples and dogwoods, and the restless fluttering of the old oak leaves
that were even now being shed in the soft breeze. He was alone, even if he still felt his skin
crawling at the memory of the beings.

The accursed page crumpled in his fist continued to run through his mind, the words echoing over and over.

> *Do not believe the lies about the Bright Night. We found another child in whom the Vael burns brightly, but the cortex within her is corrupt and has the potential to lay waste to everything around her, to cause a cataclysm the sort of which has not been seen for millennia. Do not allow her to be apprenticed to Black Temple, or the sickness that is in her soul will soon fester again.*

The warnings were not forgiving, and he wondered over the Defector's other claims. Truth or none, the words still put ice in his belly. He had the foul feeling he might have gotten himself involved in something far more dangerous than his master's contemptible ambitions and false promises. That there was more happening than his own agenda, or the criminal intentions of Five Tower, or even the creatures' unnatural presence in this world.

Lukas wrung his cloak and shrugged it back on, and then he retrieved his bag before hurrying away from the riverbank and fleeing into the woods.

He calculated his chances of escape once more, angry he'd lost the gun he'd taken from Taeryn the night before. He'd left the sword in favor of carrying less because the gun would have been easier to conceal and because it hadn't weighed as much. Now all he had was his collection of badly forged and deteriorated, mismatched knives. He should have grabbed the sword and belted it to himself despite its weight.

He thought of every scenario in which his pursuers found him. How to fight them off, how to deceive them. His arsenal was broad enough, and he devised a plan to throw them from his tail if they got too close. It was important that he be free of them before he reached the post.

Lukas pulled from his pack coverings for his feet which would change the size and shape of his prints, and he tied the bag about his chest and belly and filled it with enough sand and rocks to change his weight. It made the tracks he tested with the weight deeper, and it changed his apparent posture. He even made a staff from an ash tree's fallen branch, which he'd pulled from between two large boulders. He ensured he walked differently. Made his steps heavier and clumsier, like that of a tired old man whose feet dragged the ground. And the moment he was no longer on softer ground, he changed direction to throw off any tracker that might have been among his pursuers. And surely there was, because he'd only barely escaped those men.

Lukas spent no time foraging for food along the way. Instead, he ignored the gnawing in his belly as he rushed toward Crow Post.

At the edge of the road some hours later, his cloak finally dry and the day warmed by the midafternoon sun, he finally began to calm down and take his time. He took out a canister of white-gray ash and paint, and he dusted his hair with it. When that was done and his hair hung over his face and his yellow beard was likely a sufficiently dulled, straw-tinted gray color, he lowered the staff until its heel dug into the earth with his practiced wobble. He clawed loose the topsoil and scrubbed his hands with it until the soil was in the quick, under the nails, and in every crease across his hands and his shoes. He rubbed the filth onto his face, his neck, his arms, his ankles, and the uneven toenails peeking out from his holey shoes. Then he bent low, until his cowl draped about his neck like loose skin. His eyes squinted, until he could hardly see through the lids.

He knew he looked like an old man. It was a practiced disguise he'd used many times and with great success. No more convincing could an old man be, for even his body was padded and weighted where it needed to be. The deception had saved him many times before, and with never a hiccup.

Lukas had finished with his disguise just in time, for to his surprise, a faint sound drew his ear. Horses galloping. Several of them, and they were gaining quickly.

If these men were the same as the ones currently chasing him, they knew the land even better than he'd expected.

They were upon him too soon, and circling, like vengeful vultures.

He feinted an elderly falter as the men prepared to pass him after one scrutinizing circle, and he raised his head the way a palsied old man might have done. "Wh-what is it?" he cried, choking on slobber he inhaled in pretend fright, and nearly falling backward when one of the men reached down and ripped back his cowl. His matted, disheveled hair fell over his face and blocked part of his vision, and strings of the greasy, dirty mess caught upon his lips. "Why're you badgering an old fella like meself?" His croak was a broken, winded, wheezing noise, the sound of an aging, skeletal old man ready to keel over if a spook shook his rickety old spine even once more. "Who're you?" He squinted at them as though he couldn't see regardless of the squinting, and his chin jutted out as though he had no teeth, and his lips smacked. He sucked on his cheeks and glared at the men looking down on him.

It was a young, fiery-haired man — built almost as broadly as his own horse — who spoke first. "Have you seen another on this road at any time in the last day? Tell us true, or you'll — "

"I seen none," said Lukas, his wobbling staff supporting him as he leaned on it and peered up at them all. "None as much as leaves an' ghosts, an' this tattering cough rattling my windpipe, until you lot came crowdin' about me an' pissin' on my sunshiny stroll into Crow Post. Let me be on my way, you. My knees wait for no man, the ache they give me. I'm in need of a doctor. Lest any of you can rid me of this smattering of blisters all down my belly an' back. Got worms comin' out every hole, an' pus as green an' smelly as my late sister's blackened foot." Lukas shifted to lift his robe as though to show them, but one of the men had gone green.

"No! No, we don't need to see that," said the youngest among them, gagging. That one was hardly older than a boy.

"Thomas," said one of them, an older man. This one's head was shaven and tattooed, marked with symbols and kill counts. A warrior, from the look and the familiar scowl. But not a commander. This one had been a mercenary. Odd, since Black Temple did not often work with mercenaries marked like him. They preferred assassins. And Enforcers, who were quite loyal. Enforcers were supposedly incorrigible. *Supposedly.* Although he'd met a few who'd gone to the wayward side.

The fiery-haired man glowered at the bald one.

"Let's go. If he hasn't seen him, he's likely already gone on to Crow Post, probably heading to Lairen."

"It's *him*, Robert," said another, younger man, whose dark blue eyes blazed with rage. This one drew a gun and pointed it directly at Lukas's face.

"But he's an *old man*, Reid," Robert sputtered, startled. "Our quarry is too spry to be his age. Too quick. *Look* at him, Commander. He's got the shakes. Can hardly stand, let alone run."

"I am looking," said the other. "And I am saying it is *him.*"

Lukas felt the blood drain from his face. But he shook his head deliberately, and he continued to act in character. He refused to be brought low by Reid's piercing, fiery stare. "I beg your pardon? Who am I? I am Wilhelm. Who, may I ask, are *you*? Are you planning to rob me, you, you *burgling purse snatcher*?" That stare promised retribution, and Lukas did not want the type of retribution it promised. "I tell you, I have nothin' worth taking but boils an' creatures I want gone from my body. Do I look like a man with a pocket deeper than my gnarled thumbs?" That stare promised to break the law, to do something terrible to him, and ever so slowly. That stare became angrier with every word that came out of Lukas's mouth. *Reid*. He recognized the name suddenly. He opened his mouth to speak, and his hand tightened involuntarily over the note he clutched.

Reid saw the motion. Nothing seemed to escape him. Not the ash. Not the dirt. Not the note. The man's jaw ticked furiously. "I am the son of the man and woman you murdered last night," said Reid. "*That* is who *I* am. And you are no old man."

Lukas gasped. "M — *murdered*, you say? By my mother's beard! I tell you, I — "

Robert moved to dismount.

Lukas abandoned his lost cause and darted to Reid's left. He swung his staff up and shoved the man from his midnight horse with it. The gun fired just above the horse's head, and the beast reared, screaming when the bullet rent its ear. Reid tumbled to the ground, and Lukas used the confusion to dart from the path. He descended the slope as quickly as he could, darting through thickets and hopping over deadfall, and trying not to twist an ankle on the rocky ground.

Too soon, as he tumbled into a pit that served as some local's boar trap, he could hear the men drawing their weapons and surrounding him. He was revolted by his luck, that he hadn't seen the trap among the dark green firethorn and the fading yellow witch hazel and the ivy. He hadn't recognized the skeleton of branches beneath the heavily scattered deadfall.

He tried to crawl out of the pit, but his leg caught in the stinging firethorn and the ivy growing there.

A loud screech startled him, and the wild flurry of leaves kicked up within the pit had him cursing his luck as a wild hog, stuck in the vines as he himself was, wriggled and squirmed and tried to gore him with its tusks. A cloven hoof caught him in the shin as he drew his knife to cut himself free of the thorny vines and stinging wild shrubs. Reid and Robert appeared over the edge before he managed to avoid a second vicious kick from the animal, or even a slicing of his forearm by the animal's tusk. He continued desperately to saw at the vines and tangled firethorn about him as the beast continued to scream and screech and writhe against its prison.

The vines and flexible branches snapped in quick succession as Reid and Robert moved toward him.

Reid's ire shone hotly in his blue eyes when Lukas shoved the missive into his mouth and scrambled to avoid the man as he hoisted himself from the pit. He had jumped over another shallow gully when suddenly an elbow jutted out from behind a tree and caught him in the jaw.

Then three men were upon him, and as his jaw throbbed fearsomely and he wrestled against them, Reid pried open his mouth and took the missive. "*Search him!*" Reid grunted as he stepped back, and the two pinned him down as a third and fourth began to search his pockets and his pack.

Lukas choked on his laughter. "Better a prisoner than a godforsaken slave," he proclaimed. Robert's fist collided with his chin. It did not deter his laughter. "Take me to see Black Temple's justice! Go ahead!"

Reid exhaled when he looked up from the paper. His face had gone white. "Why do you have this? Why was it important for you to take this?"

Robert put his hand on Lukas's throat and squeezed when Lukas struggled against them. "None of your business — " He choked when Robert squeezed harder.

"What is that, Thomas?" asked Robert. The man who must have been Thomas removed Mr. Ivan's ring from his pocket, and the others began to bind Lukas's wrists together. They were not gentle, and the rope burned and ripped the flesh. He struggled and fought them, still laughing.

Thomas glared down at Lukas and snarled when he uncurled his fingers. He spat in

Lukas's face. "It's Mr. Ivan's ring. The one that allows him to pass into the main posts without a summons."

Reid had holstered his gun and pulled out his knife, and now he pushed Thomas out of his way and knelt over Lukas. He slid the sharp edge dangerously against Lukas's left ear, and he held the paper up. "I asked you why you took this, and you have not answered me, you murderous thief. *Why this?!*"

"For my master," Lukas hissed. "There was a shard with it, glowing that unholy violet color. He'll send men to find that child."

"Who is your master?" Reid snarled. "Why are they looking for my niece? To everyone else, she is dead."

"So *your* family has claimed her." Lukas grinned wickedly at the revelation. "That makes that particular part easier, doesn't it?"

Reid struck him and then knelt low and sliced off the top of his ear. Lukas's bark of pain only invited another fist to strike him.

"Commander, be careful not to cross that line," warned Thomas.

"Yes, Reid, follow your precious little rules," sputtered Lukas, laughing. "Even though I killed your parents. *Slowly.* First your mother, just as she opened her mouth to scream, as your father watched, incapacitated. And then your father mewed for her as he died. I thought Black Temple guarded their guests better. Or is that because you had already left a week before to get to Cyan, taking all your armed men with you? I guess no one thought they were important but me." Lukas smirked when he saw the rage beating beneath Reid's temple, roaring for release as the man clutched the dagger and brought it close, under Lukas's chin. The blade scraped away some hair as it slid up and under the ashy blond there.

"Means he's been watching for weeks," Thomas said to their commander, to prompt him back from the edge. "What did he have in his teeth?"

Reid held the paper out and dropped it, his scalding blue gaze never leaving Lukas's, his trembling blade hand never pulling away.

Thomas exchanged a glance with Robert and then bent low to pick it up. "Oh, dear," he said simply. "Well . . . oh, dear." He ran his hand over his chin and looked at Reid. "He can't leave her behind now, Commander. You know this as well as I do. She won't be safe at Crow Post, not with everything that's been happening lately."

"This is bigger than my niece," grated Reid after a long moment. The blade inched back. "He is desperate, this thief. Fearing for his life, by the look of him. All of you, get back to the road and give me some time alone with this murderer. I have some answers to get out of him, and I would rather not implicate any of you in what I am about to do to him."

"I'd like to stay," Robert said.

"I'm not going either," Thomas began to say.

But Reid bit his lip until it bled, and then he hissed between his teeth dangerously. "That is not a request. That is my command. Do it, or you will regret defying me." He glared over his shoulder and pointed to the road with his knife. "*NOW!*"

CHAPTER FIVE

STONES

THE INFLUX OF NOW HOMELESS, frightened people who were kept just outside of Crow Post was adrift with rumors of Wolfshadow cult raids, and mass murders, and missing children. It was difficult enough to keep the peace and treat the wounded without the citizens of Laurel picking fights with the people of Dry Port, or the upper classes of Cressen provoking others with their accusations of alliances with the dreadful cult. And to make matters worse, the Enforcers had not stepped in, as was their sworn duty. The people had no protection.

The supplies were dwindling fast, and with so many people who were in such close quarters, disease could break out among them and spread quickly. It would turn the already terrible situation into a dire one. And it was never spoken aloud, but there was a thick apprehension among them all because the people of Cyan were not counted among these fortunate survivors.

In the meantime, John imagined very few of the leaders who were at the meeting truly knew how close they all were to disaster. He'd returned to this mess, and when he'd seen the state Crow Post was in, he'd immediately begun to snap orders to help ensure that chaos would not erupt. Then he'd advised the posted doctor here to call this meeting to order. There was a lot to discuss, and there was a lot more to do — and it all needed doing before the fast-approaching spring rains flooded the basin to the north. Before those rains turned heavier and overcame the roads and began to wash them away again this year. These people could not be allowed to idle until the waters trapped them here. It would end badly for everyone.

The meeting itself started very well, and everything went according to the agenda they had set . . . until the lead mortician, Dr. Ellie Mae, stepped in.

"I don't know what has come over your daughter," said Ellie Mae as she stormed inside, her fist clenched tightly about a small leather purse. "First, that hair-raising screaming of hers in the night, waking me out of a dead sleep next door. And then that bloody, *creepy* song that sent those poor mourning mothers into hysterics after the deaths of their children. Now *these*." There was a clinking sound as Ellie Mae emptied the small leather pouch onto the table. Six jaggedly broken, glittering glass shards spilled across the polished steel. The candlelight flickered near them, as though the glass had stolen a breath from the room.

For a moment, none among the thirty field doctors, apothecaries, botanists, attendants, brewers, emissaries, or even Crow Post's leaders, said a word. Silence had gathered, thick and heavy as a thundercloud, ready to split wide open with deafening sound.

The back of John's neck prickled as one of those shards slid across the table. The glassy item stopped merely a centimeter from his fingers, where his hands clasped each other tightly.

A single gunshot thundered outside among the hordes of refugees, and an angry scream slithered after it, and then a wolf's howl, just outside the refugees' camps. They ignored the noise, knowing the situation would be handled while they were busy getting their affairs in order.

Meanwhile, on the table before them, the shards seemed to begin to glow from within. It was faint, but a violet radiance flamed there. Men shifted uncomfortably in their seats, and Sean Heinzrich fell silent; he was unsure whether to proceed, given the hostility in Ellie Mae's glare as she directed that anger at John.

John struggled to keep his expression impassive. "We are busy, Dr. Mae," he said evenly.

But another man had leaned forward, shocked. "Are those . . . ?" It was John's friend Amos Shipwright, who was Crow Post's assigned doctor. He was the man in charge of the post. The man was more often referred to by the pseudonym of Nails.

Ellie Mae looked at John expectantly, still clutching the now empty coin purse. "Haven't you anything to say, John?"

"By the apocalypse — I've never seen so many at once," said Nails. "Nor so bright an' purple. Where did yeh get 'em?"

"Jeana," the mortician said coldly, "just retrieved them from among their daughter's things." John cringed inwardly at Ellie's accusatory look, and he wondered, what, in the broken chain, she could be angry over. Then she revealed that particular detail. "Along with the walkies that went missing last week," she vented, "and several of his brother's tools."

John lifted his gaze from the glittering stones and listened intently. His heart beat furiously against his ears, but he withheld a certain stream of words which might provoke her further. His daughter's many eccentricities made for an unwelcome topic, given the current state of affairs. "I do believe this is the last thing we need to be discussing at present," he warned instead.

Far be it from Ellie Mae to take heed in such a dark time, however. "I couldn't disconnect any of them without destroying the walkies," she said through bared teeth. "I'll have Reid or one of his men repair them as soon as he returns. If Nymeria doesn't run off with more of his tools by then. He may not have any left by the time he gets back, at this rate." Her scowl deepened. "You said you would do something about these growing problems of hers."

Sean Heinzrich cleared his throat and opened his mouth again to redirect the conversation to their previous topic. "As I was saying, Amy Nacanth, the Lady of Cressen, claims to have evidence there will be more attacks. More people will be displaced, I am afraid — "

Nails held up his left hand to silence Sean, then dug into his left breast pocket for a scratched pair of spectacles. He scraped one of the stones across the table with his long, herb-stained claws, then, and he held the thing up. Sean looked helplessly to John, and John returned his silent frustration as some of the others in the meeting began to grumble over the interruption. They quieted when the surprise on Nails's countenance deepened, when he palmed the shard and peered at it through the shadows in his closed fist. When he *harrumphed*, John's own brow creased. "I see," said Nails. "Quite interesting. Truly. From among Nymeria's things, yeh said?" he asked.

Ellie Mae nodded, her expression most grave. "Do you know what they are? Why would she be doing this, destroying our equipment to attach them?" She was more than impatient.

"Aye, I do summat know what they are," said Nails. But he rebuked her. "But yeh shouldn't have disconnected any of 'em." He eyed her good and hard. His lips smacked together several times, rolling over things he thought to say next, then settled. "Are any of 'em still intact an' workin'? I want teh see 'em. The radios, that is. Now."

Ellie Mae was taken aback by Nails's reaction. She sputtered. "What? *No!* Absolutely not! That equipment has already been distributed back to its proper owners, and I'll not have them without their radios again — "

But Nails had already moved on to another question. "These shards of glass . . . these . . . these *stones* — where'd Nymeria get 'em?" He was looking at John now.

John studied the small slivers of purple glass glittering on the table as he scratched his wiry-haired chin to keep from spitting curses. Faintly, he recalled he was in dire need of a fresh shave. "I don't know," he said, glaring, in turn, at Ellie Mae. "But I will find out."

Across from him, Taiir's face remained devoid of any glitch or twitch that might betray some sort of knowledge on the matter. "Have we forgotten tha agenda, then?" Taiir asked.

Nails waved off that question. "This is more important, I assure yeh. Of all the blabberin' mongrels here, I'da had a mind yeh'd know the trouble these pieces of glass could bring, Taiir. Yeh should know better'n any here, this hue of forbodin'."

"*When* will you be finding out?" demanded Ellie Mae. Her bow hand flexed, as though she'd just released another arrow.

John would have ordered the mortician out of the room to discuss his daughter's startling sins in private after the meeting, but he knew by Nails's reaction that it was out of the question. John was disappointed in his eldest child for the theft and the tampering, but he could do nothing about it right now. All he could do was offer the mildest thread of damage control, and then try to get them to return to the emergency at hand.

"Ellie — " he began.

"Don't you dare *Ellie* me," she said venomously, shaking the empty purse at him.

John said nothing else as he contemplated the situation as well as how best to deal with Nymeria's serious offenses. He wanted all of this pushed quickly out of the light so they could concentrate on the agenda tonight; he did not understand why Nails seemed to think these stupid stones were important.

Curse you, Ellie Mae, he thought.

Then the smell of coffee filtered in on a breeze as John's wife and brother pulled aside the canvass of sheer linen that hung across the doorway. Both entered quietly. Reid's footfall was as silent as ever, and two of his men stepped in after him and maneuvered to the right. Reid moved to the back with a solemn expression upon his countenance. He didn't look directly at John, and he said nothing, either, which was unusual. But John was preoccupied with Ellie Mae's current, rageful interruption and could ask nothing of it.

Sean again tried to make his case as others murmured their aggravation also. "I don't understand how they could be more important, Dr. Shipwright. We're soon to run out of certain supplies if that train from Edantine doesn't get to us in a couple of weeks. If more refugees — "

"Shut it, yeh noisome ferret," growled Nails impatiently. "Let me think, damn it! There's a whole baloogy I remember 'bout 'em, but what they're called an' some'a the details . . ."

Jeana's dark boots crunched over gravel again as she moved to the left and lifted her steaming cup to her lips. In the dying daylight, several of the doctors who'd been awake more than a full day stared longingly at the cracked mug in her hands, with bloodshot eyes and downturned, practically salivating mouths. Jeana winked at them as she savored its fragrance. Then she signed to John that their son was sorting herbs they'd harvested from the low tunnels for Adam, one of Crow Post's busier and more talented apothecaries. The last she'd seen of Nymeria was in the lab, asking Adam for a few things.

Ellie Mae's eye twitched. "What kind of things?" she asked. Her sassy, soul-filled *harrumph* might as well have split the earth, for all John thought. It still would not have elicited the smallest outcry of rage from Jeana. Not even a scornful, pursed lip. Jeana was most often quite patient with angry people. Calm despite it. Perhaps *in spite* of it.

John interrupted, afraid to allow another topic involving his daughter to take light. "Where are we on the water situation?" Any distraction, to put off Ellie's wrath, even if it was only for a moment longer. Jeana grinned as though she understood already what was going on, and why he was avoiding Ellie's questions.

Jeana signed to him that Adam was enjoying Nymeria's company, even though he was still finding it difficult to understand their daughter's strong, foreign accent — her unusual accent had not faded yet, and John suspected it might never.

Jeana also told him the water would hold for another year, even if the refugees doubled — or another five years if the rains continued north of them even two days more.

Ellie began to repeat her question, but at Jeana's look, she realized Jeana was not going to answer her regardless of what she asked, or how. Ellie would get absolutely nowhere. So she quieted, seemed to at last put her anger on the backburner. Jeana had always commanded that kind of respect among her peers; she was small and quiet, but her presence was fierce and her will was to be obeyed.

"Something's wrong, I know it," Ellie said at last. "Your little girl is in a fright like nothing natural, John. I've never known that child to scare for anything in the least. She started taking the walkies after she started having those nightmares that set her screaming last week."

"I don't want any more questions about my daughter right now," John said to her. "We are in a meeting, Dr. Mae."

"But is she *okay*?" Ellie demanded.

"She's *fine*," he said flatly. "She always is, always will be. Nightmares, nothing more, Dr. Mae. Now, are you done? Can we get back to the more important conversation at hand? Like Black Temple's upcoming request for more apprentices? It is getting close to the traveling season, and there are too many trips to plan to waste on discussions of my daughter's waywardness. Or perhaps we should immediately turn to another better topic, such as the attacks and who the culprit might be. Laurel is gone. So are Dry Port and Cressen. And no one really seems to know who is responsible. There are just rumors of Wolfshadow uprisings all over — which is strange, given their reclusive nature and relatively small numbers, which will never likely increase much because they eat their children. And there is the fact that their groups are scattered across the forests around Five Tower, *to the east*, and *they eat their recruits' children, too*. Several posts have been attacked nearby as well, and some of those are gone, too."

John felt his eye twitch. "Or, perhaps we should talk instead of the desperate lunatics who've been trying to rob our caravans lately, trying to find golden liberties, of all things. There are a great many things more important to discuss than my wayward daughter, with whom I *will* be speaking later today about what she's been up to — "

"Aha! They called 'em *memories* — that's the name," said Nails suddenly, bringing the conversations back around to the damned stones on the table. John felt his blood pressure rising and looked up helplessly at his brother. But Reid's eyes flashed with something when for the first time, he saw the six purple shards scattered across the polished steel surface. John opened his mouth to ask his brother how his journey had gone, but Nails continued before he had the chance to do so. His gut churned even as Nails began to speak again. "Never seen one quite so bright," said Nails. "Worth a lot in Five Tower. They were tryin' teh make 'em a'fore — " Nails looked up at John and frowned. Then he tossed the glass memory back onto the table. "Yeh know what I mean. That."

"I have seen slivers of glass like those before," commented Taiir. "Caol used to ship them. Those, he would have destroyed after tha Bright Night. Tha color became a grave offense to him."

"But what are they?" Nails's son Mark set down the knife he was sharpening and reached for the stone Nails had returned to the table.

"Keep yer grubby hands off 'em, *boy*," said Nails. "Yeh can ask yer questions. But yer eyes aren't learned enough teh discern what they are, an' yer greasy fingers better not touch 'em."

Mark scowled. "My eyes know what they see, you fat, old, plunky senile. An' my fingers are clean." Mark plucked the stone from the table, and then he kicked Nails's groaning chair out from under him when the old man's hairy upper lip quivered at him. There was a great crash, and curses billowed upward on a plume of Nails's fat, flailing limbs.

Nails roared as he folded up his spectacles, placed them carefully upon the table, and drew his axe. "Why, yeh ungrateful whelp! I'll show yeh, teh kick a chair out from unner yer elder — "

Taiir and several others moved to separate the father and son, but Jeana had already darted forward with footsteps that whispered almost as soundlessly as a wraith, and she placed a delicate hand upon Nails's shoulder as he wiped the spittle from his fat, bloodless lips. His head turned wildly, and he took a breath to shout another curse when he realized it was small, frail Jeana who'd reached out to calm him. Her flat expression tottered the old man's wrath. "Eh . . . sorry, sorry. My son irks me, is all. Just like 'is mamman. No manners, 'im."

Her thin brow arched humorously, a razor thin line of bright auburn beneath loose, chin-length locks. Nails had gotten her to raise her eyebrow, having raised his weapon. That eyebrow was — in a way — equivalent to Jeana having drawn her slender pugio and placed it beneath Nails's chin.

John swallowed against the dryness in his mouth. The smell of her coffee had made him thirsty.

Jeana cocked her head ever so slightly and wagged a finger at Nails. She clicked her tongue once, and when she nodded with her chin determinedly, her expression warned he should brook no argument.

Nails scratched at his wooly scalp. "Aww, come now, Jeana, don't make me apologize teh my mannerless boy."

Her brow rose higher.

John chuckled under his breath as he leaned to pick up the chair and set it back at the table. It was bent at an odd angle, but even as it sat on three of its four legs, he did not doubt whether Nails's weight would press that last leg back down. "My wife is fierce when it comes to one's own children. She believes parents should set the example," said John.

"Are yeh saying I am a rude, mannerless man?" Nails blubbered, his eyes wide and round and insulted. "But I wash my hands, an' I respect my elders, John. Even if most of 'em are dead. An' I don't talk with my mouth full. Why, I even say please an' thankuns! Mark, here, does none of it! Yer lucky not teh have 'im shovin' live turkeys in 'is gullet like a mad dog, or spittin' in yer coffee when yer not lookin'. He does mine, that boy! He's disrespectful, a *wild 'un!*"

Ellie Mae, arms still crossed, was still glaring at John. Still waiting. Her damned foot kept tapping against the earth, even though the sound was soft and difficult to make out through the sudden commotion.

Mark forgot he sat to Taiir's immediate left, closer than he should have, to mock Nails next. "Yes, Da," smirked Mark. "You should be a better leader an' set a better example. You — "

John nodded, and barely a fraction of a blink passed before Taiir had smacked the younger man in the back of the head. The movement was a little too eager, as though Taiir had uncorked the bottle on some great and unbearable pent-up annoyance.

"Shut it, Mark," said John. "Nails is sorry. And Nails, Mark will be sorry tonight when my brother catches him falling asleep on watch again." Mark, still holding his head, cut his gaze at John.

John motioned to his brother, and suddenly Mark realized Reid was, indeed, back. To John's humor, Taiir threatened to smack Mark again if he dared open his mouth one more time. Some of the other doctors and attendants chuckled heartily at Mark's misfortune.

When the younger man sat straight and resumed his knife sharpening, John nodded sourly with approval. "Problem solved, Jeana." Now for the next issue. He and Ellie stared at each other in a silent standoff. Her jaw ticked. So did his. Her claws tightened over her arm.

His blood pressure rose higher, until it was pulsing dangerously from his neck to his temple. The arteries felt as if they were about to pop. Damn her tapping foot. Damn that tic of hers.

He swore. She'd already opened the can, and the worms from that can were already on the table, still drawing the eyes of every man and woman present. He noted the continuing glances of curiosity, of interest, littered among even those who were as annoyed as he was. He dreaded learning more, but it was the way Nails had allowed the conversation to turn. There was no *out*, no return to the previous topic of the changing season and the journeys it entailed before the rains hit hard, or of the growing threats to the uneasy, increasingly frightened and desperate civilian population. No, their attention had been hooked like fish, and they were being reeled in. Ellie had already won with those stupid rocks.

And most unyieldingly, he wouldn't admit that he was curious as well. Not even a tiny bit. He knew next to nothing about those shards. They'd perplexed him much the same, but he'd already dismissed them in the past, preferring not to dwell on them when more important things were always at hand. It was not so easy now, not with thirty other curious faces about him. Not with Nails's obvious interest.

He sighed. A damned headache, this was. He was going to end up with an aneurysm before he ever received his first gray hair.

John leaned forward then, and he held out his hand for the delicious coffee Jeana was hoarding. "Give me that, will you? Making me thirsty, smelling those freshly brewed grounds. Haven't had a good brew from this sorry, flea-ridden lot in three days. You would think these two could boil water right and cook for themselves on the return trip from Cyan. Not so. The coffee was undrinkable, and I'm sure nothing will ever grow where I poured it out, or where they pissed on the shrubbery. I'm surprised it didn't burn a hole in the ground."

John took the cup as his wife smiled knowingly, and he inhaled the potent aroma, ignoring Taiir's and Mark's wounded expressions — and especially Ellie Mae's more furious one, for his having made yet another attempt at steering the conversation away again. "Goes right to the soul, that does," he said before throwing his head back and gulping down half the scalding cup. There was a resounding *thud* that made Mark jump and Nails take his seat as John slammed his fist onto the table.

On to it, finally. Get it out of the way so that he could get everyone to focus on what they should *still* be discussing.

"Nails. Tell me what these things are. How do you know anyone in Five Tower was trying to make them, and what are they for?" He wiped clean the dark coffee that had spilled down his chin with his collar, and when he glanced sideways at Ellie Mae, he noticed that some of the tension had finally cut itself from her rigid posture. Hopefully, it meant she accepted his acquiescence, that he was willing to ask about the damned stones.

That woman knew how to pick her moments, damn her. Just like Jeana. Whatever obstacle she aimed at, she shot down.

"Back teh the heart it is, then," said Nails as he folded his stained hands together and then unfolded them to tap on the table instead with his nails. "I don't know how they work, just that they do. Magic, I s'pose. Somethin' like it. I don't have the right equipment or trainin' teh begin teh figure 'em out an' give yeh a more scientific answer. I just know tha — "

"That's the extent of your knowledge about them, Da?" Mark exhaled, exasperated. "*Some kind of magic?*"

Nails glared at his son for a long moment, then continued. "They're usually precious stones, teh start with. Or some kinds of glass," said Nails. His fingernails tapped at the steel again. "Doesn't truly matter what is used teh make 'em, I think, as long as they're made from some kinds of clear material — somethin' yeh can see through, a'cause light passes through 'em an' holds true better. An' they're dangerous. Verily so."

Taiir grimaced. "Indeed, they are. They were a guarded secret in Five Tower, and Caol forbade tha use of them after tha Bright Night."

Nails shrugged. "Yet 'is son Eiran still got 'is nasty hands on 'em after it. Rumors of the experiments unner Five Tower spread through a certain grape vine, an' I was able teh pick some'a that such info when I was posted there. Even got meself involved a bit, a'fore the bastards ran me an' my boys off, harrassin' us as much as they did. I examined some'a his slaves — they were crazier'n crazy, but they all said the same lunatic things, they did, a kind of symptom of the shards. An' later, Eiran hired some doctor who was inteh weird sciences an' even stranger medicines, supposedly inteh magic an' souls an' all maniacal manner of other things — he's the man who took my post from unner me. I'd heard Eiran worshippin' the man's know-all as if he was some kinds of witch doctor. Never met that bastard, though. I'da given 'im a piece of my unhappier thoughts if I'da met 'im. Things changed after yeh left, Taiir. An' for the worst. Yeh were good an' lucky yeh got fed up with the corruption an' left when yeh did."

Taiir nodded gravely. "I am well aware, Amos."

"The shards shatter if yeh touch 'em, usually. Eiran still traded unusual prisoners an' slaves for 'em, though. That wacko doctor was the supplier when they got rarer'n diamond trees, but none'a them shards of 'is were as bright or stable as these. The shards he got, he had teh have 'em handled careful-like. They called 'em memories a'cause of the hallucinations they made 'is slaves start havin'. On top of that, my vine even rumored these shards teh be cursed. The thieves an' killers in the Gray Halls called it the *Violet Curse*. The *Violet*, for short." Nails shook his head, his eyes round and twinkling with admiration. "That bag should'a been filled with nothin' but sharp, lightless slivers by the time yeh'd brought them inteh here, Miss Ellie Mae. Eiran would'a paid heavily for 'em."

Sean Heinzrich cleared his throat. "How are they dangerous? And are you sure you should be handling them so casually if that is the case?"

Nails chuckled heartily. "Taiir would know more'n I would, how they're cursed."

"What else do you know on the matter?" John asked Taiir.

The warrior shook his head. "Only that Caol and Eiran took slaves deep into tha recesses of Five Tower to condition them behaviorally. It is where he had had tha stones taken also. Too few knew what tha stones were for, precisely, or what they could do. If Eiran is still experimenting with them, he has found them useful in some ill capacity."

Mark went back to sharpening his knife. He glanced once more to the glittering glass and sucked on his canine with a look that assessed the value such shards could bring them versus the cons of dealing with someone from Five Tower. Mark was more aware than most here how shady some of the councilmen were in that city; he'd commented about the ill things he'd seen when he'd lived there with his father and his brother.

The slithering scrape made by Mark's blade on the whetstone was the only sound for a moment before John's brother broke the silence.

"I want to see them closer." Reid moved a couple of the men to the side as he made his way to the table. When he touched one of the shards, the candlelight flickered, and the purple radiance again became a bright, brilliant color in the temporary darkness. When the flame flickered lively upon the candle wick once more, however, the light in the stones began to fade. Reid sucked in his breath, perplexed by what had just happened, and he let go of the shard.

"See? The stones seem teh adhere teh an' mimic circuits an' data an' the like," said Nails. "Five Tower had some old tech they'd dug up from some councilman's collection. These beauties supposedly got 'em workin' when nothin' else would — but only temporarily, mind yeh. My vine said even the shoddy shards they had did some use, but none'a them ever lasted very long. They were tryin' for quite a while teh fix that problem, teh see why these damnable shards worked — an' then why suddenly they wouldn't. An' I don't know where they came from, neither. None but Caol an' 'is innermost circle would."

Nails scratched at his fat, bearded jowls and readjusted his spectacles to peer down at the one pinched between his thumb and forefinger. "These shards don't work the way old tech did. Don't need no batteries or green chips, don't even need no wiring, not really. Some'a them caused electromagnetic pulses, from what I heard. Weird stuff about 'em. Weird. As I said. Sometimes the lights'd explode a'cause of 'em gettin' too near. Stranger rumors'n that, too, I'd heard. Yeh want a load of liberties, or more knowledge about 'em, take 'em teh Five Tower. Eiran would pay yeh well for 'em. If he didn't kill yeh an' just take 'em instead. But yeh'd be wise teh keep Caol from hearin' about 'em, that'd be a death sentence waitin' for anyone as stupid as much. 'Cept Eiran, I'd s'pose, bein' his son an' all. Surely the man wouldn't kill his own son for that trickle of defiance."

John shook his head, though. "No one is taking them to Five Tower," he said. "I am not willing to send another into that dangerous city just to find out more about these rocks. I think they should be destroyed when and if it becomes safe to do so." He looked about, studying the other faces among them, and he saw Taiir nod at his wisdom with approval. "I'm sure none of you want to deal with the leaders there, anyway, just as the lords there want nothing to do with our guild." There was a murmur of agreement from among them all, save Reid, whose dark expression only became graver.

Ellie Mae's foot had finally fallen silent. Perhaps she was also perturbed by the idea that the shards were more than just glass. That they were something alien, something not many people understood.

The thing that struck John the most was that there were men supposedly willing to kill for them. Usually Nails's intel on Five Tower's goings-on was quite on the mark, so he didn't feel as though he needed to question the validity of it now, even if it was strange. And Taiir's invaluable knowledge had helped them avoid conflict since the day he'd arrived, seeking employment at Crow Post just months after John and Jeana had rescued Nymeria from the horrible city.

"Dishonest men," nodded one of the apothecaries among them. "City's full of them. Overrun with killers, and slavers, and thieves. It would be best to destroy those things."

Jeana snapped her fingers, and Nails turned in his chair. It groaned, threatening to collapse under his massive weight again. "What is it, yeh mighty, scary little woman? Goin' teh frighten poor old Nails again, that it?"

John took another swig of the deliciously aromatic beverage she'd brought in. Then he translated the quick motions of her hands. The others usually understood her, he knew, but not quite so easily when caffeine had her hands fluttering faster than hummingbirds' wings, as it did now.

"She wants to know . . . If they have figured out how to even remotely get these shards to work with old tech, even if only for a little while, then why haven't they tried to sell them off?"

"I wouldn't know," said Nails.

"There are people who would shed blood to have some working tech from the Modern Civilization," John pointed out. "All we have left of that bygone era are books that are next to worthless because it took old tech to build the tech in them, walkies and radios that only a handful of tinkerers know how to fix or make, a few thousand working vehicles it takes forever to get scrap parts made or salvaged for, and not enough guns to fight any kind of large-scale war. There are not enough smiths with the equipment or knowledge to enable such a war, either."

"It seems to say that greed and fortune are not on tha agenda in Five Tower this time," agreed Taiir, "even though that is usually tha soul of its stain."

"So what, then, is their intention with the shards?" asked John. But no one seemed to have an answer. "Why the secrecy? Why be willing to shed blood to obtain them, or to become so paranoid as to want to kill to be rid of them?"

Jeana nodded, approving of his added questions toward the end. "And if they aren't trying to jack away poor merchandise for a quick liberty as they do with everything else," he wondered, "what are they really doing with those things? Reviving old tech can't be the extent of it."

Thomas, who'd been silent until that moment, decided to remind them of something more dangerous. "Keep in mind, there are other sinister things which could, in some way, be related to the rumor of this 'violet curse.' The forests around Five Tower are sacred to the Wolfshadow cult, and they have rarely ventured from them before. Perhaps whatever is going on in Five Tower is driving them this way. They won't take children they think are cursed; they wouldn't dare risk it, as they are a superstitious and paranoid folk. What isn't eaten of the dead become their clothes, their weapons, their baubles, their coin."

Thomas continued as John pondered what he was saying. "And Five Tower has always enjoyed some twisted relationship with the cult, so they've never bothered to try to drive them away. They've even traded children to them to keep them near. That fact has been proven several times." Thomas's gaze flickered to the stones on the table, briefly. "The sightings and the attacks upon the refugees and their homes is worth the same questioning as the shards on the table. What has caused their movement? Did it begin after the Bright Night two years ago, or is this more recent? And are *they* really the ones stealing children? Could it be Five Tower instead, looking for more victims? Or could it be someone else? And children are not the only ones missing."

John's gaze flickered to his wife. She'd paled at the reminder of the wolfmen, and her fingers clutched the handle of her slender pugio tightly. She did not try to add to the conversation, however, but simply stood there, listening patiently, waiting for some clue that would tie all of this together. Just as they all were.

He hated that Nails had been correct, after all. The stones had brought up some important points that might otherwise have been overlooked.

"All right," said Nails. "So then we'll destroy these shards away from camp. An' Ellie Mae, yeh can do me the favor of lettin' me examine yer own radio after we're done here, as I imagine it's also been tampered with by Dr. Ivan's little one. Back teh the agenda, then. Sean. Where were we? Yeh'd said somethin' a'fore our chief mortician walked in earlier, somethin' of the water supply bein' contaminated upriver, near the Cyan fork — "

"We already took care of Cyan and its riverside division during our cleanup assignment," John said. "Which is why I am present in Crow Post in the first place, and why I asked you to call this meeting. We have other issues to resolve, the first of which — "

Reid cleared his throat as a darker cloud seemed to descend upon him, and John allowed him to speak. "Before we move on entirely, Amos. John. I think I may have someone who can answer another part of this puzzle about the shards. Or, at least, why anyone would want the dreaded things."

Nails considered his request and then allowed it. "If yeh can tell us all a bit more'n we already know, I'd welcome it. They're a conundrum — an' I don't like conundrums that are of no medical or helpful value. I like 'em worse when they are dangerous, an' I know these things *are*. Or *can* be, at any turn. What's whispered about 'em is dreadful, in any right."

Reid turned his head as he stepped forward, and he nodded to his men near the room's opening. The men were Robert and Thomas, both of whom were very big men with scowls that could shatter mirrors — and send the pieces flying, too. "Bring him in," said Reid.

The command startled John. Perhaps this had something to do with Reid's perplexing mood, he thought.

There was a murmur along the table that spread throughout the enclosure as both the warriors under Reid's command obeyed. Both warriors disappeared for a bit.

"Absolutely," said John, and he placed his hands calmly upon the table and then clasped his fingers tightly. "We'll just talk about the glass and Five Tower all night, then. Why not? The plans for the travel season can wait, and so can the supplies we are supposed to be dealing for. Everything else can wait, too, while we're at it."

There was a short-lived, raucous commotion outside, and then there was the hoarse voice of some young boy whose voice cracked with approaching manhood. "How many times do I have to tell you, I *wasn't* trying to steal anything, fellas? Can't we make some kind'a deal? I — "

"Be quiet and go in," hissed Thomas.

Mark kept sharpening his knife, but his head had tilted a twinge with renewed interest. Taiir's brows drew together, however. He seemed to recognize the voice, and by the set of his jaw, he didn't seem too happy about it, either. And Ellie Mae had forgotten her anger entirely. Her hand rested instinctively upon the leather-wrapped grip of the bow she always carried, as though ready to pull it from her shoulder and arm it. She and Robert shared a look — hers questioning, his gently telling her to wait.

"I'll have you know, I am a nobleman's *son*. My father can *pay* you — "

The *boy* fell through the awning and collapsed at the end of the long, curved table. When the sack over his head was yanked back, greasy, dirty, blond hair fell past his chin and obscured his black eyes. Small prickles of blond beard poked through as he lifted his filthy face. He raised his dirty hands and wiped away the fresh blood coming down from his nose. Then he spat in the dirt and looked up. He smirked comfortably at them all, seeming to think his game wasn't yet over. It was a slimy expression, and his dark eyes glittered, seeming to drink in everything about the people before him. "To what do I owe the honor, fine doctors and cohorts of the Glass Chain?" He bowed as though he was in some court, although he was already upon his knees and could not bow much lower.

"This man," said Reid, his voice low in his throat and more menacing that John had heard in a long time, "has some interesting things he can tell us about what's been going on."

"Ahh," said the blond man dejectedly when he recognized Reid. He wasn't a boy, though his voice had previously cracked like one. Now he cast the falsetto aside, and he lifted his shoulders higher and studied each of them, until they grew uncomfortable under his cutting black gaze. "Well, I'd hoped I could persuade a softer heart or mind, but *you're* the one who's here, Range Commander . . . It *was* worth the try." The haughty, irritating note to his speech crawled under John's skin and scraped his nerves raw. Instantly, he did not like this man. Judging by the faces of his equals, this captive had a similar effect upon them all.

"Who is he?" Nails demanded, his hand upon his axe again. "He ain't one'a ours, I'd know a mop like that, runnin' 'round camp. He follow yeh from Edantine an' Hagenhold? Has the look of a weasel, all right. I bet he'd cut an' run first chance he gets. Has that look about 'im; cut throat, then ghost."

"Gentlemen," said the blond man. "I — " Reid's knife was under his throat before he could murmur another word, and so it was that John noticed Reid's knuckles were caked with dried blood. Then those thin, long fingers of the stranger's curled in the air, although they were not quite bold enough to clasp the blade. The blond man's healthy teeth flashed in a grimace of a smile, and he made a sound in the back of his throat. "Please remove that . . . ? It doesn't do the nerves any good, you know — "

Reid did not release him. Instead, he knelt close and whispered into the man's ruined ear. The knife pressed deeper, until it drew blood. "Best be cautious with your next words. If you try to beguile anyone here with another lie, this knife will enter your mouth and exit through the back of your skull, and I will do it so slowly that your screams will gurgle and weep. Do not dare doubt my sincerity or my sense of judgement. Remember how little escapes me and what I will do again if you do not cooperate." He then addressed the men and women in the enclosure, but he did not look at John. "And all of you be careful what you say or do in front of him. This man is called Lukas. He is a spy, and a murderer."

"A *murderer*, have we?" said Mark, his features twisted with menace.

"A *spy?*" Sean Heinzrich was equally disgusted.

Reid nodded and released Lukas from his knife.

"I should guess," said Lukas, his tone unduly polite as his hands came together slowly. He rubbed at the chafed skin beneath the bindings on his wrists, but he left the blood upon his throat to ooze, wary of provoking Reid's blade again for too sudden or extended a motion. "You want me to tell them about my dealings with Five Tower. I'm sorry — Two Tower? Twin Tower . . . Whatever it is they are being called now by outsiders. They should be, anyway; there aren't five towers anymore about the proud bastards. Their name should be Franken Fingers." Lukas chuckled, amusing himself despite the threats and having very obviously been beaten. "Crippled Fist." Another laugh bubbled up from the lunatic's throat. "Broken Teeth? I can keep going. Bastards deserve the worst names. *Crooked Fingers*. That's the one . . . Do you know how hard it is to rename a city properly . . . ?"

Reid sheathed his knife, quite aggravated. "You will tell them everything." A look passed between them, and Lukas hesitated despite Reid's baneful expression.

John shifted in his seat. A sinister feeling that was laced with dread began to pool in him. He didn't want to believe this was going to go where it seemed it might go.

Then Reid approached the table and bent forward to speak to John and Nails quietly. The blond man watched them warily, but there was no way for him to hear as they spoke in low tones. "Most of what he has to say somehow has a lot to do with Nymeria. It's bad. It's very, very bad."

The startling revelation set John's stomach to roiling.

Mark objected. "But they don't know about John's daughter, not unless — " Mark shut his mouth when he saw Taiir's threatening look. Then he remembered Lukas in the vicinity, and he said no more on that matter.

"No one there besides Timothy knows," said John quietly. "Taiir trusts him greatly, and I trust Taiir. The two of them have many times given us intel that has kept our guildsmen from harm by any of Five Tower's ill-intending associates, so I have no reason to question either of them."

"Then what could he know that has something to do with Nymeria?" Mark asked curiously.

John shook his head. He wasn't sure he knew how to handle that news.

Nails waved the expectant prisoner on. "Go ahead, yeh right worthless rodent." Even as Nails spoke, John felt his gut twisting further with that slithering dread.

"We're listening," John added, his voice hard.

Lukas did not look at Reid directly when he made his next disgusting proposal. "I'd be more willing if I received some form of *payment* for this information — "

Nails drew his axe and pointed it at him. "Get teh talkin', yeh rotten, pale-haired fidget. So we can hurry up an' toss yeh teh Mercy's dogs. They're hungry, 'em dogs. Leathered strip of scrawny, yeh are, won't feed 'em much. But it's better'n naught, an' they'd have somethin' teh chew on for a mighty bit."

They heard the sudden vicious barking of the guard dogs on the other side of the camp then, and Lukas strained at the bonds on his wrists uncomfortably as the cacophony continued to rage. Several men shifted uneasily. John did as well, although he was more worried about his daughter than the idea of the dogs eating the killer alive.

"Of course," said Lukas. His head tilted very slightly to acknowledge Nails's steady, polished axe as it gleamed in the candlelight. "Eiran and his league of cursed hunters are about to kill all of you, and the Enforcers won't be helping you. You're on your own."

No person was left inattentive after such a dreadful statement.

Mark's dark gaze lingered on the stones again, and Lukas's followed. The blond man's jaw unhinged, but he snapped his mouth shut and looked away from them quickly, as though he knew exactly what they were and what they could do. He acted as if even looking at them could set them off. He didn't seem to be in any hurry to speak again.

"An' just what do you mean by that?" asked Mark dangerously.

Lukas offered a cold, unfeeling smile. "I meant exactly what I said." To Reid, he then said, "I am sorry, but your friends here seem to know only the barest touch of Five Tower's great and many schemes. May I have a chair? This may take a while."

"You can lie in the dirt like an animal or sit on your own feet," said Mark. "Now let's start over from the beginning. What are you doing working for Eiran? An' how much could he be paying you for that dangerous sort of treachery, for it ever to be worth any sort of trespass against Black Temple? I know he's into slavery an' killin', an' thievery an' worse. Who did you murder, an' what secrets are you trying to steal an' sell?"

"Secrets?" Lukas asked innocently. "You have the wrong idea. I'm no *ordinary* spy. My specialties are . . . *niche*. I was a merchant from Tallil, and an emissary who negotiated with both Black Temple and Five Tower before I became what I am. And you would not precisely understand my occupation as it is now. It is not a path any man would have chosen for himself."

John doubted the murderer's claim, but Taiir verified it. "He was what he says he was, and more," Taiir said quietly. "He is one of Caol's crazed servants now, though, not Eiran's. I saw tha change in him firsthand. Before, and after."

"Before and after," hissed Lukas. "You're the one who dragged me down into the dungeons for them to do what they did," snarled Lukas. "I — "

"You have not found tha golden-eyed one Caol sent you after yet, have you?" Taiir asked. "Rhael, that is?"

Lukas gritted his teeth but said nothing. The question had infuriated him.

Taiir prodded further. "I did hear you were tha one responsible for tha man's escape in tha first place, Lukas. That it was intentional, to spite Caol and his son for what they had done to you."

"I don't know what you're talking about." Lukas glanced at Reid again, hesitant to continue. Reid simply glared back at him. There was so much hatred in Reid's eyes that John couldn't for the life of himself understand it.

"Go ahead. Explain it to them," Reid commanded.

"Caol has unfinished business with Rhael. And Eiran wants more of *them*," said Lukas. "More hunters, loyal without fault. He has more of a twisted mind for getting his wishes, and he isn't as conservative as his father Caol. He's not afraid of the consequences his father learned the hard way. He does what he pleases, and what he pleases is . . . not even in Five Tower's interest. He'll break every last link in the Glass Chain, flushing out every member of your guild to execute or to turn to the slavery of the Blood Light. Eiran's obsession with the strange energy in those pieces of glass will eventually earn him a throne if he is not stopped. And everyone, including the Enforcers, will have to bow to him as a king."

"He would have to try to remove the entire Enforcers' Alliance for that to work," Ellie Mae said sourly. "They would stop that sort of madness. And we're here to serve the wearyworn. That includes Five Tower, despite its many wicked citizens. Why would he, or anyone else, want to destroy us?"

"*Why* doesn't matter so much as *how*, unless it is to motivate others to do your work for you," Reid said with a grimace. "But they've already implemented part of their plan," he said. He paused to let those words sink in. "It's been years in the making, and the beginning stages of the takeover have already been carried out. Strategic attacks have begun all around us. The refugees outside are proof of the stirrings of his desire for war, and the evidence I've seen suggests it is all tied to Five Tower. Why else would the cities who have been attacked only be the ones who most strongly support and work with Black Temple? I'd already suspected this for a few months now. This only confirms my suspicions."

Thomas spoke again. "In every attack thus far, we've found nothing left of our guild at all. Even the banners were burned away. The hospitals and apothecaries and plant nurseries were utterly demolished, as though whoever attacked wanted Black Temple's mercy to be forgotten. Everything related to us was set to flame."

And then Reid dealt another harsh revelation to collaborate Lukas's heinous claim. "I've also learned that at every place that has been hit, the Enforcers were recalled a week before for various reasons. My men and I are concerned by the amount of evidence there is to support everything Lukas has told me — even some of the more unnatural things he has claimed."

Reid nodded to the stones then. "Unfortunately, the stones on the table in front of you seem to play a major part in everything else that has been happening. We need to worry about this problem before everything else that is on our plates. No one will be safe this season, the apprentices least of all."

John sighed. "How does Five Tower plan to kill us all if they lost over half their population on the Bright Night two years ago? Thousands more were injured. They couldn't have recovered so quickly. It would have taken generations."

Lukas shook his head, smirking to himself as the faces of the men and women among them stared blankly at him. It was as though he felt he should not have to answer that question, as though the answer was obvious. The smugness upon his visage hinted he still had some master plan for having ever been brought here at all. He seemed too comfortable as he sat before them, even as he was bound and bleeding and playing the role of a thief who'd gotten caught.

John felt a strong urge to unsheathe his knife and gut him. It was uncanny how the smug man irked him.

"Well, isn't *that* a nice question?" Lukas grinned. The expression was foul upon him.

"We'll have to get back to that one," said Reid. His jaw ticked, and those blood-crusted knuckles of his cracked. "There is more." His scuffed boot tapped Lukas's bruised leg, and the blond prisoner cringed as though the appendage were broken.

John had thought that was all of it. He felt sick, hearing there was more.

Lukas cut his black gaze sideways. "When Eiran's hunters get a hold of me, they'll figure out I've told you everything." He held up his hands at Reid's murderous look. "You'd better keep me under heavy guard after this in order to ensure my protection."

"You're lucky I have enough restraint not to have gutted you myself," said Reid. "This man is my brother. How do you think he'll take it?" When Lukas blanched, Reid's fists curled again.

"How will I take what?" John asked.

But his brother tapped Lukas's injured leg again. "Keep talking. Tell them the rest."

Mark stopped studying the tip of his blade for a flawless edge and pointed the weapon at Lukas. "What he's said doesn't explain why *he* is *here*. An' I don't mean that he was caught, either. Could have been a robbery, could have been some bounty hunter after him . . . If he knows all this, an' it's true, an' he's chasing down some ghost they've sent him after, why is he *here*?"

"I commanded you to tell them everything," Reid said again. "So go ahead and tell them how you got involved in this mess to start with."

Lukas hesitated to say anything.

When Reid glared at Lukas and touched the handle on his dagger again, Lukas cringed. "All right." He held his hands up, surrendering. "All right. I will tell them everything I told you, Range Commander." There was silence for a moment, and Lukas sat on his heels. He spat crimson on the ground again and then flung his filthy, curling hair from his face. His upper lip sported a nasty cut — a fresh one, too, for how it bled still. "It started years ago," began Lukas. "It's why *everything*. Caol and I were still allies, not master and servant. He hadn't turned on me yet," said Lukas.

Then he began to tell them a tale Reid seemed to believe was true, but whose details were too incredulous to be so. "Some obscure group had set up a heavily guarded dig site. Their weapons were strange — not like ours but better. We wanted them, and we made plans to steal them. My men and I remained above while Caol and his friend, this golden-eyed freak who went by the name of Rhael, went in with a small group of their own men to scope our mark. They returned, gathered their forces, and then moved into the deeper levels of the excavation for a proper attack. We were to guard their backs from the surface. But several hours later, the ground began to tremble, and then several hours after that, they all emerged from underground, like cockroaches escaping the light. None even cared to fight one another. They were all running from something *else*."

Lukas paused for a moment to wipe the blood from his throat where it had begun to congeal. "Some of them had clawed their own eyes out, we saw," he continued, "and many had killed themselves, we later learned. Some attacked everyone and everything around them in a blind, mad rage, and some began screaming — and some of those went on screaming until they died. The half-mad ones who survived it said there were monstrous creatures down there — demons, as black as jet and as tall as trees nearly a decade old. The creatures had swarmed the pit they'd found down there and had attacked the others, and more than a hundred men had died. They told us an ancient wall had collapsed during the excavation and revealed some kind of unholy tomb, with pillars engraved in glowing glass runes, and bright, violet lightning arcing and striking man, tomb, and demon alike. Several said the pit itself was filled with cursed magic, that the unstable energy had burned a lot of men alive, and many others had been turned into red-eyed flesh eaters by the demons there."

Lukas wove an enrapturing tale, and even John found himself drawn into its horror. It was worse for him than most because the creatures were the same ones his daughter described. The coincidence was too frightening to consider. Reid *had* told him Lukas's confession had a lot to do with her. Was this that something?

"Caol lost his nerve over whatever he witnessed down there, but Rhael led them all back to the surface. When they reached us, they had something contained in a chest that was large enough to hold some kind of creature. The chest was covered, but I saw the violet light emanating from it, and so did a few others among us — we were fools to think it was something valuable. The light it gave was the same as that violet in the glass before you. We should have realized that it was the color of a promise of death, of madness. Whatever was in that trunk, they took it to Five Tower. And Caol was nearly as mad as the rest of his men. He was never the same after that night. He still employs men to guard him from the darkness at every hour of the night. We dismissed it as hysteria — we weren't down there, after all. My men and I eventually made light of it all; it was a mistake we didn't think we'd regret later. But Caol never forgot it. Neither did Eiran."

Lukas was angry now, but Reid kept his hand upon the dagger. "Don't quit now," said Reid. "Tell them everything you told me, and not a word less, or I will keep my promise and cut open your throat and toss you in with the dogs myself. It'd be fitting retribution for what you've done."

The murderer shook his head, disgusted with the order but heeding the warning. "It was Rhael's idea for Caol and himself to work together. Then Caol decided I was worthless and betrayed me. My men were slaughtered in the middle of our next weapons deal — those who survived were dragged into the depths of Five Tower alongside me, and they put those unholy shards of glass inside our flesh."

Several of the doctors seemed befuddled by this, as they did not understand what putting glass in flesh could accomplish besides a splinter and an infection. Many were only slightly less than outraged that Lukas had been dragged in to tell such a bizarre tale. But Nails seemed to believe it. Reid was heavily concerned over it. And John and a few others had an idea what Lukas meant, and it chilled them when Lukas confirmed it.

"I survived," said Lukas. "None of my men did, and neither did hundreds of others they later betrayed, or captured, or bought. They experimented on us with the glass and the energy in it, and like me, the others screamed because of the visions of the blood and the death and the agony. Then they found some of the survivors from the first night, from the pit. And then more strange people began appearing with violet eyes, people who'd been cursed by the Blood Light. So they took them, too. All of them. Called us *Violet Cursed*. Everyone who was cursed to see the creatures in the shadows, to hear the voices in the visions and the dreams and the night itself — they took anyone who could feel the beings in the darkness or hear the voices that were always hissing, calling for some *one* or some *thing*."

"Dear skies above," Nails exhaled, and he folded up his spectacles and put down the shard. He pushed the shard away from himself with his glasses, now quite mindful and wary of the thing.

Lukas went on, and he stared at the bonds on his wrists as he spoke what he remembered plainly, no fancy words or nerve-curdling haughtiness.

"Later, Rhael wanted out because his agenda had been different from Caol's from the beginning. He decided to leave, but he was the only one who understood whatever it was they had. He was the one who'd kept the experiments running properly — and from what I could gather, he wasn't an evil man. I believe he truly wanted to help everyone who'd been affected, including *me*. But he couldn't work with Caol because that bastard's heart is as black as the creatures they said were in that pit.

"After Rhael escaped with his life — and with whatever he took — Caol tried to continue the experiments. He failed, and badly. That failure caused the Bright Night, and it killed his wife when the experiment backfired, and he's cursed the color ever since. Blamed it on everything except for the truth. Violet offends him. It used to be his wife's favorite color supposedly, but because it killed her and destroyed his city, it was completely purged under his order. Violet is the color of the Shamed now. He's even gone to have the color removed from the banners of his own family name. To wear it or to keep anything of its color is to invite torture and then death."

Lukas twisted his wrists under the ropes again, trying to loosen them for a more comfortable fit, and he continued. "But Caol's son Eiran never gave a smidgen of pig sludge when Caol himself washed his hands of it all and settled for those bloodier, more practical solutions to his goals. Eiran continued the experiments in secret, and now he has a new supplier, one who was a Black Temple doctor slimier than Caol himself ever was. The man's name, I do not remember. But he bears a moon-shaped scar across the left side of his face. His left eye is blue, and his right is black. He's taken women and children and done things to them. And the screams that come from his chambers in the dungeon put what was done to *us* in a *kinder* light."

"A moon shaped scar, you said? One blue eye . . ." Sean Heinzrich exclaimed. "But that is Abel Orthwit — and he's a murderer. He was supposed to have been executed at the Reformation fourteen years ago when they found him guilty of the crimes charged against him. He murdered a whole village, releasing a disease among them — just like what happened in Cyan recently. He'd been paid to do it by a man from Five Tower; my cousin found the evidence. And Abel had the dread cult's worship paraphernalia in his home in Cressen. There was even a pair of hands, cooking in a pot on the stove."

Lukas shrugged. "Then he escaped, and another was executed in his place. If it is the same man, he's under a different name now. And he wouldn't be the first from Black Temple to skip his sentence that way. Or the last. Hell, the doctor who helps him is equally wicked. We saw what was left of the victims they experimented on. One or two *may* have survived it. And the rest of us? We only wanted to be free of the curse. Many killed themselves because *promises* of freedom were not good enough. The rest of us felt that an end committed by our own hand was the final stain that would give us entirely to the creatures. We preferred the desperate, mad blindness that drove us to trust the word of those men, that they would free us at the end of our loyal service. We believed ignorantly that if Eiran and his father knew how to curse us with the Blood Light, surely they also knew how to reverse it. They had already claimed to have freed others who had served them well. We were fools to believe them — I was, especially.

"So that is why I've been doing Caol's dirty work for longer now than I would ever have wished. And now I'm free of the visions, and yet it is not because of him. Something else is happening. The paradigm is shifting. The creatures in the darkness are waking up, one at a time, and together they are calling louder. And even though the brunt of it is gone from me, I know in my bones that I am still cursed. Why is it, do you think, Commander, that I said it was better to be a prisoner of Black Temple than a servant of Five Tower? I would truly rather perish in a cell or work a lasting and miserable penance than return to the hell I've seen in Five Tower. I would certainly be safer at the Reformation, and I would no longer be receiving orders to kill or hurt anyone for the false promise of freedom."

"We don't give a damn about your fearfulness or your yearning for freedom," said Reid. "Tell them why Eiran and Caol wanted the shards, what they were using them for," said Reid.

"To build an army, of course. Men loyal to the death, desperate to outlive the madness forced upon us — what more could such a man want? No one is more driven than a madman with cause to avoid his darkest terror. None can be more cruel, more uncaring, or more desperate to obey. Myself, I was never a man of bloodshed. The most I'd ever done was cheat and lie in the name of money and glory. I didn't risk lives, or take them. I'd never harmed another man, woman, child, or even animal. I shrank from the idea of killing. I was, in every sense of the word, as honest as a politician could get. But those ethics meant nothing against the Violet Curse. Honor means nothing in the presence of the Blood Light. Nothing is more terrifying than watching these creatures search about for you, getting closer and closer every time you commit a murder and receive its shadowy phantom mark — not after seeing what those things have done to others like me, whom they *have* caught."

John leaned forward. "So Eiran is creating an army?" he asked gravely. He was not interested in the paranoid, paranormal claims. He was interested in the real threats. "How many others like you are working for Eiran?"

Someone cursed under his breath over the ridiculousness of Lukas's claims, and Nails cut his eyes icily in the angered doctor's direction. "Shut it," Nails said, "or I'll cut yer tongue out, too. Anythin' come out'a the Gray Halls, I think twice over. Been fierce, terrifyin' rumors same as these for years, though they rarely got farther'n the gates of that city. Yeh'd be a stupid man teh ignore even this crazed fidget's weaselly, odd words 'bout it all." Nails turned his head back to Lukas and narrowed his eyes at him. "Answer Dr. Ivan's question, yeh brawny waste of a talkin' corpse. How many others?"

"Each cursed man is worth fifty seasoned warriors," said Lukas slowly, his lips drawn tight over his teeth. "And there are well over a hundred of us, plus the horde of the stranger ones who went missing before the Bright Night. The deranged are the most dangerous. The worst of them have lost the ability to speak, and when they're released, they kill indiscriminately. We are all loyal — of sorts — to Eiran. None serve Caol directly, except me. I am the last of his hunters. One of the longest surviving, and one of the sanest."

Taiir shrugged. "I admit, I am surprised tha other lords decided to proceed with Caol's mad plans, after all. I had thought they had put Caol in a corner where he was unable to carry out tha promises of his crazed rants against Black Temple and tha Enforcers' Alliance. I thought they feared tha idea, believing it would bring attention to them all and ruin their prospects in tha slave trade and their other . . . interests."

Lukas snarled at the dark warrior, and then he spat in the dirt again. "The other lords are all dead, Taiir, except the ones Caol has paid or frightened into submission — or those who were more powerful than him but already liked the idea anyway. And I never dealt with *those*. But no, these recent activities are all Eiran, the repugnant torturer. Caol removed himself from all the paranormal treachery after the Bright Night. And as I said, I do not *quite* serve Eiran. I still serve Caol's wishes, but only because Eiran does not stand in the way of it. Eiran has the rest of the hunters to command, and he sees me as broken and useless, as do the rest of the hunters he's made. I haven't yet completely lost my mind as they have. Only a fraction . . . It's a struggle. So I do the killing, the murdering, the enslaving, and the thieving for them both. But most namely for Caol, if it does not interfere with the other hunters' objectives."

"So explain why the Enforcers aren't stepping in to help," Mark said.

Lukas laughed. "Oh. *That.*" He wiped blood from his nose again and leaned back lazily. "If the High Commander Avery Ramont had ever suspected what was going on, he would have easily put a stop to all of this before things had escalated to where they are now. Caol already planned for all of it decades ago, what with how little love there was between him and the leader of the Enforcers' Alliance. He did not want Avery to be able to be tempted into the fold. He was discreet about it."

Ellie Mae choked back what sounded like a strangled mew as Lukas continued.

"He knew it was impossible to organize a direct attack on Black Temple or the Enforcers, even if it was a quiet one. Both are too large and too well distributed across the continent," grinned Lukas. "A direct attack on either would have been a few small skirmishes, and then the flame that was Five Tower's objective would have been extinguished. Snuffed out in but a few quiet battles. He always said the most effective enemy is your closest friend; the blade you never see coming."

"Are yeh saying High Commander Avery Ramont is dead?" asked Nails.

"I'm saying worse," replied Lukas. "The whole alliance has no idea it's been compromised. Caol's allies are among them."

"I am going to be sick, I think," murmured Ellie Mae. "I didn't realize the glass would lead to all of this."

"It's not too late to cut out the rot," said Reid. "The wise choice for Caol would have been to place a handful of men he trusted in their ranks, in crucial places. I've a few men with the same kind of training who know what to do to pinpoint the infiltrators, as well as how to quietly get rid of them. We must avoid outright confrontation or blatant accusation, and pretend we know nothing. This will ensure we remain discreet. My men as well as our contacts among the Enforcers will help flush these rats out and get them arrested by their own."

"So yeh already have a plan then?" asked Nails incredulously.

Reid nodded once. "I always have a plan. In the event I don't, I know ways around ways. My job is to be the ear, the trap, and the dagger. It's my job to ensure the safety of the guild, its members, and those who help us."

"Next, we'll be worshippin' *yer* know-all," chuckled Nails as he breathed for what seemed the first time in half an hour. "Yer a bloody witch strategist if yeh have it figured out already, I tell yeh."

"There is one major pitfall," said Reid, and he looked at every face in the dark room with an intensity that made them stir. "We have to avoid starting a war with the Enforcers over anything trivial, even if one of them tries to provoke us into action. We cannot risk upsetting their entire order by allowing ourselves to act without weighing those actions very strenuously. Our steps will need to be cautious, and we will need to coordinate with Saura's instructions diligently in the matter, whether it becomes personal or not. We will work together most tentatively." He then added. "If any of you don't think you can do this effectively, remove your signet now and leave the ranks. You should rejoin the refugees and focus solely on doing what you can to keep them from squabbling among one another. They'll need the guidance."

"We overlooked something with tha Enforcers," said Taiir.

John closed his eyes to regather himself.

"What is it?" Nails asked.

"What do we do in tha event that High Commander Avery Ramont is not dead but a prisoner?" asked Taiir. "What if freeing him alerts these infiltrators?"

"If that is the case, we will not free him," Reid commanded. "We will do what the guild did for Saura's great grandmother a century ago when she was taken hostage by the angered nobleman of Feilmein during her pilgrimage through Arsennia."

Nails smiled warmly at that. "Ah, now that's a clever thought. Aye, it is. Excellent point." His thoughts then turned to the opposite scenario. "An' yet, what if Avery is alive, takes back 'is guild, an' decides teh rampage? Are we goin' teh take our business teh 'im, then? He'll end up causin' a lot'a innocent deaths in 'is anger, an' I doubt he'll be workin' with us easily if he's all focused on that wrath. Too proud an' arrogant on a normal day, anyway."

"Tha foulest fortune," sighed Taiir. "What a dangerous time, it is."

John and many others nodded quietly, no words in their mouths. And none removed their signets. All were willing to face difficulty.

Ellie Mae pulled at her braid worriedly. "We'll need to send a messenger to Saura immediately." She eyed the stones on the table with new respect, and wonder. "And we need to find out where your daughter got those."

"I agree," said Nails.

Then Old Jacobs, one of Ellie's morticians, said he would send his son the moment the meeting adjourned.

Mark addressed Reid aggressively, then. "Now why was he where he left *corpses*? What brought his chase across your path?"

CHAPTER SIX

CHILD

REID CONSIDERED HIS NEXT WORDS carefully — John could see the hesitance. He swore he saw a pained shadow roll across Reid's expression, but it was just a brief flicker, there and then gone before he was absolutely sure he saw what he thought he saw. "I found Lukas rummaging through one of our inbound supply trains, our men dead about him. He had this in his teeth, trying to hide it when he fled from us."

Reid removed from a satchel belted to his waist a rolled-up bit of paper with a broken seal depicting a silver feather upon it. The seal was similar to the mark of the secret order within Black Temple's upper echelons, used only by a select few who were graced with leadership . . . But it was oriented differently, more like . . .

But it couldn't be.

John then noticed the canister was gone, and half the page was missing. He took the missive and read it, and dread and anger washed over him in great waves as the words crashed through him. He passed it on to Mark, who tensed as he read it and then gave it to another.

Mark's blade paused dangerously against the whetstone in his other hand when his anger nearly got the better of him. Reid's warning look made him restrain his animosity. "You didn't mention what they found was a little *girl*," said Mark as John continued to reel.

Something about that letter didn't add up to John. It seemed to mean there were more children like Nymeria. But that wasn't it. Something else was wrong about it.

Lukas only grinned that evil grin of his. "I saw a *box*," he claimed, feigning innocence.

"Were it not for your being under Reid's protection, as his prisoner," spat Mark to Lukas, "I would flay you with a hot, dull, broken knife, with the women an' the children present, to let them all see how your kind ought to be treated. I would, an' I am not a violent man. I have no taste for blood, but I would do it, an' I would be glad to do it."

There were several hard looks passed between those in the room as the missive circled. Thomas met John's gaze but looked away, saying nothing, as though he'd already read it and knew what it meant. Sean expressed his outrage, however. "What — is this saying the child they found had some kind of deadly power . . . ? And that these glass shards are directly related to it? This is nonsense! All of it!"

John agreed, but instead, he spoke what truly plagued him about the letter. "By all that we've learned, the time frame does not fit for it to mean my daughter is that child, Reid," John said angrily. "How could you tell me this is directly related to her?"

"I know," said Reid. "But the relation is in the coincidences. Do you not see those? The description of the girl they found."

"This letter is suggesting there were other children like her in Five Tower who we had no idea needed our help as well — "

Nails placed the torn page upon the table. "That particular child is probably dead now. Were yeh teh say that, too, Dr. Ivan?"

John stood abruptly. His chair crashed loudly to the ground, and Jeana took a step forward, worried over what he'd read.

"I did tell you," Taiir said quietly. "Two years ago, I warned you. I do not blame tha child now as I did then for what happened in Five Tower, but now you know why Caol ordered her abandonment and death — "

"*Shut up!*" John snarled. He ran his hands through his hair and pulled at it until it was standing on end again. His angry gaze leveled with the prisoner's gleaming, triumphant one, and he wanted to throttle the man for the satisfaction he saw in his face. "How long ago did they find that pit?" John demanded.

Lukas laughed wickedly at some joke he saw, one that none of them seemed to understand.

John lunged at him, and his fist collided with the blond man's face once before Robert and Taiir pulled him back. Lukas fell backward and onto his side, but he kept laughing as he pushed himself back onto his heels and swayed dizzily.

"How long ago?!"

"Thirteen years ago, give or take a few."

John sagged, and his breath returned the same as it had torn itself from him. "Nymeria's hardly four," he spat. "It could have been one of her relatives. One of the other slaves."

But Lukas still smiled as though he knew something John did not.

"John," Nails said gently. "Yeh've come teh call her daughter. If the letter isn't talking about Nymeria, it's a mighty strange thing teh be a coincidence. Even if the age isn't right — somethin' other's amiss. We'll figure it out. Either the letter's wrong or somethin' else we're thinkin' teh understand is. She may have had an older sister. That sister may still be alive."

Robert and Taiir let John go, and he placed both hands on the table and stared at the glittering, cursed glass. "But what if that girl was instead her mother? Thirteen years is long enough for her to have come into womanhood and had a daughter Nymeria's age," he said. "The letter didn't say how old the child was when she was found. And many women become mothers as young as fifteen. Some younger — it happens to most of the female slaves in Five Tower." It hurt him unexpectedly to say such a thing, to know his daughter belonged to another parent. It hurt worse to consider that saving the child may have resulted in her mother wondering where she had gone and mourning the loss. John and Jeana knew firsthand how painful it was to lose a child, even if only one yet unborn.

Reid placed his hand on John's shoulder, and John looked at him as the jagged pieces inside himself shifted painfully. He took a deep breath to try to gather himself and calm the overwhelming and sudden grief he felt. "Regardless," said Reid. "Nymeria herself is still connected to it all. Even you know that, whether you deny it or not."

John shook his head.

"Where is she getting the glass from? How does she know what to do with it?" said Reid. "These are our main questions about her right now. And you cannot forget she *was* blamed for the Bright Night and cast out into a blizzard and left to die."

John gritted his teeth. "But why would the author of that letter say they found her? This bastard claims that was thirteen years ago. Yet the letter says the same child caused the Bright Night, which was only two years ago. Surely, he meant it was her mother, or some other relation . . . We took her with us, Reid. We thought we were protecting her because she had no family — "

"You had no idea regardless," Reid said. "None. You did the right thing, saving her in the face of crisis. Don't you dare question it. If her family didn't get out, *that* isn't your fault."

Mark's brows furrowed as John quieted the chaos that had erupted in his mind, and he took his seat again. His blade remained pressed dangerously against the whetstone a moment longer, and then he resumed his sharpening with a disturbing calmness about him.

For a beat, there was silence.

Mark then added another thought. "So, all we understand is some speculation on the shards' magical abilities to attach to tech an' swirl with some pretty light, an' some more fantastical claims from a murderer. An' by the way, this trash in front of us is a sick criminal, one who's got a few guts too many, an' a tongue too loose to trust. What does he really gain by telling us things, an' why is he so willing? Does he expect a painless transfer to the Reformation, where he's already expressed a preference? That would only be giving him what he wants, if even that much is true. He might have allies at the Reformation waiting to free him, or messengers who can forward the knowledge he's obviously attaining from us."

Mark licked his canine again, eyeing Lukas warily. "My da's a fool, listening to you so easily, forgetting what you are. But I saw the look you tried to hide under that scraggly pale hair of yours when you heard us talking about John's little girl after he lost it over that letter you stole. You were trying to figure out who had her, weren't you? Who she is. Where she is. Maybe even *what* she is, if you're as touched in the head as I think."

"Mark," said Reid to rein him back before things got any uglier — he was obviously afraid the questions would provoke John into attacking Lukas again. Or worse, Jeana, who was trembling with growing anger.

"I don't believe in curses, or supernatural powers, or magic stones," Mark spat disgustedly. "But I do believe that glass is probably some kind of weird technology, an' that it may even be a bit unpredictable. That much I can surrender to, but not much more. I don't trust any word this prisoner may have spoken because it could be attached to any level of lie or manipulation — truth being among the stain of his words or not. One can tell the truth to manipulate others, Reid, just as he can tell a lie to the same effect. My twin brother was a prime example of its mastery."

"Lukas's claims have been verified. And that letter cannot be fake," Reid reminded him. "The seal is, in and of itself, classified. Something like that wouldn't be floating around where someone like him would just happen to get access to it. Someone extremely important carried this message, and it is *from* someone even more important. You cannot ignore the evidence, which is the mark itself. And that my niece had these pieces of glass in the first place raises some serious questions."

"What about violet-colored magic being inside a person?" Mark swore. "That is insane. How can you believe a word of that? The man's a lunatic, an' half of you believe his every word!" There were cautious mutterings of agreement among several of the other attendees.

Reid exchanged a look with John and Jeana, and then he shook his head when John grimaced and gestured for Reid not to expect him to side with him in that argument.

"As far as I am concerned," John said, "I am of the same mind as Mark when it comes to the paranormal. I've seen men believe crazy shit from hallucinations and mental illness and cultural upbringing. Like Mark, I am not susceptible to such claims."

"I wouldn't dismiss this if I were either of you," Reid said. "I've seen stranger, and my instincts have only on the rarest of occasions ever failed me — or any of you, for that matter."

Reid sighed when Mark scowled more deeply. "Mark, I am not telling you to trust his reasons for telling us what he knows. It is wise to be wary of this murderer's reasons. It's why he isn't getting a trial to get sentenced to death. He knows a hell of a lot more than what he's told us — and I am well aware that he's only told us what he has in order to do exactly what you said. I know he wants to gather information from us, but I am just as interested in trying to figure out *what* he is trying to learn. I warned all of you before I let him speak not to trust him, to be careful of what you said. You must realize this is also why he is getting sent to the Reformation, where he can be detained properly, and where he may be questioned much more thoroughly. He will never be released. Never regain his freedom. He has committed too terrible a crime, and he knows too much about our predicament as well as about too many other things."

John stared at the glowing glass upon the table before them, his teeth clenched tightly as the muscles in his jaws continued to twitch. He was fuming still over what he'd read, over everything that had been said and learned tonight as a result of those rocks. He remained silent.

"But you do realize I am right, don't you?" Mark asked. "That they're simply magical rocks . . . Do you realize how ridiculous it sounds? How will Saura react to such a thing? How will the Enforcers?"

"So what? So what, if these things are unnatural to us, or alien to our understanding?" `Reid interrupted.

"You mean as alien as Nymeria?" snapped Mark. It seemed the argument had reached its pinnacle. "That child is the only unnatural thing I have ever witnessed with my own eyes, Reid. The things she knows, an' the things she does — an' the man before us let himself get caught because he plans to go after her, I know it. Because he believes she is the kid the letter mentioned, the child who has dark power an' unstable light inside her despite his claim the dig site incident happened over an entire decade ago. Doesn't that alone tell you his mind is broken? He believes it's her! So how about we stop talking about the damned shards an' talk about who an' what this is really all about — "

John felt ready to explode at the deliberate stab.

But it was Jeana whose lips drew back, and Reid's hand darted out to grab her wrist so that she could not draw her knife and use it on Mark. It sang as it left the sheath, but the blade's trajectory halted midair.

As vehement as Jeana's reaction was to any sort of perceived threat of her young, John felt equally provoked. He might have had more impulse control now, but his own rage was written plainly on his face — he knew it was. He met Mark's fiery gaze with his own icy one. "Say something else about my daughter," John hissed, his face feeling suddenly very, very purple. A vein pulsed in his forehead. "Tell me how unusual she is. Tell me, and let this murderer in front of us witness it and get all the information he wants or needs on the matter. I would like to know how very strange it is that you think she is so that we can put it out in the open and scrutinize her as if she is some kind of *specimen*."

"I didn't mean it like that," Mark resigned at last. "An' besides that . . . you know it as well as the rest of us that the child is not normal. Admit that she isn't, an' I may actually ignore how the rest of these imbeciles here obviously believe in magic an' curses an' the like. Then we can both move along to other, more important arguments, just as you've been trying desperately for all night."

Mark was ready to rise to blows. "Just know that this man before us is the kind of man who will steal knowledge from the mouths of others an' use it for something ill. This man has a pathological glean in his eye. A sickness that I recognize, John. He will do an' say anything to get information an' use it against you. My brother Tyler had the same sickness in him before I had to kill him for the trouble he caused, using my name to do his wicked bidding. If it wasn't for Reid's scrutinizing eye, I would have been the dead one, murdered in the name of justice. I would have paid for my brother's crimes. Reid knows as well as I do that this man is a hollow one who can do nothing but put on whichever mask will get him to his prize. I can read it in his face an' in his voice. He will use the truth in the same manner he will use a lie."

The two men glared at one another, tempers only rising as the other refused to make any sort of acquiescence.

"Regardless," said Reid. "Both of you, back down. We don't need to be arguing about his daughter or what she's done, or even how unusual she is. That is not the point we should be coming to. There are other matters to discuss anyway, as John well knows. And I need to talk to my brother next." Reid looked at John finally. Really looked. Even without hearing even a hint of it was about, John felt his insides curl coldly. "Alone," Reid added. "The rest of this needs to be wrapped up immediately."

Again, the dogs had begun snarling and barking outside. Something was upsetting them, and this time, they did not seem to calm down as quickly.

John's fist tightened around the cracked mug for a moment, and then he let it go.

"May I interject?" Lukas grinned wickedly.

Every face in the enclosure turned to him.

"What," muttered John.

"I may be but a lowly criminal," said Lukas. "But I do have something else to say, to spite you. You cannot deny them as lies, or as half-truths, simply taken from the mouths of others. You cannot say it is a mask to cover my intentions. You cannot refute this warning, because if *I* know what I am to say, you can be assured others know it. And if others know it . . . Well." He shrugged. "Trouble could truly be coming, then, couldn't it? I bear no true ill will to your guild, or I wouldn't tell you that I know this. It would be stupid, and it would place my head on Black Temple's chopping block rather than on Caol's."

Nails's chair squeaked as though its legs were about to snap. He nodded after one long, irritated moment, allowing Lukas to go on.

"My thanks," said Lukas. "Men and women of the Glass Chain. Imagine a single truckload of explosives." Several of them frowned, confused by the warning. Lukas then began to embellish it with his knowledge, which was dismaying for them to learn. Because of it, they realized Black Temple was more vulnerable than they'd ever thought. "Now imagine your enemies know Black Temple's armor is not about its heart, and that all of its major posts are gone," Lukas said. "And because they are gone, it is unable to rebuild itself after a precision attack, both coordinated and well-timed to hit Black Temple itself at every angle. A single attack, to throw it off its feet, every blow digging deeper at the heart of its armor."

Every person in the room contemplated the catastrophe.

"Even a place like Black Temple wouldn't be able to hold back that tiny contingency, if it knew *where* to strike, and *when*. The atrium is vulnerable beneath Isold."

John was taken aback to hear Lukas's knowledge of the atrium that Isold hid. But Lukas was not finished.

"The oak wall is crumbling, and the water trickling from Feilmein's shores will not be held back from the north much longer."

That was the second blow to all of them, to know that Lukas knew another vulnerable spot, which was nowhere near the heart of Black Temple itself. Yet Lukas continued.

"It takes a week to get from West Gate to North Gate — because of the ruins and the Flooded Plains, every guildsman must go underground and take myriads of tunnels just to get to some halfway — usually beginning at Isold's atrium, near Oakwall. A few others from Five Tower know these things, I will remind you. Some of them were your brothers before Caol and his son enslaved them to the Blood Light. Yet, whether you believe me or not, I tell you they did not betray their hope that they could protect your guild. These men pledged they would die before giving the information to Caol or his son. And they did. It should give you the slightest pause that I even know this. They would not have told me if they did not trust me. They knew my sins. They knew of my previous occupation, and yet they still trusted me for whatever they saw in me. However, I also must enlighten you. Caol knows Black Temple's approximate location now. He's known for nearly a year. I don't think it will take him much longer to piece together your guild's secret vulnerabilities, but I am sure he hasn't yet done so. Otherwise, he would have already made the fatal move that would have rooted you out. Black Temple needs to relocate. To move itself from the hidden dam before it is drowned."

The enclosure had become deathly silent as the fortress they had all believed would never be breached in a thousand years was revealed as breathtakingly fragile.

Reid picked up from there. "This is exactly my point. He knows a lot of things he shouldn't. It was no unfortunate accident we found him."

"Robert," Nails growled. "Get this murderer out of here. Lock 'em up with the dogs, an' don't turn yer back on 'im. An' do not tell anyone who he is, or what he's done. That he's a prisoner to be sent away for some serious thievin' is all that I allow any of yeh teh spill. Any more'n that, an' I'll personally imprison the guilty with 'im in the kennels. After removin' any loose tongues, that is. An' the dogs'd like the smell of the blood, teh remind yeh."

Lukas was wrestled to his feet by the brute commanded to detain him again.

"They call her the Bright Demon," Lukas added. "It would be kinder to kill her than to allow what is coming."

"Get him out!" Reid barked. Robert shoved Lukas outside, and Reid took a deep breath to temper himself. He paced back toward the table, then. "John."

John's shoulders slumped subtly. He looked at his brother helplessly. "She's spoken of the creatures he talked about," he said. That brought Nails's and Mark's attention back sharply. "Jeana's tried to talk to her about them, but she doesn't make much sense. She just says the *dark things* talk to her. She said these shards would help keep those things away, and she started putting them in things — I didn't know she'd started stealing walkies and manipulating them." His head fell, and he rested his palms against his eyes. "She said she would keep them from hearing us. I don't know where she got those things. I didn't know what she would do."

"Yeh've got that look that says that's not the least of it, John," said Nails gently.

"I don't know how to help her," John said. "Every time she starts talking about the creatures and the strange things she's been seeing — all of it exactly what Lukas spoke of — all I have been able to think of is how she reminds me of that little girl and her mother in Stillset several years ago."

"Stillset?" Reid repeated slowly. "That was a while back."

"Mayva an' her mother," Nails grimaced. "Brain injury if I recall correct. Swellin'. Wasn't the daughter a schizophrenic? Just needed some proper medications? Said she saw angels in the trees the night her mother tried teh kill her? Yeh were the only one who figured out what was wrong with both of 'em. I sent for one'a the counselors afterward, teh ensure they were taken care of properly once we'd gone."

John nodded.

"The mother had a worm eatin' at her brain where she'd cracked her noggin the year prior," Nails continued. "I remember. The hideous worst thing I ever watched, yeh pullin' that creature outta her head with yer bare fingers, a'cause our equipment had gotten stolen. Nasty, that was. Tasted dinner twice that day, I did. Thrice, actually. Even bein' a doctor meself, yeh'd think I'd the stomach for what yeh pulled outta her head."

"Nymeria's been having the same symptoms, but I haven't been able to help her. Nothing I know works," said John. "I don't specialize in what seems to be wrong with her, and I cannot afford to take her to any Keep, to let them look at her and prod at her as they do. And my parents still haven't arrived. They're to care for her when we head to Black Temple later this month. Saura's last messenger warned she might call for the next group of apprentices sooner than usual, and I cannot take my daughter in her current condition. My parents already know of the situation and agreed to help with her while I am gone. I don't know what else to do, especially if they cannot handle her. I can't let Jeana abandon her duties if Nymeria becomes disruptive. She's got her hands full, and it's only going to get busier with these refugees."

"I am sorry, John," said Nails. When John looked up at him, he saw the man's sincerity. "I had heard yer son sayin' somethin' about yer daughter changin' things teh protect everyone — I suppose I am also teh blame for not realizin' somethin' was goin' on. I'd just thought it was imaginin'. Youngins' mindplay, nothin' more."

John scowled. "It's quite a bit more than child's play at this point, Nails. She's been making my son afraid of the things she says she sees."

"Her sickness isn't contagious, is it?" asked Mark, suddenly more serious as he stopped sharpening his knife again.

"A'course it ain't," muttered Nails as he glowered at his son. "Yeh think John is foolman enough teh allow a contagion teh walk free in camp? This man is a master of our craft, even young as he is. Knows the most among us, he does — more'n even me, an' I've been at it far longer. Got a bright spark in 'is head, unlike yerself. Yeh couldn't even manage teh keep yer equipment in good shape till yeh knew Reid was comin' back but within a few days, yeh moron. An' at that, yeh were too late. He was already here, right behind yeh."

Ellie Mae took a hesitant step forward, her fingers clutching her elbow. "John, that's *terrible* . . ." she started to say.

John cringed. He hadn't wanted his daughter's illness to be known. "You've said enough, Dr. Mae. Now, because of you, everyone knows she isn't well."

"But I — "

"Don't bother apologizing, you'll just be wasting it on my ears. The damage is done. What we should instead try to do is salvage the original point of this meeting. We need to get our affairs in order for the sake of those refugees outside. Our jobs need getting done whether or not my daughter is ill."

Again, the dogs went to barking. This time, however, they did not return to the relative quiet of before. John could have sworn from the sound of it that another animal had made its way into their kennels and begun a fight with them to the death.

Reid raised his hands. The others quieted, but the concern among them all was palpable. "Listen, everyone," he said. "I know there has already been enough bad news today. But given the current news, we should all attempt to keep an eye out for the little one. Let one of us know if she's doing anything strange or if she has committed some offense. We will attend to it — "

There was a flurry of activity from outside, and Adam Samsinger burst inside, startling all of them. "Dr. Ivan!" he cried. John stepped away from the table as Adam tumbled over his own feet and fell forward. Nails glared at the man as he narrowly missed him. The old man shifted uncomfortably in his too small chair. "It's Nymeria, she's in trouble!"

"I thought you were watching her," snapped John, feeling that dangerous purple blooming across his face once more as he gripped the edge of the table. "I told you to watch her."

"I was, but she slipped away when I turned my back. I was setting out the scales to weigh the willow bark's salicin extract you requested for Old Benjamin Moore. Mercy had said — "

"Spit it out, already," said Mark as he clutched his whetstone in hand, ready to pocket it and already sheathing his knife with the other as he stood.

"She's in the kennel with the dogs," gasped Adam. "I tried to get her out of there, but — " He looked up, and then John saw the blood flowing brightly where Adam clutched at his mangled wrist. The radius was broken and jutting through the skin. The poor man would be lucky if he could use the hand again after it healed.

Jeana blanched and moved forward to assist him.

"Get Jamie," John told his wife. "Put him to bed. I don't want him running out there thinking he can help." He pushed through the men and grabbed Adam by the scruff of his collar. "Which one of Mercy's dogs did this to you?"

"Wasn't no dog that bit me," said Adam. "Your daughter did, when I tried to get her out."

John recoiled. "She did what?!" He looked at Adam's wrist again, horrified.

"Grabbed hold of my wrist and bit clean through, and now that lunatic Reid's got locked in one of the kennels is freaking out and trying to break out to get away from her and the dogs. The dogs haven't got her yet, though. Mercy is trying to get her out — I came to you directly. She's not hearing us. She's terrified, Dr. Ivan. Saying something is trying to get her, to steal her away and make her see the world in red — whatever it means."

"This is exactly what I was talking about," said John as he released Adam's collar. "Nails, tend to his hand or have someone do it for you, will you? I've got a half-mad daughter to fetch."

CHAPTER SEVEN

*K*ENNELS

THEIR HACKLES HAD RISEN, and their lips curled back over sharp teeth that bared at the things beyond the thick, prickly fence wire. The dogs could sense the creatures just as Nymeria could.

Mercy begged her to come out of the pin, his eyes round as petri dishes. In the cage next to her, a man with greasy, dirty blond hair kicked at the gate of one of the empty kennels and shouted. "Someone, please move me from this cage! She's brought those creatures *here*! They'll kill us all!" The prisoner's black eyes were rimmed with sleepless shadows, and they were bloodshot and wide open with fright. His screams echoed the fear that she herself felt, and so she knew she was not alone in sensing and seeing the dark things. "Get me out of here!" he screamed. "*Please!* Someone please get me out of this cage! *Please!!!*"

"Nymeria, sweet child, there ain't nothin' gonna hurt you — unless you stay in there with the dogs, and this crazy lunatic next to them. Please, now, come on out before your father comes out here and whips us both. Adam's gonna to be okay, I'm sure you didn't mean to hurt him. Nymeria, *please*."

Mercy was afraid for her, but Nymeria felt that if she moved, *they* would see her. Not the dogs, the *things*. The creatures the wild man was terrified of. They were veiled in darkness. It writhed about them like cloudy, living, breathing cloaks.

She didn't understand why Mercy wasn't afraid of them. Perhaps he couldn't see them; she didn't know. She only knew that every time she felt that *other* thing stirring within her, whenever she remembered the fiery blue color of the water from her nightmares, the disembodied creatures seemed to come a little closer. As if that memory called to them, too.

They always called for the *Bright One*. They could never see her, but she knew they were always searching. They could sense her soul, and she did not want to think why it drew them, or why they might want her. She only wanted to hide from them. Nothing frightened her like the dark things.

This time they were not speaking. There was a dull whispering sound coming from them. It was more like the crackling of flames — the sound of slag hitting water, hissing. The area was cold about them, and it drifted outward in small streams, wilting leaves, laying grasses down in a silent, slowly blackening death. Even the dogs seemed to be shivering from that strange cold.

Nymeria clutched at a shard of black glass tightly with her fist. She felt the bright violet light as it coursed through her wrists, into her palms, and into the material, and the creatures in the darkness began to screech as they whirled about. They felt the disturbance, though they could not seem to find it. But they began to draw nearer, searching, sensing.

She shut her eyes tightly and cowered where she stood, and she clutched the shard she'd picked up in the middle of the pin. She prayed the creatures wouldn't reach her. That they wouldn't *see* her, even though they had no eyes with which to see.

Tears began to trickle down her cheeks, and they were like hot, living flames against the terrible cold she felt upon her flesh and within her soul. She wanted to curl inward, toward the warmth from which the violet light came, to flee the creatures and lock herself away in the darkness which was cradled in her memories.

But then her father was there, calling her name, and her uncle was close behind him.

Her father didn't seem as worried for her as Mercy was. Instead, he was very angry. "Nymeria!" he said. He looked at the dogs when they trembled ferociously and shrank toward him, farther from her and the creatures. He looked beyond her but seemed to see nothing. "Nymeria, what have you done? Adam said you bit him. I saw the marks and the blood. You've ruined the man's hand!" She could hardly bring herself to look at him, for those creatures were drifting, ever so slowly, closer. "Mercy, why will she not come out of there?" He glared at the screaming wild man. "And someone shut him *up*!"

Her uncle's elbow found the wild man's nose, and the man staggered back and fell. He was hardly conscious after the hard strike, but even so, he stared where Nymeria's gaze was fixed as he tried to crawl away from the dark things. His breath came in ragged veils, torn like dusty, moth-eaten lace, and his head fell back against the wire and the slats of steel and iron that framed the gate. "It's *her* . . . You don't understand . . ." he rasped, shaking his head. The motion seemed to rob him of strength, and the man slumped. His chin wobbled as he tried to speak, to plead with her uncle and her father.

"Why doesn't she want to come out of there?" her father shouted. He unholstered his gun, and Nymeria flinched when the trigger pulled back and the weapon fired. The lock did not break, however; it remained intact, merely dented. Several more shots made several more voluminous dings at various points on the gate, but nothing else weakened or broke. Her father hissed and holstered his gun when there were no other angles from which he could try to fire his weapon even somewhat safely, and he took to ramming the gate with his shoulder again.

Mercy continued to wrestle the gate lock. "I don't know, Mr. Ivan. She's been sitting there shaking real bad and crying to herself since Adam ran off to find you. She's the one who's broken the lock. I couldn't get it open after it sparked when Adam fell into it and accidentally shut it — the lock's been melted from the inside! Damned thing sparked and melted when she touched it."

"Then get some bolt cutters!" snarled Reid, and when he tore his gaze from the woods, he began to beat on the twisted metal with a nervous fury that startled even John. A fine sheen of perspiration beaded on his brow.

Her uncle looked afraid, as if he could see *them*. Or feel them, at least.

"Something is out there, John," her uncle stammered. "Something is out there, among the trees. Nymeria! Come here!"

"Nymeria!" said John. "What else has she done?" he demanded of Mercy as the man started to brush past him. "Why did my daughter go into the kennels to start with?"

"I don't know! She saw something in there, went in to get it out before Adam or I could stop her — "

"Get some bolt cutters, I said!" shouted Reid. He grabbed Mercy's shoulder and shoved him. "John, help me — "

"*Father?*" Nymeria said over her shoulder. She shivered from the cold that filtered around her now, and the half-conscious man in the kennel next to hers looked up. A dazed frown twisted his youthful face, and he blinked hard, as though he was having difficulty seeing her. His mouth moved as though to say something, but still, nothing came out.

A guttural sound began to spill from the dogs' bellies then — a visceral, feral sound that made her father's and uncle's faces suddenly bloodless. The wild man whimpered, the color draining from him as his skin took on a whitened, waxy sheen. She stepped away from the fence before her, her fingers releasing the chicken wire. *"I don't want to remember what happened, what they did."*

"What is she saying?" Reid asked, perplexed. "What language is that?"

"I don't want to be the Bright One," Nymeria said.

Mercy returned with the bolt cutters, and her father took them and began to work on the thick metal lock.

"Just help me get this gate open, Reid!"

"Move, then!" The lock broke as the two of them heaved on the handle, but the gate did not give. Again, her father rammed it with his shoulder, and again, it did not budge.

"Father?" Her father flinched when she looked up at him, and her uncle began to beat on the decayed, rusted bolts on the other side of the gate with the bolt cutter in his hands, frustrated because it still did not open, and because Mercy's aid did nothing at all. Her father looked around desperately and found against the end of the kennels some iron rods much like the ones they'd used to reinforce the cages. The bars on the cage were too large for the bolt cutters, though her uncle tried to use the cutters on them anyway. It's steel jaws only marred the surface of the metal framework, clawing it instead of cleaving it in two.

"Reid. Mercy. Move."

Taiir arrived behind them. He took one look at her and at the scene about her, and he faltered. He had never liked her — never trusted her — but not a breath later, Taiir had also taken to helping her father and her uncle and Mercy. Where all four men pushed and pulled at the wire-enforced bars, the gate began to bulge in opposite directions.

The dogs' mouths foamed white and sprayed saliva as they began to bark and snarl even more loudly. Mercy's biggest dog Chaser sprang toward the fence as Nymeria took another step back. The Doberman began chewing at the wires, even tearing and rending his own flesh upon it. He lost teeth but continued to chew madly at the cage as he belted deep, hair-raising warnings at the creatures approaching the enclosure. Nymeria had never heard such a vicious, bolting noise as what came out of that dog in that moment, not even on normal days when the Dobermans three kennels over voiced frighteningly deep and angry sounds, or when the shepherds in the cages to either side tried to fight them through the fence.

Reid stepped back as John rammed iron rods into the ground on the other side of the gate at an angle and braced one against the broken lock and its reinforced frame. He and Reid grabbed that one with both of their hands and heaved and heaved, and Mercy and Taiir put their weight against the top of the gate on the other side where the hinges had bent. "Nymeria, hold on!" said Reid. "We'll get you out!"

"Stay clear of tha dogs, Little One," said Taiir.

Nymeria clutched the glass more tightly. The shadows screeched again. *"Nai!"* she shouted. *"Leave me alone!"* Then the shadows gathered and rose in defiance, until they began to form tall, hooded creatures, and their hands — scorched and charred and blackened — reached for the wire. Chaser yelped, recoiling, and he fell as though a sickness had suddenly seized him. He was dead within the next heartbeat, and his chest expelled one last frothy breath as his bleeding lips curled over a devastated, bloody, broken-toothed snarl. *"Leave me alone!"* she screamed. And then she threw the blazing violet *memory* at the creatures and raised her hands to cover her ears.

The wild man in the next cage saw the shard, and his expression filled with sudden horror as the thing flew though the wires. He turned his head away as she did, as though he knew what she knew.

The shadows screamed and went after the violet shard, and the light within it was shrouded almost instantly by the blackness of their mantle as they devoured it. And then a brilliant explosion of violet light blinded her and threw her violently back into the gate. Her head struck the protruding, bent bar, and she felt the unforgiving metal gouge her cheek. Blood trickled down, hot on her skin.

"It's gone . . ." she choked. The trees overhead began to darken as they swirled dizzily. "Father, it's gone. I saved us from it."

"*How . . . ?*" the wild man wept, his hoarse, trembling whisper like an awe-filled echo. His black eyes, she felt them upon her back, filled with fear, with reverence, with awe. She sensed his confusion. And then she sensed the murders he'd committed, and she recoiled. They were like brands upon his soul, still burning, still hissing, and just as black as the hearts of the dark creatures and the terrible world those beings came from.

She heard the metal clink of thick steel being snapped apart.

Her father knelt over her, a blurring image of motion, and he wiped the blood from her cheek. "What did you do?" he cried. "What did you *do?* Nymeria, look at me. Please look at me."

"I'm fine," she tried to say. Except, it came out, "*Tir'nieta.*"

"What? You know that I cannot understand that *odd-speak*," her father said. "Please tell me where I can understand you."

She shrank from the memory. "It's gone."

"What's gone?"

"The dark thing is gone . . ."

"You can use the curse," croaked the wild man as his fingers laced through the wire separating him from the four of them. "I have never seen anyone able to — "

"If you do not cease speaking, I will cut out your bloody tongue," Reid hissed. Of John, he asked, "Is she all right? What's wrong? How badly is she hurt?"

CHAPTER EIGHT

SILVER

THE REST OF THE DOGS RUSHED through the open gate in frenzied disquiet, knocking Mercy off his feet. "*Mercy me*," exhaled Mercy as he knelt by Nymeria and her father and uncle. He studied the woods where fire devoured the leaves and underbrush as if oil had been tossed over the still-moist deadfall. "That was quite an explosion. It'll be a stickler of a job, trying to round my dogs back up after *that*. Is the little one all right?"

Nymeria's father cupped both sides of her face with his hands. He kissed her forehead, just above either eye. "Your mother told you to help your brother and Adam," he said. "How many times do I need to tell you to stay put?" He examined her cheek where she bled, and he cleaned the wound with a gentle hand. "Nymeria, you need to realize how dangerous it is for you to wander in your condition. If we are ambushed along our route, or even out here at one of these posts — if you are left behind or taken — we may not be able to find you again. This world is a cruel place, and children are not often treated kindly."

She said nothing in reply.

"Do you not hear me? You were supposed to be helping Adam to mix and measure the ingredients your brother has been sorting. What possessed you to leave them and come into the dog kennels?"

"I already know everything you wanted me to learn," said Nymeria quietly.

Her father reprimanded her. "I do not appreciate your sarcasm, Nymeria. You were to help them regardless. And you can't have learned everything already. You shouldn't be wasting your time running off."

"I already understand it," repeated Nymeria. "But that knowledge will not make the dark things leave us alone. It is more important I keep them away."

Her father sighed then, exasperated. "Never mind your imaginary dark creatures. Look, Nymeria, you've hit your head, and you're bleeding," he said. He showed her the bloodied fabric he'd been holding to her cheek. "This happened because you did not do as I asked, and it could have been much, much worse. What would you have done if the dogs had turned your way and tried to tear you to pieces?"

Nymeria listened as she lifted her fingers to her head to brush her dark hair from the sticky wound. Her father gently pulled her hand away and continued to administer to her. "They wouldn't have hurt me," she said simply as he went about wiping the blood away again.

"How are you so sure?" said her uncle.

"They were too afraid to."

Her father's fingers curled into a fist. "A crazed, terrified dog is *more* likely to bite you. You were lucky none of them did."

Her throat closed, and she felt herself about to cry.

Mercy coughed then. "She okay, Mr. Ivan?"

"I think so. Bit of a concussion, perhaps. A small contusion and some bruising. Go ahead and see to retrieving your dogs."

"That will probably take a couple of weeks," Mercy smiled. "Not all of them were trained, and they like the taste of the hunt. They'll be getting their own food till they get lazy."

"I'm very sorry, Mercy. If you need help, Robert can put aside the time to help you track some of them before we have to leave. And we will fix the damage to your kennel and pay for your loss. I know that dog was valuable, and I am sorry he is dead."

"This was not your fault," said Mercy. "Children wander. The mistake was Adam's. He should have watched her more closely. It is a grown man's job to do as he is assigned. I will put him to work as soon as that wrist of his is tended to. He will pay for the damages by getting me a couple of good quality breeding dogs, and he will be helping me with the kennel. As for breaking open the gate, I would very much rather a broken gate than a dead child. Don't worry about helping me retrieve the dogs, I can manage. I know Robert is busy enough, helping with this mess, and you guys have been at your wits' end, trying to keep the wearyworn from fighting out there." Mercy offered Nymeria a small one-fingered salute. "Goodbye, munchkin. Be good." To her father, he added, "Take care of her."

When her uncle's glittering, fearful gaze searched the flames still licking at the trees, Nymeria *knew* he saw one of the things concealed in the shadow that moved at the heart of the blaze. It remained standing, although it looked as if it was writhing in the fire. Her uncle took a step back. "John."

Her father looked up.

Meanwhile, the creature threw its head back as the flames curtained it.

She knew Uncle Reid couldn't hear its vengeful scream, but she could tell he did feel it. The *noise*, if it could be called that, seemed to penetrate him. She knew the familiar signs, how it had been for herself to react when it had felt as though a thread in her had been brushed with something cold, as if an icy claw had slithered slowly from the crown of her skull to the base of her spine. She sensed it was the same for her uncle this time. She also knew his heart was now aflutter because of it; she saw the uneasiness that twisted through him.

Then the last of the creatures was gone. Not dead, but gone, as though they had never even been there at all. And Taiir continued to watch silently, judging her without speaking his thoughts. Seeming ready to guard *them* from *her*.

"You can sense them, can't you, Commander?" the prisoner managed quietly as he nursed his injury with the back of his hand. He was wheezing, still trembling. "I don't know how, but they didn't like whatever she just did. I've never seen any of us wield the curse before. She — "

"Shut up, Lukas, or I'll have my brother knock you flat again," said her father to the prisoner.

Uncle Reid then saw in her hand another violet shard. His lips pursed.

"Uncle," Nymeria said quietly. "Take it." She held out her hand, the glowing shard pinched between forefinger and thumb, and the dirty blond man scrambled away from the fence to get as far as he could from the small, unassuming item. She saw Lukas's expression when her uncle's hands clasped her own — as if he couldn't believe her uncle was unaware of the repercussions of touching the shard. As if it could do something to them all if her uncle mishandled the glass.

"You're a fool to touch it," rasped Lukas. "A damned *fool*."

The wound upon her face began to tingle then, and her father uttered a silent curse as he withdrew the cloth. The blood-soaked linen fell uselessly to the dirt as he clenched his other hand dangerously for a moment. Uncle Reid knelt beside her father. "Did she just . . . *heal?*"

"It's not the first time," said her father. "Look at the new scar." Her uncle examined the mark, his brows furrowed deeply. "I don't understand it," said Nymeria's father. "All my training, and I don't even understand my own daughter's eccentricities. She's different. I've told you that before."

"If you remember," said Taiir quietly behind them. "I did tell you she is not normal."

"Shut up, Taiir," Uncle Reid hissed as he examined the mark on her face as well. "John doesn't give a serpent's scales what you think about her. Never did, never will. And neither do I."

Nymeria stared up at them both. "What's wrong?" She tried to touch the mark, but her father clasped her hand and held it gently in his own, as though she might shatter. She saw stray flickers of fear in the worry lines upon his face as he studied the tingling skin upon her cheek. His lips were pursed together as though he were biting on the skin inside.

Uncle Reid sucked in a breath. *"Silver?"*

"Exactly," her father exhaled. "Silver. It fades soon after, until there is nothing. Just days, usually, with no trace hinting any injury ever occurred."

"What does silver mean?" she asked. "Is it not normal?"

"It means you are very special," said Uncle Reid thoughtfully. "Very, very special."

Nymeria smiled shyly. "But Father says . . ."

"Never mind that," said her father. "It will always be okay to talk to your uncle. He is family."

"Are you hungry?" asked her uncle suddenly, a big grin breaking out across his face. She was relieved of the change of subject, and now that he had mentioned it, her stomach was growling. "Ralleigha has Mercy's wife Enna cooking up something quite wonderful. With all the work you've been doing for your mother and Adam, it's no wonder you've decided to wander. You *are* hungry, aren't you?"

"Reid," glowered her father. "You're going to reward her for her behavior after this? She's destroyed Mercy's kennel."

"Technically we did, getting to her."

"Well, she did kill his dog."

"Are you *blind*? That dog went crazy and then keeled over, as though it choked on the wire it was trying to eat."

"The grenade, or whatever *that* was that she just threw?"

Taiir grunted and walked away without a sideways glance.

"I saw her throw a rock," sighed Uncle Reid. "It might have landed on an old mine. You know that this forest is full of booby traps left from the wars. You're worried about her, and that is fine. But don't go getting paranoid, or distrusting and hateful toward us. We'll have the boys go out and put out that fire so it doesn't end up burning down someone's home or workstation. The tents will catch fire too easily, and that'd be a nightmare when it spreads." Her uncle winked and nodded for Nymeria to come with him. "Come on, monster. Let's get something to eat together. They're gonna be cooking some really good food tomorrow for the wedding shower for Robert and Ellie Mae. They'll be married in a month or two, after the apprentices have been delivered for the season. We need a change of topic, anyway, get you out of this uncomfortable spotlight John puts everyone under. I get hives and start my itchy, scratchy dance when he gives me that look. Does it make you itch, too?"

Nymeria tittered with uneasy, uncertain laughter. "Nai. Why would I itch? And why are you doing so now?"

"Because I'm allergic to his bullshit, kiddo. Now, about the wedding that's coming. I heard Robert say that he wants the wedding to be here, at Crow Post. Do you wanna ask Ellie if she'll let you be her goddaughter so you can walk the aisle and throw flowers at everyone?"

Again, she found herself laughing, and the fear she'd felt began to dissipate. Her uncle was very good at making her feel better when she was upset. "Why would I have to throw flowers at people? Wouldn't that make them mad?"

"Oh, but to the contrary," her uncle growled. "They'd love to smell a little better. *We* would love it if they did, anyway. Lots of nasty, dirty people running around, not bathing for years at a time. You throw flowers to chase away the stink, didn't you know?"

Her father sighed, exasperated, and then he threw his hands in the air. "Fine. Take her to get something to eat. But take her to Jeana afterward so she can be put to bed with her brother."

CHAPTER NINE

PARTNERS

THE MORNING SKY WAS BRUSHED with gold, and bright yellow goldfinches and brilliant red robins chattered rapidly. Jamie laughed at their mother's silly expressions as she carefully measured the white willow and witch hazel extracts for Old Benjamin Moore, Mercy's ailing grandfather. These were medicines their father had instructed her to make for Old Benjamin for his swollen, aching joints. Hyperuricemia left him hobbling about on crutches when it was at its worst. He was often bedridden with chronic, debilitating pain, but some days he was able to walk about. Other days, like today, he slept, which was the reason for the witch hazel. It served as a mild sedative and aided the white willow's anti-inflammatory effects.

Their mother's work station had been set up just outside the tent — close enough that she could work and check on him where he slept wrapped up in a heavy blanket on a cot in the shade, but far enough to let him rest undisturbed while she dealt with other attendants who occasionally came and went. She prepared other medicines between helping the old man and amusing her son.

Nymeria was busy with her own chores. She was studying — or pretending to study — her father's journals while she crushed multitudes of different herbs with his favorite granite mortar and pestle. The current victim under the grinding stone was dried lavender. And Nymeria's wrists were tired, the muscles drawn. She stared at the yellowed pages in the light that filtered in from the canopy of live oak and flowering plum overhead, but she wasn't reading her father's sloppy, sprawling script. Her eyes burned when she blinked them wearily. She wiped the back of her hand against her left eyelid and stifled another yawn. "Mother?"

Her mother looked up happily from Old Benjamin's cot, where the old man rambled restlessly in his sleep. Her brows drew together in a silent question as she came to the doorway at once so that Nymeria could speak more quietly.

Nymeria was mindful of her mother's reason for leaving the old man's bedside, and she lowered her voice respectfully. "Can I please stop pretending to read this? My eyes hurt."

Her mother laughed silently. She set down her beaker and touched the tip of Jamie's nose, making him giggle. Then she signed her response slowly.

You need to practice reading and writing. Not everyone can. What if you must administer medicine, or make it, without either of us to help you, or anyone else about to read to you the ingredients and the dosage? You cannot remember everything —

Nymeria slammed the book shut and looked up coldly at her mother — effectively quieting her. Nymeria was aware that she had never revealed any inclination of having such a volatile temper before. She'd always smiled, and she'd even bowed her head in acquiescence. It was one of the many things that had set her apart from other young children who would have tantrums or argue with their parents. Nymeria had never even *once* outright or blatantly refused to do as she was told, and she knew it was startling for her mother to see it for the first time. "How many times must I say *I know*?" Nymeria said very thickly. "I *understand*, Mother. You don't believe me, but I *know*. I don't like to read. I don't want to read. I don't

66

want to *know* anymore. It is too much, and you keep making me do it. Again, and *again.*"

The sound of gravel crunching drew her mother's eyes upward to the open doorway at the back of the tent, where a continuous breeze blew in. Nymeria continued to stare coldly at her mother.

Uncle Reid bowed his head as he followed his daughter Marissa. He carried several new glass bottles his wife had completed that morning in a box which was also stuffed with grasses. "Hello, girls and boys," he said quietly. "Gifts for the insane." He looked worse than he had a few days ago when he'd brought that prisoner, who was still locked in the kennels. The grief from losing his mother and father still showed in the shadows under his eyes. At least he didn't smell of alcohol today. He'd been drinking lately, and only Nymeria knew why. She didn't understand why he hadn't told her father yet. He needed to. He'd even avoided Aunt Ralleigha so she wouldn't smell the alcohol or see how upset he was.

"Nymeria, look!" Marissa said delightedly as she placed her own, smaller box at the foot of Jeana's worktable. Marissa bent over the box and rummaged through its contents until she came upon something that clinked, and with her fist closed around it, she rose and hurried over to Nymeria.

"Be quiet," Uncle Reid muttered under his breath, and he stole a glance back to Old Benjamin as the bedridden man coughed forcefully in his sleep and then began to snore again. Old Benjamin snored all the time, sometimes even when he was awake. That part wasn't a medical condition so much as amusement. Old Benjamin favored the sound and often took to laughing over it when another cast an annoyed look his way. He sounded like a donkey when he cackled wildly, and he often kicked one leg out as he did so while leaning forward and clapping the other.

Nymeria set down the mortar and pestle and straightened from the book. She shoved it away from her and cast another glare at her mother as Marissa brought to the table what was in her hand. It was a glass bottle . . . kind of. It was warped, almost had the shape of a heart. The round stopper hadn't fit the angled bottleneck, so the cork had been shaved down on one side. The glass was blackened slightly on the bottom, and a hairline crack ran the length of it. "Well made," said Nymeria, giving her cousin her *nice face*, as her father called it. "Is it your first one?"

"Yes. Mom finally let me give the rod a whorl," explained Marissa. "It's ugly, so don't lie and tell me it's not. But it's only my first. She said her first one looked worse. Hard to imagine, isn't it? Mom makes such beautiful pieces. It almost looks like a heart, doesn't it? I meant to make a butterfly."

"Like a really gross heart," Nymeria agreed. Her cousin tittered with laughter.

"Exactly!"

Uncle Reid ruffled Marissa's dark red hair and stepped closer to Jeana. He'd seen the looks passing between Nymeria and her mother. Nymeria knew he had, and she saw the subtle signs he passed to her mother, belying another question besides the one he asked aloud. "What's going on?" he said quietly.

Marissa remained busy pointing out the cracks, explaining the intricacies of glass work. The bubble of glass on the rod, the pincers, the rolling and heating and polishing. Flashing and tilt, stretching and pressing. It was all very interesting to Marissa, and she was eager to explain how she would make the next piece better. But Nymeria was watching her mother's hands.

She is upset, said Jeana. *John wants her here, to focus on learning and on helping me. She doesn't want to do it. She is restless, and I don't know what to do except tell her to just be quiet and do what we've told her to do. I don't like being mean to her. I don't want to have to punish her.*

Uncle Reid's brow lifted. "She's a child, Jeana. They are all defiant. And you're her mother. Parents have to be the bad guy. They love us anyway, that's the wonderful part." She knew her uncle suspected that she had picked up on the deaths of her grandparents, though he had still said nothing. Nymeria suspected it gnawed at him something terrible when she gave him that grief-stricken, consoling look that was always shared at funerals. Her grandparents hadn't gotten a funeral. She knew it. He knew it. But no one else in the family did, and even he didn't know that *she* knew.

But she's . . . so different. Nymeria's mother turned away from the girls and continued to sign to Uncle Reid what was going on. Nymeria could no longer tell what she was saying, but she saw her uncle's brows draw together worriedly. He stole a glance to the girls and noticed Nymeria watching them discreetly. Nymeria looked away quickly, letting her dark hair curtain her face.

"Marissa?" said Uncle Reid.

Marissa turned her bright eyes to her father. "Yes, Daddy?"

He smiled gently, though there was still that sadness in his eyes. "How about you go see Uncle John for a bit? Take the new set to him and show him how you and your momma set it up. Let him know how hot it can get before it breaks."

"Really?" Nymeria's heart sank at her cousin's eager reply. She didn't want her cousin to go already. Marissa smiled when her father nodded, and she took Nymeria's hand in her own and pressed the cracked heart bottle to her palm. "Keep this, okay? You can loop a string through the hole and wear it. Put something special in it."

"Thank you," Nymeria said quietly, her eyes downcast.

Her cousin darted away, red hair whipping after her in a quick flurry.

Uncle Reid stumbled to the side, startled at his daughter's speed. "I always forget she's so fast," he chuckled. "Just like her mother." He placed a hand on Jeana's shoulder and nodded. "I'll talk to her before I head out. Try to see what's going on. Go get something to eat, you've not taken a break. We'll look after Old Benjamin Moore and the others while you're gone."

Jeana snapped her fingers, and Nymeria sat down again, her hands clasped neatly in her lap. Jamie raised his arms when their mother knelt to pick him up, and he stuck his tongue out at Nymeria as their mother carried him out. "Myria's in trouble," he giggled, his nose crinkling wickedly as he bared his teeth at her. "In so much trouble."

Nymeria clutched at the small glass piece, turning it over in her hands several times. Her uncle crossed his arms and began tapping his foot as he studied her quietly. He said nothing, just stood there and waited for her mother to be out of earshot.

Nymeria grimaced when she felt an odd spasm in her chest, right where her heart was. It was the same spasm that threatened to make the world red. It felt cold. It felt as though a small hole had opened in her, as if icy water had dripped in. She rubbed at the skin just over it, wishing for warmth. Wishing to be safe from the cold of the dark things.

Uncle Reid noticed. He always noticed nearly everything. Still, he said nothing.

Old Benjamin smacked his wrinkly old lips in his sleep and began to mutter something pronounced oddly like, "Ahm, nahat my crahkasyahwidls . . . bahstud . . . Ooohooo, buttahflahs." He swatted at something, then moaned, then went back to snoring again. "Too-fah."

Nymeria set down the precious gift from her cousin. "Uncle — "

"Don't *Uncle* me," said Uncle Reid. "Your mother only wants the best for you. You need to respect that. Your mother and your father are preparing you for one of the finest, highest-respected futures there is. There is nothing more respected than a Black Temple doctor — a field doctor, at that."

"Then why aren't you one, if you think so highly of them?" Nymeria said evenly.

Uncle Reid flinched. "*Ow.*" He laughed. "Right at my heart, is it? Your grandfather's inheritance went to save your grandmother, you know. The only one they could afford to send to Black Temple for that kind of apprenticeship afterward was John. Because he showed a knack for it."

"And you?"

"Well, I haven't wasted my time complaining about *reading*, now have I?" Uncle Reid said nonchalantly. He winked. "What is the matter? Why won't you do what your father asked you to do?"

"Because I already know what to do," said Nymeria. "Because he is wrong." She stood up, then, and she pushed the journal toward her uncle. "And because *this*. I don't like touching it."

"She said you don't seem to like to even touch the books," he said. "Have you developed an allergy to them?"

Nymeria stared at him, not comprehending.

"Are you allergic to reading, then? Come off it. You can tell me, you know. I am your uncle, after all. That means I can keep secrets and you can breathe a little. We're supposed to be best friends. It's the law."

Nymeria shook her head. "Nai."

"Then what is it?"

"I . . ."

Uncle Reid's brows knotted. He reached over and picked up the book. When he opened it and fanned through the pages, a smoky plume of dust rose from them. He choked and held it away. "Well, there's the problem — wow. What is that *smell*?" He brought it close to his nose and then quickly held it aloft. "Wow. I see. This smells like John's butt sweat. He's sat on this, and he expects you to *read* out of it? I decree this *gross*."

Nymeria felt the corner of her mouth tilt upward and she laughed a little despite herself. She had already known he'd had a handful of dust, but his attempt to lighten her mood had worked a little. "You're more of a child than I," she said. She wiped away the dust that had settled on the table.

He chuckled. "Obviously. Being a grown-up never was my strongest quality." There was still that sadness in him, but he was trying desperately to hide it. And he was more concerned about her than he was about himself. It hurt to watch him suffer so.

Out of respect, she decided not to address what was bothering him. "Uncle Reid, please don't tell them if I tell you. Will you promise?"

He grinned. "Now why would I go and do a thing like that?" He motioned at the bench. "May I?" When she nodded, he dropped the journal as he sat by her, and he picked up the mortar and pestle. "What's this, lavender? What's it for?"

"It would take an hour to explain. You would fall asleep," she said. "There are thirty-three uses, and lots of math for half of them."

"Ah. You sound just as John used to — or is that *still does*? The bloody nerd." He smiled at his morosely accurate pun. "So what did you want to tell me, then?"

Nymeria dug into her pocket and pulled out another purple shard. She put it next to the tiny glass bottle. "You saw what I threw and what it did, and you knew it wasn't a mine that blew up, even though you told Father that's what happened. But did you see *it*? The dark thing?"

Uncle Reid was no longer smiling. His dark blue eyes clouded with the memory, and his lips pursed together tightly. "I'm not sure what it was that I saw." He drew his hand away from the shard, as though he didn't want it near him. "And where are you getting those? Why do you keep picking them up? Do you want them to blow up in your *hand*? What are you going to do if it goes off on the table? And why on earth did you go and attach them to the radios? I couldn't get rid of them. And *how* did you get them to adhere — "

"Well, that is a mouthful of questions," she said matter-of-factly. Nymeria picked up the bottle her cousin had made. Her fingers closed around it. She felt that *other* thing in her stir, that *Spirit*, which was like a tingling, electric pulse and which made the veins in her wrists brighten almost imperceptibly. She was unsure whether her uncle could sense it. He was normal, like her mother and her father. Like her brother, her cousin, her aunt. Like everyone else, too. Still, he shifted on the bench and seemed to grow uneasy. "The other one blew up because I told it to send them away." She lifted her hand and held it in front of him. "Take it."

Reid looked down, not sure what to expect. "Marissa's glass?" Nymeria nodded, and when he held out his hand, she pressed it into his palm. It was warmer now, and it pulsated with energy. She let go, and bright, violet light curled within it. Ribbons of it danced within, in patterns that she knew he couldn't decipher. He sucked in his breath. "You're making them — *literally* making them. But . . . how? I've seen things that glow before, but not like this. What kind of mineral — "

"It's from me."

Uncle Reid remained silent for a long moment. He seemed to truly study her for the first time — not to look fondly upon her as his precious niece, but as someone — it seemed to hurt him to realize — he didn't really understand. This upset him, even though he struggled to hide it. But it was still in his voice. "John and Jeana don't know, do they?"

Nymeria shook her head. "I don't want to touch his books because he writes them when he is still learning from the patients. Sometimes there is blood in the pages. Sometimes there are screams in them."

"What do you mean, there are *screams* on the pages?" he asked her sickly, turning over the glass bottle her cousin had made. "John wouldn't write something like that."

"Not on them. *In* them. Just like in the ruins, in the walls. Death is still there, inside them. Pain stays, Uncle. When I look or touch where it has been, it gives me nightmares. Not just the other nightmares, but nightmares about how Father had to save people. How some of them didn't make it. Even his tears are in them. I saw Mayva's father's body. I saw her singing and then later screaming where she and her mother wept over what they'd done. Father never wrote what happened, but I dreamt it because it was in there. I saw his hand shaking when he wrote it in the pages, and I saw everything else, too. I don't like to touch the journals. Mother and Father don't understand, but that's why."

"Fallen skies," said Uncle Reid. He stared down at her. "No one has talked about the gruesome stuff in Stillset in years. You get all of that from *touching* the journal?" She nodded. "Okay . . . Let's change the subject for a bit. We'll revisit that later. Do you want to tell me why you haven't been going to sleep at night? Jeana said you're awake all night, crying. That this has been going on for weeks. Why? Are the other children being mean to you?"

Nymeria crossed her arms. "I don't want to talk about it." She really didn't.

"You won't even tell me?"

"Nai," she said sternly. "None would believe me anyway. Not even you."

Uncle Reid arched a quizzical eyebrow. "Try me. I am quite understanding." Still, she shook her head. "It can't be worse than what you've already told me. What could be worse or more unbelievable than your psychic journal thing? And I took that well, I would think." When he saw at last that she was truly unwilling to speak about it, he gave up. "Then what did you want this glass to do?" he asked.

"Nothing. Just shine."

"Really?" He seemed surprised. "How bright can you make it?"

"Flashlight bright. I've never actually tried to make one brighter, though. It is very useful when you are not allowed to waste the batteries. Father won't let me use them much. He says they are for emergencies . . . Although I still get into trouble because he does think I am using the batteries despite being told not to touch them."

He contemplated what she'd told him for a long moment, still turning the glass over in his fingers. Then he handed it to her. "No batteries, no fuel?" he murmured ponderously. "How long does the light inside these last? As long as you want it to?"

She shook her head. "Nai. Only a few hours. The dimmer ones last twelve or more. Just like the batteries."

"It won't explode if I throw it?"

Nymeria took the other on the table and let him see that it was the same as the others. "Nai," she said. Then she flung it.

Uncle Reid nearly came out of his chair, startled when it shattered at his feet. But nothing else happened. His hand fluttered to his chest. "Give me a warning, will you?!" he gasped.

Nymeria stared at him, her eyes wide. She curled up on the bench as she began laughing.

"Washit, dummy," murmured the sleeping Old Benjamin. "Gimme summnin tareat. . . . Bahs . . . Lossiff bahs . . . Fizzlin like . . . Snippy. Snippy, shnippy. Hap tar it, nah. . . ."

Uncle Reid glanced behind him, into Old Benjamin's snore-filled tent, and an incredulous look crossed his face before he, too, began to rock with quiet laughter. "The ridiculous things he says in his sleep, right?"

Nymeria nodded. "I think he's talking about . . . bass?"

"Yeah. Crackers, oyster, and bass. Mercy won't let him eat them, and that is all he wants to eat."

"Just crackers and fish? Ew."

"And oysters. He calls it *fish and chips*, but it's not even reminiscent. He stews it with some foul-smelling root, and it smells like leather and dog breath together. He thinks it's some of the finest, fanciest food — but the way he eats it, even the dogs throw up. You wouldn't want to smell it." Her uncle's head bobbed. "So yes, I agree. Ew. So what else can you do with these?"

"The walkies I tempered work better now," Nymeria said. "The glass amplifies their signal range by cutting through corrosive cross-Spirit — " He'd blinked just then. "It's a solid medium," she said. "A radiant trans-medium. It functions like a slow-moving liquid conductor, which stabilizes the optic stream. Some media and hue combinations conduct better than others, but some last longer if the exchange of ions is restricted to . . ." She realized she'd lost at least *part* of his understanding, so she quieted. "I am still trying to learn about it the way Father had to with his patients. Except I must figure it out by myself. I don't have books or teachers. Just . . . memories. Ideas."

"Corrosive cross-mediator-trans-functioning-what?" He blinked again.

"Interference, sort of," she said more simply. "I don't know where it is coming from, but I think I know why it is happening."

"The destruction and burial of the Grid would just about be responsible for the majority of the interference near the old cities," said Uncle Reid. "Everyone knows that." But Nymeria shook her head. He continued. "And a lack of towers and signal transponders . . ." Still, she shook her head. "And fallen satellites . . ."

"Actually, that's not all true," Nymeria countered. "We should already have gained back some of our ability to communicate across longer distances with the equipment and facilities the Enforcers rebuilt a couple hundred years ago before they quit trying to make them work. You know how magnetic fields work, right? Some of the loops of the opposite charge are much more elongated because some waves are more powerful — that is based on the rhythm of the push-pull cycle, and it is affected by our solar rotation. Most of the rest of the waves form a sort of continual sphere because those are the rhythmic skips between. If a liquid mass, or a mass suspended in a vacuum, has gravitational weak points and strong points, it is usually because . . ." She trailed off. "Um. This is . . . similar." Finally, she had to ask obtrusively. "What?"

Uncle Reid tapped the table. "I think I'm just starting to realize that you may be a bit of a savant . . . potentially smarter than even I."

"You mean it's hard to understand?" she asked. "Why?"

"Look. Honestly, I don't often judge others' intelligence to be comprehensive enough to throw me for a loop with a really technical explanation of something they know well. I understand the power grid and why what worked hundreds of years ago actually worked, but no one's been able to figure out why so much of it doesn't anymore — "

"But I just told you why, Uncle Reid," Nymeria said.

Her uncle nodded. "Yeah, but . . . It seems you may have a knack for some kind of tech I'm not perfectly understanding. The *confusing me* thing, that doesn't often happen. I must be getting old, or something. How difficult is the medical stuff to you?"

"Not very, but I don't like it."

"Even the big words?"

"They're easy enough, even though they're tongue-twisters sometimes. But I don't like it," she repeated impatiently. Why didn't he understand that? "What about you? Father said you don't like it, either. Is it because it's confusing, or because you don't like medical stuff, either?"

He frowned thoughtfully, and then he conceded another point. "The reason I don't like talking to your dad about the complicated medical studies he gathers is that he forgets that I can follow him despite how broad and complex his field is, and I don't like being given six-hour lectures with all the intricacies therein. His creepy, perfect textbook memory thing is annoying when it comes to talking about procedural stuff. I understand it well enough if I just skim through his encrypted notes."

"That's why you tell him to skip the details all the time?"

"Yes. Most of it is self-evident, even repeatable, with the right equipment. I don't know how these glass things work, though. Yet you really must, because this one is working. Without wires, fuses, chips, bulbs, chemicals . . . or . . . Pfff. *Anything*. Just glass. It *is* just glass, isn't it?" He held up the glass heart, an incredulous look upon his face. "You're one creepy-cool little monster, you know."

Nymeria bowed her head to hide her blush. "You think so?"

Uncle Reid saw her embarrassment, and alarm flashed across his face. "Hey." He cupped her chin and lifted it. "Look at me, Nymeria. Don't ever doubt yourself, and don't ever dare be ashamed of being yourself. Okay? You have nothing to be ashamed of. It's a good thing if you're smarter than any of the other kids around here. Don't ever let anyone make you feel less for being different. Most kids your age can't even pronounce the words you said a while ago, and more than half of the adults I've met can't, either. And you know I don't lie unless I think it is absolutely necessary and in everyone's best interest. Is there a reason I would lie to you right now?"

"Not that I am aware of," she said quietly.

"Good. I meant it." He returned his attention to the glass heart for a moment. "I may very well have a business proposition for you," said Uncle Reid. "As long as you can tolerate pretending to care to read. You still need to keep up the *appearance* of bothering with your lessons, after all. Even if it is just to keep your mother and father happy." He thought for another moment and then added sharply, "But you *will* need to actually study his notes and try to learn what is in them. No shortcuts there, or the deal will be off. I'll start quizzing you to make sure you're doing what you need to be doing."

Nymeria rolled her eyes. "I don't have to read his books to know what is in them. Please don't tell me the same thing they keep telling me. I am tired of saying *I know*, because I really *do* know. I promise."

"Pretend not to know, then, or whatever floats your boat, little monster." He smirked, then. "And don't let your father realize that we're both smarter than he is, or he'll get competitive. Now. You want to know my business proposition or not?"

"Absolutely, I do."

He frowned. "Sometimes you do not sound like a child, you know that?"

Nymeria laughed to herself and shrugged. "It makes no difference to me, but I will use that for future reference should any trouble come along. It may come in hand. What is your idea?"

"What are you, five?"

"*Almost six!*"

"Jumping apocalypse, girl, you think and act and speak like an adult, and it's creepy."

"You are getting off subject. What is your idea, Uncle Reid?"

He grinned. "Make more of these. The light ones. The walkie ones — I want to test those to see how much they help. And ensure the glass is hard to find on them so it looks as though the tech is functioning on its own. *And no explosive ones.*"

"Too late." She laughed when he glared at her. "I'm kidding, Uncle Reid! I only made one! I don't even know how I did that one yet. The patterns are very intricate, and the designs are difficult to thread."

"Well, no explosive ones. And act more like a kid."

Nymeria considered it. "What do I get in return?"

Uncle Reid's laughter was raw this time. He covered his mouth with his fist, and he looked over his shoulder quickly to assess whether he'd awakened Old Benjamin Moore. The old man was muttering incomprehensibly again. "You *are* a wise one. What do you want?"

"I want you to not tell Mother and Father about our business deal, and I want . . . Well, I've never gotten to try cake before. Mother says it's divine. *Chocolate* cake."

"Oh, you expensive little she-devil," he whispered. "Do you know how hard it is to come by cacao beans? Impossible! They're from the bottom of the continent!"

"Not my problem." She stuck out her tongue and crossed her eyes. "Is this what normal children do? Do I look like a child now?"

Uncle Reid laughed quietly against his fist until his eyes watered. "Yes, Nymeria, very much so. File that away for future reference so you can save us all from trouble with it." He pushed the journal toward her once more. "I have one more request."

She squinted at him. "*Neija.*" *What.*

"You realize I don't understand what *neija* means."

"Well, that is your loss. Tell me what your other request is so I might deny you."

He tapped the journal. "If I get more books, of greater variety, do you want to test how far this ability of yours goes? It might be useful to us all later. More than your convincing kid act might be."

Nymeria took a breath and stared at the journal for a long time. "I would rather not. But . . . if they do not have in them what these do, I think I would probably *like* them. Yes. Go ahead. Especially if they are about technology and science and creatures. And places. And histories and fairy tales. No scary ones, though. Or gory."

His brows rose. "That's all, is it? Just every subject there is, or ever was? Except scary or gory."

"I would like to learn about those things. And I think Marissa and Jamie would like it if I shared the books with them."

"All right, kiddo. This will be our secret, then. I am curious about the extent of this skill of yours. It might be the only way we can truly learn about it."

"Why?" She frowned then. "Were you and Father talking about it?"

Her uncle shrugged. "Ellie Mae found the walkies you'd taken, remember? She brought them to the meeting, and we all had a talk about them. Some bad men had some glass like yours, and they did some very bad things with them."

"Why would they want to do bad things with them? Were any people hurt?" When he did not reply to her questions, she knew the answer. She was repelled. "Uncle, that's terrible!"

He nodded. "We decided to destroy the ones your mother found because it was unanimously agreed that they were dangerous. But . . . if you can program them at will, I would like to see how they may be helpful instead. It would be good if we could use them to aid others, and to continue to improve the guild's standing among its allies in the future."

Nymeria considered that for a bit. Then she made up her mind. "They *could* be dangerous, I suppose. So I will always take that into consideration when I am putting the designs together. I will be careful to ensure nothing bad happens by them."

"I'll have a talk with Ellie Mae to ensure she does not interfere with your experiments," said Uncle Reid. "But you'll have to guard yourself to make sure you do not get into trouble with them. Just don't steal anything else. You will go directly to Ellie if you need to borrow anything from her or her subordinates. No *stealing*."

"I promise," Nymeria nodded. She smiled, feeling excited. "I will deliver your first three batches of glass for free, but you will get me books to read that are not drenched in blood and screams like Father's. We can benefit from one another. Partners, if you will."

Uncle Reid stretched out his arm for a hug. "All right, monster. I'll do that for you. Gimme a hug to seal the deal, will you? I'm leaving later today, and I want all the hugs I can get before I go because I'll be gone for a while on important business. And because I love hugs. And why do I love hugs?"

Nymeria laughed as she recited alongside her uncle, "Because you're a big, old, boring bear with a mean face. And old bears with mean faces love hugs."

CHAPTER TEN

𝒯AERYN

TAERYN FELT THE GLASS SHARD he'd wrestled from them break and lodge in the skin upon his left hand. It grew hot — and the light it emitted burned him from the inside, until he screamed brutally against the glass and the wide-open wound across his throat . . . His consciousness seemed to fall away.

And then he dreamt the shard began to glow so brightly that it blinded his eyes and began to burn him alive. He dreamt of a soft, feminine voice calling out in some foreign tongue, a cry to which he had the urge to reply but could not.

And then the dream turned to the mud that clotted the bloody opening his attacker had carved in his throat. He tasted the rotted foliage, felt a worm move against the opening. Felt the air becoming harder and harder to rake into his lungs, and felt his flesh still burning where it had been pierced. The rain soaked through his clothes and drowned his hair; it pounded against his body and rammed against his eyes. And where his eyelids cracked apart, the blood pooling into the muddy water about him carried with it small rivulets of curling, silver light. And the mud sucked him deeper in its embrace as Taeryn clutched at his throat, sputtering, spitting red at death, trying to dislodge what was no longer even in his hand as the growing darkness gave way to a pulsing, beckoning light . . .

And in the vision of the light? Snowfall . . . and majestic mountains whose peaks pierced the sky and vanished beyond a roiling sea of clouds and mist and fog. He saw places to which he'd never traveled in his own life, places too impossible to have been built by men. There were giant, imposing keeps with towers that shot upward like crystal-and-steel spears, with terraces and bridges that flowed like cloth, and with ribbons of silk which flew from one peak to another, to another. He saw war, and blood, and death — he saw the most tragic and horrific chaos he'd ever witnessed in the midst of the most beautiful place he had ever laid eyes upon. And he saw an explosion much like the one that had devastated Five Tower. Before him, it toppled the cliffs and caused an avalanche that ripped trees from their roots and bridges from the skies. It blanketed everything that came crashing down in a plume of choking, freezing white. And at the center of it all . . . a familiar child's scream, off in the distance, up the mountainside.

And then the dark, monstrous creatures hiding among every shadow and nook and cranny took form and converged toward the light in a great, black flood, as though to devour it . . .

* * * * * * *

Taeryn's eyes fluttered open. His body seemed unattached, and the voices he heard were unfamiliar.

"It is awake," said one.

The other was clutching at Taeryn's jaw, looking him over. "Yes. Awakened. It has the

75

Blood Light now. The damned thing's flesh swallowed it whole just to keep that little thing from us. Didn't know this one could eat it."

"Think they'll want it?"

Their features blurred into one another, and Taeryn could not tell them apart.

"Perhaps," replied the second one. "The Blood Light's got it now. It'll be mad as a rabid cat by the week's end. Chain it better. Won't have it breaking free, escaping. Won't have news of them spreading. The Strangers will likely want this one. This is a fresh one."

Nothing they were saying made any sense to Taeryn.

"If it starts saying it's seeing the creatures — "

"We know," said the other. "Don't touch it, now. Don't get twisted by it as well."

"It is trying to speak," said the first.

Taeryn's lips would not form any words when he urged them to. But the second seemed to know what he wanted to ask anyway, and that one replied.

"*Where* is it?" The second laughed madly. Bony fingers poked his skull. "It is captured by us. Saved from the wolves that ate its dead friend. It has a long journey with us. We'll sell it for a good profit instead of eat it."

Taeryn's heart thumped at that. They spoke like the Descendants of the Moon. Like cult priests.

The first laughed. "Wouldn't want to eat a curse, no," said the second, whose laughter was hacked with a fit of coughing.

"The hunters want ones like it — "

"It's more like the hunters than them."

"*Bakh!* Doesn't matter. Hunters will still buy it. It is most unique, limp and nearly dead as it is. We'll keep it alive long enough to get paid."

"Heheh . . . Yes. Payment. Our honor will be restored."

Taeryn's fingers barely twitched when he tried to move his hand, his arm. He could not feel his body clearly through the feverish energy still coursing through him. He felt himself still burning. Deep down, beneath the skin; beneath the muscles; beneath the bones and the blood. Somewhere deeper, there was a bright, blinding fire that kept him screaming, even though his body wouldn't scream for him. The air seemed too thick for his lungs to manage anything more than a raking, wheezing breath.

Too bad he could see nothing at all. He'd been blinded. The way his eyes burned, he knew it was so.

"It is trying to use its eyes," said one.

"That *color* again," said the other. Its bony fingers took his jaw again, pulled his face forward. Taeryn smelled the rancid odor of death when the priest breathed in his face. "What does it see?" the stranger asked. "Nothing? Then what good are those eyes if its eyes see nothing at all?"

The first sniggered. "Useless color, then, isn't it?"

"Same color as the rest, and yet the rest see more than us."

"Creatures . . ." choked Taeryn. A fear unlike anything he'd ever felt began to roll into him like a heavy fog, so thick it was nearly unbreathable. "Darkness . . . They come from the darkness . . . from a gateway." His voice didn't even sound his own anymore, the way it cracked and split like burning kindlin, barely above a whisper. "Searching for us . . . for *her*."

The first cackled and slapped Taeryn's leg restraint. "See? Cursed by the Blood Light, just like the rest. It'll be mad soon enough."

Both began to laugh together until his next warning came. "It'll kill us all . . ."

Both sobered, and the second spoke again. "What does it *mean*, it'll kill us all? It'll do no such thing. It is restrained properly."

"No . . . *That*." With all his will, he pointed toward the coldness where he could see red bleeding into the black world about him. "The shadow upon it frightens them. It'll devour us *all* — "

"What does it look like?" asked one slowly.

"Eyes, like blue fire . . . Blood everywhere, oceans of it . . . They're all screaming in *agony* — "

"Gag it," commanded the first bitterly. "Gag it *now*! Knock it out! Shut it up! Cover its eyes, and get more chains! We'll not let *Them* see us just because *it* sees *Them*!"

"But what is the blue-eyed one?" demanded the other. "The cursed have never spoken of another kind, none of them."

"It is more dangerous than the demons at the heart of their curse! Do what I have said before we are ruined as well!"

CHAPTER ELEVEN

$\mathscr{M}$ercy

CYAN WAS NOW A GHOST TOWN, yet Mercy spied a spire of white-gray smoke curling from a campfire. He heard the barking laughter of men and the tortured gurgle of some animal they prodded. The sound of a stick raking across metal bars pricked his ears. His steps turned quieter when a chain rattled; he considered he needed not alert them of his presence for risk they were of the unfriendly sort.

"It's gone thirsty," laughed one of the men as Mercy crept along the alleyways. The ash underfoot, left from the incineration of the town a few weeks prior, had begun to loosen a sweet, hearthy smell after the rain had washed away the pungent smoke.

Mercy's skin spiked with fleshy goosepimples when he remembered Taiir's troublesome description of what they'd come to, of bodies everywhere, every one of them showing signs of ravaging disease. The bodies had been gathered and burned, and the rest of the town had been set ablaze to prevent another outbreak. Now Cyan's ruinous stone structures were all that remained of the settlement.

A few towers, an unfinished curtain wall meant to keep only predators from passing, and no small multitude of now doorless, roofless dwellings dotted the eerie, soot-painted, ash-covered landscape. The willows were charred, the pond where the reeds were now wilting was black from the pollution that had washed into it, the once-enormous pines were but broken nubs hinting their species, and not even vultures bothered with what was left. There was precious little to loot, so it baffled Mercy to know he was not alone here.

The men were likely an unsavory lot. They'd probably chosen to come to Cyan to create from its corpse a twisted abode from which to base their ill operations.

And the beast in the cage, he *hoped* was not one of the last of his missing dogs. He'd tracked one of his striped female pointers here. Since the day she'd run off, he'd worried over whether she'd attract an unsuitable and masterless wild beast to her heat. Mercy had been keen on keeping her from a wasted, useless litter that could neither be traded nor be of quality use.

Mercy's fist tightened when he heard the bars raked again. Dog fighting was one likely intention of these men, unless they saw how well-trained his dog was. With a deep breath, he checked his dagger, his walkie, and his courage, and he stepped from the alleyway — and a pale, unimpressed eye met him where he'd stopped. It blinked. So did he. Then the beast snorted.

His heart remembered to beat once more, and his hands fluttered away from his mouth as the urge to cry out faded. The pony shook her mane and stamped a hoof, as though demanding he untether the great burden she'd had tied to her. Mercy nearly laughed at his easy scare and placed his hand to the beast's giant, fuzzy cheek.

"I thought I tied you well to that tree," he laughed quietly as he ruffled her wild mane. She turned her head and pressed her nose into his hand and nudged. "So impatient," he snorted. "Gotta follow me everywhere, Beasty, don't you now? If only I had a woman half as enamored of me as you . . ."

Mercy frowned when he realized the tether had been sliced clean through, not chewed or broken or frayed. His horse could not have done that.

Too late did he hear the crunching of a fallen door's blackened coals. Too late did he place his hand upon his dagger and spin to face his adversary. Just before the enemy's knife drove into him, he saw the furry cowl, the wolf's teeth strung in a necklace about the man's throat, and the bone color of the cannibal's blade. Blinding white pain seared through Mercy's flesh, and his knees buckled, his own dagger falling with a muted *thump* to the ash and burnt wood underfoot. The assassin jerked the bone blade free unhappily as Mercy attempted to gasp for a breath and could not manage to do so thoroughly.

"I missed its heart," hissed the occult priest, and his unhealthy teeth flashed in a grimace as he struck Mercy in the jaw with a powerful right hook. The bearded, cowled assassin stooped to pick up Mercy's dagger as Mercy himself clutched at the gaping slit across his side, and the alleyway tilted. Red dripped into the ash and began to form a small, spreading stain. When he struggled to regain his sense of balance, the wolfman placed a leather boot upon Mercy's chest and kicked him onto his back. Then the man eyed his horse and his belongings. "What is the cage for? The leashes. Dogs? It raises dogs to trade? Or it trains them to hunt?" The man's bleak brown eyes darted back to him. "Has it been tracking us to free its friend? Does it have the Blood Light as well? Two are better than one, we'll agree. We *can* use the profit. The children *are* easier to come by with money."

Mercy pulled the walkie discreetly from his belt as the man rummaged through his rucksacks, tossing things to the ground. He cut free the cargo, and Mercy bit out a cry as his horse skirted sideways. One of Beasty's hooves crushed his outstretched foot. "Hmm," said the wolfman. "Doesn't seem so."

Mercy gripped the radio at his belt as he struggled to rise again. It wasn't a blade, but at least it was as solid as a brick. "Why are your clansmen in Cyan?" stammered Mercy. "And what friend of mine are you talking about?"

The man growled and held up the dagger Mercy had dropped. "It meant to kill us with this unholy blade, made not from the blessed dead, didn't it? The dogs were to find us, weren't they? Who has sent its murderous hand our way?"

Again, the animal being tortured up the street rammed the cage bars, and more laughter ensued from the other Wolfshadow men.

"Was it the father's final hunter *Lukas* who sent it?" asked the wolfman who stood over him. The cowled cannibal flung the dagger and spat at it where it landed across the street. "The wicked creature will regret turning on the services his master has paid well for. Word of his treachery will be sent home, indeed. I'll have his friends deal with *him* soon enough. There are more of them than he, and all are more loyal."

"I don't know any Lukas," said Mercy truthfully. "I only meant," he paused to suck in an elusive breath, "to gather my dogs. They escaped my kennels — "

The wolfman's keen gaze darted to Mercy's arm. "What is it holding?"

When Mercy shook his head and kept his mouth shut in defiance, the wolfman grew angry. The man sheathed his bloody bone knife and stepped forward. Mercy struggled to crawl away and brought the walkie to his mouth. "Alert to Crow Post! Mercy Oscanti requesting backup at Cya — "

The wolfman kicked the walkie from Mercy's hands, breaking two of his fingers and his nose, and then the wolfman took a handful of his hair and began to drag him into the street, where he could be seen by the wolfman's brethren. "Look, Brothers," the wolfman said to them loudly as Mercy clutched at his hands in an attempt to lessen the grip. "A gift. A plaything, spying upon us like a spider. Let's kill it and eat it."

Mercy was pitched forward, and ash clung to his face and powdered and stung and blinded his eyes. The thing in the cage tugged at its chains, and through his stinging, blurry vision, Mercy could have sworn it had an almost human shape.

He gritted his teeth and then whistled.

Beasty whinnied unpleasantly and she began to circle nervously. "Come, girl," he choked. "Come on, girl, help me!"

"This one had *this*, Agarath," said one of the wolfmen to Agarath, who was currently stomping Mercy's radio to bits.

Agarath looked up as one of his fur-cloaked brothers threw something small to him. It glinted like a ruby in the sunlight as it sailed overhead. Agarath snatched it from the air with his stained, clawed fingers. As he held it up to the sun, his cowl fell back, and Mercy saw the wolf skull through which his greasy locks were braided. The skull's teeth were stained with old blood, and the cannibal's braids slithered through the eyes, like snakes, and through where the ears had been. Feathers, and small tufts of fur, and red and blue beads which appeared to have been made of human fingerbones adorned the man's dread crown. And down the length of his face were three bright smears of blood that the shadows had darkened to look like war paint.

"By the Lightless Underhalls of the Fifth Tower, what is this?" Agarath asked, his voice gravelly with displeasure. "Answer me, Tarek."

"Blood. But is it the same blood Lukas went to retrieve?" replied Tarek. "Thretirak found it upon the creature today when he was cleaning its ruined throat. The Blood Light is strong in its flesh. Already, it sees the accursed *things* of the night, as did the unholy hunters themselves claim."

"But does it understand those *things*?" asked Agarath as he uncorked the vial in his hands and smelled it. He frowned and smelled it again. "It does not smell of rot. How is this? There is no cold to keep it from the rot."

"Strange, yes?" asked the third, who must have been Thretirak. "Now, where did you find *that* creature?"

Agarath sealed and tossed the vial back to Tarek. "Keep that for *Them*. They'll be curious, I think. And this creature, it was following us. I found first its horse. Then it. The fettered beast led me to it, and she even maimed it for me."

Mercy opened his mouth to speak, to demand answers, but then another man's screams broke through the kennels, and all of them turned. It rattled Mercy when suddenly he realized the shape in the cage *was* another human being. And that man was missing an arm.

Agarath spoke again. "Looks as if it's realized we cut away one of its arms to feed the dogs."

Tarek and Thretirak laughed wickedly.

And Agarath turned and knelt by Mercy and placed a clawed finger under his chin. "This one, we can eat ourselves. No curse in its blood to aggravate our own."

Before Mercy had comprehended the wicked, hungry gleam in the wolfmen's eyes, Agarath had seized his jaws with both hands and poised himself to twist vehemently. "Beasty!" screamed Mercy — and then Agarath was suddenly gone from him. The wolfman was upon the ground a few paces from him, writhing in agony, clutching at a bruised arm where the horse had kicked him furiously. The arm was broken at an odd angle.

"Get it!" roared Agarath as he drew a breath and clawed his way to his knees. His forehead beaded with sweat from the pain that spent at his every movement, but he was too fierce to be felled by such a trap, and the injury did not slow him enough.

Fear thrummed within Mercy as the other men drew their weapons. Bone knives for each hand — some of those knives were the length of an entire femur.

Mercy scrabbled for the pony's tether where it dragged the ground as she pranced about him warily, still ready to kick. He whistled urgently, "Kneel!" he cried as she neared at his call. He spat the blood from his tongue as she tossed her mane and refused. "Kneel!"

he cried again as he grasped the tether with both hands. He was unable to hold the tether tightly because of his broken fingers.

Agarath raised his dagger as he fell upon Mercy, and Mercy kicked with his injured foot, ignoring the pain it caused him as best he could. The dagger went into his calf, and he screamed. The horse started, and Agarath fell away, losing his dagger as he rolled, and Mercy wrapped the tether tightly around his forearm as his horse dragged him some twenty meters or so. She slowed again nervously, and as he choked on the ash that she'd kicked up, she turned her head back to look down upon him.

What are you doing down there? she seemed to say.

"Kneel — " he coughed.

Beasty obeyed this time and knelt, and Mercy yanked the blade from his leg and threw it aside as he climbed her back. His shirt was heavy with blood and ash, and dark crimson bled freely from the opened wound on his leg.

"Ha!" he barked as he looked frantically behind him.

She rose as Tarek hurtled another bone knife at him. It caught him in the rib but glanced off. He hissed in pain, and Beasty reared, spooked. He was very nearly unseated by her but clutched her mane for his life.

"Ha!" he cried again.

Behind him, Agarath had already mounted another horse, and the savage look upon the man's face sent another thrill of fear into Mercy. He was going to be dead soon. He would not escape these men. They would hunt him unto his death.

The trees flew by and grew thicker and thicker with various evergreens and humongous oaks, and the light became dimmer as the forest became so dense it muffled his horse's every step. Vines slashed at his face and his hands, and widowmakers fell from overhead as the wind began to stir the bare-branched, green, and flowering spring crowns of the trees. His horse stumbled down a rocky incline where rainwater had dug trenches in the earth and exposed endless webs of sprawling roots.

Mercy's pursuers were silent as a wraith, no catcalling, no shouting. Even their horses' racing hooves barely seemed to stir up any discernible sound. Several times, he would look back to see Agarath and Thretirak gaining on him, and he would spur Beasty onward, with fear gagging him from rebuke or cry.

CHAPTER TWELVE

SILENCE

REID HELD A PACK FULL OF rations, about to toss them onto the back of one of the horses when he looked over his shoulder due to the shouting of children.

His daughter and his niece and nephew were fending off some angry refugee kids.

Reid paused and watched the drama, unsure whether he should intervene.

Jamie was the boldest and the loudest among the children as he waved a stick at an older boy with orange hair and three missing baby teeth. Two smaller boys, slender and equally red-haired — brothers, surely — hid behind the larger, and both had rocks in their hands, ready to hurl them. The oldest simply held his fists curled into balls, ready to swing them whichever way.

"My sister is not a witch!" Jamie was shouting. "She's my big sister, and you better leave her alone!"

Taiir chuckled beside Reid as Nymeria grabbed the stick by the end and lowered it while her brother still held it tightly. "Stop, Jamie," she said quietly. "They know I am different. It's okay."

"You are curious how this will end?" Taiir asked, nudging Reid's arm. Reid grimaced in reply.

"It's not okay," cried Marissa. She stood between both groups. "You shouldn't have to take any of this from them. If one of them pushes you again, I'll have your brother hand *you* that stick, and you're going to learn to defend yourself properly. They'll learn to mind their manners."

"Marissa's pretty good at sending troublemakers running off," said Reid as he secured the bags and checked again the extra battery and the hand-cranked charger for the radio he carried. Both were in good repair, and the wrappings were still intact and would keep water out. "A bit of a peacekeeper, if you will."

"I have noticed," said Taiir. He gripped the black handle of his carved staff and pulled it over his shoulder. "Should I frighten them all into an alliance?"

Reid shook his head. "They'll only regroup elsewhere to start over, and we won't be there to intervene if it is necessary. Let's see if they can resolve this peacefully. They'll need the experience."

"Listen," said Nymeria to the boys. Her hands were out in a gesture of peace. "I didn't take any food from your family, I *left* food there. And it's not cursed because I touched it. Also . . . if I *am* a witch, it is not the kind to hurt you, it is the kind to protect you. Otherwise, I would not be allowed to live here, too."

Taiir chuckled again under his breath. "Using tha logic of lesser minds to outwit them."

"You have no *idea*," Reid sighed. He finished fastening the second pack and calmed the horse beside him. He was not going to ride this one, although he did favor her. She was more surefooted than most, and she kept a steadier pace. But she was of a stronger, more enduring breed — it made more sense for her to haul the load. "Nymeria has a . . . *special* brand of logic. It's hard to argue against her sometimes. It's sometimes easy to forget she's a kid."

The soulful eyes of the sweet-mannered horse in front of him found him and blinked, as though to ask, *What about me? I have a special kind of logic, too.* Reid ruffled her mane, and she whinnied softly, content.

"But you're *not a witch*!" cried Jamie as he tried to jerk the stick free from Nymeria's hands. Nymeria did not let go. She was determined to avoid conflict.

Reid was amused to hear her confide quietly to her brother and her cousin, "They don't know that. And I shouldn't have to fight every person who judges me wrong. That's probably going to happen at every turn, and that would be a wearisome way to live, fighting everyone. I'd make more enemies that way."

"I don't understand why you won't just pummel them and get it over with," Marissa huffed. "Bullies deserve to get beaten up, and they'll leave you and other people alone if they learn they're not all powerful."

"You forget that I am smaller," Nymeria reminded her. "I am an easier target than most. And being different makes me stand apart, Marissa. They want someone to vent their frustrations at."

"So? You're not going to be that person! That is not your responsibility. They're brothers. They can vent at each other and beat each other up instead! And besides, only boys who are cowards pick on little girls." Marissa placed her hands on her hips and whipped her hair over her shoulder as she turned her head to glare at the oldest boy. She poked him in the chest and told him exactly what she thought of him. "You're a bully. And so are your brothers. You're scared, so you're mean. And if you want to be mean to someone who was just trying to help you, then you better be willing to fight. And I don't mean three on one, because that is a coward's way. Three of you, three of us. Are you willing to fight *now*? Or do you want to run home and cry to your *mommy*?"

The largest boy gulped in the face of Marissa's intensity. "But . . ."

"So much for peacekeeper," Reid chuckled fondly. "She's just like her mother. All bark and bite. She'll provoke a fight soon if she keeps it up. Also, make sure we've extra tethers, I don't like the fray or wear on these." He eyed the saddles, running through his usual mental checklists and searching for new things or things forgotten. It was always good to be prepared and to keep equipment maintained. Any less could cost a man his life at the most inopportune time.

"But there was a bite taken out of it!" cried one of the smaller boys.

Marissa rolled her eyes. "And . . . ? Did it look like a little girl bite? That dog you keep around your tent will eat anything. And besides, if she ate a bite of it, why not eat the rest? Maybe you were lucky any was left to you at all, if that was the case. If I was a witch and wanted to curse your food, I wouldn't take a single bite out of it . . . I'd turn it into *frogs* and *worms* and leave it for you that way. So go ahead and throw your rocks and hit her. See what *I* do about it. I'm not scared. My daddy and my uncle will kick you out, *and* your parents, because you're causing trouble. Then the wolves will get you. They love the taste of mean boys."

The smaller boys cowered behind the bigger one. "Wolves . . . ?" whispered one. "You mean the — "

"Yes. We keep them around to feed them our enemies. Nymeria could command them if she wanted, but she's a good witch, like she said. That's why they don't come into your camp, and that's why you had food instead of frogs and worms. You heard about her being in the kennels when the dogs went wild, didn't you? There were demons there, and she chased them away to protect everyone. Not one of the dogs hurt anyone, and no one got hurt. That's what that crazy man was screaming about. Go on and ask him. He'll tell you all about it — "

Reid's amusement faded, and he stepped in. "Marissa!"

His daughter started and whirled around, eyes wide and mouth cinched in an *O*. For the first time, she saw him. Marissa blanched, embarrassed. Her hands clasped behind her back, and she bowed her head innocently.

The three boys darted away, their rocks falling to the dirt.

Taiir belted out raw, belly-shaking laughter, and Marissa looked between the two of them, her nervous gaze darting back and forth.

"Daddy, I — "

"She did well, Commander," Taiir said as he shook his dreads from his dark face. "Quick wit, sharp tongue."

"You know better than to send other children around that man," Reid said gravely.

"But they all know he's crazy, and he's scary," she said shyly. "I only meant to scare them more. I don't think those boys would be brave enough to really go and see him. If they were scared of me, they wouldn't dare talk to *him*."

Reid conceded that she had a point. The lunatic killer in the kennel had sprouted rumors the night he'd screamed, begging to be let out. About a hundred people camped in and around that part of the forest had heard him and the explosion. "Regardless, don't tempt the other kids. That prisoner is off-limits. And you should remember that things rarely go according to plan. The weak flock to one another for strength, and bullies often resort to seeking outside help for revenge when they are defeated. Which means they can find the right incentive to recruit even your friends against you. You must consider your provocations more thoroughly and make contingencies that are easier to defend or replace, Marissa. And Nymeria — " He frowned. "Uh . . . Where did she go?"

Jamie stiffened, and his head jerked sideways. "No! Nymeria, wait for me! I wanna help with the flashlights!"

Before Reid could say another word, the stick Jamie had clutched as a weapon fell uselessly. Leaves flitted from the brush and drifted to the ground as the boy thundered through the thicket in search of his sister.

Marissa simply shrugged. "Don't ask me," she said. "Nymeria does that a lot. Can I go? I am not in trouble, am I?"

"Not really. You did well, defending your cousin. But don't provoke as many fights. Eventually you will have to actually finish what you start or try a hell of a lot harder to outsmart their next tactics. Sometimes avoidance is best."

"But you and Momma said — "

"Take advantage of tha moment and run off, little glass maker," Taiir chuckled. He swung his staff and slid it into its secondary angled holster upon his back.

"Bye, Daddy!" Marissa laughed. She, too, darted away.

When she was gone, the mood darkened considerably. Reid felt a hole punching through his chest. He craved another drink to keep what he kept to himself at the back of his mind. Instead, he removed his dagger and ran his thumb across the blade, checking its sharpness. He did the same with his sword.

"Tha girl is very aware she is not normal," Taiir said warily, reminding Reid of the other things he'd uncovered.

"I know," Reid said as he sheathed the sword once more. He was satisfied that both blades were sharp, and he checked the rest. "I am glad she accepts it," he added. It was better to listen to Taiir's contemplations and focus on preparations than to allow the memory of his parents' deaths to return. He could not allow himself to dwell on the image of their blackened, smoldering bodies.

The clips for his gun were all fully loaded, and Reid had already checked the individual bullets. Everything was in place and in good order.

There was a small moment of silence, and Taiir turned to questions he'd probably been considering for days now. The man wasn't often prone to say much unless he'd weighed what he wanted to voice heavily. As it turned out, Taiir had several questions and several concerns. The first of those was, "Are you sure you still want to try to find buyers for her tech?"

Reid scratched his head as the two of them turned back the way they'd come to fetch more of the wares and documents they would soon be transporting. "Normally, Taeryn and Davos and my parents would be doing all of this. Trade and business were their duties, not mine. I have men who can step in for me to help with the apprentices, just as others would normally be able to do their jobs. But we don't have anyone who can really take Davos's and Taeryn's places, not with the things that need looking into. I'm the only one that can take care of the extra tasks this time."

"You did not answer tha question," Taiir said.

They breathed in the acrid scent of iron and soot in the air as they passed by the blacksmith, and they began to make their way through a bustling crowd near the command station, where complaints were being made by the refugees. Beyond that would be the gates into Crow Post, and just on the other side of the low curtain wall stood the silo and the apothecary. Adam Samsinger was back at his job, his hand bandaged but hardly usable. He'd been working hard despite the injury, and thanks to several new hires from the refugee camp, he had more supplies waiting in heavy boxes. Medicines and notes, contracts, and more. Things that would need to be taken to Aelynhold, Hagenhold, Tallil, Lovael, Arsennia, Black Temple, and several other places. It would all take more than a single trip. Some of the cities would forward the information portion of it, others would require Reid's arrival in person.

Reid contemplated his answer as they made their way toward the apothecary. "I told Nymeria to disguise it. It's going to look like regular tech, but it will still be a hybridization. She'll figure more of them out, I'm confident. She's already gotten many of the lights we made a deal for done, ready to pitch. I don't think the clients will figure out how they work, or be able to replicate them . . ." He shrugged. "I hope it keeps her busy. She was excited about being able to do something useful with them. Ralleigha said she's already asked for a few odd things to be made in glass." His brows furrowed as he added thoughtfully, "I think she'll be an excellent entrepreneur someday. Besides. It keeps her from running off with others' tools, because I gave her a set, and she'll be able to trade with the junkers soon and learn some new things. And if she's occupied, it'll keep her from trouble." At Taiir's doubtful look, he added, "Hopefully."

Taiir was one of the few who had a closer insight about Nymeria and her eccentricities, and Reid didn't mind talking openly with him.

"I'm still worried, though," Reid admitted.

"You asked me to read tha rest of that letter after tha meeting," said Taiir. "You knew I would understand what it meant, and that I would agree to go with you. I will be with you even after tha end, Commander. But I trust her tha least among my allies and my enemies." Taiir broke through the throng of people first, and Reid followed behind quietly.

"Two years ago, I told your brother she is a dangerous child," said Taiir, and he slowed so that they fell in step once more. "He did not believe me. Neither did his wife. You are tha only one who is not blind to it. If she harms others tha way she did tha Bright Night, I will kill her. You know that. I told you when I arrived, when I became an ally of Black Temple and joined Crow Post and began helping others. But even with such a promise, I hope to be there when we find a way to help her. I do not believe what happened was her fault, but I will not risk another Bright Night. I want to protect your people from such a dread fate."

"I know," Reid sighed. "And you know I will fight you to the death if you ever raise a hand against her." When Taiir smiled, Reid knew they still had an understanding. "You've been valuable, Taiir. I am glad we understand one another."

Taiir voiced another of his questions then. "What will you do if you cannot find either of them? Tha ones tha letter named *Gabriel* and *Rhael.*"

"I'll figure it out. In the meantime, we're going to indulge her little business to give her something to work for, so she can practice her abilities and get them under control. We'll figure out how that letter is related to her eventually."

"That sigil should be a clue," said Taiir. "But I am unsure where to start. I saw many sigils in Five Tower, borne by messengers and traders and emissaries. But I have never seen that one before. I imagine you have already planned a route to find tha information we need to progress in tha search?"

"Tallil, perhaps, would be the best place to start," Reid answered slowly. He had, indeed, thought of the most likely sources of knowledge on that sigil's origin and meaning as well as who might be using it. "I know a man there who has an old library. He has a few really old documents from the time of Black Temple's beginning."

"Black Temple's *beginning*?" asked Taiir incredulously.

Reid nodded. "The sigil looks similar to one used secretly within my brother's guild. Not even the High Council has access or the authority to use it. Those who *are* allowed to use it are few and far between, and they do not send those messages to others outside the guild. I was surprised Lukas had gotten a hold of it, or that my parents had carried it." He rubbed at his chest where his heart throbbed deeply, and he swallowed against the tightening in his throat. Even the mention of his parents hurt. It turned his thoughts to the fire that had savaged their bodies. "I don't think it is a coincidence that it looks similar," Reid explained, and he buried the thoughts of his parents away.

He went on. "Arsennia would be even more likely for information if we don't find anything sooner rather than later. The acolytes there have the largest collection of information on this part of the continent, aside from Black Temple itself. But I'm not allowed in Black Temple's archives because I am not a high-standing guild member, and their archives are guarded strictly. In Arsennia, such information would likely be considered trivial historical text, of little import. It wouldn't be so much guarded there as hidden by the monstrous quantity of historical texts they have amassed and stored. It's still guarded, but I could more easily bribe my way. And even though the information I could learn would be older than the trees, and might not be much to go on, anything is better than nothing. I might get an idea who is using it, why, and where it hails from."

Taiir nodded, surmising, "So it might be tha approach to locating him."

"Indeed." Reid and Taiir waited for a passing cart, and then Reid changed the subject. "I've other matters to attend to as well, besides the investigation into that letter, or finding clients or healers for my niece."

"What else are you after?"

"Well, my wife will be away with Marissa to Lovael, where they'll be working with other master artisans, and she requested I find more customers and traders. John also had a list of things he'd wanted done this season while we were delivering apprentices — a trip with which I won't be giving assistance this year. His son has a love for plants that defies explanation."

Taiir's brow lifted, so Reid explained.

"My mother and father wanted to cater to the boy's love of plants, since, like his older sister, Jamie doesn't want to become a surgeon in the guild. But while Nymeria is bound by tradition as the oldest child to become a surgeon like her father, Jamie has options. John gave instructions to our traders this season to find any botanists and acquire every new species of flora and glean every bit of information about them."

"Like alderoot," Taiir nodded. "It began to sprout in my homeland in tha mountains when I was a child. Green, even in tha whitest of winter, and despite its broad, thin leaves."

"Precisely," Reid agreed. "Alderoot saved Nymeria's life. No one knows where it came from, but it's a new species, perhaps only a few decades old, and it has more medical uses than we've expected from any singular plant."

"Ah. John caters to his son's dreams and not his daughter's. You resigned yourself to cater to hers instead."

Reid grimaced. "She shouldn't have to be forced to do something she doesn't want to that would affect the rest of her life. It should be her choice. But John thinks she'll save a lot of people, and he has a perfectly outlined idea of how she will grow up and fit exactly into what he thinks she should be. He thinks it's a high honor to become a surgeon, as does the rest of the guild, *per tradition*. And it is an honor, there is no denying that."

"Yet for tha girl, you and I both know it is a bad idea," Taiir surmised.

Reid paused, then agreed. "Yes."

"And if tha letter speaks of her and not some other, or if she is in some other manner tha same as tha child they found, then it is a mightily bad idea."

Reid sighed. "Yes."

They began to smell a fresher aroma, one of woodsmoke and sweet maple, and of herbs and roasted goat flesh. Reid's mouth watered, but he didn't have time to eat now. They had things to get done.

"Does your brother know you are leaving Crow Post soon on your own agenda? That you will not be helping with tha apprentices this year?"

Reid grimaced. "He will soon. He won't be happy about it, but he'll have to understand. I'll deal with his anger when it comes."

"Why have you not told him about your parents?" asked Taiir suspiciously.

Reid took a deep breath and held it for a long moment before letting it go. "Because it isn't the time. There is too much to do, and *I* haven't even properly processed that they're gone yet."

"You are afraid of what he will do to Lukas."

"Yes. If he kills him, he'll lose his place in the guild." Reid admitted. "But he'll lose more than just that. He'll be branded a traitor. A murderer. No one will trade with him. It's nearly a death sentence on its own to a guild doctor. But it will be worse because he has a family. He would be sentenced to become a junker, and that's extremely dangerous work. Black Temple does not tolerate cold-blooded murderers among its ranks, not even among the higher echelons. If a guild member is proven to have sinned in such a manner, his entire household is punished alongside him. Mistakes are an entirely different thing. Same as self-defense. But I don't think he'll be able to hold himself back and make it look like anything except what it would be."

"You are that worried about his wrath?"

Reid nodded. "Now is not the time for him to learn about Lukas's deeds. I will not risk letting him throw his own future away, let alone the futures of his daughter and his son for one ill-tempered moment of weakness."

"Why do you think he would kill Lukas?"

"Because of what he did to Griggori, another post doctor. Griggori is the reason Jeana cannot speak more than a bare whisper most days. She is doing better, but we don't know if she'll ever recover fully. The scar tissue in her throat makes speech difficult. When she tries too hard to speak, or too often, she suffers. I've seen it send her into coughing fits that don't stop until after there's blood. Because of it, she's very vulnerable to respiratory illnesses, so she can't take on certain responsibilities that most field doctors' wives or husbands take on. She's a tough woman to still be alive after everything she went through, though . . . Griggori is the reason I am hesitant to let my brother learn the truth while Lukas is still at this post. That wretched murderer deserves to die, but we need him for what he knows, and I need my brother where he is. Doing what he is doing. His family needs him."

Taiir's head dipped. "Griggori was a case of self-defense, then. Lukas would not be considered so."

"Exactly. Even if it was self-defense, twice allowing himself to fighting another to the death would be too suspicious to forgive again. My brother is already walking a fine line with Saura's temper over the incident with Griggori."

Adam Samsinger was arguing with John when Reid and Taiir opened the creaking door to the apothecary, which was just across the winding cobblestone street from the inn from where the delicious aroma was wafting.

"You can't tell me you haven't got enough help, Adam," John groaned. He was pulling his hair upright again — any harder would mean he would be pulling it out by the roots.

"Yes, I can," Adam said sorely. "There are too many refugees. The attendants are in and out all day — "

"What is in the crates beside the shop, then? Bunnies and apple sticks? I know you have enough of everything already made. You can't be asking me or Amos for more help again. The attendants need the medications for the refugees — "

"The crates are spoken for," Reid cut in when he saw Adam's chin quiver. The man wasn't good at defending himself; he didn't like offending others, and he didn't handle confrontation well.

Reid felt his gut churn sickly when John turned to him, surprised. "That's part of the assignment Davos and Taeryn were to undertake once they got back," explained Reid. "Part of it was to go to Cyan, but Cyan is gone, so it was reassigned to Hagenhold. They needed the supplies. In return, we are to receive a higher yield of apprentices this year, the most promising among the orphans who are willing, and among guildsmen who are sending their own who have come of age."

John stepped back, defeated. "I'll have to let Nails know the news, then. We'll have to make do with what we've got until those trips are completed."

"Why aren't you attending the wounded, anyway?" Reid mocked lightly. He knew fully that John wanted nothing more than to put planning and commanding on hold so that he could return to his calling. When Reid saw John's darkening expression, he held up his hands . . . and he hoped John couldn't smell the alcohol on his breath or see the shadows under his eyes. "I jest," he said, even though he didn't really feel the energy that he tried to deceive his brother with. Fortunately, John didn't seem to see through the charade. John was at his wits' end, dealing with the chaos, keeping the peace — doing more jobs than he needed to be doing.

Their parents would have stepped into that role if they had still been alive.

The realization pained Reid, and he bit his cheek and shoved the emotion and that thought deep down.

"Can I talk to you alone for a minute?" John said suddenly, forgetting his argument with Adam and waving the apothecary off. "Go ahead and get back to work, Adam," John said. "I apologize for the inconvenience. If you have anything that can help, let me know later. I'll be heading to Ralleigha's glass shop with Reid."

Taiir sensed the brother-to-brother talk would not require his own ears, and he stepped back outside. "I will fetch extra hands to help with tha crates, Commander. They will appreciate tha meal at tha inn afterward. Join us when you are done here."

John and Reid stepped out after Taiir, but while he turned right and called to a very tired, hungry-looking pair of attendants to help him, John and Reid turned left and continued to walk up the cobblestone pathway, through throngs of exhausted morticians, attendants, and others who were making their way to various destinations for various reasons. A fire had started somewhere, and several began running toward it to help extinguish the flames, and John and Reid stepped off the path, out of the way. They took back alleys, which served as a shortcut anyway.

"What is it?" Reid said at last over the fading shouts behind them. He grew weary of waiting for John to speak his mind. John didn't usually hesitate unless something bothered him greatly, if that something was a thing he hadn't quite made his mind up about.

"I've been thinking about sending Nymeria to a specialist. A Keeper. I wanted your opinion. When Mom and Dad return, I'll have them take her. We'll all be busy anyway, and they've been looking forward to taking her on."

Reid's gut clenched. Any words that would have found their way to the surface were strangled out. He did not look at his brother because he did not want him to see that he knew something terrible.

John continued. "I think . . . maybe that strange light may have something to do with some kind of . . . I don't know. Radiation? Something of the sort, perhaps. I have never received or found much information about that kind of sickness. A few of the refugees were speaking about some other people with the same sickness from the mines. They said the ones with it were ill and it blistered them as they got worse. They kicked most of them out, worried it was contagious. I wasn't able to approach to ask any of them anything else on the matter."

And now Reid felt sicker. "It's not radiation."

"But how do you know? We don't have any way of testing for radiation here. The Keepers would."

"I'm educated lightly in the matter, and I can recommend some documents for you to read if you wish. Dealing with possibly irradiated areas was and is one of the thousands of assessment aspects of both my past job and my current one. I think some other tests might be good in her case, but at what cost? Black Temple doesn't just have machines capable of every kind of test lying around, and the nearest Keepers are too far. It would involve a lot of travel, and we can't afford any deviations from our current courses of action. There have been too many attacks. Too many people are relying on us."

John huffed. "I didn't mean send her now. I mean when the apprentice season is finished."

Reid's fists clenched as he struggled not to tell his brother the truth. He could only imagine the rage and the havoc it would cause. "I'm sure Mom and Dad won't be able to make that kind of trip, John."

"Then I could if they are still busy. I could have Nails distribute my duties among some of the other field doctors, and I could have you take over the rest. You know what to do. I could take Nymeria myself — "

"Even if you left today, it would be winter by the time you reached Arsennia. And how do you expect Nymeria to react? You found her unconscious in a crater, about to be killed by a city full of vile people. Dragging her to any kind of Keeper would bring her close to Five Tower. Arsennia is on the *other side* of that wretched city. Perhaps three months' travel, depending on your hardships. By the time you reached Arsennia, you would already be needed again here. I have too much on my plate to take over your job as well. And I wouldn't trust any other slimy, guildless doctor close to Five Tower."

"I'm sure Saura would sanction it, send her with someone — "

"You would really risk Saura taking an interest in Nymeria?" Reid asked incredulously. "Ha! That old woman is cruel and calculating. Perhaps a just leader, but certainly not the kindest or fairest with her way of it. She's called the *Pale Serpent* for a reason. The woman's like a Viridian viper."

Before John could utter another word, Reid turned from him to return the way they'd come. "I've got more important matters to handle right now. Go see Ralleigha and figure out what else she needs. She'll be heading to Lovael soon with Marissa."

Reid left his brother standing there, openmouthed and flabbergasted. Reid did not look back.

Instead of returning to the apothecary — as he'd told himself he would the moment he was out of John's sight — Reid's feet took him to the brewery a few blocks down. The rickety door slammed against the railing when he opened it, and Neathan Heinzrich dropped a glass with a start. The glass shattered, and Odessa Heinzrich looked up from a shot glass half filled with an amber fluid hovering before her lips.

Reid stalked up to the counter, his fingernails biting the edge, and he told them. "Get me the strongest poison you've made. I don't want to be able to remember my name when I wake up."

Odessa set the small glass down and slid it over to him without ever so much as sipping from it. "You probably need that instead. You won't be able to handle our strongest rightly in your state. By the smell of it, you've already been drinkin' some anyhow."

Reid lifted it to his lips, paused, and asked the gray-haired woman what it was.

"*Goldenrod*," was her reply.

He grimaced. "Like the flower?"

Her hearty laugh was hoarse from years of the burn of the strong alcohol they brewed. "Son, it ain't nice like no flower. It's gonna leave your ears ringin' enough you won't have anything left for thinkin'. *Goldenrod*. Golden color. Hits you hard like a rod, smackin' your eardrums to get them ringin'. She's hard to swaller."

He lifted the glass to his lips and swallowed the contents whole. It felt like he'd swallowed acid. Stronger stuff than what he'd been drinking. And he knew better, but he made another bad decision. "Get me a bottle or two for the road, I think I'll be needing it." He told himself he would only partake when he needed the reprieve.

Odessa eyed her son. "You gonna clean that mess up, Neathan? Or just stare at the man? That's grief possessin' him, and you're bein' rude. Get him a couple bottles and clean up." Then she leaned closer, placed her hand gently over the back of his right hand, and said in a motherly, concerned tone, "It's on the house, Reid. But please don't let what's eatin' at you take you to darker places. You have friends among us. We're here for you. Talk about it when you're good and ready, you hear?" She grimaced and barked at her son. "Neathan!"

Neathan flinched at his mother's rebuke and nodded. The Heinzrichs knew why Reid needed the drink. Neathan had been there when they'd found the blackened corpses of Reid's parents. But it seemed Neathan had otherwise followed Reid's command, as the rest of their group had. No one outside the Heinzrichs and Reid's men knew his mother and father were dead, or that he had made the decision to lie to his brother about it, to house the murderer *and* protect him.

John would never forgive him for it.

"Thank you, Odessa," he wanted to say, but he couldn't speak. Nothing went past his lips, not even the merest, scraping whisper.

She seemed to understand anyway, and her wrinkled hand patted his gently before she withdrew. "I think I'm going to go get something to eat at the inn. You're invited to come if you feel up to it, Reid. The company would be nice."

Chapter Thirteen

Testing

NYMERIA AND JAMIE HOVERED behind the boulder, their shoulders brushing against the bright, fibrous green moss that coated the swirling patterns in the rock. Their knees pressed into damp leaves and other forest litter. They were both breathless with excitement, and they whispered the way conspiring children did as the two watched their red-haired cousin.

Marissa was perched atop a stump at the edge of the gully, where a small creek bubbled with clear water. She sorted through her small basket, humming a song she'd once heard from Nymeria while she arranged tubes of different colors of sand samples and bits of very old glass. The items were some she'd found along the road when she'd gone out of Crow Post with her mother a month prior when they'd visited Avask, a village almost entirely devoted to glass making. It's where her mother Ralleigha had been born.

"Uncle is a mechanic and a warrior," said Jamie. "Is that why he left again? So he can fight? And fix things?"

Nymeria nodded as she eyed the perilous trap she'd laid for her cousin. "Father says he is very intelligent. He understands things and people. I heard him talking to Aunt Ralleigha, telling her he is going to take Davos's and Taeryn's and our grandparents' places until some matters are resolved. He's gone to Tallil first — I think he's going to do some other things this year instead of help Father deliver apprentices to Black Temple."

"I heard some of the refugees talking about a mine collapse by Tallil," said Jamie. "Is he going to help them?" Jamie's guiltless expression turned sour. "If those wolf people are behind it, I hope he gives them a lesson!"

But Nymeria shook her head. "He will send extra help once he knows more about what happened," she explained. "Remember? He assesses first, acts second. Unless there is an emergency that calls for the reverse."

"I told you he's smart."

Nymeria shrugged. "I know. Also, he promised to bring back books for me. And chocolate cake. Otherwise, I won't deliver another shipment of lights to him. We made a bargain."

Jamie's bright blue eyes went wide. "Cake?" he asked excitedly, practically foaming at the mouth. "Could I have some? Momma said it's very sweet. I love sweet things! And she said they always have cake at weddings — I bet Ellie Mae and Robert are going to have cake at theirs!"

"They do not always have cake at weddings," she corrected. "Only at some of the expensive ones." Nymeria thought for a moment. She didn't see why not. "But yes. You can have some, too. And Marissa. You've been helping me experiment, and you've given me some new ideas. And she is our guinea pig. It's only right if I compensate her for this." Jamie laughed at that, and Nymeria smirked. "Your birthday is soon, anyway. When the June bugs come out, remember?" She covered his mouth with her hand suddenly when he drew a breath to say something. She knew he'd forgotten to be quiet from the fire in his eyes. She reminded him not to project his voice. "Shh. Tell me quietly."

Her little brother nodded, and once she withdrew, he began to pull bits of his pale sandy hair upward to make it stand up in spikes. He copied their father when he did that, the adorable brat. She thought his hair was too cute when he did it. "How does Uncle understand things and people?" asked Jamie. "I want to understand things and people. I want to be a warrior, too."

"No, you don't, you want to grow plants," Nymeria scoffed. Jamie pursed his lips thoughtfully.

"I guess you're right. I do. But I could do both! Warriors can have gardens!"

"It's Uncle Reid's job to know things. He usually has a good idea when people are up to things. He also makes scoutings to ensure it is safe before we go places because Black Temple doctors could get robbed and killed if they don't have protectors. Some people are stupid enough to cross the guild like that. Father doesn't think it so much, but me, I'd watch my back even against allies. Sometimes I hear the grumbling of some of the people he helps when he isn't there, and the things they say are nasty. They blame him when someone dies because they are beyond his care. He just says they're mourning and ignores it. People get very nasty when they don't know or understand things, and it's worse when they don't want to believe you, even if you know better. That's why sometimes other people are mean to me."

"Oh."

Nymeria contemplated one of the things her uncle had said to her and finally voiced it to her brother. "Uncle said I understand things and people, too," she said. "But I don't think we do that in the same way." Even though her uncle had said she was smart, she'd seen his expression when he'd said it. His countenance had hinted that her understanding was . . . different. Special. *Alien*. But it had still felt nice to be *complimented* for something among her unusual traits, as opposed to being *scolded*.

She knew her own father didn't mean to be, but he wasn't very nice to her sometimes about those unusual qualities. Even if it was just because he was worried about her, he often made her feel horrible about herself. Because she did not fit in with the other children, she would not play with them much. And because she had some difficulty keeping her nightmares at bay, he thought there was something wrong with her. She knew he did; she was not blind or stupid.

At that thought, if her father had any idea what they were up to now, he would be making her feel a lot worse. Mostly with the use of his belt as he whipped her for her disobedience.

But Nymeria thought this could be great fun, pranking her cousin so. And she could get some new information on how to use these shards. She'd had an idea that had spawned from another unintentional event the last time she was out testing them. She believed several of them might react with one another if a central key was created to connect and coordinate them.

"Why doesn't he ever take Marissa with him?" asked Jamie. "She's not a mechanic or a warrior, but she wants to learn his job, too, like I do." Jamie pouted. "She's not even very smart. She's just mean. But I'm smart. I could be a warrior like Uncle Reid."

"We are supposed to work for the guild in other ways. We're supposed to become doctors whether we want to or not," said Nymeria, placing her finger to her lips. "And be quiet, or she'll hear us. Give me that one."

Nymeria pointed to the second of two glass jars, which had only hours ago been full of dim shards. She knew in her heart that this experiment could yield some very favorable results. The more uses she found for these small pieces of her inner light, the more she imagined her father glowing proudly one day. And her uncle and her mother. She was ecstatic, and she had planned this meticulously for two entire nights after her brother had said the thing that had inspired the idea for it.

"Have you ever dreamed about a magic key?" Jamie said. "I saw you holding a magic key when I was asleep last night. You made a glass one, and it turned the trees into doors. We played hide-and-seek in them."

The words had been the catalyst to this creation. The idea had made her think to use a central key to trigger the other stones. If it worked, she would eventually be able to use a keystone to create other shards without having to do it with her ability, which was, at times, difficult to call out or control.

Nymeria reached into the jar and pulled out a single piece of glass. This one, she had requested from her aunt. It had a very specific shape, though it did not look at all like a key. It was a thin sliver of black glass, and it was shaped like a ring. Nymeria held it in her palm and concentrated, trying to find the part of her that tingled and shook and breathed, almost like a separate entity. Right there, at the wall of it, she felt something within her coil and rise. It felt like a memory of some ancient time, although the memory wasn't hers.

The current began to pulse within her. It began in her heart and in her mind, until it feathered and rippled outward. She was careful, though, because she knew that letting it loose without leashing it with some amount of caution meant it would simply continue to spread until it disintegrated into webs of fading nothing. There was a new pattern in this one. She could tell it was there, but it was hard to discern. Hard to read. Harder to write.

"It's getting harder to do, isn't it?" said Jamie knowingly. He watched her face contort from a peaceful expression to a frustrated one.

"I don't get it," she said, putting it down. "Sometimes it's fine. But then . . ." She shook her head and then tried again. "It'll do us no good if I cannot do this at will every time. Whenever I need to."

"Can I try?" Jamie held out his hand, and Nymeria grimaced. The simple question was one she had never expected him to ask. She very nearly cringed. Then she wondered. He *was* her brother, after all. Maybe he would one day develop the ability.

"If you want to," she said. Nymeria placed it in his open palms. "Be gentle." She peeked over the boulder to her cousin. Marissa was stooping to gather another sample of sand, which she'd made room for. "Hurry, though."

Jamie's face twisted and contorted until he looked as though he were trying to push over a boulder with his mind. His face became red, and he began breathing hard. Then he looked up, flustered. "I don't know how. You try again. Maybe someday I will do it, too. Wouldn't that be awesome? Maybe when I am your age, I will finally be able to do what you can do."

Nymeria pondered for a moment. "Hold on to that. I have an idea." She poured out several of the stones from the remaining jar and began to arrange the glowing things into a pattern. First the ring, then the center, then, stacked upon two of the stones, an extra set of stones. "This is the pattern. But something is wrong. When I try to cross this core with this frequency, it only . . . I got it!" Nymeria clapped her hand over her mouth and peeked over the boulder again. Marissa hadn't heard. Currently, their cousin was labelling the tube as Aunt Ralleigha had taught her. Next, she would be marking her small map and creating a standing pillar with a familiarly shaped stack of creek rocks.

"Look," said Nymeria. "I forgot the cross-reference doesn't stop here. It's spotty, the way I keep trying to do it. The current doesn't flow, it diverges here instead. Path of least resistance, my toes," she laughed. Jamie simply looked at her and blinked.

"I still don't understand," he said quietly, his gaze downcast as Nymeria took the glass ring from him and tried once more. She grinned and pressed her finger to her lips.

"Peek out and watch," she said. "This is new. I think it will work."

Jamie pulled on his hair again, making sure it was still upright, and then he scurried around to the other side of their shared boulder. He grasped a vine of ivy gently and peered through the leaves sprouting from it. When he glanced back at Nymeria, she held the ring between her hands, and violet light — streaked with bright, flaming blue — curled around the glass. It settled in the hollow center a moment later, forming what almost looked like a lens. It emitted a musical humming sound that was nearly too quiet to hear. "Hurry," Jamie whispered. "She's getting away."

"She's going right where I want her," Nymeria promised. And then she tossed the black glass ring over the boulder, into the clearing — as might a man pull the pin from a grenade and toss said grenade. But neither of them ducked behind cover. They both watched expectantly.

There was an almost indiscernible sound of smushed scuffling and crackling of wet and dry leaves as the ring crashed into the brush. Nymeria's heart began to race, and she held her laughter tight on its leash when Marissa looked up.

Marissa searched about, clutching her basket, a scowl spread across her freckled features.

The other stones Nymeria had laid about the area began to emit a rattling, like snakes' tails.

Marissa hated snakes. *Hated* them. She blanched at the noise.

Suddenly, one of the stones shot away from the others, and a whirlwind of leaves flew up behind it. Marissa's squeak nearly had Jamie laughing. He, too, clutched at his mouth as his smaller frame jittered quietly with humor.

Another stone shot off, and again, more leaves flew into the air about Marissa, who stumbled back from the flurry of forest litter. She dropped her basket and began to look for snakes in earnest among the leaves. "No, no, no . . ." she said. "Not snakes! Not snakes again! *Mommy!!!*"

Nymeria shut her eyes and held her hand tighter over her mouth when a laugh escaped her. "Shh," she told Jamie when she recovered.

Another shot off, this time exploding into a blinding flash of light. Marissa screamed and ran — and Nymeria darted from behind the boulder and grabbed her. Marissa screamed louder, her arms and legs flailing as Jamie howled with laughter that could no longer be contained. Another shard exploded.

"You!" Marissa cried, tears streaming down her cheeks. "Nymeria, why would you do that to me! You are so mean!"

"I was only playing," Nymeria said, still doubled over and gasping for breath between raking laughter. Her hands balled into fists as she pounded on the dirt with them. "You were so scared! I bet I could scare a grown man with them, because you don't scare easy, Marissa! The look on your *face* was *awesome*."

"*Not snakes again!*" howled Jamie as he gurgled on his back.

Marissa looked at the two of them, quickly becoming angry. "All of that, just to scare me? Really? You are so immature! I'm telling your dad on you."

Nymeria sobered immediately. "You wouldn't."

"Don't tell on her!" Jamie cried. "You can't because it was awesome! She'll never get to do it again!"

"I will, and I am going right now."

"But she was going to give you cake to pay for scaring you!" Jamie said disbelievingly. "*Chocolate* cake! The rich people cake!"

Marissa's mouth fell open. "You're the one daddy's cacao beans are going to be for?" she exclaimed. "When I saw them on his list, he told me I couldn't have a single one when he comes back! He said he would put them away where I couldn't reach them." Her eyes welled with tears. "And they're going to be for *you*?"

"Yes," said Nymeria. "We have a business agreement. But I am going to be paying you for your very hard work. Those snakes were a terrible start, after all."

Jamie gurgled again. "Is your neck sore? All that screaming was very hard work, indeed. It *must* have been." When Marissa glared at him, he ducked behind Nymeria and began laughing and mimicking her earlier fright. *"Not the snakes again,"* he mocked, wringing his hands on the handle of an invisible basket he pretended to lift just beneath his chin. *"Not the snakes again!"*

"Well I found a spider. *Here!*" said Marissa, and she opened her hand and flung a giant wolf spider at him.

Jamie screamed and ran from them, his hands flailing as he tried to get it off. He disappeared into the trees, his screams hurtling toward camp. "Daddy! Daddy, help me! It's on me!!!" he screamed all the way.

Marissa and Nymeria looked at one another. Marissa's face cracked into a smile, and then Nymeria began to laugh. Marissa clapped her hands together and bowed over laughing as well.

"I know that was just a wolf spider and it doesn't bite," said Nymeria. "But I like how you think."

"So what did you really scare me with? I was very afraid of it."

Nymeria turned heel and paced back to the boulder where she and Jamie had hidden behind the log. She lifted her jars of glass and stones. "These."

"You were throwing rocks at me?" Marissa said. Her chin jutted out. "But they were rattling, like snakes. And hissing. And then they exploded."

Nymeria set the jars down and crossed her arms. "Trade secret. But it uses these. They weren't supposed to explode, though. I didn't expect that to happen."

"It's because of that light you make, isn't it?" said Marissa.

Nymeria stopped smiling. "How did you know about that?"

"Because I saw it when you were asleep one time. It was going through your wrist and the side of your face. And I heard Uncle John talking to Daddy about it yesterday. Uncle John was saying he was thinking about taking you to a specialist in Arsennia to see what it might mean. If it was harmful or not to you or anyone else. Daddy was afraid of what that kind of trip would cost."

Nymeria sat down slowly. "Father wants to send me away to be a patient?"

Marissa explained. "Uncle John was worried about you. He said he would even take you himself. He said if anyone glows like that, it usually means radiation. Daddy told him it wasn't radiation sickness, he said it was because you're special. I bet they have something in the archives at Black Temple about it."

Nymeria's chin trembled. "I don't want to go anywhere, though. Not if it means *away*."

Marissa's face screwed up. "Well . . . you can't just stay in Crow Post forever. Even we won't do that. Traveling is part of life, and it makes life better. You might not get a choice anyway. Nails said Saura is pushing for younger apprentices this year. You might have to go with your daddy before the end of the season. Especially if they amend the Summons."

"Oh."

"So why were you scaring me, anyway?" Marissa said, sitting down across from Nymeria. "Other than to be mean."

"I found out I can tie different ones together," said Nymeria. "Like receivers. I can almost triangulate motion with them now. They could serve as an alarm system at night, so we know if any animals, or the dark things, or the wolf cult are getting close to camp."

"Like a minefield?" Marissa asked incredulously.

"Kind of," Nymeria said. "I'm sorry I scared you. I thought you wouldn't mind when you realized it was for science."

"Don't be sorry. You were right. In the name of Science, I forgive you." Marissa then steepled her fingers, and she rested her chin upon the tips as her father often did. "I want to scare those other kids that were mean to you. Teach them a lesson for saying we're both witches."

"I didn't make them for revenge, you know," said Nymeria. "Just to protect. Father says the weak seek revenge, that I cannot behave or think like them. He really wants me to be a doctor, even though I don't want to be one."

"Well, *my* daddy says the best way to make people leave you alone is to make them afraid of you, or of something or someone that is on your side. Fear is the best defense, he says, so long as you stay ahead of everything they might resort to. That's not revenge, Nymeria, that's just common sense. But he did warn me to use that tactic sparingly or it will become my very strongest weakness because it will isolate me."

"I would rather just avoid those other kids."

"Well, you can't hide forever. Bad people will always find you if you try. They smell weakness, and they taste fear. That's what Momma says. It's probably why your mom almost got her throat cut all the way out, because she was too afraid to fight first, because she hesitated because of her fear."

"It's easier for you to think that way, Marissa," said Nymeria. "Your parents aren't doctors and attendants. Mine are. Father says fear, fighting, and aggression are signs of pain, stress, or madness. Everything is a symptom of something else, he says. It's enough to make your head spin, with all his explanations. I just want to do what I want to do."

"And what is that?" Marissa turned to gather her things, and Nymeria watched her for a long time.

"I don't know." She listened to Jamie's fading screams finally quiet. He must have reached the center of the camp. Perhaps he'd found one of their parents. She imagined he was sobbing, that there were great big tears and rivers of snot running down his face. She imagined her father's angry expression when her brother finally managed to tell him why he thought there was a spider on him. Nymeria promptly picked up her jars and began trying to figure out where else to hide them. Somewhere none of the refugees would cross them. "I think I wish I was an artist. A mason. A baker . . . Anything else. I don't want to be around blood and death and sickness all my life."

"Well, sometimes we don't get a choice. Better to be prepared for the worst, that's what I say," said Marissa. "What are you going to do to change your destiny? And what do you think it will cost? Daddy says big decisions always cost something, and you have to weigh the options and decide which loss is less difficult."

"Uncle Reid will be calling you freakishly smart next, you know," laughed Nymeria. "Help me hide these somewhere."

CHAPTER FOURTEEN

BELL TOWER

THE COLD, HEAVY RAIN had ended a few hours ago, but a deep fog had threaded through the valley until it had wound its ghostly white tendrils about the woods. The fog was so dense that they could hardly see or hear anything, even if it was a few yards from them. Muddy rainwater trickled down crevices carved from a long history of rains, but the sound was merely a whisper to them. The horses swished their wet tails and cast the mist from their manes.

Reid shivered at the reins, and when Taiir looked over and saw how he hunched, drenched and freezing because of the weather, the man merely grunted. The sound seemed to offer little sympathy, though Reid picked up on the humor in it. Taiir's fox coat warmed him and repelled the water, so Taiir was perfectly comfortable. Reid's coat had burned a few nights ago when they'd gone in search of more dry wood. Embers had caught in the wind of the approaching storm and blown onto his gear. He'd saved the rest but lost the coat.

"I should have w-watched where I p-put my coat," Reid chuckled. "Cold as w-winter in this rain. I'll have to get a new one in Edantine."

"Why not Tallil?" asked Taiir. "We are heading there first."

"Tallil's merchants do not make coats f-fit for travel," shivered Reid. "They make them for fancy balls and jesters, and they make them far too short for my taste. T-too many clown clothes in Tallil."

Taiir's hearty chuckle was worth that sentiment. "You would look like a proper gentleman in purple, pink, and green, Commander."

"Go to hell, Taiir," laughed Reid. "I'll never in my life wear a rainbow such as th-that." Reid signaled to the driver of the wagon behind him. "Manard."

"What." The man had had little to say lately. He wasn't always so quiet, though he was a patient, somewhat solemn sort with plain eyes that burned fiercely with suspicion and anger at the sight of any stranger who seemed to have even an inkling of ill intent about them.

Reid had known the man would be a good companion for their trip the moment Taiir had introduced Manard to him. After some inquiry, Reid had discovered Manard had been a guard at his village — a good one, from the word of other refugees who hailed from the same place. He'd saved several families from being murdered or burned alive in their homes, and he had a good reputation for his work ethic. The man had good gut instincts, Reid had observed, and he had proven trustworthy. Manard would guard their supplies while Taiir and Reid were busy. No trusting sort would do for that job.

"You still alive back there?" asked Reid.

"What kind of dumb question is that? I answered, didn't I?"

Reid laughed. "Just checking. I thought you may have been struck mute or d-dead since yesterday. Haven't heard a peep from you."

"Tha horses need to rest," said Taiir.

97

"We'll make c-camp soon. I believe there's an inn but two days fr-fr-from here. We'll rest near the river between here and th-there." Reid's ribs ached from the shivering, but it couldn't be helped. If there was some place they could gather more dry wood to burn, he'd be glad of it.

They rode for hours, until the sun began to set and the air grew even colder. Not that it made much difference in the amount of light. The forest was dark enough on its own. But the mist made it darker, only catching the golden rays every few meters when the green crowns parted in a whirling breeze.

A large shape rose from the fog, and they rode toward it until it began to shift from a murky blue shadow into a giant stone wall covered in moss and vines. Part of it was greatly eroded, and the old mansion beyond it had also crumbled away. All that remained were a few tall walls and a portion of a second floor and a decrepit balcony. The depths of the place were too indiscernible. It looked as though it could have once housed a thousand people.

"We cannot camp there," said Taiir.

"We may be able to find some dry wood inside, though," Reid suggested. His ribs ached from the constant shivering.

Taiir gave the ruin a bleak stare and turned his horse about. "I would not risk it. I can hear tha beams inside groaning. Any wood you might find inside would collapse tha rest of it on you, and that would be tha end. If you are that cold, crawl into tha wagon, take tha straw from tha boxes, and use it as a blanket."

"I can't risk the bottles br-breaking," Reid said under his breath. "And I wasn't worried about being cold . . ." A distant wolf howl punctured the fog. "*That* is what's worrying me. They've caught our s-s-scent again."

Taiir grimaced.

"You were right, though. It won't do to have the horses slow if we need to outrun those wolves. If there are more than six or seven of them, it'll put us all in worse danger. We should find a spot we can spend a full night, since we've been traveling hard for seven days." Reid sucked on the side of his cheek as he searched the murky blue shadows for movement. All that moved was the rolling fog itself. But that was nothing to believe. He could just as easily be attacked by one of the beasts without ever seeing the thing until it was at his throat. He could barely make out Taiir and Manard.

"Your orders, then?" Taiir grunted.

"We'll search about f-f-for any other spot we can defend. Turn your radios on. I'll go left, you go right. Manard, you'll stay here. Ready your weapon just in case, and don't let your guard down. We'll meet back h-here in half an hour if nothing is found. If that's the case, we'll just make camp here."

They split.

Reid was met with a very uncomfortable, eerie silence. The fog thickened as he rode on, and the ground began to slope downward. Then it began to rise, nothing else visible to him but the murky dark blue of trees.

The blue began to darken to black as he rode forward, and moisture began to fall from the ominous sky again. His skin stung from the bitter cold of the precipitation, and he could barely feel his fingers as he gripped the reins . . . Then he heard the faint sound of branches creaking dangerously overhead. There was a hard crack, a sound like wood splitting, and his horse spooked. A long moment later, leaves and small twigs began to drift downward about him. He looked up. The blackness was from some great tree.

Then his horse's hooves began to clatter against flattened stones with increasing consistency, and Reid realized he'd found a small road — overgrown and littered with dead leaves from many passing autumns though it was. He followed it as it began to ascend. A giant root rose out of the ground before him; that root looked like a monstrous, ancient serpent, as if it were held prisoner by the ground itself.

His horse circled it.

Another root, even larger, rose a few meters later. When he tried to circle it, he found that the darkness had begun to turn to blue again — and then golden — as the fading light of the sun shone over the uppermost part of the hill and warmed the ground and the air. Here, he could see a little farther.

Reid was surprised to find an archaic bell tower collapsed among the roots of the trees. The tower had been here perhaps centuries, by the look of it. The roots had grown through and over the giant tower, and the rubble itself had sprouted large butterfly and forsythia bushes with thick bases, and moonflowers were in full bloom along the stone and deadfall. Hummingbirds slept among the tangled branches, some upside down, some pointing beaks at the sky and gripping thin twigs with tiny feet. The roots of the large trees formed natural fissures and alcoves among the ruin, also.

The ground itself looked like . . . a courtyard. An old one. The broken walls of the tower didn't seem to have any deteriorating rebar or wires, which would have been an indication it was from the Modern Age. Perhaps the tower was even older. He didn't know.

But he found himself grinning. The place was perfectly defendable, and there was dry wood where widowmakers had crashed from the canopy and fallen where the rain couldn't get to them.

Reid gripped his walkie and pulled it from his belt. "I've located a good spot. Manard, stay where you're at until we come back for you."

A couple of hours later, Reid had a fire going, and the horses were eating. It was Taiir's turn to keep watch, but Reid was restless. He still ached from days of shivering, and he'd eaten too recently to get to sleep.

The shard Nymeria had given him seemed to be emitting some kind of energy, and it had been doing so for the better of two hours. He could feel it through the coin purse belted to his waist. He'd only just realized it when he'd placed his hand upon the old stone wall under one of the massive roots.

"What is it?" Taiir asked, looking up from the rabbit thigh he was roasting over the fire. "I can tell by tha look on your face that something strange has caught your attention."

"I'm not sure," Reid replied. "Now that I think about it, I think I had guidance to this place."

Taiir watched him silently, waiting for him to explain. Manard was already asleep and had no clue about any of it.

"It's strange," Reid said, and he placed his hand over the pouch. He looked down and unfastened it carefully. Bright rays of violet streamed through the opening, and he sucked in a breath.

Taiir froze midbite. When Reid reached for the shard, Taiir quickly set down his food and rose, pulling a knife from its sheath on his side. "Do not touch it," he said. "Let me cut that thing free."

Reid held up his hand to signal Taiir to stop as he himself pinched the shard and withdrew it. The light grew brighter.

"You are putting yourself in danger, holding it. It would be wiser to drop it, and then to crush it under your boot."

The glass was nearly humming, it was so alive with energy.

The stone wall behind him began to hum as well, and he and Taiir started when the stones began to shift beneath the roots. Another light, this one golden, began to crawl through the wall. A circle, it formed, and it was almost large enough to be a doorway. Some kind of writing began to sprawl toward the center, until the gold turned silver and the image of a feather appeared, bright as sunlight. Taiir and Reid shielded their eyes as the light in the violet shard synced with the pulsing rhythm of the silver.

Reid sucked in his breath and stepped forward. Taiir advanced with him, but he did so more cautiously.

Reid stretched out his hand and traced the bright light swirling outward from the stone. "It's warm," he said. "Almost electric."

"I can feel that from here," said Taiir. "Are those words?" He motioned to the changing symbols upon it.

"What else could they be?" Reid studied the mark at the center, though. "But more importantly, that is the same sigil that was upon that letter."

Taiir's brows furrowed. "What do you think it means? This ruin is ancient, perhaps even older than Black Temple for tha shape it is in. It doesn't look like tha other ruins. Tha skyscrapers, that is."

"Nymeria probably has more an idea than any," Reid said slowly. "I wish she could see this. It's beautiful. Have you ever seen anything like it?"

Taiir shook his head. "I have not."

The shard winked out, its energy hibernating once more. The light in the wall then began to fade, until all that was left was a silver stain where the feather sigil resided. It pulsed, like a beacon, from silver etched in the stone to dull, golden light, and then back again.

"Why is it doing that?"

"I have not any clue, Commander. These things are beyond me. I was never privy to tha secrets of tha Underhalls of Five Tower beyond what I have already told you. I do not know if they knew of things of this nature."

Nothing else happened but for the continued pulsing of that strange light. Reid finally broke from his enthrallment and stepped away. "I think I'll explore this place more once we're back this way. For now, I'm going to sleep. Go ahead and take watch. Wake us in the morning."

Taiir studied the mark a little longer and returned to the meat cooking on the spit. Reid threw more wood on the fire and curled up on the pile of leaves he'd made into a temporary bed.

No more howling sounded for the rest of the night, and Taiir told them the next morning that none of the wolves had appeared near their camp. Reid surmised the beasts might have killed some other animal along their way instead. He'd slept well, and the horses were rested and ready to travel again.

CHAPTER FIFTEEN

ℋEIR TO ℐSH

THE BUSTLING NOISE OF WARES being exchanged and of deals being haggled very nearly covered the sound of the horses' hooves and the rattling of the wagon's wheels. One look at the Black Temple mark upon the horses' blankets and upon the wagon itself had many merchants waving their customers aside to make way. The noise never died, and for a while, neither did the progress of Reid's small group. Mud sloshed under the horses' hooves rhythmically, and the rain continued to pound against his skin, which stung from hours and hours of merciless downpour.

Leave it to Edantine to keep the market open during a heavy storm, he thought. Business first, weather second. That was the muttered motto whenever outsiders asked after it. Many other cities closed their markets on account of the danger of the wind tearing down the stalls' lean-to rooves. Edantine merchants just went without the rooves during storms or sold them to one another after the storms abated, when damages could be repaired quickly.

Reid grimaced when he noticed several large groups of unhappy citizens; he did not discount the anger he saw upon some, or the distrust upon others.

Something was amiss in Edantine.

"Some seem less than happy to see a thing from Black Temple," commented Manard.

"Indeed," Taiir nodded.

"Something has happened," Reid hissed. "Or some *things*." He prayed they would not be kept from a quick and easy trip. He hoped it was something simple, something easily solved.

Then they came to a halt when a thin woman broke from the parting crowd. While screaming harsh obscenities, she threw a handful of mud at them. The wet, sour slop slapped Reid right across the face, right where his hood would have protected him if he'd still had his coat. It splattered over his arms, painted his saddle, and even made his horse flinch. He gritted his teeth but stayed his hand as the woman went on screaming, and he signaled for Taiir and Manard to stop behind him. As he dismounted, a disheveled man in ragged, filthy, smelly clothing broke from the mob and reached out for the woman.

"Mary! Mary, *stop*!"

"I won't have it!" screamed Mary, and she shoved the older man from her and picked up another handful of frigid, sour mud. "They cannot come here *now* and expect us to just welcome them, Ames!"

Ames caught her wrist before another sloppy insult could fly through the air and find Reid's approaching form, and Mary struggled as Ames took hold of her and wrapped her up with both arms to subdue her.

"You don't attack Black Temple, Mary!" Ames wept. "They're not the cause! They haven't done a thing!"

"Yes they have! They've done *everything*!" Mary began to weep when her fight bore no use, and her body sagged to the ground as the fire was taken from her by force. Ames lowered himself to the ground with her, still restraining her and soothing her muddy, frazzled mop.

Reid knelt before them and placed his hand upon the wailing woman's shoulder. She cringed from him, but she looked at him, nonetheless. "What has happened?" he asked. He wiped the mud from his face when she could not respond, so he turned the question to Ames.

The man shuddered. His bloodshot eyes met Reid's briefly before flickering back to Mary. "Our daughter, our sons . . ." His voice doddered as the words steamed over his crooked goatee. "Seven children dead, and the last, we have already signed to Black Temple to raise in the name of Honor. Mary, we cannot go back on our word."

"My son," she wailed. "My only living son . . ." Her thin frame shuddered severely, and Ames wrestled against his own grief as he continued to soothe her. They rocked as she wept, and Ames pulled her gray hair from her forehead where the rain plastered it flat, and he tucked it tenderly behind her filthy ear. "If they'd come sooner, my babies wouldn't be dead! You cannot let them have Michael!"

Reid now had at least some clue. "Let's get her out of this rain, she is cold as ice. Where is your home?"

Ames cast Reid a haunting gaze and opened his mouth — nothing whittled free but for the broken sound of restrained sorrow. He had the look of one whose soul had been spent, whose prayers had become whispers of old dust, drifting uselessly for eternity. He had weathered an appalling storm, he and Mary. Reid felt a lump form in his throat when Ames finally managed to speak after several uneventful tries. "It's gone," said Ames. "We don't have a home left to us. We fled Cyan — and now it's burned to the ground, and on Black Temple's orders. We have nothing left to return to but ash. That's why we have to send Michael with you. We cannot go back on our contract. It is his only chance to live well."

"Then you and your wife and your son — "

"Michael isn't *his* son," Mary hissed, her shoulders continuing to quake as she inhaled against a raw and mournful tremor. "He has no say who can take my son away from me!"

Ames shrugged as he continued to console her. "It is as my wife says," he said quietly.

Reid's mouth closed. Then he started again. "We will lodge you. The three of you. By the look of it, neither of you have rested or eaten well for weeks."

Ames's chin trembled, and then he nodded. "We thank you for the kindness, sir." He encouraged his wife, then. "Did you hear him, Mary? They're going to help us." Still, she only wept.

"Are there any other survivors from Cyan?"

"None," said Ames. "We searched for weeks. We're the only ones." The man's voice shook.

Reid motioned for Taiir to help him, but before Taiir ever dismounted, two of the merchants separated from the crowd and lent their help. "Let it not be said that I wouldn't lend a hand to an agent of the Temple," said the younger of the two as he tucked away a necklace that sparkled dully, like dirty diamond. His great, bushy orange beard clung to his chin like an unwanted cotton tumbleweed. "Maker bless yeh for not harming her a'cause of her insult. She's on the hardest of times."

"I've been sparing what I could to them, same as Hagath," said the other. "They're in dire straits. They've no useful skills, not even the housework any family could tend alone."

"They have no skills?" Taiir's brow rose.

Reid's gaze darted to the couple's hands. They wore plain signets, but the signets were ones he recognized. They'd lost more than a home, he realized. "You're both of the Cyan name?"

Hagath's bronze gaze darted tightly to the Cyan refugees, and his jaw seemed to tic furiously at the injustice they'd suffered. His friend stepped back, out of the way as he lowered his head.

Ames nodded. "Her brother was Aris Taramine. He and his wife and children are gone, with the rest."

"Then Mary's child is — "

"Michael has become the heir to a city of ash and ghosts. What good is there in raising him to be the sovereign of a dead city? You can help us if you wish, but you *must* take him with you. Send him to Black Temple and honor us. It will be a blessed new beginning for the Taramine line."

"I'm not sure sheltering them would be wise," said Hagath's merchant friend. "What would others think of this family living *there*? In a house where the infirm are kept?"

"We are well aware," said Taiir, "that it is improper for nobility to house where injury and disease are tended. But judging by their haggard appearance, they have not been met properly by any official at all. We will offer any assistance we can regardless, until such time as tha noble hospitality of their stations are accorded. It is better they come to tha guild house stationed in your city than be offered but crumbs and *nothing*."

The man grimaced but accepted Taiir's rebuttal.

At the Temple's guild house, Reid was met by the posted doctor himself, an awkward, short, freckled, constantly-smiling, auburn-haired man named Linel Virien. The man was a very warm-hearted sort of fellow, quick to embrace and eager to help.

As it turned out, Linel had heard of the three Cyan refugees and had sent men in search of them a week before. Thus, as they sat opposite the fire, Reid and his company learned why the last of the noble house of Cyan had been treated erroneously. Linel was an emphatic storyteller, and he told all that he knew as the attendants brought them each food and drink and dry blankets.

"Turns to the right, you found these three where I never would have looked," said Linel. "I sent scores of men to scour the city — no mind to the homeless district. Nothing but shabby crevices there, where the infirm and the gamblers and the thieves try to blend with the unfortunate. I thought, *surely*, no sovereign's direct blood relation would have sheltered there."

Ames shuddered.

"You are surprised to be wrong, Dr. Linel?" Manard asked. Sardonic mirth curled his lips. "Why? Are you never?"

"Oh, to the contrary! And put like that, I should have guessed the most unlikely. I am often wrong!" Linel leaned back and slapped his left leg with a hearty laugh. "Cyan's twisty little tree sigil is not widely recognized here in Edantine. I'm sure it was mistaken as common jewelry, something just handed down from an old family line — maybe even bought from a junker. I discovered only yesterday that these poor, pitiful creatures were turned away by the guards themselves at Ragan Crostor's manor an entire week ago — they should have been admitted immediately when they presented their house sigil. They should have been allowed to plead their case and inform the leadership here of what happened in Cyan! It's almost as if that Crostor wanted nothing to do with it! And what threat could they be? They've lost everything!"

Linel stood as one of the attendants returned from another room, and he rushed over to greet the young man, taking the steaming blankets from him. He unfurled it and quickly wrapped it about Ames's shoulders. "There you go, there you go, sir. Get you nice and warm. I do hope the clothing isn't too large or too small. We don't often take citizens who are not injured or who aren't Temple members into this guild house. Most have their own clothes brought with them, at that, never a need for a change. Some leave a bit behind for others, though. Never fits, none of it." Of the attendant, he requested a few more things. "The boy will need fresh, clean shoes, Nathan. He's walked *miles* in his others, and they weren't made for travel. They've shrunk, they've split, and they're all but fallen off. Same for the mother. Ames's shirt is torn to shreds? Well, see the seamstress next door, even if you have to wake her from a dead slumber. Until he has something appropriate to call his own, fish him out one of my more formal shirts — it's still garbage compared to what a lord or lady should wear, but it'll make do. I have another he can borrow tomorrow when he is ready to go to the manor and call upon Ragan Crostor."

Linel clapped his hands together enthusiastically and returned to his previous conversation with them, never missing a beat, not even as Nathan lingered a moment longer, taking in the sight of their strange guests. "As I was saying, as I was saying. They were turned away by the guards themselves. It's a travesty! Poor lad out there starving. Parents couldn't even forage, or hunt, or bargain, or work! I questioned Crostor's entrance guards myself about the family. Astin told me the family they turned away 'didn't appear to be no noble family.' A mighty travesty. Shabby and starved, he said. Grief-stricken. Said Crostor wouldn't admit trash into the manor just because they had an ugly ring, that he wouldn't bother the lord with such nonsense. I had a mind to climb up Astin's lanky, giant frame, take off his helmet, and slap that tree of a man with the sight-blinding thing! Of course, those traits would have been relevant, I told him! Such hardships. It's atrocious to even imagine. They were treated with disbelief by nearly everyone they tried to tell, until you crossed them — and thank goodness you did, Reid! We'll make sure those two merchants are hailed as heroes for helping them all this time. The guild will send their thanks, truly. Those men will be blessed."

As Linel spoke, Reid watched the family. Mary had dozed, comfortable and warm after the bath and the food and drink. Ames sheltered her beneath his arm, still shivering himself but seeming to finally be settling. The color had come back to him, little by little. He looked exhausted, on the verge of falling asleep for a true rest himself. Michael sat politely beside Ames, on his other side, and he ate his food slowly. The boy was wide awake, but he never interrupted them.

Reid noted how calm young Michael was. And the boy had the darkest hair, like Nymeria. And Michael also had the most unusual eyes. One blue, one green. Neither quite human in color. The green was similar to Nymeria's own, though it was a shade darker and the color was somewhat less saturated.

The boy had a knowing, quiet stare, the kind that whispered he had seen the hideous, secret faces of the world's worst cruelties. He reminded Reid very much of Nymeria, which made him remember his worry and his urgent search for information.

As though the thought of her summoned its energy, the shard in the pouch on his side again grew warm.

"Are you not tired?" Reid asked, concerned for the haunted boy. Linel paused.

Mary sniffled in her slumber.

"Pardon?" Ames asked quietly.

"I don't often sleep the way others do," Michael said simply. He blinked, and then he offered nothing more.

"Oh . . ." said Ames. "I am afraid he is telling the truth. I've never heard of another who does not sleep, only rumors of his . . . *father*." It appeared the subject was a painful one to Ames. But Reid was curious.

"I hope you don't mind my prying . . . but was Michael the oldest or youngest of the children?"

"He is both, now," said Ames quietly. "But he was the youngest."

He seemed such a soft-spoken man, not prone to exercising authority. It made some sense to Reid why the guards at the manor did not believe Ames and his family were of high birth. They didn't fit the normal profile. All of them were sullen, their eyes downcast, and they were quite resigned. They behaved more as servants than as leaders. None exhibited the haughty pride that hinted they were used to getting their way, as would have been the case among one from the leading families in a city the size of Cyan. Some level of commanding expectancy or some bitter ability to argue or to complain about their unfair trials would have been among the usual. But not even a trace of that sort of expectancy or bitterness seemed to exist among these three. There was only the desperate sorrow of a mother mourning the loss of her children, the quiet support of a loving husband, and the acceptance of a ten-year-old boy who seemed to expect nothing more than he received.

If Reid remembered correctly, the sovereigns of Cyan had been *quite* a nuisance to Black Temple. Quite commanding, demanding, rude . . . All of them. Apparently, he'd never met these three — or their incredible loss had changed them mightily.

Ames's spoon scraped the bottom of the bowl. "I don't mind much, to tell you the truth, even if it is difficult or painful to speak of it. Your guild will soon become his new family, and aside from that, all of Cyan knew of her affair."

"She had an affair?" asked Taiir. "Did Cyan not punish infidelity with death?"

"Normally, yes, they did," Ames admitted. "Our circumstance was . . . strained. I lied for her until I could not. And then I bargained for her life."

"Even though she betrayed your marriage?" Taiir stared incredulously.

"I love my wife despite it. And I love Michael. They are all I have ever wanted, and all I will ever need. What we had and what we lost taught me that much. It was a hard lesson."

"If loyalty was gold, she'd be a beggar and he'd be a king," shrugged Manard through a slurpy spoonful of stew. "And I'd still be right where I am because I'm not foolish enough to bother with marriage at all."

"What happened? If you're willing to tell us, that is," asked Reid.

Ames grimaced. For a moment, he didn't speak. He looked at Mary's sleeping expression — grieving, even in her slumber. Tears glistened in her graying lashes. "The seven children we've lost were *our* children. Mine *and* hers," Ames said finally. He looked up to Reid and Taiir, and his jaw was stiff as he spoke, as though he would fight them if they condemned her for her grave sin. As though he felt himself to blame for what she had done. "We had a good marriage. A respected family."

Ames scraped at the bottom of the bowl again. He sighed heavily. "I thought she'd lost her mind when she spoke of the man who came calling to her dreams night after night. It started just a year after our wedding, at the beginning of a spring much colder than the one now upon us. I told her he wasn't real, even when she was convinced he was. She spoke of him more than once, concerned over his intentions. She thought him a demon, a witchling. I teased her about the man for years. Called him her dream prince, told her it meant nothing but that she was wild at heart."

Ames dabbed at his cheeks with the back of his hand. "I didn't realize I was losing her to him. Seven years, and she never let it go; she wouldn't admit he wasn't real. We finally had a disastrous argument over it, and I didn't notice something was wrong between us until after I told her she should see *him* and let him console her because I wouldn't . . . She wouldn't look at me afterward. She tried to keep it a secret, but I pried it from her that she'd been with him. I'd laughed about it, thinking it her imagination. When she became pregnant with Michael, I thought nothing of it . . . I thought he was my child she carried, an eighth to my blood and my good Hullen name."

Ames cleared his throat. "Then she told me she thought she'd made a mistake and married the wrong man. That hurt, yet I still couldn't believe the man was real. I thought she had gone mad. Imagine my surprise when that very man came strolling into Cyan, into our hall — right in front of my entire family, and in front of all of hers — and challenged me for her. Where he came from, a man could take another man's wife by fighting him to the death. And that's when I realized she'd fallen in love with him. Yet she begged *him* not to kill *me*. She was fearful he would anyway. But also, she would not leave with him. When I convinced him

I would not entertain his mad scheme to usurp my marriage and my family, he set my house afire and vowed he would return for her, and for his son — the child she had yet to give birth to. He evaded arrest. Then he was found dead in the woods just outside of town, his throat torn open, all the blood gone from him as though someone had drained him of it for some kind of sick ritual. Several other men were dead there, too. Twenty of them. All the same."

Ames placed his palm against his eye as his silent grief spilled into the firelight. "Eight months later, Michael was born, the most beloved of her children for his eyes, for how he reminded her of that man. I lied for her until I could not, that the child was mine. When her family saw the eyes, they knew the truth . . . I've never treated Michael or Mary ill, mind you. And I blame myself for her betrayal. I was cruel to her when she'd always told me the truth. I drove her away when she'd asked me for help. And it's never been Michael's fault. Honestly, he's been a delight, considering the other spoiled brats before him. Michael is a wise thinker. He could have become the greatest leader in the history of our city if he'd been given the chance. If he'd been allowed to compete among the family for the title."

Ames's smile was ghostly when he lifted his head again. He put his arm about the boy and hugged him close. A few tears had run through the crevices gouging his cheeks. "I persuaded Mary's family to spare her life. In turn, we became indentured to the rest of the family. They made sport of it, having her 'learn the sword' so they could bruise her whenever they felt, and having my children and I make desperate attempts at rebuilding the crumbled portions of the old house ourselves, without any knowledge or skill on the matter, and without the help of any who did have such a skill. All we'd known before were the political trading of information and the management of Cyan itself. We'd always done well enough on our own never to have needed to cook or clean, or sew, or any of it. She didn't mind the change too much, to be honest. Neither did I. Nor Michael. Our marriage grew stronger despite what had happened. Our other children . . . that was a different story. But Michael's been a wonderful, patient child," Ames said. He sighed sadly. "Even though it isn't easy for him because he isn't like other children."

Reid had never thought to cross another child whose circumstances were as unusual as Nymeria's.

Nathan had returned at this time, and he was, again, lingering. It seemed the attendant felt great sorrow for them and wanted to do all he could to help. He seemed most intrigued by their tale while most of the other attendants simply rushed about, providing their services and ghosting before they became too noticed.

"He can divine truths from dreams, he says," said Ames. "And I've believed him after I've seen his abilities myself. Obviously, the gift is from his father. He inherited that as well as his unusual insomnia. The closest I have ever seen him to a true night of rest is to shut his eyes for a few minutes. He says he doesn't like to experience his own dreams. He prefers to watch others' dreams."

"Your niece is like me," said Michael. "She is not ordinary."

The statement startled Reid.

"I would like to meet her," Michael said.

"Your niece?" Ames was also surprised.

Reid was unsure how to reply.

"Tha commander has come in his parents' stead in search of information that might help her," said Taiir. "We have more business here than just Black Temple's work."

"What kind of information are you looking for?" asked Linel. He rubbed his palms together, stood, and stirred the dwindling flames, and then he began pacing again. "I'm sure I could help."

Reid shrugged. "I am to complete quite a lengthy list this visit," he said. "Business for my family and for the guild . . . For my niece, I am in search of books. It seems she can . . . how should I put it . . . read *more* than what is in my brother's medical journals."

"She is an inpath," said Michael.

Reid frowned. "Inpath?"

The boy nodded. "Telepath. Empath. There is more than one kind. But I think she is open to more than one thing. She internalizes quite a bit around her, and it isn't restricted to living things. I thought that's what I had sensed." Michael held out his palm. "You've something in your pocket that is emitting energy. What is it?"

Taiir stood and walked across the room, cringing. He placed his empty bowl on the table and crossed his arms. "I will not be near tha thing when you take it out again. Be careful. And do not be leaving more golden rings around, it could well invite some questions from tha wrong sort of people. Or have us booted from Edantine for witchery."

Reid removed the shard from the satchel and balanced it upon his palm before them. The stone glowed brightly at first, and then it began to dwindle in the presence of the firelight.

Linel sucked in his breath. "What, beneath the skies, is *that*?"

"A magic stone," laughed Taiir darkly. "Cursed, *I* say. From what little we have learned, as well."

"Shut up, Taiir," Reid snorted. "What we talk about tonight will remain a secret to those who are in this room and in this house. That is the only command I will give under this roof, Linel. You have my word on that. And it is the only condition for which I will take Michael into the guild, Ames. If you cannot agree to it, I will not allow any man or woman from Black Temple to take him on."

Ames nodded in agreement. "You have my word. We have kept Michael's gifts quiet to keep him from the judgement and suspicion of others also. We understand the need for silence."

When Reid looked at Linel, Linel raised his hands. "Of course, of course, as you wish," said Linel emphatically. "I will ensure my attendants do not say a word, or they will be threatened with being ostracized and worse."

"Good." Reid sighed. He nodded to the stone. "This is the result of one of my niece's many gifts. It is just glass, but she's turned it into a light. She is now experimenting with her ability to make other items like this, and I've told her I will find customers for the lights. Each does not require a battery. It is its own energy source. The rest I've brought with me are made a bit differently. They've been fused to metal casings to appear as though they are powered in some other manner, but they work the same. Do not share that her gift is the source. It was her request, and it is mine."

"Something of this paranormal nature could well be dangerous knowledge, I imagine," said Linel. "How does it glow so brightly if it's just glass? There is nothing inside it?"

Reid shook his head.

Ames simply stared at the shard, both perplexed and pleasantly surprised. Some of the life seemed to have come back into the man as he leaned forward fractionally. "I know a man who would be very interested in these. He would pay well for them, at that."

"Seems you already have a prospect for her," Manard said through another slurpy spoonful of stew. It was his third bowl of it, and he was about to ask for a fourth, from the sound of the spoon scraping the wood. "That didn't take long."

"Nymeria and I have made a deal," explained Reid. "I think the business will help broaden her career spectrum so that she will have something to fall back on. Besides, she's been defiant recently about any sort of reading at all. She has agreed to make these if I get her more books — nothing medical, of course. She seems to despise those."

Michael's lip curled up at the corner, and he uttered a small, boyish laugh. "No inpath would ever touch something so drenched in death and suffering as a medical journal. Does her father not know she is gifted with such a grim ability? That she would know every horrible detail of the dying patients whose demises were written into those books?"

Reid steepled his fingers. "We are not used to . . . *unusual* children."

"Ah." Michael seemed to understand. "She is the same as I, then. Her father is not her father. But perhaps her mother is also not her mother if *you* are the one trying to help her." It was apparent Michael *did* understand. "Where did they find her? What happened to her parents?"

Ames looked at his wife's son. "Michael, it is rude to ask such personal questions."

Reid sighed. "You've told us your story, and it was a personal one. I don't mind, as long as all of our secrets remain here. We've never met Nymeria's parents. We're not sure if they are alive or dead. My brother and his wife found her in Five Tower just after the Bright Night — "

Michael gasped. "The *Bright Night*, you say?"

Ames seemed confused, however. "What is it, Michael? What do you know of it?"

"I've seen the strange fires in their dreams. That was a harrowing time." Michael bit his lip. "Was she the little girl in the crater? They dreamt of a young demon queen, lying broken and unconscious, and covered in white, in a black crater. Ash and glass. Snow and fire . . . Everything was muffled by the eerie silence and the broken towers. Was that *her*?"

"Dear God," muttered Taiir. "Mary's son is just as eerily knowing as his accursed *niece*."

Ames began to laugh. It started quietly, bubbling up like the wind stirring before a storm, and then it broke into a mad sound. When the raw sound died out, Ames clutched at his sides gingerly and took a great, gasping breath. "It seems Mary's son and your brother's daughter should become the best of friends someday. My god . . ." He began to cry, then. Great, heaping sobs of relief. "I thought Michael was the only one. I never thought . . . Skies above, but I am *grateful* that he will be near another like himself at the Temple."

"One could hope they would become friends," Reid nodded. "But her father might not approve. He's a picky, stubborn man who can barely see past what he readily understands." Reid leaned forward, clasping his hands patiently. "So where is your contact, the one you said might be interested in these?"

"Aelynhold," Ames said. "He is a tech merchant. A right good one, at that. He knows some about odd tech that appears here and there. He doesn't sell often, or often buy. But he has money, and seemingly no end to it. He was in Cyan the night before the outbreak. Some men had harmed him gravely, but Mary's brother Aris had helped the man himself, ensuring he had the means to flee to Aelynhold. Aris had known the man for a while. Mary knows more of that, something about a family debt."

"How would I know him if I were to find him?"

"For a start, he has the strangest golden eyes. There is no mistaking the color. The color is an unusual shade, like Michael's."

"Silver-blond hair, too?" asked Taiir. "Long, plaited?"

Ames nodded. "Perhaps you've dealt with him before. He doesn't meet with just anyone. He's an elusive sort of man. Trusts very few. He has a brother I have only ever seen once. They're built like great, mighty warriors — you wouldn't think them as tinkerers or the kind to be generous. Supposedly, the brothers are healers of some kind as well. I remember Aris once mentioning they had some ancient connection to Black Temple."

Reid realized he was holding his breath, and he released it quickly. Could the men Ames was speaking of be Rhael and Gabriel? They had to be. "Do you know their names?" asked Reid.

But Ames shook his head. "No. Only Aris did, and he never called them by name." Reid's heart sank. But then Ames said something else that sent him reeling. "He preferred to call them by odd titles."

"What were the titles?"

"Something about death and something about traitor, detector . . . I don't remember."

"*Dead One* and *Defector*."

Ames frowned, and recognition sparked in his dark eyes. But it was Michael who spoke. "They're very kind but dangerous men. I've read dreams of them, dreamt by those they've helped. They're cursed, both of them. I couldn't even track those they cross because they cross too few."

Ames grimaced. "Cursed? Why would you say such a thing?"

"Death has shunned them," said Michael simply.

"Surely you aren't saying they're *immortal*?" snorted Manard.

"That is not what I said," said Michael. "Their presence *means* death, most often." He frowned and looked at his mother. "She's dreaming ghastly things again. Ash. Blood raining from the skies . . . It's about my sisters and brothers."

Mary let out a breathy wail in her sleep, shuddering, and she began to cry again. "*Setha . . .*"

Ames grimaced painfully. "Setha was our oldest. Our daughter," he explained. He hugged Michael then, and he told him, "Go ahead. She shouldn't have to go through that again every night. I'm going to catch a breath outside — I can't breathe in here. It isn't *home*." Ames got up and walked out of the house without another word. A heavy gust of cool air fanned the fireplace, and the smell of wet earth and the sound of thunder rolled into the house like a weighty hand. No one else, save Michael, said a word for a long while.

Michael placed his hand upon the side of his sleeping mother's face. His face went slack, and his eyes began to glow intensely, until he shut them. "Mother, remember us," he said. "We're still with you. I will visit you when I am gone. You will not lose me the way you lost Father."

She seemed to say something else, but none of them could hear it. Then she settled, and at last, her delicate features became serene and her breathing became even.

"How did you know I had a niece?" Reid asked.

"Your dreams last night, before the three of you came into Edantine, were unlike the rest drifting about in this city. I was interested in them, so I looked. I saw your concern for her. She isn't well, is she?" Reid frowned but said nothing. Michael sighed and scooted forward in the large chair. "Sir, I know more than I ought. I am aware it makes others uncomfortable. It happens to anyone who becomes aware of my gifts. I did not intend to cause offense."

But Reid just shook his head. "That's not it. I am not insulted."

"You are worried she is going to die."

Reid steepled his fingers. The child was right about that. "What did I dream that caught your interest? I don't remember it."

"The creatures in the shadows took her and killed her in the forest," said Michael. "I saw your brother, John. He was angry and blind to everything, even her death. I saw you trying to help her, but you were held back by both his wrath and his denial."

Reid was troubled by the scene that was repeated back to him. It brought the memory of the dream back vividly. "Ah . . . That wasn't a pleasant dream."

Taiir made a sound at the back of his throat which Reid was sure meant disbelief.

"Have you ever seen those creatures outside a dream?" Reid asked.

Michael denied it. "I have not yet seen them, but I know you and your niece have. So did the man you threw in the kennels. They're real. But you've been blessed by her. You've been given an extra sense to be able to protect your family, and you have been given her protection. That's why she gave you that stone. The creatures cannot see you, and they do not like what is in that stone. It is sour to them."

"What is in the stone?" asked Reid.

"Her love for you, and for the rest of her family. And a warning." Michael looked away, and his hair curtained his glowing eyes. "I won't pry again unless I am given permission, I promise."

Taiir yawned. "Rest is an excellent idea."

"I'd like another bowl, if you don't mind, Linel," said Manard.

CHAPTER SIXTEEN

THE NOXIOUS SMELL OF FUEL all but choked him as it pumped from the large metal housing that had been built to hold it. The housing itself was a large tank made from scrap metal, and from and to the tank were several other sizes of similar tanks, all smaller — all were connected by boundless arrays of tubes and hoses and wires and cables. The cables balanced across ladders and beams, and they formed massive webs that spilled over crumbling partitions of the ruins. They spilled into various pits in the ground, and they hung through crumbling walls eaten alive by different kinds of ivy, creeping succulents, and multitudes of edible plants that were midharvest.

This centuries-old, ruinous section of the city had been left untouched by the rest of Edantine, as the area had been long ago cordoned off as uninhabitable and much too dangerous to navigate. Reid had heard the soil here was still poisoned, but with all the green thriving and providing the family here with food, that was very clearly no longer the case. Reid recognized multitudes of leafy root vegetables and herbs, all growing from every pot, ledge, recess, and protrusion. In his immediate vicinity, he saw Redbor kale, purple cabbage, collards, rutabaga, bay leaf, sorrel, leeks, brussels sprouts, and even rosemary and purple cauliflower. But the various edible plants crossed the entire ruin, and they blended with the ivy that seemed to hold sections of broken walls and upper floors together and which also seemed to keep the structures from disintegrating.

The family who lived and worked here seemed to know every weak structure, how much weight each could carry without collapsing, and where to step and when — as even the weather could limit each structural vulnerability's weight load.

Reid admired the endless tangle of sky-high cables and the scattered network of family members navigating every crevice and shadow with what seemed to be a sixth sense. The place looked dangerous to live in, but this family was thriving instead. The fuel itself was always under close supervision, its quality and quantity scrutinized, and the tanks were always under heavier scrutiny, each being repaired as needed.

Crow Post would need the fuel being made for the travel season, and Reid was pleased to find that Edantine's secret fuel makers were done with most of the quota they'd been asked to meet. Their own drivers would soon send the commodity back to Crow Post, so he would not have to worry over that particular detail.

Linel knocked on the shop door, out of breath from climbing the ladders and platforms to the crow's nest, where the operators lived and worked and watched for trouble that might approach their own. The fuel was an expensive commodity to come by, and the operation here was so secret that it was only known to a handful of Black Temple's reps, Edantine's posted doctor — not his attendants — and the reclusive family of fuel makers. Not even the leadership in Edantine really knew they had a golden machine in their midst.

The family was an odd one, and a large one. Forty-something cousins, all grown — plus their children. All were under one roof, and all were wearing goggles. Most wore leathers about their hands and torsos, their feet wrapped heavily, their breathing masks tapped full of hoses. They looked very nearly like giant-eyed, landbound fish.

It was only the second time Reid had met any of the fuel makers in Edantine, and he was familiar with their cover story, that the few among them who visited any place outside the secret hideaway were unsuccessful tinkerers, and junkers, and foolish lovers of unstable explosives. To be looked upon as a smelly, poor, crazed, fire-starting wanderer prodded others into leaving them be, except where the interaction was an absolute necessity.

Linel had insisted Reid and Taiir come with him to see a patient, and so here they were, climbing the ruins as Linel became more and more weak-kneed as the ground fell far below them. Manard had remained behind to watch over their wares, and to try to find a suitable driver to take some of the supplies on to Hagenhold so they themselves could return to Crow Post sooner rather than later. Time was of the essence.

Linel took a heavy breath and choked on the fumes and slammed his fist down on the corrugated metal door once more. "Op — " He gasped and clung to the ladder above Reid. "Oh, these heights, oh . . . This will be the death of me!" Again, he choked, and he repeated as best he could for entry. "Open the door! It's the surgeon! And I've company!"

Through the dusty windows, the leather-wrapped, goggle-eyed children ducked, laughed, and scattered like roaches. One blond child with great, big, gray eyes opened the door and offered a wide, scraggly-toothed grin. "Hi," she said shyly. She offered her hand. "I'm Anna. Are you Daddy's doctor?"

The hand startled Linel. He nearly lost his grip and cried out. The short, squat man clung to the ladder bars with all four limbs and shut his eyes, tears streaming. "I hate heights, I hate them! I hate heights, I do!"

Little Anna laughed, reached over his head for a cable, and jumped from the balcony, shouting, "Momma! Daddy's doctor is here!"

Taiir laughed below, unfazed by the distance to the ground below them. Reid urged Linel up gently, one inch at a time. With a great big sob, Linel plopped onto the floor inside the over-occupied sky-high hut and curled in the fetal position as he struggled to regather his breath, and twenty-something odd, soot-covered cousins with wiry hair in shades of copper and iron and steel continued arguing and throwing papers, and none paid a lick of attention to the three newcomers at all. Children shouted and climbed the house like monkey-spiders, and faces and eyes appeared and disappeared in circles, like a chaotic tilt-a-whorl in a circus, with flashing lights and never-ending motion.

Adults and children alike scattered when a large man rose from one of the tables, coughing, and his long, wild hair stood on end and swayed with every step as he made his way to them. He sported the same goggles as the rest, although his were pulled back into his wild, tangled, soot-dyed hair. "That you, Linel?" the man wheezed. "Get up, come over here!" The big man scooped up the tiny one with a lung-hacking laugh and knuckled Linel's scalp where he had too little hair left to lose already. Linel whimpered as another stray auburn hair drifted to the floor before him. "Ha! Had the nerve to finally come up here and see us?! Who are your friends, here?"

"Never mind that for a moment," shuddered Linel as the great man closed the door. "Danny, let me have a look at you. How are you feeling today?"

The great big man slammed the door as it opened again, as he was swarmed by youngsters and arguing adults who scattered a moment later when he tried to shoo them. "Shut the door when you come in or go out!" he said as several small laughs chittered about him and three more darted in and out. He slammed the door again, and again, and again, as each new child rushed him, darted by, and vanished before being caught. The children started laughing instead, and he slammed the door again with a roar. "I said SHUT THE DOOR! Shut — " He started coughing again, and he continued doing so until he had doubled over and turned purple in the face. "No peace. No peace, never," he growled, his voice raw.

Danny at last turned his back upon the door, giving up, and marched over to retake his chair. He shooed away more wild-haired children and adults, all covered in soot and looking quite like shadow spiders with big white grins. "How am I doing, then?" he asked. "Let's see. I'm swarmed by goblin children who nearly lit the whole operation on fire this morning. My cousins keep breeding and taking in strays, and I'm managing no sort of sleep with all the racket constantly about me. No more than this time last month when I fell off this rig house and broke my rib."

"But how are you feeling?"

"Gorgeous, absolutely smitten," laughed Danny. He tugged at the breathing apparatus he'd let fall loose about his chin, beneath the braids of dangling beard. "Feel like I could fly or sing in an opera."

"Still got that cough, I see," said Linel as he fished a generations-old stethoscope from some hidden pocket. Sticking it to his ears and fondling with the drum at its end, he stepped onto the table bench and forgot about his anxiety of heights. "Off with your coat, you great, big, goofy oaf," said Linel.

"Nah . . . I won't," sputtered Danny. "That thing is cold, and I'm delicate against such things!"

"I'll warm it first," Linel promised, placing the metal against his own palms. "Now, do as I say, and then be still."

With an exasperated sigh, Danny obeyed and removed his coat, and the post doctor performed his checks upon him, poking and prodding at the barrel-chested monster of a man, where a badly mending rib showed an obvious history of trauma.

"Fourth time he's broken this same rib," explained Linel.

"I should just sit and read the way I ought, but I'm afraid of spiders and anxious of fire," laughed Danny. "Family has to pester me with both for laughs, and they know better than to light a fire in the pits, but they do it anyhow."

"Again?" asked Linel.

"I told you the place almost blew up, didn't I?"

One of Danny's many frizzy-haired cousins swept into the room, his hair still sparking, and fumes of oil and fuel and grease wafting from him. "There yeh are, yeh blasted, useless, giant, cripple-ribbed man. Danny! I swear — hello, Doctor. Guests. Danny, we cain't see for nothin' in the pits! Why do yeh keep forbiddin' the torches?!"

"George," growled Danny. He sounded like a bear, and his fuzzy brows burrowed like angry caterpillars. "I said no torches, no fire, no electric lights. One spark is all it takes, and our entire purpose helping the Temple will be ruined. And the rest of Edantine would likely stone us to death, they'd be so angry. All these years, keeping this operation a secret from our own city folk, giving all we can to the Temple to help them in helping others. Instead of sharing wealth to greedy folk. It would be our heads, and then where would all these orphans end up? Or our own kin?"

"We'll all fall inteh one o' them holes down there first, drown it in fire! The kids know teh be careful!"

"Deep breath," said Linel, listening. "Hold it. Good. Another."

Meanwhile, Danny just stared at his cousin like a naked butterfly. His fingers twitched for his coat, but he did only as Linel ordered.

"You can't see in the pits?" asked Reid. Never mind that Reid didn't know exactly where the pits were.

George nodded vigorously. "O' course we cain't. Used teh have a domed glass ceiling, but it broke an' the rain started gettin' in, so we had teh close it off."

"My wife is a glass maker. I could put an order in for you, have it ready by the end of the season, before winter comes."

"New glass ain't the problem. The frame o'er the pits is in dire straits. The new glass would only break again. A'sides, no glass means it's less cold breeze fallin' in durin' the winter an' spring, an' it's cooler in summer an' fall, too. It's jus' darker." George smeared black globs of soot from his eyes. "We look like we deal in coal, eh? Tricky teh keep 'em city folk from guessin' the truths sometimes. Some'a us don't never go inteh the rest o' Edantine, jus' stay here a'cause o' the smell of *us* is worse an' won't come off." He chittered with humor and slapped his hands together. "Right, see here . . . Yeh one o' Missus Selena Ivan's boys? Yeh look like her. Willowy fingers, slender nose. But broad shoulders, features the ladies seem teh like, and tall like her husband Anthony, though. Yer Reid, ain't yeh? How are they, anyhow? I'd expected teh see 'em in another couple o' weeks — "

"George," grumbled Danny. "I . . . I think they're *gone*. Look at him, he's grieving a great loss." Danny waved off two of his cousins. "Reid, sir." He pushed Linel from him and slung his great coat about his shoulders once more, and he rose and crossed the rickety old room. Each footstep seemed to make the house shake.

Before Reid could wave them off, Danny had already wrapped him up in a bone-crushing man-hug and was slapping him reassuringly on the back. "So sorry, boy, so sorry. They were fine folk."

"Finest, teh truth," said George as Danny stepped back to allow Reid to breathe again.

"Anything you need, we'll do our best," said Danny. "It was a pleasure, knowing them. How good they were with the children! Why, even Sobrienne decided she wanted to become a doctor because of your mother."

"Ha! That bitter child!" chittered George. "What a miracle, *her* wantin' teh help *others*!"

Again, the door flew wide open, and papers went flying as cousins ran after children who darted every which way while clutching handfuls of paper.

Danny's eye twitched, and he sighed heavily. "Might as well head on down to the pits. Quieter there than this nonsense. They're in a flurry today, plans in the works. Always, with the plans; always starting over since the plans don't always work. We've had three pumps go out, but they'll have them back to working in a day."

"Oh!" cried George. "Let's do! Let's get yeh inteh the pits, Danny. You'll see how hard it is teh work in the dark. Been ages since yeh've come down from this blasted bird's nest. Yeh haven't been down there since the dome broke. An' when we're done, I'll have some good boys helpin' yeh with yer supplies, Reid. I'd heard it was teh get teh Hagenhold, teh help the poor folk there. The good boys are brothers. Jonas an' Don Oliver. Now come along, follow me."

Linel had gone pale again at the thought of walking out the door and climbing back down the ladder, but he had no time to argue or to dig his heels into the floor, or even to go weak-kneed. Danny had already grabbed him up by the torso, slung him over his shoulder, and begun a difficult, awkward climb down the ladder with a wildly screaming post doctor. "I'm gonna die, Danny! You put me back up there NOW!"

Taiir cracked a smile. "These people amuse me," he said to Reid. "Odd ones, all of them."

Reid nodded, still sober from the reminder of his parents' deaths. "Yes, they are."

At the entrance of the pits, as they seemed to have been aptly named, the odor was far stronger. Reid's eyes watered, and even Taiir had opted to wrap a scarf about his face and nose. Danny tugged two respirators free of one of the doors and tossed them to the both of them before donning his own, and then he pried open a cellar door near one of the ruined, dilapidated buildings. "Put those on," said Danny. "You'll get dizzy otherwise. They'll only last about four hours before they'll need to be switched so they can be cleaned properly for someone else to use. The air in the pits is mighty rank."

"Operation's gotta be below ground. Keeps the most o' the smell from bein' smelled by the rest o' Edantine," explained George. George grabbed one of the lanterns.

Danny took it from his hand and hung it back up. "What did I just tell you, George? A minute ago, in the loft. No fire."

"Oh, shut yer flaming pie hole, yeh wheezy, giant coward. These men don't know the way. You want 'em dyin'?"

"No fire! No electric! No flames!" shouted Danny. "No light! We already went over this just after you blew up the first well. You can't blame it on the children, because you are the one grabbing the lanterns and passing them out, George!"

"I ain't gonna be responsible for any kin or kid dyin'! It's a terrible way teh die, Danny! Drownin', cain't even gasp for breath through this sludge in the air teh call for help!"

While the two men argued, Linel, who had finally come close to his original pallor, crossed his arms and simply waited. Reid shrugged. Obviously, Linel was waiting for him to intervene. "I may have a solution." It was apparent they would not step foot into the pits without light.

For a moment, neither man seemed to have heard him. Danny had gathered the breath to lay into George something fierce. But then he blinked. "Pardon?"

"I've come into the possession of some rather useful tech that would enable your operation here to continue without risking the place blowing up."

Linel began to laugh. "Ah! There it is! At last. Finally!" He nodded vigorously as George cast a suspicious gaze at Reid.

"What kinds o' tech? He ain't gonna allow no batteries, nor cable-fed lights. Nothin' at all. I'm surprised Danny even lets us breathe air down there, a'cause it might set the whole place teh flames!"

Danny growled. George growled. Danny twisted his beard braids around his fingers and growled some more.

"Oh, let him have the chance!" Linel fumed. "He can *help* you both to get what you want, and to end this ridiculous tirade. You'll be able to rest, Danny. The children will be busy, enthralled with the prospect of traveling the deeper parts of the tunnels. Children love adventure."

Danny's eyes lit up, and he held out his hands. "Ah, what a godsend that would be! What have you, then? What is this mystical help that could make us both agree to this at last?"

Reid produced from his pocket one of the modified shards his niece had made, and Linel eagerly began to sell them. "I am perplexed how they work, but these beauties are magnificent. I'm going to be ordering some myself, and I knew you two were in need of a solution here."

Reid tossed one to each of the men, and he took a third and tossed it into the cellar. There it began to glow. The other two remained lightless in the sunlight. "It has to be dark for them to work," he said. "My contact invented these, and he is looking to profit from them. They only last about eight hours at a time . . . the same standard for the heavy torch or the usual flashlight or lantern. But these don't use fuel or electricity, so there is no risk of fire. After half a day to recharge, you'll be able to use them again for another eight hours. I've been testing some of them for weeks during the trip here, and they've been extremely reliable. They last between one and two months before they should be traded for new ones."

Taiir turned and made a point to admire the ivy behind them. Only Reid caught the gleam in his eyes or the laughter about to steal from his throat. "Tha man who made them is a very intelligent man. He is also very fierce," Taiir said. "He drove a strict bargain we could not undercut." He seemed to greatly enjoy partaking in Reid's humorous employment of Nymeria's chosen alias. Because of his decision to embellish, Reid knew that Taiir understood the tactic. That if these men believed a grown individual made the tech — especially a fierce one — they would likely pay the full commission. If they knew a child made them, the value would plummet. Most amusing of all, the whole idea had been Nymeria's. "He threatened not to work with tha Temple if he did not receive fair compensation for his wares. Tha commander agreed to process tha initial sales exclusively to ensure fairness."

George's and Danny's eyes went round as the sense of urgency took them and riled them into a state of obvious anxiety.

"How many yeh got?" asked George. "We'll take 'em all! An' all the next ones, an' the ones after!"

"Now just you wait," said Danny. "I'd like to test to see if this is what you say it is. What are they made from, exactly? What does he call 'em?"

"Hex lights. No other special name for them," shrugged Reid. "I've brought three hundred of them, but I cannot sell them all to you. I've other customers already waiting for theirs, and many of the lights are reserved for sampling purposes to drive demand for the next shipments."

"Reid is also in need of books," said Linel. The post doctor winked when George and Danny turned their backs and paced. "Lots of them. I don't know what kinds."

Linel seemed all too happy with himself.

"Books?" asked George. "Danny, give these men yer library. Whole thing. All the books for all the lights. Every last one."

Danny glowered at George. "My precious books are going nowhere. Reading is my *life*, and I will not give that away, George. Give them your coffee instead. You have stores of it all over the place, and the strongest, most aromatic grounds in the country."

George gasped. "How dare you, sir! How dare you! They don't even want no coffee! I would never sell my beans teh no man! I am a dead man walkin' all night an' day without 'em!"

And so the men argued on, until at last, George hiccupped most mournfully. "Fine, yeh monster! I'll give up my coffee, but yeh'll give up yer old books, too! Every one that yeh have two'a!" And with that, George snagged the lantern and dodged Danny's murderous looks.

Danny barreled after his cousin, chased him into the pits, and then fell into a fit of coughing halfway down the ladder. He snapped his respirator on and called after George. "George! You bring that lantern back right now!"

"If yeh don't hurry up, I'll light it, Danny. Come on, Dr. Linel. Got a couple youngins with burn ointment for yeh, an' also, Danny's grandmother's brother's wife's niece's friend Martha needs yeh teh look at her arm. It's goin' green. I told 'em teh get her teh yeh last week an' she refused teh go . . . An' I'da jus' said *Martha* in the first place," he called over his shoulder, "but . . . well, we got thirteen Marthas runnin' about now. Last week, it were only seven. Martha Carry, Mary Martha, Martha Marta, Martha Dame Martie, an' the rest jus' *Martha*. I keep tellin' 'em women teh name their babies otherwise, but all o' them love *Martha*! Yer gonna have teh say somethin' teh 'em women, Danny! They're doin' it on purpose teh confuse us all!"

They could barely understand him for the echo. It very nearly sounded as if he just kept repeating the name *Martha*.

So they navigated the old tunnels together, and George grumbled all the way, still rubbing at his scalp tenderly where Danny had smacked him with the lantern he'd taken. The lights Nymeria had created grew very bright in the tunnels. They could easily see every squirming centipede and spider and rat retreating from the light, and the moss that crept up the stone, concrete, and rebar turned from black muck to glossy green as they passed by, and then it returned to lightless muck again in the shadows behind them. Condensation dripped from overhead as Danny squinted and led the way. Occasionally, as though confused over how it worked, he turned the light in his hand over to examine it. Whenever he looked at it, he had an expression that showed he wanted to break the item apart to figure it out.

They passed metal clanging and orders being shouted back and forth. "Not that valve, the other one! Turn it now!"

Some of the noise quieted as they turned another corner that brought them back to the strongly smelling area. A giant machine appeared, and it was covered in greasy, half-blinded people who were holding all manner of tools and feeling their way along the casing. Most of them covered their eyes and looked away from the light. An old woman with gray hair placed her hands upon her hips. "Put that light out!" she wheezed. "No light!"

"Momma," said Danny. "Fetch some volatile debris. This Black Temple rep claims these lights won't cause an ignition." Danny held his hand up to keep them from coming any closer to the rig, which sputtered to life and then died again. The ground trembled from its short, ill purr.

Reid admired the machinery. The rig was an artwork of industrial scrap.

"You're well within the flash range," said Danny's thin, frail, tiny old mother. "Boy, I will tan your hide with torched leather if this rig goes up again because of you and your rep's lights." She crossed her arms and smirked. "On the other hand, if they work, we'll be needing as many as we can get. Can't see a thing in the dark. It's all by feels. Twenty hands to the left, fourteen feet to the right, an awkward head-bump here, and sometimes a cut or two you thought to avoid. Gets infected real quick. But that ointment works miracles."

Danny's mother shielded her eyes again. "And just maybe," she said, "we'll get to the bottom of who else has been down here."

"Children said they was hearin' other voices down there," said George, and he pointed at an opening in the floor twenty paces to the left. "Cain't drop no torch or lantern down it an' look a'cause it'll explode, most like." The hole seemed bottomless, just the gaping mouth of shadow having erased the floor. "They didn't start that fire, Danny. I told yeh they wouldn't light the place on fire!"

"Footprints, voices, lanterns. I don't believe in ghosts," said Danny's mother. "Contessa, bring me some debris!" One of the women who were wrapped in cables and breathing apparatuses scampered away and began digging through the rubble just beyond the edge of the light. "Peter! Help her!" Another boy darted away to help the woman.

Contessa returned a moment later with oil-stained cloth, and so did the boy who'd helped her. Danny tossed the light in his hand and caught it. "Mind if I break this one and see if it sparks?"

"Be my guest," Reid acknowledged. "It shouldn't be a prob — "

"Not right here, you don't!" snapped Danny's mother. "Beyond the flash zone! I'll not have the rig explode, you buffoon!"

She shooed them away, and Reid couldn't help but laugh at the overzealous greed in her gaze as her dark eyes followed them, unwavering. She never moved any closer and continued to snap orders. "Remember to place it *gently* upon the ground, you giant moron! You drop that, it'll knock you against another wall, and you'll snap that same rib again and get out of even more work! I'll burn your books, Danny, I will, you lump!"

"Mother!" Danny cried. "You're embarrassing me! Shush, woman! These men don't need to hear family squabbles — "

"I'll *squabble* your hide, you mouthy lump! Hurry up! We've work to do! And I want to know whether those will help us!"

Danny sighed and eyed Reid, just *daring* him to laugh, smile, twinkle eyes, or otherwise show he found the situation funny. Reid stared quite seriously at the debris, as did Taiir. Both remained *very* focused.

A moment later, the glass shattered over the debris, and the slivers continued to glow as the casing fell uselessly to the ground. Danny's eyes glittered excitedly as he knelt to pick up one of the shards. "It isn't even warm," he said ponderously. "What a miracle. Reid, sir?"

Danny held out his hand. "We have a deal. We'll take them. I'll have the Oliver brothers help take the books to the guild house and load them up." He gave the shards to his mother and Contessa. "With proper light, we'll send some of the boys down that well to find out who's been down there." He dropped the last shard in his hand, and it ricocheted off the sides of the well and continued to fall, and fall, and fall. Finally, it cracked against the bottom of the pit . . . where a body lay, all twisted and broken. The stone itself down there was mossy, though jagged, and green spears of rusty metal and old glass protruded from the dead man's blackened flesh. The corpse itself was black as tar, the flesh cracked from smoldering heat.

Reid swallowed thickly, remembering how the flesh had slid from his parents' bodies when he and his men had tried to lift them from the carriage.

This body didn't seem very old. He was certain he could see and smell a little bit of smoke coming from it still.

"Eh . . ." said George. "Looks like he's still down there. He looks like one o' those pensive monks from the square, preachin' against the Temple o' late. Same necklace. A glass chain, it looks. They been mockin' the Temple doctors with 'em."

"Monks?" asked Reid.

"Yeah. Poison, the lot o' them." George spat down the well disgustedly. "I cannot in good conscience think 'em innocent o' harm. The Temple serves the people. It is only right we help the Temple in its duties. Every man fendin' for himself gets ugly real quick. It takes *people* teh become a nation, like in the old days when there weren't a mile uninhabited by at least one family. Every person should be workin' tehward the whole. The monks are a disgraceful lot."

"The fire got him," surmised Danny's mother as she approached the hole and saw the body. She scoffed. "We'll have the body brought up and find out where he came from. I don't like the idea that intruders have found tunnels we didn't even know about, and under our own secret hideaway. We'll have to collapse and booby trap their entry so no others can get in, or want to, neither."

"Looks like rails down there. Big 'uns," said George. "Them stairs . . . ?" They squinted. George huffed. "Well . . . I'll be. Them're stairs. Echos real good when we're this close. Looks as though it might mean there's a whole system under us. City's old, an' we're in its oldest parts, preservin' its original beauty as best we can. No one been here but us for a couple centuries. Could be some intrestin' things down there."

Others had quit working and gathered around to stare down into the hole with new interest.

"Damned monks been dancin' about under us," said George. He'd gone red in the face with anger. So had Danny.

"When we arrived yesterday, many of tha citizens seemed unhappy," said Taiir. "Are these men to blame? These monks?"

Linel clasped his hands together. "Yes, yes . . . I'd forgotten to explain the situation. These men came a few months ago and began stirring trouble about town. They blame Black Temple and accuse us of greed and hunger for power, of keeping the people from thriving. Leeches, they called us."

"We're in symbiosis," George muttered angrily. "Yeh help, we help, they help. The world isn't only about *them*. Or any one group. Yeh turn a big machine inteh a bunch a little ones, none'a them run well anymore, if at all."

Linel shuddered. "They've stirred up quite a few after news of the Cyan incident. More in the poorest districts, like where Aris Taramine's sister and nephew had taken refuge, I'm afraid."

"And the Enforcers haven't arrested them?" asked Reid. He grimaced. He would have to investigate this himself and forward his findings to the Temple as well as to Nails and the other surrounding posts' doctors.

"They couldn't. The monks are Crostor's guests. One of the monks is his favorite nephew."

"Unless *that* is his nephew," said George, nodding to the corpse. "Could be bad business for us all."

"Crostor has about had it with the Enforcers," Linel said nervously.

"I'll look into it," Reid said. "Taiir, let's get back. Business needs tying up, and matters need settling."

"When you are to leave Edantine, notify one of us first," Danny requested. "I'll send out the two who asked to become apprentices. Sobrienne and Axon. They might never save lives because of their temperaments, but . . . they will be helpful. Sobrienne can handle the roughest, rowdiest adversaries. She's slapped grown men to tears. Axon is an excellent negotiator. A bit of a whiz at it. Both are young, but their skills are set, and so are their minds. They do not want to stay here, where they will never be able to be among people outside the Family. They want to travel."

Hours later, Reid and Taiir, and the Oliver brothers, had transported a very large, very heavy collection of books to the guild house. They'd loaded all that was to go to Hagenhold into a second wagon, and the hundred hex lights Reid had been willing to trade to Danny and the fuel makers were in a small chest in the driver's seat. He was glad he had opted not to sell all three hundred in one location. Drumming up some business throughout the rest of Edantine made better sense. Business would spread afterward because of it. And he'd added a small portion, some twenty lights, to Hagenhold's wagon to whet the city's curiosity and appetite for more.

Reid had already sold every other light, and others were requesting more. His niece's gift had earned her quite a bit of coin in a surprisingly short amount of time, and he would soon be depositing every last cent of it with one of the iron banks which were aligned with the Enforcers' Alliance. One of the Temple's guildsmen would be employed there to attend to any Black Temple business.

"Those are to be delivered directly to Hagenhold," Taiir said to the coachman. "No stops along tha way."

"Yes, sir," said Jonas as he lifted the visor on a fresh lantern which he now hung from a spindle hook. The driver, his brother Don, fished a pair of old leather gloves from his jacket pocket and put them on, and he began to fasten them to his wrists.

"And to whom are you to deliver?" asked Reid as he skimmed another page of one of the old books Danny had traded him. The contents of the book were fascinating. Some of the pictures of the old cities were incredible and gave a glimpse of what life had been like over seven hundred years ago. He'd seen none but broken remnants and teetering towers in his own lifetime. Edantine had been one of the last great marvels standing from the Modern Age, and now it, too, was a shadow of its former self. In the book Reid was studying, one of the buildings had been covered entirely in smooth, black glass called 'solar panels.' Vehicles had started and driven by themselves. Great steel mills had rolled out more high-quality metal in an hour than he would ever see in thirty lifetimes. The hospitals would have been Ralleigha's glass-made heaven, with windows inside and out, and glassy surfaces making up every hallway and desk. Some of the pages showed glass that was strong enough, even, to hold entire pools of water. And the hospitals had been large enough to fit several *towns* inside, and they had looked so very clean that not a speck of dust could be seen throughout them.

The clothes were odd. Very impractical. He imagined it came from a lack of necessity. That a streamlined, clean lifestyle with endlessly available amenities had caused the trend.

One of the other books was on military applications, tactics, programming, maps of terrain he'd only heard of vaguely . . . He'd be reading that one himself. It was most fascinating.

"We are to head straight to the guild house in Hagenhold, to ask for the posted doctor Ramsay Bridger," said Jonas as he tethered the midnight horses the attendants had brought from the barn. Their previous horses were weary from a previous trip and needed to be cared for. Those were Linel's horses, borrowed and returned, all for Temple business.

"And?" asked Taiir.

"And deliver first the letter and this small box," grunted the coachman as he buttoned up his trench coat to the neck and wrapped his scarf about his high collar. "And then Ramsay will assign his attendants to an inventory. Afterward, they will relieve us of these goods. We know our jobs. I do not understand why every Black Temple rep who comes along insists upon having us repeat every line of instruction four times, ten times . . . We are not simpletons, damn you all."

Manard chuckled. "Standard treatment for any non-reps, boys. Linel himself recommended you. He said you are reliable and trustworthy."

"Linel's a bit of a trusting fool," grunted the brother, and both Don and Jonas placed their wide-brimmed hats upon their dark heads and pulled down on the brims. "But we'll get this job done. Just stop making us repeat the instructions before we tell you lot to piss off and find another driver to help Hagenhold."

"Will this Ramsay fellow be paying us?" asked Jonas. "The last one skipped over our fee, and we don't work on good faith whether it is for the Temple, the Enforcers, or the Wearyworn."

Reid sighed. "Of course."

"Most of tha wearyworn only work for money and care not for others," said Taiir.

Manard shrugged. "Such men are everywhere and have always been. Play one side as well as the other for profit. Get several benefits others don't get, like a little gold with the free room and board and the free care and maintenance of their horses and wagons, and still demand more than is fair. What amazes me is that you Temple folk always seem disappointed by it. Common sense to me, though. Play the game to get ahead."

"I am not a sworn guildsman," said Taiir.

Manard didn't care. "You think like them. Same thing. Honor rules you. Common sense rules the rest of us. All you succeed in with your *everyone is a link in the chain* mindset is making yourselves look both naïve and superioristic. Doesn't matter if you're all well-intended. It's shady and weird."

"This will cover our load, so you should not worry about the cost." Reid tossed two golden liberties to them, and Jonas caught them both. The man examined them carefully before pocketing them.

CHAPTER SEVENTEEN

$\mathcal{N}$EED A $\mathcal{D}$RINK

A BRICK CRASHED THROUGH the window, shattering Reid's restless sleep and waking the household. Doors creaked open, and footsteps came running. The door vibrated with heavy knocking. "What's happened? Are you all right?" demanded one of Linel's seven attendants.

Reid threw off the blanket with a heavy sigh and set his feet carefully on the floor, avoiding the splinters of glass. Taiir was already at the window, drawing the curtains aside discreetly. Their other roommate, Manard, was not in the room with them. His bed was made neatly, as though he'd never entered their shared quarters that night. "Beware, they are readying another, tha bold bastards." Taiir leaned back, and another brick came crashing through.

Reid glared at the stones when he noticed the twine wrapped about them. Notes were tied to them, likely containing perverse, threatening content. He didn't need to pick them up and read them to know that; the vandalism spoke for itself. Reid rose as Taiir lifted the window, and then he snagged his gun and his knife from the drawer. He tucked both into the waist of his pants. "Mind the glass," said Reid as he crawled out of the broken window.

He breathed in heavy smoke as a hard wind drove it toward him. When he turned his head, he saw that the barn was afire, and the flames had spread to the other end of the guild house. The roof was still soaked from the rain, but what was dry was catching quickly.

Then he heard the attendants shouting as they rushed about outside, trying to put it out.

Reid swore as he dusted the glass from his pants. "The house is on fire," he said as Taiir opened the door and allowed Linel's attendant Rebecca to come in. Rebecca was the most experienced and level-headed of the attendants. Reid looked over his shoulder briefly and told Rebecca, "Tell Linel those monks of yours have broken the window to our room. I am going out to arrest them."

"As am I," said Taiir, who tossed Reid his shoes, his tunic, and his belt.

"Where is Manard?" Reid asked.

Rebecca paused midturn, just after ordering a younger man behind her to deliver the message. She looked back. "Oh!" she said. "Your friend has been in the Great Room all night. Do you need him as well? I'll send Nathan, too, if you need. He's fine with a sword."

"No need. I can't wait any longer," said Reid as he sloppily donned the rest of his clothes and then his belt and weapons. He scanned the grounds for more hooded intruders and more vandalism. "Boot prints lead away to the right, toward the trees," said Reid. Taiir followed him, but before they could get away from the guild house, they were stopped.

"Wait!" cried Linel as he rushed into the room at the attendant's message saw what was afoot. A third letter was clutched in Linel's hand — likely the same as the other two on the floor. From the doctor's pale expression, Reid knew the threats in the letters were vague but intimidating. Catching the intruders was currently more important. "We need you here, Reid," said Linel from the window. "The fire is spreading wildly! And what if more of those miscreants are near?" He waved the letter he held about. "What if they kill you both? They have threatened only the two of you and your coach." When Linel held out the page, Reid glimpsed sketches of bones and sprawling letters in what looked like blood.

The notes and the burning guild house were all the evidence Reid needed to prompt the Enforcers in the city to allow him to arrest these men. Legally, he had every right to detain the intruders, regardless of whether they were Ragan Crostor's guests.

Taiir shrugged at Linel's concern. "These threats would not be tha first we have received, good doctor, and they will not be tha last."

"But what if they *wanted* you to follow them?"

"That seems exactly as they intended," said Reid as he waved at the spreading flames. "You'll be distracted, trying to put that out. Spare a man, and send him to fetch the Enforcers. They need to step in with this matter. Taiir will retreat to notify you where if we are ambushed."

"Where is Nathan?" cried Linel as Taiir and Reid left them behind.

"I thought he was with you, sir," Rebecca replied. Their voices fell aside, overcome by the chaos about the burning property.

Ames and Manard appeared outside, both fully dressed, fully armed, and ready to assist. Before Manard could open his mouth to speak, Reid threw out a command. "Ames, you will head straight to the Crostor manor to let them know what has happened. You said you have little to no skill with the sword, so you do not need to get involved in this in such a way." Ames nodded and broke away. "Manard, you should stay here in case there are more — "

"I will do no such thing, Commander. There are enough able-bodied men and women here, most with weapons. I am going with you so neither of you get killed. Three men are better than two. I saw four of those monkish bastards disappear over there — "

A loud crack sounded, startling Reid and Manard, and a hooded figure wielding a wicked spiral dagger collapsed between them. Taiir lowered his staff and used the end to pull back the monk's hood, revealing an ugly woman whose face, neck, and scalp were badly scarred by fire.

Reid cringed. "I would have asked a warning if it wouldn't have warned the devil!" He stepped aside as Taiir darted after another neither he nor Manard had seen.

"Bind her," commanded Taiir of Manard as he vanished into the brush. Manard cut a long strip from her robe and twisted it tightly as he wrapped and knotted it so that it would serve as a makeshift rope; he also gagged her with another strip of the material. They moved on after a thorough search of her unconscious form and the retrieval of her weapon, and Taiir met them in the street and told them which way he'd seen them go. They kept to the shadows to avoid being seen and stepped softly to keep from being heard.

Within the hour, they found two of the monks in a dark alleyway where the smell was loathsome — the air was a thick mixture of manure and piss, and of vomit, mildew and alcohol. Up the street was a bar, where some men went in sober and others came out drunk. Merry, off-pitch music rang out, along with laughter and with the wafting odor of the drink.

The monks were picking the lock to an armorer's shop.

Reid caught Manard by the shoulder to stop him when the man began to stride past him in his anger. But they'd already been spotted. Several hooded enemies blossomed from the shadows. Clouds drifted over the moon and cast them into the night's eclipse so that the walls became indiscernible from the ground and the men became part of a rolling sea of spasming black.

"What better place to surround us, to leave a message to the Enforcers and Black Temple," muttered Reid darkly. He found himself grinning, however. "It'll be nice to finally let loose, though." To the monks, he said, "We'll see if I've lost my touch. I haven't been outnumbered in a good while."

Their enemies said nothing, but a chorus of sheaths hissed as steel spilled from their hollow mouths. Here and there, a blade caught the distant light of a street torch or a candlelit window several stories above them.

"Reid," said Manard. The man motioned at one particular shadow which had separated itself from the rest. That one had something clutched in his hand — a heavy pouch, which set Reid to snarling even before the man spoke.

"We would like to thank you for your donation before you die. It will go to good use."

"The hell it will," Reid hissed. He felt himself trembling with rage and reminded himself to calm down and face the thieves with cold, calculating logic and controlled motion. The last thing he should do, he knew, would be to allow the monks to provoke him to fury. That adrenaline would do him no good if it overpowered his senses or robbed him of his endurance. "I'd have flashed some coin sooner if I'd known that was all it took to draw you out," said Reid evenly. "I have already wasted three days, investigating your little group — "

He twisted out of the way of a sharp jab and pushed Manard forward to avoid a thrown dagger. The dagger caught his left arm, and he hissed. It had only grazed him, but it stung, nonetheless. It would have struck Manard a fatal blow, however, if he hadn't moved the man. "Swing wildly and give them several openings. Draw them in," Reid commanded quietly. "Let them think you're useless in a fight. We'll take out four or five that way."

The monks rushed them.

He parried the lethal aims of three of their hooded enemies, but a fourth aimed low, and that monk's sword caught Reid's left calf, and he snarled in pain and anger. He managed to slit the man's belly open when he spun to avoid being sliced again. Blood ran hot down his leg, and it did so at a steady, unrelenting pace. He noted how much time he likely had until he grew lightheaded and became a burden upon his comrades. It wasn't enough time, not with the way he was bleeding. It meant he could not afford to be gentle with these men, that he couldn't afford baiting them into making mistakes. It meant he and his men would sustain a few more dangerous injuries before the fight was over.

Reid swore as another monk rushed him, and he slit the man's throat. He could barely put his weight on his injured leg. He cut another down, and another, as they sensed weakness. He parried a third and kicked the bastard back, though he clenched his teeth malevolently and cursed the stinging in his calf as he did so. He needed Manard to draw them in. "Manard!"

He wished the odds were better for gathering more information from them, but the priority was surviving. They would get themselves killed if they tried to preserve any of the monks' lives now. (He struck another with the pommel of his sword, and the monk retreated with a vicious curse.) And Manard was not great with the sword — he was just *adequate*. He was parrying the blades and being driven into a corner. He also wasn't doing as Reid had asked. "Do what I said, or we're going to get ourselves gutted by these bastards!" Reid barked as his fist knocked another monk senseless. The monk staggered into another shadow that was converging on Manard.

"I'm no good at pretending," snapped Manard as another one of the monks fell before them.

Reid snorted and spoke sideways. "Then *accidentally* drop your weapon — " The butt of one of the monks' swords struck Reid in the face then, just as he dodged another's attack. The alleyway spun about him, and he struggled to right himself as another monk fell at the edge of the ring of enemies they drove back.

"Where the hell is Taiir?!" demanded Manard. "I can't see the gloomy bastard! Is he even here with us anymore?"

"*Yes*, he's with us," said Reid. He saw Taiir for a moment in the darkness as two more monks fell behind the rest, but Taiir vanished just after. Reid was glad for Taiir's assistance, but he would command the man to retreat the moment it was safe enough to do so. "Keep one of them alive if you can. We'll be in an unsavory mess if every monk here is killed and *then* the Enforcers come down the street at us. Taiir! Retreat and report this the moment I give the word!"

Three of their enemies suddenly fell, and Manard gasped as their daggers clattered across the paved alleyway. The others halted, confused, and when Reid shoved Manard forward, the soldier *did* drop his sword as he tripped over one of the bodies. "Son of a — "

Taiir appeared briefly in the opening that was created, his staff smacking the wrist of an enemy. He caught Manard's sword as it slid across the alleyway, and he lifted it to parry another blow. His staff crunched against a skull, removing his opponent from the fray, and he clasped Manard's sword with both hands, raised it above his head, and sent it hurtling toward another who knelt to quickly retrieve his own weapon. As it spun, the blade sliced clean through the man's neck, and the severed head fell to the paved alley and rolled. The body fell upon its side, its hand still reaching and spasming.

Taiir was better and more effective with his staff than these men were with their swords, and the difference in skill was costing them their lives. That, paired with his ability to think strategically and wait patiently for the perfect moment in a high-stress, dangerous situation, was exactly why Reid had persuaded Taiir to become his Second. Few could work as Taiir did in these types of operations.

Taiir vanished again before the head ever stopped rolling.

The man was a master at nighttime warfare.

Reid laughed at the sudden uneasiness that spread through the monks. He drew his gun as Manard pushed them back, and he pointed it at the one holding the money. "I'd like that back," he said coldly. "It doesn't belong to me or to the guild. I would rather not owe such a debt."

Two men swept forward as the one with the bag clutched the money and clipped it to his belt. Reid cut the two monks down, never removing the barrel from its target. "Ten seconds. Nine."

Others closed in, and Manard rushed them as the thief stole another step back. "Seven." Reid raised the gun and discharged a bullet into the sky. The thunderous explosion caused three monks to freeze. Three more fell without their heads. Another two fell by Manard's blade, and one more fell, badly wounded. Manard sliced another's wrist before the rest converged.

The thief turned to flee.

"One." Thunder clapped their ears when he pulled the trigger.

But the bullet chased through one of the others instead of making the kill Reid had intended. The thief fled, and Taiir and Manard and Reid were quickly overrun. Reid shot another round before the bastard vanished, unscathed.

Reid was furious, and he pushed through the last of the monks to chase after the one he'd shot at. But before he'd even made it three paces out of the alley and into the street beyond it, they were swarmed by new hostiles.

"Lay down your arms!" came a shouted command. "NOW!"

The Enforcers had arrived, thirty or so in number, all of them having drawn their weapons — spears, long swords, short swords, and maces. From their appearance, the aggressive men were already at the edge of a dangerous decision: to attack unprovoked.

Reid did immediately as he and the others had been commanded. The final two monks, however, turned their blades upon themselves, and before Reid or Taiir could stop them, they ended their own lives right there. Reid's stomach coiled as though he'd just swallowed a bunch of poison, and the alley tilted as it spun about him. His leg throbbed immensely, and so did his temple where one of the monks had struck him. Reid wiped the sweat from his face —then he realized it was blood.

He took a deep breath to steady himself and lower his heart rate.

"We work for the Temple," said Reid loudly as the Enforcers approached him and goaded him roughly back to the bloody site where their fallen foes littered the alleyway. Taiir laid his weapon on the ground with great care, keeping it from the pools of blood and refuse. The smell of the blood overwhelmed every other foul scent there.

Manard also tossed his weapon when one of the Enforcers pressed the tip of a blade against his back.

Reid showed the ring upon his hand, which was engraved with a Black Temple sigil. "We were attempting to arrest these men after they robbed us and vandalized the guild house — "

One of the Enforcers, a hardened man with iron eyes and dark, well-groomed facial hair, struck Reid in the jaw. Reid stumbled backward, into Manard, who caught him. "You will keep your mouth shut until we begin to question you." The man shook out his hand and wiped Reid's blood from it, and he called to one of his comrades. "Lieutenant Cramer, put these men in restraints so they don't try anything while we investigate this vile scene. Do not underestimate how dangerous they are."

Taiir grinned. "So much for your sporting face, Commander."

Reid laughed. "The wife will have to forgive any new scars, eh?" He held out his wrists to accept the cuffs. "Just comply, Manard. I am completely confident these men will do their jobs. I've spoken extensively with Linel on the matter, and I trust his word about the state of the Enforcers' Alliance here in Edantine."

"Captain Robin," said another of the Enforcers. This one hardly looked older than a boy, perhaps fourteen summers at most. The younger man had rolled over one of the bodies as the captain picked up Reid's discarded gun and looked it over.

"Fine make," said Captain Robin. "We don't see many guns in Edantine, especially not in such good shape. I knew an old man who used to carry one just like this. Used to visit this city every year or so."

"It's a three-hundred-year-old antique," said Reid. "Please don't drop it."

Captain Robin growled unpleasantly. He scratched his chin and ignored Reid's comment. "Take these men and drop them in a cell, Lieutenant — "

"*Captain Robin*," said the young Enforcer more forcefully.

The captain frowned. "What? What have — " He froze. "*Broken shields*," he swore as the other Enforcer stepped aside. "Is that Crostor's *son*?" He'd spoken in a near whisper to avoid drawing the others.

"And wearing the robes, yes," said the younger Enforcer, who stood over the body.

"I can see that, you idiot! Damn that fool for this. Crostor must be part of their scheming, too. Cover him back up! Don't let anyone else see this, and say *nothing* about it to anyone." The captain turned with a snarl upon his face, and he walked up to Reid, Taiir, and Manard. He looked them over with an unforgiving eye. "Well? Have it out before this gets any worse. Crostor will have you three hanged if he gets wind of this. I am at the edge of a single kindness, and that is because I am drunk off my arse and because I became a father yesterday. I will hear you before you're to be executed by the imperious lord."

The Enforcer who had restrained Taiir removed from his belt the hefty pouch the thief had run off with, and Reid stared at it, astonished. Taiir's gaze sparkled humorously, and he spoke before the Enforcer could ask him where he got it. "Tha thief dropped your client's money when I sliced him."

"Thank the stars," Reid sighed. The captain looked even more peeved. "Your monks, as I said," explained Reid, "robbed me of my client's coin. You may verify the sales and the amounts with the men I sold to yesterday and the days before."

"What are their names, and where may we find them? And *what* did you sell them?"

"My client is a junker who wished to remain anonymous. He's created some invaluable tech. Lights, safe during flood or drought. Just as durable and less an issue in unfavorable conditions." Reid grimaced when the shackles dug in, but he gave no resistance, as such would have been a grave error. Manard, however, stepped forward as though to backhand the Enforcer before him with his cuffs. "Calm yourself, Manard."

Manard's jaw ticked. "If I hear one more click on these cuffs, calm won't be an option," snarled Manard. "I'll break his nose if he thinks to damage my hands with these things."

Reid held up his hand again. "I am a Black Temple rep — "

"Anyone could put on a ring and call himself a king. Give me the names," decried the captain.

"Oh, I like you. Very thorough. The posted Black Temple doctor, Linel Virien, purchased ten for twelve liberties. Ten were delivered by coach drivers Don and Jonas Oliver, who were referred to us by Linel himself. The delivery to Hagenhold was free of charge on a gamble the guild members there will incite more business. One hundred sold for six hundred liberties, plus a load of old books for my niece; the books are in our wagon at the guild house, and those one hundred lights were sold to your odd inventors here. I'm sure we could find them again. Those men stank, but they had the coin. The names were Danny Igratio and George Heckel. I met them just outside of town when they took interest. I also sold to the mason, Abbot Questrian, and to the miners' manager, Corben Schleuter . . . The log is in my quarters at the Temple's guild house. The total was three hundred lights sold for approximately twelve hundred and forty liberties, ninety-seven copper hint, and the books. We've more orders listed. Some even paid in advance."

"By tha nether regions of tha knotted oaks," growled Taiir. "You said nothing of such a sale. You should have gone straight to tha banker!"

Reid shrugged. "The tellers were already gone for the day when I closed the last sale. I thought I'd do that first thing in the morning, but the thieving bastards brought us *here* first."

The captain's teeth grated, and he looked briefly at Reid's signet.

Reid continued. "Captain, the Temple's guild house was vandalized. Cold murder was never our goal. We pursued these men to make a series of arrests, but we were ambushed. We'll attempt nothing else against the rest of them unless permitted. We'll stay out of the way or offer our assistance as requested so that you may get your job done with minimum interference."

The captain growled under his breath and waved the lieutenant over. "Get them out of here. Put them in the dungeon until we figure out for ourselves what is going on."

"The guild house is on fire," said Manard before he was shoved forward. "They may need help."

"We don't *help*," hissed the captain. "We arrest. We investigate. We execute. And we fight wars." He spat upon the ground before them. "It is Black Temple's duty to *help*."

"Your leg," exhaled Taiir when Reid staggered. "That wound needs to be seen to, Reid."

"Bastard got me good," Reid huffed. "Captain Robin."

Captain Robin paused, irritated by the request. He turned one last time. "*What.*"

"One of these monks got away. He's the one who had my client's money."

"I slit him wrist to elbow to get it back," Taiir nodded. "He may soon show his face to tha Black Temple doctor."

"We'll watch for him," nodded the captain. "A wound like that will be difficult to hide. He'll favor it and try to avoid certain natural movements to dodge suspicion."

Reid and his companions spent a week in the Enforcers' dungeon as their captors seemed to do nothing. The captain never returned, and through the tiny window that was lined with bars, they could see that many Enforcers were busier getting drunk and gambling than bringing in any sort of rabble to be thrown in the dungeons with them.

The food was stale and moldy, and Reid's leg throbbed ferociously. The wound had crusted over, and it was becoming infected. He had developed a fever, and the days were quickly becoming a blur.

Manard and Taiir grew concerned when he stopped fighting them, when they at last removed the makeshift bandage and saw the state of the injury.

He stopped drinking the putrid water by the fourth day, and through the sixth and seventh days, he continued shivering, until his ribs felt cracked.

Then the doors atop the stairs creaked open, and down came the captain himself. He had sustained a very recent injury from throat to temple, and he hadn't yet cleaned up or had it stitched. "Come with me," he commanded as he unlocked and opened their cell. "And pick up your friend. We're both going to see your guild doctor."

Taiir was hesitant, but Manard immediately grabbed for Reid and dragged him into a sitting position. "My niece," Reid grimaced as the fog whorled sickly. His tongue felt heavy and slow, and grief spilled through him unexpectedly. He shook languidly as another chill surged through him, and the next breath ached beneath his ribs. "Please tell me she is still alive . . ." Then his head fell back, and everything returned to darkness.

When he woke again, he understood nothing being said about him. Faces blurred with one another, and he was being held down, and fire wrapped itself about his leg and bit viciously. He screamed and tasted the leather of the bit they'd placed in his mouth. Michael stood in the hallway, watching him quietly.

Something was wrong; that was all he could gather. Something was incredibly wrong.

Then the darkness took him again.

The next time he became aware, Reid tasted steaming broth being poured down his throat. He choked, and his hands fluttered to push it away. A crashing sound caused his eyes to open, although his vision blurred. The attendant, Rebecca, took the wet cloth from his head and changed it for another. "Your fever's finally broken," she said. "You should have awakened yesterday sometime. That dinky dungeon did you terribly. Do your best not to be thrown in another."

"Is he awake?" cried Linel. "Good! Excellent!" Linel stood from where he'd dozed on one of the chairs just outside the patient wing, and he quickly pulled the curtain open as he stepped closer. "That leg of yours came close to needing to be amputated. The cut was deep. I believe it missed any major nerves, however. Can you move your toes at all . . . ?" Linel bent over the bed, where Reid's leg was propped up on a mound of pillows. Reid's injury was wrapped with linen, which held some soft gauze in place. The room smelled of lavender and eucalyptus oil, and of some other acrid scent he was familiar with but couldn't name currently.

Reid clutched at his leg as fire leapt from the calf. He took a deep breath. "That smarts."

"Well, you moved the toes, so that's good. You need to remain as you are for a couple of weeks," said Linel.

Reid glared at the doctor. "The hell I do," he said. "I've got work to do. Put me in a splint or something. Give me crutches. I am not going to lie here and deteriorate like a leper, or risk getting an infection or a blood clot because I'm not about. The worst thing for me would be to listen to you — "

"The worst thing for you is not to listen to me, you stubborn fool!" snapped Linel. The man's sudden aggression startled Reid. "As my patient, you will do as I tell you to do. We'll make sure you don't get a clot, but remember that you are the patient and I am the doctor."

"Damn, Doc. Got a nasty little backbone hidden under that goofy exterior, don't you?" Manard laughed. "All smiley and fidgety and soft, gentle voice, unless the patient puts himself at risk."

Linel returned to his natural, good-natured temperament and laughed heartily. "Of course. I take my work seriously, Manard. Absolutely, I do. Reid, this is for your own good."

"And it will be for *your* own good, not to try to force me to remain in a bed I will not stay in." Reid tried to sit up, but Rebecca placed her hand upon his shoulder and gave him a warning look. She didn't seem happy to be enforcing such an order. "If I were you, I wouldn't test my resilience or my temper. My wrath is more dangerous than yours is, Linel. You don't want me getting cabin fever when I have urgent matters to tend to. How long was I unconscious?"

"Four days, after Captain Robin came and escorted us out. Before that, you were delirious, in and out with a fever. Doc, here, is extremely effective. Never seen a man bring someone back so quick from that bad a wound. He saved your leg — I didn't think he would be able to."

"How long were we locked up?"

"About a week, I think."

Reid swore. "Linel," he said evenly. He waved off Rebecca's attempts to calm him. She withdrew without trying again. "Get me some splints or some crutches. Or I will set the other half of this guild house afire."

Linel gasped. "You *wouldn't!*"

"I *would.*" The growl that left Reid's throat was so menacing that Linel jerked and backed away.

The curtain slid farther along its track, and Linel disappeared beyond. Reid caught a glimpse of the captain laid up in another bed. Faintly, he recalled seeing the huge gash in the man's face. He wondered what other wounds the man might have, not to have left the guild house yet.

Manard noticed where Reid's gaze had fallen. "Captain," Reid called.

There was no answer, so Manard booted the bed frame. The captain stirred, and he let out a long, blistering curse and reached for his shoulder.

Reid suddenly realized the man's entire left arm was gone. He sat upright and set his feet gingerly upon the floor. His leg throbbed hideously. "Help me, Manard."

Manard snorted, but he did as he was asked. With the soldier's help, Reid managed to hobble over to the captain's bed, and there he took a chair. Every motion stabbed at his calf, until he found himself holding his breath and growing dizzy. He gulped several times, waiting for the throbbing to calm before he reached for the captain's good shoulder. The captain opened his angry gaze, his teeth set to shatter, his jaw ticking fiercely.

"What happened?" asked Reid.

"Same monks that got at the three of you. Your group held better against them, although I have no damned clue how, since there were only three of you to their seventeen," grunted the captain. "I took a sword to the shoulder on the way here, after I'd already taken one to the face — luckily, it was mostly the flat side rather than the sharp edge. Doctor had to remove the arm. Too mangled, he said. Was sliced almost entirely in half lengthwise — I nearly had two arms for one, he said. Blood all over the place. Only kept from bleeding out because we wrapped it so damned tightly right after. Your men fight well." The captain gritted his teeth with a rough laugh and looked at Reid, and Reid saw in the man the same very faint glimmer of humor that he himself felt over his own injury. "Recovery is going to be raw. Going to have to figure out what the hell I'm going to do with myself . . . I won't be able to investigate without strengthening my game somehow. But I'll be waving my sword about with my other hand in no time."

"Well, your fortitude hasn't suffered," grinned Reid. "Pair of stubborn idiots, already planning to go back to work, the both of us."

Manard laughed. "Seems like."

"Men who lie as the dead may as well become the dead," nodded the captain. "We verified your claims, and then some. The monks had targeted you for assassination. You were getting too close to them, it seems. They killed both of your refugees, and they tried to kill off your post doctor, Linel. Crostor is in a rage. Word got to him that his son is dead, and that *you* killed him. He wants you hanged for it. It's apparent that we have a leak in the ranks. I gave a direct order to my men to say nothing. To keep quiet. You three were in the dungeon, so I know you couldn't have betrayed one another because of it."

"Were you able to question the female we bound outside in the garden?"

The captain closed his eyes as another wave of agony shot through him. He growled, his breath catching, and he said nothing for a long time. When he finally spoke, his voice was strained. "Yes. But Crostor's soldiers set her free just after I got a bit of information out of her. He accused the Alliance of stepping on his right to secure his own city the way he sees fit. He's sent out demands to have us withdraw from Edantine. I suspect it won't be going well for either of our guilds soon. Feels wrong. He's part of something *wrong*, I know it." The captain grimaced again. "Your client's coin was taken to the bank and placed in an account under the initials *N. I.* Your own name was added as the financial handler, just as you had listed in your log. Once we confirmed you were who you said you were and that what you said happened *had*, indeed, happened, we made sure no further crimes could come against you over it. It's more than we would normally do, but I did punch you in the face. I'd rather no lingering animosity between us, considering our respective positions within the Temple and the Alliance."

"Which teller did you use?" asked Linel. The doctor seemed concerned.

"Isaac Maston, I was told."

Linel paled. "Isaac Maston? Are you mad? The man's a blatant crook! Did you ensure the paperwork was done properly? He could make off with every last liberty and hint over the smallest loophole!"

The captain sighed. "I am unsure. I wasn't there to sign the exchange. I just issued the order to have it deposited."

"Who is this Maston character?" asked Reid dangerously. "Why should I be worried about him?"

Linel's shoulders sagged. "He's a slimy man, from Five Tower. I've had enough dealings with him to know he is never to be trusted. His brother Bryant is fair enough, and I trust him a great deal more. But Isaac is corrupt. He served in Five Tower for twenty years before he moved here. He's never done anything but wrong to the people he's dealt with, and he pays bad men to intimidate his victims to keep them from speaking out against him."

"I'll deal with it," said Reid angrily. "I am not worried about some worthless, weasel of a bank teller. I'll ensure it has been done properly. And if it hasn't · · · well· It will be· Captain, my thanks for the honorable intent."

"Reid, was it? That's your name, correct?" grunted the captain.

Reid nodded, grimacing as his calf shot through with another ribbon of flame. His fingers twitched as he reached to clutch at it gingerly. "It is."

"Well, Reid," said the captain. "Let's get ourselves a drink and have another talk. It seems we have a few more things we need to discuss."

"I think you are right," said Reid. "And a drink seems to be exactly what I need."

"That leg of yours won't be healing right if you burden your system with booze," said Linel gravely. "Or your shoulder, Captain Robin. I would advise *strongly* against it."

Reid and the captain stared at Linel. Reid's lip quivered. "You keep us from a bottle up the street, you'll be wishing you hadn't. This is more than called for. I'll be a patient when I get back to Crow Post."

"Doubtful," chuckled Manard. "I've seen enough to know better than believe that lie."

"Where is Taiir?" asked Reid.

Manard and Linel both looked away.

"What?"

Manard cleared his throat. "Em . . . The boy is out of sorts. Taiir's been trying to calm him, but he's having a hard time of it. Kid loved his mother and Ames."

"How did Ames and Mary die?" demanded Reid. His blood pressure was rising.

"Ames was killed just before he reached Crostor's manor," said the captain. "One of the monks parted from the crowd and slit him from navel to throat, spilling the man in front of every citizen there. Bastard was dressed as a Black Temple rep, no less, but no one saw his face before he disappeared among some of the preachy monks that were on the street near the cathedral. The killer was probably one of them."

"And Mary?"

"Smoke inhalation the night the fire started," said Linel quietly. "She collapsed just a couple of feet from her bed. We didn't get to her in time. She never had a chance. Neither of them did."

"Why would they have killed Ames, though?" asked Manard as Reid's fist moved toward his mouth. "I still haven't figured that out. It makes no sense. The man did nothing to anyone."

"What they did to him meant he was targeted specifically," said the captain. "But your question still stands . . . Yet you look as if you know the answer to that already, Reid. Why did they target him?"

Reid took a deep breath, trying to push aside his anger and his sadness. "They killed Ames because he had just become directly allied with a Black Temple rep who could make some adjustments to this city. Because someone here knew what I used to do for a living and realized what it meant. I have more authority than most reps who come through. I am a retired range commander. I have commanded armies large enough to destroy this city twice over, and I have the connections *still* to put the leadership here in their place. Ames and Mary, and their son Michael, could have been installed to replace the leadership here if the Enforcers and I had deemed Crostor and his family incapable or detrimental to peace. The Hullens were a direct threat because they were from a very old family and they knew how to run a city the size of Edantine. All they lacked were some political connections here — and for people in their position, that wouldn't have taken long to fix. That was their trade."

"Range commander?" asked the captain, surprised. "A bit young to have been a range commander — "

"And yet I am retired," Reid said icily. He dared the captain to question his service further. The subject was one of the few about which he did not tolerate disrespect of any kind. "Have you a problem with my age, Captain?"

Captain Robin seemed to realize his mistake, and he scratched his brow. "Not at all. They're just usually so wrinkled and gray . . . Here, and I thought you were just another Temple rep. I should have been following your orders instead of knocking you on your ass and then locking you in a cell to keep you out of the way." He laughed darkly. "Crostor will find it mightily hard to hang you, then. But he might opt to send more assassins after you when he discovers the authority you wield over him. Retired or not."

"If Crostor is caught pulling those sorts of strings," said Reid, "I'll have him taken to the Reformation as a political prisoner. They'll get every ounce of information out of him there. I wouldn't even have to ask Saura for permission."

Reid made to stand, and he hissed as the wound bit. Linel handed him a set of crutches, and he took one. It helped only a little. "Let's go get that drink, Captain." He offered his hand.

The captain grimaced but took it.

CHAPTER EIGHTEEN

◌IRTY ◌NFORCER

THREE OTHER ENFORCERS WERE at the bar with them, all as sullen as he. The rest of the tavern's guests seemed to be a mixture of joyful drunkards, lunatic partakers, and a few respectable lovers of the drink. The tavern was lit by three fireplaces and an endless array of hanging lanterns, and the sweat and smoke and alcohol formed a nearly unbreathable miasma that seemed to choke Reid's joy and set it to a silent grave. His mood soured the longer he sat and talked with Captain Robin and his men, and the more his mood soured, the more he drank. He pulled at his collar uncomfortably, and his fingers dug into his aching calf. Blood had seeped through his bandage, just as it had the captain's. And the more angered he became, the more he calculated his potential enemies and how they might be tied to Five Tower's schemes.

Captain Robin verified his suspicions with the help of his fellow officers, and meanwhile, as they spoke, Reid found himself continuing to break from the conversations they were having to look at the red-hot hearths. His pulse spiked with every leaping flame, until the laughter in the tavern almost sounded like screams to him. And Reid steepled his fingers and pressed his fingertips against his brow, his thumbs digging deeply into the nerves along his eye sockets, on either side of the bridge of his nose. The pressure points relieved no anxiety, but he kept the pressure for a while as he listened to the Enforcers debate.

Captain Robin seemed in a similar mood, as the man had downed more drink than Reid and continued to roll the cup about its bottom, in circles, watching the last of his whiskey slosh about in its glassy body.

"The fact of the matter is," slurred the captain, "Crostor has crossed a line. He has too many connections to the monks. A few connections would have been coincidental in his position, but there is too much happening in Edantine for him to deny it all."

Finally, Reid spoke aloud his deepest suspicions. "Listen to me, men. Black Temple is being uprooted, and your Alliance has been compromised as well. Every lead I have trails back to Five Tower, to a man named Caol. And when is the last time any of you have spoken directly with High Commander Avery Ramont? Or seen him? You used to see him every three to four months, isn't that so, Captain? Your roster required you and your troops to report in, so reassignments could be handled, debriefings could be put in order, and new orders could be doled out."

"That ratty-haired demon ghosted the idea of having meetings with us about thirteen or fourteen years ago. Locked himself away in a rage, and started giving orders from behind closed doors," snarled Captain Robin. "He's changed for the worse over the years. We know he's withdrawing our men, but we don't know why except maybe due to his mental state. If he locked himself away a long time ago . . ." Captain Robin growled angrily. "Look, I hate it. All of it. Withdrawing, and then finding out the cities we're supposed to protect are getting attacked right after. It is not our way. I've argued against it until I've turned blue in the face. I even abandoned my post eight months ago in order to return to the Keep and confront him. He still won't see anyone. Damned near had me hanged for insubordination, even threatened my wife and my unborn child, if I didn't return to my post immediately."

"He used to hold open meetings with all of his commanding officers," shrugged another captain, a rugged, unshaven man still filthy from a fight. The man, who went by the name Thames, slammed his mug against the table, and when a tavern wench came to refill it, he pushed it toward her. He waved her off instead of paying for the drink immediately, as was the custom in Edantine's taverns. When she placed her hands upon her hips and opened her mouth to start spitting curses, Thames placed his hand upon his sword. "You know damned well I will pay when I am done, woman. Be gone with you before I decide I am drunk enough to cut out your tongue."

"The Alliance used to have so much structure," hissed Captain Robin. "It's slowly disappeared over the years, and our reputation is being destroyed because of it. We're a joke, now. Just a band of miscreants claiming to be the Sword, the Shield, and the Shackle."

Reid snorted. "Avery isn't the one giving orders, isn't it obvious? Your ranks have been infiltrated, and other men are calling the shots. Men from Five Tower who are opposed to the Temple and any order or justice among the wearyworn."

"That actually makes sense to me," said the female lieutenant, Dari. She scratched at her buzzed scalp along the right side of her head, and then she shook her long top braids back over. "I've been watching Lieutenant Cramer and his subordinates for a while. They fell into our ranks without any kind of reference, and the small cluster of commanders at the Keep who give them orders are *disturbed*. Avery's personal guards, they call themselves."

"Arrest them, then," said Reid. "Figure out a crime, and force them out before they ignite a war. Get them to sign confessions. Get the Reformation involved, if you need. Me, I'm going to see to this bank teller Linel is concerned about. Your lieutenant, Cramer, he took my client's money to him just after it was stolen and recovered."

The female lieutenant cocked her head back with a hearty laugh and leaned back in the booth. "Your money is gone, then, if it is Isaac Maston he is concerned about," she said. "The swindler. And Cramer knows better, too. He's smart enough to have been avoiding being seen making any kind of deal with that crooked banker, but one of the teller's part-time bodyguards is Cramer's lover. I've seen them together enough not to mistake that rotted love tangle. Gotta be a crooked Enforcer if his smelly little lass is fighting for slime like that. She's a piece of work, too. Contessa is her name."

Reid looked up. That name was a very uncommon one on this side of the continent. "Contessa?"

"The name familiar to you?"

"Yes. You said she reeks. How so? Like oil?"

"Some kind of oily smell I can't quite label. Almost like fuel, but acrider. Same smell as the weird tinkerers that wander the town on occasion, freaking out the citizens. Everyone is convinced they'll blow something up rather than trade, and no one trusts what they have to sell." She laughed again, and then she took a deep swig from her mug.

Reid stood abruptly, then staggered. He'd forgotten his leg, and it reminded him bitterly. His glass hit the floor and shattered, and the room spun about him furiously as his blood boiled. He knew these developments meant something, but a fog rolled through him so quickly it nearly knocked him over. And something else had struck him so suddenly that he hadn't even the time to process it before he'd reacted as though he'd been bitten by a snake.

For a moment, Reid didn't realize Captain Thames had caught him, or that they were speaking to him. "Well, what is it?" asked Captain Robin.

Reid exhaled. His tongue felt dry and swollen. Their third captain, a man whose name he couldn't recall, and who had said little thus far, lowered his glass slowly and looked up at Reid. The captain's hand tremored ever so slightly, and Reid noticed he tried to swallow but couldn't. "Nothing, it's my leg," said Reid, but he returned the third captain's glare, and he found his own hand inching toward his own dagger.

The others sensed the danger too late. That captain drew his sword and attacked. The blade swooshed by Reid's throat, barely missing as Reid's leg gave out. Instead, it caught his cheek and left a stinging ribbon. Before any of them could parry, the captain stabbed Thames in the back.

Thames gasped, and he spun about when the betrayer withdrew the blade from his flesh. The traitor shoved the injured captain into Dari and tried to escape.

But Captain Robin threw a dagger into the man's back, and it sank into the flesh next to his spine. The traitor crumpled with a shout, and screams erupted from the tavern as the fearful women and the cowards ran. Reid was the first to him, stumbling though he was. He gripped the man's hair and jerked his head back, and he tore the Cyan signet he'd caught sight of from the twine about the man's throat. When the bastard fought him, Reid took the dagger's handle and twisted it, causing the man to scream, and then he ripped it out and placed it to the man's throat. "*You* murdered the Cyan nobleman in cold blood!" he raged in the man's ear. He didn't even recognize his own voice, he was so overcome with anger. "This signet belonged to a decent man, and you killed him and took this ring as a trophy. You are in league with Ragan Crostor and these criminal monks. Deny it! I dare you!"

The man began to laugh instead. "You think you're clever, don't you?" The blade dug deeper, and the captain leaned into it, daring Reid to slit his throat. "Do it, if you think you're man enough to kill an officer in front of them."

But Captain Robin grunted. "Give me my knife. I'll do it myself when we're done with him."

The traitor sobered. "Wait — you can't kill me, Robin. You're supposed to arrest him for threatening the life of a captain — "

"What are you going on about?" said Dari. "You're fine, trying to tempt an agent of the Temple instead?" She kicked Reid's arm away, sending the blade sliding across the floor, and then she kicked the traitor in the shoulder. "You dressed yourself as a monk, murdered a highborn in cold blood, and robbed your victim's corpse — and you've done it all in public. You cut an innocent man navel to throat and spilled him for the world to trample, Hagath."

"You can't prove anything. I bought that ring from those junkers."

"Bullshit," shuddered Reid. He rolled his shoulder and let go, and Dari took over and placed the man in cuffs. *Hagath*, she'd called the murderous captain. "You and your friend claimed to have helped them in the market when my men and I arrived just over two weeks ago. I knew I thought your face was familiar. You had a beard then, and you'd dressed as a merchant. You most likely hadn't killed them yet because Crostor wanted to see what they might do and who might help them. Who was the other man with you, Hagath?"

Hagath hissed as Dari hoisted him viciously from the floor, breaking his hand with a *crunch*. "I'll say nothing more," Captain Hagath snarled.

"You gave Cramer the information and sent him to the banker," growled Thames. The man clutched at his back, which was slick with blood already, but he punched Hagath in the face with his other hand. Hagath's head snapped to the side, and the traitor spat blood. Thames tossed five golden liberties onto the counter to pay for his drinks and gave a warning glare to the men and women remaining in the tavern. "Mind your business, the lot of you, or I'll remember your faces." The music returned once more, and the bartenders ushered their clients back with a free round on the house, on account of the amount of money Thames had just given them.

"I'll have some men investigate this rat's belongings, see what else he has," said Captain Robin.

When Hagath stiffened and started to say something else, Dari twisted his broken wrist, and he howled with pain instead, and they forced the traitor outside.

Reid berated himself angrily for not having recognized Hagath immediately, for not already having put everything together. He'd seen the ring about Hagath's neck when he and

Captain Robin had joined them at the tavern hours ago, and he hadn't recognized it for what it was.

A half hour later, Thames met them in the dungeon with the incriminating evidence from Hagath's locker in his hand. There were letters directly to Crostor himself, along with forgery tools and seals belonging to Black Temple and a few other Alliance captains. Captain Robin was enraged to find his own marker among the fakes. There was a ledger to be delivered to the teller from Five Tower, and there were instructions from the Keep detailing who, among Edantine's infiltrators, should do what.

When the items were presented to Captain Robin, the man drew his dagger. "Open his cell. This man is going to start feeding the maggots tonight."

"Wait!" cried Hagath, who crawled piteously to the back of his cell. He left a trail of blood behind him. "I can get you the men who robbed the guild house. Just let me live. Please. I'll tell you where the thief is, and I'll get you Cramer and Contessa. And the banker."

"Who is the thief?" demanded Reid.

Hagath hesitated, defiance blazing in his dark eyes. But when Captain Robin grabbed the keys from Dari, Hagath gritted his teeth and exhaled, and he began to spill. "Your coachman. He gave us the money," he said. "He gave us the money, and he told us what you knew."

Reid felt as though he'd been punched in the stomach. "Told who among you?" he said sourly.

"The monks," Hagath replied. "Everyone in the alley. And the banker."

"*What* did he tell you?" Reid snarled. He grabbed the keys from Captain Robin and shoved the door open, and the cowering traitor's bladder released its contents as the man began to weep. The corrupt captain knew he was about to be executed, be it by Reid's hands or by another's. "*I SAID WHAT DID HE TELL YOU?!*"

"He said you have a niece who is a witchling, that Five Tower is looking for scores like her and the boy. Strange people. They want strange people! He said they would pay. All we had to do was kill you and your friend, and take the money, and that we could use your ring to get into Crow Post — "

Reid had already stabbed the man in the throat before he'd even realized he'd done it. Before he'd even realized that the other captains and Lieutenant Dari had leapt forward to pull him off the scum rat who was currently gurgling and gasping in shock, red spilling from his mouth in a growing blood-fall. Reid's knee struck the stone underfoot as his stitches tore, and he cried out — though it was more anguish than physical pain that seemed to gut that cry from him.

They held Reid down as he struggled to rise and finish the job as the bastard clutched at his throat.

"*RESTRAIN HIM!*" shouted Captain Thames.

"Be careful of his leg. He's bleeding all over the place!" said Lieutenant Dari.

Reid lost the fight against them, although he felt the storm within himself swirling stronger with every breath. "I'm going to kill him," he gasped. "I'm going to kill that rotten hire for talking. I made him swear upon his life never to talk about my niece, and he swore it at the guild house. He knew how important it is to protect her — "

"Commander Ivan, calm down," Lieutenant Dari said. She grabbed a hold of his face with both of her hands and rested her forehead against his so that when he looked at her, he had to look her directly in the eyes. "Listen to me. You've just killed an Enforcer, a captain from among *our* ranks. You're retired, you fool. It is *our* job to clean this mess up, not yours. And how do you know he wasn't lying about his source? He might have been hoping to hold out until we verified his claim or proved him a liar."

He couldn't breathe. His eyes found the torch on the wall, followed the merciless flames, and he shuddered dissolutely. "If Manard spilled information about my niece, he will die badly for it," he continued, gasping.

"We will be the executioners if he is involved," said Captain Robin. Robin let go, and he gazed hard upon the body before them. He swore aloud to himself. "You've robbed us of the chance at more information. Let him up, Thames. Dari, help him. We're going to the guild house right now. Have that banker dragged out of his house, and find Cramer and his smelly lover. Bring them to the guild house, too. We're going to execute them all, and then we're going to start cleaning our ranks here. And speak nothing about the commander's mistake here. We wouldn't have even discovered Hagath was a traitor, or his connections, if it wasn't for the commander. I won't allow him to undergo a trial because of what he's just done."

"What about Crostor?" sighed Dani. She let go of Reid's face and offered him her hand instead. He hardly saw it; he'd shut his eyes when a spasm had torn from his calf to his thigh.

Thames answered. "Crostor's a coward, just as his nephew and his son were. Once he realizes we're back in charge, on behalf of the Alliance, he'll let us do our job without — "

"You cannot let Crostor live after what we've learned," hissed Reid, his mind spinning through every scenario and every bit of information they had learned. "If he does, with the connections he has and how much damage he has already done, you will be found out. Your infiltrators will know that you know everything. You will become targets for assassination, same as I. It is too dangerous to reveal our knowledge of Crostor's alignment, and it won't take much for him to turn already angry citizens. The monks have done their damage and turned enough of them. All they need is a spark and the fire will spread. You can't fight a mob when your men have been compromised to such a degree."

"Look at me," said Dari. "Commander Ivan."

Reid slowly pulled his gaze from the fire. When he at last complied, he realized compassion was written upon her face despite her cold order. It was the only hint of warmth in the room.

She held out her hand.

"We are grateful you were here to help us uncover this traitor and his web," she said. "But let us do our job. Stay retired. As far as anyone else will know, Hagath tried to escape and this was the result, and it was at my hands, not yours. I will not have your name tarnished over this mistake, or ours. Let us do our job, or we'll have to lock you up again to keep you out of the way."

Reid took another deep breath, still fuming, his head still pounding. But at last, he took her hand, and he shook it. "All right."

"Why is your niece important in this? Why would Five Tower want her? And why the boy he mentioned?"

"A bigger scheme," shuddered Reid. "I need to find a healer for her. It is urgent."

"Can't one of your doctors help her?" asked Thames. Thames had settled in a chair. He was pale now from blood loss, and he was winded.

Reid's answer was a denial. "Her father is one of the best, and even he doesn't know what to do. I can't let him abandon his duties to go chasing after what he thinks ails her when he is wrong."

"And you would know better than a Black Temple doctor?" asked Captain Robin skeptically. His brows had risen with disbelief.

Reid hesitated. His heart ached with worry when he remembered the letter he'd read. The thought of his niece's possible death tore at him. "Tell me," Reid said solemnly. "What Black Temple doctor knows how to deal with cursed magic?" The Enforcers were shaken by his statement. "She's been cursed," he told them. "I am not a man who naturally believes in the paranormal, but she has been cursed. I've evidence that claims it will kill her if we can't find the person who knows how to treat it properly. She is being followed by *demons*. I saw one of them. I have never seen a creature anything like it in my life, none so terrifying. It is not a being of this earthly world, but it was as real as you or I. And I promise you, my mind is quite intact. It was no hallucination or trick of the light."

"What about the boy?" asked Dari. She'd become quieter.

"He is also special. The Lord of Five Tower sent one of his thieves out to search for some man they want dead. That thief killed my parents, and when he did, he gained access to some dangerous information that might help my niece. Things are not as they should be, and my brother does not see it or even know how to deal with it. And now, possibly having one of my own betray me — " Reid shook his head angrily. "If Manard did betray me, his death will be a slow one."

"We'll assist in the questioning," said Captain Robin. "And I'll send some men to escort you back to Crow Post when you are done in Edantine — men I trust, mind you. They will accompany you as far as Oakwall, and then they will part from there and head to the Keep. We will find out who else has infiltrated our ranks, and we will cut the deceit from our brethren. Then we will look into this Five Tower mess."

Reid exhaled. "Be careful when you do. The Descendants of the Moon are working with them."

"The Wolfshadow cult?" asked Dari, surprised.

Reid nodded. "Yes. Every clan among them, for the number and movement we've seen. The Descendants seem to be the most determined among those."

"You need stitching again," chuckled Thames. "Same as I. And when we're done, you're gonna come back here and scrub up every drop of blood you spilt. I don't want to smell it still rotting every time I come to interrogate any prisoners after you're gone."

CHAPTER NINETEEN

WHEN REID RETURNED TO the guild house with Captain Robin, they were not accompanied by the other officers from the bar. The others had gone to search out the banker, Lieutenant Cramer, and Cramer's lover, Contessa.

Reid and Captain Robin brought no reinforcements because it was yet unwise to surround the guild house. If Manard was truly a traitor, he would realize what was going on before they had him cornered, and he would run. They couldn't risk it.

But what Lieutenant Dari had said also nagged at Reid. What if this was wasted time? What if the dirty traitor captain had sent them after the wrong man on purpose? The monks' and traitors' schemes had been a great, undiscovered secret until now, so what would have kept the man from lying to them to try to postpone his own death? Causing them to search longer meant it would have been increasingly likely they accidentally exposed the corruption. That meant Hagath would have had an increasing chance of an assisted escape as well as an increasing likelihood that Reid, Captain Robin, and everyone near them would be assassinated.

So who else could have told Hagath all that he'd known? The informant could *only* have been as close as Manard.

That betrayer could be Taiir, even as unlikely as that seemed. The person could be Linel instead, or even one of the attendants.

But no one else here who knew the secrets about his niece could have had the motive to give that knowledge away.

While considering everyone he'd talked to, Reid cursed himself for having been so naïve. He had known better than this. He'd always *been* better than this. But the circumstances around the boy Michael had lowered his guard, so he'd spoken about more than a few things he shouldn't have.

He should have considered the possibility that Five Tower's schemes could have reached this city already. It had been almost fifteen years since Avery had stopped communicating openly with his subordinates. That was a lot of time for Five Tower to do a lot of groundwork for a discreet takeover. And it was very likely that Avery had been missing for *twelve to thirteen* of those fifteen years.

Reid had known Five Tower could have involved more than just the wolfmen, and the moment he'd heard about the monks, it should have raised his suspicions over any possible ties. It had been blatantly obvious from the moment Linel had told him what the monks had been doing and saying here.

Yet he had missed it.

Like a blind fool.

"How long has your friend worked with you?" asked Captain Robin as they reached the guild house.

"Long enough to know too much," said Reid. He hesitated at the door when he saw his hand was shaking. He withdrew it, and he wiped his sweating brow and scrubbed the dried blood from his cheek.

"What is it?"

"I need another drink is what," Reid said quietly. "But I am too much like my brother, and I need to *think*. Other possibilities are running through my head at the moment. A lot of things I missed that were right in front of me. No one in this guild house is to be trusted until we've found our informant. Or *informants*. There may be more than one."

When he reached for the door again, it opened. Manard held it aloft. The guard looked relieved to see Reid.

Reid wondered if the man had heard anything they'd said, though they'd spoken quietly.

Manard opened his mouth, but when he seemed to notice something was amiss, he pulled the door farther open and extended an arm to assist Reid. "What's happened?"

Reid cringed inwardly.

"We've had our drink," growled the captain. Robin did not step in immediately.

"And a bar fight, to boot, eh?" asked Manard. "Well, whatever gets you crazy Alliance types hot. Come in. We've got another problem, and this one isn't to do with an Enforcer."

"Really?" asked Reid. He watched Manard's expression carefully, replaying their every past interaction and searching for second meanings in all of it. Even for misinterpretations. It did fit for Manard to be a traitor, yet he found himself refusing to want to say it aloud. "Keep your weapon at the ready," muttered Reid to the captain.

Robin merely grunted in reply. His gaze sparked in agreement, however.

Linel rushed them, waving a rolled sheath of papers. "I told you that you shouldn't drink!" he cried. "But look at what you've gone and done to yourself! If you refuse to follow my doctorly orders again, I will boot you back out immediately!" Linel's face was beet red, as if about to pop. "Get over here, now! But how awful you both smell, at that. Like a brewery! It is an effrontery to my nose and to this guild house!"

The captain closed the door behind them, but neither he nor Reid went any farther.

Taiir frowned. He read more than he acknowledged aloud, for his hand twitched for his weapon, ready to assist. He was the one to relay the news. "Crostor sent a summons."

Manard grimaced. "It's a sham."

Taiir nodded. "I agree. He has summoned tha three of us to his manor to discuss how to deal with tha trouble stirring in tha city. He has mentioned he wishes to discuss it after tha funeral for his nephew and his son."

Linel grew redder. "I said to sit! Over here . . ."

Reid had drawn his dagger. "Crostor should have no idea about his son's death." He turned the dagger over and then gripped the handle dangerously as he stared hard at each of them. He glared at Manard the longest. "Especially not his nephew's."

Captain Robert drew his dagger as well.

Reid looked at Taiir. "Manard never knew of the nephew. Have you said a word to anyone, Taiir?"

Taiir's brows drew together again. "Only if I was a fool or a betrayer. I have already asked Linel tha same. It seems he has spoken to one other about it."

Reid lowered the dagger, surprised Linel would have done something so stupid.

"Yes, yes," cried Linel, who still seemed naïve of the suspicion upon them all. "But why would it be such a bother? We only found the body; we didn't kill the man! He died because of a fire he himself had likely caused!"

"Who did you tell?" asked Captain Robin.

"Only Nathan. And he's a good lad — "

"And you're a trusting fool," spat Manard, taking the words right out of Reid's mouth.

"Maybe I am, too," said Reid.

Manard frowned when he sensed Reid's hostility. "Pardon? Are you trying to suggest something?" The soldier grew angry and drew his weapon also. "You've both drawn your daggers. You've been told something, haven't you? What have I been accused of? I have the right to know." He threw his sword upon the floor at Reid's feet, where it gouged the wood. Then he held up his wrists. "If you believe I have suddenly betrayed you, do your job and arrest me. But you will give me the courtesy of telling me *why* first."

"You've been accused of quite a bit, Manard."

"Out with it, then," hissed Manard. "Let's have the list, shall we?"

"Have you conspired to abduct his niece and the boy Michael in the service of Five Tower?" asked Captain Robin.

Manard's surprise seemed genuine. He started to deny it, but then he broke into confused laughter instead. "*What?*"

Taiir and Linel looked at each other, concerned.

"Why would I do such a thing? And who would I give them to?" said Manard. "But go on. Let me hear more of it."

"Where were you when — "

A scream tore through the guild house, and all of them looked at one another. Glass shattered in another room, and the sound of something heavy hit the floor. Linel paled. "*Rebecca?*"

The others turned, and Reid and Captain Robin looked up as Rebecca stumbled into the Great Room, clutching at her throat. Blood streamed through her fingers and dripped across the floor. The only thing any of them could hear her choke was a gurgled name. "*Nathan — *"

"What happened?" cried Linel.

She teetered, and then she collapsed before anyone could even catch her.

Reid shoved Taiir and Manard out of his way to get to her, and Captain Robin retreated to the door behind him to guard the entry.

"Rebecca!" Linel wept. His frail hands shook immensely as he knelt by her to look for other injuries, but they soon returned to trying to help her stop the flow of blood from her throat. "Somebody, grab my surgical kit!" he commanded. His voice shook with grief and fear. Manard snatched up his sword and darted from the room, into the hall and toward the sound of more glass shattering. Flames splashed into the hallway.

"The bastard is trying to set the guild house on fire again!" shouted Manard. "Someone, put this fire out behind me!"

Reid pressed his hands against Rebecca's throat as her wild gaze darted back and forth between him and Linel. Her bloody hand fluttered between them as she tried to point to the hallway. "Who did this to you?" Reid demanded.

"Natha — " She choked, and blood sputtered from her lips. "He killed Vanessa — " She tried to gasp for breath, but she could barely gather enough air to continue without choking. "H — took Michael — "

"*Nathan* did this?" Linel was confounded. "But he's been bedridden since his injury! He took to a fever!"

"What kind of injury?" asked Captain Robin.

"His arm," said Linel. "He was cut badly the night of the fire weeks ago. The broken windows — "

"From his wrist to his elbow?" asked Taiir as he picked up his staff.

"Y . . . yes," said Linel. "You didn't know?"

Reid swore as Taiir darted from the room. "Taiir cut the man who stole from us. Wrist to elbow. He was dressed as one of the monks, helping them to break into the armorer's shop."

Linel snapped orders to two of his attendants who had come into the Great Room. Supplies, to tend to the injured woman. But both had gone pale at the site of Rebecca on the floor between Linel and Reid. Rebecca had lost consciousness. Reid hardly felt her pulse . . .

And then her pulse was gone.

"Linel, she's dead," said Reid.

Linel shuddered and began to cry, then, great, heaping sobs. "She can't be! She can't be, I — "

"She's dead," Reid repeated. "Call your people together. Captain, can you get all of them to tell you what they know? I should assist Taiir and — "

"You won't get far on that leg," wept Linel. "Shasta, get the linens." He hiccupped and wiped his face on his sleeve, and he withdrew his bloody hands from Rebecca's body. "Your stitches, sir. Let's get you in walking condition again."

"Let your men catch him, Reid," said Captain Robin. "You'll get yourself killed if you try to pursue him with that injury. Finish questioning everyone here, and then we'll search the premises."

About an hour later, Reid was using the crutch again, and he was pacing. He and Linel had gone through Nathan's belongings. There wasn't much to find, as Nathan had decidedly kept little evidence against him in the guild house. But a partially burnt letter was found in the hearth in his room. Reid tossed it onto the wooden table before Linel, who was red eyed from weeping. Linel had a glass of fire brandy, and he was nursing it as though it were the only thing keeping him alive. His hands were still trembling, and tears glistened upon his freckled face.

Linel stared ahead, not noticing the burnt page. Slowly, ever so slowly, his gaze shifted, until he was looking at Reid. He said nothing for a long time, though his mouth quivered. And then he was looking at Rebecca's body. "W-we were to be married . . ." he said. His voice was ghostly. There was no more warmth in it at all, and then the man shook as though winter had rattled his bones.

Reid looked at the blood that had dried on the doctor's hands. Already, it had begun to flake away. "I am very sorry, Linel."

"The letter is too blurry to read. What does it say?" Linel asked. He continued to stare at Rebecca's body, until fresh tears began to fall and he had to look away. "Who was it from?"

"Crostor wanted your attendant to bring Michael to him." Reid took a chair opposite Linel. "I couldn't read the rest. Too charred."

"That's a fine thing to hear," said Captain Robin with disgust. "He's kidnapping kids now." The captain didn't look well. His head hung so that his hair fell over his face, and he was leaning forward as though he was about to collapse. Even talking seemed to take everything he had. "When he is arrested, I'll see to it that he is sent to the Reformation. Keep that letter safe until I ask for it, Range Commander."

Reid nodded.

The three of them remained silent for a long time as the remaining attendants cleaned the mess in the house and tended to the bodies.

"Vanessa and Rebecca," sniffled Linel. "A tragedy, what he did. I don't understand . . . How could Nathan have hurt them? Or betrayed us?"

"Men do terrible things for money," grunted Captain Robin. He was teetering dangerously.

"Henry," Reid called.

The old man scuttled from one of the other rooms. "Yes?"

"The captain needs to rest. He's about to collapse."

"Right, sir. I'll fetch him some blankets."

"No need," said the captain. When the attendant hesitated, the captain snarled. "I said no blankets. I'm fine."

The attendant was unsure. "I'm not sure we can force him to rest, sir," he told Reid. "He fought us when we had to amputate his arm. Wouldn't rest or lie down."

"Damned right. I told you to do your worst so I could get on my feet sooner."

"He stood staring at us while we did, until he passed out," added Henry.

"Get him the blankets anyway," said Reid.

"I am not . . . about to collapse," breathed the captain. "Get me a sword . . . and I'll show you I'm fine."

Reid shook his head.

A knock came at the door, and the attendant scurried to answer it.

It was Captain Thames and Lieutenant Dari. And they had two prisoners — both were only partly dressed, as if they'd been interrupted from something intimate. Their heads were covered with rucksacks, and their wrists were bound behind their backs.

Thames and Dari each shoved their prisoners, who both fell roughly to the floor. They squirmed and cried out through the gags in their mouths, and Thames and Dari both knelt and ripped the sacks from their faces.

Dari grinned. "Got them in the middle of some kinky baby making. This one likes whips." She placed her boot on the woman's hand, and the woman screamed through the gag as the bones in her hand crunched.

Reid recognized the woman, and when she opened her eyes and looked about wildly, she realized both where she was and who was present. She shrank from them.

"Now, now, Contessa," grinned Dari. "Don't be rude." Dari put her weight on the hand again, and once more, Contessa screamed.

But the man was not Lieutenant Cramer, as Reid had expected.

"Who is he?" he asked.

"This is your banker, Isaac," chuckled Thames as he swayed. He grimaced, his hand against his lower back again. The man was one tough bastard. He'd been lucky Captain Hagath's sword hadn't sliced anything vital and left him dead or cripple. "I think I may need to have Linel patch me up, now. I'm about done for tonight, I think."

Dari crossed her arms. "Well. So that you know, I read the document Lieutenant Cramer had him draw up. It says nothing about any *N. I.* initials, or Black Temple, or financial handler, or anything relevant or even remotely related to where it came from or what it was supposed to have been deposited under. It's made out to some strange fellow, one Rickon Stantsy. I'm pretty sure I've heard the name in the same circles as I've heard among some of our less reputable Enforcers. One of Crostor's butchers, I think. And that butcher doesn't just cut up animals."

Reid stared at Isaac, who was desperately fighting his bonds and trying to talk. "You don't know me," he said. "But I know enough about you to know I need to ensure my deposit can be recognized and honored by any banker. Even in Five Tower." The banker looked at him, wide-eyed as Reid sat back. He pulled the Cyan ring from his pocket. "We'll use this to secure the money, and then some. Judging by your gaudy rings and necklaces, you have plenty to spare."

Captain Robin gave a throaty laugh. "Give me a few liberties when you're done with him. I wouldn't mind a cask or two."

Reid grabbed his crutch and made his way to his feet gingerly. He winced when he nearly lost his footing. "This is Cyan's ring. You know about Cyan, right?" The man's attention never slipped from him. "Your little slab of easy flesh here has the lieutenant we're looking for whipped. Without her involvement with the two of you, none of you would have been figured out so quickly. His dirty captain killed the man who owned this ring. He took it for himself as a trophy, and then I took this ring from him before I killed him. I understand the captain's and lieutenant's reasons for having anything to do with a crooked banker. They're traitors, and you're the purse who'll keep them free and clear of getting caught. I'm guessing she just likes the gold." He looked at the man's hand. "And the rubies." He looked at Isaac's necklaces. "And the diamonds." He snorted. "They look real. Most people can only get colored glass these days, and those are expensive on their own. Only skilled glass makers know how to make them well, or to color them just so. As for real gems, it also takes a talented sort of fellow to know where to dig up some precious stones. The Modern Age had them in abundance. Most of that is lost, and skilled glass makers are hard to come by. Expensive, as I said." He stopped in front of the banker. "You must have very deep pockets. That's a lot of victims."

Isaac writhed against his bonds. Terror washed over him as Reid knelt and pulled free his dagger. "Are you right-handed or left-handed?"

All he got in reply was a bunch of words muffled by the gag.

"Blink once for right. Twice for left. And if you lie to me, I will cut off your eyelids and instead have you scream once for right and twice for left. And if you lie again after that, I'll dig up a pair of centipedes yay big," he held his hands apart, "and I'll cut you open, avoid all the things that will make you bleed out, and let them slither around in your innards. Let them bite and sting until their poison sets you to fever and screams. I am not a man who will tolerate lies, Isaac the Banker. Henry, get me some wax. We'll just use his blood, mix that in it to make sure it has some color to it." Isaac's eyes widened. "Meanwhile, I'll figure out whether I want to put those centipedes in his belly or by his lungs. Do you know how many places centipedes can writhe around next to your organs, Isaac the Banker? Some of them chew their way through those organs. You last longer if they're in your belly. Hurts worse if they're crawling between your lungs and your ribs. They rip and claw a bit more."

"He's twisted," laughed Dari. "I like it. Can we *hire* him?" she asked Captain Robin. "We need a good torturer. This guy knows how to use the psychological stuff. Thames sucks at it. He's all physical, and that doesn't work very long before they're dead or run out of skin to bruise up or bones to break."

Captain Robin grunted. "If you ever tire of your current job, Retired Range Commander."

The side of Reid's mouth tilted, but he didn't feel any humor at all. All he felt was anger. He was going to ensure his niece's future was not stolen by this creep, even if he had to lower himself to unpleasant means to achieve it. She deserved to be able to choose her own future. One that she *wanted*. One that didn't risk her death or aggravate the curse upon her. "I'll take that offer when I decide I want to do it for a living," he said. "Right or left, Isaac the Banker?"

A wet stain spread under Isaac as he blinked twice. The smell of urine assaulted Reid's nose.

"Good for you. I'll draw up some documents and have you sign them properly, then. Dari, would you mind getting me some paper from Linel's desk? And some ink? I'll use his blood to write it if there is no ink."

Isaac was crying now. He was defenseless without his bodyguards. He was a maggot and a coward without them.

Contessa merely whimpered, her face against the floor so that her hair covered it. She continued to try to twist against the ropes binding her, and they cut her deeper.

The document didn't take long to write. Reid had read and signed enough of them to be able to ensure it was correct. Then he reached around behind Isaac, grabbed his hand, and twisted it at the wrist. The rings on the man's fingers shone brightly. Isaac fought him as Reid brought the dagger up to the man's middle finger, and the banker screamed when Reid sliced off the digit, right above the signet. He mixed Isaac's blood with the wax, as he'd promised, and he took the ring from the finger. The imprint made by the signet was clear as day on wax as red as blood. He laid out Black Temple's seal next to it. And then Cyan's signet next to that. Then he removed from Isaac's other hand the ring with the largest ruby. He pried the ruby from its setting and tossed the ring itself. "A gift, for one of my loved ones," he smirked. "A blood-colored stone seems fitting for the one." From the necklace, he took the largest diamond, which was three times larger than the ruby.

"This is no different from what you've done to countless others," said Reid. "Being stolen from doesn't feel too great, does it?" He pocketed the gems as Dari put her boot on the man's left ankle. Reid then cut the ropes at Isaac's wrists. "Take the pen and sign. If you don't, Dari, here, will break your ankle. We're being kind, not taking everything else you have. But I am a fair man. An honest man. I could have forced you to sign a confession, or to sign a document transferring all of your assets to me, or to Black Temple. I could have done worse and forced you to forge documents signing all of Crostor's assets over as well. We've got the seal we need already. Your friend Hagath had several very useful items. Unlucky for the lot of you, we're smarter about how to use items like these. Clearing the corruption from this city and the alliance will be easier. So thank you, and thank Cramer and Hagath, for being unwise and unable to cover your tracks."

"Are you *sure* you don't want to work for us?" asked Captain Thames. He leaned his head back, grinning from ear to ear.

Isaac snatched the pen, crying out through the gag when Dari began to put pressure on his ankle. He penned a signature, and Reid took the page. He handed it to Dari. "Is this his signature?" asked Reid.

Dari took the document, studied it, and then handed it back. "As right as daylight is bright," she replied. "Definitely no false hand or fake name. It's his mark, all right."

"Isaac Maston. Contessa Whatever-Your-Family-Name-Is," Captain Robin said. He struggled to his feet, his voice growing hoarse as he spoke. He was even paler than before, but he drew his sword, nonetheless. "Have you any last words that may spare your lives? Any information regarding the monks, or about Crostor's motives?"

Contessa murmured, and Isaac began to cry, to plead through his gag. Dari untied Isaac's first, and Isaac began to spill. "Please don't kill me! Please!"

"Captain Hagath said the same thing a few hours ago. It didn't work for him," said Reid.

"The monks are waiting outside of town," stammered the bank teller. "On the old eastern road. They're going to take the boy to the wolfmen in Cyan so they can take the boy to Five Tower! Crostor is going to meet them there, to give the boy over. He's going in person!"

"Well," said Captain Robin as he lifted his sword. "That was a mouthful, and it was quite useful. Thanks. Too bad it wasn't enough to save you."

"Wait! Plea — "

The man's head was severed from his body in one swift motion. Captain Robin staggered and leaned upon the pommel, leaving the blade embedded in the floor so that it could hold him upright. "Five Tower will be notified of Isaac's crimes after this is done. They will learn to keep their crooked bankers under control."

"Hypocrite," said Reid to Captain Robin. "You could have kept him alive for further *questioning*, remember?"

Captain Robin shrugged. "That was for therapy."

"Evidence was littered throughout Maston's chambers," shrugged Dari. "He kept a private ledger on those he swindled."

"I figured that out myself," breathed the captain. "Corrupt bankers love their secret ledgers the way serial killers love their trophies." He strained to remain upright, as though the room were whirling about him.

"You look as horrible as I feel," laughed Thames. "Go sit down and let Dari execute the woman."

"It is my responsibility," huffed Captain Robin. "I want to do it . . . I call dibs. He showed me up with the centipedes. It's frickin' disgusting, frankly."

Reid shook his head. "You lot are the twisted ones. What kind of sick individuals look up to that sort of wicked behavior?"

"Says the man who mixed blood and wax to color it and threatened to cut off eyelids and insert centipedes *yay big* into a man's opened belly," laughed Dari. "No one will ever be able to deny Isaac was present when that letter was signed and marked, not when a Black Temple doctor can summon an Arsennian Keeper to compare his blood to the bankers' registry in Five Tower. They have to sign it with their own blood."

Captain Robin turned his attention to Contessa as Dari pulled her gag free. "The way I see it, you're just a lass caught up in the wrong crowd," he told Contessa. "The man we just executed has a long history of wrongdoing. You're young. I can overlook your crimes and let you walk if you give us the truth."

Contessa spat upon the captain's boot rather than saying a word. So Dari stepped on her hand again.

Contessa groaned.

"Why did you betray your kin?" asked Reid. "They are good people."

She glared at him. "My kin are tunnel-dwelling trash. They want to give *everything* away to people who do not deserve that help. Edantine treats them worse than human, and they are fools to settle for the disintegrating home they're struggling to keep for themselves. My mother and my father died there, and so did the rest of my family. The fumes killed them, and everyone there has to work in it, and every time we get *anything* for ourselves, we have to give it away."

"Yet no one in Edantine knows what good they do, or how they contribute to the welfare of the city, the wearyworn, or Black Temple. Have you never told anyone any part of your family's sworn secret?"

"I betrayed them by coming and going as I pleased, not by opening my filthy mouth, you piece of garbage. I'm not cruel enough to get them all killed. I just wanted out. I wanted no part of what they believe in, or of what they put up with in the name of that stupid belief! I wanted a life of my *own*."

Reid grimaced. He could only hope his niece and nephew would never develop this rebellious, hate-filled state of mind. Nor his daughter. The woman was angry, defiant, and willing to mix herself with bad people to feel even a small sliver of happiness. At the very least, he appreciated her wish to protect her family despite following her own desires. It seemed her only redeeming quality.

"What can you tell us about the monks?"

"I'm not saying anything else. Go ahead and execute me, or torture me, or whatever you want. You're not getting anything else from me. I've had my fun, and if it's over, it's over."

Reid sighed. "Are you really sure you're willing to die?"

She snorted. "Isn't it obvious? I've got nothing else." She eyed Isaac's body and shuddered sickly. "Just . . . tell Danny I'm sorry things never worked between us. He's a good man. And tell that barren hag he married to go to hell."

She looked away, and she would not say anything else.

Captain Robin pulled the sword free from the floor and held it over her. "It isn't too late, miss. You can rebuild your life after a few years in prison. Confess what else you know. Anything that could help us regarding Crostor's schemes or his monk friends' plotting. What are they into?"

She stretched out her neck but remained silent. Her expression seemed to say that if they didn't execute her, she would end her own life. She knew a lot more but wasn't giving them anything else, and locking her up wouldn't change that.

Captain Robin and Reid shared a look. Both seemed to read the same thing in the woman.

Dari snorted. "She's so stoic, isn't she?"

Then Contessa was executed.

CHAPTER TWENTY

Wolves

REID AND THE ENFORCERS rode through the woods and into the thickest of the trees. Metal was clanging, and wolves were snarling, and monks were screaming. It had begun to rain again, and another fire had broken loose, spilling its liquid, flaming tongues across the path. The fire devoured everything it touched, and the smoke felled the men who ended up in the thickets of its fumes.

Taiir and Manard were battling them. They were barely holding their ground when Reid and the Enforcers arrived.

"Commander!" shouted Manard. "About time! These fiendish ghouls were trying to off us!"

Reid issued a command, and his horse spun about and bucked two of the monks, center-chest. The men flew back into other monks, who landed upon their own swords.

"That's gotta be a record!" Manard shouted. "Four in one fell swipe, you rotten genius! I'm going to try to steal that horse from you when we're done!" Manard laughed wildly and charged.

"That is Crostor, fighting tha wolves!" shouted Taiir.

Reid wheeled about and spied several dead Edantine guards. Three or four remained, and Michael huddled behind the line of fighting men. Crostor was between the boy and the wolves, being torn apart. The man screamed as the largest beast took a bite of his arm and dragged him from among his men, and two more wolves pounced, joining the fray.

The monks fled, and so did the wolves when Reid took out his gun and shot one of them.

He and the Enforcers who'd come with him circled the remaining Edantine guards. They dropped their weapons the moment they realized they had been defeated — the men did not seem to care that the reinforcements were mostly wounded.

"They'll die from smoke inhalation," gasped Manard. He doubled over, gulping, coughing. "Don't worry about them. The fire is raging that way. My bet is on the wolves' survival. It could be a dangerous trip back to Crow Post, though."

"Michael," said Reid.

Michael looked up. They boy's tear-stained face was covered in dirt.

When Reid leaned forward and stretched out his hand, Michael reached out to take it.

"Come on, kiddo, you're safe now." Reid hoisted the boy onto his saddle with him. "Are you hurt?"

Michael shook his dark head but said nothing as he wiped his eyes. The motion smeared the soot and the filth.

"Put the rest of them in cuffs, will you?" Manard asked. "And please tell me one of you has some water. Ale. Anything." He coughed again.

"Commander," said Taiir.

When Reid looked at his companion, his stomach curled. "What is it?"

Taiir nodded, his chin pointing to the brush where lay a dead horse and a dead man.

"What? I don't read minds, Taiir. What's important about him?"

"It's Mercy," Taiir said.

"*What?*" Reid got off his horse more quickly than he should have. His knee struck a rock, and he hissed, but he staggered over to the body. When he knelt by the body and pulled aside some of the withered leaves there, he saw and smelled an ungodly sight. The man hadn't been dead for long, judging by it. But his stomach had been torn out, eaten. More of the horse was gone, though. Yet it was certainly the kennel master from Crow Post.

Why couldn't bad things *stop happening*?! Everywhere he turned. His parents, his niece, the wolfmen, the murders — everything! It was getting to be too much.

Reid ran his hand through his hair, and then he gripped the mess and screamed until he couldn't breathe.

Taiir stood behind him. "He rode until his horse died. They collapsed here just as we found tha monks and Crostor trying to exchange tha boy. We could not continue hiding when one of our own needed us, but we could not get to him. I think he was dead before tha wolves got to him. He has been wounded gravely. Look at his arm, his leg. He has been stabbed multiple times. Perhaps days ago. A lot of tha blood is cracked and dry."

"What am I supposed to tell his wife?" cried Reid. "Why was he even *here*?"

"I do not know. He was looking for his dogs, yet it is unlikely they wandered this far. Tha horse's tethers have been sliced, also. His hurry must have been great. It seems likely he crossed something he was not supposed to witness."

Reid sighed, his pulse beating at his ears at the thought of having to tell Mercy's wife what had happened to him. "His widow will be heartbroken. She's already had a difficult pregnancy, and this will probably cause her to miscarry. Ralleigha's always loved the couple to pieces. She'll take it hard, too."

"A tragedy," agreed Taiir.

Taiir assisted Reid in getting to his feet, and Reid turned to the Enforcers. "Captain Robin. My men and I need to get home. I'll trust you to take care of the rest of the situation in Edantine. If you could spare some men immediately to get Mercy's body prepared for the journey ahead of us, I would greatly appreciate it."

"Anything you need, Range Commander."

"Taiir, go get the other apprentices. We're leaving in the morning. No later than sunrise."

Manard stood at last, and he sheathed his sword.

"Manard, go find something strong for me to drink before I can no longer hold myself together."

Reid was shaking by the time he left Mercy's body to the Enforcers.

Three days later, Reid was in such a solemn, drunken haze that he couldn't remember the way back to Crow Post. He left it to Taiir and Manard to drive them, and he wouldn't talk to any of the Enforcers. He just drank until he slept, and he drank some more when he woke. Whenever one of his own men would try to talk to him, he would wave them off and lay his head back. He wasn't ready to talk. He still didn't know how to approach the subject of his parents' deaths with John when it was time.

The trip was a long one, and he didn't want to think. The only care he bothered with was to open his eyes every time he jolted awake, to make sure Sobrienne and Michael were still alive, still safe. The apprentice Axon had never come with them. The boy had died in the underground fuel cellars the night before Taiir had gone to get them. He'd died by fire.

John would demand to know what had happened in Edantine, Reid knew. But he planned to avoid him until their special prisoner was out of John's reach. He didn't know how John would handle any of it, either, and he didn't want to imagine the fallout he knew was coming.

So he drank so that he couldn't think.

CHAPTER TWENTY-ONE

FOR NEARLY A MONTH, fires erupted among distant settlements, and the smoke pilons grew closer by the day. Refugees sprang up everywhere about the post, stretching the camp thinner and thinner. The smell grew worse, and fighting often broke out, and radios chimed warnings back and forth like gunfire.

The conditions for a riot brewed like a thick poison, ready to erupt in a killing steam.

Lukas could no longer differentiate the smell of manure from that of the meat tossed into the kennels, and the water, he drank without reserve, uncaring whether ten or more of his furry, growling neighbors slobbered first in the trough or whether they tried to eat his face off through the wire and bars separating them from him.

The worst were the carpenter ants and mosquitos. Day and night, until he'd all but clawed off his own flesh to be rid of them, the ants crawled and stung, and the mosquitoes landed and bit. And neither were picky. They went after both his wounds and his uninjured skin, and the carpenter ants left small blisters that stung and itched for the better part of several full days and nights.

Once every few days, and likely on the range commander's orders, the bastards also came for him. He would be shaken from slumber or interrupted from eating the slop their subordinates had given him, and he would be bound, often spilling the vile water. The dogs would be set on edge by his struggle against the men who came to drag him off — and those men would nearly drown him. They would cut him, or they would burn him as they questioned him. And when they were done, they would bring him back to the dogs he'd almost gotten used to, and they would toss him back into his own kennel.

He tolerated their insults, and he toyed with his torturers rather than broke. He would laugh, or bite, or spit. Even when he was tossed into his cage, still shivering and still choking, he ensured they saw his gloating victory, that their tricks were worthless because he knew they could never kill him.

These men knew not of the ways of the depraved, unlike the range commander. Lukas had experienced the unpleasantness of the commander's knowledge, and he had been unable to abide his own silence even when he'd tried under Reid's questioning. But these men were not the commander, and Lukas did not fear them. They were bound by much higher honor, and by much stricter rules. They were afraid to kill him, and he made sure they saw that he knew it. They had little of the finer knowledge of anatomy and surgery — what they could or couldn't do that would or wouldn't kill him. He knew he could provoke them and frustrate them because he would continue to survive their rookie attempts to get information from him. After all, he'd kept greater secrets intact when he had survived the darkest pits of Five Tower's wicked underbelly.

So he bid his time patiently, and in all the chaos, and despite his conditions and maltreatment at the post — as Lukas's heart beat heavier with a growing feeling of unease — his smile grew only wider. Opportunity bloomed like a sickly miasma before him, the spores spreading over every person and thing as the dire situation at the post grew steadily worse.

He heard whispers here, and sickly, hungry children prodded at him there, and the more he heard, the more he plotted.

He'd convinced some of the youth that he was a harmless fugitive, that he was being hidden in the kennels for his own protection against a family of witches. That the kennels made him appear naught but a dog to the witches. From his lies, he'd earned himself stale bread, an occasional piece of fruit, and some molded cheese. Gems, considering what his captors had been giving him.

"Witchlings, your brother said?" whispered Lukas as he grasped the bars and wire holding him in. Before him, a small refugee boy named Ben stood, his orange hair almost as matted from grease and filth as Lukas's own. "How so?"

"Paul said they took the mason's friend to Orath. 'Cause Jonna could tell what everyone was thinking. He always knew. And he was the one hiding them."

"People got sick after those witches showed up, didn't they?" It was so easy to feed children such logic.

Ben's eyes went wide as he made Lukas's suggested connection. "They were why my momma got sick and died?"

Never mind that Ben had told him that his mother had died years prior, when she'd given birth to the boy. Lukas instead reveled in his ability to mold young minds in the worst of ways. "Yes. I've seen how witches work. The creatures Black Temple is protecting here are much the same. Did you bring that file I asked for? I made a promise to you. A toy that can protect you in exchange for the things I need to know while I am hidden."

The boy hesitated, but when he dug in his pockets and produced a dagger-length metal file, Lukas applauded him. The wide tool would make quick work of the wire and the bars so long as he could get it to slip through them.

"Did you say the witch's cousin works with glass? What is the cousin's name?"

Ben nodded, watching Lukas wiggle the file through the bar and the wire where it had wedged. "Yeah. And her name is Marissa. She's mean, too! But she keeps saying her cousin is a good witch."

"There are no good witches. What about that doctor I told you about?"

"He leaves his house unattended a lot. The lady there is usually busy, too, and her son, that witch's brother, he doesn't stay there by himself."

"Could you get in?"

"Yeah, just as you explained it to me. But I couldn't find the ring you told me about. Or any bottles with blood in them."

Lukas hid his displeasure, although he itched to snatch the boy's throat from between the bars and frighten him into looking more diligently. He knew his time at the post was whittling down. A month had already passed, and they wouldn't keep him in the kennels much longer. He would be shipped away soon.

"All right," said Lukas. "You'll find it. Just keep looking. And hurry. It is my father's ring, and the doctor is hiding it to keep it from the little witch. I fear she will find it soon if you are not first about it."

"What is the blood for?"

"It is magic blood," he lied. Although he wasn't certain whether it really was a lie. The way Caol and Eiran saw it, that blood was just as valuable as the accursed glass, and that in itself gave him pause. "If she finds it first, she'll be free to burn everything at Crow Post, just like at Cyan. I have to take it far from here as soon as they let me out."

The boy nodded. "I'll keep looking, then. You and me, we'll protect everyone. But I want to go with you when they set you free. I don't have anyone left. My folks died in Orath. Will you take me?"

Lukas pretended to be compassionate, and he spun another lie. "Maybe. I do travel a lot. Before I lost my son to the witches, I used to take him with me." He pretended to be sad, and his voice cracked like that of a grieving father. "I miss my son terribly. But if you've got no one, and I have no one, I don't see how it could hurt if we became family. It would be nice, being able to teach a son to trap and hunt witches again."

"How did Joshua die? What did they do to him?"

Lukas grimaced, but inwardly, he laughed at the boy's gullibility. "Purple fire. Same as what killed all those people in Five Tower. As a matter of fact, I heard they have been developing weapons to combat the witches there. I think if I talk to the right people, we could get you well on your way to becoming a fine witch hunter."

The idiot child's eyes lit up. "Really? Me? You think I would be a good witch hunter?"

"You have to learn to be a better sneak and a better liar. And you have to learn to disguise yourself better so none can guess who you really are, not even when they look upon you. But yes," Lukas said. A little false flattery and a few false promises of hope always went a long way in sweetening the well of knowledge spilled by children. "What else have you learned?"

"A lot of people posted here are talking about a wedding. Someone is going to get married when they leave for Isold soon," said the boy.

"Isold?" asked Lukas. "How interesting. I wonder if they'll split apart for that trip, or if they'll all head there together." He almost had the file through the bars and the wire. "What else?"

The boy told him everything he'd learned, and when Lukas sent him scurrying off to gather more intel and to try again to find the ring and the vial of blood, the file finally slipped through the bars and into his palm. He held it in his closed fist and snarled. "Dumb child," he said under his breath. "He'll make himself the first casualty when I escape . . ."

The wet squish of footsteps on leaves and mud, and the change in the dogs' behavior, alerted him. They began wagging their tails, and they rose to their feet, crowding one another as they whined for food at the gate.

Lukas shoved the file into the muck, along with a broken bit of blade Ben had also managed to take for him. He pushed the mud over the items and leaned back languidly, his head hanging as though he had nothing to live for. His filthy hair hid the small grin upon his face as two of Reid's men approached.

Yet, out of the corner of his eye, at the opposite end of the kennels, he caught the startling ghost of the young face of the Ivan child. Eyes as green as an emerald held against the sun had appeared among the shadows, and he felt his pulse quicken with dread. He looked up as the men opened the cage — but he wasn't looking at the men. The men were the same as ever, the tracker with the mercenary tattoos on his scalp and the brewer, both of whom had known of his crimes the night he'd committed them.

Neither of Reid's men saw the girl. Yet she remained there among the dark things, her hair like a curtain of shadow silk, a silver scar dusting her cheek like fading white flame.

How long had she been watching . . . ? How much had she overheard?

A thread of cold anxiety swept through him as she watched him be struck by the brewer, bound by the tracker, and dragged from the kennel by both.

Hatred flamed in her eerie, inhuman eyes. Calm, bloodthirsty hatred.

He'd never feared a child before. Yet his every instinct had him recoiling from the merest ray of her emerald gaze. *Demon*, his instincts screamed.

When she bit down on her own lip, he imagined the ghastly image of a monstrous beast taking his throat and severing arteries and crushing bone.

He could not take another breath whilst she gazed upon him and judged him guilty.

"Murderer," she whispered soundlessly — and then he saw the dagger in her hand. The thing was made of black glass. Violet twisted through it like small veins of lightning.

Lukas recoiled — yet when he blinked, she was gone. His heart thundered so violently that he could hardly breathe for the pain and the tightness it caused him when he tried. Just like in the Gray Halls. The same had happened the last time, when they'd strapped him to that table. When he'd seen what they'd had inside that tank.

Lukas clutched at his chest, gasping, and he tried to blink back the blinding pain that seared him from the inside. It was like a white-hot hand, gripping his stomach, his heart, and his lungs, and also clogging his throat.

Half an hour later, once they had reached the same old, abandoned shed in the woods, the brewer pitched him forward carelessly. The refugees were not allowed access to this area, so the men were free to do as they pleased to him. The only entrance to the area began as Crow Post ended. The path led high into the neighboring hill which served to protect Crow Post's back. Three sides of that hill dropped away in steep, dangerous cliffs.

The shed was all that remained of an old dwelling, and that was where they'd many times lit fires and burned him. The natural spring that flowed down the hill was the same one they'd waterboarded him in enough times he'd already lost count.

Yet this was the first time he'd been brought up the hill shaken or fearing for his life.

Unlike before, neither the brewer nor the tracker immediately set to torturing him as they asked their questions. No fire had yet been lit, and the air was cool and heavy with the scent of approaching rain.

Robert dug in his satchel and pulled out a cigar and lit it. David took a seat on a rotting stump.

"He's terrified of her, Robert," snickered the brewer.

Robert just grunted.

Lukas realized he was quivering head to toe when he struggled against his bonds. He couldn't even grasp the rope bindings.

"What's taking her so long?"

"Avoiding her father, probably. He'd have some things to say if he caught her prying near the kennels where this worm has been kept for the past month," replied Robert. "She's that special kind of kid who thinks to investigate and be wary. Her uncle's taught her a lot, but there's no telling how much of that was already natural to her. Definitely not like other kids."

Lukas glanced between the two wildly as the brewer spoke again. "Torturing him has been useless. Are you sure this will work?"

Robert exhaled a cloud of smoke and flicked the spent cinders from his cigar. "Haven't had a decent smoke in ten years," the tracker sighed. "Hell of a trade. Worth every liberty I spent. I'll probably be going another ten years before I find another decent smoke, or before I can afford another."

A ghostly chill crept across Lukas's flesh as the wind carried the cinders away. It was as though the night had taken a breath and smote the red light.

Robert knelt then, and he used his cigar to light the fire pit they'd prepared.

"Nymeria was right," said David. "He's been busy while we've been away. Shouldn't have trusted Nails's reasons for leaving him with a tongue. What are we going to do about the boy he's brainwashed? That could be disastrous."

"The boy is an innocent bystander. He's just a dumb kid with no one left to care for him," said Robert. "We're not doing anything to him, but we'll let John know about it. They'll give him a place at the Temple, help him to become a good man. They did well for my brother, and he was a monster. He'd already murdered ten people before he'd been able to buy a decent drink in a tavern. He's saved a lot of lives since his rehabilitation, and he loves the work." Robert eyed Lukas then, and after a long moment, he exhaled the smoke he so enjoyed. "Your game is up, Stupid. We know you've been talking to other kids besides Ben, and that you've been gathering information. You didn't realize some of those kids were planted. Some of them are smarter than you, and better at the game you're playing."

Lukas laughed. "Aren't the two of you clever?" When he shook his hair from his face, he marked the contempt he saw upon them both and wondered how best to provoke them this time.

"Reid wanted us to leave it be, but that's not good enough. His parents, those people you murdered? They were good people — better than my own folks were. Practically helped to raise me." Robert grinned, then. "But I think I've figured out how to crack you. You have a very odd weakness, and it comes in a very small package, doesn't it?"

Lukas rolled his neck and shoulders, loosening them for whatever might come his way. He was ready for every weak thing they had to offer. "Doubtful. You can keep cutting away at me, keep pretending you'll drown me, and keep burning me with your cinders and sticks and hot knives. I've nothing to spill for such unimaginative morons."

Robert lowered his cigar and offered it to Lukas. "You may want to let off some steam before we begin to work on you tonight, you slithery scumbag." When Lukas refused, Robert shrugged and flicked it aside. And Robert flashed his teeth. The tattooed tracker's expression was a viciously amused one.

Lukas didn't see her at first. But he felt her. Her presence slammed through him like a wall of frigid water.

Every single breath became difficult as his heart began to pound against his chest, like a wild animal wanting to flee its tormentor. It was like being submerged in a coffin, the way her presence unveiled itself. She wanted him to know that he should fear her. That she could do worse than curse him. That she didn't even have to lay a finger on him to do it.

"What the hell is wrong with his eyes?" hissed David suddenly. "They've turned *purple*."

Lukas squirmed against his bonds, and he began to tremble profoundly as the darkness around him began to unfurl. The forest bowed over toward them, and he struggled to get away from the approaching shadows.

"What are you so terrified of?" grinned Robert. The tracker looked over his shoulder, into the heart of a darkness he couldn't seem to see. "It's just a little girl."

The shadows shifted as she bled apart from them, and they seemed to flame and recoil from her. She held in her hands the file and the broken bit of blade Ben had gotten him.

"You planned to kill my uncle," she said quietly. Her voice was sweet. Innocent. Soft. But he felt the power lurking far beneath her words, hidden from the world. She looked down upon him, a tiny, green-eyed creature — an immense, monstrous presence. She took another step toward him, lifting the blade and the file, and Lukas tried to back away from her.

"Keep her away from me," he gasped, wrenching his eyes shut when the brewer put his knee into Lukas's spine and placed a firm hand upon his shoulder, forcing him to remain where he was.

Still, he could feel the incredible, ancient corruption flaming within her deceptively young and fragile form. The unstable black energy radiated outward, convulsing wildly within her and spilling over.

Could these men not feel the ground itself rumbling? The tremor grew stronger when she took another step, as her anger deepened.

His eyes opened a fraction, almost involuntarily, as terror took him by the throat.

Dust drifted from the rafters overhead, and the pebbles upon the ground quivered. Some of them began to blacken as they turned to glass. Violet and silver streaked through several — just the tiniest slivers of light. Neither of the men noticed, and neither realized the shed was groaning dangerously.

Nymeria gave the bit of blade and the file to Robert, who shook his head in disbelief. "I have never seen a grown man so terrified of a child. She's almost too small even to be a *pipsqueak*."

"You killed my grandparents," she said evenly to Lukas, and a fiery flame of emotion cut through her blackness and sliced through him. He trembled.

Her knowledge on that matter startled Robert and David, for the tracker and the brewer grimaced. But neither said a word when she looked at them.

Nymeria turned her attention upon Lukas again. "You will never again plot to kill a child." He cringed when the emerald in her gaze sparked with rivers of violet anger. "And you will *never* lay a hand upon another in my family, or I will do worse than kill you. I will feed you to the Dark Ones. First, I will turn you to glass and ignite it with the Gift, and then I will set them upon you. Do you understand this, Thief? Do you agree to abide by my command?" The power radiating from her choked him until the edges of his vision were blackening, until he could feel it drawing dreadful paths throughout his own body. The violet threatened to course brightly through him again as it had just months ago, its grip painful and blinding and leaving him terrified of the visions that had caused the others to claw their eyes out and rend their own flesh to remove the agony of it.

Lukas never even realized he was nodding wildly. He heard himself squeak, "I swear! Anything — do not curse me with the Violet again! Please — not those creatures! Not the *memories* of them!"

"He's about to piss himself!" laughed David.

Robert watched the display curiously, however, his brows furrowed. He seemed to sense there was something supernatural occurring.

Nymeria then produced a sliver of brightly glowing glass, and Lukas shrieked. The brewer restrained him.

"Get that away from me!" Lukas screamed. The child gave it to Robert. "*Not again! Don't you dare touch me with that vile thing!!!*"

Robert palmed the shard and placed his hand gently upon her shoulder. He gave her a hug and nodded. "Thanks for the help, kiddo. Go ahead and get back to camp before your father misses you. And stay far from this man. He is not right."

Nymeria nodded, but she offered one last bit of advice to Robert and David. "If he starts seeing them, destroy it immediately. Do not let it cut you. This one is different from the others I have found within my Gift. There is anger within it. I do not know where it came from, but I know that it is terribly dangerous. Don't let it become my mistake by mishandling it. And don't tell Uncle Reid I ever made that one. I promised him I wouldn't." She looked at Lukas coldly. "But I want *him* to know I am serious. I will curse him if he tries to hurt anyone again. If he even thinks about it. I will be able to see his next murder, so he will not be able to lie about it."

Robert and David shared a confused look, but Robert agreed, nevertheless. Then she was gone, and color returned to the forest. Lukas stole a shallow breath, his chest still too tight to take a proper one, and when David forced him upright, his eyes tracked the glass in Robert's hand wildly.

"Well, his eyes are back to soulless abysses," sighed Robert as he held up the shard curiously. "You think she's the reason his eyes lit up? Looked just like the people he talked about. The slaves Five Tower supposedly lost. The ones they want back. Makes me wonder how much of it was actually true. And then about why Nymeria coming here scares him so bad."

"I'll tell you nothing more," shivered Lukas. But he found himself weeping. "Nothing more," he repeated.

The glass began to lose its light.

Lukas began to laugh madly as he tried to tear his gaze from the dreadful glass. "Nothing more!" he cried, determined not to break. But the world was blurry, and he felt the tears upon his face. He wouldn't tell them a thing. He would be a dead man if he did. He couldn't. "You cannot curse me again!" Robert lifted the shard to Lukas's cheek, and Lukas fought desperately to get away from it. He barely heard the men laughing over his horror, barely registered it. His skin crawled, and his heart beat furiously in his ears until he could barely breathe again and his chest felt as if it had been kicked in.

"We'll try the questions again," said Robert.

Lukas couldn't answer. He couldn't even think. The cold, tingling energy burned his face where the piece of glass touched the skin, and he trembled, hyperventilating as he struggled against it. He fought the memory of what it had done to him beneath Five Tower. Eiran's cruel amusement when Lukas had screamed until he'd tasted blood when the Violet had coursed through him the first time. "Get it off of me! *Get it off of me!!!*" he screamed. He stared into the blackness where Nymeria had gone. He could barely see her. "Nymeria, please don't let them curse me again! Take it back!" She didn't stop, didn't look back. "Please — "

Lukas felt the waves of agony which were just beyond his own body, and he shoved them away from him, tried to close it all off, to keep it out of his mind. He could almost hear the screaming again. The glass in Robert's hand cracked, and Lukas felt himself convulse. The Violet flared brightly in his veins, and he screamed. The last thing he saw was Robert and David as they let him go, startled and scrambling back from him. The glass fell to the ground, splintering as the light inside it tried to escape.

Lukas felt her stagger along the path in the pitch of the night. He felt the shadows that crept through her veins, making her skin as dark as ebony before they faded. He tasted the blood that pooled from Nymeria's mouth as she knelt, shivering sickly. He felt the tears in her eyes and heard her cry softly — the sound was that of a broken creature.

She was alone in a world where the predators traveled through shadows and sought to devour every last ray of light within her, and she'd just cut away some of her light and given it away, and it had been infused with wrath.

Lukas tried to claw the memory from his mind — but it wasn't a memory. It was *now*. She'd used the power within her to hurt him — but it had done worse to her.

He felt the heat that rolled from her. It wilted the leaves of the young saplings and blackened everything for several meters. Cinders drifted about in currents as the dying trees creaked and groaned. He felt her lift her fingers first to her heart and then to her head as she fought to turn away the rising tide of poisonous memories hidden deep within her.

He felt the silver scar glowing brightly upon her shoulder.

He felt her consciousness fall away as his own screams erupted into the night. She was never even conscious to hear them. All she could hear was the darkness calling out to her in that eerie, inhuman, hissing language — it was the first time Lukas had ever been able to understand them.

"*Briiiiiiiigggghhhhhttttt Ooonnnnneeeee . . .*"

Then he saw snow and death, and he felt great sorrow. Memories. Memories that he fought with everything in him —

When he was yanked from the vision suddenly, he was shivering violently, and his face was in the dirt and wet with tears. The glass Nymeria had given to them was broken, and Robert and David were both staring at him, and both men were very pale. Robert picked up the broken glass, his hand shaking. David released Lukas's hands . . . and Lukas realized he'd been trying to claw his own eyes out. Just like the others. There was blood on his fingers. His own flesh clogged the creases between his nails and the skin of his fingers, and his hands were shaking profoundly where he stared at them.

He shut his eyes, shuddering severely. "Keep it away from me," he begged. "Cutting me with it won't make me tell you the answers you want so badly. I can't . . ." He looked at Robert again, shaking his head. "You don't understand what those things *do*. I'll lose my mind. I won't be *me* anymore. They'll devour me if I don't try to devour you first or kill myself — please keep it away from me — *please* keep it away."

"That's what you meant by *Blood Light*," said Robert, his voice quiet. "I didn't even cut you with it."

"We should give it to Reid when he gets back," said David. "Honestly, I don't think I want to risk that thing cutting either one of us."

"And what are we supposed to tell him?" asked Robert. "Oh, by the way, your niece gave us something to torture your mom and dad's killer with. By the way, that curse thing is real, and he still won't talk."

"It hurt her," Lukas choked. "Don't let her make another one."

Both men looked at him, confused. "Pardon?"

Anger, more poisonous than anything Lukas had ever felt in his own life, boiled to the surface, and he felt the urge to rip out their throats with his bloodied fingers. With his teeth. Anything, even if they gutted him with that accursed splinter of glass. Even if it cost him his life or his sanity.

The desire for the taste of their blood running over his tongue and down his throat almost overwhelmed him.

He could barely recognize it for what it was, but on some level, he knew it was the beginning of a dire shift that would send him careening into madness like the others before him.

He sucked in a deep breath, but the anger wouldn't lessen. His vision started to darken at the edges again, and his jaws cracked painfully.

"What's wrong with him?"

He couldn't tell which one had asked. Their voices were beginning to sound the same. Their words were becoming difficult to understand, the meanings becoming jumbled and mixed and washed out like faded, indiscernible colors bleached in unforgiving sunlight.

The glass was too close to him still. He could hardly think. Fire raged inside his head, and he could hear screaming.

"That thing hurt her," he finally managed. The words were difficult. "She's collapsed, bleeding from the mouth and the ears, and you have no idea you're the ones who caused it to happen by trying to reignite the curse inside me . . ." Lukas broke down into tears, his head bowed. He could taste ash. Blood. Dirt. "You don't understand what it does," he said. "None of you understand how serious this thing is, or what it does to us. *But she does.* No matter what you do to me, I can't give you the answers . . . I c-*I can't* . . ."

Green eyes . . . water receding . . .

Lukas rocked violently again, his eyes snapping open, and his tears racked him as he watched the Blood Light flare faintly, tracing old history upon his skin while hinting at another's as it bled through his veins and faded. "It's always worse . . ."

CHAPTER TWENTY-TWO

JOHN WAS CURRENTLY EMPLOYING teams of refugees to help with the growing numbers of sick and injured. He couldn't even recall most of their names, but he'd made do with what was available. The Heinzrichs had come through with another brew, but it wasn't quite as potent as he would have liked. It worked to clean wounds, but not as efficiently as higher quality, aged brews.

"Harry, hold still," he said firmly.

Three volunteers who knew Harry personally were holding down the screaming man as John debrided the burns and cleansed what flesh already had the beginnings of infection.

"Harry, calm down!" shouted Harry's wife. The fat woman removed her hand from her husband's shoulder and slapped him right across the face. Harry's head jerked to the side, and John stopped what he was doing.

"Mrs. Adder," sighed John. "Slapping your husband's face off will not help with his treatment." A large, purple welt was already forming where she'd struck him. "This procedure is still going to hurt him. He needs to be calmed, not beaten."

Mrs. Adder pulled her frazzled hair from her plump, sooty face, and she pushed up her spectacles. "He'll calm down if I knock him out," she declared matter-of-factly. "There's nothing left that can put him out for this. Slapping him to sleep is kinder than telling him to stop screaming."

And with that, she balled up her fist and punched her husband square in the jaw, and with the fervent motion of a well-practiced boxer.

Harry fell still, and his breathing became even. And Mrs. Adder's sister and brother cracked up, doubling over at the table and guffawing mightily.

While the siblings could not edge a word out, John shrugged. "A valid point, I suppose." He went back to work, cutting away the cooked flesh from Harry's abdomen. "But if he wakes again during this operation, don't hit him again. You may have given him a very serious concussion."

She huffed. "What else am I supposed to do when he's allergic to your medicine? Besides. He's been bucked in the skull by a horse, mister. Thrice in a month, and it did him no harm but to make him even dumber. He's a dimwit for not caring about it, always goes back to his work the next day. All I did was make him a little sleepy. You'll see when he comes 'round."

When John said nothing, she placed her hands on her ample hips. "Fine. I'll choke him out instead. He doesn't like that as much, though. It'll be a struggle. A real one."

John chuckled, then. "I'll leave that to you, then. If he doesn't wake, it will be your fault, not mine."

The plump woman then took a chair, and she stroked her husband's stringy hair, brushing it from his forehead. "The idiot just *had* to pick a fight, knowing he could've gotten kicked from the post. He just has to keep worrying over us before everyone else, the fool."

The next flake of charred skin bubbled and bled a mixture of fresh blood and fatty oil. The smell was both sweet and rank. "Consider this your family's final chance, Mrs. Adder. I could use your help. You three make for an excellent trauma team. Your stitches were expertly done. You were able to stop any bleeding rather quickly, cleaned the wounds well, and have the strength to keep a patient from harming himself or others. Harry, on the other hand, will have to serve his penance another way, however his wounds will allow. Can he cook? Does he know anything about irrigation? We need more ditches dug, and the cooks are at their wits' end — "

"He's worthless at everything but cooking," she said. "He's always been a fine cook. Even so when he lost his hand a few years ago. Nobody does a faster, finer job, or with such strained resources. He's a whiz in the kitchen. Why do you think I'm so fat? Why do you think he's so skinny, and my brother and sister are even bigger than I am?" She nodded proudly. "He knows his wild forage, too."

"Wild grub, huh? That will help more than simply cooking. I'll assign a couple of attendants and some of the children to assist him — "

But Mrs. Adder's brows furrowed. "He doesn't like to reveal his recipes. He's hard-headed that way. That's what got him in this mess in the first place. He wouldn't let your cooks touch a thing, or let them take a look at his foraging. Or tell them where he got it, even though he told me and Bertha and Benjen, here, where he got it all. He said there was enough there to feed forty families for a month. He set his new stores afire when the order came from your post doctor, Mr. Shipwright, that he hand it over and help everyone, or leave."

"Be it as Amos ordered. Either Harry puts in and helps, or all four of you are gone. I will not allow more resources to be wasted on a man who wishes to fight rather than help during the crisis we are facing. Your family was allowed into the camp under the same agreement the rest here were given. To share and to help. We cannot serve those who remain unwilling to forward that precious gift. Our assistance only works if the wheel keeps spinning. We must *all* come together, or the amount of death you and your family escaped will only increase."

She remained quiet through his speech, as did her brother and sister.

It was her sister who agreed. "We'll make him so miserable he has no other choice," Bertha nodded firmly.

Mrs. Adder agreed at last. "Well, if you two are willing to help me whip my man into submission, I'll do it. And I'll be glad to put away my knitting and sewing to help, mister. Just tell us what to do for this trauma-team thing, and how we should do it."

Bertha added, "I know some other lovely old geese who would love to set their knitters down, too. They're restless and feel useless in this mess. Set themselves to mouthing everyone instead of finding other ways. They'll be good at giving orders, too, those old nags."

When John was finished with the surgery, he instructed Mrs. Adder and her siblings on the other three victims of Harry's fiery revenge. They were lucky none had died, but the fight had cost some valuable supplies. Not just Harry's, but some of the post's as well.

John was exhausted, but he kept working until he was relieved by Nails. "These beautiful women did all that stitchin'?" asked Nails, astonished as he looked over the wounds that had been caused by the exploding lamps. "Yer a good teacher, John Ivan."

Mrs. Adder flushed at the praise and fanned herself. So did her sister.

"They'd already done most of the immediate work before I'd even arrived," John admitted. "Cleaned the wounds, stitched them up, everything. Better work than usual among the wearyworn. These three did quite well. Set them to work again after they've had some rest and some food. They want to help. And the husband shouldn't be a problem after this. They've sworn to make him sorry, and to prove that sincerity."

"In-laws!" guffawed the post doctor. "Ain't nothin' as vicious as an angered sibling of a spouse. Yeh need teh rest, too, John. Yeh haven't stopped for a wink. I'll take the rest of yer shift. Go see teh yer wife an' kids. Jeana said she couldn't find yer daughter again."

John nodded. But before he let Nails take over, he stopped him. "Have you heard anything from my parents yet? It's been over a month since they were due."

Nails shook his head, though, and he stroked his beard. "Nah. But one'a the courier's messengers may have returned with Wylem's group. There may be news today. Yeh know how it goes with yer parents' work, though. They have a lot on their plates, same as us. Be patient, they'll get here when they get here."

"What about my brother? Is he back yet?" John was growing anxious. Angry, even. He wrung his hands on a fresh towel after he poured a bit of the Heinzrichs' latest brew over them to cleanse them.

"Not a clue, but I think one'a the boys said they heard some traffic over their radios a day ago. Sounded like Taiir an' that guard they hired teh help 'em. Should be back any day now." Nails scratched at his bearded chin again, and he adjusted his fox-handled ax, which hung from his belt rather than resting in a sheath. "Saura ought teh have sent her Summons, too. Stop at the Courier's an' check on that. The weather is closer than I'd like teh turnin'. We can't wait any longer anyhow, not with this many mouths teh feed. Those apprentices need teh get teh Black Temple as soon as possible." Both of them glanced at the heavy skies above. "A'fore 'em swollen clouds burst an' flood the valleys about."

"The rains haven't reached us yet," said John, "but it has been raining heavily to the north, Amos. The rivers are gaining ground. No one can get to the onion and garlic fields, except to take the boats and dive to try and harvest the crop."

"We're movin' as many of the refugees as we can," Nails said. "Hagenhold agreed teh take an hundred or so. We've only been able teh send as upward as seventy. Not enough wagons an' horses. But the Enforcers are arrivin' by the day. We'll be out of this mess soon enough. Keep yer faith. We'll make it yet, even if it's by the hair above our teeth. With luck, yer brother will have news statin' Edantine will take on some'a our flock here, an' help 'em out of this situation."

"Maybe my parents will have good news as well."

John thanked Nails for his assistance and left for the Courier's. He was halfway to his destination when a familiar face greeted him among the bustling crowd. Wylem's great, toothy grin cracked the solemn angles from his expression, and the huge warrior raised his fist in greeting. "John!" He forced the crowd to part as he crossed the street, and he smacked John across the shoulder as a brother might before he stood back to take in John's haggard appearance. "You look like you've been eaten alive and spat out again by something dead. Worse than a maggot trying to swim."

John shrugged. "You look like a furry tree. Are you trying to grow your scarf early for winter this year? Expecting snow again?"

Wylem laughed loudly, free of worry. "Nah, just giving those pricks something to glare about." He nodded to some of the Enforcers who were dismounting from their long journey. Wylem very much disliked Enforcers. He had to travel with them a lot, and they were too strict for his tastes. They were required to remain cleanly shaven, except for some of the officers. Wylem appreciated his freedom from such regimens, and he found their customs too wearisome. "It's unnatural to have a thousand men, of all ages, be shaved like little babies. A man needs his individuality. Too many rules, these Enforcers. Only thing I like about them is that they aren't afraid to use a sword . . . Well . . . I guess that's been changing, hasn't it? Every year, they seem less willing to help."

"Yes, it seems that way sometimes," John agreed. "But leave them be. Don't try to pick another fight."

"It's all they're good for," laughed Wylem. "Now, where are you headed, you stubborn jack rabbit?"

"The Courier's, across the street. You can come along. I wouldn't mind the company. You can tell me how it's been in your area." John and Wylem waded through the Enforcers and Crow Post's other, assorted citizens and allies. The horses they stepped too near nagged and swished their tails at them. It was all very claustrophobic. Wylem hated it, but John didn't mind it at all. It was the way his line of work went. Crises were what he had learned to deal with. Wylem could only see potential threats and ambushes, and that he could not take cover here if a riot took place. John saw people working together toward a common goal, and possible ways disease could spread which needed to be addressed and ironed out.

"I've brought about fifty apprentices this trip. Another forty-three or so were brought two days ago, from what I heard when I arrived," said Wylem. "Ender's Creek should be the last of them."

"We'll receive those after we begin our journey," said John. "Amos wants to send the apprentices ahead of the Summons, since it hasn't yet arrived."

"That would be the right choice. The raining season is here already. I'm surprised we haven't been blocked in yet."

The two of them made their way into the Courier's Office, where the messenger Zacchary Cadle — who'd been missing for nearly two months — was busy arguing with the courier. The younger man was refusing to hand over the letters he had clutched in his hands, and Bryan was demanding they be handed over so that he could have them delivered properly. Zacchary wouldn't have it and claimed he had been instructed to hand the letters in person, not to entrust them to the courier, or to any other, until Reid Ivan had received his instructions first.

"I hear you have a prisoner," said Wylem.

"That, we do."

"How does that situation work? This post doesn't have a prison," said Wylem. "Where is he being kept? Why hasn't he already been dealt with?"

"Until Saura's instructions dictate what we're to do with him, he's being kept in the kennels with the dogs."

Wylem laughed. "Do you guys take him for walks?"

John stepped forward and waved his hand between Zacchary and Bryan. "Stop! Both of you shut up!" he shouted over the ruckus.

The yelling instantly ceased, as both men were startled into silence. Neither had realized John had entered. Zacchary paled, however, and he darted from the Courier's Office.

"What on earth?" John proclaimed.

Bryan held up his hands. "He says he has to talk to your brother first, that it is urgent."

"My brother isn't here yet — "

"You didn't know?" Bryan's bushy eyebrows had risen. "He arrived last night, drunk off his arse. He's at the tavern, trying to start a fight with some Enforcers."

John was beyond shocked. *"Pardon?"*

Wylem's humor had faded.

Bryan nodded. "He's not himself, Dr. Ivan. If you're going to go and talk to him, you need to press carefully. He's drawn his sword and is threatening to kill any man offended enough as to look at him wrong. And Ralleigha's trying to calm him, but he won't listen to her."

John and Wylem were both out of the Courier's Office before Bryan could say another word.

"Move!" John shouted at the crowd. "Get out of my way!"

Wylem barreled ahead of him, but just as he reached to open the tavern door, Reid crashed through the door and Ralleigha followed. "You rotten monster of a man! You drunken fool!" shouted Ralleigha. She had his sword in her hand, and she clutched tightly at the folds of her skirt. "How dare you return and not even stop to say a word to your own wife and daughter, and come to this disgusting establishment — no offense, Mrs. Heinzrich, it's a lovely place, and you and your family have helped a lot of people." Ralleigha's rapid-fire insults returned to Reid, who, instead of getting back up under her vengeful onslaught, chose to let his head fall back into the dirt. "I married an honorable man, Reid Ivan, and I don't know what you've done with him, but you'd better bring him back right this instant! Think of your daughter, you fool! Is this the example you would set for her? What of your niece and nephew? You would want any of the children to see you like this? You're a hero to them, for heaven's sake!"

"Shut up, Ralleigha," Reid said groggily. He looked awful.

John had no words. He was disconcerted to see his brother this way. He'd *never* seen his brother in such a state.

"What did you just say to me?" Ralleigha protested. She threw his sword at him, and it swung end over end. Reid remained unbothered, unworried, as the blade struck the ground just inches from his hand. She hitched up her skirts, ready to make an example of him. "I — "

"Mercy was murdered," said Reid. "I've just told his widow. Let a man have a drink, will you?"

She staggered, her hand fluttering to her heart. "M — " She took a halting breath. "*Murdered?* But — "

Reid grabbed the handle of his sword and used it to hoist himself up. He swayed dangerously and took a deep breath, clutching at his calf as though it had received a mighty bruising from his drunken fight with the Enforcers inside the tavern. "Please, Ralleigha. I need some time. Enna just killed herself, right after I told her. Right in front of me, not even an hour ago. Right in front of her little boy. She couldn't handle it when I told her of Mercy's death. She blew her brains out in front of me before I could get the gun from her . . . I didn't even know they *had* a gun. And I'm still painted with her blood."

Ralleigha swayed, and the sound of grief that escaped her mouth was awful. She wiped her eyes, struggling to comprehend that her best friends were dead. Both of them. And their unborn child. She and Enna had been planning a baby shower that was supposed to have been in three days.

"Reid." John found himself finally able to talk. But Reid cringed from him, recoiling.

"Don't," Reid said, shaking his head and turning his back. "Go back to work, John. I've got work to do, too."

Ralleigha had begun to weep, but she wiped her tears with her sleeve again. "Reid Ivan!" she sobbed. "You come *home*! Right now!"

"I can't, Ralleigha. Not tonight. Keep Marissa busy at the shop so she won't see me drunk like this. And John, I'll talk to you soon enough. We have a lot to talk about. And you had better have something ready to drink when I come."

"Reid — "

"*NO!!!*"

The refusal was so vehement that John and Ralleigha both staggered back a step.

Zacchary appeared from the crowd, and he proceeded to stop Reid and tell him something quietly. Reid shuddered when he tore open the letter he'd been given. "Do it. Immediately. Get him out of John's reach." Reid strode out of sight without ever looking over his shoulder or saying a word more.

John was floored.

"What, in the bloody hell, is that about?" asked Wylem. "What's going on? What's happened?"

John shook his head. "I have no clue. I've never seen him like this. Never."

"I have a bad feeling it may have you in similar straits soon enough, when he's ready to talk," said Wylem.

Then Zacchary finally made his way over to John. "I'm sorry — I had orders to follow. I was kept at the Temple much longer than anticipated after the news was delivered. Everything's gone to hell. Saura's Summons." He gave John the Summons. "I know you've been waiting for it."

John was irate. "Where the *hell* have you been, Zacchary?"

Zacchary paled rather than answering.

John grabbed him by the collar. "You've been gone for *two months*! You were supposed to have met with my parents to help them! Where the hell are they?!"

Zacchary wriggled free, refusing to answer. He seemed afraid to do so. "I am sorry, Dr. Ivan. My mission was more urgent than you realize. You need to talk to your brother."

Then Zacchary was gone, and John was left even more confused.

John shut his eyes, his pulse throbbing dangerously along the side of his throat. He bit back a curse and loosened his intense, shaking grip upon the Summons. "Wylem, I am afraid we'll have to catch up later. I have some important tasks to tend to, which includes hunting down my idiot brother and figuring out what he is hiding from me. Even if that means I have to beat it out of him."

CHAPTER TWENTY-THREE

JOHN'S FINGERS TAPPED THE TABLE, and he lifted his head. The children were asleep, and Jeana was dozing. Her delicate fingernails combed through Jamie's sandy hair where his head lay across her lap.

John studied her for a long time, chewing on the end of his pen. She was his anchor, calm when he was a storm inside, patient when he was restless. He loved her for it. And she balanced him. She always knew what was needed, even when he did not. He felt better knowing she had his back when he was most vulnerable, just as he shielded her whenever it was necessary.

But what bothered him now, he knew she could not fix. Neither could he, and that was the problem. "Something has been wrong with Reid for two months now," John said quietly as he put his pen down and at last closed his journal. Saura's orders remained closed within the pages. He'd sent his reply to her Summons just hours ago. "He's been avoiding me as much as possible since the day he brought that thief into Crow Post. And I haven't been able to find him since I saw him at the tavern three days ago. He had Ralleigha extremely upset."

His wife looked up, alert. It didn't take much to wake her. The same could be said of their five-year-old daughter.

At that, his thoughts returned to Nymeria. His lips pursed, and his gaze slid to her as she slept in the other room with the door ajar. The warm light pooling from his study revealed her restless slumber. Nightmares, he knew. And she wouldn't talk about them. He regretted that he could do nothing for it, that Jeana and Reid seemed to be the only ones who could ever manage to soothe the restless child. Nymeria did nothing but defy him — day or night, awake or asleep.

He sighed. Too many things tugged at him this night. His brother, his daughter, his parents. It felt as if they were all drifting away despite his efforts to keep them together. And then there were things he knew he would never be able to stop, like the attacks, or the unrest among the people they were trying to help, or the rising of the rivers. Saura had sent her Summons much too late this year. The storms were about to be upon them. The North was already flooded, and they would be lucky if they could pass through Ender's Creek near Virien and the old ruin there. He didn't even want to think about having to track down boats, or about how many would drown trying to cross if it had already become impassable.

John could not concentrate on the rest of the orders or on updating his ledger this late, not with how worried he was. Too much rode on his shoulders at any given time, and he didn't have the luxury of blowing any of it off. And now, with Saura's orders . . . The Summons had not only been late but *modified*. She'd included instructions on shoring up at Isold and the Temple. To send more supplies and much larger numbers of workers to help defend Black Temple's most vulnerable reaches, which would strip Crow Post down to a skeleton crew and leave it daringly unprotected. Saura had placed more burdens than he felt they could compensate for in their current situation. She'd even demanded that John travel with the apprentices all the way to Isold instead of allowing him to continue to assist Nails with the management of Crow Post during their great time of need, and though it was his job to assist in crises like this one. The modified Summons meant he had to leave his wife and children behind for weeks. A month, even. And his parents still hadn't arrived, and he didn't know what to do about it. He needed their help. Even if their presence only meant some semblance of peace in his head and his heart, he needed them to arrive at the post now more than ever.

Jeana reached up and cupped his face gently, her dark, loving gaze glittering in the candlelight. Her expression seemed to say that his brother would come to him when he was ready, and that things would work out. "I'm worried about my brother," John said.

She nodded, as if understanding far more ailed him than his brother's recent avoidant activities and cruel, drunken demeanor.

Jeana opened her mouth to speak, and though the sound was merely a broken, scratching whisper, John understood her without any difficulty. "I know. He's been drinking since he's come back," Jeana whispered. "Taiir would say nothing, but I think your brother has been drinking since before he left for Tallil and Edantine. Ralleigha said he hasn't come home for several days now," Jeana said. "He hasn't even spoken to her."

John grimaced. He clasped her hand in his and lifted her palm to his lips. The back of his finger caressed the scar upon her throat apologetically. "You don't have to try to speak aloud for me, Jeana. I know it hurts you still to try. Give it more time to heal."

The scar upon her was bare and obvious without her coat or her scarf, and at the sight of it, he remembered how long it had taken the wound to close. For her to eat, or even to manage the barest whisper. He remembered how every second had ticked by and felt like an eternity of wrenching, taxing agony. Because Jeana had only clung to life by the barest of threads. Because, even though he and Jeana had married in another city, he'd been too late to get her and her things from her family. He and Jeana had meant to surprise her family, but when he'd come to them to get her and reveal the news, he'd found out they'd already given her to the detestable man who'd lusted after her for years. Who'd threatened her life multiple times when she'd refused his barbaric advances repeatedly. They had *forced* her to go with him. And when John had finally reached his wife and the bastard who'd taken her from him, Griggori had found out Jeana was pregnant not with his own child but with John's. John had barely been able to get him off her before the attack had taken her life.

They had lost more than just her voice when Griggori's rage had struck.

"I should have killed Griggori before he could have done what he did to you," he said quietly. His thumb traced the smooth skin over the phantom wound delicately. He didn't dare mention the child they'd lost, the one that would have been their firstborn.

Jeana's fingers tightened around his, but otherwise she ignored his kind reprimand not to put herself through any discomfort. Her eyes seemed to tell him that she already knew all that was running through his mind and his heart, and that she'd long ago forgiven him for his cowardice. That it wasn't his fault he'd waited to face her family and tell them. That they'd agreed together to wait . . . Her expression told him that she loved him despite the loss of their firstborn and despite everything else that had happened because of Griggori.

"When Reid is ready, he will tell you what is on his mind, I am sure of it," she said. She inhaled slowly to censure the burning itch that often preceded the coughing, and John placed one more kiss upon the back of her hand. "He does not keep things from you without good reason," she continued.

John nodded, but he wondered again why Reid had told Zacchary what he had. Why they'd had the thief skirted from Crow Post, especially with so few men and in this dangerous time. The wolfmen raids were closing in on Crow Post, and if Lukas was as important for information as they believed, then risking such a hurried trip with so little preparation would put the man's life in danger. John didn't like Lukas, but he did recognize the importance of keeping an informant alive.

Still. The way Reid had treated the man. The anger. Almost like hatred. And it wasn't just Reid who seemed to feel that way, it was all the men who had been in Reid's company at the time. Two months, and that enmity had never dwindled in any of them. What could have possibly caused that? Also, John still couldn't get Reid's threats to the man out of his head, or Lukas's reaction to them. Every time he thought about the thief in the kennels, his mind turned to that. It was almost as if Reid had tortured the man for the information he had given them all. Not questioned. *Tortured.*

Despite Lukas's jokes and sniveling, twisted personality, John felt in his gut that the man had been utterly afraid to defy Reid's command to tell them what he had. And the idea that Reid was probably capable of doing very evil things to other people unsettled John despite that he knew Reid had served the Alliance for fifteen years. But . . . to *torture* a man? It wasn't who Reid was.

Or was he wrong?

Reid had never talked much about his service, and John had never heard much or put much thought into what Reid had done to promote so quickly. But fifteen years was a long time for an Enforcer to create and then bury some very dark stains. It was long enough to become an adept killer and skilled torturer, and then to learn restraint and present a calm, patient, normal, and calculating exterior. Which was exactly what Reid most often presented.

What could have caused his brother's calm to have shifted so violently aside that he had set himself to drinking to quiet his demons?

"If he doesn't come clean soon, I'll probably have to beat it out of him," John sighed. "I'm tired of the secrets. Two months, and I haven't been given even a dribble of the truth, Jeana. His men haven't talked about it, but I heard some rumors a week ago saying they've been sneaking around, torturing that thief for more information. I don't like it one bit."

Nymeria's eyes cracked open as John stole another worried glance to the children. He frowned when he realized she was watching him, and he got up and crossed the study to kneel by Nymeria's bed. "Nymeria," what are you doing awake, honey?" he asked as he pulled the blanket over her to keep her warm. The cool front that had come through had made the house cold, and the temperature was still steadily dropping.

Nymeria said nothing as he knelt by her. She simply shrugged the blanket off and curled on her side, watching him with eyes that were such an unusual green that most strangers seemed taken aback by them. As he brushed her dark hair back from her face, he thought sadly how being different had already begun to affect her. Already, she was becoming prone to hide her face, to look away when others called to her. It hurt him to know she was suffering at an age so young simply because she was so very different. He'd long suspected the other children were no kinder because of it, either, and that suspicion had been verified by some of the attendants who'd caught some of those children trying to hurt her. But she wouldn't admit to it. And if she was not willing to speak about it, he could do nothing more than ask the attendants to watch for her, to try and chase the bullies away or find punishments for them.

Nymeria looked at the lantern hanging over the desk in the middle of his study, and she watched the moths flitting about its light like mad creatures, never able to touch the fire.

"Do not pity the moths," said John with a halfhearted grin when he discerned what she was looking at. "They are desperate and do not understand the firelight they want is deadly to them."

"Uncle Reid has decided to tell you what happened," she said quietly. "The thief saw them, too. And so did Uncle Reid." John cast a look to his wife when Nymeria shut her eyes tightly against tears that seemed to rise unbidden. She turned away from him, and she curled in on herself when he placed his hand upon her shoulder to try to stop her from pulling away. That she was upset bothered him because he never seemed to be able to make her feel any better.

"Saw what? The dark things you told us about?" he asked gently. She wouldn't speak to him. He sighed, frustrated. "Nymeria, you know the shadows are not alive. Darkness has no heartbeat, and it cannot talk, I promise you that — "

"John." Jeana lifted her sleeping son and paced across the room with him in her arms, Jamie's head resting upon her shoulder. Their son stirred, and one small hand rose to rub at his eyes before it dropped again as sleep swept him from awareness once more. Not much could wake him, John reflected appreciatively. It was far different for Nymeria. "I h — " Jeana suppressed a cough, and when she spoke again, her voice was in its last throes. It was likely she would not be able to speak again for the rest of the night and possibly well into the morning. "I hear footsteps."

John gripped Nymeria's shoulder gently because he still wanted to talk to her, but his brother's hoarse inquiry from outside changed his mind.

"John? Jeana?"

John sighed. "Get some sleep, Myria. We'll talk later," he said. He planted another kiss upon his daughter's cheek, and as he stood, he placed another upon the crown of his son's head. Jeana put Jamie to bed as John stepped away to open the door. Another quiet knock came just as his hand touched the rickety old knob. The lock clicked when he turned the mechanism, and he slid back the deadbolt.

Reid looked up when the door creaked open a slit.

John saw immediately Reid's red-rimmed eyes, as though misery had held him in its clutches earlier in the night. His hair was still as tossed and wild as it had been days prior, which was unlike him, and his clothes seemed to hang from him as though he'd lost weight. He did not stand as tall or as proudly as he normally did, and as a breeze picked up, the smell of alcohol slithered lazily in through the entryway like a poisoned, suffocating fog, and Reid swayed on his feet.

Ralleigha hovered behind Reid like a specter, hardly visible in the darkness despite her fair skin. Usually she was busy into the dark hours of the night with her glasswork, but that was not the occasion tonight. She looked just as ruffled and undone as Reid; her hair was frayed and tangled and thrown quickly into a topknot, where wild curls broke loose like a den of angry red snakes. But her eyes were clear where Reid's were glassy and barely present. Their daughter was not with them, and every alarm went off in John's heart as he gaped at the two of them, flabbergasted. He opened the door wider. "Blistering coals, Reid, what is it? Come in." When Reid said nothing and did not move, except to sway where he stood, his chin quavering, John motioned to his brother. "The children are in bed, just be quiet," said John. "Come in. Please."

Reid's throat bobbed, and his eyes lifted at the sound of the screech owl that had made its home in the oak that towered over the house and the veranda. Its song was woven with ominous, solemn notes tonight.

Ralleigha nudged Reid's elbow to urge him forward. Finally, he nodded, and he followed John into their small house. Ralleigha closed the door behind him. Her expression seemed to let John know the conversation with his brother was going to be a difficult, painful one. She locked the door behind herself, but she remained standing there, the heavy wood at her back as though it was the only thing holding her upright. Her thin fingers pulled at several locks of her red hair as her gaze returned worriedly to her husband.

Jeana shrugged her shawl on over her shoulders and greeted her brother-in-law and his wife with a kiss upon each cheek, and a hug. Her hands fluttered in a focused, ready manner. *Sit down. I'll get you both something to drink.*

Reid shook his head. "It won't be necessary, Jeana, but thanks." His speech was sure, although he swayed dangerously where he stood. His breath reeked of cheap booze. "Ralleigha, go on and sit, honey. You've been working day and night while I've been out of sorts, and I'll not have you fainting after it."

Ralleigha nodded. "That would be a bit unfortunate," she admitted. "Coffee would be nice, if you don't mind, Jeana," Ralleigha said quietly. "Not much, though . . . I'm afraid I won't be able to drink much. Reid's only *just* told me . . ." Tears glistened in her red lashes, and she took a deep, quivering breath. She shook her head and held up her hand. "I'm sorry. I'll let the three of you talk about it. I just need to sit."

What happened? Jeana demanded.

Reid watched her hands, but he did not reply. His mouth snapped shut, and his gaze fell to the floor. A ragged breath ripped from his shuddering frame, and a grimace carved itself deep into his face as he stood there, unable to talk. He ran his hands through the tangled mess upon the top of his head and continued to stare at the floor, utterly lost, his fingers clutching at the sandy mess.

Reid looked haggard and broken, and it was all John could do to keep his mouth shut and not push at his brother. He didn't want to press for answers when Reid looked so obviously ready to ignite. Or shatter. He didn't know which idea was worse, and his stomach knotted when Reid's ragged, pained inhalation shook his tall frame.

CHAPTER TWENTY-FOUR

FIRST VISION

NYMERIA TURNED OVER ONTO her back, her eyes wide open as her mother pulled the door to her room shut. A single ray of light swept under the door as the restless footfall that was her father's traversed the study. She already knew what her uncle was to tell, and her heart twisted and beat an unbearable rhythm beneath her ribs. His mourning was like a shroud about him, and it burned through the walls to meet with her own. She had seen the haunted anger written upon his face before her mother had closed the door, and she had seen the look of apprehension in her father's own visage, inviting the bleak breaking of news. This was the night her parents would learn the truth about her uncle's deceit. She was afraid it would tear their family apart.

The pool of light bleeding under the door rippled with shadow as her father passed before it. Still, her uncle said nothing. But she could hear how difficult it was for him even to take a breath to speak. She listened to the sighing of the floorboards where her father at last stopped moving and simply stood still.

Beside her, Jamie's breathing was even; he remained peacefully unaware of what was about to be said in the other room. She pressed her face against her pillow as she uttered her prayer, and the linen soaked up the tears that had gathered in her lashes. "Just tell him, Uncle. Tell him what he did. You have to."

The walls began to close in as she shivered and cried quietly to herself. A long strand of her hair slid over her shoulder, and her skin prickled.

Someone breathed, and the sound echoed in a prolonged, hissing chorus, as though the walls and the floors had become stone. It was an agonized sound, and she heard it as clearly as she felt it, as though it had been her own, rattling breath . . . Except it hadn't been.

For a moment, she was no longer home. She was in a dark place, in a cell in the deepest pit of a dungeon somewhere far away. The air was cold, but the floor was colder, and the chains . . . yet colder.

"*Iyutha . . . ?*" he asked. Nymeria felt the words raking over her own throat as his voice poured out like a viscous liquid. *Who is there . . . ?*

The language was the same as the one she sometimes spoke when she forgot others could not understand her, but the voice was not her own. She knew she'd never heard his voice before . . . and yet it was familiar.

"*Aiya tzedaket'hae ian.*" *Please help me.*

He drew another agonized breath and pleaded louder, his shredded voice cracking the way a sick, dying creature's might. Fire trickled down his throat, and the coppery taste of blood followed it. Miniscule beads of moisture burned the blistered flesh that continued to quiver over more broken, corroded words. "*Aiya tzedaket'hae ian . . .*" *Please help me . . .*

Such agony wove his plea, and Nymeria shook as the man in the cell began to weep, as long slivers of black hair fell over his own face and into her vision. She felt the filth that was caked to his skin — hardened, like scales. It pulled on his flesh with every tremor, until it felt as though he was being stung over and over. And then she realized the filth was dried blood, for the smell of it when his tears wetted it. Weakness stole through him as the cell continued to spin, and his head fell forward. The world continued to pool in and out of focus as it swam closer and then receded in waves of waxing and waning consciousness.

The voice . . .

Nymeria opened her eyes. No one was there. Just her little brother Jamie. Just her. The wooden walls were where they should have been, and they did not radiate that breathless, unforgiving cold. A soft bed was under her, and the blankets over her kept her warm. She was not upon an uneven, filthy floor with naught for warmth but torn rags that served as inadequate clothing, and she did not feel the creature's presence any longer. It was gone. His voice was no longer in her throat or in her ears. There was only the sound of her own frightened, muted sobs.

How profoundly hungry he'd been. Her own tummy was full of the night's dinner, but a knot now curled there, and she felt sick because of it. How his wrists had ached and burned, as though they'd been put in a hot fire and left there to blister the way his throat had from thirst. Her own wrists felt strangely cold and strangely numb in the absence of the grisly pain that had plagued his.

Her whole body quaked as she tried to shove it from her mind, to push it far, far away.

Though her grief had not subsided, another emotion washed through her, and with it, confusion came whirling in like the first monstrous breath of an odious beast as it ascended into her mind.

The voice . . .

Her heart skittered fearfully as her eyes darted about her room, and she prayed the walls would not abandon her ever again. She did not want to know how such a memory had come to her when it had never been her own. She did not want to ever know another thing about him. There was a blackness, a despair, about him, and it frightened her because she sensed that it could swallow her if she drifted too near it.

But the voice —

Then her uncle chased the harrowing thoughts and memories and fears away as he opened his mouth and spoke at last. Nymeria listened quietly, feeling alone, even though her brother slept peacefully beside her. She wanted to be away from the dark. Anywhere that was safe would do. Mostly, she wanted to be in the study with her mother and her father and her grieving aunt and uncle.

CHAPTER TWENTY-FIVE

*T*RUTH

"THE NIGHT WE CAUGHT LUKAS, I sent Zacchary Cadle to deliver a message to Saura," Reid began, his mouth downturned. He said nothing else for a long moment, and John held his tongue, knowing not to interrupt his brother. He'd never seen him in such a state, and he didn't know what else to do but listen. So he paced as he waited.

Jeana handed Ralleigha a cup of coffee, and though Ralleigha lifted it slowly to take a sip, her hand convulsed suddenly as she struggled to quiet a sob, and the cracked mug fell and shattered. Jeana took Ralleigha's hands in her own and squeezed them. Neither of the women said anything as Reid continued.

"I didn't write the message I sent, because I couldn't risk it falling into the wrong hands. Zacchary was to relay my inquiry directly to Saura — he was the only one I could trust not to forget what I wanted said word for word, and he was the fastest among us. He was to tell Saura what had happened the night we caught Lukas," Reid explained slowly. His fingers curled into a fist, but he did not look up. "Three days ago, he'd just returned with Saura's commands. I gave him the order to get rid of Lukas immediately, according to her instruction. Two days ago, that order was carried out, and Thomas was among that charge along with a few of our fiercest men. Lukas is being taken to the Reformation. Saura did not want him to be brought near any of Black Temple's other holdings. She didn't want *you* to have access to him, because of what he's done. She didn't want you to have the chance to kill him. Frankly, I shared that fear."

John felt a deep disturbance over Reid's lacking explanation. "What are you not telling me?" he said quietly.

Reid did not answer the question. "I won't have you exiled from Black Temple for killing him. He knows too much, and that makes him valuable. I knew that's what she would command, and I made the right call. Because I was right." He shuddered as another wave of anger rolled through him, and he choked on it. "I wanted to kill him. I made him suffer when I interrogated him." He looked away. There was a twitch in his expression that nearly resembled a twisted, humorous smile, but it was so filled with anguish that the agonized ghost of humor fell from his face. Still, Reid wouldn't look at John. He stared at the coffee that had spilled on the floor, at the broken fragments of Jeana's favorite cracked mug.

Reid lifted his hand, and his fingers uncurled from something small, something that glinted in the lantern light. John stepped closer as his brother held it up in his fingers, as he held it out for John to take.

It was an emissary's signet, like the one their father wore. The black quatrefoil glimmered where silver etchings rose from the center, which marked it as belonging to a highly respected courier working for Black Temple. It was about the same size as their father's ring, too. John shook his head when the weight in his hand felt heavier than it should have. He opened his mouth to speak . . . and he found that he could barely utter a word. "Whose is it . . . ?" he managed after some difficulty.

"I didn't tell you everything," said Reid. "I would have sent him off sooner, but Saura had

170

to approve it first, considering the nature of what happened and everything it entailed." He lifted his chin and looked John in the eye.

Then Reid pulled the second half of a torn bit of paper from his satchel and gave it to John, as well as another, familiar torn page that was about the same size. The two were separate halves of a whole. The tear along the middle was a perfect match. "Dad was approached by a man named Rhael who knows exactly what those shards are and how they work. I don't know exactly how to find him or his brother Gabriel, but I found a few leads in Edantine that point to Aelynhold. I don't know where the letter is referencing, but I did come across an old map keeper in Edantine who said he'd seen a place like it once, a long time ago."

Reid grimaced and looked away for a moment before he could bring himself to continue. "The place exists," he said quietly. "I think I know where to look for it. In Tallil, I was pointed to some Keepers in a secret library in Balthora who know historical signets like the broken seal imprinted on this letter. They should know more about the places described in the letter."

The ring in John's hand felt icy. He found it difficult to focus on his brother's words.

"If they don't," said Reid slowly, and his voice shook minutely. Grief. It was grief that John was hearing in his brother's voice. "If they don't, they have access to others who might be able to point me in the right direction . . . It means I have to leave again to track down one of those brothers. In that letter, Rhael said Nymeria will *die* if she isn't treated. It's some kind of cursed magic that comes from the souls of certain people. Nymeria is one of those people, John. Doctors can't fix this. *You* can't fix her."

"There's no such thing . . ." John's voice trailed off as the meaning he was trying to reject broke through to him. Jeana touched his hand tenderly in a silent offer of support. His knees had buckled, and he'd abruptly sat in his chair. The ring shone dully up at him. It was still covered in soot. There was *dried blood* caked in one of the grooves on its face.

The ring had the same scratch their father's had, along the lower left corner of the quatrefoil. It had always been there.

John's hand began to shake intensely. *They're just late*, he wanted to say, but nothing formed on his lips. The sound would not reconcile as his throat constricted.

"Why didn't you tell us before?" Jeana tried to say as she signed the words to Reid. "*Why?!*" Her voice only broke the merest whisper for but a second before it failed her. She was angry as she rose from John's side. She stepped past John and put her finger upon Reid's broad chest to push him. He staggered back a step, as he had not braced himself.

Why?! Two months ago, we could have had a decent funeral for them!

"You know why," Reid said quietly. "Because John's grief would have turned to vengeance, and he would have gone too far, just like he did after what Griggori did to you and your baby, when the bastard found out you'd already married my brother. When he realized your baby was John's, not his. You may not remember what John did, because you were bleeding from the throat and clutching the dead baby girl Griggori had cut from your belly, Jeana, but I know very well what John is capable of. I've seen the carnage."

Jeana recoiled as if he'd slapped her, and her hand fluttered to her belly, over the serious scar hidden beneath her clothing. Tears shone in her eyes even as her expression twisted fiercely with anger and grief.

"Your husband would not be given a second chance if he was to attack another man and do to him what he did to Griggori," said Reid. "Both of you would lose everything, and he would be executed or exiled." Reid crossed his arms as if he could ward off a sudden chill. "John, I am sorry I had to keep this from you. I am. But you need to read the rest of that letter. You need to know what it says, and you need to remember that Lukas Maverick has also read every bit of it. This knowledge makes him more dangerous to Nymeria's safety, and to Black Temple's security. That is why Saura wants him incarcerated at the Reformation, in one of the units reserved for protective custody. I had to have a letter of authorization for Lukas to be given that level of security at the Reformation. He must be protected until we can learn what else he knows."

"How am I supposed to head to Isold and then make my way to Black Temple if our parents are dead and you are going away to chase down some ghost you have no idea how to contact?" John said quietly. He turned his head to look at the closed door where Nymeria was supposed to be asleep with her younger brother. Part of him knew that not only was she awake but she was likely crying to herself as well. She'd already known. She must have overheard Reid telling Ralleigha before dusk, before she'd come home to have dinner and go to bed. She'd been quiet since earlier in the evening. "What am I supposed to do with my daughter, Reid? She is in no condition to go to Black Temple. It's unsafe even to bring her as far as Isold! I cannot risk her doing something irrational or dangerous there. Her hallucinations are worse than they were two months ago — she'll barely even sleep by herself anymore! I can't pawn her off on anyone here, not with this crisis about us, and especially not after the insult she caused with the walkie incident. You and your wife are the only other people who understand her, or who can take her on properly if I must go. And I must. Saura has finally sent her Summons. She has modified them so that every resource we have here is going to be stretched to its limits!"

"I cannot take her with me," said Reid. "I won't risk running into any of the Descendants of the Moon with her in tow. With Lukas gone, I must leave immediately if I am to have any chance of finding Gabriel or Rhael. You'll have to figure out what to do with Nymeria on your own."

A strange sound scraped past John's throat as he shook his head and clutched the ring in his hand. He was quaking, and his mouth had gone dry.

This couldn't be happening.

"Where are Mom and Dad?"

Reid grimaced. He took another deep breath, and it seemed to hurt him to do so. "They died quickly, the way it looked. I swear I wouldn't have kept this from you this long if — "

"YOU LIED TO ME!" John shouted. "You didn't just keep this from me, Reid! You *lied* to me. And even while knowing that, you've sheltered our parents' *murderer* in our home for over two months. My daughter was merely a meter from him where you had him locked up! Where are our parents?!"

Reid chewed on the inside of his cheek for a long moment, his gaze flickering to the door where the children were sleeping. They both knew Jamie and Nymeria were likely awake now, and they were both waiting silently for the children to begin crying. Not a single noise was to be heard in the study, save for Ralleigha's sniffling.

John shifted as his anger rose. "You lied to me, and then you ran, and in so doing, you avoided not just me but your own wife and child, who needed you. And now you're going to abandon all of us again for a fool's errand." He turned the ring over in his hand and then flung it across the room. It hit the inkwell, which shattered. Black dripped onto the floor and stained the throw rug. John gripped the armrests of his chair tightly, until his fingernails felt as though they would either tear through the wood or rip right off his fingers. He took a deep, deep breath, and then he rose from his chair, quivering. Everything was tinted with red, and his temple throbbed with his rage.

"John — " Jeana cried urgently, trying to calm him. "J — " Her voice failed her, but she still tried to say his name as she reached out to stop him.

"John! Stop!" Reid commanded desperately.

But the door was already open, and John was already halfway to the stable before his brother grasped his shoulder to try to stop him physically.

John's fist struck true, and mercilessly, and Reid staggered and fell. "Don't you dare try and stop me!" John shouted.

He processed little beyond his anger over his brother's lies as he saddled his horse furiously, and then the doors to the stable exploded outward when he exited it on horseback.

Rage beat at him. He ignored his brother's protests and his sister-in-law's pleas as he rode out.

Soon, though, Reid was gaining on him. Reid reached out to grasp the reins to John's horse to rip them away, but John pulled away and lifted his foot from the stirrup, and he kicked at his brother's leg. Reid caught his foot and tried to hold on to it, but John bellowed with rage and clawed him across the face. He shoved Reid back so hard he was nearly unseated. Reid veered off the path, crashing through the brush and cursing vehemently. "Ralleigha!" Reid shouted. "Get Robert! We've got to stop him from murdering Lukas! *HURRY!*"

John's horse collapsed by the time he caught up with Lukas's transport. It was nightfall of the second day, and his entrance startled Thomas and the others awake. The man on watch duty, Baron, had already drawn his gun and started to aim it before he'd realized John was the one who'd come.

"It's the commander's brother!" shouted Baron as the others roused.

"Stand down!" John commanded as he approached the cage Lukas was imprisoned in.

"Dr. Ivan, we cannot do that," Thomas began. "Your brother has made it very clear that this piece of garbage is to be delivered *alive* — "

"Stand aside!" John shouted. Thomas's hands rose, and the man stepped back carefully as John's knife pressed against his throat, threatening to insert itself. John stepped with him. The others were wary of moving against him for fear of risking Thomas's life. "Tell your men to stand aside and let me revenge my parents' deaths," he told Baron, "or I will gut every last one of you here. Not one of you will survive the night if you try to get in my way."

"John," said Baron. "We cannot — "

John roared, and he threw Thomas into the older man. Both men toppled, and John spun wildly as the others looked at one another, drew their weapons, and put their backs to the murderer's cage to protect him. John would never forgive any of them for that betrayal.

"Don't kill him!" cried Thomas, who rubbed at his throat with a shaking hand. "Just get him under control!"

As they rushed him, John took each man down. Some bled, others bruised. One lost the use of his hand for John's crippling, maiming aim, though John had managed just enough restraint not to kill any of them. Baron, John pinned to the cage itself when he stabbed the man through the shoulder and grabbed his belt and tightened it about the bars and Baron's neck; John buckled it where Baron could barely reach it, and he leaned into Baron's face and glared at the man as he snatched the key to Lukas's cage from the ring on that very belt. "When I am through here, you'll all haul his murderous carcass back to Crow Post, and then I'll be on my way to give my parents a proper funeral."

"John — "

"DON'T!" he shouted.

He thrust the keys into the lock, glaring madly at the murderer.

Lukas only grinned back at him calmly. The killer spoke as John entered the cage, "If you kill me, you will face unimaginable retribution — "

John took him by the throat to silence his lies, but the bound thief managed to break free. And when John's fists found Lukas's face, the thief only began to laugh. The murderous thief continued to laugh, even as John struck Lukas again and again.

The laughter only became madder and madder as he beat the man.

"Why did you kill my mother and father?" John demanded. "Why?! What could they have had or done for you to have murdered them in cold blood?!"

"You'll never find Avery if I'm dead," Lukas warned. His blood was everywhere, and one of his eyes had swollen shut. His mouth was filled with blood and mucous, yet he merely laughed when John tried to beat the answers from him. "I am the only one who knows where he is."

And then stronger arms wrapped around John from behind, and he was dragged back from the murderer. Reid slammed the cage door shut and locked it, and he shoved John away from the murderer's cage. No spark of kindness remained in Reid's expression, and the darkness in his gaze was a livid, deathly storm that was very clearly used to killing and *worse*.

Baron took the keys from the door and tossed them to one of the others as he nursed his wounded shoulder.

"What the hell do you think you are doing?" Reid asked venomously. He shoved John again. When John dove at him, Reid side-stepped and slapped him so hard his head rocked sideways. "John, calm the hell down before I have to injure you!"

Thomas had seized him from behind, and so had another of the men.

John struggled against them both, and Reid stormed up to John and grabbed him by the hair. "John," Reid snarled. "*John!* You know what you were trying to do was wrong. Yes, he killed our parents. But think of your kids, you fool! Your wife! If you manage to kill this man, Saura will clip your rank, and you will be booted from the guild or executed. You *know* this! How can you take care of your family if you get them thrown out while Five Tower is trying to start a war?!"

"You have no right to lecture me, Reid!" John swore.

Reid slapped him again, even harder than the first time.

Everything spun wildly. Thomas and the other let him go, and he staggered in the direction everything tilted, and then he hit the ground.

"You wrathful fool," spat Thomas. "Your brother's a rabid madman, Commander. He shouldn't be using a scalpel; he should be wearing a sword. He's not a healer, he's a natural-born *killer*."

"Get this murderer back to Crow Post *now*," hissed John. He was out of breath, and he felt sick to his stomach. "*NOW!*"

"We cannot do that," said Thomas.

John glared at him. When he spoke again, what he had to say startled them. "Never mind that *I* want him dead or that I took my anger out on him. What are you going to do if some one or other of his enemies or ours comes along and tries to kill or free this bastard? Tell me! There are not enough of you to defend against the kind of attacks that are destroying entire villages right now. The last raids we got word of were only days away — we're in the middle of enemy territory here! Twelve haphazardly prepared men will not survive that kind of attack. He needs to be delivered with the Enforcers' help. Never mind his safety. The lot of you are in danger here."

Reid gave pause. "Holy hell. You *can* think when you're in a murderous rage."

"I still say you should give me back my knife so I can cut his damned throat, but at least I managed to beat that vile grin off his smug, satisfied face." John snarled at his brother. "I will *never* forgive you for lying to me about what he did."

Reid shrugged and shook his hand out; he had bruised his knuckles when he'd struck John that second time. "I made my decision knowing what the repercussions would be. But we're still not going to let you touch him again. Saura wants him alive. I told you that already. Come back to Crow Post with me. We'll have a drink, and we'll perform Mom and Dad's last rites. Then I want you to read the rest of that letter I gave you. It concerns your daughter's life." Reid held both pieces up in his fist. John had left all of it behind in his fury; he'd never even read it. "Your daughter is still *alive*. It isn't too late for her yet. A man's priority should always be his children, above all else, John. I would think you, of all people, would have learned that lesson a long time ago, when your first was murdered before her first breath. Mom and Dad are gone. Nymeria isn't."

Reid sighed and turned to the men, then. "I really hate to say it, but my brother does have a point regarding this scumbag's transport. It will be safer to take him to the Reformation if the Enforcers are involved with the trip. Go ahead and take him back. I'll put in a request for some of them to be assigned to help us guard him and keep him separate from the kids and John and his friends." Reid swore, clutching his hand, and then turned it over to look at it.

CHAPTER TWENTY-SIX

Funeral Rites

TWO NIGHTS LATER, Reid and John both tumbled into John's home. Ralleigha had met them halfway to the house, and she'd been mortified at the state in which both had returned. Reid had a black eye, and shallow claw marks slithered across his face. John's jaw was as purple as Reid's knuckles and eye, and he was nursing the wound and still feeling vengeful. Neither brother had spoken much on the return trip into Crow Post. And Lukas was still alive, though his face was far more skewed with bruises and swelling. The men escorting Lukas weren't in much better shape, given how John had taken a knife against most of them despite their loyalty. He knew no apology would have sufficed among them, so he had never bothered to waste one.

Jeana opened the door for them, and she scowled when she, too, saw the shape they were in. But she saw Lukas's cage rolling past, and she grimaced as shadows of fiery promise danced across her darkening eyes. She turned from the sight of the carriage and the murderer within its cage, and she said nothing as John and his brother came inside.

"Get me something strong to drink, and then I'll take you to see where we buried Mom and Dad," said Reid finally. "At least you didn't have to see what the fire did to what was left of them."

John flinched. He knew very well what fire did to flesh. He'd tended too many burn victims to be ignorant.

He studied Reid's hand for a long moment, remembering the marks that had been upon his knuckles the night he'd had Lukas brought in at the meeting two months ago. At least now he understood what had happened.

For a long moment, John choked back all the questions that wanted to rise. He was still too angry with his brother to voice most of them. Finally, he allowed one to part his lips. "It wasn't how they died?" He could hear the faded horror in his own voice.

Relief flooded him when Reid denied it.

He followed his brother's gaze to Jeana's knife, where it hung upon the wall near the door, and he flinched as though it had plunged into him instead. His eyes began to burn. "I hope the bastard screamed when you got a hold of him," John said.

Reid lifted his knuckles and curled his fingers, remembering. "It wasn't enough," he said simply. "I wanted to do far worse, as badly as you tried. The men reminded me to think first — that's something you need to give effort to more often when you're angry. I realized more was going on than the unpleasant business of what he did to Mom and Dad. Saura said the Reformation will take care of Lukas. I thought three days was enough of a head start before telling you. Obviously, I was mistaken. You're lucky I stopped you from killing him."

John's intent hadn't been murder but vengeance. Yet he felt no need to clarify.

"Do you remember how he screamed in the kennel when we got Nymeria out of there?" asked Reid. Again, his fingers curled into a fist, until the knuckles were white. "He won't be leaving the Reformation once he's committed. Not even if one of his friends from Five Tower tries to buy his way out. He'll be diagnosed as criminally insane when they find out what he's afraid of and what he's done to be free of it. Once he is registered as Black Temple's political prisoner, only Saura will be able to send a request for his release or his transfer. And if she happens to die, he will just remain there until his own death."

John realized the ring he'd thrown days before sat upon his desk. The ink had been washed away. He'd gone off in a rage and left his wife and children to clean up his mess, and he hadn't even thought of them. It angered him, but there was nothing to be done about it right now. He would sort things out with her later.

John took a seat once more, his fingers digging into the arms of his chair, and he took a deep breath. He let it out very slowly. "If the circumstances surrounding Crow Post had been any different, what you did would have been the right thing. Sending Lukas away, that is. I've never wanted to murder someone so savagely, aside from Griggori, for what he did to my wife five years ago." He glared at Reid, then. "Were you not my brother, I would be telling you to get the hell out of my house, and to leave Crow Post for good. As I told you, I will not forgive you for not telling me the truth earlier, Reid. Brother of mine or not, you should not have lied to me. You should not have kept our parents' deaths from me."

Reid nodded. "When the last rites are done, I will be leaving."

"Jeana," John grated. "Bring the *Melancholy*. I still want to murder that man. Better to numb it for a night. Wake the children and take them to Ralleigha's for a few days, until this is over." Jeana had already twisted the cap off a bottle of *Melancholy* before John had finished speaking. "It's one of the Heinzrichs' best brews," said John to his brother as he took the bottle and drank deeply from it. "I've been saving it. Haven't yet had to use it as a wound-cleanser. Rightly fitting, though, that name." He gave it to his brother as the fiery liquid burned his throat fiercely, and he scrubbed at the stubble on his chin with his still-quivering hand. One drink wasn't going to quiet the anger and the loss he felt, and he knew it. Jeana seemed to know it, too, for she'd already pulled another bottle from the cupboards and placed it on his desk, next to his father's ring. She busied herself, preparing to leave for a few days. She understood how the Ivan men grieved as well as Ralleigha did. It was best to stay away.

Reid simply stood there, looking at the bottle he held for a long time. "I've probably already killed my liver this last month," he said quietly. "And Ralleigha's lost her wits, seeing me drink as I have been." He wouldn't look at his wife, though. "But I'll let her give me hell for it later." His back slid up against the wall as he contemplated taking another drink. The bottle turned in his hand. He shrugged and took a heavy drink, and he sank to the floor. His head fell against the wall, and he tapped the bottle against his leg several times. "I used to think Five Tower was primarily a trade city," said Reid. He took another swig and then offered the bottle to Jeana.

"I'm terribly sorry," Ralleigha sniffled. "I didn't mean to break your favorite mug the other day. I never apologized." But John and Jeana both knew she was apologizing for more than the mug. Jeana patted her sister-in-law's hand and gave her a forgiving expression.

We're not in the mood to drink, Jeana signed to John and Reid.

Ralleigha shook her head as she stood. "I need to get back home to my daughter. John, please take care of my husband while I'm away. Marissa and I are leaving in four days with the refugees who are going to Hagenhold. We'll be busy in Lovael."

"Of course," snarled John. "I'll take care of my brother, even though he's endangered my children and lied to me about that murderer. Not a problem."

Jeana grimaced. She leaned to kiss John's cheek, and then she opened the door to the children's bedroom and grasped Nymeria's arm. She signaled for their daughter to get up and follow her, and she leaned over the bed to gather their sleeping son in his blanket. Nymeria grabbed her pillow. John saw something else that glinted beneath it for a moment, but it was gone before he was sure he hadn't only imagined it. He pried the cork from the second bottle as he thought bitterly how much time he'd wasted not worrying over what to do with his daughter because he'd still expected his parents to arrive. When in fact, his brother had known they had been dead for two whole months.

Nymeria trudged into the study and walked straight over to her uncle. She gave him a hug. "Drinking won't fix your sadness," she said quietly. "But I'll forgive you this time. Next time, I'll bash your head with the first empty bottle I find, and you will know why." John laughed quietly to himself that such a sharp comment had come from such a young child. He was used to it, though it still amused him. His brother, he could tell, never grew used to her wit. "You should be with your family, not drinking. Both of you." She glared at John, too. "Father says men should not drink in their grief. It makes them do stupid, vengeful things."

John cringed at that. "Grieving men do stupid, vengeful things," he agreed. And he took another drink as he glared at her for turning his own words against him.

Reid stared after her as she left behind Ralleigha with her pillow clutched in her tiny hands, and they both looked up at Jeana as she signed to them a goodbye.

I'll be home with the children in two days. Have your heads clear then. Both of you.

Then she added one more command. *If my house is destroyed when I come home, you two are going to rebuild it by yourselves. Out of stone. And if you make me really angry, I will have you build two houses, one each. One of stone and one entirely of glass. And Ralleigha will not have a hand in your punishment. You will cast each piece yourselves. Your blisters and your sweat will create every crevice.*

Reid grimaced at that, but he did manage some broken semblance of a smile. The effort was there, anyway. "Of course. Yes, of course. Stones. Glass. Might as well be a temple, how expensive that could get. Ralleigha would certainly love to see us squirm at the heat of the rod."

Ralleigha exhaled sadly, and the women left both men to their grieving. "Reid's never been this way," Ralleigha whispered as the door shut behind them. John could still hear her through the door. "I'll make him *miserable* if he thinks he can become an alcoholic. I didn't marry a drunkard."

A long silence stretched between the brothers, aside from the occasional sloshing of the fluid in the bottles as first one brother drank and then the other.

"Why did you used to think Five Tower was a trade city?" John asked.

"What?"

"I am trying to be civil instead of using this bottle to break your ugly nose for lying to me," said John. "And I think I'm almost drunk. I'm a lightweight with alcohol, it doesn't take much. I said, why did you used to think Five Tower was a trade city?"

"Because I was an idiot." Reid bent forward to crawl to his feet. He staggered once he was on his feet. "*Melancholy*, you said? Stronger than it tastes," said Reid.

John gripped the half-empty bottle and pinched the bridge of his nose. He exhaled, trying to follow Reid's logic. "What made you supposedly stop being an idiot?"

"You remember when I wanted to leave home because they chose you to be their heir instead of me? Because you had more potential for the apprenticeship than I, and having a Black Temple doctor as a son was preferable to them to having a warrior as a son. Who wants their son to grow up to be a murderer when he could instead be a healer, after all?"

"I remember. You made it clear you wanted to go to Five Tower, and Dad wouldn't have any of it. That's the reason he cut you out of his will, not because they preferred me being a doctor to you being a dumbass." When Reid remained silent, John cut him a cold look. "Don't give me that," he said. "Why did you change your mind, anyway? The two of you argued until he was blue in the face, and I thought you might just run off and never look back. Made me angry that you would even consider it."

"Dad changed my mind. One of the things he said before I left. He'd bought Mom from Five Tower."

John sputtered at that and sat upright. "What the hell do you mean, *bought*?" He wiped his mouth.

"He never told you she used to be a slave."

John stared at his older brother.

"Yeah. That was my reaction. I still left, but because of that, I never went to Five Tower. He told me Mom went through the lowest rings. She was the only female who survived her year. He found her there and gave up most of his inheritance to get her out. They had only enough left for your apprenticeship."

"But he told me they met under the canopy of his grandparents' orchard back home. North."

"They did. But then slavers took her. She never talked about it. For years, Dad and I thought I was only your half brother. We both thought my real dad was some whoremongering bastard from Five Tower and that I wasn't really his firstborn son. I was just a dumb sixteen-year-old, twisted up with too much anger and pain when I left. I said some very harsh things to Dad that day because I felt as though they had told me about Five Tower only to make a point to hurt me. To let me know I wasn't really part of the family. After what I said to him, I didn't really deserve to be. I never really intended to come back at all. But a few years went by, and I finally got tired of wondering who my real father was. I paid for some tests from one of those Arsennian Keepers when I visited the place. We found out we had both been entirely wrong."

"Damn." John grimaced, and his brother shrugged.

"Yeah," said Reid. "It hurt a lot. All of it. But I made my way as an Enforcer, which meant they had the means to send you to Black Temple."

"Then why did you stay gone? You broke Mom's heart when you left. For the first couple of years, she cried every time one of us said your name."

"I climbed the ranks, initially intent on sacking Five Tower because I wanted them to pay for what they'd done to her. To all of us. I was good at fighting, but then I found out I was even better at investigating and leading . . . and then I had to choose between Ralleigha and my anger . . . I'm glad I am not part of the Alliance anymore, because it means I can stay home with my wife longer. And I get to see my daughter. But the lessons I learned have served me well. It taught me a better state of mind, and it paved the road for you to become who and what you are. Because I was out of the picture, they could focus on your education. You're a damned good field doctor. Wherever you go, every post doctor you work with pretty much lets you run the place from the moment you arrive. You've built an incredible reputation with all of them, and you know more than most of them. I'm sure you've saved more lives than I've taken, and that means a lot."

"I've killed men, too, Reid. I am not innocent. My hands are stained with blood. For a Black Temple doctor, it is sacrilege . . . And those tests were a worthless investment," said John. "Whoever you paid to run them had to have screwed up. A different father would explain why you're so much uglier than me." John whistled.

Reid stared at him. "Screw you, Momma's Boy."

John's mouth tilted into an irritated leer. "I still want to smash your bottle with this face — er . . . other way."

Neither spoke again for a long stretch of time. There was only the breeze outside stirring the branches, and then the first rumble of thunder groaned across the sky. Leaves quivered, and the screech owl above the rafters shared their quiet discomfort. Dust filtered down into the fading lantern light as the house seemed to stretch and groan. Sometime past midnight, Reid staggered to his feet again; the floorboards beneath him seemed to weep, the way they creaked.

"When you're ready, I'll show you were I buried them."

"Not too drunk to lead the way, are you?" John huffed.

Reid just stared at him. "Enough to stagger, not enough to be incapable. Who's the one who made that brandy again? Sits nicely. Easier than *Goldenrod*, almost as strong."

John didn't bother to lock the house, but Reid objected to it. "A proper drunk would never leave his house unlocked. Somebody would steal all his booze," said Reid as he made sure no one could slip in while they were gone. He struggled a while with the lock. "Don't you Black Temple doctors ever drink? Never sit around a fire with the men while I'm gone and celebrate my absence? Pretty sure I've never seen Nails drunk, either. And I think he's made for it. Right beard. Right belly."

He and John laughed at that image, both nearly losing their balance in the process.

"You're right," sniffled John. He barely managed to right himself. "But I don't usually drink myself senseless," said John. "I'll have you know, I've got too much responsibility to meddle with hangovers, same as you. Now get on with it. Where are they buried?"

"What did my niece pick up from under her pillow?" Reid asked suddenly. "I swore that was a knife in her hand."

"I saw nothing," said John. But he wondered. Briefly. Until he stumbled in the dark and began cursing over his stubbed toe.

"Oh, yeah," Reid said. He pulled out a flashlight and clicked it on. "Hey, don't you go cursing me. You start sounding a bit Aracanian when you get this mad, like Nails in one of his tirades. And I can't understand a lick of whatever it is you're saying. Just as bad as Nymeria with that other language I've heard from her. No wonder, she got that from you."

"Shut it, yeh windbag. Help me up."

"You've been around Nails and Mark too much."

A day and a half later, thanks to the extremely precarious trail that cut their trek nearly in half, Reid and John stood before two leaf-littered mounds in the middle of the forest. John's horse nudged him. He stumbled forward, and the reins slipped from his hand. The reality still hit him hard through the haze as his brother remained standing several yards behind him with his own dark horse.

John opened the bottle — the last half of which he'd saved for the site — and he drank deeply from it. He swayed where he stood, his head still throbbing from days before when Reid had struck him. The brandy sloshed about inside the bottle as he lowered it from his mouth, and he wiped his chin where it ran down. He had the impulse to throw the bottle, to smash it against something. But no amount of raging or breaking would lessen the grief he felt over having lost his parents and having been denied giving them a proper funeral. They were gone. They'd been abandoned to two shallow graves in the middle of nowhere, and he'd been a fool to think they were still coming.

Instead of drinking the last of the *Melancholy*, John poured it out, over the mounds. "A drink for the dead," he murmured. They needed it, he thought. "Couldn't need a drink more than if you found out you were dead. Isn't that right, Mom and Dad?"

"We buried them just after we caught Lukas," said Reid. "Couldn't stand the idea of carrion pecking away at them, or beasts dragging pieces of them off. The insult would have been worse than just having buried them here. Someday I'll dig them up and take them home, lay them to rest where they belong. Mom and Dad would have liked that. Davos didn't even get that much decency. The wolves got him."

Reid said nothing more, and John simply stood there, quaking. The bottle slipped from his fingers and cracked against a sharp rock that protruded from the roots there. Merely three months before, he'd discussed home with his parents. Of securing the future of his children and sending his parents back to the estate they'd lost, which he and Reid had only recently managed to buy back. The estate with the orchard, where his parents had first met. They had planned to build another outpost a few miles from their home so that he didn't need to travel so far, and he had intended to send a request to Saura to change his post. To assign him there rather than have him traveling every season.

His parents had wanted to start another plant nursery, and they had agreed to help with Nymeria until he could afford to take her to one of the Keeps where the specialists worked. Where the last remaining Modern World medical machines could run tests.

His family had finally had a home. And now his parents were dead. Gone. With no one to care for it, their home would become nothing but weeds and dead things. Like the rock at his feet, the house would probably be crushed and swallowed up by the roots of other things. Nothing would be left there but faint vestiges of what had been.

Home wasn't a home without them.

John pulled the torn letter from his pocket at last as he stood over his parents' graves. He held the letter up, but the words were too dark and blurry. Reid lit his torch since his flashlight had died, and he approached John so that the flickering light danced over the carefully scrawled script.

John knelt, his shoulders slumping forward, and his fingers threaded through his hair as the page crumpled slightly in his other fist. Reid said nothing as the sound of John's restrained grief raked their ears, and John could think of no words to say for their parents. Nothing. No last rites, no promises. He had just a feeling of loss, and of dread over the knowledge of having an uncertain future for their family. And his fears were worsened by that long letter, which he then read aloud, his voice quavering as he held both dreadful halves.

Gabriel:

This letter was drafted with urgency by a friend since I am currently unable to write it myself. If all goes as planned, then by the time you receive it, I should be able to contact you properly. Please understand, I would not have risked this method of communication but for the urgency of this news and the incredible uncertainty of my own survival.

To more important matters, I warn you Black Temple is in extreme danger. I am sorry I couldn't prevent this, but I have been preoccupied and severely compromised.

My disreputable allies in Five Tower intend to destroy the Temple and erase the Enforcers. They stole from me the knowledge that will enable them to do so, and already, I have seen the first parts of their plans set in motion. I can neither take back what they have stolen nor undo what they have already done. A great upheaval has begun, Gabriel. I am sorry for what it will cost us all.

Keep your distance from Five Tower. Caol and his sons are not to be trusted, and neither are the twisted hunters they made of some of their slaves. They will recognize you because of me. And do not believe the lies about the Bright Night.

We found another child in whom the Vael burns brightly, but the cortex within her is corrupt and has the potential to lay waste to everything around her, to cause a cataclysm the sort of which has not been seen for millennia. A member of your own guild now calls her Daughter. She is like

we are, the nature of her uniqueness visible in the color of her eyes. You
will know her instantly by the brilliant green, lit by heritage stranger than
our own. . . .

His voice shook. "I still cannot help but feel wrenching despair every time I think the girl
they found might have been Nymeria's mother," John admitted to his brother.

But Reid urged him on. "Keep reading. Nymeria draws the wraithlike beings Rhael and
Lukas described. One stood outside the kennels where the explosion occurred a month ago. I
glimpsed it — barely, but enough to know it was something living, not just part of the forest,
and not just part of the night. Others have seen those creatures, too. And on our way to Tallil,
Taiir and Manard and I discovered something we couldn't explain at an old ruin. It reacted
to one of those shards, like the damned thing activated it. More, the Taramine family owed
a debt to Gabriel and Rhael. They said one of those brothers was there the night before the
Cyan outbreak. He was badly injured. And the Taramines' son is special like Nymeria is. He's
got one green eye and one blue, both of which sometimes burn like flame when in shadow.
The kid knows things he shouldn't, just like Nymeria . . . I can't refute the claims of that letter,
John. Everything I've crossed so far supports it. All of it. And worse."

It was almost too much to take in. John didn't want to believe his brother, but he knew
Reid wouldn't have chosen to abandon his duties and then returned to finally face him with
an explanation composed only of paranoid lies or the second half of a letter that could never
be believed by logical men. Superstitious, gullible, easily frightened . . . *that* wasn't who Reid
was.

John returned to the letter.

But I warn you, Brother, she is more dangerous than even the worst of
our kindred. She draws the Dark Ones as though she has been scorched by
a thousand years of agony. She is very fragile, and she will need your help
since I am unable to provide it. The shadows of death and pain will stain
her and cause her to eventually lose her mind like the others before her. Do
not let them apprentice her to Black Temple, or the sickness that is in her
soul will soon fester again. She must be seen to properly and be removed
from the proximity of their professions. You are the only one who can mend
her. I beg you, return to your guild in haste. Keep her curse from devouring
her completely. She cannot be allowed to die because of it.

The letter shook in John's hand.

You will understand my enormous fear and great hope when you
analyze the glass and the vial of blood I have sent with this letter. Even
without your accusers' confessions, I am sure this might earn you a pardon
and spare your life. Do not let this curse consume her.

The Silver Ravens will fly from Tallil. I remember the sigil. I
remember the harvest moon and what it means to you to be denied the
right to properly mourn.

As a final aside, do not worry more over my life than over the life of
this child. Given time, I may be able to secure my own escape. If I do not
survive, this is what I know of my captor: I cannot name him, but he is an
Old One. I have not yet discerned his disastrous intentions, but they are
certainly far more disturbed than what the men in Five Tower plot to bring
about. The touch of darkness in him makes one even such as myself uneasy.

As for my location, I can only guess my prison to be within the Court of Feathers. It must be, for the courtyard I glimpsed bears the golden feather, and I saw the arbor of slate and granite and I heard a river. No other place could it be in my living memory.

Be ready. Protect yourself. You are the Dead One, not I. Remain true to that until you are free of this dangerous lie. And be careful, this master is the man you are accused of being.

Stay safe, Gabriel.

—— Rhael

The second half of that accursed letter crumpled in John's fist, and he took the torch from his brother. He wiped his eyes with the back of his sleeve, and then he returned to Reid both halves of the wretched message. "I still don't forgive you," he told his brother.

"I *am* sorry," Reid whispered.

"I know. Let's get home. I need another drink." He wiped his face with the back of his hand again, and he said a silent goodbye to his parents before he got on his horse. "We'll face our wives and Nymeria when our bereavement is done."

"You will," Reid muttered. "I may just elope and stay in hiding. Everyone else only sees Ralleigha's innocent side. The woman's a wraith in disguise, I swear it. Mom feared her. I never understood it until after I married her. I love her, but she can be a fright."

John laughed solemnly. "It's called a *wife*. They're all scary. Yours jus' happens to have red hair, too. Mine carries a pugio. Not just a regular knife. A damned pugio. Don't you know how many men she's killed with it? All of them were threats to our family, of course. But she's threatened me with it, too. Said she'd use it if I ever left her on account of death or another woman or whatnot."

"There you go, sounding Aracanian again."

"Oh, shut it . . . Where will you be going first? To find this Gabriel or Rhael person, I mean?"

"Balthora. I didn't find much in Tallil. The letter mentioned Gabriel hasn't been around Black Temple for a long time, but he is part of your guild. Or both of the brothers are."

"I've never met or heard of either of them," said John.

"Few have," Reid agreed. "They're very quiet, very elusive men. Hard to find. Almost impossible, from what I've learned, and Saura revealed no knowledge about them through Zacchary, even though that was part of my inquiry to her. It's possible even she is unfamiliar with them. They have been part of your guild since before she became the Lady of the Temple. That being said, it'll be difficult to find any other information on either of the brothers. But I've already learned what they look like, and some of my strongest leads point to Aelynhold. As I said, I was told the secret Keepers in Balthora have archives on old courts and sigils and the like. What is on that letter is the only other solid clue I have. I don't know what he meant by *flying the ravens* if he didn't mean sending a message or a signal of some kind. But the Court of Feathers is an actual location. Something I will find once I know exactly where to look."

"Did Lukas have the vial of blood or the stone when you caught him?"

Reid shook his head. "No. But Nymeria's had plenty of those shards. I imagine the one she gave me will work to get Rhael's or Gabriel's attention if I find one or the other of those brothers."

John sighed. "Most of this sounds mad. I can't grasp it, Reid. I can't. I am a man of logic, of things I can test for results or fix with my own hands. This is not in my path of understanding. It's not natural. It cannot be my daughter's illness. They *must* be wrong."

"I don't blame you for that. But if this cursed magic thing is true, it's worse than serious. And more immediate than the danger Black Temple is in. Mom and Dad wouldn't have had that letter if they didn't believe in it. They wouldn't have agreed to deliver it. You know Dad was a bigger cynic than Mom ever was. You could say something was blue, and they'd still give you that frickin' *eye* saying they wanted you to prove it."

"What else haven't you told me?"

"Lukas's master is trying to find Rhael as well. I got that much out of him. It was Rhael for whom he was searching when he got a hold of that letter. Some kind of ongoing feud that is worse than what Caol has started with the Alliance and Black Temple. With Rhael, the dispute was personal. And it all has something to do with this cursed magic thing. By that letter, it means absolutely everything has to do with Nymeria. If she gets worse, you may have to give her to Gabriel or Rhael. We don't really even know much about her from before, such as where she came from — "

"Nymeria is my responsibility," John snapped. "*My child*. And you would have me give her away?" His brother's words had touched a nerve, and before Reid could say another word in protest, John continued his rant. "I would never give her to anyone. Not to these brothers, not for any claim or curse or other crap. I don't care where she came from or what happened to her before. She is my daughter."

Reid recoiled. "Understood." He swung himself into his saddle and nearly toppled back out of it. "Easy does it," Reid told his horse as she pawed at the ground, and he gripped his left calf as though it still hurt him. The horse tossed her head as though to tell him to straighten himself already. She didn't seem to like the swaying weight that was upon her back. It was unfamiliar. "There, now." The horse calmed, and Reid looked at him. "Pick up your bottle," said Reid. "I'll get it to Ralleigha so she can repurpose it."

"Fine."

"You know, you're a sorry enough bastard even when your head *isn't* so far into your own job and your own worries," Reid said coldly. "If it comes to you giving Nymeria up to save her life, I'm not quite convinced she'll survive. Not with you making the decisions. And I wasn't suggesting you *give* her away to Gabriel, you idiot. Obviously, he's a doctor of some kind. I meant let him treat her."

John was about to open his mouth to defend himself again, but Reid already had another thing to say that he hadn't told him before.

"Taeryn's been missing since the night Mom and Dad were killed, by the way."

John frowned, so Reid explained.

"The driver of their carriage? What the hell, John? Pay more attention to the outside contractors in your employer's transport. That'll get you killed one day. Taeryn. He's been missing for two months now, and no one has seen him anywhere or heard from him. Zacchary found a bullet casing from a gun of the same caliber as the one Taeryn carried, and later Robert found the marred tree trunk that showed where he'd pulled the trigger, trying to shoot whoever had attacked them. We found enough blood there to know whoever had been injured should have been dead, but we found no body, and Taeryn was nowhere to be found. We never discovered whether the wolves dragged him off. We had already walked the area too much for Robert to read anything more."

"You mean Drunk Terry?"

"That's the one."

"Damn it. I'll have to let Saura know that as well when I see her."

CHAPTER TWENTY-SEVEN

GIFTS

REID STOOD BACK WHILE his daughter and his niece and nephew studied the books with the voracious appetites of children who'd discovered something new and wonderful. It was the first time he'd seen Nymeria truly smile in a long time. And his daughter Marissa was delighted to see her cousin so happy. They were poring through the ancient pages of an old work of fiction written by some obscure author.

The book was nearly a hundred years old, but the sketches in it were vivid and quite whimsical, and the tales within it were sweet. They told of dragons and riders, and of castles and adventurers. Even Jamie had taken to it, and he could hardly read his letters yet.

Reid pulled from his satchel three other gifts. "Marissa, come here for a moment."

His daughter looked up delightedly. "Daddy, these books are *wonderful*! We love them! Are you going to bring more when you come back?"

He nodded. "Come here, sweetie."

She rose from the dining room table, where Ralleigha had begun cleaning their dinner dishes away, but she gave Nymeria a long, inescapable hug first. "Thank you, Myria! Jamie said you asked him to get us books, too. I love you so much. You're the best cousin in the world! Did you see the one with the crystals? The pictures look *real*!"

Nymeria smiled shyly. "I'm glad you like them," she said. "I knew you would."

"The plants one is mine," Jamie chimed in. "I'm going to write *No Girls Allowed* on it."

Marissa laughed. "You can't even *write* yet. Just draw a circle on it, and then put your face there. We'll know it's your book if your face is permanently attached to it."

Ralleigha chuckled and kissed her daughter on the head. "Nice one, sweetie. You're such a clever little wit. You make me proud to be a mother."

Then Marissa rose and rushed over to her father, and she jumped up, into his arms. "Thank you, thank you, thank you, thank you!" she screeched.

Reid held out the ruby he'd taken in Edantine. "I've one last gift for you, little girl."

Marissa's eyes lit up. "What kind of glass is it? It's beautiful!"

"It's not glass at all," said Reid. "This here? It's a gemstone. A real one."

Ralleigha rolled her eyes. "That's what you tried to tell me when I asked what you'd brought. Some beautiful selenium ruby or chromic oxide for one of my finer bottles would have made me a very happy wife," she pouted. "But you forgot. You're too busy trying to spoil the girls."

Reid stuck his tongue out at her as he set Marissa back upon the floor. "It's still on the list, Ralleigha." He walked up to the table, and Jamie grabbed the book about plants and ran away with it. Marissa returned to her seat, where she placed the ruby on the gemstone book before her and spun the stone slowly to watch the light within it change. Reid placed the diamond upon the table and sat down in front of Nymeria. He took his glass from Ralleigha, who'd picked it up from the counter and handed it to him, and he drank from it. His head still hurt from the drinking he and John had done, but he did not complain. He just drank the juice his wife had prepared for him, and he went about the only normal family day he knew he would be able to have for a long time.

"What is it?" Nymeria asked. She was perplexed. "Another gemstone?"

"This one is a diamond. I took both gems from a crooked banker because he tried to steal your earnings."

Nymeria picked up the diamond. "My earnings?"

Reid placed the Cyan ring upon the table. "Your earnings," he repeated. "You've made a considerable amount of money with your lights, and there are a lot of customers waiting for more. This ring belonged to the Taramine family that ruled Cyan. Their son Michael is now to become an apprentice, and he didn't want the ring because their name is what got them killed." Michael had told Reid to melt it down when he had tried to give the boy the Taramine ring.

"Then why are you giving it to me?" Nymeria asked, perplexed. She picked up the ring and studied it. "Is that a tree?"

"Yes. Except for Michael, the Taramines are gone. Not even distant relations remain. Cyan itself is also gone, so another contract will never be made with or by the city which will require their signet. The ring is still an official signifier, however, and Michael signed a document giving you possession of the ring and all that it would accompany. After that, around the same time I took those gems from that corrupt banker in Edantine, I obtained a certified copy of an account where your earnings have been deposited. The document has been forwarded to Saura already, and it will remain in the archives there for safekeeping. It has been marked with the banker's ring, my own ring, and the Cyan ring, which is now yours, and only yours. Only you and your family will ever be able to access that account. Your brother could if you or your father gave him permission. But they don't even need to know about it. That is up to you to decide."

"Does that mean I don't have to be a doctor . . . ?" Nymeria was starting to cry. But the tears seemed to be joyous. Hopeful. "I really won't have to be?"

Ralleigha stopped washing the dishes. She hadn't known about the girl's aversion to her father's occupation. "Does John know she doesn't want to become a doctor?" she asked worriedly.

"He knows, all right," Reid said. "She has always made obvious her loathing of it. What would *actually* surprise me would be to find out he has no idea even Jamie doesn't want to be a doctor. That boy loves plants. But Jamie is more likely to get his way because . . ." He looked at Nymeria and changed what he was about to say. "Well, you know. *That.*"

"Can I look at yours?" Marissa asked as she picked up Nymeria's diamond. She was awed by the way the light changed colors, and by the beautiful, angled cuts. "Daddy, these gems are so beautiful! I want a bed made of them!"

Ralleigha burst into laughter. "Dear heavens, child! You would have to own the entire continent to afford such a thing. Let's just stick to one red ruby for you, and one diamond for your cousin."

"Rocks are stupid!" hollered Jamie from the study. "Plants are the future! Plants are alive!"

"He's dumb," sighed Marissa. She fanned herself and rolled her eyes. "What do you expect from a boy? No taste whatsoever." She climbed back up to sit by Nymeria. "We girls know what's really important. Isn't that right, Myria?"

Nymeria smiled and cupped her hands together as Marissa dropped the diamond there. "It's beautiful."

"Truly," agreed Marissa.

Reid was pleased that the girls were happy with their gifts. His nephew amused him the most, however, when he stole back into the room, knocked over the rest of the books, and chose another to disappear with. Jamie merely growled the entire time, like a young beast fighting for its newest, most favorited toy.

Reid was going to miss the kids.

He put his hand atop Marissa's head and roughed her hair up so that she fought him. "Stop!" she cried. "Momma! He's messing up my hair again!"

"Then bite him, you silly girl!"

Reid laughed. "*Bite me?* What are you teaching these girls, Ralleigha? We're still trying to get Nymeria out of that habit. Don't you remember what she did to Adam's hand?"

Nymeria ducked her head. "I told him I was sorry."

"He's still terrified of you. You've traumatized that man. He has a stress disorder now because of it. He pales at the sight of smiling children."

"Honey, I'm going to miss you so much," Ralleigha said. She slipped up behind him, wrapped her arms around him, and rested her chin on his shoulder. He leaned into her, appreciating the warmth and the closeness, and he grasped her arm and held her.

"I know. I would go with you and Marissa if I could. But I have to find him."

"I know," she said.

"Get a room," Marissa chimed, and Nymeria started laughing so hard she slipped from her chair, which cracked Marissa up. Jamie came rushing back to see what he'd missed, and he just stood there confused and pouting because he'd missed whatever had the girls laughing.

"What are you going to do with your earnings?" asked Reid when Nymeria finally managed to get herself righted. Marissa kept prodding her, trying to tickle her back out of her chair, but she defended herself well.

"Nothing yet. But I do have more hex lights for you to deliver. And thank you, Uncle Reid. I really appreciate your help. Thank you for caring. My father doesn't."

"Yes, he does," Reid said firmly. "Don't ever question how much your father loves you. Ever. He just doesn't know any other way. He wouldn't give you up in a million years, or for any reason. That's how much he loves you."

"Even if I get worse?" she asked.

The question struck him hard. She was too young to ask such a serious question, or to understand the meaning behind it. Yet she did.

It was a terrible thing.

"Even if you get worse," he agreed. "And if he ever made a mistake, Nymeria, or if you were taken away by anyone, I would come and get you myself."

"Would you adopt Nymeria so she could be my sister instead of Jamie's?" shrieked Marissa. She'd practically jumped onto the table in her excitement. "We could be sisters! I've always wanted a sister, Daddy!"

Reid blanked. He had no idea how to respond, but Ralleigha apparently did. She burst into another fit of laughter and then took her time to answer. "There are other ways to get a sister, you silly child. For one, you could just wait. But yes, we would always adopt your cousin. I would in a heartbeat if John and Jeana were ever in trouble. She's a delight. And I would have no problem with her biting people as long as it wasn't me her teeth sank into."

"No sister would ever be as good a sister as Nymeria," Marissa beamed.

Jamie yawned and made a face. "Sheesh. You've never had to sleep in the same room as her. She's scary at night. Her stories make me wet the bed. I get too scared to get out of bed at night because of them."

Marissa cracked up. "You're such a wimp. I love scary things. Her nightmares are awesome! And besides that, you're afraid of *grasshoppers*, you little weirdo! Of course, you can't handle her if you can't handle a grasshopper."

"You are both weird," Nymeria sighed. "But I'm glad you are all my family. I could have had worse. Or I could have had no one."

Reid said nothing to that. Neither did Ralleigha. It would never be their place to tell her where she'd come from.

It seemed as if she didn't even remember anymore, even though it had only been a couple of years since John and Jeana had rescued her from Five Tower.

CHAPTER TWENTY-EIGHT

JOHN GLANCED INTO THE side mirror, back to the rest of the envoy behind him. The armor on the main vehicles was thick enough to keep most any injury at bay, but their field of vision was limited here. The land buckled and curved, but there was no other way to get to Raven Trail, which led directly to Isold. The ancient levies which stretched on for miles were no longer suitable to drive over, and at only one place where they had crumbled away could they be crossed covertly. The opening the envoy would need to cross was in Oakwall, and that was still several days away. It was far enough that traveling toward it always risked drawing unwarranted attention, especially with the loud rumbling that came from the vehicles, and with the dust they kicked up about them. And there was that unattractive smell of burning fuel.

The only thing in their favor was the darkening of the skies and the ever-increasing thunder. A storm would provide excellent cover. The rain would prevent clouds of dust and cover shallow tracks, and the fierce winds would cut the smell of campfires and prevent the circling of any scavenger birds hoping for scraps from the hunting along the trail.

Nymeria put her hand on the glass and rested her head there as she stared out at the passing trees and broken old buildings. John imagined she was thinking of the people who used to live in those buildings, that she was letting her imagination run wild with both beautiful and unnerving things.

The way her fingers pressed into the top ledge of the door panel when the wolves began to howl again told him she *truly* didn't like the look of the decrepit structures they passed.

Riding ahead of them on horseback, Wylem was arguing heatedly with one of the Enforcers who had come to Crow Post to assist them during the traveling season. The Enforcers had recently been recalled from a village called Anarat, and Wylem was accusing them of cowardice for it. Captain Makam — a lean, grizzled man with a cold, severing smile and a scar crossing his lips from nose to chin — was not taking kindly to Wylem's objections.

The captain was the Enforcer Reid had attacked in the tavern in Crow Post.

John grew more uneasy about the tension between the two guilds. If Wylem kept it up, a fight was sure to break out. Apparently, he hadn't received Reid's instruction not to provoke any suspicious Enforcers for fear of losing the support of those who were still loyal to the Alliance's true code of ethics.

John turned his attention back to his daughter in the seat beside him; he'd had no better luck in communicating with her. "Tell me again the different stitches for a suture," he said to her. She didn't respond.

The engine roared as he pressed the gas to urge the wheels over the rocks. They were far too exposed here, he thought, but the woods were growing denser by the mile. While that meant better cover, it also meant less visibility and less maneuverability.

Another peel of thunder sounded from the heavens. It echoed for a long moment, like a slowly moving avalanche. The horses were spooked by it, and Wylem pulled back, anger flashing hotly across his face as he retreated from the smirking group of unsavory Enforcers under the captain's command. Wylem was attempting to help John and Mark and Robert fill the gap Reid had left in his absence. But none of them were Reid, and none commanded the same results or the same respect. Reid had a way of pulling others together that neither John nor the other present members of his guild possessed.

"You are worried," Nymeria observed.

"That's a gross understatement, Myria. This journey is often perilous. This year, we're so late getting out that the weather is starting to turn on us. The wolves are staying just out of sight, too, as if they're waiting for the first idiot who goes off on his own. And — "

"You are worried because Uncle Reid left."

His grimace carved itself deeper. He studied the piers where something flashed in the shadows beneath. There used to be bridges and boats and floating cities around that area. Now, nothing but barely moist marshland stretched for hundreds of miles — save for the rivers that cut across it. And numerous caves pitted the rocks where the shallows used to be.

"Your uncle is busy," he said. "He's been called away for some important errands. The stitches, Myria."

"Continuous, simple interrupted, mattress, and subcuticular," she said coldly. "The stitches." She stared out at the wasteland, where the grasses rose in a sea of gently rolling green, where flocks of birds started and then settled and vanished in the undulating color. Where some of the wolves prowled day and night. Where soon the late spring rains would flood again, until the tops of the massive, centuries-old cypress trees currently dotting the winding fields were all that were visible.

"There used to be so much more water here," Nymeria said. John noticed the pensive note in her voice.

"One of your uncle's books tell you that?" He looked at the two old books she had put in the floorboard. They lay atop his medical journals as though to keep the journals out of sight. She'd devoured the writing in the older books with a fervor that had surprisingly upset him.

John's gaze flicked to the fuel gauge for a moment and then returned to the rough, broken road that stretched before them. The vehicle groaned, and the sloping ground hissed as he maneuvered around the trees that had grown through the old concrete there.

He had no idea why she was interested in a stupid book about the types and properties of all the kinds of rocks, stones, gems, and soil. It irritated him to no end to discover she wanted to read about geology, which was next to worthless, when she could be learning more of his field to secure her future and help a lot of people.

The other book was an affront to him altogether. It was as though Reid had deliberately done it, giving her access to such obsolete material. Computer chips, drones, programming, communications, energy production . . . What the hell had Reid been thinking? And the book was humongous. It was *far* ahead of her comprehension level. It was beyond the comprehension of most anymore. And yet it seemed to be the most precious gift she'd ever beheld, the way she'd pored over it night after night, day after day.

"*Nai*," she said, bringing him back to her comment about the water. "I have seen it."

He tried not to roll his eyes and tried not to feel uncomfortable over what she'd said. "Sure, you have." He didn't understand how she could be so matter of fact, as though she knew she was right.

She was always so sure of things, and John always struggled to remind her that she was still a child. That adults were to be listened to. Especially mothers and fathers.

"What do we usually use for the sutures? And where do we get it?"

Nymeria wasn't finished with him, though. "You're upset because Uncle Reid wouldn't stay so that he could come with us. It has something to do with me, doesn't it?"

John took a deep breath, and his fingers gripped the steering wheel. "We don't need to go into this right now," he said. "It has nothing to do with you, and there is nothing to be worried about. I said he was called away."

"I'm not the one worried. You are." She turned her green eyes upon him for a moment, too intelligent not to see through his defense, and then she shook her head and stared out the window again. "He will be okay. So will we. Isold is just a week away, remember? You said that yesterday."

"As long as Wylem doesn't provoke these Enforcers," he grated.

"I don't like the one with the scar," she agreed.

"The Enforcer?" John asked. When she nodded, he added, "That's Captain Makam."

"I don't like him. Or those three officers he talks to all the time. They keep hanging around grandma's murderer, just like that girl from Edantine. Every time we stop to camp, that's where they go."

John clenched his teeth. How had she known about these tidings and he hadn't? "Every night we camp, you say?" When she nodded and laid her head back against the glass, he tapped the steering wheel. He would deal with that later tonight.

"He's a killer, and a good liar," she said coldly. "He's already learned a lot because of them. But they keep telling him more."

"He's gagged. How can he ask them anything?"

"He knows sign language."

John refrained from swearing aloud. "How do you know?"

"I've watched." Nymeria then sighed as if she was impatient with him. "You would learn more if you stopped running in circles and watched, Father. Instead, you assume, and then you get angry when you are the last one to find out what everyone else knows."

"*Does* everyone else know?"

"Not everyone. But Wylem does. He's been watching them closely. That's part of why he doesn't like them."

"Why else doesn't he like them?"

"Because he doesn't like any Enforcers. Those four are worse, though. I like the others, the ones in the back. They're nice. But they have to obey Makam."

"Fair enough," he said. "I'll speak with Wylem tonight, and I'll make sure Robert and the others know to watch him."

For a long, silent moment, John contemplated what it might mean if the captain turned out to be a traitor in his own guild. The idea was unsettling. For now, he decided, it was better to be aware and to watch the Enforcer to see what all he had his hands in.

"If anything happens," John said at last, "stay out of the way and just observe. And no more running off, unless I tell you to. Which I won't. Unless your life depends on it."

She looked at him again, and this time she was angry. "*Really?*"

He almost laughed at her, but the situation was too severe. When lightning shot brilliantly across the sky, he looked up. A strong gust of cold wind rushed them, bringing the smell of wet earth from just ahead of them.

"Nymeria, you're not old enough to be an apprentice yet," he said honestly. "I'm not ready to give up my only daughter, either. But if Saura decides she wants to have you taken on for an early mentorship, I will be unable to do anything about it. She knows intelligent children when she sees them. And you, Nymeria, you blow them all out of the water. But you're still a child — *my child*. I'm not yet ready to send you off to train. And I will never admit how smart you are again, so wipe that ridiculous little smirk from your face. This is not the time to let your ego catch fire. Your uncle has done enough harm there, as it stands. You're too independent and willful for your age."

Nymeria's expression soured, and she clutched the seatbelt. But she said nothing and seemed to at least be listening.

He thought of the second half of the letter his brother had given him, and his insides curled sickly. "Do not tell anyone a word of that crazy stuff you've been scaring your brother with. You know what I mean. About those dark creatures. And if you start acting strangely, and others ask questions, just tell them it's Tourette's. Okay? It's nerves. You're not crazy, you're not cursed, there is no magic, and you don't see things that aren't there. No one will believe if you do, anyway, and saying otherwise could ruin your future. If Saura or anyone at the Temple thinks you aren't mentally sound — "

"But — "

"Zip it, okay?" John asked. "This is important. You *are* special. But let's play it down so your quirks don't draw the wrong sort of attention. Okay?" He glanced at her as she pouted. "No more imagining. I don't want a word of it coming back to me through anyone at Isold or Black Temple. And if I catch you with even *one* more of those glass shards, I will tan your hide. Do you hear me? And you can tell your mother afterward, I don't care. Jeana will not oppose me in this. She already agreed that you are to stop disobeying us, and that you are to learn to discipline yourself. You have the mental capacity for strict focus already, which puts you leaps and bounds ahead of other apprentices and attendants several times your age."

"How about you just shut up and keep pretending to be a considerate adult," she exploded hysterically. John's mouth fell open, but she held up her hand to silence him. "And how about you let me pretend to be listening while I pretend to be a kid who is pretending to be normal. I don't care if Mother knows, or if Mother agrees!"

"Nymeria!"

"Father!"

John forced his frustration down as he backed off. Arguing with a five-year-old, he reminded himself, was already an impossible thing, usually. Most adults lost against most five-year-olds and then just told themselves they'd won. It was easier that way.

Yet his daughter had to offer the most difficult battle of them all. It was much harder to win against a child with higher logic and an even more intense stubborn-headedness — she also happened to be more difficult to distract than other five-year-olds. And she had a knack for creating distractions that ensnared even him.

He loved her, but moments like these just made his teeth crack.

Nymeria picked up the book Reid had given her, the one about technological advancements, and she opened it deliberately, as though to tell him the conversation was over.

The first drops of rain began to fall as the envoy settled into camp among the ruins of a long-dead city. The horses had been tethered in various broken buildings where the walls could protect them from the predators who were still on the prowl, and fires had flared up at intervals where individuals had grouped with favored familiar faces.

John had ordered Lukas and his cage to be removed from the back of the truck which had been traveling several vehicles behind them. He'd had the murderer placed in a dark corner among a pile of rubble where the last vestiges of a garage pointed skyward and made its failing stand against nature. As the rain fell harder, bits of rubble groaned over Lukas's cage. The prisoner had no shelter against the elements.

The man was gagged and hidden in shadow, and no one could visit him without Robert, or Wylem, or John, or someone from their guild knowing. John had also had a sack tied around Lukas's hands so that he couldn't sign, either, and Wylem had discreetly pointed out the captain's attempted secret visit as well as the displeasure upon the man's face when he'd seen what had happened with Lukas's hands.

The Edantine girl had never appeared to try a visit, however. She'd likely only been the victim of a mild case of curiosity, anyway. It was unlikely Lukas had managed to corrupt her the way he'd tried with those refugee boys in Crow Post. She was a very strong-minded child.

Ellie Mae sighed, fiddling with her radio. "You know, I really was wrong about these. I was mad when your daughter took the radios, but I haven't had to charge the battery once since she's done it. The storm doesn't affect its range the same, either."

Wylem grew interested. "The girl fixed them? Were they broken?"

"No, they were fine," said Ellie. She turned the dial on the radio until some semblance of music came out of it. "Hear that? That's from a music station. A *music station*. My grandma used to tell me there was a place somewhere near Virien, an old building that still played tunes on a loop. Never knew what gave the place power, but she'd heard it when she was young, when this junker came through, trying to sell his stuff. He'd told her it always played when he passed through. She never could get that stupid radio to work after he left, though. . . . I'm surprised the station is still playing music. Never thought she'd told the truth about that place. I just thought it was another of her tales."

"It does sound a bit like music, doesn't it?" Mark said. "Color me intrigued. Mine's worked better than it ever did, too. I used to have problems with it. We've been testing the reach over the last two an' a half months."

"Good news?" asked Wylem.

Mark nodded. "The kid's a bleeding genius. We counted seven miles' distance, even in that strong storm that blew through Crow Post five weeks ago. Used to be only one to four on a good day."

Ellie smirked. "Remember how angry I was?" John just shrugged and took another sip of the disgusting coffee. "I shouldn't have complained. Nails was right that I should have let them be. I shouldn't have been so angry. I hope I didn't scare her over that. She's talented. She could make a living at it."

John felt his face twist unpleasantly. "Don't give her any ideas. Her future is decided, Dr. Mae."

"Just saying. If she wanted to make some extra money on the side to build something for herself, or even to improve the guild's standing, she could do that as well. She could help a lot of people."

John glared at the mortician. "Stay out of it, I said."

The others looked between the two, and a heavy silence fell as Ellie Mae backed off.

"So. Ender's Creek tomorrow, eh?" asked Mark. "Scouts said the waters are high but not uncrossable yet. We're lucky this late in the season. Rains held back much longer than usual." He'd settled at the fire and was sharpening his knives again. He'd always favored occupying himself that way when nothing else was to be done. Reid had taught him well, to keep his blades sharp and himself alert. Because of it, he'd saved John's life during the last season, when a wanderer carrying an unpleasant disease — his mind gone — had attacked them off the beaten path.

"Very fortunate," John said as he pulled the coffee pot from over the fire and poured himself another cup. He was going to be taking watch tonight, and he didn't want to do so without the boost. The coffee was hideously gross again, as Mark had made it. But it was worse when Taiir made it. Thankfully, Taiir was with Reid and couldn't burn it any worse. "But yes, Ender's Creek is next. We'll receive the last apprentice haul for the season without incident, hopefully. And if it keeps raining like this, we may just be stuck in Isold for a few months. Otherwise, we'll have to take a boat back home."

Mark snickered. "You can't swim?"

John shrugged. "Nope. Fear of deep water. But it doesn't matter if I'm not anywhere I'd need to be taking a boat."

Wylem paced about behind them, watching for Enforcers. Whenever he saw even one, he would snarl and reach for his sword, and the Enforcer would leave.

"Wylem, stop chasing them off," John said. "Not all of them are suspicious."

"They're all suspicious to me," said Wylem. "I don't like any of them. Not one. They shave their heads funny, leaving nothing on the sides and too little on the top. Most of them have babies' chins, they shave so close, and they have weird rules. They're all unworthy of trust. A man's beard is a man's pride, John. No beard, no pride, no trust."

"I'm clean-shaven most of the time, too, Wylem. So is my brother. Just like the Enforcers."

"Sometimes you and your brother have a little patch on your face after traveling. So sometimes you're a little trustworthy," countered Wylem. The men snickered. "I'm serious. Those Enforcers are not *men*."

Robert laughed, smacking Wylem on the shoulder as he walked toward them to join them. He took a seat near the fire. "Wylem, you're sore as always, I see. Are you going to take them all on by yourself again? We're bored of just watching you growl at them and touch your sword oh, so much."

John glared, and Mark and Ellie Mae snickered. "Stop trying to provoke him into starting a fight with them. They are our allies."

"They're *your* allies," grunted Wylem. "I will gladly fight them. All of them. You cowards can sit here and relax."

"Cowards, now?" laughed Robert. "Aww. Go on and touch that sword again, big guy. I might shiver in fear. Cry to myself after."

Mark cracked up again.

Wylem smirked, and he raked his boot across the log Robert sat upon, causing it to roll. Robert nearly fell but caught himself.

The rain fell harder as they huddled under the shelter of rusting, corrugated sheets of metal which hung over the piles of rubble and murky old glass. The fire flickered madly for a moment as the wind gushed in. Then the direction changed as the storm continued to rage outside.

"Ender's Creek tomorrow," said Wylem as at last, he settled himself at the fire. He was convinced he'd kept any Enforcers from joining them in their makeshift shelter, although there was room for twenty more. "We've one last haul of apprentices to run back from Lirien and Virien. We'll split at the fork and should meet again just past the riverbend. Should be separated from the main envoy for just two hours if they've already sent the kids to the waypoint. So you won't have to wean yourself from my love for long, Robert. You and your *crying* after I play with my sword *oh so good*. Don't you forget, a gentleman buys his lady dinner first."

"Who's the gentleman, me or you?" cackled Robert. "You're the one with the longer hair — even if it's only on your face and not your balding crown."

"I'll be whichever gets me a free meal in an expensive town," smarted Wylem. "You're paying."

John laughed. The innuendos among the men seemed never-ending during their journeys. Wylem usually remained latent with his comments until he'd been prodded a few times by Mark or Taiir. This time it was mostly Robert.

It was certainly a brotherhood all of them appreciated.

"So what were you an' Makam arguing about this morning?" asked Mark. "An' don't go getting mad again. I don't want to be dodging or taking cover when your roar brings them to fighting with us."

"Ah. I told Makam the plan, and that coward said they wouldn't be joining our temporary departure from the main envoy. Even though some of his men had previously come from Virien because they'd been withdrawn — which also means we won't have any reinforcements to or from Virien. The withdrawal was under the High Commander's orders. *Re-appropriation of resources*, they'd called it."

"So they're expecting us to share our rations, but they do not have to do their job?" asked Robert.

Wylem snarled. "Of course. And Makam has ordered the rest of the Enforcers to sit on their arses if anything goes down. He told me any conflicts would be our problem, that it isn't their responsibility."

That displeased John greatly. "It is tempting to threaten the captain, but we should not. The fact that they are with us at all is still a hell of a deterrent to anyone who would think to attack us. Thanks to Saura's modified Summons, we've actually got valuable items with us this year. A robbery would be most unfortunate at this time."

Robert rolled his eyes, and when he turned his head, the tattoos on his scalp seemed to slither in the shadows as if they were alive. "Yeah. Well, your brother could have gotten away with speaking or thinking like a pacifist. But you're not Reid. The commander knew what buttons to push. He wasn't afraid of offending them. He would threaten to make them take off on foot on their own instead of hitching a ride with us no matter the valuables we were carrying. These Enforcers don't want to do their job but want to take our rations without exception. It's uncalled for."

"It is ill enough that the Enforcers haven't prepared themselves for this journey," said Wylem. "It speaks volumes about Makam's poor leadership. John isn't much of a negotiator, but he is a damned good prepper. And he cares about everyone's health, not just the lives of his own. But his temper is something I've learned not to try to provoke. I only hope Makam has enough sense to realize that, and before I have to gut him to keep John from doing *worse*."

Mark laughed wickedly. "Yeah, I'll admit that, too. John, you really are worthless at negotiating. There, we've all said it."

John shrugged. "I negotiate with the Maker every morning I wake: *Give me the strength not to smack Mark in the head again for his dumbass remarks.*" The men snickered when Mark scowled at him. John held up his cup and toasted them. "Just like this nasty coffee. Every day, I negotiate with my taste buds, begging them to die so drinking this burnt crap isn't so atrocious. I'll have cancer in my gut in a few years because of it." He took a swig and choked on it, and he felt his face contort in awful ways. The men just laughed.

"It'll keep you awake, though," said Ellie Mae. She'd kicked back and shut her eyes, and now she smirked. "Function before flavor," she added.

"That's . . . Ooh." Wylem cleared his throat. "Robert, handle your woman. I'm not touching that comment."

"Nah, just your sword. All the time. You have problems, Wylem. You need a counselor."

More laughter ensued when Wylem blushed at last. He just shook his head at them and refused to reply.

"If we sent the captain off, he'd order his whole outfit with him," said John, turning the conversation again. "That would be bad for us if we crossed anything more serious than wolves. I think, ultimately, the captain will do his job in the event of an attack because it would jeopardize their lives also if they did not act. Nothing short of a traitor would ignore his sworn duty."

"I think he's a traitor," Wylem growled.

"He is," Nymeria said behind him. Wylem and Robert had both forgotten her presence, and her comment startled them. Robert fell from his log; Wylem nearly came out of his skin.

John noted she held what almost looked like a sliver of glass. "What is that?" he asked gravely.

It vanished. "What is *what*?" she asked. She stared hard at him, as though daring him to try to find it. Then she turned the page of that damned book she held. The medical journals were nowhere to be seen.

The horses grunted as though they had been spooked, but there was no thunder to have caused them the uneasiness. He frowned, but he heard nothing else.

John opened his mouth to speak again, but Nymeria's head snapped up. She was looking outside, as though she'd been startled by . . .

Then the rest of them heard it. It was a guttural sound, and vicious. The creature had come upon them without any other warning. Rainwater dripped from its oily coat, and its bloodstained fangs glistened in the firelight. Its golden eyes stared at the child hungrily as it approached, one dangerous step at a time.

Nymeria stood slowly — but instead of backing away, she also moved forward. One dangerous step at a time.

John's hand reached for his belt — but his gun was in the truck. He took a breath to call out to her. "Ny — "

But he was interrupted by Ellie Mae, who'd already drawn her bow and stepped forward. "Shhh . . ." Ellie Mae said urgently.

Nymeria was snarling back at the wolf, her fingers curled. If the child had been a wolf herself, her hackles would have risen, and her tail would have been low. Her ears would have been back, and her teeth would also have been dripping saliva. It was the oddest thing he'd ever seen her do, and yet, with his heart in his throat, he couldn't even cry out. All he could think was that the animal was going to kill his daughter in front of him, and he'd left his gun in the truck.

The wolf lowered its belly to the ground as though it was going to pounce. Nymeria did the same, and she hissed something animal-like to the creature.

The black creature stopped just as Ellie had drawn an arrow.

"What the . . . *hell* . . . ?" Robert said quietly.

The creature side-stepped Nymeria, circling her, but it seemed to calm as she turned with it, never putting her back to it. Nymeria stepped forward again, and the beast quivered and sank lower. It cringed from her when she reached out to touch it. The contact was brief.

Nymeria looked away, frowning. "She doesn't want to hurt us," she said. "She's lonely."

John was as speechless as the rest of them when the wolf stopped snarling and its tongue lolled from its mouth. The creature laid down next to his daughter, shivering, and its tail began to wag nervously. And then Nymeria did the next most outrageous thing. She gave the creature the blanket she herself had been wrapped in. The wolf snuggled closer to her and laid its head on its paws.

Ellie lowered her bow as the giant creature whined. "Uh . . . John . . . ? I'm not sure if I should kill it."

"Me neither," said Robert.

Wylem's head cocked sideways. "That's a wolf. A real one . . . That's not a dog." He couldn't seem to process what he was seeing. "John, your daughter just tamed a wolf. It's a giant wolf. He could eat her in one gulp."

"She," Nymeria corrected. The girl then settled back to her book and placed her hand upon the wolf's giant black head. The creature's tongue ran across its teeth and nose, and it yawned. Its ears pricked backward and twisted about, listening to every sound about them. The beast seemed only to trust them because of Nymeria. Its tail ceased its nervous wagging and curled up under the creature's belly. The tail flopped occasionally after.

"That wolf just let her put a blanket on her," said Wylem.

John's heart was still beating furiously in his ears.

"There's a really big rabbit under the back tire, if you're still hungry, Dr. Mae," Nymeria said nonchalantly, turning the page as she read on. The wolf took a great, deep breath and sighed. Then the creature nudged Nymeria's hand, whining.

"Um . . ." That was all John could manage.

"By the storm, there is!" Ellie laughed. She released the arrow. The giant hare hopped once and fell, dead, her arrow sticking out of its eye. It had been a nearly perfect shot.

The wolf didn't even bother to take interest. It just closed its eyes and went to sleep.

"I seem to remember that she wasn't afraid in the kennels, either," Robert said thoughtfully. "Looks as though we've got a new dog trainer. The search is over."

"I don't want to be a dog trainer," said Nymeria.

Wylem began to laugh. Then so did Robert and Mark. At first it was soft, a ripple of disbelief. Then it turned into a fit of raucous humor. "That wolf is almost as big as your truck!" exclaimed Wylem.

"I'm at a loss," John admitted. He threw his hands up in the air, and he gave up. "Don't even ask me to explain it."

"Maybe she had an owner once," said Wylem as he seated himself to watch the wolf in case it suddenly became feral again. " Hell. I'm in need of some music. Robert! They tell me you're a singer and a meddler in music."

"No!" cried Mark. "He's already got the stupid thing with him! He didn't even leave it in the bed of their truck."

Wylem smirked as Robert opened the case and removed a stringed instrument that had a set of keys across its face. "What sort of instrument is that? I've seen flutes and strings before. That looks old."

"It's a hurdy gurdy," Robert shrugged. "My fiancée, here, was so terrible at it that she gave it to me. A killing blow is all the music she can play with a string."

"True," said Ellie Mae. "His fingers make magic with that thing." She'd grabbed the rabbit at last, still wary of the wolf, and she gutted and skinned it. "But mine make magic with knives." She flashed her gutting knife and then wiped the blood from it and sheathed it. "That's why I'm a mortician and he belongs in a ballad's tights."

Wylem cracked a grin. "Sing for us."

"What do you want?" asked Robert.

"Anything is better than that beast's whining."

"Well, being that she's taken the spotlight tonight, I heard Nymeria and Marissa humming a song once. Could never get it out of my head, so I meddled with it — "

"Don't you dare play that creepy song, you — "

Robert threw his hands in the air when Ellie Mae drew her knife and sent it hurtling into the log, where it imbedded in the wood right between his thighs — a few centimeters lower than would have cut him. "*Woman!*" Robert shouted, pale as smoke.

"Sing that one," Mark laughed. "She's no longer got the knife!"

Robert eyed Ellie Mae and gripped the hurdy gurdy. "You almost took my manhood from me! I'm playing the song!"

"Don't play it," Nymeria said.

Only John seemed to have heard her, though. Robert struck a few chords as he adjusted the strings, and then the tune began.

It was, indeed, quite creepy. The melody was ghostly. Yet the words were worse.

As Robert sang, John no longer wondered why the song had upset those grieving refugee mothers in Crow Post — the ones whose children Ellie had prepared for burial.

"Sleep as if dead
And burn in bright flame.
Reach out to the dreams and remember the cursed man's name.
He will hear you; he will find you · · ·
For memories of monsters
Awakens a demon.

"Blood will change
And Mother will know
The black in our bones as great sorrow flows · · ·
And our mourning
And our pain
Are memories of monsters · · ·
That
Awaken the demon.

"So sleep as if dead
And face not the lies.
Oh, sleep as if dead
In your grave of bright fire.

"And when you wake, show the devil our home.
Show the demons the black in your soul.
Remember the dead man's name
Oh, cleanse with blue fire.
All sins cast into bright and violent flame · · ·"

John had enough. The song was worse than Ellie had described. He considered what else he could go and do to prepare for tomorrow, and he stood to leave — he realized Nymeria was gone. So was the large wolf.

"Nymeria?" he called. The anxiety he'd felt earlier returned. That creature had behaved so unnaturally with his daughter that he wasn't beyond believing it might have turned on her just as suddenly as it had appeared or been calmed.

But there was no blood, and neither had made any other sound.

Yet her book lay upon the dirt, the wind turning the pages.

John strode out into the rain after her, and he caught a glimpse of a small form walking away from their shelter when lightning flashed overhead brightly. The trees bowed over, and mud sucked at his boots as he followed her. She returned to the truck, and the door slammed behind her.

He tried to open the door, but she'd locked it.

The wolf's paw prints led away, back to the forest around them. "Nymeria?"

He realized he heard her crying.

"Leave me alone!" she said. "Go away!"

"Nymeria, please open the door!"

"*Nai!*"

"Open the door! What's wrong?"

"I don't want to ever hear that song again!" she said. "It made me remember bad things!"

She wouldn't open the door.

"Bad things?" He wiped the rainwater from his eyes. "What do you mean, bad things? Just open the door!"

He could hear her crying, but she still wouldn't open the door, and he didn't have the key. He'd given it to her earlier when she'd gotten their supplies for the camp.

John pulled upward on his hair, frustrated. His forehead touched the glass, and he tapped the window again with his palm. She refused to change her mind still, and John finally let go of the handle. "Fine. I'm going back. When you're ready to talk, I'll be with the others, okay?"

"I'm not coming back!"

"You're going to get cold. The fire is warmer."

"I don't care!"

He didn't know what else to do or say to console her.

CHAPTER TWENTY-NINE

THE STORM ABATED an hour before dawn. The first rays of warmth broke through the clouds and the old ruins, and the chirping of the birds became a loud and noisy chorus. All that remained of the angry weather from the night before were gently cascading veils of mist and the pitter-patter of water droplets still gathering and rolling from the leaves and the ledges.

John's eyes felt full of sand. He'd kept watch all night, and now, as he yawned, he shut his eyes tightly against sleepiness and rubbed away at the stinging that blurred his vision. He'd roasted another fistful of coffee beans to near perfection, crushed them, and brewed them, and now his mouth watered at the smell. At last, a decent pot of coffee hung tantalizingly close to him, and it was nearly done. It was well worth the damp clothes and cold breeze. And it was all his, because the men were still asleep.

He kicked Wylem's foot. "Sun's coming out," John said. "Late start today."

Wylem sighed. "I know. I was thinking about that killer you've got locked up. He still looks a bit rough." That was because John's fist had fractured some of the bones in Lukas's face. "You would have killed him, wouldn't you? Who stopped you? Your brother?"

John said nothing. Lukas was shivering in his sleep. Even from across the enclosure, John could see it. He smirked. The cage had been placed perfectly under the opening in the roof, letting the bastard suffer the entire night. The rain had washed most of the smell of him away, too, so it had been a doubly wise decision.

"Don't even think it," said Thomas, who strode into their small camp. "The look on your face," Thomas explained as he reached for the hanging coffee pot. "I can see the wheels turning. He's my responsibility, John. I don't want you to even look at him."

John raised his hands guiltlessly. "No further scheming here, Thomas. I've attacked enough of our own men over him. I'm only wishing the weather hadn't begun to warm yet. The bastard would have suffered some more. Frost on the ground instead of dew would have been most satisfying."

Thomas gave the coffee pot to Wylem as John reached for it. He became aggravated at that because he hadn't brewed it to share. The others were rising now, on account of the smell of it, and he was determined to have some before it was gone. But Wylem gave it to Mark, who then gave it to Robert and Ellie Mae.

The damned thing had only a quarter of a cup left when he got it back, and too little time remained to brew more. As it was, his supply of beans was running low.

It was possible he would have to resort to dandelion root coffee —though the flavor of that was nice, it had no caffeine in it. Dandelion root coffee was therefore worthless at waking him or giving him the burst of energy he needed after a long night on watch. It was more of an herbal tea, and he was not a heavy tea drinker.

John growled. "That's the first decent pot of coffee that's been made in this camp all week, you worthless scoundrels," he muttered as he stared at the dregs in his cup. There was no filter, and he hated getting the last cup. The first half of the pot was always the best.

"Mmm," said Mark and Robert. "That is nice. What'd you add?"

John snarled and emptied his cup into the fire, and he got up. "It's not a matter of adding, Mark. If you cleaned the burn from the pot first, and didn't burn every bean you touched, you'd be making the same quality."

"Doubt it," Mark chuckled. "But I'm surprised you have hope in me yet."

"I don't."

The envoy was moving again an hour later, and everything seemed to be going per usual. One odd change had come about, however. The wolf Nymeria had calmed stayed close, appearing occasionally beside them. The beast trotted along as though it had always done so. It seemed to soften his daughter's mood, to put her in a better state of mind and heart. And John still could not explain why the beast had taken to her. All he could guess was that it had once lived among other people. It was the only rational explanation.

"She's beautiful, isn't she?" Nymeria asked. She never looked at him. Instead, she'd lowered the window and was holding her hand out, touching the low-hanging leaves of the trees they drove under.

"She's still a wild animal," John warned.

"She likes me. Marissa wanted a wolf, but Uncle Reid said they're dangerous, too."

"You're not keeping her." He prayed she would not start to cry and beg him to let her keep the creature. Jamie had already cried about taking in a stray dog once. An old, blind thing eaten up with fleas and ticks and worms.

Nymeria's answer surprised him, though. "I don't want to keep her," she said.

He looked at her. She was still playing with the passing leaves.

"She likes being free. She would have to change if she came home with us. And I wouldn't make her change."

His eyebrow rose. "Your mother would be having a heart attack if she saw you with that beast. She's following you like a lost puppy."

"I told you she was just cold. She lost her pack a while ago. You didn't see the dead wolves, did you? They were on this side of the trail." She shook the rainwater from her hand and reached out again. "They were all killed barely hours before we passed them."

"How do you know that?"

Nymeria looked at him as though he were stupid. "The bodies were not bloated, and there was no smell yet. They weren't even stiff when one of the Enforcers rolled a couple of them over to see what killed them." She shook her head. "I know I say many things that you think are strange, Father, but I'm not stupid. That beautiful mother wolf came to us because we were camped in her home. And I'm pretty sure I smelled like one of the other wolves to her. Probably like one of her babies."

Nymeria pursed her lips, then continued. "I thought she might try to eat me, but once she calmed, I knew why she was there. She missed them. It was terrible, her losing her whole family. And then all of us, strangers, walking around her home. Now it doesn't even smell like her home, and I'm the only thing that smells familiar to her. I'm the wrong shape, but I'm not a threat to her. She likes me."

"Hmm."

"What?"

John shook his head. "I'm just thinking that you've actually made the smallest bit of sense there. Scent is important to animals, and mothers are protective of their young." He laughed. It was still odd and still ridiculous. "So you're a wolf whisperer, then, on top of everything else. Jeana isn't going to believe a word of it."

Nymeria smiled. "It would be fun if I were. I would have her scare Uncle Reid to ribbons. Or Jamie. Jamie's funnier. He runs in circles screaming when he can't get away, or he jumps and climbs things."

"Well, don't name her. You don't want her following you everywhere for the rest of your life. Or hers."

Nymeria shook her head in agreement. "She wouldn't remember her name anyway. Only we would."

He said nothing else about it, and neither did she.

A little while later, Robert rode up on horseback and knocked on the window. John rolled it down. "What is it?"

"We're heading off to Virien's waypoint. The easy trail hasn't washed out yet, so we'll take it. We haven't gotten any intel on the state of things in Virien, so we're hoping they haven't had any incidents. We should have gotten a reply, at least. Wylem and his men have ridden out several times trying to get in range to reach them, but they've had no luck."

John nodded. "All right. Radio if you have problems. Take extra men with you who can fight. I'll see if I can spare someone to scout the roads ahead for us to check the rest of Ender's Creek. The rain may have flooded the first crossing."

"If we're taking extra men while you're sending out scouts, the envoy will be even more vulnerable. You've got supplies, and there are a lot of apprentices to protect. And with Makam in charge, the Enforcers don't seem willing to assist with any defense."

"Trust the Enforcers to do their job. Focus on the care and protection of those apprentices from Virien. We will handle this end. Just be quick. And be safe."

Robert nodded and pulled on the reins to turn his horse about. "We'll meet at the creek if all goes well. Be careful." His horse resisted the reins with a short protest. "By the way. Wylem's been asking why you would risk bringing Nymeria if you knew it was going to be so dangerous this season. He's just heard about her condition . . . Robert and Ellie Mae were discussing it, and it's got him tense. You know how he gets when he's worried, especially when it involves children. Just giving you a heads-up, he'll probably have a word or two with you when he gets back. I told him to talk to you about it. He doesn't trust the way things are going. And he's got a good instinct for danger, almost as good as Reid's."

"Tell him it's none of his concern," John said.

The next two hours grew tense. They'd crossed the body of another wolf, at the sight of which their new furry companion began to whine. She'd drawn closer to the truck. "Father," Nymeria said. Nymeria was also more tense than usual. "They're being followed."

"Hush, Nymeria. I need to hear the radio."

The creek had risen because of the rain, and it rushed the bank mightily. The tires ground against the riverbed, and the horses struggled against the current. Water still dripped from overhead. Several droplets hit his arm and bled downward, where they dripped onto the door panel.

A cold breeze made the willows' long, weeping branches sway, which made the route ahead vanish for a moment. John could not see the vehicles ahead for a few minutes as he maneuvered the truck around a slippery bend where the water deepened.

The water bubbled into the cab and flowed against his boots as debris washed from the bank about thirty meters up the creek. One of the trucks before them began slipping.

"Father." Nymeria gripped the door frame and pulled herself into the window so that she could look out better. He wanted to pull her back into the truck, but she said something next that caught him by surprise. "I hear screaming."

"What? Screaming, you say?" John tried to listen, but all he heard clearly was the roar of the water and the struggle of the engines. Beneath that, all he caught occasionally was some arguing among the Enforcers and the guildsmen who were struggling to keep their trucks on course. Mud and large, broken branches swept against the side of his rig, and the vehicle seemed to float off course for a gut-wrenching moment before the tires gripped the riverbed again and pushed them forward. Their wolf friend had already crossed and was waiting on the far bank, pacing and whining incessantly. "I don't hear anything — "

"Father," Nymeria said again. "I hear *screaming*." She grabbed the secondary radio that was charging on the dashboard and turned it on, and before he realized what she was going to do, she'd climbed out of the window and on top of the truck. "We've got inbound hostiles! Regroup and defend the trucks!" she said loudly over the channel. Her voice projected over the roar of the water. It was a child's voice, but it surprised him because the intensity in it promised she would one day wield great authority. That she would, perhaps, even command armies. "The scouts are dead at the bend! They've been ambushed! Keep your eyes open!"

"Nymeria!" John shouted. He nearly hit the brakes, but he didn't want to cause her to fall, and he didn't want the current to sweep them away. "Get back in here before you fall off and are swept downstream!" His heart rose into his throat at the thought of losing his daughter to the current. He wouldn't be able to reach her if she fell. He wouldn't be able to let go of the steering wheel, because the apprentices in the back would drown and the supplies in his charge would be lost. Even he himself would likely lose his life if he tried to get to her.

But Nymeria clung to the tarp over the back of the truck as she looked out over the vehicles ahead of them. The water began to let go of them, and the truck crept closer to the water's edge.

The wolf began to growl as she circled in front of the emerging truck and fell back just a couple of feet from his door. The wolf's golden eyes flashed at him, alarmed, and then at Nymeria. The beast's lips curled as John withdrew hastily from the door.

They were clear of the water at last.

"Arm yourselves!" Nymeria continued. "They're approaching from the west — "

The first arrow whistled by, and John swore as the mirror by his hand exploded. A couple of shards sliced his hand, and the steering wheel jerked. He gasped in horror as he heard his daughter fall onto the roof of the truck. But she climbed back into the window a moment later, uninjured. "Stop the truck!" she commanded.

"Sit down, Nymeria! I cannot stop or the others will be washed downstream behind us! Get your head down! Get in the floorboard — "

A gunshot rang out, and John saw one of the doctors fall from his horse as red mist exploded from his throat. Chaos erupted before he could process what the gunshot meant.

"Daddy!" screamed an apprentice from the back of the truck directly ahead of them. A young boy tried to climb out to get to the dead man, but he fell when a knife flew from seemingly nowhere and imbedded itself into his belly. The boy screamed in pain and writhed where he'd fallen as John swerved to avoid running him over. Their own truck almost toppled, and cries of fear erupted from the children in the back.

Nymeria shut her eyes and grabbed at the door handle. She looked sick, as though she was about to throw up. She was pale, and she was afraid. "We have to drive them away," she gasped. "They'll kill everyone."

John tried to stop her, but she was already out of the truck and running. The wolf took off, racing behind her, growling as though ready to kill anything that got close to either of them.

"Nymeria!" he shouted.

Then he saw the first of their enemies. The savage line of wolfmen held their approach as they crept through the decayed city, their daggers dripping blood, their cowls reflecting the occasional ray of sunlight that filtered through trees and murky glass. The red painted upon their faces looked like blood, and the bright blue and red feathers and bone beads clung to their hair like dread crowns.

More gunshots entered the chorus as the Enforcers took up arms, and John hastily took his gun from the glove compartment as the truck skidded to an abrupt stop. His gaze flickered to the broken side mirror as he shoved the shifter into park — and he realized one of the trucks was losing ground. Bullets ripped across the side of his truck. He jerked back, leaning away from the ripple of impacts that rammed the side of his door. One bullet made it through and bit his shoulder. He hissed at the stinging it caused, but he knew when he glanced at it that the projectile had only grazed him; the wound was so shallow he wouldn't even have to worry.

He had to get to his daughter. But one of the last trucks was going under.

He swore.

John reached up and slammed his palm against the glass behind his seat. He ducked to avoid another barrage of bullets as the glass and the reinforced steel window behind it slid open. The cries of the twenty children in the back of his truck grew louder when that window opened. "One of you, get me the rope!" he cried. "We're going to lose one of the trucks behind us if you don't hurry!"

"I wanna go back home!" wept one of the girls. He didn't know which one. He'd hardly spoken to the children he had been delivering other than to ensure they were fed and had plenty to drink. "I don't want to get shot, Dr. Ivan! I — "

"What is your name?" He braved sitting up and glanced out his window. Thomas was currently fighting off two of the wolfmen, who seemed to have the upper hand. He aimed his gun, but before he could pull the trigger, another arrow flew through his open window and out Nymeria's side of the cab.

"Sobrienne, sir," she said.

John cursed as another bullet ricocheted off the steel window frame and ripped him again, this time across the abdomen. "Sobrienne, you're going to have to be brave, okay? These men are bad men. If you want to get away from them, get me that rope. Have you ever driven?"

Sobrienne's small hands reached through the window, and her oval face peered out at him. Her eyes were puffy, but a spark of indignation flickered there. "Of course, I can drive. I wasn't raised as stupid as these other children. I'm an inventor. I worked on these kinds of engines in Edantine."

The Edantine child. John sighed. His brother had gotten a useful one from that city. "Get me the rope. I'll have you drive. You can be brave for that, can't you?"

"Yes, as long as you promise that I won't get shot."

"I'm not going to promise something I cannot ensure, Sobrienne. But the truck is armored. That means bullets and arrows won't tear through its sides."

The child climbed through the window, and as she did so, she began to shout orders into the back. "Ashton! Langry! Get me the rope!" Her lips pursed. "Where is it?"

John shielded her from gunfire as he turned the truck about. They skidded to a halt as he unbuckled his seatbelt and grabbed his other gun from under the seat. He prayed it wasn't a mistake to let the girl drive his truck, but he had no other choice. And she looked tall enough to just barely see over the steering wheel. "Hanging to the right of the back door, just above the tailgate. The box welded there. It'll open without a key."

"Get us that rope!" she screamed angrily. "Or I'll beat you into a pulp like I did that jerk from Winhelm!"

The commotion in the back sounded of desperation, and Sobrienne nodded satisfactorily as she grabbed the rope and handed it to John as he climbed out of the truck. He took it as he told her what he wanted her to do. "Back up to the bank just by that tree — "

He clung desperately as the child grabbed the shifter, changed gear, and then shoved the truck into a wild, weaving path that abruptly spun and stopped when it hit the tree. He fell and rolled, and his shoulder struck the base where the gnarled roots rose. The girl could drive well enough. She hadn't even given him the chance to explain where the shifter, the gas pedal, and the brake pedal were. "Get ready to drive forward!" he shouted as he hefted himself from the ground. The truck fighting the raging current was beginning to drift away.

Captain Makam stood near the water under the cover of a cluster of old ironwood trees, an angry look upon his face. His horse was dead, and he was shouting commands to his men. "Put your weapons down, you fools! This is not our fight!!!"

John wanted to pummel the man right then and there, but he could not. The driver of the troubled truck was Ellie Mae. She was pale as a ghost, and she was gripping the steering wheel and screaming. "ROBERT! ROBERT PLEASE HELP ME!"

"Ellie!" John shouted. He tied the rope to the reinforced bumper of his own truck. "ELLIE!"

"JOHN!" she screamed. A frothing wave of water flooded into the cab, and she sputtered. She let go of the steering wheel and tried to climb out of her seat. She was too terrified to realize she was being restrained by her seatbelt. "JOHN, GET ME OUT OF HERE! I DON'T WANT TO DROWN!"

"ELLIE, FOCUS!!! KEEP YOUR WITS TOGETHER FOR THOSE KIDS!!!" He was already wading into the raging river, and despite the icy fear that tried to overwhelm him the moment he'd stepped into the water, he kept moving. His heart was in his throat, and each and every step and motion was a battle of will. But people were going to die if he let his fear of the water overtake him. The truck that had been between his and Ellie's was struggling to pull them out of the water and was being dragged backward, toward the river. John had to get to them as fast as he could. There was no time to consider the scathing current or the thought of himself drowning.

Bullets sprayed across the bank, and three more Enforcers were killed as they retreated. Some of them had begun to argue with Captain Makam because he'd ordered the retreat. His lieutenant shot two of the Enforcers who refused to obey.

The water was icy against John's skin, and he struggled to stay afloat as he fought the current to get to the truck. The turbulent water nearly pulled him from the grip he'd taken on the ropes already connecting the other truck to Ellie's. Hastily, he tied his rope to another anchor point as the vehicle on the bank groaned and its tires skidded backward some more. Mud slung, and rocks flung at him. One struck him in the head, and he felt his fingers slip. His face went under the water, and he fought to reach for another hold as panic gripped him. When he came up again, he was choking. Water sprayed from his mouth, but it also clogged his lungs. "SOBRI — " He coughed.

The girl looked out of the truck, fear upon her face when she realized what had happened.

"Now?" she hollered. He kept choking, and the water almost tore him from the truck again. His shoulder struck the corner of the bumper, and his fingers slipped again. This time, he found no purchase.

He glimpsed Nymeria upon the bank as he tried to claw his way to the surface to gather another breath. She was staring after him, fear glittering in her brilliant green eyes. He saw her mouth the word, "Father."

And then more water rushed into his lungs.

When John struggled to claw his way the surface yet again, there was black fur everywhere, and snarling, vicious white teeth. And beyond that, a wolfman stood behind his daughter, wielding a knife that seemed to be angling upward, toward her back. Wolfmen didn't care whether their victims were alive when they took them.

He tried to scream her name, but the water had him again, and then so did the foaming teeth.

He heard a scream, and when he tried to fight the wolf and the current, it all gurgled together.

Then he was on the bank, and he was coughing and sputtering as he emptied his lungs, and the wolf trotted away, still snarling and growling.

Sobrienne pressed the gas, and the engine roared. The second vehicle on the bank caught ground at last and pulled from the water, and with both lines taught, Ellie's truck also found purchase as it was dragged toward solid ground.

Another crack of lightning rolled across the sky, and thunder groaned through the bellies of the graying clouds.

John rose, gasping, and he reached for the guns he'd tucked into his belt. He didn't see Nymeria. He didn't see the wolfman, either.

Where was his daughter?

John's temple throbbed, and he lifted his shaking hand to touch the tender spot. Blood came away, thinned by the water. He blinked hard against the spinning, and he stepped forward.

He saw one of the children being carried away by one of their attackers; the child was kicking and screaming wildly. John aimed and fired his gun, and the man fell, dropping his prize. The kid crawled away, terrified and shrieking even louder. John's lips pulled tight against his teeth. He had to find his daughter.

"Father!" she shouted. "Get away from the water!" He heard her over a walkie that had been dropped near the water's edge. She was giving directions not only to him but to others as well. Some part of him recognized how bizarre it was that no one was shouting at her to get off the radio as she continued giving directions. "The enemy's line has split along the middle of the envoy! Several of them are sweeping toward the last of the trucks where the prisoner is being kept! Those of you near the third truck, flank the wolfmen there and keep them busy. The rest of you, regroup and head them off before they get to the end of the line!"

He scrambled toward the walkie as one of the men replied, "How many have split for us, kid?"

"Twelve in the trees, twenty on the bank behind the truck already. It looks like they already had lines out. They're moving fast!"

John grabbed the walkie and lifted it to call out to her, but someone struck him from behind. The walkie slipped from his grasp. He hit the rocks on his back, and he rolled over onto his side dizzily. He fired his gun again, and the Enforcer who'd struck him stumbled back, surprised. It was Captain Makam. "I thought you were one of them," the captain stammered as he held up his hands. "Apologies — "

"Order your men to help!" John hissed, and though he struggled to hold the gun steady, he kept it pointed roughly at the captain's face.

The captain snarled, his surprise vanishing. "This is not our fight. And why would I help you, when it's your fault my men are dying? You're the ones who set this course and walked us all into this ambush!"

John clenched his teeth, although it caused his ears to ring. He shook his head, trying to rid himself of the spinning. He staggered when he clambered to his feet again, yet he kept the gun — for the most part — still aimed at the captain.

"Your job is to defend us on this journey. That is your sworn duty. That is the contract between Black Temple and the Enforcers' Alliance, Captain Makam. Order your men to help us."

"Avery has recalled us. Our job is done," the captain grated. "Our new assignment will determine who we are to protect. Your men should have been prepared for this. *You* are the one who chose to travel while there is unrest. That means every life lost here is *your fault.*"

It had been Saura's decision which had caused the traveling season to begin so late, not John's. The responsibility did not lie with any man or woman from Crow Post. John glared at the Enforcer. "Captain Makam. If we'd stayed any longer, there would have been worse to pay. Countless more would be dead. The refugees at the end of this envoy have no homes left to them. The refugees we sent to Edantine and Tallil, and to Lovael and Hagenhold and elsewhere, also had no place left to turn. If we hadn't left when we did to get these apprentices to Isold and those refugees out of Crow Post, all of us would be rained in. Do you think this creek, or the others, will still be crossable at all in even another week? One more week, and we would have been too late! More lives would have been lost! Tell your men to help us!"

Another rapid burst of gunfire erupted as it pummeled the side of his truck. His heart leapt. He had to get back to that truck, to get those children out of the line of fire. At least he knew his daughter was alive, because she was still on the radio giving orders. And not one person was objecting to it.

He couldn't believe she had taken charge of the envoy's defense; she was coordinating the moving components the way Reid did. But John didn't have the time to question further. He had to get moving. He abandoned the Enforcers among the trees. "You're a coward!" he shouted over his shoulder, and he rushed back toward his truck.

Sobrienne was pale when he pulled the door open. Tears streamed down her face, but she clenched her teeth and pushed at him when he started to climb up. "I've got this, Dr. Ivan! But a little girl is in the tree up there! I think she's the one on the radio. They're shooting at her."

John's head spun about, and as he abandoned Sobrienne to her promise, he saw more of the wolfmen surrounding them all from every street corner. The broken buildings had provided their snipers with good cover.

"Another wave of them have split for that last truck!" Nymeria shouted. "There are about thirteen of them, and they have guns! Be careful! Shoot their feet out from under them if you have to! And someone, climb on top of it, the snipers can't see the top of it from this angle! Shoot them at the back corner when they get close enough!"

John tackled one of the wolfmen, took his knife, and shoved it deep into the man's gut. The man gasped in surprise as they rolled, and he tried to grip the knife. But John twisted it and then pulled it free and ran at another. "Get away from my daughter!" he screamed. Blood seeped into his eye, and he tried to wipe it away.

The truck behind him roared as Sobrienne pressed the gas again, and he heard the children in the back screaming. "Shut up, you idiots!" shouted Sobrienne. "I need to hear the radio! They're in the middle of saving us and I need to hear what's going on! Ashton, give them something important to do! Get them ready to attack any wolfmen if they try to open the back! Grab whatever you can find, and tell them what to do!"

Thomas had killed several of their attackers, and he met John halfway to the tree. "Glad to see that little psycho girl from Edantine saved Ellie's life. And your daughter is one loud little shit, John. She gave everyone here enough warning that I think we may be able to pull through. The brat is coordinating the entire defense the way your brother does."

"I noticed," John hissed. "She's painted herself as a target, though." He pistol-whipped another wolfman.

"Lukas is in that truck. I'll help you get Nymeria to safety, but the moment I'm done with that, I'm heading down there to get rid of those wolfmen," Thomas said. "And I thought you couldn't swim. I thought you would drown down there."

"Oh, I can swim, but barely. Her damned wolf pulled me out — "

One of the wolfmen began screaming as a black shadow shot through an opening behind him in the closed ruin and began to maul him.

"I swear, that's the most unnatural bond I've ever seen," Thomas stammered. "A wild animal looking after us, and all because of her." He shook his head and leaned against John for a moment as he attempted to regain his breath.

The battle lasted for a full day and night, and every muscle ached in John's body.

Nymeria had scurried from the tree and rushed to the truck to assist Sobrienne when the Edantine girl had gotten shot and started screaming. John hadn't been able to get back to them, but the wolf had defended the truck from any of the wolfmen who'd tried to get to it.

When it began to rain again, the mud made it harder to maneuver. The trucks weren't able to move beyond the site of the ambush. Lukas's truck was still stuck in the rising creek, where more debris had lodged the vehicle between the willows. The wolfmen got a hold of the thief and dragged him and his cage downriver twenty meters while he tried ineffectively to fight them off. Some of the remaining wolfmen began to attack their own as they, too, tried to get at him. Because of that infighting, Black Temple's guildsmen recaptured him and brought him back. The cage had been wrecked, but the murderer was still bound and gagged.

John toppled the last of those wolfmen with his sword and pulled Lukas from the muddy bank, and he ripped his gag free. "I can tell you recognize some of them," he snarled. "Who are these men to you?"

Lukas shook his head, sputtering as he tried to expel the remaining water from his lungs. "Don't let them take me back!"

John gripped the man by the collar. "Take you where?"

"They're going to take me back! Don't let them get their hands on me again!"

"Who are they?!"

He could get nothing else from Lukas. John shoved Lukas back to the ground, where the man curled, disjointed and still coughing and choking.

The Enforcers were arguing back and forth now. A lot of them were angry. More of them tried to help, but Captain Makam's goons rounded them up and arrested them for disregarding his direct orders.

Some of the children had been killed. Some of them had been taken.

And Nymeria continued to evade John and put herself at risk. She refused to stay where she could be protected.

Then the wolfmen began to retreat.

At last, John made it to the truck, and he helped to move Sobrienne. She'd only been grazed, but she still cried. The wolf continued to circle the vehicle as he opened the door and pulled Nymeria from the cab. "Thank god," he said as he held his daughter against him. "Thank the heavens you're okay. You're okay, aren't you? You haven't been hurt?" He looked her over, fearful she might have been fatally wounded in his absence. "Nymeria, you scared the hell out of me!"

Robert's palomino whinnied behind him as more of the wolfmen broke from the engagement to retreat. More than thirty of their number were dead in their immediate vicinity. More than double that number of the refugees and children and guild members were dead. And several more Enforcers had been killed. Bodies littered the ground everywhere, and blood ran toward the river behind them as the rain fell harder.

John turned and looked up. The pale horse Robert sat upon pawed at the ground nervously and pranced a bit. It was still uneasy from the rumbling thunder and slowing, rhythmless bursts of gunfire. Nymeria gave John another box of bullets, and he took it gladly. He loaded his empty clips as she scrubbed the blood from the seat compulsively, trying to clean it away.

He leaned on the door, shaking, and stray rays of sunlight filtered through the rain and the clouds. Some of them blinded him.

He shifted. "What is it, Robert? How bad?"

Robert dismounted. "Because of the ambush," he said, "we've lost a lot of apprentices. We ran into a line of wolfmen from behind while they headed here for the attack."

John sighed. "Damn."

"We managed to get through, obviously," said Robert. "But all we have left is seven apprentices. The two from Acreage and Savannah are dead. Virien sent thirteen instead of the full haul. Some of the other families there needed the help and wanted to keep the kids on as their own. They grew attached. It's good for the kids, but eighteen apprentices in total were killed. And one of them is hurt. He was stabbed in the leg when they tried to kill off Wylem."

John cursed. "Is Wylem okay?"

"For now, yes. He wasn't far behind me. I think they got cornered just a few miles back. The scouts never saw anything on their first pass. We've been cursing their blind stupidity and crap luck since. Where is Ellie?"

John grabbed the walkie Nymeria handed him. "She nearly drowned," John said. Robert paled and started to open his mouth, but John quickly assured him she was okay. "The Edantine girl helped to save her and the children she was hauling. They're all alive and uninjured. She was so frantic she couldn't get out, because she forgot to undo her seatbelt. But she's okay."

Robert rubbed his eyes. "Okay. All right. Wylem's going to need help. I rode ahead to get here fast as I could to see if you needed help here. I was completely out of bullets, and my gun got shot out of my hand, so I just hauled ass as fast as I could to drop off a couple of kids and get help."

"I'll need a horse."

"I'll get Ellie's mustang. He's quicker than lightning, and he's rested long enough."

"Here." John gave Robert one of his other guns, and then he reloaded the other and its clips and stuffed the remaining bullets in the extra pocket against his outer thigh. "Nymeria," he said. "Stay here. Get in the back with the others, and lock the door. Keep them calm."

"But — "

"You will do as I said!"

Nymeria jolted, startled by John's fury.

"You have put yourself at enough risk. Get inside!"

Robert nodded. "For once, I agree with your dad. These men are still trying to kill us."

"I won't let them hurt the others," she agreed finally. "I'll have the other kids help to get your equipment and medicine ready so we can tend to the wounded quickly."

John frowned. Had he just heard her correctly? That was the first time she'd ever expressed any desire to help him with his job. He looked back, but she was already climbing into the back of the truck.

"Adorable," Robert sighed. "I wish I had a kid that damned adorable. John, she's a natural-born leader. Why in the hell would you want to force her to be a field doctor? All they do is follow Saura's orders, and they serve every post doctor's whims and deliver things and do surgeries. She would be a much better Enforcer. Hell, she'd probably climb as high as Avery's position with her fortitude and her surprising skill in strategy. She directed the defense. We heard it over the radio when this shit-show started."

"Shut up, Robert. Get Ellie's horse for me, and I'll get what I can for Wylem and the others."

When they got to Wylem, the battle had already been whittled away. "Why the hell did you come back here?!" shouted Wylem as he decapitated one of the wolfmen. "I've got this, I told you!" Then he saw John.

"Where are the kids?" John asked, and he tossed a couple of packs of ammo and a canteen to the man. Wylem drank from the canteen deeply and then held it up in silent thanks.

Wylem then withdrew from the decayed concrete path, leading John and Robert into one of the decrepit buildings with him. "They're hidden for now. Safe. We heard Nymeria on the radio. How bad is it?"

"We'll survive the trip," John nodded. "But we've had losses."

"Did the Enforcers pull through, as you thought they would?"

The savage expression on Wylem's face told John he shouldn't answer. But his silence told Wylem what he wanted to know.

Wylem roared. "I'll wring that captain's neck! I told you they wouldn't do anything!"

"The battle isn't over," Robert said. "We've got to hurry with these kids so we can help defend the envoy, Wylem. It's way worse than we thought. Nymeria did a hell of a job coordinating everyone, but there are a lot of wounded. Worse, it doesn't seem like those wolfmen are finished. We can deal with Makam when this crap is over."

"Sonya!" Wylem stormed off into the dark, cavernous depths of the building, under old cables and broken walls. Dust slid from the ancient hanging lights when his broad shoulders brushed against them, and a spark of electricity shot outward, catching nothing. The brief flicker of light was all that came from the cable, but from it, John saw several small faces.

One of the heavily armed refugee women who'd gone with Wylem moved forward. "Here," she said from the darkness.

"Get the kids ready." He then spoke to John. "We don't need you to stay and fight with us. The bullets you gave us will be enough. And from the sound of it, you're needed more there than you are here. We've only got one more sniper, and he's across the street. I've been luring him out, one trick at a time. Dominique's got his sights on him right now. Soon as he raises that gun to shoot at me again, his head's going to explode. Dominique's a good shot. The rest will be easy to deal with."

"Are you sure you're good?" John searched the darkness and the emerging, filthy faces. The children were frightened. He only saw six. The seventh whimpered in the shadows.

"You can seat two of these youngsters with you on Ellie's horse," said Wylem. "Robert can seat two more. That will help more than anything. Go. We've got the other three — "

The hidden boy cried out, and Sonya disappeared again. "It got my leg!" cried the boy. "Something bit me! Something bit my leg!"

"Shhh . . ." Sonya coaxed. "Shhh. We'll take a look at it soon, okay? What got you? A snake?"

But Antonio kept crying.

"Scorpion," hissed Sonya. "You'll be fine. We'll get you out of here soon."

John reached for the first child Wylem lifted to him. The boy was barely eleven, by the look of him. Blond hair, brown eyes, which were full of fear. The second boy was a bit darker, and larger. "Hold tight," John commanded, and he took the reins firmly. "Wylem, you'd better get back in one piece." Once Robert had two more apprentices, they rode out.

A bullet ricocheted off the stone just behind them, and Wylem stepped out, waving his sword and shouting insults at the sniper.

* * * * * * *

At the main camp, the apprentices were quickly taken into Ellie's custody. Another dead wolfman lay on the ground below the tailgate, and Ellie was withdrawing her knife from his torso. "I'm getting sloppy with my knife work," she said. She had dark circles under her eyes, but she kept her guard up as the four apprentices disappeared into the truck. She watched warily, even as she drank deeply from her canteen. "I'd rather cut them up *after* they're dead, but a girl's gotta do what a girl's gotta do." She looked John and Robert over. "You both seem fine. Where is Wylem? Is he still alive?"

Robert took the canteen from her and kissed her deeply. "Wylem's fine, love," said Robert. He drank from the canteen next. "John told me what happened at the river."

"He saved my life," Ellie said. "I'll owe him that debt for the rest of my life."

"The Edantine girl saved your life, I just tied the rope."

"You let a little girl drive your truck?" Robert laughed heartily. "You're crazy!"

Ellie filled them in. "Most of them retreated this morning, but the scouts said they've regrouped. They're going to be coming in hard, this time from the east. Captain Makam is still hard on his refusal to help. But I've talked to a few of his men. They're about ready to throw him into the river themselves. Him and his goons."

"Best news since yesterday," said John. "What about the wounded? The dead?"

"We've got most of the wounded being tended to. We'll get a better idea once this is over. No one else seems in critical condition, though. Everyone should be able to travel as soon as this Wolfshadow trash is dealt with." She took the canteen and drank again from it. "I swear. That wolf your daughter enchanted? That wolf has been killing left and right. She's taken probably thirty of them down."

"Is the wolf still alive?" asked Robert, amused. "I figured they would have shot her a while back."

"They did," Ellie nodded. "But she's quick as shadow, and tough. She's protecting Nymeria and the children as if they're her own. I don't know if she'll make it, though. She was bleeding pretty badly last I glimpsed her."

"So how many of them are left, and where?"

"Just up by the church — I think that's a church, anyway. Stained glass. There are trees growing from it. Yellow leaves."

John squinted in the direction she'd nodded. The heavens rumbled angrily with the promise of more rain and high winds.

"Your head hurt?" she asked.

John shook his head. "I can still fight. The captain tried to kill me. He thought I was one of the wolf cult — "

"That prick tried to kill you?!" Robert was aghast.

"He backed off when I put my gun in his face. We'll deal with him when this is done."

"That gutless Enforcer," hissed Ellie Mae. She shook her head and refilled the canteen with the rushing water at the creek's edge, and then she passed the canteen into the back of the truck. Small hands took it. "Drink up, kiddos. We're about to face another wave. We'll hold them off, so just be brave."

Ellie Mae patted the truck loudly, and several quiet *thank-you*s poured out from the confines of the armored bed. The thanks sounded like prayers.

True to Ellie's word, as the Enforcers regrouped on the other side of the envoy — taking cover on the lower bank under Captain Makam's command — another volley of arrows and gunshots interrupted the peace. Where the Enforcers had regrouped, John could hear shouting. Swords flashed in his peripherals. Some of the soldiers were fighting amongst themselves. But John and the guildsmen and the refugees were too busy fighting off the wolfmen to do anything about it.

An explosion startled the horses and the wolfmen, and fire erupted along the trail, even though the trees were soaked. "*Back off!*" Nymeria hollered. And she hurled another something. The wolfmen scattered as another explosion erupted. "*Leave us alone!*"

"Where the hell did that girl get *grenades*?!" shouted Robert. "*Holy Mother of the Dead!*" Robert and Ellie both recoiled from the shrapnel and took cover.

Something screeched in the forest, and scores of birds took flight. The wolf yelped in terror and fled by them, leaving a heavy trail of blood behind her as she disappeared into the woods. The screech came again, louder than a bomb, and the ground itself quaked as though waking from a deep and disturbed slumber.

John clung to the boulder before him as rubble came crashing down from the teetering ruins about them. He wanted to cover his ears, but he feared letting go.

The children cried in the back of the truck, and wails of terror echoed from the forest and the ruins.

The entire creek slithered sideways a few meters before it crept back.

Then Sonya appeared alongside other warriors, several of whom were wounded and weary but who clutched their swords and rode toward the wolfmen anyway. She dropped from her horse and slid beside him as the others rode into the fray. "The rest of them are coming. Wylem's men have flanked them. This side and that. We need more help, though."

John looked behind him, beyond the trucks. The Enforcers' voices had risen. Captain Makam's angry shouting was the loudest. He heard Wylem as well.

Wylem had abandoned his horse and rushed into the thick of their encampment. John got up, swearing. He knew this wouldn't end well at all. "Wylem, don't you dare!"

By the time John reached the warriors, Wylem had already fought his way to the captain's inner circle. The man was ordering his men to get rid of the guildsman. "Get him out of here!" shouted the captain. "How *dare* you — "

"You're a bloodless coward!" Wylem roared. "What kind of Alliance captain abandons his sworn duty to defend and to protect?! Never have I met such a frightened, gutless captain in all my years! A man who hides behind his men and calls them to protect him while these wolfmen attack his charge is not a man! And all of you. How *dare* you obey the ramblings of this man! You who follow the orders of an obvious traitor!"

"Do as I have commanded!" the captain said to his men. "Remove this garbage at once!" Captain Makam's snarl was a nasty one.

"Wylem, leave them alone before you start something we cannot finish with the Alliance," John said desperately.

"I'm not leaving until this man is arrested for treason." Wylem said. "He's betrayed his own! They should clean up this mess before I take that job into my own hands."

"Wylem! I'm ordering you to back down!"

Wylem spun wildly and faced John, rage written across his face. The man was a ticking bomb, and he was ready to kill anyone that got in his way. "Stay out of this — "

The song of another sword leaving its sheath cut Wylem off. Wylem swung about, dodging the captain's blade.

Captain Makam's loyal officers dove toward Wylem and caught him by the arms.

"You're a dead man," said the captain. The wicked satisfaction in his eyes turned John's stomach. "You've accused me of treachery for the last time. Your intent to incite rebellion among my men will be your last insult to me."

John drew his gun and shot the wet ground between the two men, startling the captain and the other Enforcers. Four among them also drew guns and pointed them at John and Wylem, though they seemed nervous over the idea of aiming at him, or of pulling their triggers. He was a Black Temple doctor, and he was in charge of the entire envoy. His rank was technically equal to the captain's, if not a hair higher.

"Stop this nonsense!" John commanded. "Both of you! We don't have time to be fighting each other." Wylem tore free of his captors with a roar before John could say a single other thing.

Wylem picked up one of the men who'd restrained him, and he threw the man at his comrades. Then he went after the captain. Captain Makam swung his sword, ashen at the sight of Wylem's rage and berserker strength. Wylem simply twisted out of the way again and again as the captain swung madly.

The Enforcers seemed unsure whether to intervene or to shoot, but the situation was too dangerous to let bullets fly. John's fist clenched, and he lowered his gun with a curse. He had no chance of stopping the two men from fighting until an opening appeared. It wouldn't be long before Wylem had the upper hand anyway.

"Get back!" the captain screamed at Wylem. The coward stumbled, and Wylem grabbed him by the wrist, halting the sword as it slashed through the air at him. He snarled victoriously and crushed the captain's hand. Captain Makam screamed again, this time in pain, and Wylem jerked him forward and grabbed him by the throat. He threw the captain to the ground and kicked him hard. The Enforcer rolled down the embankment, and Wylem went after him, shouldering off the Enforcers who tried to stop him. Every one that tried lost his sword or got punched in the jaw so hard he collapsed, unconscious.

Wylem was unstoppable when he was angry. "Tell your men to help! If you don't, I will kill you!"

The captain staggered to his feet and tried to run. But then his own men stepped in his way. His lieutenant and two other officers tried to order them down, putting swords or guns to some of their throats. But more of the Enforcers turned on the captain's officers. Captain Makam's goons dropped their weapons. They were angry, but they were also outnumbered.

Captain Makam tried to dart away, but Wylem caught him and hit him again. Harder. John heard bones crunch.

The captain collapsed, barely conscious.

One of the sergeants stepped in front of Wylem and held up his hand in a gesture that requested the warrior calm down. "We're placing them under arrest. We're tired of his callous, suspicious behavior. He'll answer to the High Commander."

Wylem snarled but smoothed his beard. "And who are you? I maybe can work with you."

"Elija." Elija grimaced as he clutched at his bloody abdomen, but he offered his other hand. "Please accept our apology. We should have done this yesterday when he started ordering us to murder our own simply for trying to perform their duty. It didn't sit right with any of us to stand back and do nothing."

"You'll be executed for this," the captain snarled as he struggled to get back up. He seemed too dizzy. As if he'd been robbed of his strength.

Elija put his boot on the captain's ankle and put his weight down on it. The captain cringed.

Wylem snorted. "Can I just hit him one more time?"

Elija grinned. "Men. Help the captain to his feet."

"It is very nice to meet you," Wylem said. And he shook the Enforcer's hand. "Grow a beard, and we'll be good friends."

"I'll have you all executed," hissed the captain.

Wylem swung again. The captain's neck popped again, and he crumpled. Some of his men dragged him away alongside his officers.

Elija ordered the rest to assist with the defense, and the Enforcers gladly parted the confines of the coward's camp. Blood seeped from the captain's lips as his head bobbed.

John grimaced and holstered his gun, thankful he hadn't had to use it after that initial shot. "I think you broke the man's neck, Wylem."

Wylem laughed. "He deserves it. He didn't want to fight. Now he *can't*. If you'll excuse me, I've some more anger to express with these wolfmen."

Wylem headed for the defensive line with the Enforcers.

Barely an hour later, the rest of the wolfmen had either fled or been killed. And Lukas remained Black Temple's prisoner. The murderer seemed angry to see the distraction gone, and his cage was repaired, and he was put back in it. That seemed to anger him more.

Good riddance, John thought.

CHAPTER THIRTY

$\mathcal{B}$LADE

MOST OF THOSE WHO had suffered major wounds had died in the night, though many of the remainder who'd survived had been sewn up and medicated. The rest of the injuries seemed to be composed of a few concussions here and there, a few broken bones, and scrapes and bruises. He was relieved the death toll hadn't been higher, but to see so many murdered was still appalling. They'd lost nearly a third in their company, Enforcers included. But it would have been worse if Sergeant Elija hadn't stepped in and taken command of the soldiers.

John tended the injured as quickly as he could. The sooner they were able to move the envoy, the better. The dreaded cult had fled hours before, and none of the scouts had seen even a print suggesting they were regrouping again. But it didn't mean they were free of them completely.

The wolf hadn't returned, either.

Nymeria had escaped uninjured. As far as he knew, anyway. The way she healed, it wasn't likely he would have found anything wrong. But he saw no new silver markings upon her, and none of her clothes were torn or bloodied in a way that suggested she'd been hurt. She was just wet from the rain and uncomfortable at the sight of the blood and the dead all around her. She wouldn't look at the bodies. He didn't blame her. She was young, and seeing the dead strewn about upset her.

It was wrong that any of the children had to be exposed to it, but the lesson would sober them and teach them the reality and the importance of Black Temple's calling.

Robert had approached. "Most of those men weren't wolfmen," he said. "They were just dressed like them."

John had already put that together. "I know. I figured that out after the first bullet grazed me. They don't use guns."

"Do you think they were hired by Five Tower?"

"It would explain a lot," he said as he wrapped up an Enforcer's ankle. The man had broken it in three places, and one of the bones had gone through the skin. He was lucky it hadn't been worse. The break was clean, and John hadn't needed to pull anything from the wound. Sewing it up had been an easy job. "Stay off this foot as much as you can," he told the Enforcer. "Also, the sergeant requested I send you his way the moment we were done. Take these with you." He handed the Enforcer the vials and the gauze he'd set aside. "Make sure that wound of his doesn't change color. Keep an eye on him and let me know if anything changes." The Enforcer nodded and hobbled off.

"That last kid Wylem brought isn't doing well," said Robert. "That injury of his is infected and oozing, and he's got a fever. The blade may have been coated with poison. They were afraid to pull the damned thing out until about an hour ago. It was stuck in him good. Bled all over when they'd tried the first time, Wylem said. They didn't try again until Timothy joined them."

John groaned. "If he's been poisoned, it's more proof that none of the cult were involved. They wouldn't risk it. Have you seen his leg? With your own eyes?"

Robert nodded. "It looks bad."

"Any bite marks, or odd coloration? Puffy and oozing, or is it rotten? And what manner of tainted smell has it? Almond? Foul? Also, what color discharge? Thick or thin?"

Nymeria placed two cold bowls of food on the table for John and the next refugee in line for his care. The woman grabbed hers and ate heartily, thanking her. John was too busy to even think about eating yet. And Nymeria stood by, listening.

"That's too many questions at the same time. Give me a second to answer them before you ask too many more," Robert scowled. "The boy just has a prick from a scorpion, they said. You and I were there when that happened, though. That was yesterday, about midday. It didn't start the problem, but it may have made it worse."

John nodded. "It is still possible he's allergic, though such a delayed reaction isn't quite so common."

Robert growled deep in his throat, clearing it, and then leaned to the side and spat. "His leg is swollen twice the size it should be," he said. "Has a sickly-sweet smell, but not of almond. Didn't you say almond meant cyanide poisoning?"

John clenched his teeth. "Yes, Robert, but rarely does it pertain to the wounds I tend. Most of the time, cyanide is ingested, not put on a blade. Did Sonya tell you what kind of scorpion it was? I never saw it. She did."

"Run of the mill, nothing dangerous."

"And the exudate?"

"Well, kind of blackish around the edges — "

"What kind of knife cut him?"

Robert slid a wrapped object from his satchel and unbound it. "Timothy was able to get it out without the boy bleeding out." A dull, six-inch metal blade reflected the sky faintly through the dry, flaking blood that clung to the worn, crusted threads of the cloth that was peeled away.

John took the blade as he stood straight, and he examined it carefully. "A ritual knife. Looks like a slaver's brand. This mark here, etched into the end of the pummel. This is a slaver's knife, not a wolfman's."

"That's what I thought." Robert's hand went to the back of his neck as he squinted into the sunlight. "I'll have Wylem bring that kid by as soon as they are able to move him safely," he said. "Looks as if you've already got a line of people waiting on you, so I won't make you come to him. Do you need anything?"

"I'll have another kit brought from the truck. Make sure you give Elija my thanks for stepping in and having his men help us. I am incredibly grateful for their intervention."

"Of course. But you should have been the one to step in and spur the Enforcers to action. You're supposed to be the lead on this trip, not Wylem."

John grimaced but overlooked it. "I've only got a couple more surgeries that need my immediate attention. Once we've moved into the ruin and fortified ourselves to take a full inventory of the damage, send the boy to me. Should only be a few hours. I'm told we've already got an ideal location."

Robert nodded. "Whatever you want, boss. I'll forward the message."

CHAPTER THIRTY-ONE

Death's Touch

NYMERIA FOLLOWED HER FATHER'S uneasy gaze up the hill, where another crumbling mansion stood over them like a haggard stone wraith in a cemetery. Generous sections of it had been layered with years of growth in the form of tangled vines and giant aerial tree roots, just like the rest of the city.

About them, the rooms of the decrepit cathedral were spacious — almost cavernous; such was the nature of buildings which had been built during the Modern Civilization. Time had taken its pleasure in eroding the cathedral. The ancient structure's walls pressed inward, and several species of young trees sprouted through the last bits of roof. Shoots of green caught stray flickers of sunlight which turned them an almost blinding, golden yellow.

The ruins around them formed a perfect cave, which was lined occasionally with the wrought iron frames of long-ago shattered stained glass windows.

This part of the old city gave her father the creeps. But Nymeria only sensed the history within its limits, and then a yawning emptiness passing by a brief and grieving sickness. The entire city was littered with ancient bones, most of which were buried beneath the forest litter and the city's decay. She felt them all for the briefest moment when she stopped to look about.

Her father placed one of his guns back in the door of the truck, but Nymeria saw him remove another from the waterproofed box under the seat. He holstered it. Her gaze flicked back to the ruinous city and the thick forest which stretched out around them, and then she turned to walk away.

"Where are you going?" her father asked.

"Don't tell me to stay out of the way," she said. "I'm helping. I know what to get."

"Knows, does she?" Robert chuckled under his breath. "Ares! Go and see if Wylem needs help getting that boy to John. And make sure the water is refilled while the creek is running high and heavy. Make sure you're not followed back, either."

Ares leapt down from the back of one of the trucks where he'd been giving out food, and he darted away.

"Walk on feathers, not leaves, Ares!" Robert called after him. "Don't give any of those wolfmen a path back to us!"

Nymeria climbed nimbly into the back of her father's truck and was struck immediately by several pairs of curious, wary eyes. Her face reddened as she threaded through the other children, all of whom were several years older. She was smaller than them all, but she felt especially miniscule under their quiet, expectant gazes.

"What's wrong with your eyes?" said one of the tallest girls. It was the girl who'd recently been shot. Sobrienne. The fierce girl had an oval face and short, dark hair, and her brows were high and arched, as though she were permanently suspicious.

The others squinted in the sunlight that filtered through the darkness inside, and those nearest Nymeria shifted in their seats uncomfortably.

Nymeria did not answer Sobrienne's question. She knelt before her father's trunk and unlocked it. Inside, among his paperwork and other essential items for the journey into Black Temple, she found his medical bag — the one with the potent anti-inflammatory medicines and a few of the more exotic fever-reducing remedies. It had several other things, too. He'd already had other supplies on hand, but he'd used quite a bit of medicine with the injuries he'd been tending. And this chest was always kept under lock and key because the contents were valuable and could be perilous in the wrong hands.

But he didn't think these children could pick that lock. She was quite sure one or two of them could, and she would never have trusted them with it. But her father was the doctor, not her. And she didn't want to become one, either.

Nymeria locked the trunk when she had his bag, and she turned around to leave, the key clutched in her fingers.

Sobrienne stepped in her way and grabbed her by the hair and yanked, forcing Nymeria to look up. She shut her eyes tightly and clutched at her father's bag.

"Why are you closing your eyes?" demanded Sobrienne. "Why are they that weird green color?"

"I was born with them," Nymeria said quietly. "Please let go. One of the new boys is hurt. Wylem is bringing him. My father needs to help him."

Sobrienne let go, but she did not move out of Nymeria's way. Nymeria looked up, and she felt her bottom lip tremble.

"I've never heard of them taking a girl as little as you to be an apprentice before," Sobrienne huffed. She placed her hands on her hips. "You probably think you're special, don't you? I heard you on the radio telling everyone what to do." When Nymeria said nothing, Sobrienne lifted her fingernails to study them. "Well, you're not special. I am, though. I saved a lot of people yesterday. I got to drive. A lot of kids would have died if I didn't."

"I'm glad you saved them," Nymeria said. "You were very brave. Can I go now?"

Sobrienne rolled her eyes and looked Nymeria up and down, as though scoffing at her. "Can you get us something else to eat or drink? The dinner they gave us was stale, and we're still hungry."

Nymeria shook her head. "I can't right now. But they will be serving more soon," she said. "The hunters have been gathering food to stretch the rations." She turned her gaze to the floor as she made her way toward the sunlight again. But she felt their eyes bearing down upon her with every step. Then she heard Jasper as she was crawling out of the back of the vehicle.

"She's the one I was telling you about. That wolf followed her. That's what Robert said. Isn't her dad the doctor driving us?"

Sobrienne began to whisper as well, but Nymeria could hear them still, even as her toes touched the rocks. "Of *course,* he is. I already told you that."

"I heard she was a science experiment," said Jasper. "They mixed her blood with dragon blood. That's why her eyes are that color. They almost glow because of it."

"There's no such thing as dragons, Jasper," proclaimed Sobrienne. "If you're going to be a doctor like me, and not just an attendant or in a support field like the rest of these dumb kids here, then you're going to have to get stuff like that out of your head. You need to live in the real world. There are no dragons or fairies."

"But dragons are real! My dad and me, we saw one. She has the same eyes as it did. And you heard that roar, too! That was a dragon roar! That was the sound of it waking up real mad."

"She has that color because she's dangerous," said another, more quietly. Nymeria couldn't quite place the voice, but she thought it belonged to the one still sitting in the darkest corner. The Edantine boy. Michael. "Some people are born like that. Even if it's pretty, the color is a warning."

The others snickered. "Pretty? Really, Michael?" huffed Sobrienne. "What? Are you going to marry the weird girl some day?" When he said nothing, Sobrienne crossed her arms over her crinkled woolen tunic. "You're gross. You not denying it means it's true!"

His reply was still quiet. "I had a dream about her. The night after I first saw her." Sobrienne started to laugh, but he wasn't through. "The darkness was alive, and at the darkest part of it , a man was chained to her. And the light that came from her burned him, even though it kept him alive." Sobrienne's laughter died. "When he looked at you, he wanted to kill you. But instead, *she* took your throat out with her teeth. While you tried to scream, she tore your heart out and held it before you while it was still bleeding in her hand. And there were dark demons that were tall as trees and made from the shadows themselves. They were hissing something in another language. I don't know what they were saying, but it sounded as though they had told her to kill you. When they got angry, they sounded just like that creature that roared in the forest yesterday."

Sobrienne had taken a step back, and Nymeria peered up into the truck bed.

"She's not like you. Or even me," said Michael. "My dreams don't lie about what people really are. There is darkness in her, and you should not provoke it. It'll get you killed."

Nymeria wiped the moisture from her cheeks, and she picked up the bag before they realized she could still hear them. She wanted away from them, and badly.

Nymeria hurried back to find her father, but he was not where she'd expected him to be. She suspected he'd already gone farther down the line, inspecting more injuries and talking to the other drivers and the Enforcers to ensure the rest of them would coordinate with each other should anything else unexpected happen. The defense preparedness stuff was her uncle's job, she knew. Her father's priority was supposed to be health and safety, but with Uncle Reid's absence, no one except the Enforcers seemed as alert as they should have been. Not even with her father's help. Things were unorganized at best.

She wished her uncle had come with them. She also missed her cousin and her brother. She had loved those last days, sharing the books her uncle had brought her.

Nymeria gripped the handle of her father's bag once she'd wiped her tears away, and she gritted her teeth. There were things to be done. Her father was angry enough that she'd not hidden herself away when they were attacked. She didn't want to give him more fuel against her. She could still prove that she could be useful without his forcing her to become a doctor.

The other two vehicles Nymeria passed were crammed. The children were less than comfortable among the supplies with which they rode, and she heard the grumbling among them. There were also armed men from each of the posts hurrying to and fro as they made repairs, reloaded weapons, and carried out other tasks. There was little time to rest or eat for any of them.

Several of those armed men were from the same places from which the apprentices had hailed, and only fifty Enforcers remained. The horses seemed to be doing fine, however, as were the rest of the refugees, and they hadn't lost any of the supplies or documents.

In all, their number now totaled just under three hundred fifty. Most were apprentices, a fifth of the remainder were refugees, and the rest were split between guildsmen and Enforcers. Nymeria was sad so many had died, and she tried not to think of the blood or the screaming from the battle. Instead, she turned her mind to the idea that had struck her from having read through the largest book she'd brought with her. She thought deeply about it as she avoided most of the envoy to keep from drawing more attention to herself. She already knew she was being whispered about among some of them, and that it displeased her father to no end.

Nymeria found herself along a wall of thick foliage and old rubble behind the cathedral. The trees here were so dense she could not see far into them. The peace they offered seemed to beckon to her. It was quieter out there. There weren't any wounded or murdered people. If she went and hid by herself, she wouldn't have to worry about trying not to hear or see what had happened to them.

She slowed when she felt another tear slide down her cheek, and she scrubbed it away. She didn't want anyone to see her cry.

Nymeria stared out into the trees. "It's not my fault I'm not like everyone else," she whispered to herself.

For the first time in her life, she thought about just leaving. She'd never had such a thought before, and it made her want to cry even more. But she couldn't help it. Everything around her felt tremendously and overwhelmingly wrong all of a sudden. She knew she was too young to consider it, but the path was before her. An opening that snaked away from the city, into the depths of nowhere. She knew it was wrong, but the thought had pushed its way into her mind, as if trying to convince her she *needed* to leave. Before it was too late.

But she didn't know why.

Another thought followed the first: What if her family was happier and safer without her?

She stared ahead, gripping the bag and fighting tears. She was ashamed of the thought, but it had ignited a storm of confusion and sadness in her heart, and she didn't know how to shut it out. She remembered the bright red blood she'd drawn when she'd bitten Adam. She always remembered the bright red blood. Always, it was the bright red blood that drew her, as if whispering, as if promising . . .

Something moved, as if provoked by the storm within her. Nymeria stepped back as a veil of uneasiness rippled through her. She saw a small murmuration of starlings, but the birds were not what had caused the sharp crack of thick wood breaking.

The noise rooted her in place and set her heart to racing. She tried not to let her imagination run wild. The sound had not been that of a widowmaker falling. A widowmaker would have thundered and crashed in a different, more careless sequence of sounds. What she'd heard had been a long, slow creaking sound, like the deliberate footstep of some creature stalking prey. And from the bright green sea of leaves, she felt its senses reaching out for her with a twisted hunger that was born of the darkest of torments.

Even the female wolf had never rang the same fever of alarm within her. This was a dangerous creature, whatever it was. It had no human emotion, and from it, a tainted aura crept through the woods.

A few leaves floated downward, and Nymeria shivered as the twisted presence drifted nearer. She stepped back, but its tendrils seemed to wrap around her and hold her still.

Her throat closed on its own. It felt as though the being intended to slowly steal away and devour her will. It pulled her toward the trees, though she resisted it as her fear grew stronger.

The presence felt familiar. She could almost remember the feel of its twisted emotions, whirling in a raging sea of chaos — almost remember the sound of its heartbeat within her mind. She could almost feel the shadow of the agony that swirled within it. She remembered its need for her presence, and the gripping, rending sensation as her soul was constricted within her until it was about to be snuffed out.

Glowing blue eyes in the water's reflection . . . So much blood in the water . . . Despair, as black as demons.

The fractions of memory were so stark that Nymeria gasped, recoiling. She did not hesitate another moment. She hurried toward her father's voice as she fled the memory and the presence. It seemed to flicker and die away behind her, slowly unraveling, until she could breathe again.

Within the hour, rhythmic hoofbeats thundered through the camp, and several attendants rushed forward to greet the emergency head-on.

Nymeria's father looked up from his preparations as she handed him his medical kit. He didn't seem to notice her hands trembling, or that she tried to hide it.

"Get out of the way!" Wylem's voice was deep and gravelly, and he commanded her attention whenever he spoke. She watched his long, plaited, oak-colored hair swing to the side as he slid from the saddle. He was not as massively built as Robert or Thomas, but he was perhaps a foot taller, and he was much quicker. He was a frightening man with an even more frightening temper. She had seen him fighting with Captain Makam the day before, and he was savage when he was angry. She'd never seen anyone else in such a rage, not even her father.

None of the other ill-intending Enforcers had dared to challenge Wylem after the fight. He'd been such a brute that the other disgraceful men had lost their nerve when they'd seen how he'd dispatched the captain. Especially because Wylem had walked away without a single scratch or bruise while fighting the armed Enforcer with his bare hands. Captain Makam had sustained several broken bones and lacerations.

But now Wylem was favoring his left knee. Someone had hurt him, and Nymeria couldn't imagine who could have bested him in any fight.

"What did you do to your knee, Wylem?" asked her father. But the darker man scowled and then reached up and pulled an unconscious boy off the back of his giant, excessively furry horse with a single hand.

"Antonio, as requested," grunted Wylem. "He'll be dead by sundown unless you can perform a miracle. Never mind my knee. One whiff of weakness, and those frickin' Enforcers'll have a heyday with me, so say nothing of it."

"I'll take a quiet look once I am through with Antonio," her father said as Wylem placed the boy on the cot. Nymeria's nose crinkled at the smell.

Nymeria bit her tongue thoughtfully while her father argued with the attendants and Wylem, who had simply tossed the unconscious boy onto the cot. The motion hadn't been gentle enough, according to her father.

She studied the bloody handprint that stained Antonio's shirt, right over his diaphragm. It was the size of Wylem's hand, as though he'd tried to stanch the bleeding when the knife had been pulled from Antonio's leg. The wrappings on Antonio's leg also seemed too tight.

As Wylem made excuses for the poor hygiene afforded to the boy's bandages, saying he'd had to leave Antonio with inexperienced refugees until Timothy had arrived, Nymeria realized that Antonio also lay too still. His skin was pale, and his lips were tinted blue. She opened her mouth to interrupt her father and Wylem, but she paused when she noticed the gray color creeping slowly through his veins.

Wylem was telling her father that Antonio had been conscious the last time he'd seen him, and that he'd given instructions for the bandages to be kept clean. That it had only been hours since then.

Her father continued to rant about Wylem's brutish treatment of the boy when Nymeria tugged at his sleeve.

"He's not breathing," she said.

Her father looked down at her, startled, and then his gaze darted to Antonio. He retreated from the argument with Wylem and bent over the unconscious boy to check his pulse. He put his ear just over the boy's mouth next, and he frowned when Nymeria reached out to touch the bright red coloring Antonio's pant leg. The color was hypnotizing where a ray of sunlight pierced it. It seemed to grow brighter, as though to dare her to touch it — as though it might hold a memory of what had happened to him.

"Nymeria," said her father, "get back. Stand over there, out of the way."

Wylem grimaced. "I thought you wanted both of your children to become apprentices. Teaching her is going to involve getting her hands dirty."

"She is too young to assist in any surgery yet, Wylem. And she isn't traveling as an apprentice this season, not yet. She is here because I have no other placement for her." Her father took his knife and slit Antonio's pant leg and bandages open to look at the leg. "All that festering, and in just over a day?" He swore under his breath, and then he spoke to one of the attendants. "Anise, bring Robert or Ellie back here for me so one of them can help me to clean this boy's leg up. Ellie would be better, she's got quick, steady hands . . . Actually, get both of them. He'll need to help Wylem to hold the boy down, probably. This could have been prevented, Wylem. The refugees you left him with are not trained. Just giving them instructions does not always cut it. Regularly, I *still* have to explain to the wearyworn that coffee grounds mixed with human saliva is *not* how to get a wound to clear up quicker. The remedies some of these people are passed down through their families and some of their local doctors are just insane."

Nymeria's father gritted his teeth as he prodded and poked carefully about Antonio's wound. "I may have to amputate his leg. Hold that filthy bandage on him while I get the rest of what I need ready." He then opened the bag Nymeria had collected and began placing certain vials upon the temporary table behind him. Whenever he paused to think with an urgent, calculating look upon his face, he pulled his hair upward, until it stood on end. Just like her little brother. Then her father selected another item. Some of the things he set out were surgical tools. Others were various pain relievers and medicines. He then opened the disinfectant and poured it onto his hands and into a shallow bowl, which he dropped the tools in. He wiped the bottles and the table as well. "All sorts of opportunistic pathogens could settle in that wound. More than what's already taken hold," he muttered.

Wylem looked after where the attendant had scurried away as he held the bandage to Antonio's leg. He sucked on his tooth for a moment and then leaned against the gurney to ease the pressure from his knee. "Why don't you have any placement for your daughter? This is the most dangerous trip we've had in years. And you knew it was going to be so before we left Crow Post. I wouldn't risk it for my own children, no matter their ages. It's bad enough the apprentices must travel this season, what with everything else going on."

"Jeana is tending to my patients in Crow Post and Old Crow Town during my absence. She has her hands full helping Nails and the brewers care for and send off as many refugees as they can. It's enough to watch our son on top of that. My brother is busy out of town, and his wife Ralleigha left with her daughter to Lovael. The artist guild there doesn't allow more than a single apprentice per artisan. You know how they are about what gets sold in their city, and who sells it. They're even picky about what *doctors* come and go. So Ralleigha can't look after my daughter, either."

"But why can't your wife keep her? She is the girl's *mother*. A tiny dove like Nymeria shouldn't be dragged into any unnecessarily dangerous situations. This is unnecessary."

Nymeria's father set down his stethoscope and met Wylem's dark gaze. His jaw ticked, and he glanced at Nymeria briefly. "I really don't want to talk about this right now, Wylem. This is the worst time. Antonio's got a strong enough heartbeat, but she's right. He is hardly breathing. The blue in his lips is because he isn't getting enough oxygen. His throat is swelling, just like the leg."

"Was it the scorpion?"

"No way to tell for sure yet, but it certainly appears that way. Although such a delayed reaction is less than common. A few other things could have caused this amount of swelling and the constricted airway. It may be a compounding issue instead, but it's getting worse by the hour. I don't think he'll be able to walk again if he recovers, even if I don't have to amputate. That knife severed the tibial nerve and . . ."

Nymeria's father veered off into incomprehensible mutterings, as he normally did when he was working and thinking, and when Ellie Mae joined them, she added to the wordy conversation.

Nymeria was torn. She knew that something else was off about Antonio. His skin looked bloodless. And the gray color creeping through his veins had advanced, and they'd darkened where the vessels showed through the skin. The gray was creeping through his neck, along the sides of his face, through his wrists . . .

When her father lifted Antonio's eyelids, the boy's eyes were red, as though the veins had burst. Blood seeped down his cheeks in dark rivulets. And Antonio's jaws clenched while he was unconscious. The muscles never relaxed.

Nymeria's heart wrenched beneath her ribs once more. Impulse took over, and her foot moved forward almost as if of its own accord. She reached out, until the tips of her fingers hovered just over Antonio's wrist, where his arm had fallen over the side of the table. She wanted to heal him, to burn away the sickness festering in him. She wanted him to walk. She wanted him to live.

But Wylem saw her reach out. He also saw her hesitation.

She began to pull away when she sensed something else in the boy, something darker. Something that slithered within him, as though stirred from the shadows by the light within her. Something was inside of him, waiting for her to touch him. She felt its hissing aura, its evil stain upon him, and she started to recoil from it.

Antonio's body convulsed.

Her fingertips grazed the hot flesh upon his wrist. She jerked away, but it was already too late. The dark thing hiding inside of him had bitten the light within her. Suddenly, she was unable to breathe. Her throat constricted, and her body felt paralyzed. She found herself trapped within her own mind as the world began to spin about her.

It kept spinning.

For a brief moment, she felt the scathing fire radiating outward from Antonio's leg, and she tried to push it away. Then the boy's pain overwhelmed her and began to wash the world away.

"Nymeria!"

Her father caught her before she hit the ground as the tremor struck, and she felt the Violet creeping through her veins, stretching for the surface and wanting desperately to be released as the chorus of vile whispering began again.

"Oh, no, no, no — Nymeria, will you please, please breathe? *Breathe*, honey!" Her father's voice was frantic, and it was growing harder to understand him as the whispering began to rise in volume. "Ellie, hand me that before she bites off her own tongue! No, no, no . . ."

"The shield which protects her is gone. He has left her to us. The soul of her kindles with warmth, Brothers . . . Give us her life. Annnnnnswer usssssss, Briiiigggggggghhhhhhtttttt Oooooooooonnnnnne . . ."

The words were in that other language again, and the noise was loud and unbearably near. The malignant sibilation rippled over her like water, until she began to sink beneath its volatile current.

Faintly, she heard her father's frantic voice. "Robert! Hurry!!!"

On the backs of her eyelids, dark, ghostly silhouettes flashed by. Voices echoed down a long, dark tunnel. The faint rays of sunlight were blinding, and it made her skin burn and her head hurt. She felt the Violet swirling vehemently beneath her skin. She also heard that strange man's voice again, heard the same earth-shattering, heart-breaking plea she'd heard him cry out before. The sound that scraped past his cracked lips was hardly recognizable anymore as belonging to someone living. He'd been locked away in that dungeon for so very long. *"Aiya tzedaket'hae ian."*

Please help me.

"Aiya . . ."

Please . . .

The plea called to her very soul the way the presence in the woods had earlier, and when she recoiled from the rising beast that was his endured horror, she felt her body jolt, as if encasing and restricting a lightning storm. She recoiled from the voice, from its cold, wretched pleading, and *he* began to scream in agony.

"NAI!!! Kretu henna ian avae'ue!!! AIYA!!!"

NO!!! Do not abandon me to them again!!! PLEASE!!!

"Caaaaasss — "

CHAPTER THIRTY-TWO

*A*waken

WHEN NYMERIA WOKE, the protective bulwark that was the cathedral's failing walls was gone, and the rain had ceased. The golden sky had turned black, and sparks and ash now drifted toward the glittering crystals suspended in the heavens.

The heat from the campfire made her skin feel as though it were about to crack and break open. Some of the men were arguing quietly nearby; Robert simply stood there, a silent creature with haunt written in his eyes, his arms crossed to bar any attempted conversation. Dark, disturbed anger carved itself deep into his features as he chewed gravely on the inside of his cheek.

A small body was being bound on the other side of the fire, and her father was staring into the flames, lifting a wooden spoon and placing it in his mouth absently. He didn't even seem to taste the stew he was eating. The motion seemed more mechanical than anything as he stared blankly ahead. In his eyes, the golden flames danced solemnly.

His eyes were bloodshot, as though he hadn't slept for days.

She looked once more to the body just behind her father. Antonio's sunken face looked as though it were made of wax, and dark, dead hair dragged the dirt. Nymeria's eyes widened. He was *dead*. The realization made her stomach curl in wretched ways.

She hardly heard the small mew that escaped her mouth as she shrank from the sight of the dead boy.

Her father jolted at the sound, and his wooden bowl slipped from his hands as he let out a gasp. He rose from his place opposite the fire and came to her. She took deep, wheezing breaths as the back of her father's hand touched her forehead.

"How are you feeling?"

She could hear the fear in him, for how his voice trembled.

"What happened to him?" she asked.

Her father looked over his shoulder, where Ellie Mae stood with one of the attendants. "Cover him and get him out of here, will you?"

Robert shook his head as though to tell Ellie to continue as he stood there, between Nymeria and the dead boy.

"What did I do?"

"You fainted," her father said as he gathered her in his arms and held her against him for a long time. The hug did not dull the strange emptiness in her, even though she sensed his torrid fears disintegrating as he held her. "You had a seizure," he said. His voice was raw, and it cracked upon his next command. "Robert. Ellie. *Please*. Take the boy's body away. Just get him out of her sight. I don't want her to see him."

Robert shook his head and grabbed a fold of the canvass the men were using to bind the boy with, and he flipped the last corner of it over Antonio's sunken, waxen, expressionless face. The tracker then grabbed the part of the bundle where the body's feet were, and he began to drag the dead boy behind him by the rope. Ellie Mae said nothing, although her eyes flashed with anger as if she disapproved of this disrespect to the dead child.

Nymeria shrank from her father's touch when he tried to cup her face to make her look at him. "Don't look away from me," he commanded quietly. He sighed when he was satisfied with whatever he saw in her eyes, and he told the others to go about their business. Only Ellie remained, worry pulling at her expression.

"What happened?" Nymeria repeated.

Her father refused to elaborate. "Exactly what I said."

Nymeria stared at the overturned bowl as Ellie reached for the ladle to fill another. It smelled . . . off. Strange, even though it was still familiar. "When did he die? What happened? Why is everyone looking at me that way?"

But her father shook his head. "I don't . . . I'm not sure exactly what happened," he said slowly. "One minute, he was crossing into death. The next . . . he just started screaming. You scared me when you collapsed, Nymeria. And I told you not to try to help. Why do you never *listen* to me?" Nymeria shook her head, upset that he wanted to turn whatever had happened to more anger and more blame. His voice shook. "Why can't you just be like other children . . . ?"

The comment stung. Her bottom lip wavered, but he hadn't answered her question. "Father," she said. "When did he die? Stop avoiding my question. *What happened?* Why was he *screaming?*"

"I don't know!" her father snapped. Nymeria winced, her eyes wide. The grief and the anger on her father's face hurt her. "Okay? I don't know. I don't have a good explanation. That damned violet light — " He gritted his teeth for a long moment and then exhaled loudly, as though he was close to breaking into pieces in front of her. "You need to eat," he said. Again, his voice raked with emotion. "You haven't eaten anything solid in *days*, Nymeria." Ellie handed him the bowl, and he held it out for her.

"It smells rotten," she whispered. She cringed from the smell of it when it neared her. "I don't want it."

"That's not a good sign, if she isn't hungry," Ellie commented. "It's not even an hour old, Nymeria. It's not rotten." Ellie lifted the ladle and smelled it, and she shook her head. "It's fine."

Nymeria's father dampened his anger and his fear, but she could still sense both broiling in him. "The last time you ate was two days ago. We're only two days away from Oakwall. You've been unconscious since that seizure."

It hadn't been a mere seizure. She knew it. She'd touched *Death*, and it had shown her things she hadn't wanted to see. She couldn't get that man's screams out of her head, or what the dark things had said.

"Here. Take it and eat." Her father clasped her hand as she reached numbly for the bowl. His hand tightened over hers when he realized how badly she was trembling, and then he set the bowl down. "Nymeria . . ." He didn't seem to know what else to say, and he looked up at Ellie as though hoping *she* might have an idea what to do. "She's shaking terribly," he said, lost.

Thunder rolled across the sky from far away.

"Go get some sleep, John. I'll stay with her," said Ellie. "Never you mind, let me take over from here. She needs her mother, but I'm sure I'll be fine in a pinch. A man is never as good as a woman when it comes to young children."

Nymeria's father pinched the bridge of his nose the way he did when he was exhausted. With a contemplative sigh, he agreed. "All right, Ellie. Wake me if anything else happens." He kissed Nymeria's forehead and ruffled her dark hair. He held her longer than normal before letting go and standing to leave. "Be *good*," he pleaded. "Please, Nymeria. *Please* be good."

"Shoo!" said Ellie as she slid onto her side next to Nymeria. "Be gone!"

Nymeria's father grimaced and went back to his truck, where he'd parked in the clearing at the edge of their camp.

The moment he was out of earshot, Ellie rolled onto her stomach next to Nymeria and placed her head on her hands. "So let's cut to the truth here. I know you're not going to stop asking because you're just like your father and you can't let something go, and I don't want to see this argument drive you two even farther apart." Nymeria stared up at her. "When you touched that boy's wrist, I saw that freaky light leave you and flash through Antonio's body. Same light as what was in those pieces of glass. I saw it battling the shadow beneath his skin. It closed his wound like it had healed him, and both of you were unconscious for two days. Earlier today, the light ran through him again, and he woke screaming. He didn't stop screaming until it killed him."

What she'd described was horrible. Nymeria's bottom lip trembled again.

"The kid is dead, and it is because of whatever you did to him," said Ellie. "To everyone else, we're saying the infection killed him. Now you know. Don't ever ask your father about it again. He's spooked over it, and he is terrified of what it means for you. I've never seen that man unable to handle anything, Nymeria. He can't handle the thought of anything happening to you." Ellie changed track as Nymeria struggled to comprehend what she'd just been told. That it was her fault Antonio was dead. That they were covering it up. That her father was terrified. "Shift of topic, honey. You are not to breech the other again. Let's talk about some girly things. Do you know how to braid?"

Nymeria stared at Ellie as a confusing whirlpool of emotions opened up in her.

"I can teach you. Yours is long enough to make some incredibly beautiful braids. There are all sorts of them, and I don't even care if you turn my hair into a nest of knots as you try to copy."

Nymeria looked into the darkest part of the night, where her father had vanished.

Ellie pulled an ebony comb from her hair and pulled her braid free of its leather ribbon, and she tossed her bountiful spirals over her shoulder. "Come here. Let me comb out that pretty hair of yours. It could be housing a couple of squirrels right now." Ellie scooted closer as Nymeria's head fell into her hands. "That father of yours is a mess, isn't he? He's doing his best, but he's lost, by the look of it. I'm glad your mother's got his back, though. He needs a good knife-wielding woman to keep him in line . . . He's downright handsome when he's clean-shaven, though. Nearly as cute as Robert." When Nymeria wiped her eyes and looked up to the mortician, Ellie smiled. "Aww, don't tell me you've got no crushes, now. All those cute boys in the trucks, come on."

"I'm five," Nymeria declared. "Of course, I don't have a crush yet."

"Five? Good lord, child. I thought you were a dwarfed twelve-year-old. Good to know you're going to grow up able to climb a horse without a ladder. It'd be hard to be a doctor if you had to make all your patients kneel or lie upon the floor, now wouldn't it?"

Nymeria nodded. "Yes."

"I bet your mother ate books while she carried you. What do you want to bet? As smart as I've heard you talk?" Nymeria burst into tears, unable to hold them back any longer. "Oh . . . that's it, go ahead and cry, kiddo. Come here. I'll hold you until you feel like talking and braiding hair. I've got all the time in the world, and no terrible questions for you." Ellie held Nymeria as though she would slip away, and the warmth she offered was genuine despite Nymeria's past offenses.

"I don't know what's wrong with me," Nymeria wept. "I didn't mean to kill him. I didn't."

"Shhh. I know you wouldn't ever have meant to hurt anyone. Everyone knows you wouldn't ever do such a thing. You're a brave girl, and kind. We've all seen how much you try to help, and how much you care about others."

"My father doesn't believe anything," Nymeria protested. She shook indelicately with tears. She hated that she only disappointed or upset him.

Ellie stroked her hair, pulling it from her face, and leaned her cheek against the crown of Nymeria's head. "He loves you more than anything, Nymeria. He's just afraid, and he doesn't know how to help. We're all going to try to help him, though, and you. We'll figure it out, okay? No matter what. The both of you mean the world to all of us."

"No one can chase the dark things away, though, or make me *normal*."

"You don't really have to be normal, Nymeria," said Ellie. "That's the kind of choice none of us has. Just do your best to be true to yourself. If you're special, be special. Be the best version of yourself, and don't let anyone hurt you for it."

Her tears seemed to have no end. It felt as if she'd buried an ocean of them, as if all of her grief were now bleeding toward the surface. But Ellie did not protest as she held Nymeria. The fire continued to make Nymeria's skin sting, and the overturned bowl of the off-smelling stew caused her stomach to curl in wretched ways.

When the sea of sorrow finally seemed to empty itself, Ellie shifted to another conversation. "I have a question for you."

When Nymeria said nothing, she continued. "Do you want to attend the wedding when we return to Crow Post after the traveling season is finished? Robert and I would love it if you and your father stood with us as our honored. I'll have several maidens, but you would be my favorite. Wouldn't that be lovely?"

Nymeria nodded, sniffling. "No hurdy gurdy, though."

Ellie laughed. "Of course not! I'll break that dumb thing if he ever tries to play it again."

"Will there be any chocolate? Uncle Reid said he would find some cacao beans. Will my uncle be there? Or Marissa or Jamie?"

"I'm sure we'll make do without them. How are we going to do your hair, then? Do you want it braided?"

Nymeria shrugged, and she wiped the tears from her face as she sniffled again. "I don't know."

"Will you eat for me, then? I'll show you a few pretty hairstyles if you do."

Nymeria shut her eyes against a fresh wave of tears, but she nodded slowly.

"Good. Your father will be pleased at that. He's not slept for days, worrying over you. Robert and I have practically force-fed him to make sure he's eating enough. And Wylem's been helping to drive. It's keeping him and the Enforcers from arguing, so he's been glad to help."

"What about Wylem's knee?"

"Oh, your father patched up that knee well enough. Wylem's fine, don't you fret."

CHAPTER THIRTY-THREE

Oakwall

THE OAKS WERE MASSIVE. Rows of them stretched on for miles, creating a monstrous grove that stood like sentinels above the rest of the thick woods about them. The walls on either side of the grove were formed by the old levies, whose ancient faces were covered in vines and moss and decay. Spilling from holes where the stones had been pushed aside and crushed by centuries of growth, exotic ivies grew thicker than a horse's thigh. The flora barred the hollow interiors, although sunlight filtered through the occasional crevice and wind howled through and echoed within the walls.

Nymeria watched the people here as they worked, flitting here and darting there. All were dressed in black and in shades of the forest. Many of them carried woven baskets upon their heads, most of which were overflowing with various herbs, and bark, and other things. Some of their heads were covered with netting, and even their hands and feet were barely visible — what *did* show was most often covered in more shades of green paint. Cloth wrapped nearly every inch of them, until they themselves seemed to be a breathing part of the forest.

"Father, why are they dressed so strangely?" Nymeria asked.

"I take it you're feeling better," said her father appreciatively. He didn't look at her. His finger still rested on his upper lip, and his elbow braced on the frame of the door where his window was down. His gun lay in his lap, unholstered. He looked worried, but at least he seemed to be feeling better, too. "Don't let any of them see you. There is a man here I don't want to find you."

Nymeria pursed her lips, but she did as she was told and lowered herself in her seat. She peeked out at the strange people. Her father grabbed the rough, woolen blanket that lay on the seat between them and tossed it over her quickly. It was itchy from the moment it touched her skin. But she did not move.

"Your wolf has come back," he said. "She's keeping her distance, but we can hope she'll still help the way she did at Ender's Creek."

"She's back?" Nymeria hadn't seen her. Her heart fluttered. She was glad. She'd worried the wolf hadn't made it. "Is she okay? She was hurt when she left. They got her in the shoulder, and her back paw got cut."

"As far as I can tell, she isn't limping," said her father. "Now curl up small, and don't move an inch," he commanded. "If I tell you to run, head beyond the wall. These people are forbidden to set foot on the other side; they know that if they do, they will be shot on sight. The path is under the ivy behind their longhouse. That's on the right. The vines that begin at the ravine just after it are thick enough to climb, but they'll break from the wall easily. You'll see the entrance to the Haunted Road from there. You will wait at the entrance for us. Promise me."

She heard the gun click against the dash where he placed it. He wanted the strangers to see that he was armed and brooked no patience. "Yes, Father," she whispered, determined to obey him so that he would not get angry. She wanted to ask what was going on, but she did not want him to get in worse trouble. He was afraid, and that meant she had even more reason to be so.

"The refugees and the Enforcers will head north, and Lukas's escort will split as soon as we're all permitted through Oakwall and its forest. We'll be on our own with the apprentices and guildsmen after that, so we'll have to be more careful, all right? But we should be fine as long as no more of those wolfmen pretenders find us."

Her father quieted. Leaves crunched, and twigs snapped near her door as the armored truck slowed. Nymeria kept still, as she was asked.

Other men shouted, and rapid bursts of gunfire erupted. Nymeria winced.

"Guns down!" Wylem roared from his furry horse. "We are passing through peacefully! If any of you dumb goats shoots one of theirs, I will take you by the neck and crush all the bones there."

She heard Robert acquiesce politely when he was told to get out of the truck behind them by one of the Greenmen. "I've no other weapons on me."

"*Kneel*," said the Greenmen.

The leaves that crunched near Nymeria's door and her father's door quieted.

"Get away from my truck," her father snarled. His gun scraped across the dash. "Just tell me what you must, and let us move along."

The person outside her door cleared his throat. Somehow the sound was menacing, and she felt it when the man leaned on the door. She felt his hands dangle over her; his fingertips just barely touched the blanket over her head. "That's no way to greet an old friend, Jonathan."

"You are no friend of mine, Irkov," said her father. "I said, *What do you want?*"

She recognized the man's name. Irkov was the name of the brother of the man who had taken her mother's voice a few years ago.

"Your men did not pay their way last year," said Irkov. "We have not been treated fairly, in accordance with the Pact. We were cheated, and we want recompense."

"I should kill you where you stand. You have no right to bar us from the Haunted Road, Irkov. We've always paid our dues."

"Ah-ah," said Irkov. "I wouldn't if I were you."

Her father hissed. It sounded as though he'd been struck by someone. He moved cautiously, probably to lift his hand to the wound. She smelled his blood. Nymeria gritted her teeth when she heard the strangled pain in her father's voice. "This extra toll of yours is a farce. If you really believe we didn't, then your men counted wrong."

"Regardless, I did not see what we were owed. So. You are not to pass through our home again without making up for your last insult." Irkov whistled, and the door opened next to her father. He was dragged from the truck, though he struggled against them. Nymeria shut her eyes tightly. Her heart knocked hard against her ribs, but she kept still.

Irkov opened her door as well. The breeze carried the smell of smoke on it, and of maple.

"Irkov, stop!" Nymeria's father cursed.

Irkov paused. "You have with you over a hundred children," he said. "Give us half, and I will not gut you when I am done searching your trucks. We don't want the refugees. Grown men and women have a mind of their own. They're harder to control, and they weigh too much to climb the highest branches." He flipped open the glove compartment and removed her father's ammunition and spare gun. "I'll add these to my collection. It's rare to come across working guns. Seems as if Temple guildsmen and Enforcers have the only decent smiths, and too few at that." He put them on the seat next to her. "The money we are owed as well. I want that. The last two winters have been too mild for us, and because of it, the locusts and the webworms and the loopers have been eating everything in the groves. We can eat the locusts and dampen their numbers. We cannot eat the loopers or the webworms. So we need the money, and we need more hands to scrape away the eggs, and the webs, and the worms."

The men who held her father made no sound, except to viciously tell him to shut up when he groaned against the painful holds they had upon him.

The glove compartment shut. "Make this easier for all of us, Jonathan. Which trucks have the children?"

"You're not having any of the children," hissed Nymeria's father. "If you want apprentices of your own, you'll have to send a requisition to Saura and receive her approval for the next season. These are not yours to take. They are to be apprenticed to the guild — "

Nymeria flinched when Irkov's hand rested on her knee as he leaned forward to search under the dash and under the seats. She knew he would lift the blanket soon and see her.

The knife she carried for the *dark things* slid from her boot, and she pulled a hidden shard that she'd been working on from her sock. She placed the glass against the metal and felt it begin to heat up. She didn't know what to do with it, but she knew she needed to do something if he found her. She didn't want to be one of the kids he took.

Nymeria heard her father's cry when one of the men struck him again. There was a wet crunch, like bone being broken. "No!" he gurgled. "Irkov, *stop*!"

The blanket was yanked away, but the man who stared down at her made no other move. He hadn't expected to see a child beneath the ragged blanket. His gray eyes went wide. His lips drew back into a snarl, and he reached out to grab her. He sliced through the seatbelt with the knife he held before reaching to take her arm. That was enough of a delay for her. Nymeria twisted out of her seat before he could touch her, and her own knife went deep into his left eye. He screamed and recoiled as she jumped out of the vehicle. But he caught her by the wrist and dragged her back not a moment after her feet had hit the ground running. Blood was everywhere, and she wrestled free to avoid touching it.

"Nymeria!" cried her father. "*Run!*"

Irkov's fist crashed down against her temple, and the world shuddered. He staggered back, his hand over his eye.

Nymeria's knife was on the ground beside her, just inches from her fingers. But her fingers wouldn't move. Tears clung to her lashes as she tried to move her arm, and her skull pounded furiously as her head lolled. She wanted to cry, but her fear for herself and her father kept her from doing so.

Irkov was still there, and he was furious.

His meaty fist wrapped around the hot makeshift blade, and he ripped it out and flung it deep into the woods. Then he cackled madly as he bowed over and clutched at his face. "This little creature has taken my *eye*!" His laughter continued to bubble forth like a river of madness.

Nymeria rolled over onto her side. Her fingers dug into the leaves and the dirt, which were still wet from the morning dew. The shard pressed against her palm.

"I can take your other one, too," she managed to say. Her tongue felt like a slug in her mouth. "Come closer, and you'll never see again." She looked for the building her father had mentioned, but she saw nothing but small lean-tos where green canvasses were stitched together and draped over bent branches. Smoke rose from several fires beneath the little canopies —

Captain Makam had crept behind Wylem and was pointing a gun at his head, his finger twitching over the trigger. He'd only stopped because of what she'd done, because of Irkov's screams.

Behind Wylem and Captain Makam, she saw the crumbled roof of an old longhouse, and she saw the great, massive vines her father had described.

Nymeria scrambled to her feet, but before she could run, Irkov said, "I think you and I should come to some kind of agreement, Little Creature." He was talking to *her*. "Seeing as how you've shown more balls than the grown-ass men in your company. How about *you and I* strike a bargain? We can put this feud between him and me to bed for good. Him in a grave, that is, if it is necessary."

As Irkov spoke, Sergeant Elija slipped behind Captain Makam and placed his knife against his throat. The captain dropped the gun, scowling. Wylem realized the danger he'd been in. He kicked the gun away, allowing one of the Greenmen to take it, and then Elija slit the captain's throat and let him go.

Captain Makam went to his knees as he sputtered and clutched at his throat. His eyes were wide and round with shock and anger. Nymeria looked away, not wanting to watch the Enforcer die. She could still hear it, though, and it was unpleasant.

"He's been a problem," explained Elija to the Greenman who aimed his gun at him. "He was placed under arrest the last time he tried to kill this man. His attempts will occur no longer."

The Greenman nodded approvingly, and he lowered the gun as the sergeant lowered the knife. "Wicked men should always be ended by their own. Now give me the knife and be a threat no longer. I want to go to bed tonight *not* counting how many corpses I had to haul out of Oakwall myself to avoid the smell of them days later. We've more important things to do than waste the season cleansing your stain."

Nymeria looked at the ancient wall, and then she looked at her father. He was struggling to keep the Greenman's dagger from cutting his throat. His nose was bleeding, she realized. The skin had split over the bone. The sight of the injury angered her as nothing ever had, and she forgot caution. She forgot about running. "I should take your other eye just for having them hurt my father," she hissed.

"Nymeria!" snapped John.

"Shut up!" she shouted. "All you do is tell me to obey and be quiet, and hide, and that I am a bad child! I am sick of it!"

Irkov began to laugh again. "She's your *daughter*?" said Irkov. "Scrappy little thing. Like a small, wild demon monkey."

"What is your bargain?" demanded Nymeria. "Money? What did you want money for? Treasure will bring nothing but misery. Others will come for it."

"Not for riches," Irkov said. His smile was revolting and snakelike.

"If you anger my father's guild, Oakwall will be burned to the ground, just like Cyan. No one will survive. Whatever glory you are seeking will only cause your fall."

"A fierce little demon, are you?" laughed Irkov. "I am not interested in glory. This is about respect and necessity. And your father, with his men and on behalf of the Temple, has gravely disrespected us."

"Why does he have to respect you? Because he killed your brother, and that offended you? Your brother was a killer, and a worthless, unskilled blob of smoldering pony dung who thought only of himself and his ego. He tried to kill my mother. Your brother had no right to be called a *doctor*."

"Nymeria, shut up!" commanded her father. His eyes were wide, as if he was horrified that she would throw such insults directly into Irkov's face. Rightly so, because Irkov's expression became savage. "There are other children with us who must get to Black Temple, and these people will kill or enslave them!"

"*Bakh!*" snarled Irkov. "That is not the way of the Men of the Forest. We have no respect for slavers. But my brother was a well-ranked doctor, and your father stole his wife. You're the right age to be Griggori's kid. Black hair, too." Irkov finally drew his hand away from his ruined eye. Nymeria had to look away. Looking at it made her queasy. Blood still pulsed from the wound. It trailed down the crevices etched deeply into his grimace, and it even coated his teeth where it ran over them. It dripped from his chin and stained his green shirt black. She couldn't look at it. "I have never seen eyes like yours, though," said Irkov. "Not in my family. There were none in Jeana's family, either. All of them had almond or blue, and only in natural colors. I've never seen eyes that were such a color."

The shard Nymeria still held fused with energy and pulsed malignantly. *No explosive ones*, she remembered, and she felt the knots within the energy dissolve. She would never break that oath to her uncle again, not unless she had to — and even then, she would tell him why. Uncle Reid would understand. But in the present moment, she could blind Irkov's other eye, and she would never feel bad about it.

"You're prattling," said Nymeria impatiently.

Irkov's brow rose. "Excuse me?"

"I asked why you wanted what you have demanded. Tell me, then. Let's bargain."

Irkov's brows drew together. He stared at her for a long time, then looked at her father. "How old is she?"

"I'm five. You're about to be outwitted by a five-year-old, you dumb ogre. You've already lost your eye to a tiny child. Let's bargain."

Irkov's men began to snicker — until Irkov snarled and cast his one angry eye at them.

"Ferocious little demon child. Bargain it is, then. The money would be for supplies."

"What kind of supplies?"

"Lights."

Nymeria cocked her head. *Lights?* That was the stupidest thing she'd ever heard adults fight each other over. They were pointing guns at everyone because of *lights*?

"Batteries," he added. "They are among the most expensive things we need. We cannot go into the groves and risk burning down our livelihood with the torches. We will lose Black Temple's aid by the time the leaves yellow if we cannot harvest this entire grove and our fields by then, and there is not enough daylight. Our equipment never came when it was supposed to during the last season." He snarled at her father over that one. "We don't have enough workers. We would work through the night to make up for it — but we cannot do so without the lights."

"That's all? All of this, for lights and batteries? They're that difficult to find, or to make?"

No wonder her uncle had expressed so much interest in her items. And no wonder her father had always valued batteries and lights so, and with such a temper.

"Watch your tone, little Demon Monkey. But yes."

She interrupted him. "The simplest batteries and lights are easy to make. There is copper everywhere in the old ruins, and the other ingredients are cheap and easy to come by."

"They are easy and cheap for others to get. Not so for us," he glowered. "How do you propose we get them, other than by exacting this new toll in order to make up for what we are owed?"

Nymeria crossed her arms. She couldn't believe this was so *stupid*. "First, you can let my father go. Second?" She clutched the shard tightly. The solution was *stupidly* easy. "I'll get you the lights you need."

"Ha!" choked Irkov. "You. *You* will get them. Why don't we just take them instead?"

She knew he saw the knowing behind her smile. It caused him to hesitate. "Because we have too few good ones left with us. They're almost completely used up, or they are broken, you imbecile. Go ahead and search. You will find children and wounded refugees and Enforcers in the trucks, and medicine you will not know how to use without dosing up and killing yourselves on accident. Even if you stripped our trucks to create what you might need from the scraps, your crappy craftmanship would last barely a couple of weeks. And you would be back to needing lights and batteries, *and* you would have offended Black Temple and lost its aid. I doubt the Temple will take kindly to having its envoy robbed."

Irkov nodded to the men holding her father. They struck him hard, and he hit the ground. "Search the trucks," commanded Irkov. He was displeased. "Take anything we can use to our end, but leave the trucks intact."

The men backed away and did as they were told.

"Why don't you ever *listen* to me?" her father groaned. He lifted his head as he rubbed at his throat where the knife had pressed dangerously deep. Irkov glared at him, and he became angrier at her father's every word. "You're going to get yourself and other people killed — "

"You keep talking, I'll kill this cute little ballsy kid in front of you," said Irkov. Her father paled. "I'd rather not because this creature is adorable. She has a hell of a backbone. But I will to make a point, you wayward-minded piece of shit. And keep your eyes on the damned ground, too, or I'll kill all the other kids and refugees. If we're doomed to be cast aside by Black Temple, we may as well go out with our finest middle digits pointed skyward. With our dignity and honor intact as Men of the Forest. Not as brittle-boned wife-stealers such as yourself."

"You can't step in unless they start killing the apprentices and refugees, can you?" Wylem asked Elija unhappily.

Elija shrugged. "Not unless we are willing to cast our honor aside and destroy our treaty. This is simply a dispute between your people and the wearyworn, and it is a resolvable one. Your doctor should really shut up. He's making this worse." Elija smirked. "I think the little *Demon Monkey* is handling this quite well. She has my respect . . . I'm glad it's not *my* eye she's taken."

Some of the Greenmen chuckled under their breaths and immediately feigned it was not themselves who'd laughed but others.

Irkov glared at Nymeria's father with his single good eye and paced as he waited, and he and Nymeria stared at one another, neither willing to back down. He wiped more of his own blood from his cheek and his chin, and in so doing, he smeared the three dark green stripes upon the side of his face. The blood glistened wetly against the green.

Irkov whistled sometime later, even as he continued to pace. "Elsir? Anything?" He looked quite impatient. There was no answer. "*Elsir!*" Irkov barked.

"Irkov, there is nothing usable. Their lights are half-dead. Maybe an hour or two left in them. The chargers are shit," said another man who was draped head to toe in the colors of their forest. The only thing that stood out about him was his very red mustache. The green could not dull it. It looked like a fuzzy red caterpillar, curled up just beneath his nose. It wiggled when he spoke. "Just the things she's said were there. Not even money, aside from the usual amount, which seems to have been for us. The box says, *Green Troll Toll.*" That garnered another quiet snicker from one of the Greenmen.

Irkov growled deep in his throat. "Usually the children are the honest ones. Scare them enough, and they always tell the truth. This one's different. *Akh!* There always has to be *one defiant brat.*"

Nymeria shook her head, showing her annoyance. "Do you have any glass?" she asked. "Anything with glass that can be broken and not missed? I will also need my knife."

He stopped pacing. "Are you telling me you were actually serious? How are you going to get us what we need with just *glass* and your *knife*? By stabbing my other eye? I don't think so."

Her fingers uncurled from the shard, and she cast it at his feet. The light that shone from it was blinding. It was unlike the other lights she'd made before. She'd incorporated new properties inspired by her books. "I intend to make these for you," she said. "Or does the half-blind ogre not want them?" Then she gave him another deserving threat. "No one else can make hex lights, and I will never make them for you if you anger me again. Take this bargain or walk away with nothing. I will not negotiate again if you refuse."

Irkov lowered his hand finally as the light dimmed a little, and he knelt to pick up the shard of glass. "What . . . *magic* is this?" he grated.

"It is not magic," said Nymeria, although she wouldn't know whether it should be classified as such. She chose not to let him think it in case the idea would inspire the same fear as it seemed to in others. "The Modern World did not operate on magic, did it? Of course not." She shook her head. "I will never teach your people how these are made because you harmed my father and threatened the lives of the others who have come with us. That is the punishment for your cruelty. However. I am willing to make this bargain with you. But it may cost you more than you are willing to give. How desperate are you for these lights?"

"By the Oaks, you're a damned *witch*!" laughed Irkov. "This is made from one of the forgotten sciences?"

She nodded as he turned it over in his hands incredulously. As he studied it, she dared a peek at her father. He was daring to look as well, and confusion was written all over his face. He hadn't known what she'd thrown, or what Irkov held, except that it was bright.

Her father had threatened to whip her for those shards.

Nymeria tried to swallow her fear. She offered a faint smile instead. Then she nodded for him to continue staring at the ground before Irkov made good on his promise to kill the other children.

"How long does the light last?" asked Irkov. "And how do I turn it off to conserve its energy?" There was a childlike glee in his voice. A note of wonder. Some of his questions were the same ones her uncle had asked of her.

"Every hex light lasts twelve hours and will recharge itself once it has been depleted," she said. "The lights will last for several months before they must be replaced." Irkov turned the shard over in his hand, as perplexed by it as he was excited. "You will not be able to replicate them, but they will get you through to the next traveling season."

Irkov looked up as Elsir held out his hand, and he gave the glass to him. That red caterpillar wriggled up and down on Elsir's face. "I've never seen this before," said Elsir. "There are stories, however. Glass, with light inside it, and not like our flashlights or lanterns but in the glass itself. It was common centuries ago. I've heard of these *hex lights* showing up in Edantine. My friend wrote me about them. He asked me to send our entire savings so that he could order them for us. A man working for Black Temple was selling them before he got caught up in some trouble there."

"This is the same?" Irkov asked.

"*Nai*," said Nymeria. "These are better." Her lip curled when Irkov glared at her. "Forty hex lights, or none. Take it or leave it. I will promise more to come on the condition that you will never harm anyone from Black Temple again, and if your people will never tell others where these lights came from. I don't care if you tell them some junker man from Arsennia came through, or if you dug them up after part of the levies collapsed during a storm. I don't care. I don't want anyone else coming to me or my family for them. This will be kept a secret, and if you break that secret, I will come back without my father, under the veil of the night, and I will not only take your other eye but also your tongue."

Irkov stared at her. "I think we have a deal, Little Creature. Just don't take my other eye, and leave me my speech."

"One final thing," she said. "I want my knife back. I will not tolerate being given a different knife, either. You will retrieve the one you threw into the trees."

Irkov chuckled as he pocketed the shard. "As you wish, Little Creature." He held out his hand to her father, then. "I respect your daughter more than I have respected most men. I believe she has earned a truce in your behalf, Jonathan." He shook his head in disbelief. "For you to have raised *that* and still have both of your eyes . . . ?"

Irkov spat some of his blood upon the ground at their feet. "We will keep this deal, and there will be no more animosity between us," he said. "My brother was garbage; I will concede that. He did not deserve to be called a doctor. But I *will* kill you if you ever harm another one of mine. And even though my brother is dead, your wife is still considered part of my family because of my brother's marriage to her. Because of Jeana, I claim this child as my family. Keep that in mind if you ever intend to insult me again. I will take the girl from you and raise her *properly*. She will become a great, proud warrior, and she will learn what honor and ethics truly are."

Her father was stunned.

Nymeria bowed her head respectfully and kept her proud grin to herself. Her father *had* told her, after all, that it was not nice to gloat over a victory.

After she was done creating the hex lights a few hours later and had pocketed the pen-like tool she'd fashioned to create the lights, Irkov's men let them be.

The Enforcers prepared themselves to part ways. Several removed and buried the captain's body, and others tightened the bindings on his goons to ensure they could not escape. Meanwhile, Nymeria's father warned the sergeant of some of the quiet dissent Nymeria and other guildsmen had noticed among some of the Enforcers. Elija had already known about it, but he did tell her father that they were going to question Captain Makam's most loyal men about the nature of their recent actions and about the validity of the orders they'd been getting recently.

So her father had told the sergeant quietly, away from the ears of the others, about the High Commander's disappearance and Lukas's hand in all of it. Elija had been displeased, but he'd nodded as though he'd suspected something of that nature for a while. He promised he would help root out any other traitors, and he also told her father that he and his men would look into what was happening in Five Tower when they were done. They didn't want an outright war to deal with. Not another one.

After the Enforcers left with the refugees who'd not wanted to stay in Oakwall to help the Greenmen, the remaining envoy of guildsmen and apprentices headed for the wall, to Isold, which lay beyond.

Her father never said a word to her about what she'd done in Oakwall. He seemed to struggle to find the words.

She was unsure whether it meant he had been humbled or become angrier.

CHAPTER THIRTY-FOUR

ꝯSOLD

THE OLD ROAD TWISTED AND turned underground as they drove through the tunnel and kept a tight line. Sometimes they would cross another old, broken-down vehicle filled with another family of skeletons and cobwebs and covered in centuries of undisturbed dust. *Wheeled coffins* was the adage. No one wise ever opened the ancient vehicles to loot them. It was one of Black Temple's stranger taboos, but it was rarely dishonored. The last time anyone had disobeyed and desecrated one of the wheeled coffins, John had been a child, and his friends had died from the sicknesses still lying undisturbed in them.

Most of the old vehicles were on the shoulder of the paved tunnel road, but some, they had to drive around.

The walls of the tunnel were still smooth, though in places, the concrete had given away, and they would have to navigate that carefully. The water that at times rose to almost door level smelled as stagnant as he remembered it last, and the horses disliked wading through it. The torches and the headlights never seemed to shine far enough. It was too dark to tell if there were any new blockages in their path until they were atop them already.

They would stop and eat without the sky above them, sleep without the sight of the stars or the sound of the trees or the birds or the insects, and then travel another full day without even a ray of sunlight. Time became an abstract notion in the tunnel, too easily lost in the enduring depths. Two days and two nights, it took to travel, and only if one didn't stop for rest along the way. The road curved this way and that, bent upward, fell downward — but it never forked. At times, the air was difficult to breathe, and at times, they would swear they were not alone.

One's inner demons would always come to haunt a man down here. That was why it was called the Haunted Road. And John's own demons rode him hard during their journey through the huge hills.

His daughter had done well — she'd done something even he had never been able to do. She'd earned Irkov's respect. And his forgiveness. She'd turned the dangerous man into a cooperative ally. John recalled how Irkov had grinned at her, how he'd gotten her to laugh herself silly after the deal had been struck and the lights had been given to the Greenmen. John always had a difficult time trying to make her laugh. If he was honest with himself, he felt a pang of jealousy over Irkov's easy manner with her when they'd left Oakwall.

John looked at his daughter. She was fast asleep, but he saw tears glistening in her lashes as Ellie Mae rode up to the door on horseback.

"How is she doing?" Ellie asked quietly.

He shook his head. "I don't think she's having a nightmare. I guess that means better than usual." He gripped the steering wheel. "I'm frightened of losing her, Ellie. What if my brother is right?"

Ellie Mae looked at him, and her braid slithered over her shoulder. "About what?"

"What if my daughter really is cursed? What if it's killing her?" He cleared his throat, remembering what had happened to Antonio. What had happened to *Nymeria*.

Ellie's expression softened. "You and I both know that curses aren't real. Your brother is chasing a desperate dream. He might or might not find someone who understands what is happening to her before we do. But that doesn't mean she's dying or that she's cursed. It also doesn't mean that we won't be able to find a way to help her at the Temple. There is a reasonable answer somewhere, and we will find it."

Ellie had never seen the other half of that letter, though.

"I just — " He couldn't speak for a moment. He took a deep breath and then exhaled, searching for the words. Instead, he felt his heart squeeze with grief. "She's so unhappy. And all I do is say the wrong things to her."

"She knows you love her. She just wants you to trust her, and to believe in her. She thinks you are disappointed in her."

"But I'm not." He shook his head. "I know that she is special. I do. And I've told her that. Maybe I was wrong to forbid her from playing with those pieces of glass, since she was able to help Irkov and his people with them, but . . ." He didn't know anything anymore. What was wrong actually seemed to be right, and what was right was turning out to be the worst. "I don't want anyone from Five Tower finding out we rescued her instead of letting her die. I don't want them to come for her to finish the job. And how am I supposed to be okay, letting her do things that are dangerous? Or things that upset everyone?"

"That's part of being a parent," Ellie said. "It's hard to protect kids from themselves, even I know that. But you'll both figure this out. It'll be all right if you let it be. Show her that you believe in her even while you are guiding her. She's going to grow up wanting to be herself regardless, but you have a choice between making her ashamed of it or guiding her to become the best version of herself. You remember what your mom did to change Robert around, don't you? He used to be a really bad kid when we were younger. He was worse than his brother Raegan in many ways. Think about how she dealt with this kind of stuff. Selena changed a lot of people for the better. It takes patience, and you have to communicate with your little girl. Otherwise, you're going to push her into a corner until she lashes out, or you are going to push her away."

He nodded, and then Ellie rode forward to talk to Robert, who was driving the truck before him. John looked over at his daughter again and pulled her blanket over her to keep her warm. It was still cold, but it was finally beginning to warm up again. That meant they'd passed the halfway point. They would emerge from the tunnel in another day. Maybe less, if they'd made good time.

He glanced at the floorboard. He couldn't see the books in the shadows there, but he knew they were there.

He wondered.

Maybe his brother had been right about that, too.

John sighed, frustrated. Reid was a far better father. Maybe things would have turned out better if he'd let Reid raise her. Reid seemed to understand her in a way John could not.

He blinked hard, and his temple and his nose throbbed acutely at the exerted motion. The bruising from his broken nose was at its darkest and would take about a week to fade.

Nymeria uttered a small cry in her sleep, saying something he couldn't understand. He'd been wrong. She *was* having another nightmare. He reached for her and threaded their fingers together. Her hand tightened over his as she slept. "Hang in there for me, baby girl," he breathed. The words almost lodged in his throat as he spoke them, and he squeezed her hand back. "Please don't give up on me yet. I'm never going to let you go, not without a fight. We'll find a way to get you better, curses and illnesses be damned."

When they finally emerged from the Haunted Road, the dawn's golden crown was breaking over the steep hills and turning everything golden. Isold's black towers rose from the trees along the path snaking ahead of them, looking like giant spikes on a serpent's back. Black flags waved along their skeletal crowns. John advised the others to display their banners, to roll them over the sides of the trucks so that Isold would know the envoy was their own and withhold their attack and stay any traps.

A mixture of Isold's couriers and warriors rode out to greet them. They guided the envoy toward the post, as they did every arrival. Four other envoys had come before them, he was told. Three had fared better, as they had avoided any confrontations. The fourth had lost more than half of their apprentices. All the Enforcers had died in that group, and so had most of their guildsmen. They'd even lost their field doctor, a man John had met a few times and liked.

As they drove over the highest point of the last hill, John looked into the sunrise, squinting. He thought he saw dust or smoke along the shore of the large lake high in the hills there. He couldn't tell for sure, though, and then the tree line blocked the lake from sight. He thought back to what they'd learned from Lukas, and he hoped what he thought he saw was for the good of Isold and Black Temple. If it wasn't, they wouldn't survive what was to come.

"What's wrong?" Nymeria asked, yawning. She stretched and sat up. "Father?"

He shook his head. "It's nothing, Nymeria. Don't worry about it. We're nearly there. Those black towers down there? Those are the first of the towers. Our guards here, you see them?"

Nymeria looked out the window curiously, and she got up on the seat on her knees to get a closer look when she saw the archer in black riding on a midnight horse on her side of the truck, a few meters ahead.

"They've got a nice camp set up for us already. They'll be helping everyone. I'm going to have to go with some of them so we can get a proper inventory and figure out what Saura wants done first. You won't be going with the apprentices once she sends them off, so stay near Ellie or Robert until I send someone for you."

"I can't go with you?" Nymeria asked.

"No, honey. I have adult things to take care of. I'll come and get you just before dinner tomorrow, probably. Then we'll spend some time together before I have to get back to work. I'll be able to keep you with me for some of it." Then he remembered. "Ah. Pull the window open for me, will you?" Nymeria obeyed quickly, shifting so that she could open the window behind them. "Climb back there and get into the trunk." He gave her the key again. "I need that box, the little one from Cyan. Be very careful with it. If you drop it and the vial in it is broken, everyone in this truck is going to get sick and die, just like in Cyan."

Nymeria's eyes widened. "Are you *sure* you want me to get it, then? Why would you be carrying something like that?"

John laughed. "That is part of my job. Outbreaks are part of my specialty, and containment is part of Reid's. I had Nails look after it for me in Crow Post. Seems the boy Lukas brainwashed was picking the lock at the house, trying to find it. Don't worry, though, I trust you not to kill us all."

Nymeria just shook her head. "You are crazy." She disappeared through the window, and a few minutes later as John pressed the brake, the box shot through in her hand. He took it. She crawled back through and slammed the window shut. "Absolutely crazy," she hissed.

He snorted. "I am responsible and very busy. Now. Over there, Ellie is already unloading the children. Go harass her. I'll be back later tonight." She opened the door. "Wait." He was exasperated. "No hug? What the hell? Your uncle gets hugs, but I don't? You even gave *Irkov* a hug before we left Oakwall."

She chittered and pulled the door closed as she crawled over to him. He wrapped his arms around her, careful of the dangerous box. John kissed the top of her head. "I love you," he said.

Nymeria nodded against him, and then she wriggled free. "I love you, too."

As she was scrambling down, he called after her. "Nymeria! *Behave* while I am gone! No glass, no crazy, no rumors, remember? Just normal!"

"I know!" she called back. *"Tourette's!"*

Good. She remembered. Although she needed to work on the attitude.

John turned in his seat and opened his own door. He searched the area for the right tower, and then he headed toward it. A small building made of stone, and only a few years old, stood at the nearest tower's base. The horses stabled outside it were for the next part of his trip. He was glad he'd be riding one of them for a little while. He needed to move. Sitting in that truck day in and day out had made him irritable. It always did.

"Jonathan!" The voice was familiar. He looked around, searching. "John!"

By the tower's ground-level door, one of the couriers waved him over. The woman had the blondest hair tied back at the nape of her neck. She was tall and built like a man, with hardly a feminine feature about her. One of Reid's old comrades. She was better with the mace and the crossbow than most were with swords, but she was funny enough to disarm most if one bought her a pint of *Old Roman Brandy*.

She met him in the stockyards and wrapped an arm over his shoulder. "By the night's fading toes, you're finally here! You're late, Jonathan. You've shamed us all with your tardiness. I'll have everyone in Black Temple buy you a clock so that the ticking drives you mad. That will be my vengeance, you ugly, unshaven heathen!"

She grabbed his facial hair and pulled on it to make her point.

"You look like a caveman."

"So do you," John said, shoving her off. "Is that a patch of mustache catching the morning light, Laura?"

Laura snorted. "Still manlier than your scruffy lady face. But no, it's my beautiful skin. Hairless as a baby's bottom, unlike yours. Looks as though you had a good fight recently. I'm jealous. How have you been? And how is your brother? I heard he didn't come with you this year. I also heard about your parents. I am sorry about the loss, my condolences."

"Of course."

"What's in the box you're holding?"

He held up the box. "It's from Cyan."

Laura recoiled, suddenly pale. "Baby Savior, what a way to warn someone. Why are you carrying that thing so casually?"

"Must I explain?"

She rolled her eyes and steered him into the doorway at the bottom of the tower. "Yes, yes, I know, I know. Rules and whatnot. If I had a ruby for every one I'd broken — "

"You'd be rich?"

Laura cut her eyes at him and mocked him. "Ooooooh, he's psychic now, is he?" She scoffed. "Absolutely not. But it would be one hell of a start, and I'd have one hell of a lot of bruises. Saura's a beast with her punishments. Even in her old age, I am skittish of offending that woman. Go ahead and stick to your anxious little non-rule-breaking-ways." She snorted, smirked, and then prodded him. "Coward."

He hissed. "Same rib as ever. Perfect aim, every time."

Laura moved the other guildsmen out of their way and ordered the guards out. "Get out. I need to be able to breathe, and there are too many of you! Out, out, out!"

She took a seat, and instead of offering John the only other chair by the desk, she propped her feet up on its back. John shoved her feet onto the desk and took the chair anyway. She just kept her sarcastic smile, unbothered. "Your manners never change," he sighed.

"Your face does," she shrugged. "It goes from this," she mocked him, expressing anger, "to this," she made the expression more extreme, "to bare-assed ugly. I'd smooch ya if you weren't married, John. You would cry, but it would still be a sexy kiss." He couldn't help but laugh when she looked at his bruise over his nose again and added, "You might bleed at the end of it, though. But a little blood never stopped me from a good smooch."

"You're mad," he said.

Laura picked up one of her papers, then, and she scooted it across the desk. "Sign this, that, that, and there, and tell me when you'll be ready to see Saura. I'll send one of the couriers ahead to let her know."

"I'll be ready as soon as the inventory is done," he said. "The papers are in my truck, and I've got some new surgeries documented that she may be interested in. We've had a new outbreak of Scales, and a new vector which I've pinpointed as the source. Not easily avoidable, but there are a few ways to treat it."

"*Scales*?" she said. She took an apple from the window basket, polished it with her black tunic, and crunched down on it. "That's a nasty one. How did you figure out where it was coming from?"

"Fleas," said John. "The first cases I found were always traced to animals. Deer, specifically, just like wasting disease. It transmits to humans who are bitten by the fleas."

"And the treatment?"

"Wouldn't you want to know."

"What, short of fire? Nah. Not really. I prefer to light everything on fire. Kills most diseases."

"And people."

She took another savage bite. "Eh. Got me there. I'm a savage. The mace is more fun, but crossbow's good, too."

John took the pen from her desk, and Laura uncorked a bottle of ink and slid it toward him. He dipped the quill and signed where he needed. She leaned forward, grabbing the red sealing wax she'd already prepared, and she poured some of it onto the paper. He pressed his signet into it as she leaned back and took another bite. "How's the wife?" she asked. Her chewing slowed, and she lowered her voice. It was her way of expressing sympathy. "Is she still unable to talk at all?"

"Sometimes she can manage a little," John admitted. "The scarring along her trachea restricts her ability to speak much. Still causes her pain when she speaks for an extended period. Throws her into a coughing fit."

"I'm sorry." Laura put the apple down, then. "She used to have such a lovely voice. It's a shame, what Griggori did to her." She took the papers and rolled them up, tied a black ribbon about them, and looked outside. "Berry!" she shouted. She tossed the letters to the first balding face that popped into the doorway. The man squeaked as he tried to catch it, nearly fell, and smacked his face into the door frame. He howled in pain, covering his face, and snatched the letters. "Get that to Saura immediately. Tell her John's ETA. He'll be there tonight, in about twelve hours."

"She's not in Isold?" John asked, surprised.

"Nope. But she will be soon."

"Where is she?"

"Working on that project you got her all stirred up with."

"What project?" He hadn't heard of any project.

Laura stared at him. "The rumor is, you caught your mom and dad's killer, and there's an evil plot against Black Temple . . . Hmm. Haven't heard of it?" She snorted. "Come on, John! The whole guild is talking about it! Everyone is freaking out. Saura has pretty much decided they need to shore the dam up the hill, among everything else. She arrived there three days ago, then headed back to Black Temple in one hell of a rush. She was going to come here and greet the lot of you, but she's been busy. That old woman is spry for her age. She'll outlive my great, great grandchildren."

"You're not even married."

"Don't have to be married to have kids."

John stared at Laura. "You don't have kids."

"I have imaginary children. They have wings, and they're evil little shits." She laughed heartily. "Actually, I got married two years ago, and I've had a son."

He stared at her, still. "Now . . . Laura, I can't tell if you're serious or not."

"That's the beauty of it, hon. No one can. My son's name is Isaac. My husband's more of a female than I am. Cooks, cleans, does laundry, can't breastfeed the baby, though. I think he's jealous there."

John laughed. "You don't make it any easier to believe you. But every man is more feminine than you are."

"Eh. Is what it is. At least I get to save damsels instead of be one. Saved my hubby from a mouse once."

"I have missed you terribly."

Laura slapped the desk when she laughed. "Yep. You, too, dear old John. I don't think anyone laughs at my jokes as you do. Everyone thinks I am always serious."

"No, they're too scared of you to laugh, Laura."

"I'll admit that." Laura threw the apple out the door, and it smacked one of the other guards in the jaw as she stood.

"Laura! Quit that!" the guard outside said as he wiped the bits of apple from his face. "I swear, this has got to stop!"

"I throw food at him every day because he's too scrawny." She laughed. "You can throw it at them, but you can't make them eat it." She scooted the chair back in and grabbed another apple. When she offered one to John, he declined. "Well, come on. I want to look at this rag-tag bunch you've brought. Any refugees?"

He shook his head. "No, the refugees split at Oakwall. We had some problems with a few of the Enforcers. I'm not quite sure if any of them were traitors, but some of their leaders were cowards. They took care of their own, though."

"Did you face any other problems?"

"We were under attack at Ender's Creek. Lost a lot of people. Several apprentices, several refugees. Dania's dead, and so is his son. He got shot in the throat. The boy got a knife in the gut when he tried to get out of the truck to help his dad. I almost ran them both over. And the creek was almost too high to cross, but the little girl from Edantine helped."

"By *helped*, how do you mean?" Laura cut him a suspicious look, and her brows crinkled.

"Moving on," John said. He didn't want her to poke fun at that, too. She would never let that one go. Hell, she'd probably go find the girl and adopt her just to parade her about. "Our attackers weren't wolfmen, but they were dressed like them."

This got Laura's undivided attention. She stopped midstride and looked at him seriously. "Are you sure? How do you know?"

"Have you ever seen one of them use a metal blade, Laura? They're strictly against it. Every knife we've ever found in Wolfshadow hands has been made from the dead they have killed and eaten themselves. Everything they have, and everything they wear — it's all made from the dead. It's disgusting, but it's sacred to them. The blade we pulled out of one of our apprentices was not bone. It was metal. And they also had guns."

"*Guns?* Are you kidding me? Where the hell would they get guns?"

"They weren't wolfmen," he reiterated.

Laura whistled. "Did you capture any of them alive?"

They were walking again, toward his truck. "No. Unfortunately, we didn't. They killed their own when we tried."

"Is the boy okay? Did he survive?"

John shook his head. "No, he died a few days later from complications." He didn't embellish on that, and he trusted neither Ellie Mae nor Robert or any of the others who had seen it up close would say anything more than that, either. They knew John's opinion about his daughter. That he didn't want Nymeria to catch Saura's attention.

"That's a shame," she said. "Did you at least manage to figure out where they came from? Or where they went?"

"They came from the west at Ender's Creek. They fled east. But several more appeared in the old city just north of it, where we took shelter. Between Raven Trail and Virien. That's where Wylem and his men killed several of them. It's where that boy took the knife to the leg."

"I'll write a report, then. I'll send it to her."

"What about the other envoys? I heard one of them had worse troubles than us." John pulled upward on his hair, until it was standing on end again.

Laura put her hand on his back. "Wolfmen was the report. Now I wonder. It might have been some of Edantine's friends."

John slowed. "Edantine's friends? How do you mean?"

"Your brother ran into some bad ones there. The nobleman who was supposed to be running the city had joined a group of monks who wore glass chains and spread nasty stuff about Black Temple's intentions. They were trying to besmudge our good name."

"Reid never told me about any of this," John said gravely. He was beginning to wonder how much his brother omitted regularly. "What happened?"

"Long story short," said Laura, "Lord Crostor lost a lot more than his title, and your brother cleaned the town of the monks. He's damned effective, I swear. That man makes friends in the right places wherever he goes. He could have wiped out every one of these fake cult members in a month if he was still an Enforcer."

"Reid's already working on our problem with the wolfmen, trust me," John said. Even though he was unsure how much Reid had going on, he at least knew Reid would always do everything he could. His brother never really abandoned his post, not even when he went AWOL. Reid still found ways of accomplishing his duties, and then some.

But knowing that didn't make John feel any better. Reid hadn't told him a single thing that had happened in Edantine. Instead, he'd gone and gotten himself drunk, and then he had picked the fight with Captain Makam that had caused the Enforcer to become a problem during their journey to Oakwall.

At least John didn't have to measure himself against a perfect older brother. That would have been worse.

"Tell him I said *'Tsup?* next time you see him, all right?" Laura said. She bobbed her head awkwardly, and she tried to pose her large body in a cool, almost feminine manner. She even propped her hand on her hip and flipped her messy hair over her shoulder, and she laughed. "You have to do it just like that."

John laughed. "I am *not* . . . Nope." John raised his hands and shook his head vigorously when she tried her best to pout. It looked quite gruesome on her face. "Absolutely not, Laura."

"Come on. Do it. You can do it." She bumped his elbow with her own. "Do it, John. I wanna see you do it. *I said do it!*"

"Nope."

"You, sir, are a *chicken*. A chicken! I'm going to teach you to master your feminine wiles one of these days. You'll be able to pull off being a female better than me. Your undercover game will be superb."

"Laura, can we focus on work? I have to get back to my daughter."

Laura's dark gaze glittered with glee. "Your daughter?" She shrieked and began to dance from foot to foot excitedly. For the first, and most aberrant moment, she actually sounded and behaved like a truly feminine female. "I wanna see her! Please, John! Please! I heard she was the most adorable little bloodthirsty, sharp-witted, Irkov-blinding warrior-monster! I want to steal her from you! I want a terrifying little monster child of my own! Mine just cries and wants hugs! It's so . . . lame! He *eats flowers*, John! Eats them! I want him to smash beetles and scare big dogs . . . *He coos*."

He had no idea how she'd heard about Nymeria's actions already, but he had an idea whose neck to wring first when he was done. Robert. Or Wylem. Maybe both. Neither had shut up about it since Oakwall. In fact, he was sure he could hear Robert's hurdy gurdy going across the grounds. The man had already written a song about it.

CHAPTER THIRTY-FIVE

THE RAUCOUS LAUGHTER warmed her. The men told anyone who would listen how the youngest child in an envoy of three hundred had tamed a wild she-wolf with a blanket and a look, charged a dangerous enemy and taken command of the defense, and even bested the most feared Greenman at Oakwall. The tale of Oakwall's bargain was their favorite, and it was told most often.

"And she plucked his eye out, and he screamed like a young girl!" guffawed Robert. His face twisted with humor. "The man clutched at his face and danced around, almost to the tune of Billy Whistle!" The cackling went on. "I've seen Irkov take a bolt to the shoulder and pull it out, and then solder the wound with a hot knife with his own hand without so much as blinking," said Robert. His arm went around Ellie Mae's waist, and he pulled her close and kissed her on the cheek. "That child bested him by taking that eye, and then she called him a one-eyed ogre afterward, not even with the merest hesitation or guilt, either!"

"No! You're mad!" objected the guards who'd come to greet them from the nearest of Isold's black watch towers. The one called Lucien bowed over the fiercest. Others were in various stages of choking, gasping, or just outright roaring at the irony and humor of it all. "The smallest child!" Lucien sniffled, straightening. "Where is this child? I want to meet her!" Robert laughed, took a drink, and then waved his mug at Nymeria, who was attempting to sneak away. Lucien stood and held out his hand. "Come here, lemme look at you!" Nymeria was coaxed forward, but she wanted to go the opposite direction. "Is this the girl?" he asked, and glee glimmered in him as his grin grew broader, revealing crooked teeth and a missing canine. He knelt before her and held her by the shoulders. "You *are* a tiny thing, aren't you? I'll bet you wouldn't even be able to knock a flea over!"

"But it's true!" Robert said, and the firelight sparkled in his mirthful eyes as he wiped the tears from them. "He started calling her *Creature*. He called her a wild demon monkey! That man was terrified of her, I say! You could ask any man near John's truck or mine. Every one of them will tell you the same."

"It's a shame I couldn't see around the trucks, or hear any of it very well," said Ellie. "I didn't dare move much, not with that many weapons poised to kill us. Every year, they've gotten worse, demanding this and that. John's put up with it every year. Irkov was determined to find an excuse to kill him this time — it didn't happen because of her. I think they'll be friends now, after what she did. He couldn't believe John still had both his eyes, raising her."

"Ha!" Robert refilled his mug with the small cask that was being passed about.

Wylem snickered. "Oh, I got an eyeful *and* an earful, Ellie. And I don't blame Irkov for being afraid of her. I fear for both of my eyes, now. I'll never underestimate a child again. I've got three of them at home I'm going to be very concerned about with knives from now on."

Nymeria tolerated the frame-quaking pats on her back, their way of showing their utmost respect and their fondness. She heard a lot of, "Good job!" And among those who'd come from Crow Post, "You did your momma proud, you little rascal! Wait until Jeana hears how you've taken after her! A knife-wielding natural, just like her!"

Robert was not finished with his tale, though it was difficult to understand him between his laughter and his drink. "What's more, she threatened to take his other eye, too. And his tongue! I swore he looked suddenly made of wax."

"Ha!" Wylem slapped his knee, then winced and rubbed at the injury he'd been trying to keep from the others. Fortunately, they were too busy smashing canteens together and drinking and barking at the humor of it all to notice.

"She had him thinking she was some kind of dwarfed science witch, and then she left him wanting for more. He took to her like a lost dog after, tried to spoil her, and even asked if she wanted to stay in Oakwall. The man didn't want to see her go!" Another round of laughter. "He was jealous as hell of John, having such a daughter. That girl is going to go places. I tell you, she will make a queen of herself one day. A *queen*. No one else would dare what that tiny little stick of a girl dared! She's worse than her uncle, that child! Reid'll roll over dead when he hears what his little prodigy's done. I have *never* seen such a little thing frighten such a dangerous man so. That green bastard was whipped. *Whipped*, I say!"

Nymeria listened uncomfortably, savoring her sweetened tea. The tool she'd made to make Irkov's stupid lights sat in her hand, dancing with its own shadow in the firelight. The diamond her uncle had given her glistened at its end, where she'd affixed it to the metal handle with some wire . . . She wasn't looking at the tool anymore, though. Black Temple's major hub, Isold, loomed ahead. The towers surrounding it were like jagged torturers' cages. They were just the frames of buildings, some of them. At the tops, long, black banners caught in the wind and were tugged sorrowfully awry. She couldn't see the quatrefoil or the scalpel and bleeding-heart emblem woven upon them, but she could see the silhouettes of the archers whose weaponry occasionally glittered with reflected firelight.

Something felt wrong within her. And as the men shared stories and praises, Nymeria's mind returned to the boy she'd killed. She couldn't stop thinking about his screams, or about the way she'd caused his unnatural death. She'd killed him. No matter what anyone else said, she knew that was the simple truth. Even if Ellie Mae hadn't told her what had happened, she would have known why he was dead.

As the darkening skies graduated into a black and starless heaven, she found herself drifting closer and closer to the dwindling fire. She didn't want to sit near the edge of the night, where the rest of the unknown opened up behind her. She wanted to remain warm, to stay cocooned in the safety these people offered. But she felt separate despite the many smiles and fond glances her way. She felt cold inside. Cold with a fear that came crawling from every shadow the fire couldn't extinguish, from every breath of memory clawing at the edges of her mind. The laughter in the camp began to lose its warming effect upon her, and she began to shiver.

She finally walked away and put her back to a gravestone whose faded letters said some terrible words.

DEMONS CLAIMED THIS GOOD MAN.

NEVER WAS THERE A BETTER BROTHER, FRIEND, OR FATHER.

THIS WORLD NEEDED HIM. BUT IT TURNED ITS BACK UPON HIM INSTEAD.

O.S.M. . . .

The rest of the name had worn away, and she could not read the date. The epitaph looked centuries old, though.

Nymeria stared at the tiny old church at the center of the complex, which was surrounded by thousands upon thousands of gravestones. Most of them had been laid upon their faces to serve as the road on which the envoys traveled. Very few gravestones had been left untouched, such as the one she currently leaned against.

She'd thought Isold would be like a castle, with archives of old scrolls reaching high, vaulted ceilings. And corridors lined with rooms filled with screaming, bleeding patients. The archives were yet to come, Wylem had promised. He'd said that part was underground, closer to Black Temple itself. But they'd already come from underground. They had entered the old cave just behind Oakwall's massive levies, and they'd not seen the stars or the sun for two days — not until this morning had arrived. It was hard to imagine how much more was beneath the ground.

This place felt unholy, and she didn't know why. She didn't even know whether it was really the place itself, for it might instead have been whatever she felt was closing in on her.

"Nymeria," said Ellie Mae. Nymeria jumped. She'd been staring across the fire, watching the trees sway with the wind at the edge of the clearing. She'd been imagining them drifting away, into nothing. The flickering light had made it look so. "Nymeria, sweetling. Have you ever met any of Black Temple's techs?"

Nymeria pulled her long hair from her face as the damp breeze caught it. "Nai, Dr. Mae. I haven't."

"Well, my friend Tessa sent a message earlier this month asking if any of the kids this year were interested in working in her field. Becoming a tech, that is. It's support work, but it's important in its own way. They've got several openings for special apprenticeships. I've told her already about the radios you improved, and she said she was interested in seeing them. After everyone is situated, would you like to go and see her? I thought you might like something to do besides roaming the archives, since your father will be meeting with Saura. Knowing Tessa, she'll want to pick your brain and figure out what you've done to the radios. She'll want you to show her how you've improved them, and she'll probably even invite you to fix some more equipment. Tessa also said several of her techie friends are very excited to meet you. It may turn your father's opinion if he sees how many are interested."

"I don't know. Maybe." Nymeria glanced over to some of the other children. They were enjoying themselves thoroughly. The laughter in the camp had infected them all. The kids were glad to be free of the trucks, and some of them were playing a weird rock game. Others were singing, or chasing one another, or finding other merriment. She only saw the Edantine boy remain apart, as somber as herself. And he was watching her. He'd been watching her for a while, as though contemplating whether to try and talk to her. She just hadn't paid him any attention until then.

Michael put down his own cup and stood when he realized Nymeria had seen him, and he walked toward her and Ellie. He picked up the pen tool Nymeria had left near the celebrating adults and carried it over.

Ellie ruffled his dark hair, and he shuffled on his feet as the mortician smiled down at him. He leaned away and pushed her hand from his hair. "Can I talk to Nymeria alone?" he requested. "Please, Ms. Idathet? It's important."

Ellie grinned secretly and winked at Nymeria. "Oh, absolutely. I've forgotten my tea, anyway. I will see you tomorrow, Nymeria. I'll send a courier tonight to let Tessa know you're interested." Before Nymeria could protest, the mortician was gone.

Ellie Mae hadn't been drinking tea, either.

Nymeria drew her arms around her legs and rested her chin there. She pulled on her other necklace, on the ring her uncle had given her, until she realized that Michael had seen it and seemed to recognize it. She pulled it free and offered it to him. "You're the one from Cyan, aren't you?" she asked.

Michael's features shifted with sadness, but he did not take the ring. "I told your uncle I didn't want it. Keep it."

"He said your mom and dad died," she said. She wanted to cry for him when he said nothing in reply. "I'm sorry you lost them." Yet she remembered how he'd spoken cruelly of her to Sobrienne and the other children. She didn't know what he wanted, but she didn't want to hear anything else he might have to say.

Michael seemed to know what she was thinking. "I didn't mean to make you cry that day," he said.

Nymeria wiped her face and looked away. "Well, you did anyway, didn't you?"

Michael held out the tool she'd made for a long time, but she didn't take it. So he crossed his legs and sat. He waited, and when she didn't say anything else, he lowered his hand. "Look at me."

She shook her head. "I'm not going to listen to any other mean things you have to say about me. Go tell your scary stories to the other kids and keep making them afraid of me, just as every other kid does. I killed that boy from Virien because I'm cursed, and I don't need you to make me feel worse about it."

He let her rant, but he never interrupted her. He also did not get up and leave. Instead, he brushed his hair from his face and put his hand on her ankle. "*Look*. We're not the same, but I'm not like anyone else, either."

Nymeria frowned. She didn't know what he meant, not until she finally looked up at him. She bit her lip. One of his eyes was unusually blue, just past the range of human color — the other was almost as green as hers, and it glowed almost as brightly. "Your eyes are different, as mine are," she said, surprised.

"Except we're not the same," he said again. "I never meant to make you cry. I was trying to warn Sobrienne to leave you alone. She's very stubborn and very rude. And bossy. And full of herself."

Nymeria played with the ring, turning it over. "You weren't just trying to scare them?"

"No. Just her." Michael said nothing else for a long moment. She studied the unusual color of his pretty retinas. "The colors of my eyes are my inheritance," he said at last. "When I am older, I will also inherit everything my father knew. Everything my kind has ever known. I've known that since I was about your age. It might kill me, it might not. I might forget who I am, become lost in the Archive of Dreams. I might not be *me* anymore after that."

"What are you?" Nymeria whispered.

He shrugged. "I don't know yet. My mother called my father a dream demon, though."

"But . . . aren't all demons bad? How could she have loved a demon?"

"He wasn't a demon. He was just different, like us. But why she loved him, I have no idea. I don't know if what I am is good, or bad . . . I don't even know if it is dangerous. But I do know I have an affinity with dreams. I know certain things others would never understand, just as you do. And I have to wait to understand what I am, just as you do."

Nymeria fiddled with the Cyan ring. "Your eyes are really pretty," she said quietly.

"Thanks." His smile was a small one. "Yours are, too."

Nymeria's face reddened, and she blurted, "Stop being weird."

Michael didn't say anything else.

Nymeria looked up, then. "Do you see them, too? The dark things?"

"Only when I close my eyes and Search. But I know the *Shadei Ra* do not like my kind. We're worthless to them. We have the wrong kind of power. It's not what they want."

"*Shadei Ra* . . . Hell Souls? That's what you call them?"

He shrugged. "It's what they are called, not what I choose to call them." He picked up a handful of dirt. It sifted through his fingers. "They're older than even the earth. They're older than the world on the other side of the Vael, too. They came from black fire." His hand fell.

"Why do they call to me?" she asked. "They call me the Bright One."

Michael shrugged. "I don't know that. I'm not sure if that is knowledge I will ever be permitted, either. But I do know that whatever is wrong here is what is drawing them." He pointed at her heart. "The light inside you seems to have something to do with it. The more you use it, the more I see them at the edges of everyone's dreams."

Nymeria shuddered. "My light is the reason they're here?"

"I don't know. It's either your light or the darkness under it," he said. "Part of you is just as deadly as they are. I already told Sobrienne that." He shook his head until his hair covered his brighter eye and obscured the bluer one. "But both of those things inside you are fighting each other. Even wide-awake, I can feel it. It's waking up your other soul."

Nymeria didn't know what he meant by that. "My other soul? I have more than one?"

"Yes and no . . . I don't know how to explain it. They're almost just one, but they're not."

"But how do you know?"

He didn't answer the question. "Everything is about to change for you," he said instead. "I wanted to warn you about that before it is too late."

"But how do you know?" she repeated.

"The memories you're fighting? You'll lose against them. You'll be overcome by the ones that are from your Other." Nymeria shut her eyes fiercely against tears that came unbidden. "It's getting more frequent, isn't it?" he asked. "The visions? The memories? The ones about the man in the chains. There is blood in the water, and his eyes are like blue fire even in the dark. Brighter than your green."

Nymeria's chin wavered, and she nodded slowly. She wanted to cover her ears. "I don't like when the other memories try to wake up. I don't want them in my head because they're horrible. They're not even mine."

"I know," he said. He tapped her knee gently. "Hey. You're a good person, even if you don't think so. But you need to be ready because this is only going to get harder when the *Shadei Ra* get closer and the shadows inside you try to destroy your bright gift."

"I don't want to think about the shadows, Michael. If you don't want to stop talking about them, then just go away, will you?"

He grabbed her hand to stop her from turning the ring over and over. "You'll have to keep fighting, even when you've lost. You have to be stronger than them to be able to drive their voices out. But let the memories in because there is a reason for them."

"The memories are bad, Michael. I don't want to see them. Stop talking about them," she whispered as her fingers curled tightly around the ring, and she pulled her hand out of his. She didn't know how he knew about her nightmares, but she didn't care, either. Now she just wanted him gone. The things he said were awful.

"The boy from Virien didn't die because of you, by the way," he added. "You saved him from worse. You burned it away so it wouldn't change him into a monster. And a lot more of us would have died if you hadn't helped at Ender's Creek, too. If you ever need my help, just come see me. I want to be your friend."

Then he got up and left.

Nymeria sat there, dumbfounded. She sniffled as she put her cup down, and then she curled up to go to sleep. Ellie Mae hadn't come back, though Nymeria wished she would.

She rolled onto her back, frustrated, and then she looked at the little pen-like rod she'd put together at Oakwall. Michael had left it for her.

She picked it up.

The rudimentary sharp end pointed outward at the tip, and where her fingers touched the diamond between the split stem, faint trails of Spirit pulsed. It wasn't bright enough for anyone else to glimpse in the dark. She didn't want it to be.

A better way to make one had to exist, she thought before sliding it into her boot and gazing up at the stars that had begun to appear. She tried to fill her mind with ways to fix the problem at hand. The lights she'd made in Oakwall had been much better than the ones she'd made for her uncle to deliver, but several of them had blown up in her hands when she'd tried to use the . . . the *pen*.

When Nymeria drifted off, the detailed, careful schematics for her next prototype were going through her mind. She was going to need her cousin's help when she returned to their home in Crow Post. She really, *really* wanted to go home. She missed her uncle, her mother, her aunt . . .

Chapter Thirty-Six

Lady of the Temple

THREE OF THEM HAD BEEN summoned to visit Saura within her headquarters at Black Temple. They'd ridden hard to arrive by late evening, just as the sun was sinking over the hills. Over the steady course of the next half hour, they descended curving stairways which cut through the steep hills. The path they took led them to the trees that hid the entrance into the temple; then it led them through various mazes of polished old floors, and high ceilings, and pillars that were as wide as John's truck in diameter.

The journey through the structure eventually led them to a hallway with only a ceiling and a floor. The windows had long ago broken away, and a cool breeze filtered in occasionally through the trees just outside. Long banners of silk drifted in the wind in the moonlight, streaming in great, serpentine ribbons of black.

John glimpsed the courtyard below, and he saw the bridges and towers being constructed on the opposite side of the monstrous ravine. The sheer scope of the labor involved dazzled him, and it humbled him to be reminded how much power Black Temple truly wielded. The wall they were constructing would become a second dam, and a very big one at that. Saura had been fortifying the place heavily. She seemed to have overlooked no detail and spared no risk.

The bridges would allow crossing if the old or new dams broke or the ravine flooded. And more of the upper floors of the ancient structure were being excavated, stabilized, and made livable by the day — the evidence of her endeavor was all about them, even in the window hall.

John hadn't yet seen any of the contents of the archives, but he imagined Black Temple's extensive libraries would be getting moved as well. And that would be an unbelievably laborious undertaking.

Their path eventually veered away from the window hall, until it spiraled deeper into the earth and through massive rooms and suites that were still as dark as night. A few candles burned throughout the halls in the hands of other doctors and support staff.

They continued into the oldest part of the complex, where the walls were made of stone and wound this way and that, forming a massive catacomb. Saura's quarters were in these dank, dark halls.

The torch John held above melted away cobwebs that hung low as he passed under their drifting gossamer bodies. His steps no longer echoed through the tunnels, for beneath his feet were woven grass rugs that dampened the sound. Not even a wraith would have been disturbed by him as he treaded through the oppressive, dark caverns.

Upon the spacious, twisting walls that now extended far enough above not to be threatened by the flame hung the temple's oldest tapestries and curtains. Most of the tapestries here had been hidden away to protect them from damage, and many were awaiting repair. They hung in every color — from the blue of the sky to the green of the fields. A great number depicted the history of the Temple, and in most of those, there were men and women and children dressed in apprentices' robes. There was also the Master, a fictional man robed in white and silver and whose face, peculiarly, was never shown. He always held a silver raven's feather, and he was often difficult to find among the scenes woven throughout the tapestries. But he was always present.

John paused as a wave of uneasiness passed over him. He had stared at these tapestries as a boy, and never once had he put much thought into the tale. No living person in service of Black Temple remembered why the figure was in the oldest of these detailed pieces. The only thing they knew was that the man had supposedly imparted much knowledge to the guild. He was said to be the reason Black Temple existed. Supposedly, the man was also immortal, and the tapestries warned that he was still watching over the Temple, still teaching in his mysterious, discreet ways. Supposedly, only the rarest of Black Temple's holy matrons had ever met him.

It was all nonsense, yet the stories returned to John's mind this night as he walked through these halls. Upon several of them, he noticed the Master hidden in plain sight. He'd never found the figure so easily as a child, when he and the other children he'd trained with had snuck into the catacombs and made a game of finding the Master in them. The silver feather struck John as an odd thing. *Silver Ravens.*

He thought of his daughter again, and his breath came out in a quiet, sibilating oath. Cursed magic. In this familiar environment, as he traversed Black Temple's catacombs, he was able to center himself and to shake off the doubt which had begun to fester in him of late. Cursed magic was nonsense, even if his brother had run off to find it. There was no way that someone in Black Temple couldn't find a way to help his daughter.

John stepped back from the tapestries and continued through the tunnel, his temple throbbing as they approached Saura's hall.

The breeze filtering in through the natural archway was a lovely reprieve from the rest of the catacombs. He did not like the sweltering, mildewed humidity of the underground, and he was grateful for the night's breath as it washed over him in cool waves and dried the perspiration upon his prickling skin. Saura did enjoy the deep, dingy darkness. He'd often speculated that she'd been a pale den serpent in another life, as her nickname suggested she was, in some sense, in this one.

Facing the water garden stood her solemn figure clad in gray-and-silver robes. Golden hair, streaked with white and braided tightly, fell down her rigid back. Her fingers, which were clasped behind her, were tipped in black and copper claws.

She'd always worn those copper adornments. They inflicted as much pain as they did healing.

John stepped forward and knelt, and his companions knelt behind him. "Lady Saura."

"Good evening," she said. "You're late." Her voice was, as always, that slithering, cold whisper that belied her age. She watched some apprentices from her hidden window, assessing them, as always. Below, the fourth-year students were undergoing the grueling process of not only performing resuscitation, but also undergoing a mild drowning. Once every week for a month, ten from a class would be forced under the water down there, and ten classmates would perform the task of saving a life. Sometimes a student died or developed pneumonia — which always instilled more grave lessons. Those who became sick were treated by their peers, under the watchful eyes of their instructors. The dead were cut open to teach the young apprentices more about their own bodies and the bodies of the patients they would later care for.

John still held a strong aversion to water because of his own experiences in that garden. He shuddered. He, like many before him, had experienced each brutal lesson that traumatized and toughened the apprentices in various ways . . . although certain situations still shook him. Those usually involved crises where his own family was concerned. The rest of the time, it was easy enough for him to compartmentalize.

"Where is the vial?" asked Saura. She continued to watch the apprentices below.

John put aside his dark thoughts and held the small wooden box out to her. "It is undamaged," he said.

Saura turned to him. Her sharp nose wrinkled when she saw him kneeling upon the floor. "Rise," she said. "Bring it to me."

John did as he was bidden.

Saura turned the box over, and then she opened it. The vial caught the color of the flames. "Smallpox," she said. "Unpleasant business, although it isn't the most gruesome thing. The proper rites were conducted?"

John nodded. "Yes."

"Good. That you are in good health pleases me. If no others have contracted it since, then you've served the Master well."

"It is an honor to serve in the Master's stead," John said, although he did not believe in the Master. Neither did she, but the phrase was a common formality, and it was rude not to say the prayer over such a catastrophe.

John frowned as a stray flicker of memory brought back to mind the letter his brother had given him. A stone and a vial of blood, it had said. Somewhere, another vial of blood had held similar importance, and that blood *might* have been his daughter's. He wondered whether it had been lost. Lukas had never had a stone or any vials in his possession. Not that John was aware of, anyway. He had never thought to ask his brother about it. And he was more hesitant to ask such a strange thing of Saura. He had no idea what could have been special about it, but if it had held Nymeria's blood, he would be able to simply draw more from her to give to one of the Keepers. He would ask Saura about it when the time was right. They might be able to figure out what was really making his daughter sick.

"Wylem, why is that hideous snarl making your handsome young face so ugly?" Saura said.

Wylem growled deep in his throat. "A recent injury, respected Lady of our Temple."

Her smile was warm, but it pulled many fine lines across her face that John did not remember having been there. She placed the vial back into its box delicately, and the box disappeared into the folds of her robes. "I've never known you to be slow enough to be injured by any man, woman, or beast. Are you getting *old*, little Wylem?"

John kept his face expressionless. He was not going to be the one to provoke the man. He already saw the displeasure written plainly across Wylem's face.

"Absolutely *not*."

"Then how did you come to that?"

Wylem shifted awkwardly where he still knelt, his head still bowed out of respect. "I slipped."

"Bird startled him," Robert chuckled wickedly. "He fell and cracked his knee."

John fought his amusement but failed to stifle it completely. This was the first time he'd heard of the reason for Wylem's injury. He received Wylem's murderous glare, and he offered his sympathy. "Now I understand why you did not want the Enforcers to know," John said.

Wylem went back to growling.

"He is a big man," explained Robert. "That is a lot of weight to come down on a poor little knee."

"I am fine," Wylem hissed. "And you two had better shut it, or I'll knock your heads together."

"First order of business," said Saura. "Where are the apprentices you have brought me? Has Laura not already sent them? She was to take charge of that."

John sputtered. "Already? But they've had not even a night's rest." He could not believe that she would already be asking for them — and in the middle of the night. "It isn't yet midnight, and they have been traveling hard. Give them a few nights to regroup. A single kindness. They've been through a lot."

"Absolutely not," she said. "They can rest in a few days, after enjoying the ceremony for Ellie and Robert. I've heard rumors of some natural talent, and I want to sift through them myself before we get them to work. I am told some of them helped to perform a few minor surgeries when your envoy was attacked. Laura should already have sent them."

"You've never before taken away my authority and given another person my duties. What have I done to deserve this? Why is it important for Laura to do my job for me?"

"What bothers you about it, Jonathan? Is there a particular reason my decision upsets you?" Saura asked. Her glittering black gaze settled on his men next when he realized he'd stepped beyond his station in questioning her authority. "I've read all of Laura's reports, including the one about that beast you allowed to endanger the apprentices. Am I missing something more?"

"Problems with his daughter," Robert explained. "He's had to bring her, and he's afraid you'll apprentice her before she is ready. Or more like . . . before he's ready to give her over."

Saura's head tilted fractionally as she studied John carefully. Her claws clicked together as she pondered. "What sort of problems would worry you? Is it not a high honor to give your children to the very calling you came into yourself? To serve the wearyworn, and to keep this delicate peace we have brought about? Your hesitation is unusual, Jonathan."

"His problem is the disobedient genius kid kind," Robert laughed. "Have I got stories for you."

John groaned. "Robert, I gave you explicit orders regarding her." He approached Saura and raised his hands. "Saura, my daughter is too young to be apprenticed — "

"You will take heed before you try and say anything you may regret. I will decide if she is too young," she clipped. "Always, that temper. You and your brother. I told you that your incident with Griggori will never be repeated, did I not? And on that matter, how did you offend Irkov this year? When your reports make you look a saint, I always know they are incomplete. You always leave incriminating details out of your reports when it involves something you've done that you should not have done."

John stared at the construction towering over the courtyard and the water garden, and he bit his tongue as Saura motioned for Robert and Wylem to rise. Wylem clutched at his thigh as he struggled to his feet, but he made no noise and his face showed no other sign of pain. However, the bruise, John knew, was still black as could be.

"Everything went well, Saura. Our feud has ended," John hissed finally. "There will be no more problems between us."

Saura stared at him hard, and her claws clicked again. "What have you done to him? Am I going to have to worry about another war? Besides the one your prisoner already promised to us?"

John swore. "Lukas is a liar and a murdering manipulator, and he is useless but to waste the air we breathe." He opened his mouth to say more, but he was interrupted.

"I know what you did to your own men to get at him." Her black eyes cut through him coldly. "He may be a good liar, and he may have committed other crimes, Jonathan, but everything your brother has relayed to me has been verified as true. And Reid has been dealing with the problem accordingly, unlike you. You've been digging your feet in and trying to sabotage my orders, as usual. Now. What happened between you and Irkov? Stop skating the subject."

John clenched his teeth. "I already told you that you have nothing left to worry about between us. Is that not all that matters?"

Saura's eye twitched. "I will get to the bottom of what happened in Oakwall. For now, you three will accompany me to the atrium. The rest of Laura's reports ought to be complete by now. And when we are done, we will make a visit to Isold ourselves. Perhaps we will meet the apprentices halfway."

"What else has Laura to tell you? She has already picked over every detail of my envoy." John grated. He controlled his voice carefully as Robert and Wylem fell into step with him. Neither of them dared to join the argument. They preferred being in her good graces and would not call a light on their own mistakes.

"Laura is assisting in the coordination of the reinforcement of Isold's towers and bridges. It should keep the Descendants of the Moon and the other Wolfshadow clans from attempting to gain access to Black Temple. Some of the traps on the Haunted Road will soon be moved to fortify the tunnel better. We will discuss the rest when the others are assembled, however. The wolf cult has been up to no good."

Saura then slipped her arm through Robert's, and she looked down her nose at him. "Explain about his daughter as we walk," she demanded. "If she irks Jonathan so, I want to meet her. He's always been too calm, too serious, and too angry when he forgets to be the prior. A little defiance is good for him."

"So you were asking about Irkov," Robert snickered.

Wylem burst into laughter. "Ha! That Greenman has met his match!"

"Has he? You mean to say the child?" Saura was very, very interested.

John was very, very irritated.

"I fail to see the importance of discussing my daughter, Saura," said John.

"Oh, but it is very important," she scoffed. "It's not to worry you, though. I'll have her sent to the archives when she's brought with the rest of the apprentices. Tessa has been asking about the girl, and she is abnormally excited about her visit. All her junker friends are, which makes me wonder what your daughter has got her hands into. Your brother also sent us a peculiar document from Edantine. It is marked with the Cyan signet, next to his and Black Temple's. Her initials are upon it, and it is very official. To have come by a noble house's marker is . . . exceptional. Even Five Tower would have to abide by it. She's got her hands into something, Jonathan, and I will find out what it is." John's stomach curled wretchedly. "Tessa will look after the girl until the ceremony. While you are busy, and after. I'll need the rest of your men for the duration of your trip. We have been very busy, and every set of hands will make the work go faster. The apprentices might not be able to do much, but their number is crucial at present."

"I noticed the court has been cleared," said Robert. He sounded wary.

John was relieved. The tracker had finally decided to rescue him from her scorn.

"Yes. It was meant to be a surprise. The lovely ceremony will be my gift to you and Ellie. I know you wanted to marry at Crow Post after the traveling season, but the rains have come late this year, and the season was delayed. I think the distraction would serve a better purpose here by giving everyone something to look forward to. The courtyard will be ready the morning of your wedding. We'll make a wonderful spectacle of it. Everyone will be glad for the reprieve from their work, and if the celebration goes smoothly, every man, woman, and child will be more motivated to finish preparations for what may be darker times ahead."

CHAPTER THIRTY-SEVEN

*M*URDER

THE SMELL OF THE SMOKE kept Lukas awake as the animal's flesh sizzled and spat over the flames. The blood of his escort's successful hunt wafted through the air, the iron in it as intense as the smell of the human blood shed in the Gray Halls. Every second breathing it in reminded him more and more strongly what had been done to him, and what he'd done to survive. Every moment, the dark marks hidden in his flesh festered and burned him. Occasionally, one surfaced. A shadowy mark, just beneath his skin. Crawling through his veins. And he felt the breath of those abhorrent creatures, even in the daylight. And he dreaded the coming night with every fiber of his being. He could not concentrate on anything through it.

Lukas shut his eyes against the buzzing in his head, trying to dull the roar that now never seemed to end. It had been getting louder and louder, day by day, since that girl had visited them in the forest just outside Crow Post. The child had given Robert and David the only tool that could have made him fearful of them. They'd tormented him with it endlessly, trying to pull information from him. Now Robert was gone, but David had included another familiar face in the questioning. Thomas. Another of the men who'd been present when Lukas had been captured. And Thomas was more ruthless than Robert had been.

But Lukas had kept his knowledge from them, knowing that even a word would mean his life was over. He could play prisoner, just as he could play many other roles. But he could not act the part that would end his life, not until Caol and Eiran were dealt with accordingly.

It was at great cost that he kept to himself what was most valuable to him. His head whirled with the cacophony of screams that he struggled to keep out. In the pool of water in which he sat, he saw the dark shadows under his own eyes and deathly colored skin that was so unlike his old self. It had been no wonder he'd managed to elude Eiran's hunters and Caol's fury for so long. He was unrecognizable. And now he had barely the strength to keep his head up, let alone pick the lock.

The glass itself was almost a sort of poison to him, sedating him, stripping his faculties away one at a time whenever it was brought closer. Every time they cut him with it, he would glimpse another passing silhouette, or he would hear more screams in the back of his mind, always trying to claw their way to the surface.

His fingers dropped the small pick and rose to his temples, and he clawed at his scalp, trembling. Everything whorled about him, and he heard snarling, as though he were still in the kennels. But it wasn't a feral animal sound . . . it was more threatening than anything he'd ever heard or felt. He shut his eyes tightly against it, barely registering the laughter among the men as they stirred the fires and tended to wounds caused by Lukas's hunters.

Some of the wolfmen had been real wolfmen, for their filed teeth and the many missing fingers. But some of Eiran's men had been among them; Lukas had seen the curved swords and the wild madness in them. Yet some of those wolf-cowled men had belonged to neither group. Those had carried guns, and they had nearly drowned him when they'd taken him from his cage. It meant his enemies had allied with one another to take him out, and they would not stop coming. They may had fled Raven Trail in defeat, though he knew they would soon discover the small group of men with him were now without their previous protection.

Yet his fears of any of those men taking him were now the least on his mind. That the time allotted him to find Rhael was over and Lukas was to be killed instead of being returned to Five Tower because he hadn't found the man . . . All of it meant nothing.

His schemes, his plans, his lies. Those things were nothing against the pressure now in his skull, threatening to rip open his mind as it had the minds of his friends, his brothers, his comrades. What Caol had done to them had been a torment he'd outlived, yet he was again facing the splitting visions they had faced before they'd gone mad and killed themselves, screaming for the things they saw to be taken away from them.

Lukas concentrated. One breath at a time. One. Another. Slowly.

Slowly, the tremors seemed to recede, until he was able to manage another breath. He never heard the movement in the camp or noticed the horses fidgeting nervously. He never saw Timothy rise from his place at the fire to reach over and cut away at the meat.

Lukas fumbled for the pick he'd dropped, and he dared to open his eyes a slit. The shard lay just feet from his cage, and it was slowly cracking, slowly blackening as it seemed to absorb the darkness. Such darkness . . .

Lukas forced himself to look away from the preternatural object and the whispers it was projecting into him.

Blue eyes, glowing in the water. Molten silver veins, crawling across the monstrous man's face.

The brief hallucination sent a thrill of horror through him, and he jolted in his cage, his legs kicking out as he struggled to get away from the monster in the reflection beneath him. For a moment, the pool seemed to be of blood rather than of muddy water.

Every breath he tried to take seemed to drift just out of reach, and panic consumed him. He found the pick and tried desperately to hold it steady.

Whenever he blinked, he kept seeing an image of her, drifting in water — the very vivid image of death. Tall shadows curling around the cryotank in the Gray Halls. Violet lightning arcing through the glass. He kept hearing her screams. Over and over, he heard them, until he wanted to curl inward, clutching at his head, and just scream with her.

The shard continued cutting away at his sanity.

He never saw Timothy walk away from the campfire, never heard Thomas ask for whatever it was Timothy was after. Timothy never saw or heard what Lukas was doing, either.

The lock clicked.

Lukas fell as the bent cage door swung open. The cage leaned to the side as he scrambled away, still clutching the pick as though it was a dagger that could ward off the effects of that shard. He blinked hard, realizing he was lying on his back, gazing up at the stars and wheezing. He could barely breathe. His throat had closed too tightly . . . He felt chains around his wrists . . . about his throat. Blood was everywhere. Screams . . . so many screams.

Lukas could taste the blood, the awful, awful blood.

He scrambled back with a cry, and when he rose, Timothy stepped out from behind the vehicle, drawn to the sound. The young man had a kindness about him — normally it would have stayed Lukas's hand. But tonight, just as the night he'd murdered the Ivans, instinct and mad terror gripped him. He shoved the pick into Timothy's throat and yanked it sideways with a ferocity that startled himself. Timothy's face slammed into the door, and blood trailed down the side as the young man slumped. For a moment, Lukas felt the urge to take the man's throat with his own teeth. The smell of it almost drove him to his knees with craving and hunger, but he pulled himself from the darker impulse inspired by the madness coming from that shard.

Every muscle in Lukas's body shook violently as he looked at the blood upon his hands. So much blood. So very much blood . . . He staggered back, away from the body, and then he realized he heard a commotion from the fire pit where the boar hung, roasting. A gunshot brought him out of his shock.

Lukas fled from them. The girl was the key. She would be his bargaining chip. Caol and Eiran would have to accept.

The farther he fled from that shard, the clearer his mind grew. The night became increasingly full of life. Crickets, birds, coyotes, deer. Trees, creaking as the wind brushed their limbs. Wood frogs and early cicadas singing. But the impression that the shard had pressed upon him haunted him. He never wanted to see what his men saw. Like them, he would not survive it.

* * * * * * *

"No!" Thomas shouted as he saw Timothy turn from the truck. He'd just looked up when he'd heard something he'd been expecting but had been hoping they would have been better prepared for. Timothy had only just stepped around the truck to see what the noise had been when Thomas had jumped to his feet and Lukas's ghoulish form had appeared. The murderer had looked mad, his eyes bloodshot and wild. He hadn't even hesitated. Like a snake, Lukas's hand had shot out, and then Timothy was on the ground.

David swore, unholstering his gun — but the murderer had already fled into the night. The others in their camp dropped what they were doing as David and Thomas slid to Timothy's side and tried to assess how badly he was hurt. "He's just a *kid*!" David swore.

"GET THAT BASTARD NOW!!!" Thomas shouted as the rest of their men raced after Lukas. Thomas and David desperately tried to stop the bleeding. "Timothy!" Thomas cried. "Kid, you look at me, damn it!"

David shook his head. "Thomas, he's not going to make it. That wound is bad. It's really, really bad."

Timothy's bloody hands clutched at Thomas's. The kid was scared to death of his imminent end. He knew he was going to die, and he was crying. Thomas's own vision blurred as he gripped Timothy's shoulder and his hand. "I'm sorry — we can't save you, Tim." He wiped his eyes on his sleeve.

Timothy convulsed, and hot blood bubbled from his lips. He tried to gasp for another breath, and he inhaled the bubbling red foam. His eyes went wide. "Stop — him," he choked. Every attempted breath brought more struggle from him. "Nymeri — Tell John — "

Timothy was dead just a few moments later. David gripped his gun, and he reached out to close Timothy's eyes with his bloody fingers. "Thomas. If we don't catch him by dawn, you should ride out to warn John and Jeana. Your horse is the fastest, and you know the way best."

"I'll send Aaron to John to tell him, and I will return to Crow Post to warn Jeana and Amos," Thomas said. He rose from the kid's body and unholstered his own gun. "The bastard is on foot. We'll circle him. If we don't catch him, he'll show his face again soon enough. Let's just hope he doesn't have more up his sleeve."

David knelt and picked up part of the broken pick. "Isn't this . . . ?"

Thomas snatched it, and he hissed a stream of oaths when he recognized what Lukas's pick had really been. "This is one of the Edantine girl's hair pins."

"You think he took it from her without her knowing?"

"No. I think she came back and gave it to him, probably during the trouble at Oakwall when we were all preoccupied. That silver-tongued serpent tricked another child into helping him. If it wasn't important for him to talk, I would cut his tongue out."

David gritted his teeth. "Didn't he have a letter when Reid caught him?"

Thomas realized what David meant to say. "Good point. He can read and write. So we'll cut out his tongue anyway. The serpent won't have the chance to beguile anyone else after we're through with him."

CHAPTER THIRTY-EIGHT

Explosives

SAURA FLIPPED THROUGH THE PAGES, her expression pensive. The doctors were all drained and drawn. Not many of them were in the mood to smile despite the growing beauty of the courtyard below. Wreaths of pale, tea-tinted, and cotton-hued flowers across many sizes and various species adorned the lovely scene slowly blooming for a wedding. Dogwood flowers, rhododendrons, white viburnum, and white irises were among the varied bouquets. Great veils of spidery white lace also swayed where the wind caught them on the bridges.

The excitement buzzing below was in complete opposition to the gloom upon the shaded balcony.

The smell of the feast roasting in the kitchens was mouthwatering, but John had already drunk cold coffee and eaten quickly on the way back from Saura's thorough examination of the children they'd brought into Black Temple. She'd merely paused over Nymeria admiringly, quite taken with her uniquely beautiful eyes the way everyone seemed to be when they first met the child. But she had asked only the usual questions to test the child's knowledge. Nymeria had surprised him, answering every question directly, correctly, and without sarcasm or attitude. But he'd been soured by Saura's command for one of the junkers to watch his daughter while they were busy. The junkers were to find out what else his daughter understood.

Below, he watched more and more of those wretched, mad tech junkies bring their scrap and crap inventions to his daughter to talk about them. She seemed delighted, although uncertain. And then she began to pore over their inventions with a hunger he'd never seen in her when he'd tried to have her learn the various healing remedies and dry surgeries that would save more lives than the junk currently brightening her smile ever would. They gave her wrenches and screwdrivers, although he knew she had the steady hands that would far better wield scalpels and other, more delicate, medical tools.

Then she produced her strange pen tool. He couldn't quite tell, but it seemed to be somewhat different than it had been in Oakwall. It glistened more, like an ice dagger.

She bent over some small, smooth item they brought, and she began to work, taking in her other hand a pair of tweezers and dissecting the thing before her. Seeming to carve away at its insides, and to pull things apart and rearrange them the way a surgeon poured himself into his task at the operating table.

He growled at the intolerable sight. The longer it went on, the worse it was for him. It seemed even Saura was fine with allowing Nymeria to be swayed so.

Never before had Saura been so lenient.

He tried to let it go because his daughter wasn't an apprentice yet. But he couldn't. He didn't want to be angry at his daughter for being happy and enjoying her hobby, but it felt like open defiance, and such that everyone seemed to encourage. And what if her behavior influenced his son later? What if Jamie chose the same path away from Black Temple and dishonored them also? It would bring great shame to their family if neither of John's children took up his occupation.

But John's fear wasn't just about honor. If Nymeria chose to be a tech and was allowed by Saura to do so, she would struggle to earn a respectable place for the rest of her life. She would have to visit far more dangerous places than he'd ever had to, and she would have to dig through ancient rubble in collapsed old cities for lost knowledge and rare and almost irreparably damaged machinery. A lot of techs died working those sites. Dislodging capsules of gas left from the old wars often caused them to erupt, killing everyone for acres, and . . .

The journal flew across the table.

The members of the High Council leaned forward, and so did several of the doctors and escorts in the room as Saura raised one clawed hand and pointed and wagged her finger at Wylem. "Bring me your radio. Place it on the table, where I can hear it better. Something is going on at the old dam."

They'd all heard the crack of a gunshot over the radio when one of the men there had called for assistance. John and Wylem knew not from where the broadcast had originated. Many of the others seemed to have come to the same conclusion as Saura, however, as though they had a fuller picture than any man who'd come with John's envoy.

"Where is Alex?" John asked. Alex had helped Five Tower just after the Bright Night, after John and Jeana had left. He was a good friend, and his was a face John had been looking forward to seeing again. Alex often traveled to Arsennia, where the Keeps housed and used very old and powerful medical machinery.

"Dead," said Saura simply.

He looked at the journal. "What happened?"

Joshua, a blond man with a gray mustache and pale green eyes, lit his pipe. "There's been thirty attacks in the last two months," he said. "What do you think happened?" Joshua had come from Lovael's envoy. He had taken to their finery, and by his manner and tone, it was obvious he thought he was superior merely for the glistening clothes he wore. John knew, however, that Joshua was very lacking in his medical knowledge, and that he did not listen well to his patients. He'd worked with the man before and did not like his lackadaisical work ethic.

"Joshua, the attacks are not how he died," Saura clipped. "I sent him to the dam three days ago, along with as many good men as he could spare, to help reinforce the walls and continue digging out the new channel. He was killed by a large animal. When his men recovered the body, there wasn't much left. And when they were hauling his remains back, they were also attacked. Only one of those men survived, and only because he crawled between the boulders and hid there. Conveniently, he never saw what manner of beast killed the rest. We will need to send more men to the dam, and this time, they will need to be better armed and better prepared."

"What about the archives?" asked Mark. "Aren't they more important than the dam? The archives are the soul an' the mind of Black Temple. The knowledge kept there is what we are built on."

Saura rose, and her white-and-silver robes trailed behind her. She clasped her hands behind her back as she paced. "We cannot spend that kind of time for the archives yet, Mark. The catacombs stretch for miles underground. It would take months, trying to empty all of them. It is quicker to reinforce the weakest parts of the new and old walls, and to dig a trench to divert the disaster from any future breakage. This project will keep the water from washing over these hills and will direct it south. We may still receive some flooding, but we can survive a river. We cannot, however, survive a lake."

"Have you told everyone in this room that not all of the wolfmen who attacked us were actually wolfmen?" asked John.

There was a murmur of surprise. Saura quieted them, her claws dragging circles across the table. "From Lovael to Hagenhold and Cyan, to Wicker, to Ardimond," she said slowly, and just so, she'd dismissed John's question. Instead, she pondered something else that seemed more important to her. "The lake is extensive, with its most massive tendrils stretching toward and beyond Arsennia. What we face, unfortunately, is upon higher ground. Our forefathers thought to disguise our home, putting us near the dam. But it is also our greatest weakness."

"Did you not tell them, Saura?" John repeated, tempting her fury.

Her claws raked across the table absently, forming another circle as she looked up. She glared at him, and then she acquiesced. "What John says is accurate. Moreover, it seems many from the cult have abandoned their sacred beliefs. They've taken up guns, and they're wielding metal instead of bone, and they're resorting to poisons. None of these things are permitted by their clans, as you well know."

Wylem shifted at the uneasy looks among the other field doctors.

"The attacks have been ten to fifty men strong. People are being taken. But the cult is not our only problem. Captain Robin, an Alliance officer who was stationed in Edantine, sent this." She nodded to the journal. "This journal was one of *many* that belonged to Ragan Crostor. The questioning of Crostor's wife, and certain other individuals, meant the captain was able to trace the ledgers' detailed contents even farther. They have taken down scores of insidious monks who are causing dissent among the wearyworn and inviting members of the Wolfshadow cult into the cities they are infiltrating. The alliance between the two groups seems uneasy at best. From Captain Robin's intelligence report, both groups have broken into battle with each other at multiple locations, even though the majority are still working together toward some ill goal."

Saura continued. "These monks wear glass chains as though to mock our guild, but they've hands in worse things. Crostor's wife revealed the correspondence between her husband and the monks in both Edantine and Aelynhold. The glass chains were forged in Lovael, sent to Aelynhold, and disbursed from there for new members. Eight hundred chains. *The Merciful*, they are calling themselves. *The Brotherhood of Mercy*. They are responsible for the abduction — and possibly murder — of Avery Ramont, the High Commander of the Enforcers' Alliance. Avery has been undeniably confirmed as missing for over two years, though it is suspected that he's been missing far longer. An impostor — or several — have been giving the orders."

No one said a word.

Saura nodded. "Our enemies are everywhere, ladies and gentlemen. John's brother has had a great hand in our successful investigations thus far. That we have even learned as much as we have, or had Captain Robin's help at all, is thanks to the retired range commander Reid Ivan. Apparently, he is the one who uncovered the initial corruption in Edantine, and he has since then found and forwarded information from other cities, and he has coordinated several other cleanup operations to protect Black Temple's guild halls and the uncorrupted Enforcers who had been targeted for assassination. The monks in each city have direct ties to Aelynhold. Many of them are violent, twisted fanatics. Others are close-lipped and unbreaking in their questioning."

She paused and looked about the room. "However. I will repeat to you the warning I forwarded to Dr. Ivan a month ago. When you leave here within the next few weeks, do not provoke the Enforcers. Keep quiet about the infiltration by the monks, and send your ravens and messengers back to the Temple with information about any suspicious activity. Keep radio silence on the matter. We will notify Captain Robin and his men directly. Do not confront these infiltrators yourselves, and do not let them know that we are aware of the situation. Our greatest asset is their belief that we have no idea what is afoot."

One of the Council members spoke. "Holy Matron, who has been pulling the Alliance's strings and ordering them to withdraw from the people they are supposed to be protecting?"

Saura's claws clicked on the table. "They do not yet know, Councilor Alyssa. Captain Robin's men have been searching for Avery while trying to figure that out."

She eyed everyone gravely. "Listen carefully, Brothers and Sisters. We have two invasions currently underway. The Brotherhood is at the root of the Alliance's trouble. Five Tower seems to be at the true root of ours. Both enemies seem to be working haphazardly together, but that is only for now. We do not know what the Brotherhood's endgame is, while the truth of Five Tower's endeavors and weaknesses are becoming clearer each passing week."

"What else?" asked another council member.

"I have been forwarded reports of secret messengers coming and going from the Alliance's citadel, always in the middle of the night. The captain said a few hundred good men have been executed by what is being claimed to be Avery's orders. But each of these men are those who have spoken out against certain unusual orders they were given, and in most cases, these Enforcers demanded a face-to-face confrontation with Avery Ramont. They were denied the right, rounded up one by one, accused of treason, and then executed. They were allowed no customary last words, no rites, nothing. Even their families were killed, as though to wipe away a stain. It is very serious."

"What about the fugitives? The rumors?" asked Councilor Alyssa.

"Our informant has verified the intentions broiling in Five Tower. He took money to return to them what they claimed were fugitives. Caol and Eiran have moved not only against Black Temple, but against the Master. This cannot be permitted to continue. So I am calling the banners. Council Members. Representatives. Have every doctor under each of your commands Raise the Vial in preparation for catastrophe — "

"*Saura, you cannot!*" John gasped, shooting to his feet as horror washed through him. "You will kill more innocents than the wars ever took! Our apocalypse did not come by fire, but by disease, and you're threatening to release it *again*?!"

"I did not say I would give the order to *Break the Vial*," she said coolly. She looked out over the courtyard below. "But we must protect our people. We are immune. By our rite of passage, it was made so. Half of ours may fall — the old and the young, and anyone who is not inoculated. But *all* of theirs will fall if they dare try to destroy the Temple."

"If you truly intend to release another plague like the one that almost drove humanity to extinction centuries ago, I will turn traitor," John said angrily, and he pulled his knife out and tossed it onto the table. It slid across the polished surface until it caught the sunlight where the blade hovered over the opposite edge. "I will *not* serve a guild that murders for its own gain, or simply to intimidate. We are healers, Saura! We are not murderers!"

"Do not lecture me about bloodshed," Saura said. "You, who have soiled your hands on more than one occasion. You defied me to go after your parents' killer. And you caused the death of another doctor, whose station and skill had been much higher than your own. You preach and cling to your words of peace and healing when you are the least innocent among us."

"What I have done, and what you are talking about doing, Saura," said John, "are two *very* different things — "

"We are not only healers," she hissed. "We are also *assassins*, Jonathan. Have you forgotten the Black Oath?"

The threatening words of their guild returned to his mind. Every doctor, regent, and holy matron uttered the Black Oath with conviction as they performed their rites to become a member of the Glass Chain.

She spoke the words of that oath aloud even as he heard them in his memory.

"*Wrath* and Mercy shall draw blood for both the Bloodied and the Bloodless. When the Wound festers, *we* cut the Rot. *We* bind the Bleeding at the Source. We *Break* from Death, and we *Deliver* unto Death. We see the First Breath, and we see the *Last*. In warning, our Banners fly, and upon retaliation, our Vials break. Until the Fever is gone. The Glass Chain will not shatter but by the Master's hand . . . Our words, Jonathan, are binding. But it is only our last resort. Take back your knife. I will not accept any reneged vows or threats of betrayal. Have faith in my judgement."

John felt sick. She'd spoken only half of the oath, but still it haunted him.

Wylem stood slowly and unsheathed his knife as well. He rolled the ceremonial dagger between his thumb and forefinger, and then he placed his on the table also. "Saura . . . I cannot think of doing it, either. Maybe in my youth, I could have had a thought to be so cruel. But I have a family. The many doctors under my command along the east shores have families also. They do not have the immunity that we do. My wife and my sisters have no immunity, and my children are not inoculated. Only my brother would survive the Breaking of the Vial, and he is a cripple, and a rotten man. It would be a mockery if only he and I survived such a catastrophic blackening of our purpose."

Saura turned, and sadness flitted through her visage and settled there. She looked exhausted. "I understand your reservations, Wylem," she said. "But I promise all of you, I will not give the order unless it is necessary. Our enemies know what it means, even to utter a whisper of it. They will understand where the power truly lies if they dare. They will be reminded, even to see the banners rising, that we will not tolerate a threat against us."

"My son and my daughter are not inoculated," John said, and he shook his head, dismayed that she could consider such a command. To threaten to clear the map of any person not immune to what was contained in those insidious vials deep in the archives. "Even to threaten such a thing, I won't have any part of it."

"You will not be permitted to leave our guild — "

"Oh, I have no intention of *leaving*," John laughed angrily. "Are you kidding me? I have worked my entire life to build what I have, to earn my place, and to help the wearyworn. I am working to rebuild a broken world, Saura!" John pulled on his hair and stepped back. "I would never dare to leave the Temple or abandon my calling. When I said I would turn traitor, I meant I would work to rip from you every shred of power you have seized over the years, and I would have you taken to the Reformation and locked away like a criminal. And I would leave you there to rot while I cleaned up your mess."

This sparked the anger he'd been dancing around for hours. Her claws curled as she slithered toward the table and reached out for the blade. "Take heed to say nothing else, lest you offend me while your blood is still hot, Dr. Ivan." The blade slid back across the table to him. No one else dared say a word. "Pick up your dagger." They stared at each other. "*Now.*" He shook his head and leaned on his side of the table.

"No. Not unless you decide to undo what you've commanded of these good men and women. They may not have the guts or the temper to challenge a direct order, but I'm not the coward they are. I *defy* you, Saura. Decided and intentional defiance. Flagrant disregard."

"This is your last chance — "

The door burst open, drawing them both from their heated argument. A man covered in blood and gore was dragged in, and he struggled against his captors as another was brought in behind him.

They had been armed heavily. The number of empty sheaths caused John to step away from the table as alarm stole his attention and Saura's.

Both men were thrown to the floor, where they rolled indelicately. The tumble might have bruised or fractured a rib or two, the way they were bound. One of them groaned, wheezing, and blood spilled from his mouth when he opened it. He blinked, dazed.

"Where were these men found?" Saura demanded, putting her quarrel with John aside for later.

John snarled and took his dagger, and he handed Wylem's back to him as well. "Who are they?"

The guards had stepped back from the men, and they were, even now, aiming crossbows at them, ready to kill them, even though the two were unarmed and beaten and bound. Laura, John realized. Laura was one of the guards. There was a bloody gash over her left brow, and she was struggling to keep the blood from her eye. The snarl upon her rough features looked hungry for vengeance. "Mercenaries," said Laura. "Hired by Five Tower. They had a large haul of explosives with them."

John's pulse quickened. He sheathed his dagger, forgetting his anger entirely as this new development invited dreadful possibilities.

"Well?" demanded Saura of the mercenary who was still trying to blink away the haze and looking about. "Out with it!"

The authoritative bark seemed to draw his attention. "What . . . ?"

"Who sent you? How many more have come?"

Laura wiped the blood from her eye and then aimed the crossbow again.

The man's scarred face twisted, and his lips pulled back into a grin. "Enough to do the job without us, eventually."

"We've scoured the walls," said Laura, "and found nothing else."

"His judgement is fierce," continued the mercenary. "You've harbored the traitor's bounty hunter. His time is up. He is a dead man. And your people kept us from him. You've brought judgement upon yourselves — " The man convulsed, and a vulgar snarling sound ripped through his vocal cord. When he looked up, his eyes were violet. Then he started laughing madly and thrashing against his bonds. "You can't keep me tied up," he taunted.

The ropes began to fray as they creaked under the strain. They cut into his wrists, sawing through flesh, and his blood dripped onto the floor as he wormed.

"*Stay down!!!*" shouted Laura. Her deep voice boomed through the hall. "*Or I will shoot another bolt into you!*"

His strength waned as the violet faded. "Help me . . ." he choked. "Please kill me. Make them stop . . ." His voice cracked, and more blood seeped from his lips. "Ple — " His screams tore through the hall, and he began to writhe as though on fire. Laura jumped, her finger twitching over the trigger.

His comrade seemed less possessed, and when the screaming one lost his voice, he spoke quietly. "It never stops," he said. "He said he could take it away. He said he could end it. He could cure us. He lied — He lied, he lied . . ."

"They're coming . . ." hissed the other. His ropes had broken, and he was crawling across the floor, leaving a trail of blood as he gasped desperately for a breath. "They're coming . . ." The mad one looked behind him, as if terrified, as if seeing something there. "They're coming . . . They want the light . . . Please, kill me. Destroy the dam, break it, drown them all — "

Laura pulled the trigger, and an arrow shot through the mercenary's skull. Then she shot the other. "They were like that when we came across them." She wavered on her feet where she stood. She lowered the crossbow finally, and she wiped her mouth where she'd been struck. "I've never met men so strong — I don't know what was wrong with them. Am I crazy? Was there a purple glow in his eyes? I think I've got a concussion . . ." She shook her head and took a step toward one of the empty chairs — her knees buckled, and she hit the floor.

John was the first to her side — and he was the first to realize the wound that had toppled her hadn't been from her head. She'd been sliced open from the base of her spine to the nape of her neck. However she had made it from the dam, all the way through Black Temple, and to the balcony over the courtyard was beyond him. She should already have been dead . . . She wasn't likely to survive, either.

Laura turned her head as the crossbow slipped from her hands, and she smiled at him. "Stupid way to go, I know . . . My back was turned," she said. Her eyes grew heavy as her blood pooled the floor about them. "I wish I'd been a damsel instead of a prince." She grimaced. "My son won't even remember me for the . . . whimsical beast I have been . . ."

Her eyes glazed over, and she breathed no more.

"John."

He looked up, and then he realized Aaron was there. But Aaron had gone with Lukas's escort, with Timothy and Thomas, and with David and the others. Why was he in Black Temple? Aaron looked worse for wear, and the look on his face had John shaking his head.

"He escaped a week ago," said Aaron. "I rode hard to ensure the news got to you as soon as possible. We lost him when he headed north — "

"I have to go to my daughter," John said. Panic struck him like a dagger in the chest. "Saura, I have to get to my daughter. I cannot leave her alone."

"You will not," Saura snapped. "She will be fine there, with the others. Wylem, I need you to take charge of this. Gather some men, and be careful of your knee. I am going to send more to help find the rest of those explosives. Go to the dam. Jonathan, I need the rest of you here to take over the — "

"I need to go to my daughter! The man who murdered my parents is loose!" John shouted. "If he gets word to Caol — "

"I FORBID IT!" Saura roared. "Gather your wits, you fiery imbecile, and help the rest of us. Think of someone more than yourself or your own family. If they've more explosives set to detonate, getting to your daughter will mean nothing. You'll both drown along with everyone else in the catacombs!"

CHAPTER THIRTY-NINE

TEMPLE SHADOWS

NYMERIA'S EYES WIDENED WHEN she looked up. In the time she'd spent poring over all of their beautiful old machines, figuring them out and tinkering with them to gather ideas and impart her knowledge on how to fix them — it usually boiled down to damaged or uncharged parts — the court had sprung to life with a vivid beauty. Before, when Tessa had introduced Nymeria to seven of the techs, there had only been white bouquets and streamers as well as the predominant black slate and stone that made up the architecture of the towers and unfinished bridges overhead. But now, candles and pale-yellow roses — hundreds of them — lined the dais. White archways had been created at every entrance, and white ravens flew about in massive gray cages made of the most beautiful wrought iron patterns of feathers and leaves.

A bloodred carpet had been rolled out, and everyone who ran back and forth through the courtyard had also transformed. No longer were working clothes worn, though the wedding was still three days away. There were shades of black and white, and of cream, soft yellow, and gold — all of it adorned those who fluttered here and there. Instruments had been set strategically about the court to give the bride and groom the center, and also to allow the musicians to be heard and seen by all so that they could lead in the celebration.

Michael and Sobrienne, along with a few other children Nymeria had never seen before, hovered nearby and helped to sort the dinnerware and candles. Michael smiled at Nymeria, although Sobrienne scoffed.

Dusk was fast approaching.

She looked up, where her father and the other field doctors and morticians and warriors had gathered to meet with Saura. She couldn't see any of them near the open windows, but she hoped the meeting was nearly over and that it had gone well. She looked forward to showing her father how she had helped the techs.

Nymeria held up the small mech, and when she pressed the button to activate it, the small machine came to life. "It's incredible!" Tessa exclaimed. "I always knew they would be useful, but I'd never gotten them to work!"

The small mechanical spider's front legs rose as if it was waking from sleep, and then it twitched. Then it began to walk across her hands as if it was curious.

"Oh, it has the cutest eyes!" squeaked Tessa. "They're like starlight! I wonder if he can sew as he was designed to. Or if his programming has been corrupted — "

"The programming is intact," said Nymeria, and Tessa pulled from her overstuffed pockets a spool of twine and a torn cloth. It took both items. Its lengthy, slender legs unspooled the pale thread, then respooled it, and then it wrapped strings about Tessa's fingers, setting a web as a spider might before it slipped down one long thread and hung there, working on the cloth.

The white thread looped in and out of the cloth quickly, and in seconds, the torn cloth was once again whole. The stitches were better than the weaving of the original cloth.

Nymeria was impressed by its programming. Whoever had designed it had done an amazing job. The techs were delighted as well. "My brother hates spiders," she said wickedly, wanting a weaving spider of her own. She wondered whether she could design one herself. Its motors and internal machinery were microscopic, though. Recreating them, or changing them, could be next to impossible.

The techs laughed mischievously when Tessa looked about and held the spider as if to hide him from prying eyes. "So does Saura," she whispered. "She's deathly frightened."

Erin and Micah grinned at one another. "There's a book in the archives on them, if you want to read it," said Erin. "It was dug up from an old library ten years ago, buried under the rubble in Anise. The spider was with it. The book has design specs for all sorts of drones."

"Drones?" Nymeria asked excitedly. One of the books from her uncle, which she'd read most diligently during the trip from Crow Post to Black Temple, had been on drones and other things. It had been her favorite. "I would love to read it!"

Tessa adjusted her glasses. "Well, then. Let's get going. We've got three days before the wedding starts."

They set off toward one of the blackest towers — and before Nymeria entered, a wave of uneasiness washed over her again. She looked back, to the balcony that she could barely see through the streamers, and she wondered whether the scream she thought she'd just heard had been imagined. The techs didn't seem to react, however, so she pretended she had heard nothing. *Tourette's*, she repeated to herself, and they began their steep descent into the depths of the catacombs of Black Temple.

"Those doctors always roll their eyes at us," said Erin to Micah. "It gets so old."

Micah sighed as she exchanged the dying torch for a fresh one on the stony walls. It flared to life, devouring the flames hungrily. "No matter. If we can get the parts for that box and get it running, they'll forever call us heroes. Anyone can stitch a wound. But only the brightest can fix the things we find."

Nymeria found herself grinning at the reversal. She was unused to the idea that *techs* were the superior ones. It was all very exciting.

"That tool you've brought," Tessa asked. The archways grew taller and taller, and the smell of old volumes of books filled with various inks became stronger. "Why does it only work for you? And how do you get it to work? I've never seen anything like it, and I've perused the library for forty years. Not even a mention of the glass tech, either. I never knew glass could become programmable, or that it could become a source of energy and light."

"It's not really converted into a source," Nymeria said. "The glass is clear, so data penetrates it better. Glass just serves as a conductor."

"So . . . water could technically do the same? Or precious stones? Or even clear plastics?"

Nymeria bit her lip, thinking. "I hadn't really thought about most of those. Precious stones seem to amplify it. Water . . . I don't know."

The idea made her uneasy for some reason. But as they entered a giant antechamber, the thought fell away like a frail cobweb torn by breath. There were so many books. Shelves and shelves of them. Shadows clung to every dusty, moth-infested crevice, and the rows and rows of aisles faded from the torchlight but echoed their steps back to them. The books were the most beautiful things she had ever seen.

Micah and Erin laughed softly. "I think she's quite taken with the books," said Erin.

Nymeria breathed. "They're *beautiful*." She stepped apart from them, her hand trailing along the spines. Images and emotions drifted through her like colors, and in every shade and hue and tint. The bindings upon most of the books were made by hand, and some of the oldest jackets were covered in amazingly detailed art — though they were very fatigued and faded. Her hand drifted to the glass heart she wore about her neck. "Marissa would have loved to see these books," she said, awed.

"The first forty meters of the archives are full of fables. Then there are seventy meters of history, and of languages. Forty more meters traverse topics in the medical field, and then one hundred meters of books discuss technology that predates, meets, and was lost during the Modern Age. As you see, the most important section is the largest. No books there are alike, and there is no rubbish kept among it. And could you believe Arsennia has archives — more than one — which are more than three times this size? Our shelves are nearly fifteen meters tall — and theirs are higher."

Tessa was very proud of their own library. "Forty years, and I've never been able to read them all."

They waited for Nymeria as she perused the titles in the fiction section . . . She closed her eyes, letting the lovely tales wash over her. Some were scary, some were beautiful, some were joyous and inspiring, some were everything . . . Horses, spirits, wolves, angels, families, creatures of the seas and skies, magic, music — her father had read so many of them, she sensed. She felt him there . . . as a boy, a long time ago. So many others had come and gone over the years also. Nymeria opened her eyes, frowning. Her father's sadness had moved him from his love of reading for sheer entertainment . . . It led him away, deeper into the catacombs. She could not see where he had gone, but he'd given up on that joy for whatever knowledge he'd sought.

Nymeria didn't want to become as serious as him.

So many apprentices eventually abandoned reading for the same reasons. It saddened her.

"What is it?" asked Tessa. She'd seen Nymeria's face fall.

Nymeria bit her lip again. "Nothing. I was just thinking how most people who loved reading abandoned the joy it brought them. My father used to come down here all the time, didn't he?"

Tessa was quiet for a moment as she pondered why Nymeria would bring up the subject of her father. "Yes, he did," she said. She gave her torch to Erin and knelt before Nymeria. "He's had a hard time, Nymeria. A lot of people have. But he's done remarkably well for himself, and for a lot of others."

"He stopped reading the books he loved so much when his friend died on the Haunted Road."

"It was a long time ago."

The spider climbed into Tessa's messy hair and began combing it madly.

Nymeria laughed at Tessa's startled expression. "Well, look at that. It grooms, too." She cringed. "My skin is crawling. I may put it in a cage later. Come on, sweetheart. Let's find that book."

Nymeria nodded and followed, and they walked along with her father's old demons, into the depths of the archives.

The dark feelings didn't lessen as Nymeria and the techs came closer to the portion of the library Tessa had said they needed to reach. Instead, the scent of old blood seemed to seep into the dark, musky air. The echoes of their footsteps seemed to begin to mimic the sounds of whispering and distant whimpering. Nymeria's heart began to race when the shadows appeared to writhe apart from the torchlight, as if one of the dark things hovered just out of sight. She crept between the three techs, getting as far from the blackness about them as possible.

The smell of the blood grew stronger, and Nymeria found herself holding her breath.

"*Aiya . . .*"

Abruptly, Nymeria stopped. The voice was the same as before, from her frightful vision of the cold, dark dungeons.

The dungeons had been much like these archives. Stone floors and cold, musky, blood smells.

Tessa and Erin and Micah nearly toppled over one another when they realized she'd stopped. "What — " Tessa looked back, confused. "Nymeria?"

None of them were moving anymore, but the whispering still sounded loudly — they couldn't hear it, Nymeria realized. Just like her father, and like her brother and her mother and everyone else from Crow Post, the techs could not hear the voices. The sound began to rise in volume, and Nymeria took a step back, swallowing hard. She shook her head when she tried to tell them what she heard, but she couldn't. When the shadows moved again, warping in a manner most unnatural against the firelight behind the three techs, Nymeria shut her eyes.

She felt water all about her. Drowning, drifting . . . A blinding ray of blue light —

She found herself cowering against one of the shelves when she opened her eyes to stop seeing the water and the shroud of light.

Blood and screams were in the books here — in all of them. Tears, and death, and rot, and anger. Everything vile, everything filled with sickness. The medical journals branded her where she touched them, and she flinched away as if she'd been scalded, even though she could feel no marks left upon her.

Her head was spinning, and the bright energy inside her began to shift. It seemed to crack like glass, and a darkness that was colder than ice began to seep in through the fissures.

She could not breathe well, and she was fast growing dizzy.

When she looked up, she realized she hadn't heard a thing Tessa was saying as the old woman approached worriedly. She couldn't hear her say it, but Tessa's lips mouthed the words, "Are you all right? You're pale dear, and you've cut yourself — "

The hissing sound of flames and sizzling flesh flickered into her hearing, and then one of the shadows detached from the room about them and slithered toward her as though alive. Nymeria bolted with a cry of terror.

For a fleeting moment, it seemed as if her feet were bare and the ground were ladened with snow, and she saw drifting white snowflakes about her, and a sea of white, and mountains — and then darkness washed the vision away, and she wheeled away from the wall she crashed into. Nymeria fell, her chest heaving. The doorway had been here. She was sure it had been. She'd never taken a wrong turn. She couldn't have.

Firelight flickering dully up the passage drew her, and she looked over her shoulder, desperate to be out of the archives and away from the journals that were so filled with so many unpleasant things. Her skin crawled as though there were thousands and thousands of spiders upon her, all biting and stinging and pricking. Her scalp prickled, and her breath came in great, heaping sobs.

Tessa and Erin were calling out for her, their voices frantic. They sounded a very long way away.

Then she felt the warmth prickling upon her wrists. She turned them, and when she did so, she saw her own blood smeared there. The wound was closing, and the mark was turning silver. She didn't remember ever cutting herself on anything. Had it been the shadows? Were they now trying to harm her?

What would her father say? Would he believe her? Would he get her out of Black Temple before they hurt her worse? Was what Michael had told her coming true? The thought frightened her.

Nymeria wiped her arm upon her shirt, desperate to rid herself of the revolting red, and she stepped toward the torchlight, rounding the wall that divided the hallways. A tapestry hung there, blocking the opening. The torchlight came from the other side, and it illuminated a giant silver feather that was hidden in the weave. She crawled under it and found the tunnel narrowed and shrank drastically, but she could hear music from outside. The melody was beautiful, entrancing, mournful.

She stumbled as again the thing within her shifted. The Violet seared everything it touched as it bled through her veins and outward into the stone around her, and black marks traced after it before fading. Her knees buckled as weakness stole through her. Nymeria's fingers raked her scalp as another wave of screams found their way into her head, and she began to cry. She shouldn't have gone into the archives. She should have known so many of those journals would have been down there, so many documents drenched in death. She wanted to be away from it. Away from all the blood and all the horror. But she couldn't seem to get the strength to stand. Every breath was raw against her throat.

She felt the *other* one, the creature just on the other side of the wall of flaming energy within her. He was darkness where she was light. He was a seething cauldron of foreign *memories*, though she was a breaking soul of the fading *now*. And every moment she knelt, incapacitated, those creatures were drawing nearer. She looked behind her again, and the tapestry began to decay before her very eyes . . . and then it seemed to drip with blood.

Nymeria clawed her way to her feet, using the walls, and she staggered toward the music. *"Nai . . ."* she wept, trying to get away from those shadows. Her heart drew hard against her veins, and the stony walls about her groaned. Dust drifted down over her, cascading as rubble fell about her. Another painful beat, and cracks appeared in jagged lines across its surface. She choked back another cry as the candlelit courtyard opened before her, and she fled the tunnel.

Thousands of candles lit the courtyard, and the music screeched against her ears as the slithering whispers of the dark things' voices began to fade. Michael saw her, and he abandoned his tasks immediately and hurried toward her. Sobrienne looked up, startled.

Nymeria's knees buckled, and she began to cry into her hands.

And then Michael was kneeling by her, looking around as though hoping no one else would notice. He grabbed both sides of her face. "Hey," he said quietly. "You have to calm down, Nymeria."

She couldn't talk, couldn't tell him what had happened. She looked over her shoulder, her skin crawling, fear still making her heart shudder like hummingbirds' wings. She clutched at her necklace when she looked at him again. He understood. She could tell he did. She sensed it.

"Calm down, and they'll fade again," he said.

"I don't want it to get worse," she shuddered. "There's so much in the archives. Everything in the journals down there — it's horrible."

"Come on, so no one realizes what just happened. I don't think they'll see the walls in the air shaft."

Nymeria looked over her shoulder again. "Are they still in there? I got lost. They were following me."

Michael shook his head, though. "I'm not talking about the Shadei Ra. You changed the walls."

Then she saw the black glass. The violet in it was fading, but the glass veins remained dark and glistened threateningly.

"I did that . . . ?"

"Yeah. Come on," he said again.

She nodded. "Don't tell my father. Please. Or anyone."

"I won't. I promise. I have to keep secrets from people, too. People like us scare them."

CHAPTER FORTY

A POISONOUS BLACKNESS THREADED the woods here, as though once a thousand terrible deaths had drenched every tree, every rock, and every inch of this part of the forest. As though the trees themselves grew from the bones of the dead and still possessed pieces of restless souls within their heartwood. Some of them bowed, as if in eternal agony. Some of them bent, as though casting a defiant scream to the skies. And some of them stood, solemn, ever staring, never daring, as though knowingly watching men race from their demons but to no avail.

The trees flew by, young foliage raking across the stolen horse's flanks and scratching Lukas's face. The satchels were empty of rations, with nothing left but crumbs and a few golden liberties, and the horse was fast approaching uselessness when Lukas caught his first glimpse of the giant, vine-laden levies near Oakwall. He had nearly been caught when he'd fled north, and now that he was near the home of the Greenmen, he was unsure whether he'd lost his pursuers by circling back, or if he would be caught here.

Lukas wondered for a moment if he would have to do the unthinkable, but then he decided against it furiously. He'd gotten this far on his lies, so he would continue to trust them to work. Either way, he wasn't going to settle for simply *surviving*. Caol and Eiran deserved what was coming to them, and that alien-eyed demon child was going to help him to ensure it.

Lukas wiped the perspiration beading down his face, and a depraved smile split fractionally over his teeth. He finally had enough information to outmaneuver the first of the men who'd betrayed him. The murder of the Ivans' parents had turned out to have been his most blessed of unfortunate events — immediate repercussions aside. Having gotten caught by their son Reid had been exactly the luck and the source of knowledge he'd needed to get back on track with his own grand scheme.

How exhilarating it was, to be the liar.

His horse stumbled, and Lukas thought he saw a sliver of shadow beside him. He turned his head to look, startled, and another slender branch raked across the side of his face and ripped at his ruined ear. Lukas cursed as the wound tore open and hot blood spilled down his neck, onto his collar. But the wound kept him thinking, and thinking was good when it came to those dark creatures. It kept the thoughts of them out and the doorway calling to them closed. It kept the beings from sensing him so easily.

He was grateful the whirling madness brought about by that sliver of glass had finally begun to recede again, and he was determined to keep it that way. Determined to survive.

The smoke from the sheltered fires rose, and Lukas rode hard around the thick of Oakwall's dwellings, toward the levies where the road curved back toward Raven Trail. His pulse quickened when he saw Enforcers on the road there, and he kept a wide berth, hiding his face from them. He knew some might recognize him. He'd already been through this place too recently, and if they realized who he was, it could spell disaster.

A flash of movement occurred among the green. "Halt!"

One of the Greenmen, a fellow with a red mustache and green painted all over his body and face, held a rifle pointed at Lukas. Lukas's horse reared as the man rushed in front of them from the side of the road, coming from seemingly nowhere, along with several others dressed and painted the same. Lukas wheeled the horse about, searching for a way around them. "Out of my way!" he snapped. His teeth clicked hard against one another.

He looked over his shoulder and realized some of the Enforcers had stopped. Cursing under his breath, he held out the liberties that had been stored in the horse's satchel. "Take it. Just let me through. I have urgent business!"

Two of the Enforcers had pulled away from the others, and when Lukas looked at them next, a familiar face had begun to frown. But the frown quickly turned to shock. "*You?!*"

"I SAID HALT!" commanded the Greenman.

The Enforcer was riding toward Lukas now, determination in his angered eyes, and Lukas's horse pranced, ready to throw him.

"GET OUT OF MY WAY!" Lukas bellowed, and he kicked the horse in the sides aggressively. The horse bolted with a grunt and an unpleasant whinny.

The Greenman's gun fired on him as the horse ran them over, and they scattered to avoid broken limbs.

The Enforcer raced after him, although the others remained behind, confused. "Come back!" the Enforcer shouted.

And then Lukas's horse staggered and fell. She rolled across his ankles, and he gasped, trying to crawl out from under her as the Enforcer gained ground. Her wild eyes blinked as she cried out, and then he saw the blood. She was not going to get back up. Lukas struggled harder. The Greenmen were still racing forward when the Enforcer dropped from his horse, just as Lukas's leg came free.

"C — "

"Stay away from me if you know what is good for you," Lukas hissed. The Enforcer blinked. "I'm not going back. There is nothing you can do to persuade me to turn myself over."

The Enforcer's expression clouded over as anger flooded him, and he drew his weapon. "That's how it's going to be, is it? You would rather face the sword as a fugitive?"

"I will not live the rest of my life waiting for a dagger to find my back," said Lukas. "I'm not going back yet. If you press this, I will kill you. Do not pursue me, and this won't end badly for you." Lukas looked behind him. The wall was so close. "Let me go so that I can do what I must do." The Enforcer took a step toward him. He bolted, and the Enforcer charged after him.

Lukas grabbed the ivy and hefted himself up the thick trunks. He was much faster than the Enforcer was on foot. He'd been hardened in ways none of them could have fathomed, and survival was much dearer to him than catching him was to them. The Enforcer began climbing after him, sheathing his sword to do so, and then the first of the Greenmen joined them in the race.

"Elsir, don't kill him!" shouted the Enforcer. "Help me get him down!"

Elsir grimaced. "He's a dangerous fugitive, James. He's the one they had locked up, and he's got a stolen horse and a wild look that says trouble. And he's trespassing! We can't let him get over this wall! That is sacred ground, and letting him over it is a breach of our contract with Black Temple!"

"He was Black Temple's *prisoner*?" exclaimed the Enforcer. James looked up. "What the hell have you been into?!"

Lukas dodged the Greenman's aim several times as he climbed, until the two men had to put away their weapons to climb after him. Lukas yanked free handfuls of stone where he could reach them through the vines, and he flung them downward. James and Elsir hugged the wall, taking refuge below the thicker trunks below him, and Lukas scrambled upward. Other Greenmen were gathering to join the climb, and Lukas paused briefly to look below himself as he wiped the perspiration beading upon his forehead across his sleeve. He continued to climb.

He found a ledge hidden in the vines where the stone had been carved away by centuries of rain and ferocious winds. The wooden trunks created what seemed a walkable path in the hollow structure. Lukas tested his weight there. Small bits of stone and broken leaves fell, and they knocked against the insides of the levy's belly on their way down. But the trunks held.

Lukas scrambled across and found on the opposite side of the abyss a small ledge made of old, decaying concrete with rusted rebar jutting from its crumbling edges. He backed into the darkness there, his breathing labored from the exertion of the climb. His hands were scratched, and his middle finger bled where a portion of one of his nails had been torn free, and his ear itched fiercely.

He had no weapons on him, but he felt no concern over that particular detail. "James, is it?" Lukas called. He laughed then, and he rested his head against the wall as his voice echoed through the tunnel. The wind groaned in the structure the way a dying man's voice might rush from a pair of old, corroded lungs.

The Enforcer had reached the ledge and drawn his weapon again. The Greenman struggled to balance as he pulled his rifle from his shoulder. The ledge they shared was narrow and did not permit Elsir much of an opening to shoot around the Enforcer. "You should know," James warned as his sword caught and reflected a sliver of bright afternoon sunlight into the cavernous ruin, "I have to take you back. Whatever you're into, you can't keep running."

"You know him, then?" Elsir asked.

Both men were as breathless as Lukas was, and as they took the moment to regain their composure, Lukas peered out through the cracks in the wall, where the light washed against and bleached the stone. Dust fell when he put his weight on the wall to get up again.

"He knows my face, all right," Lukas swore. "I'm not letting you take me back, I told you. I don't care what kind of glory you think it may earn you by turning me over. I'm not dying because of you, or because of anyone."

"*Dying?*" laughed James. "You're mad if you think your situation would be so simple."

Elsir seemed to be processing their back-and-forth. Lukas could see realization dawning in those pale brown eyes of his.

The angle of the sunlight was advantageous for Lukas where he hid in the shadows; it pierced their eyes, and even though they squinted, they couldn't see him. And the trunks he'd crossed were groaning under their combined weight.

Lukas looked about, hoping for any other means of escape should the vines break because of them. He saw nothing obvious.

"What is it between you two that I am missing?" asked Elsir.

Lukas's blood thickened. James said nothing for a long moment, and then, as he opened his mouth to speak, a fierce gust of wind tore through the tunnel and drowned out what he said.

"*What . . . ?* Are you *certain*?" asked Elsir. Realization dawned on the Greenman. "So that's why they were taking him to the Reformation. That's quite serious."

Lukas swore. "Shouldn't have done that, James," he snarled. "You realize now I have to kill you both. I cannot have them discovering who I know, or where they are. You are a very stupid man."

James grew uneasy as Lukas stood to his full height and rolled his shoulders in preparation of a fight. Elsir's fingers gripped the gun, but as Lukas had noted, the Greenman still couldn't raise the weapon to aim it. The Enforcer was simply in the way, and there was no room.

"I'm going to have fun killing both of you," said Lukas. "Shadow creatures be damned. I can't have my lies getting found out, now can I?"

"You can't kill me," James smirked. The Enforcer braced himself and raised his sword. "You wouldn't, not really. That's not who you are — you couldn't permit yourself to do it."

"Boy, you cannot imagine the things I have had to do to survive since Caol betrayed me. And what you just told him is something I cannot allow. So your bodies are going to feed the maggots. No mother of yours will ever know what happened to you. You are *not* going to be the thing to cost me the only chip I can use to bargain with Caol and Eiran."

"Since when have *they* had such a hold over the likes of *you*?" asked James, laughing. "How can Five Tower's lords be so dangerous to a man they don't even know?"

Lukas's knuckles cracked, and as James rushed him, he relied on the instincts that had allowed him to survive years of hardship and bloodshed. Lukas planted his feet, and as James attacked, he stepped forward, into the Enforcer. The motion was quick, practiced, and brutal. Elsir was shoved out of the tunnel and caught himself at the stony mouth by just a handhold when James staggered backward and into him. Elsir's gun fell and slid toward the abyss between them as the Greenman himself tumbled backward.

James clutched at his throat, shocked, and Lukas slung the blood from the sword he now held. He knelt, watching the Enforcer process his own defeat. A wicked grin tilted Lukas's lips as James tried to speak and blood came out instead. "Thanks for the sword, you worthless fool," said Lukas. "You should have borrowed the Greenman's gun." He turned the sword over and then shoved the tip into the woody vine, and he picked up the gun and watched as James lost his balance and fell into the black abyss below. "Not that it would have stopped me from killing you, either." The man's descent took a while before a hollow crash shuddered through the walls, dislodging small bits of dust and stone. Elsir clutched to the vines for dear life, but he was slipping.

"What should I do with you, then?" Lukas asked. "Offer the maggots more food? Or have you another use, I wonder?"

"Let me help," gasped Elsir, even as he was about to fall. "I can help."

Lukas laughed darkly. He admired the guts of the man. "How can you help me? You're about to fall to your death."

"I know you can't do what you're trying to do alone. And I don't want to live the rest of my life in Oakwall, painted like the forest with nothing to call my own. Let me help you," said Elsir. "Pay my contract, and I'll be in your service until my death. I know you can afford it. You're a rich man. It would be nothing to you."

Lukas laughed as he pulled the magazine and checked how many bullets remained. Plenty. The magazine clicked back into place easily. "Money, is it? That's all it takes for you? A mercenary, you fancy yourself." He stood, then, and he approached Elsir as the vine he held began to creak and groan. Below, Irkov was shouting at the Enforcers. He was fiercely against setting fire to the wall to either trap Lukas or smoke him out, but the Enforcers were determined to capture him. "I have unfinished business," said Lukas. "Revenge being chief among them. You may be useful to me, though, if you're so desperate." He watched the torches being lit and sucked on his tooth, and he wiped away the blood from his ear. "Tell you what. Prove to me that you are willing to work for me, to risk your life. Then I'll pay that contract. Get me some supplies, and ready yourself to deliver a message for me in haste."

"Yes, whatever you want," Elsir gasped. "I can do that." Elsir finally caught a solid hold on the wall, and he began to climb back up. Lukas held out his hand, and Elsir grasped his forearm.

Lukas pulled him up. "The moment you are done here, you are to ride fast for Aelynhold. Do not draw attention to yourself. Draw this on the door at the guards' barracks, and take care not to be seen. My friends there will know what it means." Lukas drew a symbol in blood upon Elsir's palm, and then he grabbed the man by the collar. "When I see my men, I will know you have been faithful, and your contract will be paid. You will be indebted to me for a lifelong service, with a handsome pension if you survive it. Also . . . we don't want your people down there thinking we have become friends." Just as Elsir started to protest, Lukas shoved the man from the opening.

The fire the Enforcers set below had begun to spread along the dead foliage. The Greenmen tried to put it out, but their attempts were useless.

Lukas backed away from the opening. "Getting down is going to be a bitch," he swore. He laughed, however. Twisted luck was, *indeed*, turning in his favor. His stomach growled fiercely, and his mouth was dry. He searched the tunnel for some hint of moisture while doubting he would find a damned thing to eat.

His canteen had only enough water for a day and a night, but he did find a bird's nest. He took the eggs and held them up in the sunlight streaming in there, and he found from the translucence that they were still edible. Lukas cracked them open and swallowed the slime, and he took a measured swig from his canteen. He felt the urge to pace impatiently but conserved his strength instead.

Elsir had survived the fall, and he was limping away now, hopefully to retrieve the things Lukas had asked for. Hopefully, the desperate fool could beat the flames that were licking the vines.

Lukas looked at his wrist as a shadow of gray coursed through his veins again. His fingers curled over the gun, and he shouldered the strap.

James. That was the reason for gray this time. Every time he committed another murder, he received another mark. How many more could he accrue before he could no longer block the creatures out or hide from them?

Then the gray in his flesh faded, and he shuddered sickly. "Every time I kill someone," he said aloud to himself, and angrily. "As though my sins must confess themselves upon my own flesh. It's probably how she knew."

He pondered the girl and her situation again.

The creepy little Ivan girl had managed to chase the creatures away, unlike anyone else infected with the Violet. She had transferred the Blood Light into the most unlikely of weapons also. It was frightening . . . yet . . . it was also incredible. She'd protected not just herself when she'd cast that stone in the kennels. She'd saved Lukas's life as well, and her uncle's, since the man had sensed the creatures, too.

Yet Lukas had a strange feeling that the curse was harming her even now, even if she handled its power better than any other he'd ever met. Some small part of him recognized it was devouring her from the inside.

And that same part of him cringed at the idea that such a young child had been cursed with the Violet, that she had been forced to live with its dreadful cost.

Stranger, in his soul, he felt and recognized an instinct to bow to her, as though it was his place to offer his life before hers, to protect her from the creatures . . . He feared that instinct almost as much as he feared the creatures themselves. It was confusing and illogical. He didn't understand it, and he didn't think he wanted to, either. It was *unnatural*. And he would need to take precautions if he had to get near her again.

Moreover, Lukas had never before been able to fathom how anything could have been worse than what he'd gone through in the Gray Halls, but whatever had been done to her to curse her had been worse than what had been done to him or to his men. Instinct whispered to him, slowly filling his mind and heart with warnings — like small droplets of horror, leaking from some catastrophic, monstrous ocean of Violet.

The delicate web he was entangled in was growing more complicated as time trudged on, he knew. But soon enough, the dangerous tendrils would dissolve, and he would become the spider, and his prey would face his hungry wrath.

Over the next few days, Lukas warded off the attempts to climb by the few Enforcers still in Oakwall, and he also hindered the attempts made by the other Greenmen and the group of Black Temple men that he'd escaped. The rifle was more deadly in his hands than the sword, as they well found out. He felled both the brewer David and a fellow he believed was called Baron with a single, well-aimed bullet, and he wasted little other ammo to make the point that he had the upper hand with that gun. He'd also allowed a couple others to climb, only to behead them when they reached him. And that had made a second point, that he didn't need the gun to defend himself from them. He was just as deadly without it.

So the Enforcers resigned themselves to their fiery siege, disregarding the Greenmen's protests, and the last of his Reformation escorts who'd pursued him were injured in the fiery chaos below.

Lukas stayed holed up in the impregnable alcove high in the levy's timeworn face, and he ate and drank what food had been smuggled to him that first night by Elsir, before the flames had deeply charred the humongous ivy and spread to the rest of the woods about them.

The food and drink had been his new ally's final gesture before his departure.

Lukas had enough to last for a couple of weeks as he waited for his men. He had only to rest, to ration his limited supplies, and to wait while occasionally reminding the warriors below that he still had the upper hand. He knew his men would arrive before the Enforcers would receive reinforcements.

CHAPTER FORTY-ONE

REID HELD HIS BREATH AS he watched from the obscurity of the collapsed bell tower and the towering oak that had grown up around it. Droplets of freezing rain pattered against his skin and soaked into his clothes. The water ran in rivulets down his fingertips where it dripped over his boots. He held still, his body tense. He feared taking a breath, for the smallest motion might draw their attention to where he hid. He could not see Taiir, but he knew the man was nearby, also staying hidden. Neither could fight them. There were too many of them, and they had already killed Manard.

Most of them wore old traveling cloaks and carried awkwardly curved swords that marked them as soldiers from Five Tower. A few of them had guns as well, which surprised him, while others were arrayed in the dreaded cowls of the wolf cult. These men were traveling lightly, except for the packhorses at the outer fringe among their two groups. A prisoner was bound in a cage there, and he was chained, gagged, and seemed unconscious. Reid could not see the face of the poor soul they'd imprisoned, but he could tell the man had been a prisoner for a while. Months, perhaps. There were other prisoners as well, all chained, all bound, all gagged and blindfolded.

Among those delivering the caged prisoner were three wolfmen. Descendants of the Moon. Real cult members, not posers — for they carried only weapons made of bone and spoke the way only the wolfmen priests did. "How good, it is, for us to meet them *here*, in this accursed ruin," spat one of the real wolfmen, who stood next to the one who seemed to be the leader of the three.

Another of the three spoke, and he was just as angry as the first. "And to see so many creatures wearing our faces, as though to be one of us." That cult member was very displeased as he pulled on the wolf skull through which his dreads were woven. "A dishonor we will rectify with each one's blood upon our skin, and each one's flesh within our bellies. Only the *unworthy* carry blades of iron and steel. Unholy beasts, as they are. True Wolfshadow do not wield such weapons as these reliant cowards wield."

"Thretirak. Tarek. Cut still your tongues," said another of the three real wolfmen. "Forget not that we are accused in our making as well. Our own kin will not take us. These men are now our allies whether they dress as we do or not."

"Agarath," hissed Thretirak. "It is most unholy — "

"Forget this withering animosity, Thretirak." Agarath held out his blade of bone, but he winced as though his arm gave him pain. "Or I will make you eat the arm which our charge has defiled with his steel, and so keep from you the Blessed Land of our Dread Fathers. Retrieve our prisoner."

Reid stifled a shiver, and into his view walked two other men who stood out among the travelers. These two men were dressed most strangely. Their clothing wrapped about them like armor molded to their bodies. The color was black, and it was patterned like fine mesh. Their cloaks were finer yet, and they seemed to catch the shape and color of everything about them so that the two strange men blended into the darkness in the most unnatural way. If the two Strangers stood still for a second, Reid swore they would vanish and then reappear, like flickering spirits.

The spikes jutting from their shoulder armor made them look monstrous, like demons come from the nether world. The silhouette cast by them made the men's upper bodies appear disproportionately large, as though they could wrap their arms around each root of the giant bell tower oak — and simply snap each one. Their cloaks swept outward when caught by the wind, until the ribbons of black appeared to be scaled, serpentine tails, lashing in the rain. Their hoods made them seem to lean forward, as though they simply drifted over the ground. But he saw the armored boots, which made no noise above the rain.

Reid wondered in quiet horror whom they worked for. What sea they'd crossed to come to this land, and why they were here among these inferior warriors.

For a long moment, he almost thought the two odd ones were unarmed, for there lacked obvious weaponry upon them. Then one turned his back to him and drew a long blade from a sheath upon his back. It was not like any blade Reid had ever seen before. It was a wicked weapon — it shone in the rain, caught the moonlight in the most menacing manner. The runes upon it seemed to glow on their own, as though they devoured the silver rays cast from the sky.

The others, who had been speaking unto one another in hushed tones, quieted when the Stranger who'd drawn his sword began to speak. The language was unfamiliar. But it reminded Reid of the language his niece had spoken months ago in the kennels at Crow Post. Its cadence was elegant, flowing — but at times, it was also sharp and guttural and twisting. It prodded the senses the way no other language did, until the hairs upon the back of his neck rose on end and he felt his muscles cord and tense involuntarily.

The meaning of the words seemed just out of reach. It was as though, if his mind would just obey, the meaning would begin to slip right through him and begin to carve bleeding paths wherever the words went. The words were angry words. Promising words.

The man who had drawn his sword waved the blade in the rain and slung from it much of the water that had gathered upon it. The light within it pulsed brighter, and the runes began to change as he held it out, the sharp tip pointing at the faintly glowing golden ring and silver feather still pulsing on the stone wall. The Stranger seemed to know exactly what the mark was, and when the sword grazed the stone, the mark lost its light. It remained silver within the rock, however, like a permanent brand.

The wind hissed through the crevice, and the water dripping from the wall before Reid lashed at his face and his hands. Reid denied the impulse to shrug his coat tighter, to pull his bare fingers into his sleeves or to tighten the collar about his neck. He kept his fingers still though they were numb and stinging from the temperature. He let the cold seep about his neck like a noose, let it drip down inside his coat where the cold bit at him. Nasty little bites. Painful ones.

The others resumed their quiet argument, but again, they fell silent when the other strange one in the armored black attire held up his hand to the first. *"Khevakh neija?"*

The first, who still held the sword aloft, nodded. *"Inak muori nuot Vaelania. Neakh mekan'yath krethan."* He lowered the blade, rested the edge against his palm as though he was to draw his own blood. Then he sheathed the sword, his flesh unmolested. "He is close, this one," the man said in English. "The mark is recent. Two months ago." The accent was thick; it was the same as Nymeria's. When he drew back his hood, eyes as green as jade soaked up the moonlight and cast it back into the night. The color cut through the darkness with the coldness of a man who took pleasure in killing. Pale hair flamed about his head in defiance of the rain.

Reid's jaws clenched involuntarily. The Stranger was not quite . . . *right*, he realized. Something about him was tainted, in a sense. Twisted. Unholy. It wasn't just the eyes, it was everything about him that felt . . . not right. Reid knew to trust his instincts. They had always been correct, and they were warning him that Taiir and himself were in serious danger. They were telling him they needed to get out of the area before they were discovered — but Reid couldn't move an inch. He was trapped, and moving even a muscle would be enough to get caught. His heart thundered in his ears, nearly loud enough to drown out the storm as the rain pounded against the stones and beat upon the leaves.

Agarath had not yet interrupted the Strangers from their investigation. He waited calmly, quietly aside, warily watching the mark on the wall.

"He is *close*?" snapped one of their other travelers.

"Shut up, Eerin!" said one of Eerin's comrades.

But Eerin did not listen. "The hell he is, Rhaeven." Eerin was very angry. "We've been searching for years now, and to what avail? You told Caol and Eiran the Violet could be used to their purposes — and instead, it almost took out Five Tower. Everything that creature has touched has caused death and destruction. The Bright Demon is dead, and still, the effects of its existence are ever reaching. Eiran still believes every word you say, but I believe you merely have us searching for ghosts. *Ghosts*, Rhaeven! And you think some magic marking on a wall is from one of them. I have not been paid in months. My men have not been paid. And that traitorous, worthless leech Lukas has yet to surface. His time is up. Eiran wants his head, since he's failed to find Rhael himself, in the time Caol allotted. We could be going after him instead. Eiran has assured us — "

Rhaeven had but to turn his head and look at the raging traveler — the other man like Rhaeven had already committed to the silent command and slit Eerin's throat, and then he had flickered back into the night where he'd previously stood. The other travelers — twenty or more, counted Reid — drew their swords, afraid of the two men. The only three who were unaffected by the unnatural display were Agarath and his two wolfmen companions, Thretirak and Tarek, who were dragging their prisoner from his cage. The prisoner had but one arm, Reid saw. He grimaced at the gruesome wound.

"What other complaints have you?" Rhaeven asked of them. When he was met with silence, he crossed his arms. "We are an impatient breed, Sol and I." The traveler clutching at his throat and choking on his blood went to his knees and looked up. His hood fell back, and thick locks of black hair soaked up the rain as his mouth twisted with hatred, and as blood, blackened by the night, spilled from his lips. None of the men said anything. Rhaeven lifted his finger, and Reid saw the claw that extended from the tip of the one he placed upon the bleeding traveler's forehead. The traveler went white at the touch, and his eyes glassed over, and he fell. He was dead before he ever touched the ground.

"I have no quarrel to offer," said another traveler who sheathed his curved sword cautiously. "Spare me, I ask. I do, however, have questions I hope do not offend either of you."

"Ask them, and be done."

"Why is this mark important? What is it?" The others began to sheathe their own weapons as well. They seemed to want the same answer. One death seemed easy to forgive among them, as though the dead traveler had not been a valued comrade among them.

"This mark is ancient. From a family long forgotten. It was created by two brothers, one who was a traitor, the other who went missing." Reid nearly forgot to breathe. These Strangers knew about the mark. He couldn't believe what luck he had. He'd found men who knew what it was, but . . . they would kill him if they found him, just as they had Manard. They hadn't given Manard a word, or even a thought; they'd just killed him. It meant Reid and Taiir would be treated accordingly. It meant he couldn't just approach them and ask what he needed. "This is unimportant to you, but it is to me, and it is to my masters," continued the Stranger. "The mark is a corrosive beacon. It will shut off the communications of any who are in the vicinity, yet it will allow only this family to coordinate how they wish. That it has been activated means much to us. Continue to work with us, and you will be rewarded accordingly. Your masters understand what is at risk. So abide by their orders if you wish to keep your lives."

"Another question," asked Eerin's friend delicately.

"Ask, and then ask no more."

"Why are you after Rhael and his brother? We know why Caol wants him, but not why you do."

"That is not for you to know," said Rhaeven. The Stranger turned to his friend, then. "Sol, contact Alitran Aharet and tell him of this find."

Sol's hood bobbed once, and he seemed to vanish completely as the rain washed over them in torrents. Rhaeven looked down at the dead traveler, then moved past him. His steps brought him back to the silver marking. Reid saw the snarl that pressed his lips thin as he pulled his hood over his head, hiding his ruthless features and eclipsing that illuminated jade color in his murderous gaze once more.

"The murderous fiend," Rhaeven swore. The curse barely scraped past his teeth, and the rain muffled the sound that was a promise of retribution.

Reid eased back, until parts of his spine pressed into the massive root that rose from the ruined tower. The travelers had drifted closer to the boulder, and Rhaeven stood literally inches from him, on the other side of the wall. Reid prayed they would not realize he was there, peering through the cracks.

Rhaeven and Sol seemed to see very well in the dark.

"Did you hear about Raven Trail?" asked one of the travelers.

Rhaeven made no reply, not at first. He stood there for a long moment, his back to the decrepit wall. Reid watched the freezing rain rolling off his cloak. That strange sword was so close that the sheath scraped against the crumbling stone. Reid's fingers twitched involuntarily. "Ender's Creek. Yes," Rhaeven said at last. "Your operation was a failure. Your disguise was a sham from the beginning, and Lukas recognized you. He alerted his captors, who took him back from your men. If you hadn't been quarrelling among yourselves and your thief friends over killing or retrieving him, you would have succeeded in one goal or the other. That was your mistake, and the loss was yours, not ours. He does not know where Rhael or Gabriel is. He is worthless to Sol and me."

"What about Edantine and Hagenhold? Do you know about the devices they've found there?"

"Yes," said Rhaeven.

"You told Eiran the shards do not work for our kind. Was it a lie? How did they come into possession of them?"

"It was not a lie."

"Then why do they work in Edantine and Hagenhold," asked the traveler, "but they would not work for us in Five Tower?"

"Illegal modification. Sol tells me the devices are quite sophisticated, even though each kind is of a rudimentary design. There are more in Oakwall that are even more advanced. Whoever is making them has access to power that we do not."

"So . . . your people are not responsible for them?"

"No. The Dead One has old knowledge, but he refused to submit it to our archives. When he fled, we were unable to reproduce his other experiments. He is a dangerous man, even to us."

"You think he's the one who has been selling them?" asked the traveler.

Rhaeven did not respond for a long time. He finally let out his breath slowly. "I do not. The hybrid tech we have been finding is different. It is a combination of our old tech, and your primitive type. And the Dead One is in hiding. He has no need for your money. He wouldn't have successfully hidden himself from us for so long if he was the kind to risk selling such illegal devices. Someone else has created them, not him. Which marks the question. *Who?*"

Sol had returned, and Reid shrank even further against the roots. The man faced the wall where Reid remained hidden. He said nothing for a long time; it seemed as though he was peering at the crevice from which Reid watched. He could feel Sol's gaze, saw the minute movement of his hood as his head turned, ever so slowly.

"What is it?" Rhaeven asked impatiently.

"I've let the Alitran know. Aharet does not think the mark is relevant, but he has logged it. There has been activity north of this forest, however. Another creature with violet eyes. Possibly one of the many who escaped Five Tower near the Bright Night."

"Destroy the mark," said Rhaeven. "Make it harder for him to communicate with whomever this was intended for. I want one of you to remain here to watch discreetly. If you see anyone approach who seems to be searching for this mark, kill him as well. And when you are done, you will return to Five Tower and let Caol and his sons know of our progress. Tell him his thief has escaped his captors again. His next course of action is likely to return to Oakwall, or to head to Aelynhold. It is likely what remains of the inactive sect of the Brotherhood will be impelled to action there. Be on your guard against them. They know everything about our arrangements with Five Tower, and with the wolfmen, and of our search for the Dead One and the Defector. Not every monk is our friend. Consider them all with suspicion because their sleeper agents are dangerous. Even to us."

Reid was reeling from all that he'd heard. And then to hear that Lukas had escaped, to know where he would likely go, set aflame his desire to leave immediately, to hunt down the murderer again. But still, he could not move. And he needed to learn more.

Agarath stepped forward, and he held something up in his hands. Something small and red. A vial. Rhaeven took it from him.

"What is this?" asked Rhaeven. He held it up and examined it. "Why have you given me a vial of blood? What manner of insult — "

"We offer no insult to such dangerous ones," said Agarath as Thretirak and Tarek at last wrestled their prisoner from his cage. The one-armed prisoner growled, and hissed, and fought in his bindings, and he was shoved toward Rhaeven, where he fell at the Stranger's feet. "Open the vial," said Agarath. "It does not rot."

Rhaeven uncorked the vial and raised it slowly. His hand quivered at the scent of the blood. "Powerful," he said. In his voice, there was wonder. "Where did this come from? What manner of creature?"

"This one had it when we caught him. It also had one of the shards," said Agarath. "It cut him, and its body drank from the well of the curse and claimed it. The Violet is still strong within this creature. It sees the Dark Ones. It sees other things as well, which are more unusual. Blue light. Water. A monstrous, jaded presence, to frighten even the *dark things*. Vile things, it has spoken."

Rhaeven handed the vial to Sol. "Take this," he said. "Test it." And while Sol removed his blade and turned the vial so that a drop touched the blade, Rhaeven knelt before the prisoner. He took the man by the hair of the head and forced him to look up, and he examined him carefully. "Interesting," he said. "Spirit, coursing through his veins like fire. And yet the Spirit within him it is not his own. It is of the color of the Vael, and it is strong yet. Where is the shard?"

"It is only glass again. The creature's body has absorbed every ounce of the shard's light."

Sol's blade sparked brilliantly with blue light, which crawled across the metal like veins of data. Sol hissed a curse in that other language. "Pure," he said, examining the blade. "Rhaeven, the blood has markers for *immunity*."

"Are you certain?" Rhaeven reached up abruptly and snatched the blade away to examine for himself. "That cannot be correct." But as he examined it, he, too, seemed to come to the same conclusion. "Now I think I understand why the Defector betrayed Caol . . . In all our years, this has never been." Rhaeven took the vial again, returning the blade, and he was extremely careful as he sealed the bottle again. "I will send this to Red Coven. He will be most pleased."

"It is female," said Sol. "The scent is . . . like siren song."

Rhaeven nodded. "Indeed. Where did you get this intriguing specimen, Agarath? The Blood Light is the strongest in him." He examined a fresh wound upon the prisoner, where the blood streaked with faint rivers of Violet.

Blood Light, Lukas had said. Reid suddenly made the connection. And supposedly, Lukas had been infected with it, though he had claimed it was now gone.

These men were gathering prisoners with the Blood Light.

"We won't need the others you're keeping in Cyan if his blood is an accurate indication. In the rest you have given us, the Spirit has degraded. This one carries a stronger, more consistent power within him, and it isn't likely to fade soon. Before you protest, however, yes, we will still go to Cyan just in case. But this one will be taken to Red Coven immediately."

"Our thief tried to kill this creature," laughed Agarath. "We had nearly cornered him when we found this one. He'd slit its throat. We took this one when Black Temple chased Lukas and apprehended him — "

"I'll kill him — " choked the prisoner. His voice was nearly gone, like Jeana's. The sound had no strength.

Agarath laughed again. "This one does not quit."

"Kill whom?" asked Rhaeven. Even he seemed amused.

"The man who did this to me. It is his fault, and I'll kill him for it after I kill *him*."

Agarath bowed before the prisoner and poked him in the chest with the handle of his bone dagger. "It is delusional. Our thief is in Oakwall, and that is not where this one is being taken. This one will be taken back to Cyan, to remain with the others. The Strangers have interest. It will die a glorious death, if it dies at all. If they do not come for more, then this creature has done well."

The prisoner shivered banefully, and then he began to laugh, as though he knew something they did not. "Cursed by the Violet yourself once . . . I can bring it back. I know who can bring it back."

Agarath jerked away as though he'd been scalded. "It will commit no such unholy deed!"

Rhaeven put up his hand. "Stop badgering him. I want him to conserve his strength."

"This creature sees *them*, just like the others. Just as we three once saw. What else does Caol and his servant wish, False Brothers?" Agarath had turned his attention to the fake wolfmen. "We shall deliver."

"More of *them*," said Eerin's friend. "And for the love of all that is not cursed, put him back in that cage. I don't want him running free, putting us all at risk of catching the curse."

Agarath chuckled. "That is not how the Violet is caught, False Brother. Ask its friends behind itself. Eiran's hunters *know*."

Three more men stood there, silently. They hardly seemed to follow the conversation.

"Ah . . . they've forgotten how to talk, I have forgotten," laughed Agarath. "Madness has taken their tongues and turned their brains to worms. Thretirak. Tarek. Take this creature and put it away. Then go with the hunters to the north, and find those infected with the Blood Light. I will go with these men to Cyan."

Reid and Taiir met again after the enemy cleared from the fallen bell tower and its ancient court.

"Could you hear what they were saying?" Taiir asked as he examined Manard's corpse. Reid looked over their wagon. It had been destroyed, and what the wolfmen found useful, they'd taken. "I could not move from tha wall down there, not without being seen or heard. There were too many of them."

Reid nodded. "We need to go to Oakwall," he said.

"I disagree. Aelynhold is more important. Before those strangely dressed warriors moved to that mark on tha wall you activated tha last time we were here, I heard them talking about Aelynhold. Tha healer you are looking for will be there at tha cemetery. If you value your niece's life, we need to go now. We both read that ledger in Balthora, Commander. Our time is running out."

"Lukas is in Oakwall," Reid said. He stood, wiping the blood from his hand. "He'll go after her himself."

"Let Black Temple deal with their trespassers. This time in tha season, your niece and your brother will be in Isold or Black Temple itself. If not already, then in only another week or two. We are closer to Aelynhold, and Aelynhold is more important. I do not want to see her destroy another city, but I do not want to kill her, either. That means that healer is our only option, Commander."

Reid sighed after contemplating Taiir's point. He checked his weapons and his radios. "Fine. We'll go to Aelynhold. But first, we need to set that man free."

"And do what with him?" asked Taiir. "Best to leave tha wolfmen to their business with those foreigners."

"Taiir, they have more innocent people imprisoned in Cyan. They're using it as a base to gather and transport people who have been infected with that violet light. The man they had caged up here? With one arm? *Lukas* tried to kill him. That's what they said. I want to know when and where this happened. And I want to know if that man knew anything else."

Taiir moved from Manard's corpse and toward the old building where they'd kept their horses down the hill. "I already took care of that just after they emptied tha cage of him and turned their backs upon it. Tha cage is compromised, Commander. It is up to him to free himself. I left him Manard's knife."

"Then I need you to go to Cyan and work on setting those people free."

"I am not going to Cyan," scowled Taiir. He was quite insulted.

"You need to go," Reid reiterated, but Taiir refused.

"I will not. If there is trouble in Aelynhold, you will need me to save you, will you not? Your eyes only see so much. Mine see farther. And I move more quietly than you do. This is tha only way, Commander."

Despite the seriousness of the situation, Reid laughed under his breath. "Fine. But when we get to Aelynhold, we will need to find someone who can deliver a message directly to Crow Post, so they can get someone out there as soon as possible. It isn't likely they'll even reach Cyan in time to help those people."

"If it is a base, they are not going anywhere soon. They will have more of tha cursed there."

"They said there are a lot more of those monks in Aelynhold," said Reid.

"So we will kill them all, if we must," Taiir shrugged. "We will find out how deep tha rot is, and cut it, as you said. Maybe we will make some new friends while we are at it. I quite liked tha huntress in Tallil."

"You dog." Taiir's eyes twinkled, and Reid shook his head, humored greatly. "But business first, as always."

"Of course," said Taiir.

CHAPTER FORTY-TWO

AN ARM FOR AN ARM

TAERYN STRUGGLED AGAINST his captors as they pulled tight the gag over his mouth and then hauled him back to the cage. They threw him in, and he landed awkwardly on something sharp. He winced, and as the world spun round and round, he lay there bleeding. He felt under himself, and his only remaining hand came across the handle of something hard. Something metallic and heavy. He shifted, confused by it, and then he saw the flicker of a shadow, a dark man sliding behind the walls. He stared after the ghost, wondering whether he was hallucinating again, and his hand still clutched whatever the stranger had left him. As his captors hefted his cage to haul him back to the horses, he pulled it free. A knife. A strong knife, made of blessed *steel*. Not of weak and splintering *bone*.

Taeryn shoved the tip of the blade into the lock at his throat, and after some scraping, the chains fell free. He sawed through the bindings on his feet as the cage broke apart, and he scrambled to his feet as the startled wolfmen turned to face him. He struck and gutted the first hunter who lunged at him, and then he darted for Agarath, screaming with all the rage he'd been holding inside, with energy he hadn't known he'd had. Agarath raised his arm to defend himself as Taeryn drove the knife into him, and he yanked it free and stabbed the monster again, and then again. He pulled away, then, and he fled into the night. He already knew they would be coming after him. So he found the first tree he could climb with just his one arm, and he pulled himself up, using his chains and bracing his feet between the trunks.

Agarath, bloody and shouting orders as he always did, sent the hunters after him and then took up a horse himself, with Thretirak and one of the fake wolfmen.

Taeryn waited until they were just below him and leapt from the tree, killing the fake wolfman on his horse and holding desperately to the pommel on the seat as the man fell. Taeryn gained his balance, adjusted himself in the seat, took the reins, and kicked the horse in the ribs. The horse responded, protesting as it leapt over the body and took off.

He offered a silent thanks to whomever had given him the knife as he rode toward vengeance. Toward Oakwall. His capturers had taunted him, telling him where the man who'd tried to kill him was. Where he would be if he'd fled Oakwall. He was going there to end the man's life. It was all he lived for now. He no longer cared about Black Temple. He no longer cared about helping the wearyworn, or duty, or honor. No one had been there to help him when the murderer had taken a knife to Taeryn's throat. So vengeance drove him, and it was the only thing that kept him from falling into the madness coursing through his veins. Vengeance was the only thing keeping him from hearing the screams in the back of his mind, or seeing while awake the bloody fields from the nightmares he'd begun to battle. Thousands and thousands of deaths. So much blood. So many screams . . .

He would have one death more before the madness took him, and that would be Lukas's.

Agarath and his men pursued him through the pine forest, over the raging rivers, and through the vicious rain. Occasionally, he clutched at his shoulder, where his arm had been cut from him. He prayed Agarath would have to have his own amputated. He'd stabbed him enough times for the man to either bleed out or be left with an equally useless appendage that would only serve to slow him down.

But Agarath and Thretirak were closing in on him.

Taeryn held the knife with the reins in his hand, expecting them at any time to catch up to him. Hatred ran through him like blistering siren song, and he welcomed their attack. He would fight them to the death, and he would be glad to do it.

But first, Lukas was going to die for his crimes.

As night fell on the final day when Taeryn approached Oakwall, Taeryn saw the strange lights, and the fire eating at the great wall. He drew his horse back, slowing the beast.

He slipped from the horse and left the tired beast untethered behind him, and he began to sift through the small dwellings there. Blond hair . . . Blond hair . . . *Blond hair.* He searched every painted face as well as every unpainted face. None of the men he saw were blond. Their hair colors varied from oak to pine, to pitch, to mud, to salt, to blood. None were blond. None. He headed toward the fires, where scores of Greenmen were fighting with warriors clad in Aelynhold's colors — the armor those men wore was similar to that of the thieves and murderers of that city's criminal underground. Those men also wore glass chains about their necks as well as dark fur cloaks much like those the wolfmen donned. Strewn about them upon the ground were many dead Enforcers and Greenmen, and some of their own men were also among the dead.

The Aelynhold warriors fought as if they were trying to get to something. Or someone. The wall where the ivy had been scorched — where flames still licked with incinerating fury — seemed to be the center of the fight. Taeryn looked up.

At first, he saw nothing but the great opening in the levy where the wall had crumbled and vines had grown through the structure and created a cave. And then the blond caught his eye from the depths of the structure. Taeryn snarled and clutched at his knife, and he made his way toward the wall. He didn't care that the fire burned him. He couldn't feel it, not after what the shard had done to him. He put the knife in his mouth and began to climb, even as the flames licked at him and his skin blistered and boiled. Violet coursed through his veins, and the fire seemed to cringe from him, to die in his presence.

The blond-haired man above approached the ledge as the other armed men fell away from Taeryn, retreating from the vicious fire that lashed them yet couldn't seem to kill *him.* Above, it was Lukas who stared down at him, horror blooming across his twisted face for the first time as he recognized Taeryn. Taeryn's snarl clamped down on the blade. His fingers dug into the wooden trunks and stone walls, and both gave under his strength.

Lukas paled as alarm crashed through him. "You were dead," he shouted from above. "I killed you."

Taeryn began to laugh when the vines began to give away under him. He didn't care how long it took to get to Lukas. He laughed, even as he fell into the fire below, and rolled, and felt his bones creaking in protest. The cinders seared his flesh, and soot painted itself across his skin.

Agarath dragged Taeryn away from the wall. The knife lay in the belly of the fire there as the two fought, and then Thretirak lunged at Taeryn and knocked him to the ground again.

"I'll kill him for what he's done to me!" screamed Taeryn. "Get off me!" His teeth sank into Thretirak's wrist, and he felt the bones snap between his teeth. Thretirak screamed, recoiling, and Agarath stepped back warily, searching for the knife he thought Taeryn still held.

Taeryn felt the Violet pulse through him again, and he began to laugh madly. Tall specters flickered at the edges of his vision. "Death is coming for us all anyway. They cannot see him. *I can.* He is *there.* And I will deliver his soul unto them, so that he can feel the agony of eternity with them. Do not try to stop me!"

Agarath was breathless and exhausted, and he looked up. He stood, then, cradling his injured arm. "Let us come to an agreement, then. We shall work together to get that traitor down from there. When he is subdued, we will resume our disagreement." He sniggered, then. "I admit my respect for its willfulness, Creature. The curse has made it strong. Had it been born among the Wolfshadow, it would have brought us great honor as a Descendant of the Moon."

The three of them were again surrounded by the armed men from Aelynhold, even as those thieves and murderers guarded themselves against the Greenmen. A sword touched Taeryn's throat, and he snarled at the man who held it there, moving forward to dare the man to try and use it. "What are your intentions here?" demanded the Aelynhold warrior.

"I intend to kill *him*," said Taeryn, and he nodded to the blond man above who took refuge in the burning wall. "What do you prefer I do first? Cut off his arms and his legs, or his head?"

The warrior shook his head, and the blade pressed against Taeryn's throat. "I cannot let you do either. That man is under our protection."

"Then you are all dead men," said Taeryn. "As dead as the men you have yourself killed." The world spun, and he staggered forward as the Violet again poured through him. All he could hear for a long moment were screams. He didn't know how he'd gotten his knife again, or how he'd killed the men between him and the wall, but Agarath defended his back as he began to climb again, and above, Lukas had begun frantically searching for a way out of his predicament. He was trapped, and Taeryn was again climbing through the fires, and again he felt none of the burns as his skin blackened from the flames and began to peel.

"Come down here, Lukas!" shouted Taeryn as he climbed. "Come out and face me!" He cackled madly as Lukas backed away from the opening and began trying to kick out the side of the wall above, farther in his tunnel. "Come and face the monster you have made! You tried to kill me. They've taken my arm because of you! I've come to kill you, Lukas! Come out and be a man, and let me feed you the hot steel upon this delicious knife!"

"I'm no fool!" shouted Lukas. His voice echoed through the structure and reverberated in Taeryn's hands. "You're infected with the Violet! You've gone mad. I don't know who's done it to you, but I want no part of you! You stay away from me!"

Taeryn laughed until his throat was raw. "Come out and play, you filthy murderer! Come and finish what you failed to complete in the first place! Let's have a second round! They're calling your name, Lukas. I can hear them. Over and over in the dark, the sound hissing among the thousands of screams, rippling over the oceans of blood, and piercing the forests of crackling black flame. How they hunger for you, for the sins upon your flesh, for the shadows of murder hidden within your skin. I can taste the fire in it, Lukas. I can smell the burning in it. I can see the deep blackness within it, as they see it. They demand your sacrifice, Lukas. Come and play with me, so I can open the door to them, and throw you in."

More rubble came crashing down from the side of the levy, and the men below dodged it desperately. The Greenmen drove back, attacking them while they were distracted.

* * * * * * *

"You need to go *now!*" said Cory, one of Lukas's friends. The man rammed the wall one last time, and moonlight filtered into the dark cave with them. "It's been good seeing you, friend. But I'll fight off this possessed lunatic so that you can escape."

"You won't be able to win against him, Cory," Lukas said. For the first time in a long time, someone else he cared for was about to die just so he could survive. He'd already lost too many men. Too many friends. "Whoever got a hold of him turned him into a hunter. He's half deranged, and he'll overpower you. Pain does not affect him — look at him! He's being burnt alive! It will be much harder than you think to kill him. He's got only one arm, and he's still scaling the wall as if it's a gentle beach walk! Come with me, and we'll set things right at home."

"I must buy you time, you idiot. Your life is more valuable than mine. Go. Remember what I told you about what's been going on. We've tried to keep Caol's men out, but that fool has caused more problems. You'll see when you get back to Aelynhold."

"What about Avery?" Lukas asked. "Does anyone else know about him?"

Cory shook his head. "Only the lord's wife."

"The lord's wife?" asked Lukas. "To whom has he pledged himself? He was only ever interested in — "

"*Your* wife," hissed Cory with a brief, stiff nod. "You'll need to sort that out yourself."

Lukas felt his heart almost explode as rage bled through him. "You're saying he's taken my wife as his own?" He roared, kicking another hole in the wall. "Meet me in Aelynhold, then. *Don't get killed!*"

Lukas crawled through the wall, but when he put his weight on the ledge, it broke away under his feet. He fell.

He reached out as the vines struck him, and his hand caught a rough ridge, which left splinters, and his face slammed into the side of the levy. Above, an enraged roar from Taeryn had Lukas frantically climbing across the vines, parallel to the ground far below himself. Occasionally, he slipped.

Cory was dead. He'd stood no chance against the new hunter.

Lukas scaled the levy in the darkness, and some of his men broke away to meet him, to help get him out of Oakwall.

When he finally reached the horse, Taeryn was raging from above. Lukas cringed from the angry curses. Some of the Aelynhold warriors helped him onto a midnight horse, and Lukas nearly fell as his exhaustion shook the strength from his grip. "Are you all right?" one whose name he vaguely remembered to be Abraska asked. He barely felt himself nodding.

"Let's go," he said. "As soon as my wife and her lover answer to me, I will leave Aelynhold again. It is not safe for me to stay, not with Caol and his son trying to have me killed."

"We're ready for them," said Morris, and Lukas clutched the man's forearm, exchanging a welcomed greeting. "It's been a long time, you sly, murderous devil."

Lukas nodded gravely. "It has," he said. "Have you forwarded the message, as planned?"

Morris nodded. "Yes. Caol and Eiran are going to be furious. We'll walk away rich men yet."

Lukas laughed. "Always, money with you. Over a decade a prisoner and a servant to a vile master, and I am *still* surrounded by sycophants."

"I wasn't born a rich man," Morris said.

"Neither was I," Lukas scolded. "I have killed, and maimed, and lied, and cheated for what is rightly mine, even if everything I've earned has done nothing but injure both my allies and my enemies. But what is mine is *mine*. Sins and karma included."

"You've done a lot more than kill people or cause harm," said Morris. "No one knows the good you've done, or how much you've sacrificed."

"All that really matters is that no one knows where Avery is," said Lukas. "We'll keep it that way."

"The Brotherhood — "

"I know. Cory told me. I'll look into it when we're there. Stay low when we arrive, and I'll investigate it myself. I don't trust word of mouth alone. You know my ways."

With that, they fled into the night, the five of them.

Taeryn continued to rage as he crawled out after Lukas and slid down the wall, his fingers digging into the vines as their trunks scraped away at his flesh.

When he emerged from the thickets at the base of the wall, Agarath and the Greenmen and the remainder of Lukas's soldiers all cringed at the sight of him. None of them wanted a thing to do with him as he strode among them and demanded a horse. Most of them thought him a demon . . . and he wondered whether he had become one. When he roared again, the Dark Ones shrieked with him, and the ground shook, and every man, woman and child covered their ears. The birds nesting in the trees started into flight, and the animals jolted and tried to break free. Violet-colored fissures erupted in the earth, and Taeryn looked about madly, searching, searching, searching . . .

The Dark Ones wanted blood. He wanted to deliver Lukas to them. They demanded it. It was all he wanted. It was all *they* wanted. Death. Vengeance. Agony. He would find Lukas again, and he would finish it. They would have their sacrifice.

Taeryn staggered forward, his blackened flesh flaking and bubbling. Blood began to well in his vision, and everything began to turn red as it faded in and out, between colors and hues of blood and black. His jaws hurt, as if he'd fractured them. Shadows were crawling under his skin like snakes, swimming through his veins.

A horse was abandoned to him by the nearest man he approached as that man fled in fear.

Someone tried to talk to him, but he could only hear the screams from the other side of the *Violet*, from the red and black abyss beyond . . .

CHAPTER FORTY-THREE

Aelynhold Retaken

THE SUN FILTERED SULLENLY into the Great Room, perfecting Lukas's transformation into an old man with a crooked spine and an odd limp. He and Morris stepped in through the seldomly used servant entrance. The heavy cobwebs and thick layer of dust on the dead lichen told him no one had found or used this secret entrance in years.

Something important was happening in the Great Room, and he was displeased by many of the things he saw as he and his shorter comrade threaded slowly between the gathered citizens, the traders, and the staff serving the house of the lead family in Aelynhold. What at first appeared to be a normal town meeting was, in fact, *not*. His cousin Drake Normane was pacing back and forth, exhaling voluminous poison about loyalty and debt and the wicked codes of honor to be followed at all times by those who wished to rule above lesser men. About them, very few seemed happy. In fact, the people looked downright pinched, spent, and in disagreement.

In his memory, the city had been known for its revelry, its vibrant colors, and its numerous obese families. But the color was gone, and glass chains hung from the necks of viciously smiling men who appeared as sinister as Lukas knew his cousin's heart and greed to be. None of the monks' faces were familiar to him. And it was not joyous, drunken song ringing throughout the halls at the end of Drake's raking speech but a woman screaming when her daughter was dragged from her within the crowd.

The girl's hood was yanked back by the monk who'd dragged her forward, and the mother was restrained by more religious zealots.

Lukas's cousin turned from the crowd and held up his hand, waving over another of his consorts from the shadows. "Akarat." From amidst the dark pillars, Lukas saw a small company of wolfmen, apart from which the one named Akarat strode. Lukas crept slowly closer, wary of the vigilance of the monks and wondering why none of them were his own men.

"Mmmph!" hissed a woman to Lukas's immediate left, and she shoved him. "You've stepped on my toes, old man!" She never raised her voice above a whisper, and those he stumbled into hissed much the same and shoved him back toward her.

He held up a hand that shook as if palsied, "My eyes are not what they used to be, young miss," he said, emulating the voice of the older Ivan man he had killed. He weakened the voice to add age. "I only meant to see."

"Stupid old man," she said. "Do us a favor and go die somewhere outside before the Brotherhood chooses us as his next example. He's already given one of my sons to those wretched cannibals. Get lost!"

Several of the monks shifted and again scanned the room when she shoved him once more. Lukas and Morris lost themselves among the crowd.

Akarat reached the girl who'd been separated from the rest. She kept her eyes shut, her fingers gripping her ragged, faded-blue skirts, and she cringed from the wolfman's proximity when he circled her slowly. He lifted her tangled red locks, and then he let her hair go. He traced her jaw with the back of his hand. And then, when he stood before her, he gripped her jaw and squeezed until she whimpered. "Open its eyes, young pup. Let us see the color. It will be valued for whichever it is."

When she refused, Akarat unsheathed a dagger and pressed it to her throat until the point drew blood.

"We will kill its mother."

"Do as Akarat says," commanded Lukas's cousin. When the girl refused, Drake shrugged and held up his hands. "Fine. Kill the mother."

The girl's bottom lip quivered, and she tried to rip away as her mother called out to her. "Eneska, don't let these bastards — "

The mother gasped as a blade cut her stomach deeply. Another plunged into her back, and Eneska began to tremble as if she knew what had happened. When her mother's body hit the floor, the thunderous sound echoed, and Eneska began to cry. She could not seem to bear her struggle any longer. Her eyes opened, and violet shone so brilliantly the wolfman recoiled. Lukas felt his stomach turn to writhing knots at his own memory of the strength of the curse.

Eneska saw her mother's body, and the blood pooling beneath, and she screamed as her knees gave beneath her. But Drake yanked her head back and looked upon the color for himself. A wicked smile crawled across his thin face, and he kicked the girl forward with a laugh.

"The creature is cursed," hissed Akarat, and his fingers curled as if having touched her had made his hand unholy.

"Take her outside and put her in the cage with the other three," commanded Drake. "Take them to Five Tower in the morning. In a few months, we'll see what Eiran has to offer. I'll expect the wolf cowls from your men before you leave, Akarat. It's much better to throw suspicions on a people who do not stay long in one place. We cannot have the monks traced back to this city, after all."

"Eiran will ask it to become an ally," agreed Akarat. "Its sheep will earn such honor, as equals among the Descendants of the Moon."

"To glory and wickedness and riches," laughed Drake, and Akarat dragged the girl away.

Drake continued his religious preamble next, and then he pointed to a man among the crowd. "You. Come forward." The wretched, balding man obeyed eagerly, coughing a great fit as he did so. "I am told you are the one who got them here after you gave us the information about her." The man nodded wildly, still coughing. "Kneel and receive your chains. Become one of us."

"Thank you, sir, thank you."

One of the monks placed a glass chain in Drake's outstretched hand. Another wrapped a black cloak about the kneeling man, and another placed a dagger on the stony floor before him, which seemed would become his own.

Drake held out the chain. "Brutality is justice among the strong. Do you not agree?"

The twisted man nodded eagerly. "I agree."

"The weak deserve to stay weak, to serve, to suffer."

"Yes."

"Do you wish for indulgence? For prosperity? For honor among the Worst of Men?"

"I do."

"Are you willing to kill for the growing strength of our people, and to root out the weakness festering in our city and in our land? To lie for our cohorts, to risk all in the name of defiance?"

The man cleared his throat, seeming ready to cry. "I am."

"Do you wish Black Temple's false and inhibiting mercy gone so that we may become who we were truly meant to be? Masters among the lesser of men?"

"Yes! I am willing!" cried the man. "I will be written in the book as a prophet, sir. I will enslave and kill and maim in the name of the End of Days, so that I may be reborn an unbreakable, undying warrior of stone in the Kingdom of Fire."

Lukas blinked. "What, in the shadow fires of the seventh *hell*, is he telling these people the Brotherhood is about?" Lukas whispered to Morris. He was utterly confused at the twisted purpose his cousin had devised. He hadn't remembered Drake being so . . . *insane*. Power hungry and a little overzealous, he remembered. Mad hadn't been something he had ever foreseen. "The Brotherhood was started by *thieves*, not by killers and maniacs in want of strange . . . *occult lunacy*."

Morris shuffled on his feet. "He has corrupted our purpose. We did warn you. He's had many good years to do so. There are many fanatics like this one. Twisted men, all of them. Even if they don't believe a lick the mad part of it, they're more than eager to embrace the cause. They want anarchy. They want power. And they like the bloodshed."

"And?"

"Only his closest men know about you, or even to be looking for you."

Lukas snarled. "More than a few must be quite close to him. There were more than fifty of them trying to take me on Raven Trail, near Ender's Creek. All were dressed as wolfmen. And I'm not sure they cared whether I was alive." Lukas bit back the urge to curse loudly and challenge his cousin's insanity. "Many things have changed in my absence. I know none of these monks. But we will be changing things back — "

"Anna, my love." Drake's words snapped Lukas's attention, and cold hatred washed through him like an arctic river.

One of the monks stepped forward, and Lukas frowned, surprised. Drake gave her the glass chain. When she spoke, her voice was almost unrecognizable. None of the warmth he remembered remained in it. It was clipped, murderous, and cold. "Cut your hand," she commanded. The man before her obeyed. "Cut your wrist." He obeyed. "Cut your cheek." Again, obedience. She gave the new servant his glass chains. "By the Mother of the Lost, welcome to the Brotherhood of the Merciful. Let your blackest deeds darken our stain and stir terror into the hearts of the weak."

Anna was the monk who had killed the young girl's mother. Lukas blinked hard. She'd never been a killer, not even a thief . . . never once a criminal act. How could she have turned against their marriage and their people? Her own ideals? She wasn't supposed to have joined the Brotherhood, let alone become one of its twisted priestesses. She *never* would have joined them. She would have eradicated it —

Drake held out his hand, and though she'd despised and loathed the man, she now took his hand with the soft countenance of a lover and stepped close to whisper something suggestive into his ear. Lukas's blood boiled, and he trembled banefully as he attempted to read the words upon her blood-colored lips. Drake chuckled and drew a finger along her hip, up her back, and to the nape of her neck, and then he pulled her close and kissed her deeply.

They were all over each other, and it made Lukas nauseated to see it.

"Come along, then," Drake dared her. "I can finish talking to the wolfmen when we're done."

"Not in another filthy hallway," she scorned. "I require a proper bed, and candles. Perhaps some silk rope." She held up her hand and examined the blood upon it coolly, and Drake tucked a long, braided lock of her black hair behind her slightly pointed ear. "I do think a bath, and maybe dinner, are in order first."

"The blood never bothers you," Drake growled. "How many times have we shared passion with blood from a kill still hot upon our flesh? Why deny me my right? And why be shy before this lovely congregation? That's never stopped us before."

She simply pulled away. "I'm going to check on Ramos and Carston. Finish your business, Husband. Tend to your wicked flock." She pulled her hood back over her head, and then she slipped out among other monks who followed her every move the way bodyguards would.

Lukas did not let her from his sight. He followed from a distance, his pulse thrumming in his ears, rage gripping his heart. Nothing was supposed to be this way. Caol's schemes had infected his home. His cousin was a murderous madman, his wife was in bed with him, the Brotherhood had been twisted beyond what he'd meant for it, and he was left trying to bargain for his life. Men were after him — his cousin now confirmed as being among them. And he had too few friends left in Aelynhold. That his wife was no longer among his allies meant disaster.

Her guards slowly dispersed as she whispered to them her orders, one by one. The last monk to step away, Lukas snuck behind, and he stabbed him in the throat while simultaneously reaching to cover the man's mouth. He wrestled the body toward the secret access, and Morris assisted in the heavy, awkward work. They stripped away the chains and the robe before either showed too much or smelled too strongly of blood.

Lukas donned the attire and took the dead man's knife.

"She isn't in league with him," Morris said as Lukas strapped on the knife belt furiously.

Lukas didn't trust himself to speak.

"She's the only reason the rest of us are still alive," explained Morris. "She lets Drake recruit his fanatics, but the man who was inducted today was another fake she's planted. I've known him for a long time, and he dislikes everything Drake has done. His act was scripted. Hers is well-practiced."

"She wrapped herself around my lunatic cousin. They were entwined like diseased snakes, and their tongues were fused together like slugs in rotting slush," shuddered Lukas. He was finding it difficult to control the volume of his voice. "For *years*, I have worked toward this day, toward coming home. Toward keeping Caol's fingers away from my family. And when at last I see my wife, not only do I watch her participate in that revolting public display, I also watch her *kill* a girl's *mother*. My wife was never a murderer! Never a thief, or a whore! That woman — that is not my wife. She is Drake's creation, and they are both soon to be dead for what they've done with the Brotherhood. Gather what few remain of our *real* brethren, and tell them to clean house. I am assuming command tonight, and it will be over those two traitors' bodies."

"Did you not expect Anna to get involved when you told us to tell her *everything*?" Morris exhaled disbelievingly. "She never betrayed you."

"She's married to my cousin. The most vile, corrupt — "

"You had to have realized his mind was not right, Lukas. You gave him this leadership. And your orders were to ensure she could manage him, to keep him under control."

"You call this under control? She's become his murdering occult priestess! She has betrayed even the memory of me. And she is going to die with him for it."

"What about their children?" asked Morris.

Lukas froze. "Excuse me?" The knife's sheath hung from his belt, still empty.

"Twins. Three years old. Innocent. Are you going to leave them to the streets because you cannot stand what she's done?" asked Morris. "Are you going to kill your wife and cousin and leave those children as unwanted orphans? Or are you going to kill them, too, so they can't avenge their father and mother? Are you a child-killer? Are you as low as Drake and the rest of his fanatics?" Morris paused while Lukas tried to process that. He was vehemently against killing children. Always had been, even if he'd assumed the role of a criminal who had no such morals. It was something never to be done. It was a value Lukas and Morris had in common. It was a secret truth that even the creepy little Ivan girl had misread in him.

Just before Lukas at last formulated a reply and opened his mouth, Morris continued.

"Drake forced her into their marriage, Lukas. She resisted his flattery and tolerated his abuse for the first nine years after your absence, and she got nowhere trying to control him. The marriage and the children have allowed her access to ways of dulling his grip and distracting him. He is disarmed because she plays the depraved lover well. When she appeared to enjoy everything he was and all that he promised, he let her in. And now she is in a place of power. She is at his side, where the most damage can be done."

"But to *be* with him! Did she not know I was alive?"

Morris shook his head. "Lukas, you were always a master manipulator. I've been there to see the magic you weave with your lies and half-truths. I have seen how sly your hands can be, taking things from the very necks of your prey, planting them into the hands of unsuspecting fools in your way. You have staged revolts and sent strong allies to war against one another, and you have done the reverse. But your wife has become a better manipulator, and you are a hypocrite if you cannot bear to see it. You are letting your judgement be clouded by jealousy. Step back and assess this situation properly. She is the only reason the people of this city do not revolt. She is the reason the wolfmen do not get to stay in Aelynhold and revel in their rituals within the walls, and she is the reason that young girl out there and the other prisoners like her are going to escape."

Lukas shook his head disbelievingly. Morris handed him his own knife.

"Don't go to see her tonight. It is too risky. And do not kill her. You are going to need her if you want to get the Brotherhood back to its original purpose."

"The destruction of Five Tower's slave empire."

"And keeping Avery's whereabouts unknown," Morris reminded him.

Lukas growled. "Damn you. You do realize that when they finally find out where he is . . ."

"You'll be a dead man, I know. Because you're the one responsible for what happened."

"No. I'll be worse than a dead man, Morris. What happened — "

"As long as we are the only ones who know where he is or what he knew."

"Where are his things? There is no way to trace him here?"

"They are buried in the deepest, darkest dungeon for none to find. Same as what you did with the rest of him . . . You might should visit him sometime, see what he has to say." Morris exhaled slowly and met Lukas's gaze firmly. "I've heard he was quite wise. He might still help you to think of a new tactic. You've obviously begun to lose your touch."

Lukas snarled. "Keep pressing my buttons, and I'll leave your body in this unused entrance as well, Morris." He sheathed the knife.

"I'll have the men take care of Drake's followers tonight. We've been underground for a while, and most are growing weary of waiting for the perfect moment to strike and take back control. Every day is worse. He adds rules, and he becomes more vicious. And the fanatics become more and more cruel to our own people. Most of our people are going hungry, several have lost their homes, and the merchants can't leave."

"How do you plan to end them tonight?" Lukas asked. "What makes it an opportunity?"

"We're following the journal your wife copied. Your cousin has an odd obsession with *time*, and a compulsion to document things in nonlinear, encrypted frames. She spent months copying his schedules, and we've been poring over them religiously, looking for openings. The first and greatest opportunity was two weeks ago. But we were unable to get our hands upon the supplies we needed. We have another opening tonight, when the monks are to gather at the old clock tower in the middle of the town square. We have already staged the ambush."

"It isn't likely Drake will be there. He's gone insane, but he isn't stupid enough to leave himself open to strike. You should be aware he would know there are traitors in his midst. He'll have a double participating in any special rituals where they are all exposed."

"Then where will he be?"

"I'll take care of Drake," said Lukas. "But I am going to see my wife first."

Morris grew frustrated with him. "Do not let her know you are here. Wait until we are finished with our *coup d'état.*"

Lukas ignored him. "How many of Drake's monks are operating where mine should have been among the Enforcers?"

"A few have ended up in the higher echelons of the Alliance, though it's not enough to damage our ultimate end. They still know nothing about the operation we began when we started the Brotherhood years ago. Anna has helped see to that. But they've been trying to increase their number. A lot of Enforcers have been executed wrongly because of it. If they keep it up, we'll be found out. If we haven't already been."

That was the worst news Lukas had heard yet. "And the monks who are disguising themselves as wolfmen are only doing so on orders from Aelynhold. Under my cousin's command."

Morris glanced at the wall.

Lukas grew suspicious of Morris's hesitation. It always meant worse tidings. "What?"

"There is something else you should know."

Lukas placed the glass chain about his neck and lowered his hood.

Morris continued. "None of us knew you were alive. We just knew Caol turned on you and killed half of the men. The rest of you disappeared. No word, nothing. We had no idea what had happened. And then two years ago, we heard a rumor that you had been sighted, and under your own name. Then the wolfmen and some cursed men came asking about a thief, who fit your description."

Lukas shook his head. "What are you leading to?"

Morris hesitated. "Your wife suspected it was you. She was the one who sent our brothers to Raven Trail. But Drake also knows you are alive. The men your wife sent were supplemented with his own. He still has others out looking. His orders are that they kill you on sight."

"That explains why they were fighting one another when they had me at Ender's Creek."

Morris scratched his head. "All of our problems would have been averted if you'd just come back sooner."

"I could not," snapped Lukas. "Were it not necessary, then even now I would not have returned. But I finally have a way to peel the target from my back for good. As long as we can fix what is happening here, I may yet manage to avert death." *And the creatures waiting for me*, he thought darkly. He shuddered when he felt a cold whisper of their presence.

Morris stared. "Sir . . . Was that what I think I saw?"

Lukas ground his teeth, knowing fully that Morris meant the Violet. He'd felt it blaze dimly in his eyes. The warmth was familiar. "It is nearly gone," he lied. "It is nothing to worry about."

"What did they *do* to you . . . ?" Morris exhaled. The man was deeply disturbed. "Is that why you were gone for so long . . . ?" Morris seemed to be worried, as though breathing the same air meant he might also become a carrier.

"Worry not, you cannot catch this thing like a cold. What you see is only the faintest traces of this wretched affliction. Every day that I become stronger against it means every day those demon creatures grow more distant to me. None near me will die because of them."

"Demon creatures?"

"Nothing. Never mind them. Go tend to the job I have given you."

A few hours later, Lukas watched his wife read to her children, two lovely black-haired boys with eyes as dark as could be, their hair braided like her own. She did not recognize him under the cloak and hood when she stood from their crib, leaving them to sleep.

She became instantly hostile toward his presence.

"Why are you in my sons' room?" she demanded. "Has Drake sent you?" A dagger appeared in her hand before Lukas ever opened his mouth. "Answer my question!" she demanded. Her almond gaze sparked in the candlelight, fueled with cold anger as she gripped her weapon.

"Anna — " he said as she rushed forward to strike him dead.

Her expression flashed from anger to shock, and her attack faltered. She stumbled, and he caught her wrist. The knife pricked his shoulder when the swing lost its strength and missed its killing mark. He looked down at her as heat bloomed from the wound, and he studied her for the minutest lie. Her lips opened and closed several times as she tried to speak. She only seemed able to sound wordless gasps. Tears welled in her kohl-rimmed eyes, and she blinked them away disbelievingly.

"My god . . . You look exactly the same," she whispered, and her head shook almost imperceptibly.

The comment struck him strangely. He twisted her hand gently, and the knife fell. It struck his foot and slid off with a dull ring. His quiet anger became muddled with a sense of grief. He couldn't bring himself to let go of her. Years, he had been away. *Years*. She was still so very beautiful, and it hurt him that she had moved on. To his cousin. He started to say her name again, but he didn't know what to say.

She jerked away and slapped him. "You've come home too late, you fool." Oh, how angry she was. "All these years, thinking you were dead, and you've just been running around causing havoc. I've been stuck here believing myself a widow while cleaning up your mess. You should *never* have allowed your cousin anything to do with overseeing this city."

Lukas let her vent and only spoke when the first plume had dissolved. And he did so gently, testing her. "Where is our daughter?" He was still trying to read her, but she was very guarded. He knew this woman was a cold killer, but their daughter should have brought out some trace of old sentimentality. Instead, her features became cruel. Hate-filled. Blameful. And then he knew she was not just a manipulator. Something had happened to drive her to become what she was. He found himself dreading her answer. And he had to remind himself that this woman was Drake's Anna, a serpent who would bite sharp and wouldn't mind the flavor of poison. The glare she gave him told him she was ready to strike again.

"Carry is dead," she told him flatly.

Lukas felt as though he *had* been struck again. Pain bloomed inside his chest, much like it had when she'd pierced his shoulder. For so very long, he had not allowed himself to think of his daughter or his wife. And Carriah was dead? His silver tongue seemed not to want to move. He could think of no manipulation, no lie, no way to provoke Drake's wife into revealing anything more than she would reveal on her own. He was exposed by the blow. Laid open. His daughter was dead. And he couldn't even ask his wife how long ago, or how it had happened.

His face still stung. His shoulder ached. His chest hurt. And Lukas just stood there, completely disarmed. A liar who could not lie was simply a floundering, vulnerable idiot, and so he was as he fought his despair.

He saw that Anna read how defenseless he was. He saw the victory flash across her angry gaze. Her face twitched, almost with humor. "She has been dead since your cousin chopped her head off and gave her body to the first wolfmen who came to Aelynhold eight years ago. She was hardly more than a child." Anna read him like an open book, reveling in what her words did to him. And yet she saw even through the grief and the weariness, and she found another way to cut him. "I ought to cut you into pieces for running like the coward you are. The mess you left for me has almost completely destroyed Aelynhold. But you *had* to go behind my back with another lie and play arms dealer with them, and then you got yourself captured. I told you never to trifle with those men from Five Tower. Yet you've always chased the money, as if you could not have enough of it."

She spat at his feet, then. "Once a thief and a liar, always a thief and a liar." She eyed him, then, and saw the blood on his cloak. "Apparently a cold-blooded killer now, too, same as I."

At last, Lukas regained some hold on himself. She seemed utterly angry, but she was more bitter about her situation. That was something he could exploit. "Well, the cat is out now, isn't it?" She rolled her eyes at his weak statement. "If you dislike things as they are, then the question is, Dear Wife, what are we going to do about it?"

Anna snorted. "First, we are going to cut my husband's head off," she said. "Second, you're going to pay *dearly* for betraying me. And you are going to help raise my sons as if they are your own. I don't want them to remember him. I want him *erased.*"

Lukas was both amused and angered by her suggestion. She was playing this as though she was on *his* side . . . But then everything Morris had said returned to him. What if she *was*? He grimaced. "I can make no promises regarding your sons, Anna. I am here for only one reason."

But she was not having that. Anna's anger flared. "Oh, if you don't," she hissed, "I will sing to every city and hold what you've done with Avery Ramont. *Everyone* will know, including the Alliance and Black Temple. And they'll have your head on a spike for it. Or you'll be taken to the Reformation and tortured for the rest of your living days, you cowardly, criminal scum — "

"Anna, calm down. You'll wake the children. I doubt either of us wants the attention that could bring into this room right now."

She quieted and offered him a cold, serpentine smile, and her eyes glimmered like hot glass. "Oh, but of course, my *love*," she said almost sweetly. But the vehemence upon the last word gave him pause. Anna looked him up and down, from head to toe. "I should be respectful of my elders — you are supposed to be an old man, aren't you?" Anna flipped her braids over her shoulder, and she stepped forward again, her fingers rising to wipe the grime from his face with an almost tender caress — it ended with a scrape of her fingernail. "I cannot take you seriously in this ridiculous disguise. How has no one recognized you? Even your old man hobble speaks of you. You still carry your shoulders the same, and the way your head bobs is utterly false."

Lukas stepped back from her with a frown. He hadn't continued the old man act since he'd donned the monk's robes. She reached into a wash bowl with slightly reddened water and drew from it a rag, which she wrung out. Anna threw it at him, and he caught it. "Clean it off. I want to look upon the face of the man I married for love and then lost to lies."

"When did you marry Drake?" Lukas grumbled.

Anna's lovely face turned cold. "Why? Did it break your poor heart to see me with him?" She watched as he cleaned the disguise away. He paused again as what she said struck him as odd. "I bet you have many angry questions for him." She sneered at him most coldly. "Is he a better lover than you are? Yes. My first night with him was far superior to any of ours. I never thought I would enjoy a man I hated so, but I did. Thoroughly. He's aggressive. Beastly, compared to you and your weak gentleman's caress." She made herself appear to study her nails as anger rocketed through him again. The worst part was, he *knew* she was playing him for the fool, and yet he could not seem to help falling into her every trap. She wanted him angry, and he was. She wanted him hardly able to think through it. He couldn't. "Did I miss you ever? Not after I married him and bore him two lovely sons," she continued. She enjoyed manipulating his emotions, hurting him. "Was I ever loyal to you at all? Once. But that time is gone. And I wish it never *was*."

Lukas was trembling with anger now. His shoulder throbbed fiercely, and his head spun. He needed to calm down, to take back control, to push *her*.

"Did I know all along your lies and pretend not to have known . . . ?" Her sharp, icy glare rose and pierced him, then. "Did I know you were coming home?" Her lips curled in the same vile way Drake's did when he had cornered his prey. "Did I copy some documents Drake and I wrote together and then present them to your men so we could kill all of you in one night?"

Lukas stepped away from her and prepared himself to escape. He stumbled, suddenly dizzy. Why was he dizzy? She watched him look at her knife, and she smiled knowingly at him.

"Did I know about the reward for your head and ensure the knife I carried for you was poisoned so that Drake would not spend a dime of our money on your death?"

He felt more than heard the footsteps that approached from the hallway behind him. Lukas twisted away from the strike that would have killed him, and Anna stood still, smiling as Drake stepped into the dim candlelight, his sword gleaming.

"Hello, Cousin," Drake said lightly. "It's been quite a long time. I had to come and greet you myself when our wife told me you would be visiting her tonight." He winked at Anna, who continued to smile coolly. "I do hope you enjoyed our display in the Great Room. Nothing gets in the blood like watching another man touch the woman you love."

"Or when she enjoys it," added Anna.

She'd *poisoned* him; that was all Lukas could think. It was a struggle to stand erect, and it was quickly becoming difficult to follow anything they were saying at all.

"Before I kill you, I want to thank you in person for all that you have given to me, dear Cousin." Drake stepped forward. Lukas stepped back, cursing his fortune. This was not how he was going to die. Drake and Anna were fools to think it. "Anna, you've done exceedingly well. I knew you were a devious snake when I first laid eyes upon you, and I've loved you since that day. I vowed to bring you into the woman you were meant to be, and you have surpassed those expectations." To Lukas, he added, "The rest of your loyal friends will be gone tonight when they think to ambush ours at the clock tower. There will be no more division among them afterward. We will know the heretics from the unholy, and then our progress will no longer be hindered."

"Take care not to wake the children, love," Anna said sweetly, and she shrugged her shawl free as she stepped aside with her bare feet. She wore nearly nothing underneath, and Lukas's eyes bulged when from the corner of his vision he saw the red serpent tattoos sprawling across her body. She'd never been one for 'such distasteful things,' as she'd put it years ago. The markings only reaffirmed she was now as much his enemy as Drake was. It cemented who she now was.

As Lukas feigned full distraction — implying Anna's intent had been successful — Drake rushed him. The sword was lifted high for an overarching swing. Lukas tried to draw his dagger — but it was stuck in its sheath. He barely dodged the blow, and as he struggled still with his dagger, his wife silently attacked. Her leg swept under his, and he fell backward. His head struck the wash basin's table, toppling it. He hardly heard the crash, or her sons' startled cries. He saw the glistening red paint upon her toenails, and then he felt Anna place her foot upon his throat. Lukas blinked against the painful warmth spreading across his scalp as she stared down at him. His hand was not quite responsive when he tried again to grip the dagger, and Drake stepped forward triumphantly.

Anna took Drake's hand in her own and leaned forward to kiss his cheek. "Kill him," she whispered softly.

Drake's wicked grin . . .

Violet in the darkness . . .

Lukas blinked — and he thought he saw Anna's expression change ever so slightly. Hatred, he swore he saw. Hatred for Drake. Victorious, unadulterated, rankling resentment.

As Lukas struggled to force his body to respond and failed, a blade ripped through Drake's chest. Shock erased Drake's triumphant glee, and his mouth opened and closed. Another dagger reached around and ripped across the wicked man's throat, and his sword slipped from his hand as he gripped at the air. Anna caught it easily, still smiling sweetly, as though nothing was happening at all, and she offered the sword to whomever stood behind him in the darkness.

When Drake went to his knees, violet eyes shone in the dark beneath a monk's hood. Drake's own sword swung in an arc . . . and then Drake's head and body tumbled to the floor. Separate from one another and pooling blood.

"Is this pathetic man on the floor really my father?" asked a young woman. "He looks barely older than me."

Anna looked down disapprovingly at Lukas. "Unfortunately, yes."

"I thought they said he was a Master Thief. An Arms Dealer. A Genius of Disguise." The violet eyes studied him disapprovingly. "He's clumsy at best, and easily disarmed. And quite gullible for someone supposed to be so smart," said the young violet-eyed woman. She pulled down her hood and spat upon Drake's body, and Lukas stared. She was the girl from the Great Room. Eneska.

Eneska was his daughter Carriah.

He hardly recognized her. She looked almost nothing like she had when she was young.

And she was *cursed.*

Lukas convulsed, and he rolled over sickly. Drool seeped from his mouth when his stomach curled in vile ways, and everything spun vehemently. He wiped his mouth with the back of his hand, his head pounding. It stung fiercely where he'd struck the table, and he knew he likely had a concussion. "You said he killed our daughter," Lukas managed. Speaking increased the painful pressure in his head. He touched the back of his scalp, and blood came away, coated his fingers.

Anna shrugged casually. "We let him think he did. He was not the one to swing the sword."

"How did Carriah come by the Violet?" Lukas demanded. His head throbbed harshly, and when he struggled to his feet, he nearly toppled again.

"Looks like the sedative is already flagging," smirked Carriah. "Didn't last long. Should I prick him again?"

"No, Carry, let him be. We've rattled his brain enough for one night." Anna returned to the crib and pulled her crying sons into her arms to soothe them.

When Lukas felt his scalp, his hand came away covered in blood. "Carriah, who did this to you? And why is your hair that ridiculous color?"

"Honestly, love," sighed Anna. "You are a bore. What do you think happens when we learn to fend for ourselves? We use every weapon and every tool. And your hair is far more ridiculous than hers. What on earth did you use to dye it? Blond was the only thing that looked normal on you. You didn't even touch your eyebrows with it. Or your mustache. Or your goatee — is that goatee fake? Oh, what a lazy — "

"How did our daughter become cursed?!" shouted Lukas.

At last, Anna's sour sarcasm left her, and she flinched.

"I did it to myself," said Carriah.

Lukas shuddered in horror, his mouth falling open. "You did *what*? Do you have any idea the repercussions of such an action?"

Carriah twirled the bloody dagger in her hand and leaned against the wall, bored. "Like father, like daughter," said Carriah. "I went to Five Tower looking for you a few years after you disappeared, just after we faked my own death. I learned about the stones and the curse, and I managed to find one. You're a fool to think we wouldn't employ everything to our advantage. I am just as you are — except smarter, obviously. I wear disguises. I kill people that are in my way. I am good at lying. I see some crazy, scary creatures when it's dark. And my hair only looks *almost* as stupid as yours does right now. At least this is a natural shade of red, and I remembered my eyebrows, and I thought to add freckles. You didn't even put a single age spot on you. It was rushed, lazy work, Father. You really thought you looked so convincingly old?" Her brow rose. "You look like a badly painted mime. You should really carry a mirror."

"He was more convincing when I saw him dressed as a woman," smiled Anna fondly. She held out her hand, and Carriah returned the knife — it returned to a sheath upon Anna's thigh that Lukas had never realized was there at all. Anna shrugged her shawl back over her shoulders and paced near the crib as Carriah laughed at what her mother had said about him.

"You devious women," groaned Lukas.

"Oh, that is not the least of what we've been into," said Carriah. "You'll never know the depths of our schemes."

Anna grew silent as her sons began to calm, and sadness seemed to descend upon her.

Lukas grimaced and opened his mouth to speak, but Carriah held up her hand to silence him. "We already know you didn't come home for us. I've already made arrangements with your men, and they're ready to depart to deliver whatever other messages you intend to send to taunt the son of a bitch who caused you to obtain the Violet. I am glad you had the sense not to return home sooner. The crossfire that would have erupted from that would have destroyed Aelynhold completely. As it is, you'll be able to start sending orders to your men in the Alliance properly now. They've had to tolerate some level of Drake's decisions for quite a while, and he's even sent wolfmen as messengers to the Alliance capital. I'm sure even Black Temple has caught on by now. Morris probably already told you that some of Drake's men made it into the higher ranks and started having men executed for asking questions or demanding to see Avery. Now that you're back, we can put an end to all that and do what you intended in the first place."

"She's developed a gift because of the Violet," said Anna. "It's not quite a curse to her. She's connected to some of the others who carry it; she can find them like none other. And her gift has been our edge over Drake and the wolfmen. You could learn a few things from her."

"So what tipped you that Drake betrayed your orders, anyway?" asked Carriah lightly. "Obviously, that was part of why you returned." The Violet blinked out, and when she opened her eyes again, the light flared brightly in them.

"Eiran's hunters and the wolfmen were gathering the others who escaped Five Tower," said Lukas. Still, the room spun about him. "The Brotherhood I started was helping them. I thought when they came to Raven Trail that they were all under Drake's orders."

"I told ours to be as rough as they wanted," laughed Anna. "Make you fear for your life. A little revenge for all that you put us through when you left. I selected them personally so you wouldn't know their faces and realize you were in the midst of a rescue attempt." She laughed once more at his aggravation. "I heard you nearly pissed yourself, thinking you were going to be killed or taken back to Five Tower. But Drake's monks were not supposed to be among them. I had no idea he'd sent his own until after."

"Some of our brothers *have* tried to kill me, Anna. That day, I thought they meant to hand me over to Eiran's hunters. His hunters will carry out the execution order regardless of imminent danger, peace, or any other impediment."

Anna gasped, her head jerking. *"Execution order?* Just what did you do?!"

"What I've done no longer matters. There is a little girl in Black Temple right now who can actually wield this curse like a weapon. I've seen it with my own eyes. She's a demonic, terrifying little thing, and I suspect she can very nearly read others' minds. The girl is unnaturally intelligent, with eyes unlike ours, even though she, too, is cursed by the Violet. They're green. An unnatural, glowing shade not easily missed. Caol and Eiran would kill even each other to get their hands on her. I intend to use her to bargain with them, to remove the execution order from my head. And then they'll wish they'd never double-crossed me."

Carriah started laughing. "I'm in. How are we going to get her from Black Temple? I can slip in and take her if you want."

"No. That little girl is very dangerous," warned Lukas. "She said she removed the Violet from me around the time it finally left me, and then she proved she could ignite it again. Every instinct warns me against getting near her again. The power hiding inside her is unimaginable. You should take the same precaution. Avoid contact."

Carriah pouted. "No fun."

"I want you nowhere near her," he said. "She knows what the curse does to us. She's used that knowledge against me, and it was not pleasant, Carriah. I have other components in motion, however. Family means everything to the Ivans. I want them all distracted, and from every side. Every angle. I want groups of men to take our hidden paths to Black Temple and begin to harass them. I also want men to ride for Lovael to place Reid Ivan's wife and daughter in danger. His capture will draw the doctor and his daughter, and then she will be ours for bargaining — "

"You mean to use the underground?" asked Anna, surprised. "Your father closed and locked that place just after the Fuel War to keep the Enforcers from ever finding out about it. The location and the keys to it have been lost. And even if you know where it is or you can open it, is doing so something you want to risk having taken or destroyed?"

Lukas grinned. "If I was not willing, I would not have had the Greenman paint that symbol upon the barracks. It is already open. Carriah, the moment I give the command, you will take your men to the east wood outside the city and use that subway tunnel. Oakwall is six miles to the north, and then you will ride quickly for Isold and give them reason to bring that girl. Abraska will lead the way."

Carriah's twisted half smile did not soften her face at all. She still looked as cruel as before. There was none of the innocent daughter he remembered left in her.

"Caol and Eiran will rescind their execution order by the time this is done," he said. "Even if only temporarily when they realize what I promised is real. Their hunters will withdraw. Otherwise, they won't get a single stone the girl touches."

"When it is all settled, is the coverup about the demise of the High Commander of the Enforcers' Alliance going to be released?" asked Carriah.

"Maybe. I won't need that secret kept any longer. The girl is my endgame. She means my freedom, and she is the key to my vengeance. Avery Ramont is the last thing that should be on anyone's mind."

"Well, I'm glad you have some kind of plan," shrugged Carriah. "Now that we're a family again, you'll be resuming your rightful name."

"That I will," agreed Lukas. "Anna, you will tell my men to gather in the Great Room in the morning. The King of Thieves has retaken his throne."

"I gave it to you," smirked Carriah. "You just stumbled about, drugged and in a daze, with a scared look on your face."

Lukas growled, annoyed. "Don't word it as such."

"Why? They already know you had no idea how Mom and I were operating under Drake's nose. You were gone for a very long time. Years. Did you expect us to be damsels? We're serpents, and we have teeth. Mom? Dad's an idiot."

"Of course, he is. But at least he means well. Your uncle, however, was a bright idiot *and* an evil disgrace."

"As long as my brother-cousins don't become like him . . . It's so gross that you married Dad's first cousin. I would have found some other way." She shrugged and nodded to the decapitated body on the floor. "You know. *That* was rather effective."

Anna's irritation flashed hotly over her face. "Mind your tongue, Carry. Your father placed him in charge of the Brotherhood because of his connections in Five Tower. You know very well why we couldn't just kill him off and take over."

"We still could have easily learned everything we needed to know about Caol's operation. Now I have two hideous brother-cousins, and for what? Nothing. That's — "

Lukas held up his hands again. "Be quiet. Both of you. Anna, tell the men the King of Thieves has retaken his throne, that the rightful Lord of Aelynhold, the cousin of the recently deceased Drake Normane, has returned."

Carriah snorted. "Whatever. Good luck with your nephew-sons. They puke a lot, and they smell loathsome. They're already as crazed and contentious as Uncle Drake was. They'll rip your hair out, so don't hold them."

Over the course of the next few days, Lukas spent time reacquainting himself with his guild in Aelynhold and setting his affairs in order. The bodies in the tower yard were cleared away, and he was greeted by eager men who celebrated the eradication of Drake and his most devious fanatics. Morris brought his oldest supporters back into his halls, and they were anointed places of leadership. He rewarded the devout handsomely for their trying tribulations and long-enduring loyalty.

Lukas only visited the dungeons once, where Avery Ramont's hidden cell was. And when he returned, he was more determined than before. Messengers were sent out, and the Brotherhood was called to order. All that was left to do was idle and wait. Neither of which could he do well, but his wife and daughter made both easier for him.

But there were still enemies who could reduce his efforts to a wasted affront. Anything could go wrong, even though the end was so near. He had to get his hands on that little girl, and soon.

He had no idea whether her uncle was already heading for Aelynhold, or if he was clear across the plains, near Tetroya. But he trusted that news of family endangerment would draw him. Wherever the retired range commander appeared, Lukas's men would work to bring the bastard down.

How great to be the Liar.

CHAPTER FORTY-FOUR

SETUP

IT WAS MADDENING. The retired range commander and his friend had already been walking Aelynhold's back alleys and hidden dens for fifteen days without being noticed by Lukas's men. The two had arrived before he had, in fact, and he still had no clue how they'd known he would arrive in Aelynhold eleven days after them. He had only this morning been alerted to their presence.

Because they were within his grasp so soon, Lukas had immediately sent his daughter from the city with fifty or more of their men to carry out his orders. Anna had taken over his other schemes when he'd left the manor, and now Lukas watched the two men from the rooftops, taking every advantage of his knowledge of Aelynhold's layout to remain undetected by them. They were very suspicious of every glance from strangers, and of every movement and every sound.

His men trailed them through the alleyways, waiting for his signal, but he waited to give it.

Lukas himself remained close enough to them to hear some of what they said to each other, but he was careful that he was never near enough to be seen, or smelled, or sensed. He let Reid and Taiir ask their questions of the old historians, the map makers, the shopkeepers, and the small number of street thugs who were willing to trade a few words about Aelynhold's secrets and less agreeable activities for a few copper hint. Or, on some occasions, for a golden liberty.

Lukas let them think they were discreet, and his men would hand him scraps of intel along the way. Which items they'd requested or purchased, which historical texts and pages they'd perused, which underground tunnels they'd learned about and planned to search. Their secret quarters had been discovered only an hour ago, though it had offered little to rummage. Yet he suspected they had found other hiding places for the evidence they'd likely collected. The two were infuriatingly ahead of nearly everything he'd planned or expected.

It was also now apparent to him that they were after some*one* rather than some*thing,* and as he let them hide in his city, asking their questions and gathering their intel, Lukas anticipated well enough where they would go, and he learned much about what they'd already known when they had first arrived. He was well aware that what he learned was likely but a drop of the wealth of information they'd gathered. It meant they'd become incredibly dangerous to him. To his brotherhood of thieves. To his city. To his family.

Reid Ivan and his mountain warrior friend knew the secret of Avery Ramont's murder was buried somewhere in Aelynhold. They'd known Lukas would come here long before he'd ever arrived, and they'd been aware of it the day he had entered the city gates. They knew he had more than his own fair share of guilt in the uprisings stirring in the land. They even knew he was directly involved with the *Merciful.*

But he was most deeply disturbed to realize that Reid had other things, more dangerous, upon his mind. An old seal had been inquired about at the previous shop. A healer had whispered dreadful things in the range commander's ear, and a name, most notably familiar to Lukas, had been forwarded to him by his spies: *Gabriel*.

Lukas had never met Gabriel. He *feared* meeting the man. Yet Gabriel was also in his city, and both Reid and Taiir were *very* close to finding him.

Currently, Reid Ivan was rummaging through the wares of another of the merchants, his voice low and his hood drawn lower. His Black Temple signet was not upon his finger, which kept his association with the guild a secret from scrutinous eyes. Neither were either of the men dressed in their normal attire. They had arrayed themselves like Aelynhold's citizenry, and they had chosen the blandest clothing and head coverings, at that.

Neither man seemed to realize yet that they had just this morning been recognized and brought to Lukas's attention.

"She said a man by his description was in this city," said Reid. "He bought nothing but did ask after some odd mountain root. I think she meant alderoot. He left after she told him she didn't have it, she said. Supposedly this exchange occurred several weeks ago."

"Not according to her private ledger," said Taiir, and he flashed the stolen item. Reid took the blue leather-bound journal from under the shelf and flipped through it. "He did not come for alderoot but blood, taken from one of Five Tower's violet-eyed refugees," the mountain warrior explained. "She was paid well to give up these refugees — she has turned in several, according to this, after they came begging for a cure. And this was not weeks ago but *hours*."

Reid's fingers trailed across the pages, and Lukas leaned closer to peer down upon it, careful not to disturb the foliage that trailed along the wall. Neither Reid nor Taiir had noticed Lukas had been just beyond pocket-picking distance for a half hour now. All he had to do was reach out, around the wall and between the barrels stacked there, and whatever was in Reid's pockets would have been his for the taking. But Reid's pockets contained nothing he wanted. He'd already checked. What he really wanted was what else was in their minds. He needed to know what more they knew as well as what else they were looking for.

The page turned, and then Reid's fingers paused halfway down. "The seal," he said. "That's the same one from the forest. The one Nymeria's glass activated, where they killed Manard."

Lukas frowned. Had they found the beacon Rhael had instructed him to find? And the naïve bastards had activated it. That explained why the Dead One had shown himself. It meant Rhael was dead or missing. That Gabriel was searching for him.

Lukas cursed under his breath, and a cold chill spread down his spine. The Dead One was *not* a man he'd wanted involved. That man was the only thing he believed worse than the creatures. The creatures would make quick work of their kill. Gabriel . . . would not. The Dead One had the means to extend a man's life, and to torture him for the whole of it.

Lukas wanted nothing to do with it. He would embrace the Violet first.

Taiir produced another document and passed it to Reid discreetly, and then he took a jar of beans from the shelf and pretended to study the product. "Correct. He does not sign with any name," said Taiir under his breath. He looked sideways, over his shoulder, and Lukas held still so that he would not be detected. "That letter was in her desk, tha seal yet unbroken. It is from tha Lord of Aelynhold."

"Why would some shopkeeper from the poorest part of the city — huh."

"These monks have a new leader now, Commander. There has been a great change in them tha last four days. I could not get tha other letter from tha desk without notice, but she has some rank within this brotherhood. Tha other letter contained a list of names of men to be slain. Their glass chains were to be broken. Or recycled. It seems they want them shipped, broken or otherwise, to a smith in tha nicer market nearer their temple."

"The monks are to kill their own?" Reid looked up, through the shelf. "Well, that's unusual. It sounds as though the whole regime is undergoing a change of management. And

Lukas is likely very much involved."

"Indeed," said Taiir. "I believe they have only just begun to clean house. I have no idea what it will mean for Black Temple or tha Alliance."

"Neither do I. It could be good or bad. Or worse. What do you think the chains are actually for? They seem to have a purpose beyond the obvious mockery of Black Temple's honored address of its members. My gut says they're more than a mere symbol."

"I could not say," said Taiir. "Perhaps a threat. If those chains were to ignite with tha Violet, they would become a vile weapon."

Reid sighed. "That's bloodcurdling. Eight hundred chains, all lit with the curse and able to infect anyone . . . That's incredibly dangerous."

"A dark thought, I agree," nodded Taiir. "A worse one if each link were explosive." He placed the jar back on the shelf and moved it toward Reid, who stood on the other side. "I believe your niece asked for this sort of bean. It is tha only one of its kind on tha shelf."

Reid picked up the jar, opened it, and then smelled it. His nose crinkled, and then curiosity drove him to sniff it again. "I think . . . Maybe. But it's labeled wrong. And smells of other things also."

Taiir chuckled. "An expensive mistake we will not help mend."

Reid dumped one of the beans out into his palm and pinched it between his forefinger and thumb. He smelled the jar once more, then the bean he held. "You're right. They didn't even clean the jar. Chili, coffee . . . anise? But these *are* cacao beans. What kind of nasty merchant doesn't clean his jars before refilling them with something else?"

"A slovenly one not expecting or caring if his wares last long," nodded Taiir. "Tha dust and tha rat droppings upon tha outside should have been tha first clue. At least tha jar was sealed well. What have you discovered about this King of Thieves?" asked Taiir.

"Honestly?" Reid shrugged. "At this point, I wouldn't be surprised if it was Lukas himself. It would fit the silver-tongued murderer. Everything else his name is mixed in aligns with it. And unfortunately, what we've discovered seems to confirm that my parents' murders were actually a fluke and not something he intended at all. More like a job gone bad, even though he spoke as if he'd done it intentionally."

"You think he meant to push you over tha edge and kill him."

Reid nodded. "It was almost as if he was masking something almost *honorable* with his desperate vendetta . . . I picked up on the strangest things from him . . ." The range commander closed the jar. "Regardless, he got whatever information he set that dangerous gamble on. The man is scared. I don't know of what, but it's not just Caol or Eiran, or even the Violet. He's willing to die not to face it."

Lukas felt his skin crawling. Reid's instincts were nightmarish.

"Some men prefer death to penance," said Taiir. "It is not unusual. If it was a gamble for information, tha man is ruthless, and a force to be reckoned with. That sort of risk-taking means tha danger we are placing ourselves in here is greater than we thought. Especially now that he has joined his hooded brothers."

"Correct. The foreigners at the bell tower weren't interested in him, but the wolfmen certainly were. I imagine this city is sacred ground for him. He wouldn't have come here if he had no friends here, or informants or other elements needed for his master plan. We should proceed with extreme caution, Taiir. We've been here fifteen days, and he has been here for four of them, and already, we are finding evidence that he has power here. Things shifted the day he entered this city, and I don't know if it is for the better or for the worse that they have done so. The sooner we bind our criminal and get the hell out of Aelynhold, the better. This place is too perfect a trap. We are outsiders, and we have no allies here, and I would presume every mouth we've paid to speak thus far will eventually carry messages back to places we don't want them to go. Those monks are everywhere, and Aelynhold's city guards are worse.

If we don't get out soon, I think something bad is going to happen to us."

Lukas grinned to himself, admiring Reid's intuition. The man had a sense about him that very nearly defied the natural way of things, and it allowed him to strategize and predict what Lukas's own criminal mind would do. Unfortunately for them, they were already too late to have figured this out. Only a few hours too late, but it was enough for Lukas to maintain the advantage.

"Do you truly think one of these brothers will speak with you?" asked Taiir doubtfully. "Rhael and Gabriel have gone to incredible lengths to hide themselves."

Reid shook his head. "The only way to know for sure is to find them first." Reid gave the ledger back to Taiir through the shelf.

"What is wrong?"

"I'm worried about my niece. My gut tells me things have gotten worse for her — I don't know why, but I can feel it. Something is very much wrong." He grimaced.

Taiir nodded. "It is that shard, isn't it? Tha thing tha Little One gave you?"

"I don't know . . . I think so." Reid's fingers curled, and then he shook his head. "Taiir, I saw one of the things Nymeria told us about. One of the shadow creatures Lukas described in Crow Post. Last night. I woke from a dead sleep, and it was standing over us in the graveyard. I don't think any creature has ever frightened me so badly that I could neither move nor scream. I could *hear* it. Its voice was like a whispering, hissing sound. Some strange language. Like slag hitting the water. It didn't do anything. It just stood there, looking down at . . . I don't know. It was as though it was asleep, or in some kind of trance. Parts of its cloak extended into the shadows, as if it was controlling them, reaching out. Searching, I think. But it moved on when her shard began to glow, as if it couldn't stand whatever was in it . . . I'm not sure my niece's illness is entirely a curse or an illness, though I do think she's connected to them somehow. They *want* something from her."

Lukas's skin crawled again, until he had to check the urge to claw at it.

"If these dark creatures are real," said Taiir, "they are not something we know how to battle. I would not trust tha shard to protect us, tha same as I will never hold that accursed thing. How do you know tha thing is not responsible for its presence manifesting in tha first place? Or that it caused you to hallucinate it?"

To that, Reid had no answer. He held up the jar one last time and then ensured the lid was tightly closed. "We've been here too long. I'll buy this, and then we should go. I need you to get that map."

Another of Lukas's monks tugged on his sleeve in passing, and Lukas followed. The moment he knew they were out of earshot, though he could still see Reid and Taiir, he faced his subordinate. "It's taken you long enough," snapped Lukas. "Is it done?"

"As you have commanded, sir. They have no idea, but they will be unable to deny."

"Excellent. I've already planted the weapon."

"Are you certain this should be made public?" asked the monk.

Lukas's ear twinged with phantom pain. "When they leave this shop, have them arrested. Anna knows what to do afterward." When the monk did not leave immediately, Lukas frowned. "What?"

"That dangerous ally of yours has asked after you," said the woman. "He requested an audience with you."

Lukas's jaw ticked nervously. Then he shook his head. "I won't be visiting him in the dungeons. I don't care what he has to say. And you would be wise to stay away from him, before you get thrown down there, too. Now get about what I've set you to, Nazaeh."

Nazaeh hurried away, and Lukas stood there, thinking. He heard the clomping footsteps of the city's guard, and he heard the horn blast. He gripped the lid of the barrel before him, and he felt his lips curl wickedly when Reid and Taiir looked up, startled as the shop they were in was surrounded. Captain Morris Ramsey Bourgeois, clothed in his uniform instead of his glass chain and his Brotherhood robes, stepped apart from his soldiers. "Remove yourselves from this establishment at once! You have been surrounded!"

Lukas nearly laughed when he saw the apprehension that spread across both of their faces. And as he'd expected, they thought only to comply, to clear any mistake with a mask of honesty and innocence. Reid and Taiir stepped outside with the confused shopkeeper and several other customers. The guards opened a path for the shopkeeper and her customers as Morris's men blocked Reid and Taiir from leaving.

"Might I ask why we are being surrounded like criminals?" Reid asked.

"Remove your weapons at once," Morris commanded. "All of them."

"Of course," said Reid. "But may I ask what is going on?" He received no reply as he unbuckled his sword belt. The sheath clattered to the stonework underfoot. And he removed his gun cautiously, handling it so that they might not mistake the motion for aggression. He dropped it also, and then he began to remove his daggers. He paused when the last dagger came loose, its blade coated in vibrant red blood, and he and Taiir shared startled expressions. The dagger fell among the others, and the men looked up and saw the anger in Morris's face. They knew someone had set them up.

Lukas laughed inside as he saw the cold calculation in Reid's glittering blue eyes turn to helplessness. They could do nothing at this moment. The archers would shoot them if they managed to fight their way free and run. Twenty soldiers against two. The odds would not favor their lives if they fought.

Yet Taiir gripped his staff.

"Don't," said Reid. "It's too late for that, Taiir. We'll sort this out peacefully. It is our only choice."

Taiir held out the staff, and it was snatched away.

Lukas slid out of the shop behind a few of the soldiers who shoved the two men against the wall. One of Morris's female guards tore the hood back from Reid's and Taiir's heads. "Fits the description, Captain Bourgeois," said the woman. She searched Reid first, and when he attempted to follow Lukas's movement, she slammed his face back into the wall. "I did not tell you that you could move," she said sourly.

"What are our crimes?" Reid was as calm as could be.

"Murder," said Morris. "You are a servant of Black Temple, are you not? Your name is Reid Ivan? And your comrade here is Taiir Eskat."

Lukas reveled in the surprise upon their faces when their names were asked.

"We have been set up," Taiir snarled to Reid, but he remained otherwise silent.

"Yes, but we must not give them reason to add more crimes to this arrest," said Reid, and he turned his attention again to their accusers. "Who has been murdered?"

Morris held up Reid Ivan's Black Temple signet, which was covered in blood also. "Your dagger is coated in blood, and your ring was left at the scene of the crime. In your victim's hand, no less. You know very well whom you've murdered."

"Your city is full of thieves and killers," said Reid boldly as his calm began to slip. "And pickpockets, who are as capable of placing things as they are of taking them. I'll ask again. *Who has been murdered?*" Reid repeated. "My blade was not an hour ago clean of blood, and now it bears the signs of a murder I have not committed. I request an answer — "

The woman placed a dagger to Reid's throat, and he fell silent. His eyes closed as he struggled to remain composed. He did not resist as they were cuffed behind the back. But when her knife moved from Reid's throat to his ear instead, and sliced him there, just deep enough to draw a little blood, his eyes opened, and anger stole him. He swore, and the guard woman smiled wickedly.

"Your friend sends his regards," she said simply, and then she shoved him hard.

Reid stumbled and hit the ground. He checked the urge to reach for his weapons, which were near enough he could simply retrieve them. Instead, when he looked up at the archers and the many soldiers around them, he ground his teeth together and began to get up. Morris's boot caught Reid's jaw, then, and the man's head snapped sideways. Lukas saw the blood spray as Reid fell again to the ground and rolled onto his back. He did not move again, and when the others picked him up by the arms and began to drag him away, his head sagged forward, and blood pooled from his mouth.

Taiir's lip pulled back in a snarl, but the mountain warrior did nothing. He had the same calculating look Reid often wore, picking his moment. He knew now was not a good time to defend his friend.

Lukas followed them, and when they were taken into the lower levels of his home, he slowed, until he stopped on the lowest steps of the spiraling stairwell. Anna slipped past him on the stairs, and she strode into the echoing room. It was dark but for the flickering of the torches on the walls, and Reid and Taiir were both manacled and chained to the walls. She stepped apart from the men and knelt over Reid, gripping his chin to tilt his head back and look at him. "Oh, he's a handsome one, is he?" She laughed. "Aside from this ugly bruise and some blood, he's quite the looker." Her lips hovered over his, as though she wanted to taunt Lukas by threatening to steal a kiss from the man. "What a shame," she said with a smile as she pulled back.

Lukas rolled his shoulders, aggravated when he saw her hand trail over Reid's broad, muscled chest. He knew she was doing it intentionally to anger him. He remained silent, anger boiling in his belly, and held his disguise. "I bet his passion is just as beastly as Drake's was," she said slowly, her words almost caressing the man's skin as her painted fingers had. "He looks stronger, though. I would love to try him out. See what he's made of."

The sultry note in her voice had become somehow venomous, and Lukas began to wonder what she really meant. Whether she was as depraved and bloodthirsty as that tone had sounded.

Anna's fine black braids fell over her face like snakes when she leaned forward. "Wake up," she said against the range commander's bloody ear.

Reid remained unconscious.

Then her dagger was in his shoulder, and she was twisting it with a startling vehemence. "I wonder how bad that'll hurt when he wakes," she laughed. She rose, and she turned her attention to Taiir, and her eyes traveled first up, and then down. "My, what a calm, collected one you are. Not worried a bit, are you?"

Taiir blinked once. He did not flinch when she lifted the dagger and placed the point against his belly.

She licked her lips. "No fear of me? How cute." The blade pricked, and he bled. But he leaned forward despite it.

"You smell nice," he said against her hair. "Cinnamon. Smoke. *Blood*. Seems you have already bathed in death recently."

She looked up, her serpentine smile never fading. "Oh? So you know already what I've done?"

"We are to be your scapegoat," said Taiir. "It is obvious."

"Sorry to disappoint, but you handsome devils are both much more valuable than that," Anna said. And she pulled the knife away. "I think we'll start a war together. The three of us. The Enforcers are going to come because of your crimes. Black Temple is going to disown you or fight for you, or they'll try to cover this up. But with both in the same city . . ." She smiled. "How delectably easy it will be to ignite that fire." She touched the point of the blade to another point on his belly, an inch lower. "If everything." Another inch lower. "Goes." The blade touched just below his navel. "Just. Right." Anna brought the blade back up, under

Taiir's chin, and then her nails brushed his jaw. "They'll be so busy with each other that we'll take what we want in the midst of it." She leaned forward and kissed the assassin briefly, and Lukas tasted his own blood where he bit his tongue in anger. His fists curled until his fingernails were digging at his palms dangerously, and he forced himself not to reveal his presence as Anna played her game.

The assassin captured her bottom lip with his teeth and bit lightly, his dark eyes as poisonous and full of warning as her own. "Never tempt an assassin if he is your prisoner," Taiir said once he let go, and his smile was cold, as if he'd been unaffected by her. "Especially if he is also a trained torturer."

Anna stepped back, startled. She wavered where she stood and returned her knife to his throat, and when she lifted the back of her hand to her nose and then pulled it back to look upon it, Lukas could also see the blood upon it. She wiped it away, and her voice shook when she spoke next. "Where is the antidote?"

The assassin relaxed in his chains and raised his chin. "About my neck. A gift, for a beautiful woman brave enough to tempt an *Aseai* male, as myself." Taiir leaned closer to her when she reached up to search for it, and he spoke just as she found the necklace. Anna froze when she met his gaze. "If I were you, I would have already killed us." His smile was more sinister than before. "Your men will extract very little information from either of us."

"Aseai . . ." she whispered, suddenly pale. Lukas had no idea what an Aseai was. He would be asking her later. "I did not realize what was brought to me was so rare. How did you come here?" She looked at the range commander, then. "How did *he* secure such an asset as a friend?"

Taiir said nothing.

Anna tore the necklace from him and broke the vial upon it and drank from it. She tossed the glass and chain to the floor afterward, and she withdrew. "Well, we'll see if our bit of fun is worth the danger of Black Temple's wrath. I would have liked to know everything you two know, but now it is obvious that will not be possible. At least, not with you." She nodded to the guards as she sheathed her dagger and returned to the stairwell, but she paused and looked over her shoulder at the assassin. "Your trespass was exactly what this city needed, despite that hiccup. And with my husband Drake Normane's death, nothing else will stand in my way."

"Drake Normane has been dead for some time now," said Taiir. "Four days, tha range commander and I counted."

"But no one else knows that, now do they? As far as outsiders are concerned, he is just as healthy now as he was when my daughter chopped off his head for me. It's all about perspective, Taiir. He is still alive to everyone else, until we tell them otherwise." She drifted up the stairwell, passing Lukas as though he was nothing more than another soldier.

"That sounds undoubtedly familiar," Taiir's voice echoed after her.

Lukas frowned, and he looked across the room. Taiir was staring directly at him, almost as if he knew the darkest secret in Aelynhold. Almost as if he knew whose blood was truly on Lukas's hands.

CHAPTER FORTY-FIVE

Wedding Day

THERE WERE WHITE FLOWERS everywhere. Everyone wore the color, even Nymeria's father, who was currently leaning forward to hear what Wylem was telling him quietly. Wylem handed him a document that had Oakwall's official seal upon it. Her father nodded with a disturbed frown, tore open the letter, and then crumpled it in his fist angrily when he read whatever had been written upon it. He looked down at her, and then he knelt before her. She knew the news was bad. He wouldn't be staying for the wedding.

"Just go," she said. "I can tell it's important." He opened his mouth and then shut it again, as if unsure what to say to make things any better. "That letter is from the Lady. She's calling you away."

Her father nodded slowly. "Yes. They've found more of the men trying to blow up the dam finally, and there are rumors that Oakwall is under attack also. That Lukas was sighted there."

"Is Irkov okay?" she asked.

"I am sure he is fine." Nymeria's father nodded slowly. "Will you go and join the other children? I won't be long. Probably a few hours. Saura wants to talk to me about this problem. She may want to send me to deal with the trouble at Oakwall afterward, though. I do know she won't want to divert any of the extra security she's spared for the dam and the wedding. That doesn't leave very many of us who are armed and trained well enough to effectively counter an attack of any kind."

"But you're a *doctor*. That was Uncle Reid's job." Nymeria bit her lip. "He was security detail, and he made all the extra trade deals."

"I know," he said.

"You're supposed to help sick people, and train other doctors on their jobs, and deliver medicines and case studies. Not kill people."

"I know," he said. He ran his fingers through his hair again, and then he pulled it upward. "But Reid and I are both very capable in certain kinds of . . . *stressful* situations. Saura may see us as loose cannons at times, but it's also why we are invaluable to her. It's likely she'll send me off again. I don't want to bring you into the middle of that kind of job, okay? I need you to be strong for me. Can you do that?"

Nymeria nodded, and when he reached out to hug her, she stepped away from him. It was obvious that her father thought she meant to be angry at him, but she was actually hiding something awful from him. Even when he paused to look at her sadly, she kept her face blank, her eyes hard. She didn't mean to upset him, but she couldn't let him know that dreadful secret.

"I'm sorry, Nymeria. I should be back during the reception."

Nymeria turned from him to hide the grimace that had her clenching her teeth. She kept her arms folded tightly about herself to hide the violet and the shadow marks that were fighting beneath her skin. She picked a path toward the wedding where she would be able to see Robert and Ellie Mae . . . but she really only wanted to leave. What she was looking for was the street that led away from Black Temple's main courtyard, toward the forest, where she'd seen golden wolf's eyes glinting in the evening sunset a few days before. Her wolf had been keeping to the edges of Black Temple's borders, never entering the city.

She looked at the wedding ceremony, wishing she could be a part of it in some way but wise enough to know she should not be. Others would begin to notice what was happening; she knew she could not convince even a single soul it was just *Tourette's* after that.

Robert stood at the center of the square with Ellie, and they were so lovely, both adorned in gold and white. Ellie's voluminous hair was crowned with the brightest ribbon and with small white rosebuds, and her dress trailed behind her as she walked the aisle toward her husband-to-be.

The dusk was softened by the mist, and the deepening darkness was made pale by the candlelight that illuminated it. Musicians played harp and violin, and cello and flute and drum, and it was the most beautiful thing Nymeria had ever seen or heard. But she couldn't focus on the wedding, not even as the veils of mist and white flower petals drifted down from the archways she passed beneath. White petals littered the red carpet and the courtyard about them, until almost no surface remained untouched.

Every man, woman, and child held either a golden candle or a white bouquet, and golden light softened everything it touched, washing everything in warm hues. Every street glowed brighter as the sun fell farther beneath the valley's small, mountainous crown. Every person, every building, every step glowed warmer. There were smiles and quiet, joyful tears everywhere.

Nymeria still felt cold as she sensed the *other thing* within her, as fear tugged at her with every small shadow's movement. Keeping the violet coursing through her wrists hidden was becoming more difficult as night descended, because even the faintest light seemed much brighter. She fought to keep it down the way one might struggle against drowning, but it burned her every time she pushed against its pulse. For a week, it hadn't let up, and the voice in the back of her mind had grown louder, calling out to her. She'd sought solitude to hide what was happening, but being alone made it harder to remember where she was. *When* she was.

Even as she threaded through the people here, trying to warm herself with their joy and their candlelight, she shivered as though the weather had not turned warm at all. She closed her eyes as a wave of dizziness stole over her . . . and when she opened her eyes again, the ground was covered in great drifts of snow, and she saw large white snowflakes drifting all about her in a beautiful, rolling veil. The small mountains forming the walls of Black Temple's hidden valley had transformed into majestic formations that stretched so far that their tops were hidden by clouds and their bases disappeared into an ocean of fog. She was surrounded by giant white granite pillars, which lined a road leading down from icy balconies of some grand, hidden structure that was buried beneath the snow and the ice. She heard children's laughter, as clear as could be . . . And then there was an explosion . . . Bodies of men turning to stone . . . Blood, eating through the swords upon the ground . . . And then she heard the hissing of the dark things, and then everything was blindingly violet, and then there were screams . . .

Then darkness washed the vision away.

Nymeria's chest heaved now as she leaned against the stairwell, out of sight of all but one.

"Are you okay . . . ?" The mean girl, Sobrienne, had approached her. Nymeria was so disjointed that she hadn't even sensed Sobrienne until the girl was looking down at her, hardly a foot away.

Nymeria sensed the older girl's caution. She shook her head, nearly in tears. "I can't stop it," she wheezed. "I keep seeing them and hearing them."

Sobrienne's brows scrunched together. "Who?"

Nymeria choked back a sob. "The dark things and the man in the dungeon and the dead people — " Nymeria winced as another bright pulse of Violet streaked through her, and then she clutched at her head as she began to cry.

Sobrienne's apprehension spilled into the stairwell with them when the older girl saw the light. "That light in your skin." The girl stepped back, becoming afraid. "Lukas said it meant your family is a bunch of demons."

Nymeria staggered toward the music as the shadows around her seemed to ripple and writhe. "Nai . . ." she wept, looking for a way away from them. Her heart beat hard against her ribs, and the stony walls about her groaned, startling several guests. Dust drifted down over them in cascading sheets as rubble spilled about them. There was another painful beat, and cracks appeared in jagged lines across the stone's surface, and people fell, as if pushed by some invisible force.

The courtyard opened before her, where thousands of candles formed a sea of light. The music seemed to screech against her ears as the slithering whispers of the dark things began to call again.

At first, none among the wedding crowd seemed to notice her. All eyes were on the bride and groom. But all Nymeria could see was blood, and it was everywhere. Then the court before her flickered into the darkest, scariest part of the archives, where new names were being added to a book of Black Temple's dead, and the story of the men from the wall was being added to another of Saura's ledgers. Nymeria breathed in the dusty volumes that smelled of mildew and tears and blood. "Hello . . . ?" called the uneasy voice of an acolyte.

She stumbled forward blindly as fear rose into her throat. She wanted away from the archives, away from the people, away from the dark things. Anywhere but here.

Then the archives dissolved into forest, and when she felt herself sob because she was alone, she was returned to the courtyard that was so full of people, of warmth, of light. But those offensive shades of red and blood and black discolored everything. There was no gold or white left, for it had all been corrupted.

The screams she'd started hearing in the archives days before grew even louder.

She fled the courtyard to get away from everyone, and then the powerful Spirit within her stirred.

Glass shattered behind her, and several people cried out as they were pushed into one another and away from her. The overhead arches began to crack and twist dangerously, and then the tall shadow creatures began to appear from the night, their flesh blackened and still hissing from dark flame, their eyeless faces yawning as though they were silently screaming.

The music stopped, and as Nymeria fled, she saw Ellie Mae suck in a breath fearfully. Nymeria knew they couldn't see the creatures, but the devastation scared them, too.

"Nymeria?" Tessa's voice rang out from above, where she and a few other techs stood pale, gripping the railing for support.

She hardly heard Tessa at all. She ran from them all — and then she tumbled into Mark, who caught her and kept her from slipping away. "Woah, there!" he laughed. "Where are you rushing off to?"

"Mark!" cried Tessa from above. "Don't let her go. We're coming!"

"What's got you in a frenzy?" He knelt as Nymeria tried to claw his hand from her wrists. She shut her eyes tightly, trying not to see all the blood, but the image of glowing blue water compelled her to keep them open. She couldn't answer him through her tears. And then Mark realized she was terrified, and the humor fell from his face as she struggled against him. "Nymeria, what is it? What's wrong?"

"They're here!" she tried to tell him. She couldn't get any other words out.

He grabbed both sides of her face, trying to calm her. "Breathe for a second, okay? Tell me what happened."

"They're in the books," she gasped. "They're everywhere. I can't make them go away! They just keep screaming!" She was again blinded by the vivid scenes that kept stealing the world away from her. She couldn't see Mark's face anymore, just the blood and the trees and the creatures. She shrank from every unusual sound and every alien sight that cascaded over her, even as they overpowered and overran her desire to keep them out. "They're all dead, but they keep screaming, and the dark things won't leave me alone!"

For another brief moment, she was standing atop a hill, looking down at her hands — but they weren't her hands. They were that *man's* hands. They were covered in blood, and they were trembling as badly as she was. And she heard and felt him rasp in horror, felt him take a breath to scream.

She didn't want to see it!

Just as quickly, the image was gone. Mark gathered Nymeria in his arms and began to carry her away from the wedding. "Come on, let's get you to one of the doctors," he said. His voice shook as though he was afraid for her. "That light of yours is brighter than it's ever been. I've got you, just hold on." He called over his shoulder to Tessa, then. "Tessa! Go get John! Nymeria's sick! Saura needs to know what is going on with her immediately!"

Above, Tessa faltered, and fear rippled across her features. "What's wrong with her?"

"Just tell them I'm taking her to the Sick Hall! They need to come *immediately*!"

Tessa disappeared among the crowd.

In the next moment, Nymeria felt chains upon her wrists and cold ground beneath her feet, and she felt a gruesome hunger and a hideous thirst that had her curling inward, gasping. She felt the stranger in the prison cell shivering, and her body racked itself with his aches. She saw the blood leaking from his wrists, where they were chained to posts on either side of him. She felt a fingernail, a claw, rake slowly across his face. "*Wake up, Mihai. You're not allowed to die,*" a woman whispered against his ear. The voice was so cruel, so abhorrent, and Nymeria shuddered sickly to feel the woman's breath upon her ear, to feel the woman's malicious intent radiate from her like a hot knife.

And then she was in the alleyway with Mark again. Her cheek rested against Mark's shoulder, and she buried her face against him, sobbing. "Please make them stop . . ." she wept. "I don't want to remember them. I don't want to hear the screaming anymore."

The Violet burned her from within, and Nymeria cried out.

Mark cursed when her fingers drew blood where she clutched at him, begging him to keep her from the memories. "Hold on, Nymeria. Tessa's getting Saura. We'll see if she'll send you to the Keepers to figure out what's wrong, so they can help you. It may be a while until your father is finished dealing with their emergency, but he'll be there, too."

Again, she felt the stranger's hands, reaching out. This time, he was younger, and the light was whirling violently all about him. He was trying not to let go of someone, but she could see nothing except for the burning violet-colored light. He started screaming when the light storm pried their hands apart . . . and then there was blue water all about her. She was drifting . . . and she couldn't move.

Nymeria pushed hard at the terrifying memory — not knowing whether it was hers or his — and again, the Violet burned her for it. This time, most viciously. She recoiled from it, willing it away. The volatile energy sizzled within her body, like lightning, ready to strike from the clouds and burn a hole into the first thing it touched. "I don't want to use it anymore. The light hurts us! Please make it *stop*!"

The walls of the towers they passed under began to crack and quake, and Mark shrank from the debris, startled. He nearly dropped her, looking up as he dodged the rubble that fell. One entire tower crashed, and the people beneath it were crushed and killed.

Nymeria screamed the next time the light coursed through her. Mark struck the wall with a yelp as it bit him also, and she hit the ground when he dropped her. He crawled quickly toward her, his cheek bleeding fiercely where shrapnel had sliced him, and he looked up as more rubble showered them. Mark cursed.

Nymeria curled on her side, weeping, and he pulled them both from the next large slab that began to fall. Sinister cracks raced across the walls about them.

"I don't want the shadows to take me away!"

He rocked with her, trying to calm her. She sensed his thoughts, felt his harrowing fear. He was afraid for her . . . *of her*. He perceived that what was happening was because of her. There was no other explanation. He saw the violet light ripping everything apart. *She was cursed. The magic within her was real. And it was killing people* —

Nymeria wept at his thoughts, but she tried to focus on them instead of the shadows and the jarring memories coming from the man in the dungeon. It was a whirling storm of confusion and chaos, and she could not overcome her terror of it all. So she clung to Mark as if he could save her.

"He was right," Mark whispered against her hair. "This thing is going to kill her, if it doesn't kill everyone else first." He stared at the walls she'd almost destroyed completely, at the bodies crumpled beneath the broken archways. "Your father should never have brought you here," he said. "Nymeria, just focus on me, all right? Hold on, until we can get you to your father — "

Violet light crept into the gray slate underfoot, and the ground began to blacken and shine, like lava glass. One of the veins splintered against Mark's back, and several of the shards embedded into his shoulder. He cried out as the Violet bled into him, and he gasped as the curse filled him, as it opened his eyes to what she saw and what she knew. He cowered against the wall as the dark being turned, searching blindly for her. And then she *knew* he saw the tendrils of shadow curling through the streets and ripping through everything. She *knew* he was looking at the dark thing that stood hardly half a street away from them.

The *shadei ra*'s eyeless face turned toward him. Its blackened foot broke the glass when it stepped toward them, and the violet light that spilled from the splintering seemed to confuse it. Those sparks of light bought them precious time.

Mark pulled Nymeria with him as he eased back from the creature, but then he doubled over with a cry, and Nymeria looked up at him as his eyes glowed brighter. His hands, trembling, went to his temples as he let her go. His eyes had begun to bleed. "Run . . ." he choked, blinking hard against the fog of red that clouded his vision. The dark thing reached out for him, drawn toward the light inside him.

Nymeria shook her head. "*Nai*, I can't!"

Mark staggered forward, his hand on her shoulder, pushing her. "Get away from it before it finds you — " His knees buckled, and he hit the ground, and Nymeria grabbed his hand and pulled at him as she begged him to get up and come with her. She was too petrified to run from the creature by herself. She was too afraid to leave him alone with it.

"Not without you!" she cried. "They kill everything and everyone that has the light!" He pushed her away, and she trembled when the Violet burned inside her veins.

Mark convulsed, and he began to scream. Vision swarmed him, and he began to see gruesome, horrendous things. His fingers went to his face, and he began to claw at his eyes — but he stopped when Nymeria grabbed his hands. The touch seemed to have pushed away the worst of it, and he took great, rasping breaths, shuddering sickly. "The water . . . they can't enter the water — "

And then one of the dark things' clawed hands was upon his shoulder. Nymeria staggered back as Mark's eyes rolled back in his head. The tall creature pulled him closer, smelling him, and then it hissed in displeasure.

Then Nymeria saw her father and Tessa racing into view from behind them, from where she and Mark had fled. Another dark thing separated itself from the night from another alleyway beside them. Its great, broken-antlered head slowly swiveled toward her, until she could see the empty black abysses where its eyes should have been. Its long, clawed fingers gripped its sizzling staff, and the burned thing hissed and sparked, and the being stepped toward her.

Nymeria fled in terror. When she looked over her shoulder, the creatures had abandoned Mark in favor of other sources of light, and Tessa was kneeling by him, horror-struck. Mark's skin had been burned badly by the creature's hand, and he wasn't responding to anything. He was just staring, as though his mind had shattered. "*Demons,*" she saw him say. It was all he said before her father saw her and cried out her name. He took off after her, fear stricken.

Nymeria ran into the tree line, and her wolf joined her, whining fiercely. They fled together, and her wolf began to snarl as the insidious presence grew closer and closer. Then the wolf yelped as though she'd been hurt. Nymeria ran faster as her heart squeezed tightly beneath her ribs. Trees flashed by and ripped at her hair and raked at her face. And then something behind her roared. Her wolf screeched as though she'd been attacked, and then Nymeria knew she was alone, and the night grew more imposing.

Nymeria kept running until she tripped and tumbled down a ravine. When she got up again, she was dizzy, and she'd lost a shoe. She staggered forward, holding her hand to her forehead where she'd struck the edge of one of the rocks that jutted from the tree roots. She spat the dirt and the leaves from her mouth as she reached out to grasp the young saplings before her. She nearly fell again, and desperation surged through her. She had to get away from them, or they were going to get to her. She had to keep going!

It was so very dark out here, away from the candlelight, away from the wedding. There was only a sliver of a moon, and the sparse rays were devoured by the forest. The rocks hurt her foot.

Something moist dripped from her chin, ran down her lips from her nose. It looked like blood — but everything looked awash in it.

Nymeria's lungs ached, and her leg hurt, and her head continued to spin as she staggered forward.

Then she saw a silhouette of a man ahead of her. His was a familiar presence. A warrior. Someone safe. Someone she knew . . . She stumbled toward him, crying. "Please make them go away," she cried. He reached out for her, as though to protect her; she never realized he was nothing more than the ghost of another memory. She only knew he needed her, and she needed him to protect her. The distance between them disintegrated, and she reached out for him — and embraced nothing at all. The shadow of him overtook the night around her and blotted out the dim moonlight. His presence swallowed her whole, and everything became wintry. The violet within her flesh winked out as if devoured, and a tremor ran through her as she drew a breath.

She lost all concept of time. Death became everything about her. The agony within the blackness never seemed to end. The centuries she experienced within his mind broke her and burned her, and then it shattered her again. Eyes, as blue as the bluest fire, reflected to her from the waters of his insidious memories, time and time again. Rivers of blood drenched the earth wherever he went, and always, the blood would turn the water red when he tried to wash it away. Fear slashed her, and memories marred her, until she forgot who she was or where she'd come from.

She tasted his blood, and she felt his heartbeat, and she became him as what he was engulfed her like black flame. The screaming cacophony in his head unleashed itself from her mouth, and Nymeria was taken by the night.

The *other thing* within her awakened in response, and it hungered . . .

For revenge.

For death.

CHAPTER FORTY-SIX

Missing

THE WEDDING HAD HALTED immediately. The reception had been forgotten, and the joy and the music had turned to silence, and to grieving. From the attendees at the wedding to the security detail throughout Black Temple, to those sleeping off their last shifts building the support structures along the ridge near the dam, every person available was now busy tending to the wounded and digging through the rubble to get to those who were still trapped.

The quaking had subsided, and there was no word yet whether the dam had suffered any breakage. The known casualties were already quite high, and quickly climbing — and veins of black lava glass were stretching across nearly every city block, still hot to the touch, many of them still radiating violet light. The scene was alien, yet familiar. It was like a less devastating version of whatever had happened in Five Tower two years before.

All of this had to have been caused by another of those strange bombs. John knew there could be no other explanation. He'd seen what had happened in Five Tower, and though he was grateful the scale of the damage in Black Temple was far less, it was still a fearsome thing to see. His heart had lodged itself in his throat at the sight of those black glass veins, which were still hissing with heat and steam as the mist fell across them.

Whatever had happened to Mark had caused Nymeria to flee into dangerous territory — directly toward the area where another throng of dead Five Tower soldiers had been found between the dam and Black Temple's highest towers. Moreover, John knew the creature that had killed the men at the dam still hadn't been found. He knew Nymeria could not defend herself against such a beast.

His heart felt as though it might explode. He'd known the moment he'd seen her look over her shoulder that something was *extraordinarily* wrong, that her life was in danger. He'd followed after her. Others had also abandoned the streets to race after her, to try to help. But they'd lost her quickly among the trees and the steep incline.

And then he had heard his daughter's bloodcurdling scream from the forest.

John hadn't been able to breathe right since the silence that had followed that scream. He couldn't even give anyone orders to send them in the direction he'd seen her fleeing. His legs burned, and his lungs were on fire as he cried out her name, and he pleaded that she was alive and unhurt. But her scream had not been one only of fear. Something had happened to her — he knew it, and he tried desperately to deny it . . . to believe he was wrong.

"NYMERIA!!!" John screamed again. Others echoed his urgent call, and he tried to blink away the moisture that threatened to blind him. He wiped his face with a frenzied motion, and a moment later, he nearly tumbled over the roots of an ancient leaning oak. Every mist-dampened breath he drew was too heavy, too fear-filled to feel like an adequate, full breath. Everything about him spun dizzily as the fear within him propelled him forward. The forest flew by as he raced deeper and deeper into its blackness. *"Nymeria! Please answer me!"* he screamed.

There was never a reply. His heart flipped wretchedly beneath his ribs. There was just that awful silence where he wished her voice would arise, and the unending night, and the echoed cries of her name from others who were searching for her. Barely a ray of moonlight shone down upon them, and the torches the others held cast not enough light to see by. If she was hurt, they would easily miss her. They might never find her —

John's right knee gave out when he saw just ahead of him a deep, wet red, glistening across the ground. He tried to inhale to call out, but his entire being shuddered in sickened dread. The smell of the blood was overwhelming . . . and then he saw a familiar string of braided leather tied to a cracked glass pendant which was shaped roughly like a heart.

Nymeria's necklace lay in the mud just out of his reach, and yet she was nowhere to be found. He couldn't get up. His legs wouldn't respond. So he knelt there, gasping, denying what he was seeing.

There was so much blood. Pools of it. Small rivulets of water diluted it slowly as it trickled downhill.

The red grew brighter as Tessa slowed behind him, holding her torch aloft. "Oh, no . . ." Her voice trembled at the sight of the blood.

And then the torchlight uncovered from the night's grip a huge print in the mud. Claws, larger than that of any creature he'd ever seen, had deeply gouged the large roots in what looked like a single swipe.

"John," said Wylem, who approached from the brush just to their left, slightly above them. "You need to see this."

John's mouth opened and closed. Tessa leaned down and placed her hand on his shoulder. "She's not here. Whatever happened, she's not here. She probably didn't even come this way — "

"Her necklace," he choked out. Tessa stepped away from him as she turned and saw the item he was staring at. She picked it up gingerly, as if it might shatter. He could hardly speak. "Her cousin made it for her . . ."

Tessa looked up, and tears slipped down her freckled cheeks as the hope in her eyes dwindled and died.

"John, it's Nymeria's wolf. She's been . . ." Wylem looked over his shoulder, into the trees above, and then he grimaced and looked away sickly. "I've never seen a creature able to do that to another animal."

Tessa's tech friend approached curiously, and fear glittered in his eyes. His torchlight illuminated the blood as it dripped from the leaves overhead. The wolf's head dangled from a series of broken tree trunks — all freshly splintered. The animal's body was unattached . . . and . . . almost unrecognizable. Just fur, bits of bone, and blood and sinew and entrails.

Horror gripped John at the sight of the slaughter.

He threw up.

To know his daughter had been here, to know some creature was capable of such a bloodcurdling kill —

"*No,*" he wept. He spat the vile regurgitated matter from his mouth, gasping, and he clawed at the mud until he was scrambling through the bloody water. Chest heaving with panic, and heart beating wildly, he snatched the necklace from Tessa's hands. He staggered forward, looking desperately for Nymeria's tiny footprints. "She has to be alive," he wept. "*She has to be!*"

* * * * * * *

Two weeks later, Jeana arrived in Black Temple with their son. She stormed into the complex, demanding to see Saura. Even with hardly a voice, she posed a serious and startling threat, and her cracked, broken words reached nearly every ear as they were spread by every person who heard. If their daughter was not found, she was going to cause great and lasting strife within the Temple — she swore she would set all of Black Temple aflame herself.

John knew more than anyone how far his wife would go to ensure their children were safe — or what she would be capable of to avenge them. It was why he did not step in her way when she barged into the meeting hall, why he did not blink an eye when she slipped gracefully past every guard who tried to detain her — even while holding their son — and why he said not a word to stop her when she placed her slender, elegant pugio to Saura's throat.

Saura backed into the windowed balcony, her hands up. "Jeana, we are sparing every person we can to look for your daught — "

The blade pricked, and a bead of blood rolled across its silver surface. John merely watched, making no move to intervene. He'd already made his demands, and he'd failed to achieve results.

"Dr. Ivan," Saura said coldly. "I would recommend you order your wife down."

"She is not a dog, trained to obey my commands, Saura," he said coolly. "If you hadn't ordered off the search last week, my wife wouldn't have decided to take this into her own hands. You should have listened to me."

"Nymeria has been missing for over two weeks. You *know* I cannot continue to pull so many people from the work that needs done. There are a lot of repairs to be made. We were extremely fortunate the dam remains intact despite the explosion, and we still haven't found any remaining evidence of what type of bombs were detonated at Ellie's wedding. We already had security increased for the event, but it wasn't nearly enough. We need *more*. We need every available hand, and that means recalling the search — "

Jamie began to cry. The blade pressed deeper as Jeana's hand trembled in response.

Then Thomas, who had been among the group taking Lukas to the Reformation, slipped into the hall. He was out of breath. "I'm sorry — " he rasped. He held up a hand, begging a moment to gather himself. "She dropped everything when I told her the news about Lukas, and we nearly drowned at Ender's Creek. Your wife is a madwoman! She — " Then Thomas realized what was going on. His jaw dropped. "A-a madwoman — Jeana! What kind of example do you think to set for your son?! You cannot put a knife to the leader of Black Temple and think to just . . . *walk away*! Saura, please don't hold this against her — "

Jeana's glare turned upon him, and the giant mercenary staggered back, pale, his hands raised. "I'm sorry! But . . . come *on*! At least *one person* in your whole family has to have a level head!"

"You should have stayed home, Jeana" John sighed. "Crow Post needed your help."

"Recall your wife before I have all of you removed from Black Temple entirely," Saura hissed.

Jeana snarled, withdrew her knife, and then punched Saura square in the face. "You're a *serpent*," said Jeana. Her voice cracked, but she continued her tirade. "How dare you order an end to the search for my daughter!" She turned from the shocked room, tears welling in her lashes. And then she slapped John as well. "*You* brought our daughter here. You should have stopped your brother from leaving. His wife should never have left in the middle of the crisis at Crow Post. You know that Nymeria needs extra care. Our family should have stayed *together* — " She choked and began to cough again, even as she snarled and held his gaze and tightened her grip on that dagger. John took their bawling son from her as he pulled her close to comfort her. He knew it did nothing because their daughter was still missing, because Saura had given up trying to find her.

"You just want life to resume its normal course here," he accused Saura. Saura glared at him. "There are over thirty children missing now, including my daughter. You are more worried about that stupid dam than anyone below it. All you care about is the temple itself! Not its people."

Jeana's coughing had subsided into tears. She tried to say more, but her voice was too mangled to unleash her sorrowful condemnations.

"Your entire family," said Saura slowly as she pressed her clawed fingers to her throat, "is unbalanced. But damn it all if you aren't some of my very best. I ought to have your entire family exiled. Now, I am trying my best to be patient with you. You have lost not only your parents, but also your daughter. Dr. Ivan, I have let you two get away with more than *any* other leader over our guild has ever allowed among its subjects. But I am done. This is *the* last chance I will give to any of you. Get out. Before I change my mind and decide upon something worse. Go find some time to grieve for your losses."

"My daughter isn't dead," said John. "And I am not going to grieve when I should be out there looking for her, and for those other kids. I'm taking a team whether you like it or not. We're gathering as many people as we can to keep looking. I don't give a flying snake's fang if you want those hands rebuilding or reinforcing anything, because in case you have forgotten, the primary goal of Black Temple is to protect *people*. Not walls, or books, or dams. *People.*"

"I said *get out*. Leave this hall," commanded Saura. "We will continue to debrief weekly without you. You will not be welcome to join another meeting until I send for you *specifically*. Get out!"

"I'll help look for her," said Thomas. "And I'll ask around to see if there are others."

"You will do no such thing," said Saura.

Wylem stood from his seat and shoved the chair violently back in. The entire table shook when the chair slammed against it and then bounced back and hit the floor. Wylem gripped the table for a long moment to regain his composure before he let himself speak. His voice was calm, but there was a certain crackling intensity just beneath the surface of his words. "We've got a lot of kids missing, Saura. They're all infected with the same violet light that's made Nymeria sick."

Saura paused at that, wary. She opened her mouth to ask over it, but Wylem did not let her speak. "There is no way Lukas could have gotten a hold of her," he said, "but I do know he is connected to the others who are cursed with the Violet who are being taken. I know she is out there, and I won't risk Five Tower getting their hands on her. Or the wolfmen. Or even those monks." He looked around the room. "I am not going to stand by trying to protect a damned temple when our *kids* are being taken. These kids are our future. I will not abandon them. If you won't support the Ivans, Saura, then I'm afraid I'm going to have to step up and wave my authority as a member of the High Council. To initiate an official challenge against you in this hall, at this moment. As the Eighth of Thirteen, I demand an Assessment. You are an unfit leader, bound by as many secrets and lies as Caol himself." Wylem looked about the room and dared the men and women there with them. The other twelve members of the High Council said nothing against him. "We cannot continue on this path of ignoring our own and involving ourselves in suspicious — even *hostile* — politics and behavior. Stand with the Ivans and me if any among you are of like mind. That our young should come first."

Seven of the thirteen members of the High Council rose as well. And then ten of the representatives and doctors. And then another twelve, mixed between the remaining High Council and the rest of the men and women in the room. Only two remained seated. Every High Council member who stood followed Wylem's gesture and placed their ceremonial daggers and their guild rings upon the table, and the other standing doctors and representatives followed suit.

Each High Council member vowed the same sentiments with little variations in their words, "Challenge acknowledged by the Fifth Regent," said one.

"Challenge acknowledged by the Third Regent of the Temple," said Councilor Alyssa.

"The Thirteenth acknowledges."

"Challenge accepted by the Seventh."

"Challenge acknowledged by the Ninth."

"Acknowledgement by the Second Regent."

"The Fourth acknowledges."

"The Eleventh acknowledges."

"The Tenth as well. It's about time."

"The Sixth applauds. And acknowledges."

All but two. The First and the Twelfth. None but those two expressed any desire to be part of a guild that wasn't willing to search for or protect its own children.

John looked at Wylem and the rest, startled. Grateful. He hadn't realized he wasn't the only one who was so unhappy with Saura's policies.

Saura's face became the deepest shade of red.

John clenched his daughter's necklace in his fist, grateful to the men and women who'd stood with them. "I think we've overstayed our welcome," he said. "Jeana. Tessa and the others have refused to give up, especially Ellie Mae. And forty of our apprentices have volunteered to help look for her. More have begun to join since the others disappeared. We'll find our daughter, I swear it."

"We'll find all of them," agreed Wylem. "And then we'll deal with our Lady of the Temple."

CHAPTER FORTY-SEVEN

THE OTHER

THE DARK THINGS COULD NOT find her among his great ocean of tragic and horrific memories, for they were as lightless as the flames from which the creatures had come. He'd had a name. He'd had a home. He'd had a sister. And Nymeria watched as every single thing was taken from him, until even his mind was taken. Until even his soul was fettered and racked with agony and was no longer his own.

Nymeria stood, a ghost amidst another of the tortured man's memories. The snow bit at his skin, stinging her. He shivered relentlessly, crying out a name she couldn't hear over the raging winds. His arm was broken, and hers ached as though the injury were her own.

A small girl with eyes just like hers, and the same hair, and the same pale skin, stared up at him, trusting him to save them both from the explosions. *"Mihai, I'm scared,"* the girl said in Nymeria's other language — the one no one else but the stranger whose memories she was reliving seemed to speak. The girl appeared to be the same age as Nymeria, and she was the same height.

She was a perfect mirror.

The memory began to slip, just like the others. Violet light and screaming took its place, and young Mihai tried to hold the hand of his friend. Darkness washed away the vision, and blue light, shining through water, took its place.

* * * * * *

Mihai lay within the water, and he was unable to move. But he sensed his older sister beside him, just outside the glass walls that entombed him. He sensed his father, and in the same moment knew that his mother was dead, and he grieved the loss. But he could not choke out a sound or open his eyes and reach out to his family. He tried, but nothing happened. He remained motionless in his watery tomb.

A breath spilled into his chest and then let itself out. He began to panic. There was a respirator upon his face, forcing him to breathe. There were tubes beneath his skin pumping synthetic Spirit into him to keep him alive . . .

He was utterly alone, he realized. He could no longer hear his friend's voice in his mind, or feel her presence. She was no longer a part of him. She was gone, as if she'd never existed but for his imagination.

He tried to scream, but his small body did not respond.

"Father, he's awake," said his sister . . .

Years skipped by, barely breathing into him the memory of his father's death. The years painted into his sorrows their journey when he and his sister fled the warriors who had killed their parents.

The two of them had become members of a secretive and ancient, cursed society called the Leviathan Order. They battled monsters, and they barely survived the horrors they were commanded to drive back. Fear and anger grew in Mihai with every vile thing he saw, and he swore he would protect the last of his family from the monsters, the Leviathans, and the cursed. But those who were assigned to become his mentors abused him, and cut him, and amused themselves with his torments. He persevered in the name of his oath, defied the end which nearly claimed him many times . . .

He began to see ghosts with eyes that familiar shade of unnatural, powerful green, but no answer came when he called out. They never saved him when he begged them to. They never ended his misery when he craved it. Instead, his torments continued, and his battles continued, and his grief continued. All of it festered as he and his sister served their masters with relentless bloodshed.

And then the last person he loved in the world was cursed by the creatures they fought, and she was condemned for it. Rejected by the very beings they protected and fought for. He took the life of the man responsible for her agony, and for it, the Order threw him into their dungeons, where he grieved that he could not save his sister. He raged at what they'd done to her. But his voice was ignored.

He listened to his sister's screams when they dragged her out into the sun to burn her to death . . . and when he refused to accept the same sentence they had imposed upon him, their king ordered the dead to possess him. The souls of long-dead Leviathans entered his body and wrapped about him, and restrained him.

His soul fractured when he tried to fight their will to force him to bow so that he would let them remove from him his own head. The creatures within him began to scream as their minds merged with his, and he and they lost themselves. He became a creature that the Leviathans could not control — for even their dead could not force him to bow. His mind was gone. Words turned to ash and meaningless *nothing*. All that was left of him was violent enmity, malice, wrath. And *they* could never kill him. He killed, and he murdered, and he drank — until the screams of his victims and the shrieking of the dead within him began to grow louder and louder in his head. Time no longer existed for him but for an eternity of hell and agony, of hatred and of craving.

And then the ground caved in . . .

Darkness . . . There was darkness, and dreadful hunger . . . For so many years, he was trapped in that solitary pit where he was pinned, until even the earth forgot he'd existed, and roots had grown over him, and the light in his eyes had faded, and the breath in his lungs had become still. All that remained were the memories, the never-ending horrors — all of it slowly fading as his life waned over the expanse of his dark existence.

The Fallen. That memory always came back to him, uttered upon the lips of the ghosts of his endless train of victims. So many had whispered the accursed name to him before that last breath had faded from them.

And now, in the darkness, a single and disastrous heartbeat quavered within his chest.

The entire world shifted about him. Even the darkness about him seemed to cringe in bitter fear of him.

The Fallen sensed *her*. A creature, both of light and of darkness. A creature so filled with power that the shadow things swam about her and searched relentlessly for the fiery Spirit that was within her. Their thirst for her soul was as potent as the agony that had become his existence. Their twisted hunger invaded him, and he knew he would never rest, never die, not until he had destroyed the blinding soul that wielded that power. Not until he had devoured it whole and let it rip him apart from souls to mind, to flesh.

He would never stop searching.

Nymeria knew it.

The Fallen knew it.

Her presence pushed into his lungs his first breath in uncounted years. His soul reached out to hers, hesitant, fearful, knowing she would shatter at the touch and be beyond him forever. But she could not run. She could not hide; for his soul recognized hers. *She* was the creature whose presence had haunted him for millennia. It was *She* who had sent life into him when death had at last promised him peace. It was *She* for whom he had fought, until madness had engulfed him and created in him the monstrous creature he now was. And now he breathed anew, both of them knowing what it meant. And how he *hated* her for it. And he tasted the desire for vengeance again. It was like lava upon his tongue, like rot he could not cut away or spit out.

The darkness within him had infected her soul, he sensed. The *Shadei Ra* would never find her because of it, so long as she wrapped it about her like a cloak . . . like now. Already, the light within her was dying because of it. The last of that brightness, he would take from her, and with it, he would crown himself in Death, and he would destroy all who had cursed him.

A snarl pulled at his mouth. His fingers twitched.

His eyes opened, and blue light shone brilliantly in the putrid, soured water pooling below him. He lifted his head, and his ink-black hair pulled from the foul muck.

The taste of her soul, of her Spirit, was unlike any other, and even to sense it breathed life into him, and a craving for her soul and her blood like no other. Death, he wished upon her. The blistering flames of agony.

His fingers curled. His fangs descended. His claws cracked the stones beneath his hands, and those stones turned to dust beneath his ghastly power.

Nymeria wanted to scream, but she could not . . . She sensed she'd awakened a monster, a being more dangerous to her than the dark things she'd feared all her life. She knew it was so. No black flame or writhing shadow would ever be as dangerous. No wolfman, no murderer, no creature of the night. None were as dangerous as the *Fallen*. She had seen his millennia-long trail of bloodshed, of madness, of despicable, enduring, dreadful wrath . . .

Then he spoke to her in their shared language. "*Ki adeitus ris'viaht-eh tu, ir Kaniakat?*"

Why have you hidden yourself for so many centuries, My Queen?

His voice didn't even sound human anymore.

When she did not respond, he began to laugh.

The sound shook her. Even the roots entangling what had been his lifeless body seemed to curl away in terror.

She shrank from the presence, and she sank beneath the surface of his memories — until those memories branded her. Silver markings curled across her skin. The archaic symbols upon his neck sprawled across hers. The marks upon his arms became hers. Mark for mark, her flesh came to match his. Silver for silver. Scar for scar. Until she curled even further from him in their shared agony and his history could not write itself upon her body any longer.

The light evaporated from her like water as the *other thing* within her shifted again. It brushed off her fear as though the emotion was a nuisance. It was intrigued by the bond between them, to find that her soul and his were connected completely, one to the other. The shadow and the light were simply chains upon them both. One's death would mean the other's. Nothing could break it. And the bond was thousands of years old between them. *Her Other*, it seemed to conclude.

For a brief moment, Nymeria remembered lying within a glass tomb deep beneath the earth. She remembered the glass shattering. Men screaming as the dark things tore from them their souls. She'd once been in a tomb of her own, just like the Fallen. She'd risen from it, much the same as Mihai now rose from his.

The roots of old, dead trees snapped one by one as he clawed his way from the earth. And when he could not break them, he clawed at himself, and then his blood began to dissolve everything it touched, even the stone and the rusted sword protruding from him, which had been broken off in him long ago and had remained for centuries, untouched.

He was still reaching for her, still searching, though he could no longer sense her where she drifted beneath the surface of his memories. Dirt and stone, and ancient metal remnants crumbled away from him as he rose from the earth.

She did not want to be here. She did not want him to find her. She wanted to go home, to her mother and her father. She wanted to be safe with her family.

But the *other thing* in her writhed again, as if stretching, and the visions fell away when it brushed across her grieving wishes. She was not one, but two, and it seemed to pity her weakness. The connection between her and the Fallen fell away like the earthen tomb that had held him.

Nymeria then stood atop a broken overpass, high above Black Temple. Old wires hung like black spider webs, and more of the bridge over her crumbled as the wind picked up and the structure swayed. The people below looked so very small. They were all so very frail. And none of them lived very long. It was so strange to realize that detail. Their lives whisked away like a breath flowing across a candle's flame.

She knew not how long she stood there, watching over Black Temple like a pale spirit, and she hardly noticed or cared as the people below began to flee the crumbling bridge. As some pointed upward when they saw her. As guards arrived to clear the area of the growing crowd of onlookers to protect them from the falling rubble.

The hellish, blind creatures that crawled across the bridge, searching for the light within her, could no longer sense her. They searched every crevice, every shadow, every corner. The dark beings below looked up . . . and then they screamed as one. Cimmerian archways whirled about them, and they dissipated, one by one.

She felt her lips curl coldly in a smile. She felt *hunger*.

And then the beams groaned dangerously, and the bridge began to twist about her. The blackness within her touched and dissolved the wires and the concrete when her fingers curled with craving — just as the Fallen's blood had dissolved his earthen sarcophagus.

There was so much death below . . . She could smell all the blood. The sorrow tasted like a cloud upon her tongue, and she reveled in it.

Craved.

CHAPTER FORTY-EIGHT

REAPPEARANCE

JOHN STARED UPWARD, his breath caught in his throat, and he strained against the hands holding him back. The old bridge groaned over the pass, its ancient form causing the ground to tremble. The huge cables were snapping. The base was creaking as though it was about to come down. And his daughter just stood there, eerily still amidst the crumbling debris crashing down around her.

He had no idea how she'd gotten up there, but anxiety clutched him tighter than the men who were holding him back on Saura's orders.

Jeana skirted the guardrail of one of the old roads that led to the black tower on their side of the ravine, but a huge beam snapped free from above. When it crashed into the road before her, Jeana was knocked from her feet. The ground shook aggressively as cracks ripped across the old pavement. She scrambled back, heaving, her eyes wide.

"Jeana!" shouted John. She couldn't hear him over the cacophony. "Let go of me!"

Tessa and Ellie Mae had made it to the rocky incline and were scaling the massive supports already.

Nymeria never winced nor cried out whenever the bridge shook beneath her feet. She kept staring out, across the lake.

Robert appeared beside John. He hadn't even seen what was happening. "Where is Ellie? John, what's going on? Ellie ran this way when we heard about the bridge. Have they found Nymeria?"

"She's up there! Your wife is trying to get to her!" cried John, and he struggled against the men keeping him from going to save his daughter.

Robert's gaze followed John's, and he paled also. "Oh, god — Ellie!"

Ellie slipped, and her shirt ripped across a large, sharp section of another beam that had smashed into the frame of the bridge's failing support system. She'd injured herself, but the red blooming across her shoulder didn't seem to sap her will as she climbed toward Nymeria.

Jeana was grabbed by another guard and dragged back across the railing. She kicked and clawed to no avail.

"That's my daughter up there!" John shouted. "Let me go!" He tried to push the men who were keeping him from the road, but one of them bared his teeth and drew his sword.

"Our orders were to keep anyone else away," said Saura's guard. "It's too dangerous."

"That's my daughter!" shouted John.

Robert put his hand over John's to stop him from drawing his weapon. "Don't. I can't let you get kicked from the guild for something like that. You've already angered Saura enough."

John glared at Robert and shoved his hand from the butt of his gun. "I don't care about Saura — "

Tessa's scream shook the words from his mouth. All of them looked up as she curled against the groaning structure. And then she was falling. When she struck the ground, they knew she was dead.

Robert took advantage of the guard's distraction and grabbed the taller one from behind. He put him in a choke hold. The sword fell as the guard struggled against him.

The other turned, startled.

John's fist tightened as the guard realized what was happening.

He struck the man square in the jaw, and before any more of their friends could reach them, John and Robert were over the guardrail. They were faster than Saura's guards.

Above them, Ellie was slowing. She'd reached the bridge overhead, and they could see the pain she was in as she cradled her injury. "She's really hurt," Robert gasped. "Ellie, I'm coming!" The bridge groaned again, and more wires snapped.

They lost sight of the chaos as they reached the rubble below and began to climb desperately. John cut his hand on the shredded cable casing he used to hoist himself up to the next guardrail. But Robert was already over it and running toward his wife, where she stumbled before Nymeria.

John sucked in a breath when he saw clearly the bruises and the scratches upon his daughter. They weren't healing, either. Her white dress was covered in both dried and fresh blood — and she wasn't responding to what was happening about her. Then John, too, was running. He barely registered the falling chunks of concrete and rebar, or himself leaping over growing fissures in the old, moss-covered pavement.

Ellie staggered closer to his daughter . . . She collapsed just as Robert reached her. Robert caught Ellie, and to John's alarm, her head fell back, revealing a large, gaping wound that ran from her shoulder to her abdomen. Her collarbone appeared to have been broken, and her face was white from pain and blood loss. Robert freaked. There was blood all over her, and it was soon coating Robert's hands as he tried to stanch the flow. "Why did you have to come up here alone? You should have waited for me!" Robert cradled his wife as she lost consciousness, and John's stomach curled wretchedly when he saw the concrete above them giving away as the rest of the bridge began to sway.

"*Robert! Move!!*" he shouted.

John barely reached his daughter in time to pull her away from the deafening crash, and he held her against him, trembling. He gasped when Ellie and Robert were impaled by the debris. A terrible sound left his throat as his heart dropped into his stomach and dissolved into horror.

Robert held his wife a moment longer, and John heard the sickly death rattle that left his mouth, and then Robert's hands fell from her corpse. The rebar held them both in place; they'd been driven apart not even by death.

John turned away from the gruesome sight of the newlyweds when their blood began to pool under the mountainous pile of rubbish, and he hardly heard his own strangled grief as he blinked back tears and held his daughter.

The quaking began to subside as he shielded Nymeria from the smaller debris that still fell. Where it struck him, he was bruised and cut, and it stung viciously, and his sweat trickled down his back and arms and salted those wounds.

But his daughter wasn't crying. She wasn't saying anything at all. She wasn't even moving. He let her go and searched her frantically for injuries, casting Robert and Ellie from his mind. It was too late for them; he couldn't save them. His daughter was hurt . . . And then he realized, and he was horrified by it, that she was covered in silver markings. They were all over her skin. He lost control.

"Nymeria, who's done this to you?" he cried.

She wasn't looking at him. She wouldn't even reply. Whimper. *Nothing*. There was something terribly wrong with her, and he could barely speak when he opened his mouth, and his hands shook violently as he pulled her hair from her face.

"Please, Nymeria — please *look* at me!"

Symbols had been etched into her flesh along her neck, her wrists . . . There were claw marks, markings reminiscent of gunshots and stab wounds . . . and there were *worse*. His horror deepened with every mark that he saw.

Yet she remained silent . . . and then he realized her eyes were no longer her unique, beautiful, alien shade of green . . . They were as black as the abyss. Something dire was wrong with her. His vision blurred, and he blinked away his grief and horror. Something was *absolutely* wrong. "No, no, no, no . . . Nymeria, please! You have to tell me what has happened . . . Who took you? Why won't you speak?!"

His hands shook even worse as he tried to smooth her ratted hair back. Violet light slithered under the flesh upon her jaw. He tilted her head but could not find another trace of it.

Her obsidian gaze began to move, slowly, until he realized she was staring at what was behind him.

The hair upon the back of his neck rose on end.

She was staring at the blood that was dripping from the rebar and pooling under the concrete. The sight of Robert's and Ellie's mutilated bodies didn't even faze her. When at last she spoke, the sound was almost inhuman. The voice was completely unlike her own, as though she were possessed. Or as though she'd screamed for so long it had scarred her throat and warped the sound. Her lips curled into a bitter, cruel smile, and then that smile dissipated, like ink in water. "Death . . ." she said. She lifted her hand and touched the blood upon the bar. John snatched her hand away from it as another serpent of light crawled through the back of her hand. The scratches upon her cheek continued to bleed. They still weren't healing. "We have endured millennia of it, he and I."

"What . . . ?" John's voice shook. "Nymeria, what are you saying? Look at me, stop looking at Ellie and Robert. They're gone." She never blinked. Never looked away. He moved to block the view. "Nymeria, what happened to you? Who took you — "

Her gaze turned to him, and it was filled with . . . *hatred*. Absolute, icy hatred. There was no recognition in her as she looked upon him. "You will become the reason for our death, for I have seen it. You have driven us to relinquish control over the light that burns away the Hell Cursed. *You* have caused this rift in us, to awaken him before the Wraithes have parted him, and to set him to the hunt. You are the reason our crown becomes a deadly prison, why our protector will seek our death, why the Leviathans who created him will unlock our black truth too late. Our souls have been corrupted by *your* presence. By this . . . *fear* · · · this *love* for creatures too weak to endure the power within the Vael. When the light returns a hundred suns brighter and the *Shadei Ra* come for us again, our suffering will be on your hands, and the Leviathans will return to the Fury because of it, and . . ."

A small flicker of green returned to her eyes. She trembled feebly, and tears welled as she looked up at him, confused. "Father . . . ?" She sounded utterly broken as the smallest hint of recognition fluttered into her expression. She took a step back as fear began to bleed across her face — and then she saw Ellie and Robert. She grew very pale, and when she took a deep breath, about to scream, she seized instead and then collapsed.

When Nymeria woke screaming, John dropped his porcelain mug of freshly brewed coffee midsentence, just as he was about to lift it to his mouth to drink. It shattered and sloshed over the tiled floors of their suite as John shot to his feet and raced to his daughter's side with his wife — he faltered when he saw the claw marks running the length of Nymeria's right arm. Her blood soaked the linens as she fought them. Jeana was the first to the bed, but Nymeria fought her, clawing and screaming, and when she hit the floor on the other side of the bed, she scrambled beneath it and began to wail.

They looked worriedly at each other, and he knelt by the bed as Wylem stepped in cautiously. "I can go," he said. But it was obvious he didn't want to leave them, that he wanted to help.

"No," said John. He cleared his throat. "Just give us a while to settle her again."

Wylem grimaced, emotions whirling strongly behind his dark eyes. "How long has she been like this? Since the bridge?"

Nymeria shrank from him when John held out his hand for her. She shook her head, sobbing, refusing to come out. "Come on, Myria, it's just us," he said softly. She hid her face, and she kept crying.

"He's going to get me again," she wept.

Wylem bit the back of his fist, unable to hide his own anguish. He cared for the child as much as the rest of their group did. "Do you know if they found who took her? Has she even said who took her yet?"

Jeana's arm snaked around Nymeria's waist, and she dragged their daughter out from under the bed. Nymeria screamed and tried to grasp the floor. Her fingernails raked deep gouges into the stone. John scrambled out from behind the bed with a curse and hurried to the other side to help Jeana restrain her to try to calm her.

"I don't want to die!" she screamed. "*NAI!* He's going to tear out my throat, too! I don't want to die!!! They're going to take me away!"

"Shhh . . ." Jeana said, trembling as she rocked their daughter, trying to soothe her. "Shhh . . ." Jeana pressed a kiss to their daughter's forehead and sniffled.

"Nymeria, the dark things can't get to you, it's daytime. You said they only come out at night, remember?" John tried to remind his daughter of her own words. Tried to calm her, since telling her the creatures weren't real had never worked.

"Dark things?" asked Wylem.

But Nymeria was shaking her head. "I'm not talking about the dark things, they're afraid of him . . . They don't want me anymore." She hiccupped as she continued to cry, and John's throat closed as his emotions nearly got the better of him. She squeezed his hand, her hand shaking as violently as the rest of her. "Please don't let him get me!!!"

"Let who get you?"

It ripped John's heart into shreds to watch her cry, to be unable to calm her. "The Fallen," she wept. "They made him, and he knows I'm here, and he knows I'm alive." She took a deep breath between her prolonged, nearly inarticulate cries. "He's a murderer and I woke him up when they took me! Please don't let Mihai get me again . . ."

Hours seemed to pass before her strength finally began to diminish. She no longer fought John or Jeana, and she rested her face against her mother's embrace and kept her eyes shut tightly, as though to keep from seeing what only she could ever seem to see. John took the bandages that Wylem handed to him from the table, and he began to clean Nymeria's arm. She was going to need stitches. "She isn't healing the way she did before," John told Jeana. It worried him greatly.

"What did this Mihai look like?" asked Wylem.

John kept his mouth shut, fearing that if he said anything, she would stop talking about it again.

"He had black hair like me," she wept. "His eyes glowed like mine, but they were blue. He was in the ground, and I woke him up." She had begun to shiver wildly, and she was very nearly hyperventilating.

"Who made him? You said *they* made him."

"The Leviathans." Nymeria's tears racked her. John didn't know how to console her, and he *hated* that he couldn't do so. He kept the bandages against her arm, trying to wipe away the worst of the blood. "They're all cursed. They took his sister, and then they changed him after the Violet took his friend away. He's a *monster*! They tried to bury him, but I woke him up!" She inhaled deeply, and she choked, and her shivering worsened.

John held up his hand when Wylem opened his mouth to ask something else. "Wylem! She can't handle any more of your questions. Look at her. *Listen* to her!"

"We'll find the sons of bitches who hurt her," Wylem promised gravely.

"You can't kill the memories," she whispered, and another wave of tears smothered her pale face. "They don't die. They won't die, they never will. I don't want them, but they won't break. They just fix themselves, and they get brighter, and they don't stop burning all of us. Even the dark things can't stop them. He's the only one, but they turned him into a monster . . ."

Her head began to fall again. "Please make them stop . . ."

She fell unconscious again, depleted by the strength her fit of terror had taken from her.

"*Claw marks*," choked Jeana when John lifted the bandage again. It was the first time they had been able to inspect the wound, now that Nymeria was not fighting them. Jeana's voice was barely more than a mournful, scratching whisper. "John, she's clawed herself to ribbons!"

John nearly dropped the needle when another tremor shook him. "She's not healing," he stammered. "Something is wrong with her. Her eyes were the color of obsidian when I got to her on that bridge, and now she isn't healing the way she did before. This isn't normal for her."

Wylem watched as John managed to pull the first five stitches. "Healing? Do you mean to say — "

"Yes, Wylem," said John. "I do. These silver marks on her weren't there before. They're scars. All of them. She's always healed unlike any I've ever seen. They've always turned silver and then faded, but she's not healing anymore at all — " His voice shook when violet streaked through her arm and the thread began to dissolve in her blood. The wound began to bleed as the flesh pulled open again, and where her blood first touched the cloth he held to the rest of the wound, the cloth also hissed and dissolved.

Nymeria uttered a small cry as the three of them looked at one another and at the impossible wound.

"I need you to get Saura for me," John said. "Tell her this is important. I need her to know what is going on with my daughter — I don't know how to deal with *this*. I can't give her stitches or stop the bleeding — I don't know why there is *light* in her skin! I — I don't know how to help my own daughter." John gave up trying to sew a wound that couldn't be sewn, and the needle hit the floor. He brushed his daughter's hair from her face with trembling fingers.

"Saura's been devastated by Ellie's death, and by Robert's," Wylem said quietly. "I don't know if I will have any success, or if she'll even see me after having issued my challenge. She hasn't left Ellie's tomb for days. She fell apart when she saw their bodies, John. She's had us running things without her, and you know she's always put herself in the thick of things."

"Ellie died while trying to save my daughter on that bridge," said John. "She'll help — she has to. Tell her my daughter is infected with the Violet, and I need her help."

Nymeria shivered, and her fingers curled. "Mihai . . . ?" The name was followed by more tears slipping down her cheeks. John took her hand and squeezed her small fingers, and Jeana continued to try to wipe her wound clean. The blood still caused the cloth to hiss and decay, but the bleeding did seem to be slowing.

"I'll try," said Wylem. And then he was gone.

"Be careful, Jeana," said John. "I don't know if her blood will burn us, too, or if she is carrying some kind of organism that's responsible for this. We need to treat those wounds with care. Grab the other towel. Toss the other one away from us. We'll burn it."

Hours later, John was carrying his half-conscious daughter toward an isolated laboratory in the Sick Hall. Saura had summoned him, and when he arrived, every machine and tool had already been prepped, and Saura was already wearing her whites. Her eyes were still red from grief.

"Where are we going . . . ?" Nymeria asked, dazed. "Where is Mihai . . . ?" She wasn't quite coherent, and John held her close for a long moment before leaning forward to lay her upon the sterile bedding. "The Leviathans haven't come for me, have they?" she asked. Her head fell back. "The people he killed won't stop screaming . . . I can still hear them. I don't want to taste their blood."

John pressed his lips to her forehead, unable to say anything. When he let her go, he stepped toward the wash basin and cleaned his hands, and then he began to don the gloves and the clean cloth that served as a blood guard.

"Draw some blood when you're ready," Saura commanded. "Look at what we've got going there, and I'll stitch her up. Tell me of anything you find. Now, how bad is this wound?" She leaned over the bed and took Nymeria's small arm. "Ah, very nasty."

John drew Nymeria's blood while Saura attempted to sew the wounds upon her arm. Neither said anything to the other, except what was medically necessary. Occasionally, Saura would stop what she was doing and step aside to gather herself. Meanwhile, John ran Nymeria's blood through a battery of tests that Saura had already set up to have done.

"How long has this wound been open like this? What caused it? I've never seen anything like it — her blood is just dissolving every organic thing that touches it. I've tried five different types of sutures already. The needle is the only thing not dissolving. Turn on another lamp. We may have to try stapling the wound shut."

"Four hours ago," he said, his voice strained. John turned on another of the blindingly bright lamps, and he moved it closer. "She clawed herself."

"Your little girl didn't make these claw marks, Dr. Ivan," said Saura. "These are to the bone. Fingernails wouldn't lacerate so deeply." She looked up when he made no reply. "Since when have you nothing to say? What is it?"

"Look in the microscope," he said. He felt light-headed. "And then look at the sequencing on the monitor."

Saura frowned. "What is it?" She moved forward. "Keep an eye on her. Watch her vitals for me. That bleeding has finally almost stopped." Saura peered into the microscope, and then she withdrew with wide eyes. She looked again. "What on earth . . . ?" Then she slid over to analyze the screen where Nymeria's blood had been run through another of the machines.

"I'd hoped it was a-a virus, bacteria — anything," John said numbly. "Her hormones are off. More than that, her red blood cells are encased in a bioluminescent, spiked membrane. The light is visible whether the light on the microscope is on or off. I don't know what those other things in her blood are. They're not leukocytes or thrombocytes . . . All of her biochemistry is wrong."

His daughter's wound began to stitch itself closed again in front of them. The Violet raced through the new silver scar as it faded, and Nymeria convulsed. He and Saura both riveted their attention to the screen monitoring her vitals. One large spike marked another, singular convulsion. Her heart stopped for a few beats, and then it continued beating normally. John held his breath as Saura returned to the other screen and began to cipher what she was seeing. She switched to other data, and she let out a long, slow breath at what she saw.

"A third helix . . . ? I've never heard of any living thing having a third helix," Saura whispered. "She isn't infected with the Violet, not like the others were. These membranes around her red blood cells seem to be generating it . . . It looks as though some of these ruptured erythrocytes are disintegrating entirely."

"But it cannot be possible," John said. "None of it."

Saura looked at Nymeria's arm, and then she reached out to trace the new scar. "Those anomalies may be concentrated where she's just healed." She stood and reached for the lamp.

"Why do you say that?" he said.

"A hunch. Some species of mycelium send nuclei through their cellular pathways to the site of an injury. It's something I've only recently read about, although this is in so many ways something else entirely. The immediate, high-volume transferal of healing cells is something I would never have expected in any other living thing, but . . ." The lights switched off, and the energy within his daughter's body curled through her new silver scars faintly — more brightly in the newest one. "Bioluminescence," she exhaled. "You certainly called it correctly."

The light within his daughter's arm began to fade, until they were completely in the dark. Saura flicked the lights back on.

"What are they?" He wondered if what they'd found had anything to do with Nymeria's hallucinations or fear.

"I don't know, but I do know someone who may be able to run some more appropriate tests. He told me about this phenomenon once, about a year ago. I wouldn't even know what to look for to treat her. At least her wound is now completely gone. Why didn't you tell me about her condition sooner?"

"Because everything has been in the way," he said honestly. "And then you and I haven't seen eye to eye lately. It's hardly an easy thing to bring up when our tempers have taken the field."

"This does explain why you've been so ready to cross me," she said. "I can't imagine how much has been riding on your shoulders, or for how long. How long *has* she been dealing with this? The side effects, I mean? I was told she was hallucinating at Crow Post."

So Saura had already known. "The delusions started a few months after we brought her home," said John. "Then she started finding those shards I wrote to you about. That light started showing itself in her only in this last month. She's deteriorating. She's losing her grip on reality, Saura. Now, more than before. Since we found her on the bridge, she hasn't been herself. She hardly sleeps at all, except when the episodes leave her like this. Now her blood is doing *that*, and we couldn't sew those cuts closed. And she's having so many nightmares that I don't know what to do to ease them."

"Have you given her any sleep tonics to ease the nightmares? Anything for her anxiety?"

"I've tried everything. She's had adverse reactions to all of it. Rashes, hives, fever, throwing up . . . Some of it has made her episodes worse. She's hardly even eating. She says the food smells rotten."

Saura's copper claws clicked on the metal railing. "She was in Five Tower during the Bright Night?"

John nodded. "I've already told you everything that happened in Five Tower. Saura . . . I want to take her to Arsennia."

Saura shook her head. "I cannot, in good conscience, send you there with her. The trip is too long, and it is too dangerous."

"They can run more tests than anyone else. They have better, more advanced equipment stored away, and larger medical archives. There is bound to be an answer in Arsennia. Surely, there have been other cases like hers. There *have* to have been."

"I am not sure your daughter can handle such a trip. What will you do if she is hurt and you cannot close the wounds again? We need someone a lot closer, and I have someone."

"Who?"

Saura looked away. "Never mind who. He's grown familiar with this unusual epidemic. I've received several reports from him about it. I'll contact him. It'll only take him a day or so to finish his work. He was going to head back to Five Tower immediately, but — "

"No," John snapped, startling her with his absolute vehemence at the idea. He held his hands up. "Saura, you have got to promise me not to invite a soul involved with that wretched city."

"He is loyal to Black Temple, and he has worked hard to rebuild relations with some notable men there, Jonathan. He never even stays in the city. He only trades with them."

"No doctors from or near Five Tower."

Saura stepped back when he moved the lights away from Nymeria's sleeping form. "You're not taking her to Arsennia."

"Tell me who your contact is, then. Because I will not entrust my daughter to someone I don't know and don't trust."

He saw her restrained anger. A flash of her grief before she turned away from him. "At least you still have a daughter. Tell me if her condition changes. If you need me, I'll be in the conference room. Lovael, I am told, has come under attack, and so has Crow Post. And we've found some of the missing children."

"Wait."

She stopped at the entrance. "What is it? I am so very tired of arguing with you about *everything*. I have just buried my daughter and her husband, and I want to be left alone to grieve them."

He grimaced. "Where did they find the children? Who took them?"

"They were never kidnapped. They contracted the Violet during the quake, and they left of their own free will. Sort of. We found ten of them. They were in a trance, all of them heading north, toward the lake. '*To keep the Fallen away*,' that's what I was told several of them said. I don't know what it means. It wasn't just kids that went missing, either. Some of them were doctors who'd also contracted it. Mark knew where to find them."

"Is Mark all right?"

She shook her head. "His left eye is now blind, and he'll have some hideous scars, but all of that is superficial. He's hardly functioning. Whatever she is terrified of, he said it's all real. He said a great many things, but little of it is coherent. I'm afraid I don't think he will ever recover fully. His father will be heartbroken." She turned to go.

John sighed. "Saura." When she paused, he finally put down his anger. "I am sorry about Ellie. She was a good friend. Our best mortician. Just as hardheaded and stubborn as you."

"Well . . . I am glad she knew how to get under your skin," Saura said. "You need to be reminded often that you are not in charge."

Then she was gone.

CHAPTER FORTY-NINE

SAURA'S CONTRACT

NYMERIA DIDN'T LIKE being in the sick room, but her brother was curled up on the bed with her, and her father and mother were sitting beside her. Jeana was brushing the tangled mess from Nymeria's hair while she read aloud from a book from the archives. Jamie was enraptured by the story, and he loved the pictures.

Reading gave her something less terrible to think about.

Occasionally, Nymeria's hands would tremble as she turned a page, and she would reach to clasp the necklace her cousin had given her, unsure why it soothed her. Her other necklace, the one with the Cyan ring, remained hidden, but it, too, gave her solace. It was like having a piece of the rest of her family there with her, as if they were still together somehow, even though they weren't.

"I like that one," said Jamie, and he pointed to one of the dragons inked on the page. "He's a baby dragon, but he's the fiercest. He's not afraid of anything!"

"He's rude," Nymeria said. "And he has an ugly temper. But he is brave, isn't he?"

There came a knock. Nymeria winced when the sound penetrated the room and exploded in her ears. She let go of the book, her ears ringing as her mother and father turned curiously to see who their visitor was. None of them seemed overcome by the noise . . . When she closed her eyes, holding her hands against her ears, she felt another ghostly memory draw at her mind.

The room was dark beyond the glass encasing her. She drifted in the tank, in and out of consciousness, pale blue light arcing through the water and through her flesh. The thunderous sound of the grand chamber's doors shutting brought a taste of sorrow to the water around her, but she could not turn her head or see beyond the encasement . . . A respirator forced air into her lungs . . .

She sensed him.

The walls began to lower as the water drained, and when she opened her eyes, she could see nothing but the faintest glow of the unnatural green from his eyes . . . an expression of horrible despair as he looked down at her, as the shadows rose behind him, reaching, reaching . . .

The blue light in the tank arced with violet, and then she was falling into darkness — She could no longer feel her body as she drifted away, waiting. Always, waiting . . .

Nymeria's stomach growled as the sound of her father's voice washed away the strange memory. It wasn't Mihai's. But she didn't know when, or where, or whose, it was. Her own? She did not understand it.

"Michael, isn't it?" asked her father.

Nymeria looked up as Michael entered the room. "Yes. May I come in? And Sobrienne? Mark brought us."

Sobrienne peeked shyly from around the corner, and then she stepped out. Her eyes were violet.

Nymeria sucked in a breath, trembling. She knew somehow that it was her fault that Sobrienne had the Violet. And Mark. "Mark?" she said.

"Yes, come in," her father said suddenly, shaking his surprise. "Mark. You may come in, too."

"I don't want to frighten her," said Mark from the hallway. He remained out of sight. "The sight of me may trigger her to have another memory."

Nymeria's mother and father looked at one another, confused. "W — "

"Mark," said Nymeria, and she sat up. "Come here. I'm not afraid of you."

Michael reached beside him and grabbed Mark by the wrist and dragged him into the room.

Jamie's eyes went wide. Their mother stiffened. Their father looked away, grimacing at the sight of him.

Mark's left eye was pale, but violet arced within it, almost as brilliantly as it did in the right. The claw marks upon him were still raw, though they'd been stitched closed. His right shoulder hung lower than the left, as if he was in pain, and dark shadows rolled through the blackened flesh. Red arced beneath the bare skin as though the wound were burning from within still. As though the shadow creature still touched him.

Nymeria blinked back sudden tears. "Does it hurt?"

He clenched his teeth and did not answer the question as he entered. Jamie whimpered and held on to Nymeria, afraid of Mark.

Instead of merely stopping short before them when Mark reached her bedside, he knelt to her, his head bowed. "The only reason that creature's touch did not kill me was because your power burned its deadly hand, Nymeria. I owe you my life, an' more. So I will place myself in the Dark Ones' way if they ever try to harm you again. I will step into any gate that tries to take from you your crown. Your gift has opened my eyes to what awaits your destruction, an' I will not allow it. I will not cower from death again, not if it means saving the *Bright One*."

"Her *destruction*, Mark?" her father asked bluntly. "You're delusional if — "

Mark's hand was at John's throat quicker than any of them could even blink. The motion had been barely a blur — faster than Nymeria had ever seen anyone or anything move in her life. And her father's eyes were wide, and his feet were dangling from the floor, and Mark was choking him, his expression twisted with malice.

Jeana sprang to her feet, mortified.

"*Never* have I seen the world so clearly," hissed Mark. Red sparked through his shoulder, and the nebulous burn began to spread, like ink, under his skin. "I can see how your presence defiles her soul, for her love of you. How it weakens her — " He let go when Nymeria reached out and touched his wrist. His entire being shook when she took his hand in hers, and he let out a breath. He looked down at her, confused, and then he realized John was sputtering. Mark then looked at his own hand, as if he didn't understand what had just happened. "What . . . did I do . . . ?" he asked, dazed.

The mark upon his shoulder had receded again, the red sparks becoming dull once again.

"Don't listen to their whispering," Nymeria said. "Don't let them feel the brightness of the gift."

"But . . . they cannot see it. Their eyes have been burned away."

"They feel its warmth," she said.

He frowned slowly, trying to process what she'd told him, and then he squeezed her hand. "Thank you," he said as his one good eye settled upon her again, and he let go of her hand. "I didn't mean to do what I just did. I don't quite know or control what I do or say half the time anymore." He blinked hard as the Violet flamed momentarily brighter in his eyes. "It's difficult to sort it all . . . I'm sorry, John."

"Mark — " Nymeria's mother rasped. But John touched her hand, signaling he was okay.

"He's not himself, Jeana. And I'm fine." Nymeria's father rubbed at his throat. "Has it gotten any easier for you lately?" John asked him. "Saura said she feared you wouldn't recover, that you were half mad — I just didn't expect . . . *this.*"

"I am resigning from the guild," said Mark.

Nymeria bit her lip when her father stammered. "What . . . ? But why? Mark, you're one of us. You've trained for years, assisting your father and becoming one of Reid's best men. And only Robert was better than you at tracking. We need you. Once you heal — "

Mark shrugged. "This isn't an illness, or neurological damage. An' it is permanent for me. I've had direct contact, unlike the others." His violet eyes blinked. "There is no going back for me. A new calling has been given to me by your daughter. A blinding storm of power awaits her ability to command it, an' worse things than evil men are after it. I don't care if you think I've lost my mind. I know what I know. I can no longer be of use to Black Temple, despite anything you or Saura have to say about it."

"But . . . Where are you going to go?"

Mark stared off, into the darkness, his mind beginning to desert him again. "The Reformation. So that I might help protect her . . ."

"Mark," said Sobrienne. She took his other hand, and he looked away from the shadowy corner of the room. "Mark, she said don't look at them. Don't listen to them. She's right. They only look at me if I stare at them."

"They're still searching," he said quietly, seeming unable to turn his eyes from the darkness. "But she's touched the Fallen's shadow. They cannot seem to find their way through it."

"Nymeria?"

Nymeria blinked and wiped away her tears again, and she looked up at Michael when he spoke next. "You'll be okay. You will become a formidable force to be reckoned with someday." He leaned over the rail and hugged her. "At least you didn't destroy Black Temple."

"Ew!" cried Jamie. "You just hugged my creepy *sister*!"

Sobrienne laughed at Jamie's outright disgust and horror. "Come on, Mark. She's hungry. I can hear her belly rumbling."

"Daddy, he just hugged Nymeria!" howled Jamie. "He's got a crush on her!"

Mark placed his hand upon Nymeria's head. "We'll hold back the worst of the memories," he promised her, "until it is too much for us."

He's lost his mind, Nymeria's mother signed as the three wandered away, and her father rubbed at his throat again with an expression that said it was still a little sore.

"I cannot say I disagree," he said. Then he turned his attention back to Nymeria. He saw the sadness upon her face, she knew. "Nymeria, he will get better, okay? He's just suffered a traumatic experience. It'll take him a while to heal." When Nymeria said nothing, he prodded gently. "Do you think you may at last be able to eat something?"

She shrugged, wiping her cheek. Her face still felt hot with embarrassment because her brother was still making gagging sounds over Michael's hug. "I don't know, but I'll at least try."

What if Saura's guest arrives while you're gone? asked her mother. *He should have been here yesterday.*

John's shoulders rose and fell. "I would say to make him feel welcome, and also to stay cautious . . . But I don't know who Saura's contact is. She wouldn't tell me."

But isn't that a little strange for her?

"Yeah, actually. I thought the same thing. She was uneasy over the topic, to say the least, and she wanted us to stay busy while Nymeria was examined. I still don't feel comfortable with it."

I am not leaving our daughter's side after having nearly lost her.

"I told her as much," said Nymeria's father. "She's not quite acted herself for months now, though. It's just been more evident since we arrived. I don't know what is going on, but I'm sure we'll get to the bottom of it eventually. I get the feeling she's more intrigued by Nymeria's illness than she's letting on. She knows something. Or everything. I'm not sure if that idea suits me."

Nymeria's mother grew obviously uncomfortable at that. *What do you think she may be hiding?*

"I don't know, but this uneasiness has been stirring in the back of my mind for quite a while now. My gut is telling me I shouldn't trust her, despite everything she's done to help us over the years. What Wylem said when he challenged her is exactly how I've felt — and we all know she didn't take that well. Eleven of the Thirteen on the High Council turned against her and acknowledged his challenge. It's unprecedented. I don't think there is a record anywhere referencing such a dynamic shift among our leadership."

He tugged at his hair until it was standing upright. "If Saura doesn't soon earn back the trust she's lost at the Table, she's going to be replaced. But the two who did not stand against her are the most powerful among the Thirteen. It's a mess, and it is the worst time for Black Temple to become divided."

Nymeria's father sighed. "I'll grab something to soothe your throat, if you'd like. Are you hungry? I can bring something back from the kitchens for all of us."

But Jeana and Jamie shook their heads. "I'm not hungry," said Jamie, and he tugged the book from Nymeria's lap.

Hurry back, love, Nymeria's mother signed.

Nymeria clutched at her necklace when her father was gone. "Do you think Marissa and Aunt Ralleigha are all right?" she asked after a long silence stretched between them. Only Jamie seemed to be occupied and significantly comfortable.

Their mother leaned forward and kissed her other cheek, and when Jamie pretended again to throw up, she grabbed him and smooched at his cheeks as well. Jeana tickled him until he shrieked with laughter. The book slipped from the bed.

The door opened behind their mother as she reached down to pick it up, and she shut it quietly as she straightened. She never heard the door, and she never saw the man who had entered. Jamie hardly cared. "Can you read me that one, Mommy?"

Their mother pointed to a different page instead.

"No!" laughed Jamie. "The other one!"

Nymeria kept looking at the man, and she wondered why he had entered as though he was supposed to come in. He wore the Black Temple signet upon his hand, though — she saw it reflect from across the room the light that was over her bed. A scalpel, a heart, a black quatrefoil, and three rubies that represented blood drops. Just like her father's. The man was tall, and he had a severe scar that crept down from his temple. It swept across his jaw, down his throat, and disappeared under his collar. It looked as though a sword had lodged into him once, and bone had split with skin.

His hair was as black as Nymeria's own, and it curtained dark, cruel eyes, and when his head tilted curiously, his angular cheekbones caught the shadows and defined years of battle and hardship.

He looked familiar to her somehow, but Nymeria couldn't place him. She had never met this man before. And he had not yet been recalled in any memory — her own, or otherwise.

She wondered why he slowed, then, as if he were seeing a ghost. But he wasn't looking at her, not much, anyway. He was staring at her mother's back, frowning as though he was trying to place her. And then he suddenly looked over his shoulder to the door, and his frown etched deeper. She saw his eyes widen with alarm. Apprehension blossomed across his expression.

Nymeria's mother pointed to yet another page, again avoiding the story Jamie wanted. "*No!*" laughed her brother.

The man backed away, and he frantically checked his pockets as though he was searching for something. His back hit the door as he looked around, and he knocked a cart over when he turned abruptly and snatched the white linen from the top, spilling the surgical utensils. He tied the door handles together with it as Nymeria's startled mother spun to face him.

The man grabbed the broken aluminum stand from along the side of the door and shoved it through the handles, and he pulled it hard, until it bent. When he kicked another cart over to bar the door completely against entry or exit, Nymeria realized he might mean them harm.

He backed away from the door, hissing a stream of curses. Then he addressed Nymeria's mother icily. "She didn't tell me *you* were here," he swore.

Nymeria's mother went rigid at the sound of his voice, and her hand curled instantly over her hip to draw her knife — but it wasn't there. She paled. She had been forbidden to wear it in Black Temple after she had threatened Saura's life.

Nymeria's pulse quickened. She'd never seen her mother afraid of anyone before. Neither had Jamie.

"Mommy?" Jamie whispered.

Their mother grabbed her chair and lifted it to use as a weapon as the man turned and faced her. His eyes narrowed angrily at Nymeria and her brother, as though they'd done something offensive. Begrudging rancor twisted his features, and he moved from the door. Toward them. His dark eyes ran over Nymeria's mother with a mixture of hunger and disgust. "Well, isn't irony a blistering *bitch*?" he asked. "It's been a long time, Jeana." His mouth curled wickedly.

Nymeria's mother shook with anger. She lifted the chair to throw at him. She tried to shout after Nymeria's father, but the only thing that came out was a broken noise.

"Mommy?" Jamie whimpered again. Nymeria hushed him and held him close.

The man skirted to the side, avoiding the thrown chair easily, and it crashed into the cart so loudly Nymeria's head hurt because of it. "What's the matter?" he asked, and his gaze flitted to her throat briefly. He laughed. "Oh, you can't talk anymore, can you?" Their mother had grabbed another chair. He held up his hands. "Jeana, I am not even here for you. You don't have to worry about what happened between us ever happening again, unless you piss me off again."

He looked at Nymeria, and he stepped closer. Nymeria's mother shot between them as if she wished she could block him from seeing her. "Come, now. There is no way that child can be his," he said slowly. "I cut that child while it was still inside you. I killed your first — the one that should have been *my* child." The last words were said with vicious anger, and Jeana faltered, her hand fluttering to her belly as she breathed in sharply at the memory he provoked.

When Nymeria looked up, she realized her mother was crying. "Griggori — " Jeana choked. "Do not — take another step toward my children!"

"I was summoned to run some special tests on a very unique patient," he snarled. "Get out of my way, or you and I will finish what we started years ago. And this time, that wife-stealing bastard of yours won't hear you screaming and come to your rescue." He looked at Jamie, and he snarled again. "I ought to just kill the kids, then kill John, and then take you home with me to start all over. It's what honor would have me do." He grimaced. "But at the thought of him having been with you . . ." Then he mused, "Although I can't help but wonder how badly it would wound you both if I did to *him* what he did to me when he took you into his bed, when he *knew* we were married."

"I never loved you! You were a monster!"

"Your parents gave you to me, you traitorous whore! You belonged to *me*. Yet you stabbed me in the belly on our wedding night, remember? You fought me, even though it was my right to have you, and then you made me think the child you carried was mine. Eight months, I boasted I was soon to be a father, and you said not one word to enlighten me that the putrid thing inside of you was not mine — and then he found us, and I caught you with him. All that time I'd spent to cultivate you into a proper wife — you threw it away for him, and you betrayed our marriage. And don't you dare tell me again, how you two had already been to another city to marry, or how I forced your parents to give you to me. You *wanted* to marry me until the day I came for you!"

"I did *not*! And you defiled and killed my sisters — "

"Recompense. For your lie about wanting to be my wife," he snarled. "I don't understand why Saura let him remain part of the guild after he attacked me and left me for dead." He dragged his hand along the unnerving scar that snaked from his temple to some place beneath his coat. "He should have been executed for this. Both of you should have died, *Wife*. Along with that child. Do you have *any* idea how badly you hurt me?" He shook his head. "Why am I even asking?! It is obvious that you never cared for me. Get out of my way so I may inspect my patient."

"You are not touching my daughter!"

He stepped forward anyway. "I beg to differ, woman. I have a job to do, and I intend to honor it."

Jamie whimpered, and Nymeria clutched at him. "Irkov still thinks you're dead. He doesn't know you're alive," she said.

Griggori paused, and then he started laughing when he looked at her. "I know. I'd hoped he would have killed John by now because of it. Irkov has always honored our way. More so than I. *I* never returned to kill your mother and father."

"He said you're trash," said Nymeria. "He likes my father better than he likes you."

Griggori's humor died instantly "I'll be putting a gag on *you* . . ." Something passed over his expression as he glared at Nymeria, and the anger seemed to lessen fractionally. He glanced at Jamie, the confusion deepening, and then he returned to studying Nymeria again. "Wait a moment . . . The child I cut from you, I did so five and a half years ago. This girl . . ." He grimaced, and his jaw ticked angrily as he clenched his teeth and swore. "I may have been as ineffective as your bastard husband at ending the target of my wrath." He turned to her mother. "She looks old enough, and I may not have done the job right. She looks nothing at all like him. Not even remotely. There is no midnight hair in his family, yet her hair is as dark as mine. Whose is she?" he demanded. "Mine or John's?"

Nymeria's mother gave him a middle finger.

Griggori had enough. He took another angry step toward the three of them, and Nymeria's mother rushed him with Jamie's book in her hands. She dodged his attempt to grab her and reared back and struck him hard across the face with it.

Griggori stumbled, and Jamie began to cry. The angry man staggered into the table beside the bed, and he reached up and caught Jeana's hands as she grabbed a syringe and tried to stab him in the throat with it.

Nymeria and Jamie both flinched when Griggori grabbed their mother by the hair and slammed her head into the table. Jamie slid from the bed, screaming, and ran at Griggori, his fists balled up. "You hit my mommy!" he shouted blindly. But Griggori ignored the little boy and grabbed their mother by the hair and dragged her toward the other chair, the one their father had sat in. Their mother's head was bleeding, and when Griggori picked her up and threw her into the chair, her breath came out in a pain-filled, half-conscious moan, and her head lolled back.

Nymeria couldn't speak, couldn't move. She knew what was happening was real, but she couldn't process it. Her mother was barely conscious. Her brother's angry screaming had her wanting to cover her ears and cry. She took another deep breath as the room spun about her.

And then Griggori backhanded Jamie so hard he hit the floor and began to wail. "Stay off me, you filthy little pest." He reached into the crash cart for some plastic tubing and began to tie their mother's wrists to the chair. And her feet, her legs, her waist, her elbows . . . Then his fingers slid through their mother's hair. He clenched a handful of it, and he brought his mouth down on hers. The kiss he gave was angry, and hungry. "You still taste the way I remember," he snarled against their mother's ear. "Now behave yourself while I examine your daughter. Unless you do something stupid again, I am not going to harm her."

He stood to face Nymeria.

Nymeria's gaze was still riveted to her mother's blood. She couldn't make herself look away. When Griggori took the last chair and sat next to her, she couldn't react. Her every muscle had frozen. Jamie crawled toward their mother and hugged her, and he continued to cry. Nymeria's vision blurred, and she felt hot tears slipping down her cheeks. She clutched at her necklace, and her hand shook.

Griggori grew annoyed. He reached over to the vials on the counter, rummaged, and then selected one. He filled a syringe with the sedative he'd chosen, rolled over to Jamie, and pricked him with it. He did the same to their mother. "Now you'll *both* remain quiet and still." He rolled over to Nymeria once more, and he placed his forearms on the rail beside her, his hands dangling over the bedding. "I can't stand babies or kids his age," he said honestly. "Too loud. I don't understand why anyone loves the little creatures."

Nymeria cringed when his hand rose, when he took a lock of her black hair and studied it as it slipped slowly through his fingers. "Your hair *is* as dark as mine," he mused. "Black as midnight. A tint of blue." He sighed. "I'm sorry you had to see all of that," he said. "They and I, we don't get along." His knuckles brushed across the tears that had reached her jaw, and he removed a penlight from his pocket. "I regretted stabbing her," said Griggori. "She shouldn't have betrayed me, though. It's just one of those things." He clicked the light on. "What is your name, girl?"

"Nymeria," she whispered. The blood on her mother's head was pooling on the floor. Her mother and her brother were both unconscious, but their breaths remained strong and even.

She still didn't know whether Griggori was going to kill them when he was done, but she didn't sense any more malice in him. There was just severe curiosity.

"I would have named you Brekka," he shrugged. "It means *breaker of bones*. But your name is beautiful. I imagine your mother chose it for you. She had fine tastes until it came to that bastard. Look at me, girl. Let me see your eerie eyes."

"You hurt my mother," she said. She looked up at him in time to see a flicker of sadness. And a thread of anger. He sucked in his breath when he saw her eyes, just as everyone else did. "And my brother."

"What a lovely color," he said quietly, and he lifted her chin and shone the light into her eyes. "I've only heard of eyes like yours *once*. From Five Tower. A friend of mine told me quite a story about a demon child who destroyed most of the city and killed thousands. They burned her alive to purify the city of the death she'd caused. Supposedly, the kid came from a slave family whose women inherited some kind of second soul when their mothers died. A beautifully morose fairy tale, but it may hold some truth. Five Tower has a place called the *Gray Halls*. Full of secrets they don't want getting out. Creepy shit comes from rumors of that place. Most of it unbelievable, more of it true. My kind of refuge."

Nymeria knew nothing of any of that. She only knew she'd lived her whole life in Crow Post, and that her parents were her parents. She had strange memories of other places, but none were places she'd ever been to, and so many of those memories weren't even her own now. They were Mihai's.

Griggori's penlight blinded her. His grip upon her chin was firm. She did not dare anger him and pull away. "Magnificent," he said in disbelief. "Just like the story, if what Saura said is true. If I'm right — even if you're my child or John's, that second soul thing may have found its way to you somehow. My clients will certainly pay quite a bit. But we don't want Caol to find out about you. He'll have you killed, just like that other girl. Just like her mother and grandmother, and who knows how many other women in that family." Griggori glanced at Jeana, and Nymeria saw the lust that flamed in him. She feared for her mother; she could tell Griggori was the kind of man who thought detestable things about women. She understood the look he'd given her mother for what it was. "As for your mother," he said to her. "Things are complicated."

He reached into his pocket and drew out a violet shard. She knew he could tell she recognized it. "Adults are . . ." he said thoughtfully, "not as smart or as perfect as we pretend to be. John's a murderous coward — and I have no respect for cowards. Jeana is a killer, and, well . . . I'm a killer, too. I've always loved it. Thrilled in it. That's why I wanted her. Because I knew what she was. But John convinced her she wasn't, that she did not want to follow the impulse. I'm still pissed about that. I cannot believe she chose a coward over me. What about you? Ever dream about killing? Death? Monstrous things that shouldn't be?"

Nymeria's lips pursed. "Yes. But you would not love death so, not if you'd seen the creatures it attracts."

Griggori's smile faded. "You know what this glass does."

It was not a question.

"It does as it was programmed," she replied. "But it doesn't feel like one of mine."

"It isn't."

"I would be careful touching it, if I were you," warned Nymeria. "The dark things might see you and mistake you for me. They would eat you alive, and then you would wish you had never held it at all. Your screams would cause them to want to keep you alive so that the black flames might extract every ounce of stain from your soul."

"Dear god, you may *be* my child," he laughed. "Twisted, aren't you?"

"I'm not your child."

"How do you know?"

"Our blood is not alike. I can smell it. We are nothing alike." She truly did not like this man.

"I may decide you should be my daughter anyway. What would you say to that?"

"I would say you were a fool, and that you would regret it. I am not an easy daughter to care for."

"But I think you are the most adorable little girl I've ever met. I bet my brother would say the same."

"He did. After I took his eye." Griggori blinked. Nymeria scowled. "He cried like a girl."

He started laughing. "*You took his eye! Truly?*"

"He called me a demon monkey after. He wouldn't talk to my father, just me."

"*Demon monkey*. That's one of his curses, all right. I think I believe you," he said thoughtfully. "Let me have a look at these tests they've run. I may have to draw some more blood. You're not squeamish about needles, are you?"

"I hate blood."

"Nah. You'll love it one day. This glorious job is the best thing that ever happened to me. I've served as an executioner and a torturer many times. It's quite thrilling. Healing is handy, too, but . . . Eh. Well, it's boring. You'll love being a doctor, I think."

"I'm not going to be a doctor," she hissed.

"Well. You could always find other ways to conceal your killings. It's easier if you're a doctor for this guild, though. Saura has a weakness for her best and brightest, the old hag." Griggori slid over to the computer and flicked it on. He stared at the screen and clicked through several of the tests that had been run previously. "Hmm. Different from the others. I would almost dare to say . . ."

"What are you going to do to us?"

He shrugged. "Likely nothing. Harming your family further will not benefit me. Your mother . . ." His fingers curled when he glanced at her. "I would like to take her back, but honestly, the fighting would get old quickly. She's not what she used to be. Much too kind. After having walked in and seen her amusing that ugly creature at her feet, I find myself quite repulsed. That is not what I loved in her when I first met her. But I won't lie. If John tries anything, I will kill all three of them. But have you anything to worry about? No. You're much too valuable. Too special. A lot of men are looking for you, or something like you, anyway. Saura will be quite happy if what I suspect you are is, in fact, what you are."

"How will you know what I am?"

"I've learned a bit from the Gray Halls, dear child. Don't you worry. Now be still for a moment, while I — " He pricked her skin with the violet shard, and Nymeria winced, pulling away. He caught her arm and held the glass up to the blood that crept from the wound . . . But he frowned when the wound closed itself. "Well, *that's* unusual."

She glared at him as he pulled away. "*That hurt.*"

"Mind your tone," he snarled, and Nymeria's heart quickened. The threat was not idle, and she believed he would try to hurt her if she displeased him. He moved to the microscope, snagged a few more vials, and mixed something with her blood. Blue arced through the glass, and he placed it on the slide. And then he hissed in surprise.

He stood and pulled something from another pocket, and he turned away as her mother's voice broke the silence. "Ny — meria . . . ? Where's my daughter . . . ?" Her head rolled forward, and Griggori took the syringe and pricked her again. She lost consciousness as he pressed several buttons on the device he held.

The device looked somehow familiar. Especially when he held it up to his ear. Nymeria remembered reading about it. A *phone*. From the Modern Civilization. And it worked.

"Saura, I have some interesting news. Some of it, you'll love, some of it, you won't. You didn't tell me she was exactly like the girl in Five Tower, down to the eyes and the lumin cells in her blood. . . . Yeah. The good news is exactly that. But after you neglected to tell me *whose* daughter she is, this won't be cheap. I want triple the usual commission, if you expect me to keep quiet over this and not kill the woman who betrayed me, their kid, and the bastard who slit me navel to brow. . . ." His brows furrowed. "Eiran would pay that, and more, that won't work. . . . *No.*"

Griggori hissed. "Saura, you worthless snake. You want her dissected to see why she heals, and how, that'll cost you, too. And extra, if you expect her to live after. And if you don't pay, a deal is a deal. The kid's mine. . . . I'll find a better buyer. . . . Huh. My dear, I have the leverage, and you know it. . . . Don't try to play me. I've done enough of your dirty work to sink this whole operation of yours. You'll be buried if you cross me, woman."

Nymeria stared at her mother's slumped figure, fearful of Griggori's attention or his wrath, and she fought the smell of her mother's blood. It was doing strange things to her. Her head hurt, her ears ached, she wanted to throw up, she wanted to cry . . . But she could do none of those things as Griggori snarled and continued his conversation with her father's boss.

He looked at her mother, and that evil smile of his returned. "I've heard rumors all over the place. How many people are after her gift, do you think? . . . Oh, quite a few more than that. . . ." He laughed. "That's better. You expel him from the guild, I'll make it a little cheaper. I want to watch his merry little life fall apart, starting with my taking his daughter from him. . . . Yeah. . . . So you *do* have some negotiation skill. . . . No, Jeana is damaged goods. I'm not interested. The other fugitives were worthless. Consider it recompense. Once you pay me, I'll give her back to you, along with my research. And if you want exclusive rights to that information, well . . . I'd better be paid handsomely, haven't I?"

He hung up.

"I'm not going with you, if you think to take me away," Nymeria said.

His look promised he would take pleasure in his cruelty. "Saura has a very big decision to make."

Nymeria felt her mouth twitch, and an icy chill crept along her spine like a prickling midnight grim spider. She shivered intensely, and a black shadow curled through the room. The light over her flickered and then shattered, and Griggori leapt back when several pieces sliced him. He grabbed the bedrail to keep himself upright — he jerked his hand away with a yelp when it burned him.

The anger within her boiled to the surface, pooled with her fear, and then overwhelmed it . . . She breathed deeply as the room seemed to tilt, but vertigo never claimed her. A cold laugh bubbled from her lips, but it wasn't her own amusement that had forced the sound from her. Griggori looked from his shaking, burned hand to her.

"*What?*" he swore. But confusion washed over him when he saw the shadows coil about her dangerously.

Nymeria felt the *other thing* stirring within her, raging like a great storm. She feared it, knowing it would take control of her if she touched it again, but she was falling into the dark abyss that was its presence within her, and it was terrifying. She was losing herself to it as words came from some place she'd been unaware existed. "The death that stains you is inadequate. Your sins are weak," she heard herself say. And when she blinked, she saw burned upon the backs of her eyelids a vision of blood and death, and of gore, and she tasted just a drop of the ocean of agony she'd felt when the shadow of Mihai had taken her. "Even the *Dark Ones* have no craving for your diluted soul." Her smile grew wider. "You shouldn't have locked yourself in here with us."

When Griggori's brows drew together and he took a step back, the *other thing* in her stirred again.

"You shouldn't have hurt them. If I were you, I would try to run."

Griggori snorted. "You expect me to be afraid of you? You're a child."

"Get out."

His brow rose.

The anger in her became stronger. "Get out."

Griggori stepped forward, annoyed, and he grabbed her hands when she tried to push him away. He tried to make her look at him, but she turned her head. "Look at me," he commanded. "Your eyes have gone as black as the abyss. Is this what you really are? Is the green to draw prey, and the black to kill?" The sound of his voice was thrilled and pleased, as if he desired more twisted secrets be revealed. It was as though the thing inside her inspired his evil stain to crave the presence of another, more twisted being. It was almost fatherly in a strange sense.

Her fingers twitched as the nerve endings in them sizzled, and the bed rail began to twist. She could hear his heartbeat. She could smell his blood. It was so sour that her jaws clenched involuntarily. *"Get out,"* she snarled, and when another wave of anger rolled through her, she looked past him, at the door. The doors began to creak and groan, and then they splintered. They blackened where the metal grew hot, and then they began to glow as red as coals in a fire.

Griggori looked over his shoulder. He let her go and snatched another syringe with a frantic curse. But the vial shattered in his hand before he could put it down. He spun.

"Get out!" Nymeria shouted.

He grabbed her arm and yanked it straight. "No, you don't, you little demon bitch," he snarled. "You're not going to be infecting me with it, too. I quite like my mind intact — "

Nymeria clawed his face — and then her teeth sank into his wrist. Griggori shouted as his blood coursed over her tongue. Her teeth snapped tighter at the taste, and her fingers curled over his wrist as she bit harder. He struck her and jerked free, and the syringe clattered to the floor and rolled away, into the darkness under the bed.

She fell to the floor, shivering, and curled inward. *"Get out,"* she hissed, and her fingers dug into her temples. *"Get out . . . Get it out . . . Get it out!"*

As the room began to drift in and out of focus, she swore she saw her father's face, pale as candle wax. He said something, and then he and Griggori were fighting. Something broke on the floor by her as her eyes drifted closed.

In the dream that arose, she stood at the center of a field littered with bodies. She was Mihai, and blood ran down his chin as his fangs left the throat of another victim. The blood was like fire, and it scorched him as his mind whirled in chaos and in pain. Bones broke in the throat he crushed in his hand as a tremor rolled through him, and the sputtering creature he held fell silent. He let go, and the woman's body joined the field with the rest, devoid of blood, of Spirit, and of soul.

And the world lit aflame — first from within, and then from without.

His claws raked at his temples until they drew blood, and he screamed as pain and rage rolled through him anew. The things in him screamed also, and the ground trembled about him. A single pale blue ribbon of bright Spirit pulsed through the air about him, crackling violently, hissing where it touched the falling rain.

And then he was clawing at his wrists, hissing, *"Kae'da vos . . . Kae'da vos . . ."*

Get it out . . . Get it out . . .

CHAPTER FIFTY

*F*LIGHT

JOHN HELD GRIGGORI BY THE THROAT. All he could think was that Griggori was supposed to be *dead*. His fist found Griggori's jaw twice more before the bastard lost his balance and fell, nearly dragging John with him.

Then John heard Jeana's moan. He went to his family, and he checked his son's pulse as he picked him up. "Thank god," he stammered, relieved as he held Jamie. He didn't see any injuries upon his son besides a very red mark across Jamie's face. That red mark was in the shape of Griggori's hand. Rage shook him as he undid the knots Griggori had tied around John's wife. He kissed her forehead, praying she would wake, that he could get his family out quickly. "Jeana — Jeana, wake up. It's me. Are you all right? Are you hurt anywhere else?" The blood still oozing from her forehead glistened, and his hand shook when he reached for it gently to check to see whether the injury extended into her hair. It didn't, but she winced at the barest touch. His teeth felt as though they might shatter against one another.

"She's on the floor," Jeana whispered. She fell forward dizzily, and John caught her. When her voice failed her, she resorted to using her hand to communicate again. *I don't think he's hurt her terribly*, she signed.

Jeana took their son and held him close to her, as if he was the most precious thing she'd ever held, as if she'd seen him almost die. Jamie was still unconscious in her arms, but he was breathing regularly.

Tears clung to their son's lashes still, and his eyes were swollen and red with grief. Jeana again forced her voice to work for her, to what extent she could. "He sedated us. I'm sorry, John — "

She struggled to force another word out, and her tears mixed with the blood upon the side of her face as she looked up at him.

If he hadn't left, he would have been there when Griggori had come in. He would have been able to stop him from harming her and their children. His throat closed. This was his fault. He shouldn't have left them all alone. And Griggori should have been dead.

"I'm going to kill him," he said, and he grabbed the microscope and broke it. He took the largest piece in his hand, and he gripped it. "After I find out why Saura kept him alive and sent him in here *knowing* our history with him. Knowing what he did to you. To our child."

"Don't you dare kill him with our children in the same room," she croaked. "I don't want them to witness his murder. You'll scar them for the rest of their lives."

John had already turned from her. Griggori was currently trying to cast off his vertigo to stand on his feet again. He staggered back as John clutched the broken scope, and the bastard held up his hands. Hands that had brought harm to John's family twice now. All that John could see was touched with red as his rage beat at the inside of his skull.

"I did what I had to do so I could do my job," said Griggori. "She should have stood aside. And I've left your family in peace for several years, have I not? I could have come back years ago and finished what I started."

"Why would you dare come near us again after all this time?" snarled John. When Griggori had the gall to laugh, John struck him. Griggori's head jerked to the side, and he hit the wall.

John twisted in time to avoid the knife that appeared in the other doctor's hands, and the two of them toppled to the floor as Griggori tried several times to stab him. The blade caught John's cheek, sliced his shoulder, and skirted his wrist, and then he caught Griggori's forearm and struck him with the scope again. He couldn't throw the bigger man off him. Griggori was much stronger than he'd been years before, and he was much more experienced fighting. He fought the way a man fought if he'd faced death more than once, and John was on the losing end of the battle.

The knife sliced John's jaw, and hot blood poured from the wound, and then the blade began to inch closer and closer to his heart. He tried to throw Griggori, and instead, the knife began to bite, and then it began to sink deeper. John gasped and writhed under the blade, pushing with all his strength. He wasn't strong enough to pull the blade back out of his flesh, and it continued to pierce unbearably deeper.

Nymeria's shriek startled them both, and the blade skirted sideways and broke when it struck the floor point-first. For the first time, since the day they had first met over a decade before, John saw something flash across the bastard's face that looked like genuine worry. Griggori looked up, letting John go as if intending to abandon their fight. "The girl — "

John kicked him off balance and rolled onto him. "No, you don't!" he snarled. He wrestled the broken knife away, trusting Jeana would care for their daughter as he pinned the murderer under him.

"The girl is hurt!" cried Griggori. "Get off me!"

John held the knife to Griggori's throat. "Why did Saura call *you* to look at my daughter?! Or who did you murder in order to take their place? What is so important about Nymeria that you would dare to risk showing yourself here?"

Griggori laughed under him. "Saura's known about me for a long while. She gave me the opportunity to use my skills in Five Tower after you tried to kill me. She's always valued my talents. I'm your better, John, and I always will be. She knows I can get results when you cannot. That I can work with men no one else can. She'll throw you out onto the street if it means keeping me alive or giving me what I want. I scratch her back, she scratches mine, so to say."

"Why?!"

"Your daughter's curse," Griggori hissed. "Saura wants to know if it is dangerous. And it is. But the stupid bitch still doesn't believe it was no bomb that killed Ellie Mae and Robert. All she cares about is the fact that your daughter's highly mutated biology is unlike any other we've seen. It's alien. *Demon.* Whatever you want to call it. Your *daughter* is a monster, John. You're raising a creature that only *looks* human. She should have been *mine*!"

"My daughter is no demon, you foul-mouthed piece of shit, and she doesn't belong to you! She's a little girl in need of medical care, and you came in here and harmed my wife and son, and then you raised your hand against her!"

"Your daughter's blood is barely human, you fool. There is magic in her. *Raw power.* She carries lumin cells in her blood, which only become visible when someone like her is unstable or dying. You don't know how to care for her, and you have done nothing as it has begun to tear her apart from the inside, out. She has the madness! That's where it starts!"

"You're a liar!" John grated as he strained against Griggori, fighting to keep the broken knife where it was, against Griggori's throat. Yet he knew he'd seen the strange phenomenon in Nymeria's blood — he just couldn't bring himself to believe what Griggori said was true. It couldn't be. There was no such thing as magic, or curses. The idea was too chilling. It whispered everything his daughter had ever said was true, which was impossible. Magic did not fit with the natural world. It defied logic, and there was no way something so unchecked could exist. "There is no such thing as magic, you maniac!"

But what he said never fazed Griggori's conviction.

"It's everywhere, you idiot! If the *others* come for her, you're all going to die," snarled Griggori. "You thought what *I* did was monstrous? I have seen horrors, the likes of which you cannot imagine. You should consider yourself beyond blessed that I would not dare subject that little girl to it. I would never give her to them."

"Do you seriously believe Saura, or *anyone*, will believe this shit?!" John asked. But Griggori laughed again.

"It doesn't matter if Saura believes me. Her master will eventually start looking into this mess, and he'll realize that little girl nearly destroyed this place. There is black glass everywhere. How could he miss it? Her power is going to keep building in her until one day it explodes, and the fallout will be enough to wipe this continent from the face of the Earth. He'll kill her before he allows such a thing to occur. He won't see the guild he built be ruined by some creature child."

Griggori felt the tremor in John and laughed in his face, even when John finally forced the broken blade's jagged point to press into his throat. "There is no *Master*, Griggori. They only tell those stories to the apprentices to — "

"Who will be to blame, do you think, when he finds out that her illness is because of *you*?"

John felt the breath rush out of him as Griggori repeated words he could never have known to repeat. "My daughter's illness is not because of a *curse*, *damn you*! Or because of me!"

"Then why has your brother abandoned his duty and gone in search of *Rhael and Gabriel*? Oh, I know all about that. I know Caol's stupid lap dog helped him get all those violet-eyed freaks out of Five Tower and smuggled his research out of the city before the Bright Night." Realization glinted in Griggori's wicked eyes, and he started laughing, even as the blade drew blood. "She's not either of ours. Nymeria is that little girl, isn't she? The little Five Tower girl was never burned alive. You must have switched the bodies. My god, this is *rich*, isn't it?! She belongs to no one! She's a demon's orphan! A creature of darkness, abandoned by her own kind!"

John turned the knife and shoved it downward, into Griggori's belly, just beneath the xiphoid process, where the pain would be felt most vividly as the blade bit. Griggori jerked, attempting to gasp as he recoiled, and blood sprang forth as John twisted it and then ripped it free. "My daughter can never go back to Five Tower, Griggori, and you are *never* going to lay another hand on her. Come after us again, and I will eviscerate you in front of everyone, and *nothing* will keep me from it. Next time, I will not care if my children watch me *violently* murder an evil man!" He then slammed the pommel against Griggori's temple, and the bastard lost consciousness, blood oozing from his belly, through his fingers and clothes.

"We're leaving," hissed John as he panicked. He rushed to his daughter and picked her up, and he helped Jeana from the chair. Her legs were unsteady, and he supported her as she carried their son. "As soon as I am sure the three of you are safe," he promised, "I'll get the men and tell them what's happened."

"Where will we go after?" asked Jeana. "You'll be kicked from the guild."

"I won't be. When I know you're safe, I'll be coming back. I'll present our case to the High Council, and they'll have Saura arrested for treason. Most of them have already acknowledged Wylem's challenge anyway. Once they know what she's done, the rest will follow suit. They'll agree it is necessary to remove her from power. But we must hurry before anyone finds out what happened here. Before Griggori wakes and patches himself up and gets back to her." He looked back at the injury he'd inflicted, and then he added. "Not that moving about will be pleasant for him for a while."

Under the cover of the darkest shadows of the night, John and Jeana crept through the maze of hallways and stairs and candlelit caverns. Their son began to cry, and Jeana attempted to soothe him. Their daughter stirred as John left Jeana and the children in a secret alcove hidden among the tombs so that he could search for Wylem. His teeth mashed together in his anger when he heard what she told her mother. When he heard the fear in her voice. "Griggori meant to sell me, Mother."

"*What . . . ?*" Jeana's whispered apprehension echoed John's own. He wanted to turn back, but he knew time was of the essence as he crept into the hallway, looking this way and that.

"He told Saura she would have to pay him more to dissect me, if she wanted him to keep me alive . . ."

John could no longer hear what else his daughter had to say as their voices faded into the echoing chasms he navigated. His heart raced, and his skin remained damp with perspiration, and anger beat at him relentlessly. He ducked from acolytes and apprentices and morticians, and he threaded a delicate path toward another of the hallways that was lined with guest rooms, and all the while, he wondered why Saura had allowed Griggori to live. He considered that she'd already known Griggori had sold children who'd contracted the Violet. She'd said so herself. And he realized she might intend as badly as Griggori, that she might be in *league* with Five Tower in some way. The idea was hair raising.

John hurried toward Wylem's quarters, knowing Wylem's room would be the closest and would offer the easiest, most discreet access. He crouched behind barrels and crawled under stacks of grates, and then at last crept through an empty hallway that was devoid of light. John fumbled for the doorknob and turned it quietly when he found it, and he slipped in like a robber in the night. He took such caution to close the door that every small creaking catch made his pulse thunder and his heart jump. But not even a mouse would have heard the tiny sounds.

"Wylem," he whispered as he turned to face the dark room. He nearly jumped out of his own skin when Wylem, standing over him like some giant, threatening creature of the night, withdrew. John heard Wylem's blade slide back into its sheath, and he took a deep breath and then exhaled.

"Not a wise thing to do, sneaking about in the dark, John. Or entering another's quarters when you are not expected," said Wylem quietly. John heard the heavy dagger scuff the bedside table as Wylem laid it down. "What's happened? Something is dead wrong, if you're here like this, and at this time of night."

"Saura's betrayed my family. We're leaving, and we need your help."

There was a long, heavy silence after that, and John waited impatiently, unsure whether he would have an ally in his travel companion. Wylem and Saura had always been close despite their most recent quarrel. To have come to him was a bit of a risk, but John knew he was short of options.

"Are you absolutely certain she's betrayed you?" Wylem sat on his bed, and John heard him rifle through his things. In the blackness, he could only make out the faintest outline of Wylem's movements, of the clothing he was grabbing. "Why would she possibly want to hurt any of you?"

"She doesn't care about hurting us, Wylem. It's about Nymeria."

"But how do you know she's betrayed you?"

"Griggori is working for her," John hissed. "He hurt my wife and son when he tried to get to my daughter, and then he hurt Nymeria. Saura's had him stationed in Five Tower all this time, knowing it is the one place we cannot go. He's been working in secret and staying out of sight when he comes here. No one else knew he was alive, either, unless they've been in league with her over it. Wylem, they have some kind of deal with some people in Five Tower, and he meant to take my daughter and then sell her. Saura was going to pay him to dissect her!"

Wylem swore. He sounded as disgusted as John felt. *"Dissect her?* Heavens — she's a *child*, not an animal! And do you mean *the Griggori*? The man who abducted your wife and then tried to kill her? The Griggori you killed almost six years ago? *That* Griggori?"

"Yes," John hissed. "That Griggori. There is no other, Wylem. He's working for Saura!"

Wylem took a deep breath, as if connections were occurring in his head. "So he's her contact in Five Tower. Well, did you actually kill him this time?"

"No. Jeana wouldn't allow it with the kids there. She's never wanted that kind of violence around them. Otherwise, I'd have strung him up by his entrails to ensure it was done. Cut off his head," said John bitterly. "He wouldn't come back from that."

Wylem growled deep in his throat as he threw on a shirt and bent to find a shoe. "You should have killed him anyway. You know he's only going to come after you again. Hell, he should have been executed years before the catastrophe with Jeana ever happened. He's a fucking *serial killer*." Wylem pulled on his second boot and stood, and he grabbed his bag. As quietly as possible, he shoved whatever he could reach into it. "I've got your back. Saura's lies are inexcusable, and it calls into question her loyalty to the guild. If you're not mistaken — and I am absolutely sure that you're not — then she's broken one of our most sacred tenets." He sighed. "I never thought there would be a day where I would be fleeing Black Temple in the middle of the night. But let's get your family out of here before that bastard kills them or does anything to that precious little girl of yours."

Wylem opened the door, and John felt the whoosh of air as he slung his bag over his shoulder and stepped out.

"Don't tell me where you'll go. After I get you to Isold, I don't want to know. I'll secure a couple of the men who came with us from Crow Post. I wouldn't trust anyone else."

"Aaron and Thomas are here," said John.

"I know. They're the first on my list. We'll need to get you out as quickly as possible. I'll accompany you to the stables and help get the horses ready, and then I'll go back for them. We'll meet you in Isold."

"If Saura realizes you're helping us — "

"If we're not there an hour after you get to Isold, then leave without us. Go wherever you need to go. We'll head back to Crow Post and tell Dr. Shipwright what's going on, and we'll help ensure the news gets to your brother, and to his wife and daughter."

"Thank you, Wylem. I'd hoped you would not turn us away. I know you and Saura have only recently quarreled."

"My closeness to Saura never meant I was her lackey. I've always held a stronger loyalty to you and your brother, even as hot-tempered as the blood in your family runs. And your daughter is special. She needs to be cared for. Not *dissected*." When Wylem shuddered, John could feel the anger rolling off him. "Oh, do I have words for that copper-clawed cow."

CHAPTER FIFTY-ONE

*A*FLAME

THEY RODE THROUGH THE whirling mist on the backs of quickly tiring horses, Jeana with Jamie, and John holding Nymeria against himself to keep her from falling from the beast's back. The towers they passed loomed over them, but under the partially obscured moon and silver clouds, neither arrows nor armor, nor other weapons, glinted with any reflected light. The only things that seemed to move in the breeze were the treetops, the rolling mist, and the great black banners hanging from the dark towers, Black Temple's sigil invisible upon them in the night.

No one rode out to stop them as they passed by tower after tower. No one shouted down to them, or rose to greet the noise of their horses' hooves beating against the earth and stirring up mud and rainwater. None seemed to be alerted by the owls and ravens that were startled to flight.

No torches were lit.

John's neck prickled with both perspiration and accumulated precipitation as he held on to his daughter, his eyes flitting about, searching every watch tower for any sign of life. Adrenaline slithered through his blood, until his heart knocked vehemently against his ribs at the sight of every new tower.

Lightning shot across the sky, and the heavens rumbled, and the wind picked up.

"They're all dead," whimpered Nymeria. She was shivering still from her last episode just a half hour before, when she'd started screaming about Leviathans trying to rip her apart. She had tried to get off the horse midstride. "There's blood *everywhere*," she wept.

John was unsure anymore whether she was talking about the towers they passed, or if she was talking about the Leviathans or the dark things, or if, instead, she meant the man who'd taken her during Ellie's wedding. Jeana kept looking over at their daughter, worry creeping through every shadow that stretched across her face as they rode toward Isold.

He was unsure whether his daughter felt him trembling, or if she heard how his breath raked against his lungs as he held her. He prayed his wife would not notice how afraid he was, because she looked to him for strength. He could not crumble in front of his family, not when they needed him to lead them to safety. But the thought of not being able to care for his daughter was like a hot knife in his heart, and it was hard to breathe because of the gripping pain. Saura had betrayed them. They had nowhere left to go, except Arsennia, and that city was months away, and in the opposite direction.

He had to get his family away from everyone who intended harm, and there were so very many who did. And it was his fault for bringing Nymeria that Griggori now wanted her. John dared to glance at his wife and saw from the moonlight that the blood upon her head was still there, still glistening and wet. Or was it sweat that made that black shadow shine? His throat closed. If he hadn't left them in that room alone, Griggori wouldn't have been able to hurt any of them.

And he couldn't stop thinking about how Saura might be involved with Five Tower in some way. Griggori worked there, and he'd sold children who'd contracted the illness to Five

Tower. She'd admitted that to John. He couldn't discard his fear, even as they rode through increasingly unguarded territory. The towers should have been manned. Had Saura recalled them? Was she taking a page from the attacks on the guild elsewhere, where the Enforcers had withdrawn? Were enemies coming? Had she invited death into the guild? He didn't know what was going on, and every fear gripped him tighter as he held his daughter and rode urgently for safety. For some place where they could hide.

Another blinding vein of lightning coursed through the bellies of the clouds that were rolling in.

As they turned about another tower and the road began to rise higher into the hills, John realized he could smell smoke. His heart dropped into his stomach, and he tried desperately to deny what he feared as thoughts of Saura fell to the back of his mind. But the smoke grew stronger as they got closer to the top of the hills. He prayed against it until he was biting his tongue and tasting his own blood.

Something was very wrong. He kept thinking about those empty towers.

And then, as the treetops revealed the sky, and they began to crest the hill beneath the highest of the towers, he saw the red and yellow glow and the smoke pouring into the sky. Their horses veered away from the thickening smoke as they began to descend. The beasts complained of the overwhelming smell of ash and the sound of battle raging. Gunfire pierced the night from a single weapon, several short bursts that sounded like thunder hitting a wall and being dashed apart. But there were no screams, no roars, no battle cries.

Then they saw many of the missing tower guards. Most of them were dead or dying, strewn about the forest and the road. They hadn't been recalled; they'd died trying to drive back an enemy about which no warning had been sounded. As Isold came into view, they saw the fire consuming every rooftop, every stable, every fenced yard. It had spread into the trees and was winding its way up the hill, and the wind fanned it across the valley and up the next hillside. The thunder that rolled next was loud and long lasting, like an agonized death rattle. A large raindrop splattered his wrist.

An arrow whizzed by, just missing John. He gasped and pulled the reins. "Jeana!" he cried. "This way!"

But another arrow soon followed the first, and this time, it struck his horse in the neck. The beast staggered and reared, wild-eyed and screeching, and John and Nymeria toppled from its back. He yelped as his knee struck the old pavement. Nymeria curled up small against him, trembling intensely, her eyes wide as she saw the fire about them. She was hyperventilating, though she seemed too afraid to scream. She winced as Jeana's horse wheeled about and circled them.

"Jeana!" John called. He tore his gun from his hip and threw it to her. She caught it as their attacker slipped from tree to tree about them, another arrow fitted and ready to take aim. John clutched at his knee when he tried to get up, to get Nymeria out of the way of any bolt that could take her life. "Get behind me, Nymeria," he commanded. "Behind me, now!" Jeana's horse pranced as she placed herself between John and their attacker.

Something glinted about their attacker's neck, catching the firelight. A glass chain, he realized. Their attacker was one of the *Merciful*, one of the monks from Aelynhold. The hood curtained most of the man's face, and John was unable to tell which one of them he was considering shooting first.

John pulled Nymeria's black hair from her cheek. "Nymeria, look at me. *Nymeria*."

She wasn't listening. Fright had made her pale, and tears flowed down her cheeks as she stared off into the flames. "They're all dead," she wept, shaking her head.

"Nymeria, get behind me! I don't want you to get shot!" He tried again to pull her behind him, but she resisted, panicked.

Jeana pulled the trigger. The shot missed, exploding instead against the tree the monk darted behind.

Nymeria cried out, covering her ears, and she shut her eyes as she began to cry again. Jamie remained silent, too afraid to cry aloud. John rolled over onto his other leg and placed himself between Nymeria and the monk. Jeana held out her hand, leaning forward. John grabbed his daughter and hoisted her to put her atop the horse, his bruised knee protesting every movement — an arrow sliced through his calf, and he and Nymeria hit the ground. The horse skirted sideways, startled, and Jeana unleashed several more shots.

"Get Jamie out of here!" he shouted. "We'll catch up!" Jeana shook her head, refusing, but John couldn't risk letting his wife and son remain in the line of fire. "Go!"

Nymeria stared at him as he grabbed the arrow shaft and broke it. She flinched when he clenched his teeth and imprisoned the curse that nearly escaped as fire shot through the wound. Jeana dropped the gun as another arrow struck her shoulder. She nearly fell from the horse.

"*GO!!!*" he roared.

Jeana gripped the reins, looking down at him, her face a mask of pain and fear, and she kicked the horse and rode away.

John drew his knife and put it in his teeth, and he scrambled for the gun, dragging Nymeria with him. The next arrow grazed the side of his throat, slicing a shallow trench that spilled just as much blood as Griggori's blade had.

Nymeria recoiled from him.

The black color flickered as the green in her eyes faded, and the fear upon her face became twisted with anger. "Father," she whispered. Her fingers curled into fists as she stared at the blood coming from his throat. "Stay here while I kill him." She took his knife from between his teeth before he could stop her.

"Nymeria!" John shouted. He tried to grab her, but she'd already darted into the flames. He snatched his gun up and used the tree to get up. He staggered as white-hot pain shot through him when he stepped out from behind the tree, and he aimed the gun, searching wildly for the monk. His entire being shook when he saw the monk pull the cord on his bow. "*NYMERIA!*"

She was looking at the point of the arrow; it was aimed directly at her.

John took another breath to scream again . . .

But something strange happened. His daughter vanished right before them, like a ghost — a candleflame, winking out of existence.

The monk staggered back . . . and then he lowered the bow . . . and then he looked down. The monk touched his throat, and when his hand came away, it was soaked in red, and trembling. John saw claw marks there when the monk drew his hood back, staggering.

Nymeria had appeared behind the attacker, and she walked up behind him, her eyes as black as obsidian. She gripped John's knife with a bloody hand and slit the back of the monk's knees as if she knew exactly where to strike. As if she'd done it a thousand times. He toppled with a gurgled cry, and then Nymeria turned upon him and took his throat with her teeth. The monk screamed.

John flinched when something wet splattered upon his shoulder, and he accidentally pulled the trigger. The monk's scream went quiet, and Nymeria recoiled as two more raindrops splattered against John's forehead. The rain was finally beginning to fall, he realized. And his daughter was staring at the blood upon her hands and backing away. She spun from the body.

Her knees struck the ground, and she threw up. She started wiping the blood away. "*Get it off,*" she said, her voice shaking with panic. "*Get if off! Get it off of me!!!*"

John staggered closer, holstering his gun, and he took her face with his hands. "Nymeria, look at me. Let me see."

When she looked up, the green had returned to her eyes and the black was gone. "Father, I killed him," she said through her tears. She was horrified at what she'd done. "I killed him — I don't know why I wanted to kill him!"

"*I shot him*," he said. "You didn't kill him, I did. We're both going to be okay, but we need to find your mother."

"But your leg, you're hurt — "

"I need you to calm down, Nymeria. Breathe, okay? Focus on staying calm and on staying alive." There was blood all over her face. She was an unsightly picture, but at least she was alive. John didn't care about anything, except that they'd killed the monk before she'd been murdered by him. "*Breathe.*" He wiped the blood from her face as she nodded. But her gaze kept slipping to his leg, and her hand kept clenching and unclenching.

She reached out and tore the arrow from his leg, and he gasped, hitting the ground. John hadn't even the time to curse or reprimand her before a scream from nearby startled them both. He grabbed Nymeria without a second thought and pulled her with him, into the brush. When he peered out into the flaming trees, he saw one of Isold's stable hands crawling away from another monk, who stood over the injured man while wielding a knife. "Don't kill me!" the young man was weeping. "Please, don't kill me — "

There was no mercy. The monk bent and began to gut him without a word. And John covered Nymeria's ears and forced her to look away. The screams intensified, until John grabbed her by the wrist and pulled her from the brush without fearing being heard over the cacophony. They raced away from the murderer as he committed to his butchery of the innocent man.

At the edge of Isold, John caught sight of his wife and his son. She'd managed to secure two horses for them. She was no longer riding her black mare, but a brown one with a black mane and tail. With a start, he realized she'd faced the danger of getting herself and their son killed so she could bring that other horse back to him and Nymeria. She hadn't listened, she'd just gone to get the other horse. His heart swelled, although he also tasted bile because she'd put herself and their son at such risk. He was relieved and angry with her at the same time.

"Be quiet," he warned Nymeria. "Just follow my lead, okay?"

Nymeria nodded, and she followed as John crept through the burning city. They followed the road where the shadows were deepest, and they took alleyways the fire hadn't yet reached.

The rain was not heavy enough to put the fires out, which spread despite it. But it did cover the squelching noise of the mud sucking at their feet.

John crept through the back of one of the shops, broke the window, and whistled out it. He saw Jeana's head turn, and he signed to her. He saw the relief that washed over her. She signed back to him that there were a lot more monks near the small tower Isold used for much of its business. Where inventory and other documents and activities were often scrutinized and managed. John moved to another widow and lifted the blinds where he knew he should have a clear view of the area. "Tell your mother to circle around, to meet us on the eastern side of the gate. It's open, and there is no one there. The monks have moved on. They're searching the rest of the buildings. We need to move while we still can."

He looked over his shoulder briefly, and he saw his daughter signing to Jeana. Nymeria nodded to him, then. "She's going. She said be careful." Nymeria wiped her eyes again. "Are we going to die? Are they going to kill us?"

"Not if we can help it."

"But there are more monks on the other side of the gate."

John shuddered, not wanting to think about how his daughter knew it. He could see nothing. "You know how I told you not to bite anyone?" She grimaced and looked away. "I'm glad you did what you did, Nymeria. You bought us time twice now. But don't you *ever* put yourself in that kind of danger again, do you hear me?"

She nodded. "I don't want to think about what I did, or what happened."

"Agreed. Let's go."

Nymeria followed him without another word, and when they reached the shack by the gate, the flames had crept along its timbers, and the roof had caved in. Jeana and Jamie arrived moments later, and John hugged her, breathing deeply against her hair. He was so glad she was alive. He then looked at her shoulder. She'd already taken the arrow from it and packed the wound and bandaged it. Then he realized the horses were saddled with bulging packs, and he was stunned.

"Did you fill those packs from the stores?" he laughed quietly. "You're a madwoman, taking such a risk!"

She kissed him on the cheek and then nodded to the wall.

He held up his hand, though. "We need to be careful, and quiet." He glanced at his daughter. "Just in case." Jeana nodded. John hoisted his daughter onto the horse's saddle, and then he took Jamie from his wife. "Stay quiet, both of you," he commanded gently. "We're almost out of danger, but not yet. And Nymeria, keep your head down."

Jeana reached up to the saddle of the other horse and drew from the bag there three cloaks and two glass chains she'd taken from dead monks. She threw one about Nymeria to hide her, and John took one and threw it about his shoulders as Jeana donned her own. He shook his head when she reached out to place one of the chains about his neck. "No, that'll catch the light. We shouldn't have to get close enough to have to blend with them." She shrugged and tossed the chains.

They made their way toward the gate, and as they did so, they began to hear swords striking against shields and swords. There weren't many fighting, by the sound of it, and then the clanging came to an end. And then they heard a woman's voice, loud and clear. "Hold him down!" the woman said.

Jeana and John emerged from behind the wall, and his heart flew into his throat as they quietly edged forward. There were perhaps thirty monks striding toward another of Isold's guards. The man was battered and bruised, and he was shouting obscenities and curses at the monks who'd disarmed him. His face was covered in blood, but he didn't seem seriously uninjured. He still fought fervently against them.

The ground was littered with dead men, and the army of monks never noticed Jeana or John, their horses, or the children they hid with them as they slowly edged by. John's pulse pounded against his eardrums, and he swallowed against the hard knot in his throat. Jeana gripped his hand as he prayed desperately that the horses would not make a sound.

Then the woman who'd spoken stepped forward from her men, and she removed her hood. John's breath rushed out when he saw that her eyes glowed the brightest violet. His hand clenched Jeana's involuntarily, and she looked up and also saw.

"*The Violet*," whispered Jeana.

John nodded and pulled on the reins as he and Jeana began to take bigger steps. They had to get out of here *now*.

The violet-eyed woman sheathed her sword as the surviving Isold guard struggled against the men holding him. "I want you to deliver a message for me," she said, and her lips curled as though she had enjoyed every drop of blood they'd shed. "I want you to go into Black Temple and tell them this, word for word. My father, the rightful Lord of Aelynhold, the King of Thieves, has killed his usurper and retaken his throne. He demands reparation from Black Temple for Reid Ivan's crimes against Aelynhold, or the range commander will be executed in two weeks' time, and the *Merciful* will move against the Ivan family."

John's blood had turned to ice. *Reid?*

Jeana pulled at his hand, but John couldn't move.

What could his brother have done? What crimes could he have committed? What he'd just heard couldn't be true. This had to be a farce!

"*John*," whispered Jeana. "John, come *on*."

"Then we will kill every last person in Black Temple, including the Pale Serpent herself. I'll wear her copper claws as a trophy. I hear they are quite beautiful, and I want them," said the woman icily.

"You won't win against Black Temple," hissed the Isold guard. "You have no idea who you are messing with."

"I saw little resistance here," she laughed. "I doubt Black Temple will be much different. More children, and they don't fight well. They didn't here."

"You can burn in the deepest pits of the Seventh Hell," swore the guard. "I won't — "

"If you don't deliver the message, we'll burn the kids we took here alive, or we'll give them to the wolfmen to eat. You will deliver the message, and in haste . . ." She frowned, and she looked up, searching the monks' faces. Her smile grew wider. "Oh, my . . . I sense a child who carries the Violet nearby."

"John," whispered Jeana.

John flinched when he felt his daughter's hand touch his shoulder. "Father, get moving. That woman is not like the others. She senses me, I can feel it. She's *looking* for me. We'll go save Uncle Reid. We won't let him die. We can't."

He took her hand and squeezed it, and he took a breath and nodded. They edged back into the shadows of the night. As soon as they were able, John and Jeana mounted, and they rode for Aelynhold. Two weeks. It was not enough time. If what the woman had said was true, they were going to execute his brother anyway.

CHAPTER FIFTY-TWO

Haunted Road

THEY HAD ESCAPED THE CEMETERY without incident in the early hours of the dawn, and by late evening, the mouth of the Haunted Road yawned before them. John grew restless as he reined his horse in, and he wiped the cold rain from his eyes. Jeana drew her mount alongside his, concerned.

"We have to go back in the cave?" whimpered Jamie to his mother.

"It's the fastest way," said Nymeria.

What's wrong? signed Jeana.

"We could make numerous wrong turns in there without any light," said John, and his horse shifted, moving sideways, its eyes wide as thunder tore through the clouds and clapped their ear drums angrily again. The beast's hooves splashed in the rainwater that bled across the road, from the steep mountain over the tunnel's black mouth. "It may be a single path through the mountain, but the Haunted Road is dangerous without light." He grimaced. "And Reid doesn't have the kind of time we can gamble with." He knew Saura had ordered most of the old vehicles inside the Haunted Road's cavernous depths to be moved about for better defense. He wasn't sure whether he should risk riding in unaided. "I may have to make a detour, head back to the last of the towers, near Isold. They've a stockpile of flashlights and torches. But we'll lose almost a day."

"Father, have you learned nothing? I can help with the light," said Nymeria. John and Jeana looked down, surprised by her openness when she removed her pen tool from a sheath she'd strapped to her leg, just below her knee. He'd never noticed it before.

The pen tool looked very different from the last time he'd seen her with it. It was now a slender, elegant tool, with a series of flowing, vine-like filigree that appeared to be sensitive to her touch as her fingers ran over them. The lines began to glow as Nymeria removed the glass heart pendant she kept about her neck.

What is that? Jeana asked when Nymeria's thumb slid over one of the beautiful silver marks upon the tool's surface. Nymeria twisted one of its golden rings, and the broken tip of a diamond shard extended, filled with bright white light. When she drew the point across the hollow pendant, like a pen across a page, the glass heart filled with the light, almost as if the luminescence was a blinding smoke that crept through the glass itself. Nymeria put the pen away and held the pendant out for her mother.

"Magic!" said Jamie, his eyes brightening. "I knew you could do magic! You fixed your pen, too."

"I had to finish it," Nymeria nodded. "I don't trust myself to be able to weave the patterns on my own anymore. But the diamond Uncle Reid gave me generates synthetic Spirit now. It's more stable than the glass, and depending on what I program with the pen casing, it should create anything I need from now on. Even you should be able to use it, if you can learn to understand it. Uncle's books helped me to figure it out." Then Nymeria held the necklace higher, until Jeana took it from her and held it aloft, befuddled by it. Nymeria then addressed them both. "When that grows dim, Mother, return it to me. I'll charge it again. And if we find more glass inside the Haunted Road, Father, I'll make another for us. These won't draw the dark things. I've removed every trace of my threads from it. That's why it's white, not violet."

John shrugged when Jeana tore her eyes from the bright glass dangling from the ribbon of leather that she held. "I don't know where she learned to make them," he sighed. "She made that tool, too."

"It's like a magic wand, like in the books," said Jamie, and he reached for the glass heart. "Can I hold it, Mommy? Please?"

"It's safe for him," said Nymeria as Jamie's fingers closed around the glass. Bright rays of white light filtered through his fingers.

John hesitated, but he finally waved his hand. "Go ahead." Then he studied his daughter worriedly. "How are you holding up, Myria?"

"I don't want to think about what I've been seeing, Father," Nymeria grimaced. "Right now, I'm fine, and besides that, we have more pressing matters than lighting this tunnel," Nymeria said.

Jamie looked up as he held the glass heart delicately, as though it might shatter. "What do you mean?" he whispered.

"Father, can you tell if those monks traveled through these mountains, or through this tunnel? Is there any evidence remaining of hoofprints? Bodies? Broken glass chains? Anything recent?" She looked at her brother. "Jamie, hold that light steady so we can see."

John nodded, for the first time appreciating the unusual depths of his daughter's intelligence. But the rain had already washed away any signs of recent travel. "She has a point, Jeana. Some of those men may still be down there, waiting for stragglers."

"Or dead," Nymeria said. "If they broke the windows to any of the wheeled coffins, they might be dead."

John hadn't even thought of that. If any latent viruses were airborne down there, they could all lose their lives.

"I'll tell you if I smell anything dead or sick," said Nymeria. "Or if I hear anything."

"Like Raven Trail?" John asked slowly.

She nodded. "Yes. Please trust me. I can help. I'm not just a child. I don't know how many times I have to prove that to you; I know things others do not, and after learning about Mihai, I know even more. I am not afraid of these tunnels, Father. I want to rescue Uncle Reid from those despicable men and then find someplace we can all be safe."

Jeana's eyes glittered in the light, and she looked away. But John had seen her chin tremble. He leaned forward and placed a kiss upon the crown of Nymeria's hooded head. Her previous declaration of intended murder came to mind from the night before, along with the gruesome horror upon the face of that monk she'd attacked. John shook himself, trying to erase from his mind having seen blood coating her teeth. "All right. I'll trust you, Myria." The words were harder to say than he'd expected, and his voice came out quieter than he'd intended.

John cleared his throat, and he gripped the reins. Gently prodding the horses forward, they rode through the curtain of water pouring over the tunnel's mouth. The horses picked up their pace as he and Jeana urged them into a trot.

Hours later, amidst the thunderous, rhythmic clattering of horses' hooves and the ever so slowly dimming light, they came upon the first of the vehicles just beyond one of the deep, murky pools of sour water which were far deeper because of the recent rain. "Father," said Nymeria, but John was already reining the horse in to avoid them.

Crystals glittered along the moss-covered pavement. Glass. The windows had been shattered.

Apprehension slithered along his spine, and John felt his heart begin to race. The air here was always amply thick, and cool. A perfect holding temperature for the ancient disease the vehicles had enclosed for years.

There was evidence the monks had come this way, certainly. One of them lay dead, his eyes like black abysses where the light illuminated him. As they came closer, John could tell the eyes were bloodshot, and dried blood was caked along the side of the dead man's neck where he'd bled from his ears. He'd bled from his mouth, his nose, his eyes; he'd died in agony. Even in death, his body was still arched in rigor, his fingers curled, his mouth open as though he were still screaming. His robes were stained and torn.

Before John could stop her, Nymeria had slid from the saddle and landed upon her feet. "Nymeria," he whispered, fearful his voice might carry and be heard if more monks were nearby.

She held up her hand and glared at him as if to tell him to be quiet, and she knelt by the body, examining him. "Not contagious anymore." She leaned forward and took several shards of glass from the road, and then she began to rummage through the vehicle.

When she crawled back out, she held — very carefully — a broken vial of blood. She didn't touch it with her fingers but used instead a long sliver of glass. John was grateful Nymeria knew not to touch it with her bare skin.

Jeana's brows drew together, and her mouth opened. But she hesitated to say anything.

"Yeah," said John quietly. "It looks as though Saura's more determined to unleash hell than she'd let on. Nymeria, please be careful with that. And watch out for more. I'm sure this tunnel has been littered with vials just like it."

"It won't hurt me," she said. "But I will still be careful." She tossed the broken vial back into the vehicle, alongside the shard she'd used to pick it up. "It had Black Temple's mark upon it, Father. And it wasn't coated in dust like everything else in there."

"She claimed she wanted security tighter," explained John to his wife. "She gave orders to call the banners. To Raise the Vial."

"Does she not care how many could die?" asked Jeana. Her voice cracked a little, and she grasped her wounded shoulder and massaged the injury gingerly.

"No." He looked down, and Nymeria held out her hand when she reached them. John leaned forward and grasped her forearm, and he hauled her back onto the horse. "Give me some warning the next time you shoot from the saddle, will you?"

"So you can stop me? Nai."

"How do you know he wasn't contagious?"

"Because I know what killed him."

Chills crawled across his flesh. "How do you know what killed him?"

"Because I know what was in that vial."

"What was in it?"

"My blood."

John was taken aback. He and Jeana shared a look, and then he prodded his daughter some more. "Your blood?"

"Yes. Mixed with something else. I don't know how she got my blood, but I would not mistake it. It turned that disease into something terrible. Your boss, Father, you shouldn't ever trust her again. I think she wanted me to come to Black Temple. I don't think she wanted me to leave."

John had the same feeling. "We're not letting her have you," he said strictly. "Ever. I promise."

"We'll see if you can keep that promise. You're only one person. She has an entire guild behind her, and a lot more dangerous friends than anyone suspects. Let's just focus on getting to Uncle Reid, and then we'll worry about keeping people who want to hurt us away . . ."

Nymeria tensed, and stared ahead, into the darkness.

John followed her gaze, just as the light winked out.

"Shhh . . ." she said quietly.

Then they heard the footsteps, and the wheezing. The steps were awkward, as though something dragged behind every other step. And the breath gurgled, as though the one breathing was all but drowning. "Help me," came a wretched, pitiful voice.

John felt Nymeria reaching for her pen tool as the horse they rode pranced sideways uneasily and knickered nervously, quietly. The beast shook her head.

John drew his gun.

"I know you're here . . . You're a doctor, right?" The person began to cough, and then continued to cough, and hack, and wheeze. "You have to be, you've come from Isold . . ." More coughing, and the footsteps grew closer.

John felt his daughter take the reins gently, and she pulled them to the left. Their horse moved sideways so slowly they seemed almost to drift. "There are more of them," she said. "They're all sick."

"Where are you?" The hoarse voice of another hissed. "We need your help."

"Help us," demanded another.

"I think . . . something is wrong," said another, whose voice bubbled, and the man began to weep. "It's inside of me . . . I think it's inside of me . . . Please take it out."

"Help us!" demanded the previous.

Jeana's horse snorted.

"It's in my blood, in my head . . ." wept the other man. "Get it out of me!"

The one walking as though he was dragging something began to wade through the water before them.

A spark of light ignited when John felt a hand brush across his ankle. He kicked it away, and he sucked in his breath when the flash of light revealed a cluster of substantially diseased, dying men. Some of them were eating their own flesh, chewing on their arms, their wrists. Some of them were walking on broken, maimed limbs, and one of the men who kept coughing expelled a bloody, mucinous mass from his mouth. Dark veins crawled across their flesh, like shadows, and writhed under their skin as though alive.

"Get it out of me," wept the man who was clawing deeply at his flesh — John could see the bones protruding from his left arm where his fingers tore through the muscle and the fibrous cords of bloody sinew.

All of it, from that single flash, John saw. And his heart rose into his throat as fear struck him. He did not know what disease had caused this, or what madness had taken them all, but they were all in a similar state, and it was nauseating, and it made his skin crawl. Even as a doctor, his only instinct was to get away from them — to kill them to keep them from touching him or his family.

It seemed his daughter had the same instinct regarding them, and so did his wife.

"Go!" shouted Nymeria.

Neither John nor Jeana hesitated. But neither did the horde of sick men. The diseased mass collided with the horses, and John felt nails rake at him, and he kicked off a man who tried to bite him. Blinding light from one of Nymeria's new shards sent the monks scurrying away and into the darkness around them, all of them screaming as their flesh sizzled and burnt from it — he swore the screams were inhuman. They were not like anything he'd ever heard uttered by a human mouth.

Ahead, the wheeled coffins blocked their path, and Jamie was crying in his terror. Nymeria hunched over the glass she held, using her pen to draw designs into the shards, and John and Jeana rode back and forth, looking for any exit among the piled wreckage.

They heard voices from the other side of the vehicles, and John wheeled about as he felt another hand brush across his leg. His hand shook as he aimed the gun and pulled the trigger, and he saw black blood spray from the wound he'd inflicted upon the diseased monk.

Nymeria threw a shining white shard toward the wreckage, and she curled up against him, turning her head away as though to protect her eyes from —

KABOOOM!!!!!!!

The explosion was white-hot, and hissing shrapnel flew by them . . . By the time John returned to his senses, he realized the horses had thrown them. His head pounded viciously, and his whole body ached, and his ears were ringing. Even his eyes were burning. A huge, gaping hole remained where the wreckage had disintegrated — hot metal glowed red and sizzled still with flame and heat, and glass shone black and pulsed faintly with ribbons of red light, like cinders among ash.

Nymeria had calmed the horses — both of which were miraculously sporting only minor cuts and some singed hair, and she stood between them, her brilliant green eyes glowing unnaturally with her inner light. "Come on, before they get any closer," she said. The tool she held was cracked.

He barely heard her above the ringing in his ears.

She gave him the reins and then knelt by her mother and her brother. "I'm sorry. We have to hurry before Uncle Reid is hurt! We cannot wait here and get trapped. Come on, Father!"

Jeana hesitated, her hand trembling when she took the reins.

Nymeria grimaced as though her head hurt, but she blinked away her distress.

John staggered to his feet and climbed back onto his horse as his daughter picked up her necklace, which Jamie had dropped; she drew light into it again. The crack in the tool hummed, and she nearly dropped it when it seemed to burn her. She turned it over and stared at the crack that ran its length, and she bit her lip, her forehead wrinkled with worry.

More screams came from the retreating sick men.

"*Get it out of me!*" screamed one of them. "Get it out of me!!! GET IT OUT OF ME!!!"

Others began to scream, then, in equal rage and agony.

John and his family fled the tunnel, racing through areas now partially collapsed or blocked, and more monks came out of the darkness — many in an even worse state. The horses were staggering with exhaustion by the time the stars emerged from the receding blackness . . . but instead of the imposing ruins of the old dam near Oakwall, they were greeted by the smoldering remains of a burnt forest. The trees had been desolated. Nothing but ashy skeletons stretched on for miles — still smoking, cinders still stirred by the breeze.

When John saw Irkov approaching, he felt he had never been happier to see another healthy person in his life.

Irkov seemed to recognize as soon as he saw them that something serious had happened to them. "The monks get at you?" he asked. But when his good eye found Nymeria, his face lit up. "Demon Monkey! Come! Come here!"

John rode closer, and Nymeria leaned out toward the Greenman. Irkov took her from the horse and gave her a bear hug.

The deep laceration to Irkov's ruined eye had closed, but the scar was still raw and angry. The eye was pale and blind. Yet the man had no fear of Nymeria. Only love. Irkov's good eye turned to the rest of them, and his expression became grave as he set Nymeria on her feet. He ruffled her hair where her oversized hood had fallen back.

"Your brother is alive," said John.

Irkov stepped back, staring at him. "Did I hear you correctly?"

"He's been working for Saura in secret. And the main path through the Haunted Road has been destroyed. It isn't safe anymore. Several of the monks who infiltrated it stumbled upon some of Saura's new traps. Nymeria thinks the vials had her own blood in them, mixed with something else. I've never seen a disease such as the kind ravaging them, Irkov. If any of them come this way, do *not* let them touch you. I'm not even sure if there is a cure. So kill them all and then burn the bodies, and don't breathe in the ash. We'll be lucky if we didn't catch it when they tried to grab us."

"I said it is not contagious anymore," said Nymeria. "It's already in them."

Irkov said nothing for a long time. His jaw ticked aggressively, and he turned to look across the ruined forest. All that remained of the trees was the oldest grove of ancient oaks. "Where are you going?"

"My brother is in trouble in Aelynhold. They plan to execute him. We're going to stop it from happening."

"Aelynhold?" asked Irkov.

"What do you know of it?" John hoped what Irkov was about to say would be helpful to him in some way.

"One of my men betrayed us and helped that murderous, caged demon you were hauling last we met. They set for Aelynhold as well." Irkov scratched at his cheek, and he looked John dead in the eye. "They have the High Commander Avery Ramont. He is being held hostage there."

John held his breath for a long moment, unsure how Irkov could have learned of such a thing. "Are you certain this is true?" If it was, rescuing his brother would be even more difficult — and he would have to extend his search for Avery as well. Avery might be his only other option to save his family. "Have you informed the Enforcers' Alliance?"

"I am more than certain it is true. Elsir betrayed us, though he confessed to little after we caught him. I tried to kill him for his transgression, but he escaped. You can be assured my brother will die a bad death if I ever see him again. There is no honor in his deception, and that he is still alive when believed dead is a stain upon my own honor. To your other question, no. We have no messengers left to relay word to the Enforcers. We're still digging graves for our dead."

"Have you fresh horses we can exchange?" asked John. "We're in a hurry. I'll forward your message to anyone I can find along the way."

Irkov nodded. "Yes, but I'm coming with you. Reid is a good man, one I have long respected." He grinned. "Once, he almost took the very eye your daughter destroyed with her knife." He grunted. "I never did like Saura anyway. Always thought she was a serpent."

"Did you find out why Elsir betrayed you?"

"I managed to get out of him that your caged dog was going to pay his contract."

John squinted at that. "He can't. He doesn't have the authority to pay a Greenman's contract. He's not the High Commander of the Enforcers' Alliance, and he doesn't rule Black Temple, either. The man was just a merchant. A black-market arms dealer. He had his dirty fingers in every pie he could get them into before Reid caught him."

"Neither is he a lord from Aelynhold, Arsennia, or Aracana," snarled Irkov. "But he knows the Lord of Aelynhold. Apparently, he whispers in the man's ear."

"The King of Thieves," swore John, furious.

"Who?"

"Lukas's friend. We had a visitor in Isold, raiding the place. Aelynhold is under new management. Or back under its original management, depending on the level of truth in what she said. And you said they have Avery Ramont?"

"They do."

CHAPTER FIFTY-THREE

$\mathcal{F}$LOODED CITY

NYMERIA'S EARS RANG, and her blood sang with fire by the time they reached Ender's Creek. The crossing where they'd been ambushed a little over a month before. She shivered, soaked, her ribs aching, her fingers stinging from the cold. And the rain kept falling. Before them, what had become a raging river was utterly uncrossable. The tops of the trees she had climbed to warn their envoy of the ambush were hardly visible under the roaring current.

Nymeria blinked hard as the ringing in her ears intensified.

Black smoke curled from the fire her mother and Irkov had built together. Irkov was helping her mother with her father's injured leg and shoulder. The bruises on her father's knuckles were black, too, and his wrist had crusted with dried blood where Griggori had sliced him. His leg was the worst, though. The multiple injuries there looked very painful.

Nymeria was glad the Greenman had become their friend. She could tell he cared about her mother — he was eager to help and argued none with her as they pulled splinters of broken arrow shaft from her father's calf, and her mother cleaned and packed the hole to draw out any stirrings of infection. It was a technique Nymeria had seen both her parents do countless times for numerous patients, and it would ensure little aerobic bacteria could breed in the wound.

Nymeria's father grimaced and shifted his weight. He was pale, but he'd said little as he tried to ignore the stinging of the antiseptic. "John, relax," her mother said quietly. "I told you yesterday we should have stopped to look at your leg. Before we ever went into the Haunted Road."

"I said I was fine."

"He's a stubborn fool, as much as his brother," said Irkov with a grin. He smiled at John's irritable, determined expression. "Jeana is right, though. What good are you if your wound renders you completely useless? You are no Greenman. Just very nearly *gangrenous*."

"I've kept an eye on it," said Nymeria's father as her mother cut the thread from a final stitch and then moved to the next laceration, just above the arrow injury. This one had been from the explosion in the tunnel. There were still splinters of metal and glass needing pulled from it. It bled heavily when they removed the bandage. Nymeria's mother placed her hand on his thigh and stared up at him. "I had another day, at least, for that injury. I wasn't worried about infection," he said, and Irkov withdrew. "But . . . thank you for helping us, Irkov. I'd rather not have required your help so we could both be spared of each other's presence. I imagine you decided to come with us for a reason more substantial than merely helping my brother. Why else did you come?"

Irkov shrugged. "Elsir's dishonor will remain a stain upon the name of every Greenman until his life is forfeit."

"What about your brother's lies?" asked Nymeria's father. His teeth clenched when they pulled another splinter from his leg. "Not willing to enforce the law upon him because he's your brother? Cut the shit, Irkov. What he did to my wife, and then what I did to him for it?

That just gave you an excuse to elevate the fights you picked with me. You hated my guts far before all of that."

Irkov growled, and Nymeria's father's fists curled when Irkov's fingers pressed tightly into the flesh of his calf, right next to the hole. It seemed he'd intended the pain, but Nymeria's father said and did nothing to him for it.

Nymeria's mother examined the wound carefully as Irkov's grip made John shift so that they could get a better look at it.

John swore quietly, blinking against the pain the grip and the pulled metal splinters caused him.

"If what you've told me is true, he will face justice. But Elsir comes first," said Irkov. "My wrath has been put in check, John. My feud with you is done. Your daughter saw to that. I would have no honor if I pursued it. I would be required by our laws to strike my own name from the forest's oldest watchers. In the case of your brother, I owe a generous debt to him. I will help where I can. Now remain still, or I will ask that little demon spider of yours if I may harm you in the hope of tending your injury." He chuckled. "In the hope she won't take my other eye, that is." Irkov's single good eye glittered with humor when he looked up at Nymeria.

Nymeria massaged her temples, wishing that awful ringing would go away. She winced when another stabbing pain rocketed through her skull, and she leaned forward.

Her necklace fell.

The humor faded from Irkov's expression, and he rose. "She's pale as a spirit," he told them, and he crossed the enclosure. Jeana started to rise as well, but John clasped her hand and shook his head.

"Let him talk to her. He has a way with her, just as Reid does. She *talks* to him. She never talks with me, and she's barely pliable with you." Nymeria's father seemed a little bitter when he expressed that last sentiment, but she couldn't really analyze why it would bother him. Her head hurt too much to focus on much.

Irkov knelt before Nymeria and placed the back of his hand across first her cheek and then her forehead. His hand was soothing and cool against her skin, and she leaned into him, wishing the ringing would stop. "You've got a fever, Little Creature," he said gently. "You're shivering." His hand fell, but he still held it out for her to take. "Why have you not said you are not feeling well?"

Nymeria pushed his hand away and stared into the fire. "I hear them screaming," she said. She winced, and the edges of her vision became touched with black. A thread of confusion drifted from Irkov, and then she sensed his concern attached to it. And then more threads of inner turmoil and emotion began to rise, and not just from him, but from her mother and father as well. Their emotions were all colored gray, and they felt heavy, like a sinking ship, filling with water and sorrow — like a current, broiling with anxiety and apprehension. Their difficult-to-discern, bubbling thoughts wove themselves between every emotion she could sense, sometimes clearly, sometimes so vague they were hardly as vivid as gossamer glistening occasionally in the sunlight. And the way the things she was sensing whirled and mingled with the memories she fought of the Violet made her head hurt worse. It all seemed to swell, to circle her, to close in, until she couldn't seem to breathe without the bitter taste of grief washing over her. It left her quaking, until her ribs ached fiercely, until her teeth were chattering and her breath was uneven and at the edge of panic.

"I need to go outside," she said, and she closed her eyes to take another deep breath and to try again to push it all away. She stood, drawing the too large monk's cape around her, and she stepped out into the rain. Irkov signaled her parents to remain inside, and then he followed her.

Together, they stared out into the whirling greenery, and silence stretched between them as the rain beat mercilessly against the leaves of the trees whose branches whipped and groaned overhead. Every drop stung against her skin as the rain sliced at her in angled sheets. She breathed in the washed-out scent of the wet ash and aging cypress, and she observed gratefully that there was not a splash of red in sight. The last time they had been here, blood had painted the various surfaces of rock, soil, and forest litter everywhere. There had been deep crimson puddles, and bright splotches of red had splattered against the white stones along the river's edge, and blood had discolored the clothing and flesh of both the living and the dead. She'd had nightmares about it since, dreams which bled into her growing cauldron of seething horrors. Their screams had been added to the stranger's memories and the dark things' hissing screeches.

Nymeria stared at the raging river.

She remembered her dark wolf growling, its golden eyes flashing when it had seen her father's hand slip from the rope. She remembered the beast's rise to action as it had darted forward to save him. Her throat tightened.

Because of Nymeria, her father was now nearly unable to walk, and her wolf friend was dead. And she had the distinct feeling that her uncle was going to die terribly, and though her father had told her Uncle Reid had left for other reasons, she knew it'd had much to do with her. Because her uncle had worried over her greatly.

The idea of losing Uncle Reid stung, almost like a dagger in her heart, wedging deeper with every breath when she thought of what he might be going through. The strange things she'd been dreaming and seeing had left her with too much imagination, and far too much knowing. She didn't want to know any of it, but it was there, and it haunted her.

Her chin trembled.

She knew her father wanted to save her uncle. He intended to leave them all behind, she knew it. And if he hadn't had to protect her in Isold, he wouldn't have been shot with that arrow. With his injury, he would be in more danger when he went to save Uncle Reid.

And if he hadn't pulled that trigger, *she* would have been the one to have ended that monk's life. She was responsible for that death, just as she was responsible for the many other deaths and injuries in Black Temple. The black glass had been her fault. More people had been infected with the Violet because of her. Antonio. Mark. Sobrienne. Other doctors. Other children. She didn't even know how many.

She wished she could take all of it back.

Worse, she knew she was a burden, and not just any sort of burden. She knew she was a dangerous, unstable one. She knew something was astonishingly wrong inside her, and it frightened her. She didn't know what to do about it, but she could feel it. Her magic was a ticking time bomb. Some days, the violet coursing through her burned like seven hells, and some days, she felt that other *thing* in her stirring and trying to claw its way to the surface. Some days, she feared what she would unleash next, and who else might suffer because of her. Whenever she wanted to act, she felt the Violet burn brighter inside of her, and whatever threads held it back grew closer to snapping. But she couldn't do *nothing*, either, because that was worse.

Yet there was one thing that haunted her above all.

Her family wasn't safe. She was dangerous to them.

Irkov placed his hand on her shoulder, and she looked up at him. At his good eye and his bad eye. "What is it?" he asked.

"I don't know what I am," she said, and her voice caught. "I'm afraid of finding out. I may be their daughter, but I am also a dangerous thing. I don't know why I have the power that is in me." She shut her eyes against another scalding wave of energy. "I'm losing control of it, Irkov. It's already hurt people. I don't know how to stop it from getting worse. What if it kills my family?" Her chin trembled again, and it became hard to speak when she imagined what her life would be like without any of them. She would be alone in the world. "I don't want to hurt anyone."

Irkov let go of her shoulder, and when he did so, she felt a little colder inside. He shifted on his feet when the rain about her began to hiss and evaporate. But he didn't flinch from her, and he did not avoid meeting her gaze when she looked up again. Instead, he knelt and took her smaller hands in his larger ones. "You are what you must be," he said simply. "Even as young as you are, you are strong enough to survive anything this world can throw at you."

"But why do I want to rend the throats of those who hurt the people I love? I don't want to just hurt them, or just defend my family and friends . . ." She shook her head. "It's as if I become someone different. Something bad is inside me. Your brother thinks I am a natural killer. That's why he didn't hurt me. He thinks death is beautiful, and he could see the disturbance in me. What if he's right? What if I'm a monster? The refugee children called me a witch and a demon. What if they're right? What if I'm something evil?"

"Let me tell you something," he said. And he pulled her hands up between them, so that they could both see the dim light that pulsed beneath her flesh, running through the scars that traced her skin in spiraling, symbol-like patterns. Her hot tears met the cold rain, and Irkov held her hands firmly, unafraid. Accepting. "None can walk the path of another," he said. "But we all have our secrets, and we all have our skeletons, and we all must face demons that seem made only for us to battle."

Nymeria sniffled, and Irkov brushed away her tears.

"Whatever this magic inside you is, you will someday master it. So never give up, Little Spider. Among the Greenmen, every man and woman is given a trial to overcome. One who betrays his vow to do whatever it takes to overcome that trial does not deserve to live well and never earns the mark of his name upon the forest's oldest trees. A man or woman who has not the strength to make such a vow has no place in that world. They are given the most unpleasant tasks as their penance. If a thing is not difficult, or it inspires in you no fear, then it is not a thing to desire, or to fight for, or to die for. Because overcoming it will neither sustain you nor bring you joy or knowledge."

"But I am terrified of what I might someday do, and of what I might become. I know my mother and my father are afraid for me, and they have sacrificed a lot to try and help me. I've made my brother afraid to sleep in the dark. It's my fault he has nightmares. It's my fault my uncle left, because he wanted to help me. And I think maybe my grandma and grandpa also died because of me. What if I'm not worth what *they* are fighting for? And what about all the people in Black Temple? Even the wolf fought for me, and look what happened to her! She was slaughtered! She was a beautiful creature, and she died because of me!"

"Child," said Irkov, and he wiped the tears from her cheeks ever so gently. "Do you want to be worth that fight? Do you want them to fight for you?" Nymeria nodded slowly, her heart aching. "And are you willing to fight for them?"

Again, she nodded. "No matter what," she said. "I love them very much. I want to be strong, and I want to be good. I don't want to be evil. I don't want to be a demon, or even a monster."

"What terrifies you most is what you were born to overcome," he said. "So take strength and confidence even where none is offered. Even when it disintegrates in your grasp, take it, and embrace it as your own. Dig deep. Make your heart a shield, and turn your will into a weapon. And even when you are overcome, keep fighting. You will see the increasing measure of your own honor as time passes so long as you do not ever give up. That is the life no other can destroy, the good that no other can weaponize against you. Even your mistakes will be unable to erase the good you have done."

Irkov shifted again where he knelt as lightning flashed across the sky. The thunder following the brilliant display clashed against their ear drums. "Griggori likely saw in you what I see. Something, it seems, even your mother and father cannot. It is not that you are a natural killer but that you were born with the strength to overcome even the worst horror — to thrive in spite of it, to create opportunity rather than destroy hope. Even such a tiny thing as you are, you are not one to bow to adversity, are you? To give up and cry as your brother might? To become angry like your father and look for and embrace every wrong answer before discovering the right one? To run and hide, and avoid and deny what is your right, and your right alone, to overcome?"

Nymeria grimaced, but she nodded again. "I want them to be safe, but I also don't want to hurt other people just to make it so."

"You are wise beyond your young years, Nymeria. You make up your mind after thinking carefully, and you speak openly and take action when you must. You've stood against your father, and you've risked your own life for others you do not know. Even most adults do not have the capacity to weigh situations before acting upon them, or to do so in behalf of others. If they do, many of them act as a coward might. They blame, or they run." He smiled, then. "You took the eye of an angered man who could not see his error in order to cause him to see a truth he did not want to see. And I'll bet you've already done many other things, each as fiercely as the thing before. So, if it is fear in you, overcome it and become the best and bravest version of yourself. Only you can do that. Use your anger, use your love, use your faith. Whatever it takes. And do not ever fall into the abyss of regret. Every failure is a lesson, Little Creature. A proud jewel, no matter its color."

"But the shadow inside me is changing me," she said quietly.

"Change will always be inevitable regardless of whether a shadow is the cause," he said. "But failure is not. Not unless you give up. You decide *how* it changes you." When she nodded, he at last let go of her hands. "But you must also take care of yourself along the way. Come back inside and get something to eat, and then get some rest. You've not slept much for days, and you are making yourself ill because of it."

She bit her lip. "How do you know I haven't slept well? You only joined us yesterday when we got to Oakwall."

He laughed and pointed to his good eye. "You left me one of these, Little Creature. I'm not all blind, not yet."

Nymeria felt the corner of her mouth tug at that. "But how did you know?"

Irkov sighed. "There are great shadows under your eyes, Little Spider, and though your brother sleeps like the dead, the moment your eyes close, you pry them open as you jerk awake. As if you are terrified of what you will see." He pulled a strand of hair out of her eyes. "You must rest. We leave in a few hours, as soon as the horses are also rested enough to travel again."

"Are we crossing the river? It will be dangerous, won't it?"

But Irkov shook his head. "Ender's Creek and beyond are too treacherous because of the rains. Much of the trail has been washed out. We will instead navigate the Flooded City, just north of here. We'll leave the horses behind, but we'll find more along the stables near Tarvet's waterfalls. We should make good time on the water. One day rather than three, for the path I know through the watery ruins."

"But isn't Tarvet abandoned?"

"Mostly, but the fields on the western hills are used by Tarvet's stablemen for raising horses. It's where the best horses are bred. With luck, they'll still be in business, and that will save us time getting to Aelynhold. Now go and try to rest, child. Before you cause a Greenman to sing a lullaby. We're not known for lovely voices."

An hour later, Nymeria had finally managed to close her eyes, but sleep only lasted as long as a brilliant flash of light and a bloodcurdling glimpse of memory before she woke screaming. She could still taste the blood. She still saw the bodies of the children and the red-eyed, humanoid creatures trying to feast upon Mihai's flesh. One of them had clawed his face when it had lunged at him, just before he had cut its head from its shoulders.

Her face stung as though the creature had clawed her instead, and when she reached for the stinging spot on her face, her mother pried her hand away, and she realized as her father tried to clean the wound that there was blood all over her hand.

Irkov held her still while she screamed about the Leviathans trying to have her killed, and her blood ate through the cloth and burned him. He recoiled with a bark of pain, and Nymeria's eyes sought the fire wildly.

She never realized she'd kicked her father from her, or that she'd wrestled free of her mother's desperate attempt to hold her still — she only felt the wound sizzling upon her face, and then the cool electric tingling sensation running through her fingers when she'd snatched the cracked pen tool from her blankets. She hadn't even known she'd gone for it until she'd had it.

The diamond seared her face when she drew it across the claw marks where she felt the shadows crawling through her skin, and the scream she heard leave her mouth next was followed by blackness. She felt the light trickling away, as if it was being drawn out of her like a poison, and she smelled burnt flesh.

In the darkness, a pinprick of violet bloomed. She cringed from it, until she realized it felt like little pieces of herself, drifting across a giant black ocean. She saw and felt all of them — glittering starlight by the thousands. People like herself, cursed with pieces of light inside them. It seemed a great sigh was released across the ocean of glowing souls, and they began to dim as one alone began to shine brightly. This one was blue, and it was very far away.

She heard a familiar voice. A woman weeping. And then, as she stood, staring into the dark ocean of twinkling lights, pillars made of old stone began to take shape — they formed dim silhouettes in the darkness of some echoing room.

"Everything that you are," wept the woman, "will one day heal this world."

"Mother . . . ?" she tried to ask. She had no idea why. The woman did not sound like her mother Jeana. Was that what Jeana had sounded like before her voice had been ruined?

The blue light began to spread, to overcome everything, to wash away the violet stars. Water entombed Nymeria, then, and she felt herself drifting in it.

The woman continued, her voice frail, her emotions raw from her heart having been broken. "I'll never tell them about him, I promise. When you find each other, save him. It is the only way you will survive. Both of you share a soul that is older than the world itself. Take care of it. Do not destroy it or you will both die. She is all that protects you. And remember . . ."

The voice began to fade.

". . . They cannot enter the water."

The next thing Nymeria heard was the rippling of water. She felt her body swaying side to side, slowly, and her brother's fingers were brushing through her hair. "Mommy, Myria's awake," he said.

Birds fluttered overhead, and the rippling sound came again as the boat they were in rocked gently.

Small rays of light pierced the blackness, and Nymeria's eyelids fluttered open. Her mother had moved closer and was leaning over her, but her father remained asleep near the bow. "How are you feeling?" her mother asked quietly, her voice barely a whisper. Everything was very blurry, and Nymeria turned her head. She was thirsty. There was water outside the boat. She rolled over, the urge to drink stronger than she'd ever felt. She needed water. She *needed* . . .

When her fingers touched the water, though, she winced, and instead of trying to bring the water to her mouth to drink, she laid the side of her face against the side of the boat, shivering. She needed . . .

Her fingers twitched under the cool surface, and the light within her scalded her. Nymeria whimpered.

And then the bright light snaked into the water and spread like ink, until it seemed to explode into a flash of brilliant, underwater lightning. The vastness of the small lake seemed to stretch on for miles, and it was littered with old trees — some dead, some alive — and the ancient tombs of buildings, and long, hanging veils of pale moss.

Irkov lifted the oars and peered out at the glowing lake and its dead city, startled. When the light faded, and along with it Nymeria's craving for the water, the breeze picked up, and the birds began to sing again. The frogs remembered their conversations, and the boat drifted for the longest moment before it began to slow down.

There was no rain, and the night was still. Calm.

From the shadowy shore under the nearest trees, a doe tested the air with her nose and then blinked. Her hoof raked the ground, and then she turned from the water.

Nymeria's eyes flickered upward, and she stared at the tall silhouettes of fallen skyscrapers all around them. She smelled the algae and the stagnant odor of the water, and her stomach groaned. She removed her hand from the water. But the light remained in every broken sliver of glass beneath the surface. Every piece that wasn't covered in muck shone brightly, until it looked very similar to the ocean of violet stars she'd seen in her dream.

No one spoke to her. Irkov had had no idea the light was so strong inside her. She knew by the look on his face. But he wasn't afraid. His lips were pursed, but he stared out, across the waters, and he wondered as their path became clear to him. He must have been afraid they were lost, or nearly so. Everything always looked different at night.

"I'm thirsty," she said quietly.

Her mother handed Irkov the glass heart pendant that had been illuminating their path and turned to dig in one of the bags. "Here," said Nymeria's mother, and she unscrewed the lid to one of their canteens and held it out for Nymeria to take. Her fingers brushed across Nymeria's jaw tenderly.

Nymeria knew the claw marks and the scar on her jaw were gone from her mother's expression. Most of them had already begun to fade completely, leaving no sign of either silver or injury. She'd noticed it when she'd been talking to Irkov in the rain. Whatever the Violet and the shadows were doing to her was erasing the marks.

Nymeria took the canteen and drank deeply, and then she laid her head on the side of the boat again and watched her sleeping father. She hoped he was dreaming well, but his brow was drawn low, and his hand clenched into a fist as he slept. His expression was anything but peaceful.

Her mother followed her gaze and smiled weakly. "He's been sleeping off his pain," she said. "He decided poorly when he ignored his injuries. He'll be okay, though." Jeana looked up when something crashed into the water in the distance. "The wound was cleaned in time."

A loud splash nearby startled Nymeria's mother and brother.

"These ruins are falling apart," explained Irkov. "It's been several hundred years since they fell. Sometimes travelers get lost here. Sometimes it's the swamp that takes them. Sometimes it's other things."

"We've circled that dreaded sculpture three times now," said Nymeria's mother.

Nymeria looked out, into the night, searching for the sculpture her mother had mentioned. The glittering light from beneath the water illuminated it and made it easy to find, and Nymeria shrank from it. It was a scary thing. It looked like something dead, and the way the weather had corroded it, it looked more gruesome. Its hood hid its face, and its staff looked coated in blood, the way the rust had taken hold.

"There are seven Dead Men," said Irkov. "We are not lost. It is not the same statue, but one similar." The Greenman shrugged. "When the war began, this was one of the first cities to suffer. The statues were put here to warn the infected from leaving the quarantine, but it spread anyway. Seven times, the warning was given, and every doctor and warrior tried to keep the peace and help the dying. Seven times, it seemed hope would prevail, and the cure was in sight. And then seven times, failure meant the deaths of thousands and the spreading of that disease as it mutated from zone to zone."

Irkov scratched his jaw. "After that," he said, "a bomb was dropped on the city. A decade later, outbreaks began across the land . . . and then across the world. Tarvet was the name of the first man to die, and it became the name of this city. Its original name was lost. Tarvet was also the name of the first man to leave the city just before the bomb destroyed it. They had been brothers, the two men. The surviving Tarvet brother became the first of the Greenman, and he led hundreds to safety. This city's history is part of our past. It is used as a trial among us, as it had been for him when he'd journeyed through the city as it burned, looking for any uninfected survivors. I know this city better than most, Jeana. Even when these treacherous waters rise during the rains. You are safe here with me, all of you."

Nymeria remembered the diseased men from the Haunted Road. She wondered whether the disease had been the same. She wondered whether her blood would make it come alive again, and she felt fear stir within her.

"Do any of your people die here?" she asked.

Irkov nodded. "Yes."

"How?"

"Falling debris. Drinking the water. Drowning." He lifted the oar, and the water rippled when he rowed again. "Sometimes thieves hide in the city, thinking to make camp. They never last long. The animals aren't all nice, either."

He drove them under the shattered remains of the largest buildings, and Nymeria's skin prickled when she saw the cavernous depths of the buildings' decrepit guts. Light shone up through the water, into the blackness inside, revealing seemingly endless floors that had fallen away, and blackened stone. Moss crept across nearly every surface, and where there was no moss, there were often poisonous ivies, or trees stretching from one caved-in wall to the nearest openings. Spiderwebs hung from every surface, and glowing eyes shone back at them from the various nooks and crannies where bats and birds and furry things nested.

A creature hissed from the obscurity of an overhead ledge.

Jamie looked up. "Is that a cat?" he asked. He thought for a moment, and then he moved closer to Nymeria, as though she could protect him. "Or was it one of the dark things?"

"It was a snake," said Nymeria, and she pointed at the slithering thing as its body twisted around branches and debris and then slid into the water.

They didn't talk much for the rest of the night, or into the morning when the sun began to rise, when golden light filtered into the maze of ruined buildings, which seemed at first to get larger and larger and then began to shrink in size again. They had passed three more of the eerie statues by then, and Irkov had told them the last would mean they were nearly there. They would find a small river leading from Tarvet. They would have only to follow it for a small while before they would hear the waterfall.

He'd been quite right. And the stable had been inhabited by well-fed horses, and smoke had curled from the chimney of the small house there.

Nymeria and her family waited outside while Irkov went in to speak with the old man inside. Her father placed the back of his hand on her forehead. "Your fever's broken," he said. "Are you feeling better?"

Nymeria bit her tongue. She didn't look up at him, though she nodded. "Yes, but I'm afraid still. What if something happens when you try to rescue Uncle Reid? You're already hurt."

"Nothing is going to happen to me."

"You can't guarantee that, Father. You can barely walk. I want to go with you."

He gripped her shoulders softly. "You will stay with your mother and your brother until I come for you. Anything else is out of the question."

"But — "

"No more arguing, and if you try to defy me, you'll be whipped. I will not have you endangering yourself, or your brother and your mother."

When Irkov came out, he was followed by a tiny, ancient man who could barely see under the deeply wrinkled skin hooding his eyes. The man said nothing, but he nodded and stood to the side while Irkov spoke with her mother and father. Nymeria listened carefully.

"My uncle said he'll let us borrow the horses on the condition we'll return them in good straits and get him another mare for breeding. He's had his mind set on a sturdy Hodshire for a while but never had the chance to get one. Aelynhold doesn't sell or trade the breed because they're too valuable to them."

"I don't really care about what is special about his preference of horses, just that we need these," said John. "My brother has only ten days left before he's executed, and the journey from here will be at least how long? Eight? Nine?"

"Almost nine, even with minimum rest."

"Then we need to get moving. What about Jeana and the children?"

Nymeria looked up as Irkov scratched at his wiry-haired chin. "My uncle said they can stay until it is over. He's got plenty of food and plenty of clean water on account of the waterfall. If they can help load the wagon and get the feed from the mill to the horses, that'll pay for their stay here."

"Jeana's shoulder is not going to heal itself anytime soon," said John.

But Nymeria's mother waved off the concern. *I'll manage*, she signed quietly.

"The wagons are already hitched, if the lady and the children are ready," said the old man finally. "I usually do this work myself. The assist would be appreciated. And when we're done, we'll dine well on the watercress and spring onion stew I've made. It's got eel meat in it. Delicious stuff. Very tender."

"That'll be better than what they've been eating for a few days," John said appreciatively. "Thank you kindly. Irkov and I will try to keep your horses in the best condition. If anything happens to them, I'll pay for the loss however I can."

The old man nodded. "You know where everything is, Nephew. Be safe, and good riddance." He turned and walked away, waving for the rest of them to follow.

Nymeria's father didn't even stop to give her or Jamie a hug. "I'll be back," he said. "I love you. All of you." Then he and Irkov were rushing toward the barn, both carrying precious little in the way of supplies or rations, and they disappeared inside.

Nymeria clutched at her heart necklace, worrying about her uncle. "How will they find him in time?" she asked her mother. "I don't think Aelynhold will just let them barge in and take Uncle Reid away from them. And that woman was infected with that curse. What about her father, the King of Thieves? What if he is, too? They'll be more dangerous if they know how to use it."

"Your father will do his best," whispered her mother. But Nymeria could see she was also worried.

"They don't know how to defend themselves against the light if it is used against them," she said adamantly. "We shouldn't be staying behind while Father goes alone. He isn't good at subtle, and if he gets caught, all he will have is Irkov. And that is if Irkov doesn't get caught, too."

"Nymeria, it isn't for us to worry about now. We will do our part to ease your father's mind so that he can put all of his energy and attention into rescuing your uncle. He doesn't need to be distracted by worrying about us putting ourselves in danger — "

"But he's just one person, Mother! And he's *hurt*! He can't even run. He doesn't know anyone there who will be able to help him, and he won't know if he is being watched, or if someone he questions will betray him."

"Is Daddy going to die?" asked Jamie, and he took a great, big, deep breath, on the verge of tears.

Their mother sighed, and she scooped Jamie up into her arms and kissed his cheek. "No," she whispered. "Come, Nymeria. Let it alone."

"But I can't. It's not right. We shouldn't be hiding; we should be helping!"

"You're a child. What do you think you can do that he cannot?" her mother's voice was beginning to split.

"I can protect him," she said. "I can . . ."

Nymeria realized her mother would not understand. Her mother had not seen what she'd done in the forest near Isold. Only her father had. Her mother had not seen the black glass, or the glass explosives. Her mother had not been there when they had been ambushed. Her mother didn't know she was capable, or that she sensed things others couldn't. She didn't realize that because Nymeria was small, she could hide in places others could not.

Nymeria made up her mind. When she saw that no one was there to stop her because they were inside the mill grabbing sacks of feed, she climbed into the wagon and untied the reins, and she urged the horses into motion.

What Irkov had told her raced through her mind, and she knew deep in her heart that she was right to defy her mother. If it was something worth fighting for, she was going to fight for it. She would never give up. She wasn't going to let her father get himself killed by going to Aelynhold without her to help him. And she could prove to him once and for all that she was both useful and resourceful so he wouldn't have to worry himself sick.

 As the mill began to shrink behind her, she looked over her shoulder and saw her mother run outside. Jeana's lips formed her name, but the sound was unsuccessful as she gripped at her chest and raced after her. Nymeria saw the look of betrayal and fear on her mother's face, and then she hardened her heart, gritted her teeth, and turned her head. She urged the horses to hurry, and she promised silently that she would make sure her father and her uncle were brought home safely. And Irkov. She wasn't going to run from her fear anymore.

The wagon bounced jarringly over the rocks, and it creaked and groaned as though the axles would split and the wheels would come undone.

She wouldn't let her father try to rescue her uncle on his own, not when she sensed the pending danger. Her uncle was near death already. She'd known that for days now. She wouldn't risk losing both of them at the same time.

CHAPTER FIFTY-FOUR

The Wall

THEY'D RIDDEN HARD TO make time, but it still wasn't enough. John had fewer than three days to find and save his brother when they broke through the forest and Aelynhold's massive stone walls appeared. The first thing he noticed was the smell, and as the trees thinned, he saw large camps of refugees milling about along the curtain wall where they had set up temporary shelters. They looked haggard, and a chorus of grief and sorrow erupted from mournful faces as their tattered makeshift homes and kitchens and infirmaries were set afire by archers from atop the wall.

It had been many years since John had last seen a multitude this size in such dire straits, and it became obvious to him immediately that Aelynhold had abandoned the centuries-old contract between the old cities and the major guilds, to keep peace and offer sanctuary to those in need.

John realized getting into Aelynhold could be much trickier than he'd anticipated, and he swore aloud. There would be no sneaking through the gates disguised as a merchant or a traveler. The gates were closed, barred, and heavily guarded.

Moreover, Enforcers surrounded the city and the refugee camps, and he noted that a small band of them had approached the wall. He could hardly hear their voices over the noise of the stirring crowd as they spoke with some black-haired woman who stood on the ramparts over the gates. He couldn't quite make out what they were saying, but the tone was fierce on either side of that wall, and both sides stood as though ready to attack and to defend.

John and Irkov looked at one another, and Irkov sighed. "Seven Knotted Oaks, but what luck?" He waved at the gate. "Maybe if they can get in without killing one another, we can, too."

"They're burning everything close to the wall without regard for any loss of life," said John. "This is probably going to go badly, Irkov. We need to be careful here."

"Your plan was to get in unnoticed," Irkov hissed. "How do you plan to do such a thing in this crisis, and without us getting killed? I am no coward, but I am not stupid, either. There is little possibility for us here. And there are so many wearyworn, if one catches fire, the others may as well, and then everyone will be running about screaming and on fire." He waved at the refugees who were rushing toward a small creek and hauling buckets of water toward the fires. None of the Enforcers were helping.

"It looks as though they're about to go to war," said John, worried about the refugees. "The wearyworn are going to get killed if no one gets them to move away from the walls, and away from these negotiations."

"I hope you don't expect either of us to do it. They don't seem to be in a listening mood, and I'm not in a telling one, either." Irkov frowned, and then he cleared his throat. "Anyway, you should realize the wearyworn do not matter to either side, here. Aelynhold's currently a hive of reclusive pricks, intent on keeping that gate shut, and the Enforcers are obviously here for something they hold more important. *Your* guild is the only one who wants to help every unfortunate soul. I can only hope your instinct to make peace does not get the better of you here . . . You aren't going to gallivant off and try to fix this, are you? I've heard of some of the things your guildsmen have to swear to."

John recalled Saura's order. He felt he should probably warn the Greenman of the pending disaster, but he wasn't sure how Irkov would react. The Breaking of the Vial was a thing feared more by Greenmen than by any other. It was why the Greenmen served Black Temple without reservation.

"We have to get into Aelynhold no matter what," John said finally. "We have only three days until my brother's execution."

"Then we should speak with these Enforcers," nodded Irkov. "If there was another way in, there would be fewer here. To be honest, I think we should just climb that wall with a dozen of these Enforcers. Let them carry the shields at the top."

John snorted. "What do you think they're dipping those arrows in to light them?" he demanded. He waved at the smoke that rose from key points atop the wall. "If any of us, shields or not, got near that wall, we'd be drenched and lit on fire. Aelynhold participated in a large fuel war thirty years ago and held off hundreds of Enforcers for over twelve months with little to no loss, Irkov. The Enforcers were completely defeated and conceded the route to them. Aelynhold's defense is nearly flawless."

"They were under siege the entire year?" Irkov's brow rose. He seemed hesitant to believe it. "Hmm." He looked up at the looming walls again, his expression brooding. "I doubt the entire city is farmland inside that wall. How did they keep from starving through the winter? Any scaled activity that enduring would need a massive food store."

"I don't know many of the details, just that they outlasted the Enforcers. Could have eaten one another." John dismounted carefully, his leg and shoulder both throbbing from the wounds he'd gotten twelve days before. The rest were minor injuries and bothered him not at all. "Easy," he said to his borrowed mount. The beast was unusually skittish and had caused him some trouble on the way to Aelynhold. Now it was all he could do to keep her calm. She skirted away from an arguing pair of refugees who came to blows over a bit of moldy bread. He glanced toward the rest of the wearyworn about them, and he noticed the growing anger as the Enforcers refused to help. A small crowd had gathered a few hundred yards behind them, and several of the wearyworn began to shout and throw random projectiles at the Enforcers' armored vehicles.

The Enforcers took defensive stances, but their leaders ordered them not to spill any blood, as they were not here for the wearyworn.

The fire at the wall spread farther outward all the while, and John became more uneasy with every passing minute.

"Jonathan Ivan! What are you doing here, you devious doctor?"

John spun about, startled, and an Enforcer he recognized from their journey along Raven Trail clasped his shoulder and offered his hand. John took it.

"I didn't expect to see you here," said John. "I thought they would court-martial the lot of you for betraying your captain and his officers."

"Nope. I was promoted to lieutenant while those bastards were executed. Captain Robin's men uncovered a whole hell of a conspiracy in Edantine and elsewhere. Our superiors think Avery Ramont may be alive, can you believe it? He's being held hostage in this city somewhere."

John was startled that the traitor Elsir had imparted to Irkov accurate information, though he was glad the Enforcers had already known about Avery. "So it's true that he's alive? Then where has the Alliance been getting their orders from?"

Elija shrugged. "They're battling every step of the way, trying to figure that out. It seems some of the commanders had no idea he was ever missing but had been paid to help create the ruse. But the ones who were caught intentionally issuing false commands refused to speak on it and then fled capture. Others really believed it was Avery's commands they'd been passing on. No one knows why, or *what* about anything, yet. Right now, our orders are to keep Aelynhold under siege, and to ensure none of these bastard monks get out." He nodded to the commotion behind them. "The wearyworn are a bit of a thorn right now, and a lot of my men want to take arms against them despite orders not to."

"I noticed the tension," said John. "They look half-starved."

"Yeah, they've been picking fights and stealing from us. We can't easily manage a siege of a city if our own supplies are dwindling too fast, though, can we?" Lieutenant Elija grimaced, and he scratched at his wiry chin, pulling at the short clump of braided hair there. He sighed. "It's a damned mess. But Captain Robin's at the wall right now, talking to Drake Normane's wife. She's the creepy, black-haired wraith over the gates there. She's denied the charges, but he's setting it straight for her as we speak. If she doesn't comply and allow us to search the city for Avery peacefully, it's probably going to turn to bloodshed. Could be months and a lot of dead men before we get those doors open. I'm hoping he'll scare her into opening them voluntarily."

Irkov grimaced. "If they have Avery, they're a bunch of fools."

"Well," said Elija. "You can't expect to kidnap the leader of a military alliance without bloodshed and major losses on both sides. War is highly likely, but our first priority is to approach them peacefully. Negotiate quickly. Time is our enemy, as always. The last time the Alliance was here, our soldiers waited out a bad winter and rough weather during the rainy season. Several hundred of us froze to death, and then others drowned, and afterward, several hundred more starved. Aelynhold's allies attacked our men from outside our defensive lines, driving in from behind us every time. We're prepared for that this time, and we're lucky we're here while it's late spring, early summer. So we won't have to deal with that sort of weather. We'll be able to fight longer, but we don't want to do so if we can find a peaceful solution, and quickly. Time is . . . Well, not on our side, as I said. The wolfmen have retreated to Five Tower, and word is, Caol's army is about to march from Five Tower. Half of his fleet has raised its sails already, in Isold's direction."

John felt sick. "Five Tower's fleet has *set sail*?" He shook his head, appalled. "Do you know if word of it has been forwarded to the guildsmen at the Temple?"

Elija shrugged. "I'm not sure. I was at the meeting this morning when the messenger arrived. This peace we've had has gotten stormy. We may end up in a very bad war that's going to last for years, if we don't stop it. But our first mission is to rescue Avery. He was investigating Five Tower when he disappeared. He'd kept the subject of his investigations highly classified — we *still* don't know what he was looking into. There seems to be no documentation anywhere. It's likely been burned, or buried, or sent somewhere far off. There is nothing at the citadel about his investigation, except faint breadcrumbs."

"Well, I don't have months, Elija," said John. "Aelynhold has my brother. They're going to execute him. They sent a message to the Temple after killing everyone in Isold almost two full weeks ago."

Elija grimaced. "So Isold's gone? Then the Temple has no defense. Damn. What'd they want?"

"They claimed he's committed some crime, and they demand reparation. And if they don't get it, then they're going after my whole family, and then Black Temple itself. The Temple is vulnerable right now. We've lost a lot of people. If what you're saying is true about Five Tower's fleet, I don't think the guild will stand a chance at all. The dam is barely holding, and the men we've had patrolling it have been finding small groups of wolfmen and deranged, suicidal soldiers who were trying to blow it up. One of those explosions turned half of the streets to black glass. A lot of people have been infected with some strange disease I've never seen before. It makes their eyes violet, and they lose their senses, a lot of them.

"I don't know if you remember Mark, but he was one of the men who traveled with us. The son of Amos Shipwright, Crow Post's assigned doctor. Mark contracted it. He damned near blinded *both* of his own eyes, trying to claw them out because of it. Some of the others weren't so lucky, and none of us have been able to cure it. Black Temple will not survive an attack at this time."

"We cannot afford to lose Black Temple." Elija growled under his breath and started shoving refugees out of their way. "Move! Clear off!" he shouted. He looked over his shoulder at John. "That little girl of yours okay? She saved a lot of lives on Raven Trail, mine included. I got a knife in the gut, but she threw a rock that hit the bastard on the head. It was enough for me to take his knife and kill him with it before he could slice enough to spill my innards."

John hesitated, and then he turned when he thought he saw a familiar face drift by him in the chaos about them. *Lukas?* Had he imagined the man's face? None of these people looked at all like Lukas.

His heart still beat furiously.

Surely, the man wouldn't have been so bold. And why would he be among the wearyworn and the Enforcers? Unless he, too, had been unable to enter the city.

"What is it?" asked Irkov, eyeing the crowd suspiciously.

John continued to scan every face he saw, searching for anything familiar. At last, he shook his head, and he wiped the sweat from his brow. It was a humid day. "I swore I saw Lukas."

Irkov's gray eye grew darker. "Are you certain?"

John shook his head. "No . . . I'm not. But I thought I did."

Irkov muttered an oath under his breath. "I'd like to kill him for Oakwall's demise. He might not have done it himself, but he *is* the reason my home is gone."

John understood Irkov's anger. "He murdered my parents in cold blood, Irkov. I'm sure the scum rat has a long line of men who want him dead for his various sins. But my brother was right. He must be taken to the Reformation. He's got his hands in far too much to simply allow some quick and useless end." He raised his hands at Irkov's glare. "Beat him as much as you wish. Just keep him alive."

They entered a large tent behind the lieutenant, who snagged the inkwell and a quill once inside and bent to scratch something on a blank page that lay upon the small desk there. But the material that hung over the opening of the tent was ripped aside, and a flurry of motion startled the three of them. A man hit the ground, and he struggled against his bonds with a ceaseless stream of muffled curses. He was covered in blood, and the number of empty sheaths upon him suggested he'd been armed for an assassination. Or for several.

A broken glass chain was flung to the ground beside the monk by another Enforcer who stepped into the tent with them. "Just you keep struggling, you worthless . . ." The man's jaw ticked at the sight of John and Irkov, and then his gaze shot to Elija.

Elija slid his blade back into its sheath at his hip and relaxed. "Go ahead, Arius, these men are friends. They're desperate to rescue another prisoner in the city. I'm sure we can use their help with *this* matter." He waved at the battered monk on the ground between them.

Arius's brow lowered. He didn't like this, it was obvious. But he spoke anyway. "The entrance in the trees where we caught him and his friends has collapsed. We believe it's killed everyone still down there. And we still haven't heard from our men who got through. They're probably dead or imprisoned. The collapse was not a natural one, it was intentional."

"Obviously, *he* couldn't have had a hand in destroying the tunnel," said Elija. "He's been locked up. Him and his friends."

"There's another tunnel."

"There are tunnels?" asked John. He and Irkov looked at one another.

"What happened?" The lieutenant crossed his arms and glared at the bound monk for a long moment. He did not answer John's question.

"Morris's other friends came. Several of them. We finally got the woman to talk. She no more than said a few things by the time we realized he'd come in, and then this bright sack of maggot rot killed her to keep what else she knew quiet. And it seems their friends value him for some reason. He was the first one they freed, and they tried to get him out after he killed her. They didn't like being cut from navel to neck, none of them. We didn't get all of them, though."

"Damn. Did she tell you anything valuable when you were questioning her?"

"Not much before he slit her throat, but just enough," said Arius. "There are several other tunnels across the woods. We got an approximate location of a few of them, and we found the one his friends came out of. Caught the rest of them before they got away, but most of them won't talk, just like him."

"Is this one booby-trapped, too?" asked Elija.

"We don't know. We haven't gotten to explore it yet. There are more monks inside, and they are blocking the entrance. Either they're planning to attack or they can't seal it properly. Not sure why else they could be guarding it for."

Elija's foot tapped the ground. "The other tunnel was a tight fit. Only a few men ever got through."

"They're most likely dead, as I said," said Arius. "This tunnel is different, though. It's promising. I don't think so many would hole up there, not if they couldn't all get through quickly when things go to the trench on them."

"How did you find the first one?" asked John.

Arius turned to him and grimaced. "We followed the cowled rats, of course. They attacked my group when we were combing the area after having spotted several of them. That was nearly two weeks ago, when we first arrived. Lieutenant, some of these guys used to be Enforcers. Some of them still are. Some were captains, lieutenants . . . Ranking officers, many of them. A lot of them knew Avery personally, and a lot of them were extremely loyal to him. Just like this one here. His name is Morris Ramsey Bourgeois. He was a captain directly under Avery's command. Seated at Avery's table and privy to his innermost circle. Everyone thought Morris was dead, but he was my sergeant when I became an Enforcer years ago. He'd promoted through the circle until he'd become one of Avery's closest confidants. I had a nagging feeling he'd fled when Avery had disappeared, but I didn't realize he'd joined this cult. I recognized him soon as I saw him.

"And what's more, these monks have been acting as if they're trying not to actually kill us. I think they're trying to protect something. I'm not sure if it's Avery himself, but I do know it is *something*. Whatever it is, some of them know what happened to him. The rest of them are loyal to their cause, whatever that really is. They just don't talk much. It's all fake *nickermather*. About vengeance against Black Temple and causing a great war, and the false crap about being superior to everyone because they're most willing to be wicked. The woman we were questioning admitted as much — and it's backed up by the journals and the documents Captain Robin confiscated in Tallil and Edantine. He found a codex that directed every sect to portray a certain set of goals, and to remain undercover among their *blackened brethren*."

Arius laughed. "I guess they had their own set of traitors. It's just poetic. It seems to have been sorted out, though."

"The monks on Raven Trail were more aggressive than these, certainly. They covered themselves with wolf cowls, pretending they were the Descendants of the Moon. They had no problem killing us when they were after that thief of his." Elija nodded to John. "So what makes these monks any different?"

Arius shrugged. "I have no earthly clue."

"Lukas didn't want to be taken by any of them," admitted John. "They seemed desperate to take him prisoner. Maybe he really did know what happened to Avery. He'd claimed to know Avery's whereabouts when my brother caught him after he'd murdered our parents. We were delivering him to the Reformation, but he escaped after we split at Oakwall."

"Aye. That thief of his set for Aelynhold," said Irkov. "And Oakwall is gone because of him. Burnt to ashes. All that's left are the skeletons of the trees, and the ruined wall. Not many of my people survived."

"Oakwall is gone?" asked Arius slowly. He studied the two of them more carefully, and John saw in his gaze a ghost of sympathy.

Lieutenant Elija contemplated quietly for a moment. Then he picked up the quill again. "Dr. Ivan, I'm not sure if Lukas's presence here has anything to do with our situation, but I'll include it in my report to my superiors. If he really does know Avery's location, then it is vital we locate him, and that we make him talk. Perhaps Captain Robin's men may find more about his other connections here."

When the bound monk laughed through his gag, they all looked down at him. Arius yanked the gag from his mouth and jerked his head back by the hair. "What's so funny?" asked Arius.

But the monk, Morris, just turned his head and stared at John. John's teeth clenched tightly.

"So where *is* your daughter?" Morris asked, and he blinked against the sweat that dripped into his eye. "You were supposed to have brought her. That was the deal."

Anger swelled hotly within John, and his fists clenched.

Irkov unsheathed his knife, but Elija grabbed his wrist and stayed his hand. "My daughter is safe," said John. "What is it to you? Why is she important to your little cult?"

But the monk shook his head. "He'll accept no plea and no trade. Give her to him, and your brother will live. If you have not brought her, you'll be given your brother's headless corpse."

The sound of swords clanging rose in volume, and the engines of a few of the vehicles roared to life. The shouting that rose outside nearly drowned out the pulse raging in John's ears.

Elija grimaced. "Who wants his daughter? The thief? He's the one who wants her?"

"He's not the only one who's expressed a desire to kidnap her," said John. "But yes."

Irkov snarled, pulling free of Elija. "How could anyone want to harm such a child? Who *else* wants to harm her?" The knife he held shook violently. "I'll put an end to them all!"

John believed him. "Your brother Griggori, for one. And Saura, and Lukas . . . I'm sure there are many, many more at this point. Caol's son Eiran buys them — anyone who carries the Violet, that is. Supposedly, he uses them to experiment on." He took a deep breath to steady his rage when his voice shook. "Apparently, Lukas owes some kind of debt to the Lord of Five Tower. But she'll be murdered if she's ever taken to that city."

Arius frowned. "What could a mere slip of a girl be worth? Why would *Saura* want anything to do with a single child? Hasn't she more to do than focus on just one?"

Irkov chuckled and touched his cheek with the tip of his blade, just under his ruined eye. "Oh, that child would surprise you, Arius. His daughter's the one who took my eye. Even if they got her, I doubt it would last long before they began to regret it. She's a fierce little thing. A beautifully terrifying little demon spider. Utterly gentle — except when provoked, of course. None escape her web unless she lets them. You would never meet another like her in a thousand lifetimes."

Arius sucked on his tooth, considering it.

"Your time is running out, Dr. Ivan," said Morris. "Get us the girl, and no more of your family will die. We will leave your guild and everything else you hold dear untouched."

John frowned. "The woman who burned Isold said the King of Thieves wants reparation from the Temple for my brother's crimes. She said nothing about my daughter. Why would he want her? And who is he?" Then he thought of Lukas. If Lukas had the wherewithal to get the King of Thieves to agree to pay Elsir's contract, the man was likely to also help him to get what else he wanted. But why? Was Avery's whereabouts Lukas's secret alone? Did the King of Thieves want the most valuable hostage in history?

That would explain why the two were working together.

But they wanted John's daughter. He could not abide by that.

This time, it was Irkov who kept John from stepping forward. When he followed Irkov's single, studious eye, he realized Arius's hand was resting upon his sword's handle. He stepped back, and Arius's hand relaxed fractionally.

Smoke began to filter in, and the shouting outside grew louder and closer. "Arius, look outside and see what is going on. That clamor is too close to be from the wall."

But when Arius lifted the curtain, all of them could see for themselves. The wearyworn had taken to revolt. They were attacking the Enforcers and raiding the trucks and the tents. They were arming themselves, and some had stolen vehicles and were driving them toward the wall. Toward the gate.

Arius retreated into the tent, drawing his sword as several mad-eyed wearyworn swarmed inside, roaring with rage and anger when they saw it was occupied by Enforcers. The candle on the table was knocked over, and the seal and pages and ink lit from the flame. The ink bottle exploded as John and Irkov recoiled from the blood-splattered blades that swung at them. John kicked the chair at the first who leapt over the monk to get at him, and the monk began to labor at his bonds, sawing at the ropes with his teeth as he rolled to avoid the fighting.

The wild anger in the wearyworn was no small thing. The man trying to kill John was gaunt from hunger, but he gave all his strength with every scream and every swing, and that strength seemed to surge forth without end. It was deranged desperation that drove him. Vengeance. Grief.

Every strike of his sword vibrated down John's arms as he blocked each blow with his own sword. The blade swiped across John's cheek, and then Irkov pierced the man between the ribs with his dagger. But several more wearyworn flooded into the tent, and John and the others quickly lost ground as the tent's flimsy walls converged behind them.

Arius sliced the rough fabric and retreated into the sunlight that poured in through the hole. Elija followed, and so did Irkov and John as the flames ate the enclosure vehemently. There were too many angry wearyworn for them to fight in those flaming confines, and as the flames devoured the tent, the structure collapsed, and those who had not followed them out or managed to retreat through the entrance began to scream as they were trapped and burned alive.

At the wall, arrows flew from the archers' bows, forming giant, smoking trails of flame, and leaving wakes of death rippling at the feet of the volatile mob. The Enforcers retreated from the area, scrambling to regroup. They joined other Enforcers nearby who fought to keep the wearyworn back, and then one of the vehicles near them exploded, knocking many of them off their feet and killing a few more.

John's ears rang, and he staggered to regain his balance, his head spinning. He'd dropped his own weapon, and now he held his hands against his ears as they pulsed painfully. His whole body ached, and his ears burned inside as though his eardrums had been utterly demolished. He could hardly hear, and his head continued to thrum painfully, every movement making it worse, every breath pushing harder against the building pressure in his head.

When he opened his eyes again, he sucked in a deep breath and held it, and a maelstrom of rage washed through him, overwhelming the initial shock from the explosion. It cut through the throbbing pain and drew his undivided attention.

Lukas.

Lukas stood among the wearyworn, his hood over his face to cover his blond hair, Morris leaning on him for support. Their gazes met, and while Lukas smiled a cruel and victorious smile, John snarled and reached for the gun at his hip. John was well on his feet before Irkov or the others had recovered, and he struggled to force his way through the crowd as it found its feet and began to surge into violence again.

Flaming oil poured from Aelynhold's walls as he pursued the murderous thief and the wounded monk through the thick of the fighting. He could not get a clear shot to maim either of them to slow them. Several times, he would think he had hit his target, but others who were in the way would fall instead. When the gun jammed, John racked it. The bullet was stuck. He smacked a palm against the chamber and the unspent round, and when the bullet fell, he aimed again.

Nothing.

Lukas and the monk were gone. They had vanished.

John's heart dropped into his stomach as he stared at a blank stone wall, where there were no doors, no ladders, and no windows . . . There were just a few tall trees now catching fire from the oil being sprayed from above. He stepped back as the heat grew more intense, and he looked up when he heard the command for the archers to take aim.

John staggered back, his heart racing furiously, and he took shelter behind the tall trees as a volley of flaming arrows were unleashed. He shouted his frustration as the arrows kept coming, but the wearyworn did not relent. They continued to rush the wall, holding up anything they could grab to block a few of the arrows from hitting them. Some hauled bodies, some hauled pieces of the armored vehicles they'd torn apart. Some hauled living shields who quickly turned into dead or screaming shields.

The screams of those who were splashed with oil deafened him. He flinched as a child ran from the wall and fell beside him, writhing and screaming under the trees. Her face was completely engulfed, and half of her body was being eaten by the flames, and three arrows pierced her back where she shrieked on the ground. And still, she kept screaming, and screaming, and screaming.

His hand jerked, and he was almost deafened by the gunshot that ended her. And then he realized he'd just murdered her. Instead of putting the fire out, he'd just killed her to spare her the agony. He'd just killed a *child*.

John's throat closed, and he lowered the gun with a shaking hand, revolted. He covered his ears, and he sank to his heels, his entire body quaking. He tried to focus on his goal, to remind himself why he was here.

But he could almost still hear her screams among all the others about him, and he choked on the smell of her sizzling flesh.

The volley of arrows finally ceased, and he dared to peer around the trunk, searching for the opening Lukas had found. *It had to be near!*

He tried to get close, but several times, he was driven back. Arrows flew at him before he could get within twelve meters of the wall. He clenched his teeth, desperate, and each time, he was driven back into cover behind the trees.

Still, he could see nothing along the wall. When he at last gathered his wits and searched the field behind himself, he grew even more sickened at the sight of the many dead and wounded being trampled by the angry wearyworn. He knew he couldn't stay here. Already, branches overhead were beginning to crack and break, and cinders and flaming debris cascaded down around him. He did not want to be burned alive or crushed by broken limbs, and he gave up trying to find the hidden door when it became apparent he would only end his life if he stayed. This was only going to get worse here.

At least there was another way into the city, and Elija and Arius knew where it was. He would be able to get into Aelynhold if he could get back to them. If they weren't dead.

John counted the time between the volleys of arrows, waiting until he knew for sure he would have the chance to get out of their reach without getting shot down. Hours passed before the archers began to call out for more arrows, and the sky began to take on the color of blood by the time the next volley ended. His heart leapt, and with a dreadful ache in his injured leg, he pushed through the mob again.

Then there was a desperate roar among the wearyworn. People shouted for one another to get out of the way. Just as he broke from the crowd atop the hill, John saw a wagon barreling along the road, its horses a blur and its driver invisible. There was a massive, blinding explosion at the gate below as the wagon plowed into people diving out of the way. He winced, covering his eyes as his head jerked in the opposite direction to appease the stinging of that bright light.

He blinked hard against the aftervision when he looked again, but before he could see another thing, the mob surged again.

John cringed as more screams erupted.

The gate had been cracked.

He returned to where he'd left Elija and Irkov and the other Enforcers, and found they were only *just* regrouping. "You're *alive*, you snake?" asked Arius angrily. "Where did you go when you went running off in the middle of our fight?! Elija, why would you speak well of a coward? How could you trust such a man?"

"I saw *Lukas*," John defended himself. "He and Morris made it through another entrance near the wall. I couldn't find the damned thing."

Arius remained suspicious. "You took your damned time, getting back."

"I was almost shot by several volleys of arrows and burned alive by the oil they poured over the wall," John hissed. "The gate is cracked. We should be able to get in."

Elija shook his head. "A cracked gate is not an open one. And we're not walking in through that gate, not with the fighting that's erupted. The tunnels are still our fairest, quickest chance. They don't know how much we know. They're unprepared. Let the wearyworn continue this distraction for us."

Arius snarled and then turned from them. He approached another Enforcer. They spoke quietly, and then they departed. "We'd best follow them," said Elija. "Whatever caused that explosion did not destroy the gate, but it did get their undivided attention, and most of the wearyworn are swarming that way. Perhaps the monks guarding the new entrance will be occupied if word gets to them about that gate. If not, at least they won't be getting reinforcements."

Irkov laughed. "You missed a good fight, you yellow-bellied lunatic." Irkov's ruined eye squirmed in its socket when he looked after the retreating Enforcers. He scratched at his chin, smearing the darker green paint and blood there. "But I agree with Elija and Arius. Let the wearyworn make their entrance. We have our own to pursue." He shrugged then. "Too bad you didn't get him."

"If I'd just managed to injure him, we could be getting some much-needed answers."

Irkov's laugh was raw. "A shit shot, are you? Good to know you couldn't shoot a cow, even if you had it suckling the barrel. I'll know not to trust you to have my back with that thing if we're in trouble." He nodded after the Enforcers, still chuckling. "Best hurry."

They followed the men for hours, until they were well in the trees and out of sight of Aelynhold and the revolt of the wearyworn, altogether. The other Enforcers paid little heed to John or Irkov, except to shove them out of the way when the ground began to slope downward into a steep gulch when the footing became treacherous. The brambles thickened, and John's foot slipped. His knee struck hard when he caught himself, and it brought tears to his eyes. Irkov smirked. "That look brings back memories. Hurt, did it?"

John rolled his eyes. "Not as much as your eye did, I bet."

Irkov grumbled, then. "Bee sting, nothing more. Just a fleshy little wound."

The Enforcers about them began to move more quietly as those ahead held up signals to approach with caution. Many of them drew their weapons.

An arrow struck the stone just inches from John's hip, and he nearly let go of the rock face in his surprise as the arrow bounced off and plummeted. Several of their allies looked up. One flung a dagger, quick as lightning, and then another arrow loosed as a body collapsed in the shadows of the thickest trees below. A groan escaped the Enforcer just in front of Arius, and Arius caught him before he fell from the precarious ledge. Another dagger flew from another Enforcer's hand somewhere along the line, and the second archer fell from deeper in those trees.

"Hold it together, Daniel," said Arius quietly. He broke the shaft of the arrow protruding from Daniel's abdomen. Daniel turned white, gripping Arius's forearm, but he shook his head and reached for the wall again with his shaking, bloody hand.

"There are about twelve more of them," said Daniel. "Before the cave mouth. Make sure everyone stays quiet, even if one of them gets shot. We don't want the rest of them to raise the alarm." His voice was strained as he spoke.

The next enemy John *heard* fall, rather than *saw*. Blood painted the ledge where it began to widen again. A body lay below, crumpled and broken. The woman's belly had been cut open.

John looked away from the body and focused on what was ahead as the rest of their group gathered. He'd never understood how his brother could be a part of this kind of lifestyle. The hunting and killing of other human beings. But Reid was . . . Reid. And he had always been partial with a blade, even when they were kids. John preferred being at the bedside of patients, battling death itself.

He shuddered, and then he shut out any memories as well as all of his worries for his brother. He also shut out worries for his daughter, and for his wife and his son. He focused on his mission, even as that very fear pounded at his head and made his heart ache. Distraction now could cost him his life.

"Arius," said Daniel. He was gripping his abdomen. Blood soaked through his fingers, and he was shaking badly from the injury. He was likely only standing because of the adrenaline still coursing through him. "Take your men straight to the trees," said Daniel. "We'll drive at them from the shelf above, just where the oaks end. That's where they'll come out. See it?"

"Yes."

"Wait," John said. He rummaged in his pockets for a moment and produced a small bottle. He held it out, and the dark blue glass glimmered.

Daniel looked down at it.

"Take this," said John. "It'll help until you are able to sort that properly."

It was the least he could do.

Daniel's lip curled. "Save it. You came here for your own reasons. Accomplish that." He nodded at John's limp. "And don't get my men killed by getting in the way."

John grimaced, but he held out the bottle, insisting. "Take it. You may be fighting much more than I." But Daniel turned his back on him and walked away, and nearly half of the Enforcers followed.

Irkov snatched it and pocketed it. "Free stuff," grunted the Greenman.

Arius shrugged. "He doesn't trust anyone he isn't familiar with. You two decide for yourselves how you are going to proceed. Help us, or help him. But you'll have no help from either if you stand by and do nothing at all. We've no room for cowards."

Irkov's chest puffed, and he stood tall. "Just who are you calling a coward?" His voice tangled with menace, and he slapped a fist to his chest. "Greenmen know no cowardice! Our honor — "

"We're with you," said John as he held up his hand to quiet Irkov's ego raging. Arius hadn't even been talking to Irkov.

A half hour later, the trees overhead creaked ominously, and the flickering forms of men moved like ghosts among the branches, casting shadows that darted here and there.

"Why aren't they attacking?" said Irkov. His voice trembled.

John couldn't suppress his amusement. "Greenmen have no fear, huh?"

Irkov growled low in his throat. "Greenmen *face* their fear."

"And what is it you are afraid of?"

"Ghosts," said Irkov. He hesitated as John stared at him. There was more. "Forests," he added awkwardly, quieter than before. But there was another confession, which followed just after, and which seemed to embarrass the Greenman the most. "Bees."

John bit hard on his tongue, until his eyes watered.

When Irkov looked over at him with his one eye, the big man snarled and held out his knife. "I will *cut* you," Irkov threatened.

"Forests, though?" whispered John, and he shook his head. "Golden skies, Irkov. You *lived* in the largest of them all!"

"And saw ghosts aplenty, and was stung by many bees. A Greenman faces his fears, and I faced mine every day. I have earned my place, and then some, among my brothers and sisters . . . Though I'll admit freely that your daughter's wrath frightens me the most." He touched his eye with the strangest fondness, as though his ruined eye was a badge of honor, a priceless, treasured gift. "I shall never disappoint that wonderful child. I will never have the courage to anger her, I fear. I would kneel and call her *queen* first. I do not want to become a blind mute."

"You are a very strange man, Irkov," sighed John at last, and he shook his head. "I will never understand the absolute simplicity of your people."

They fell silent as the men in the trees unleashed a volley of arrows. Each one struck the ground at an angle, until a circle was formed about their group.

"Turn away so we may not shed blood," a man called out from the forest about them.

When Irkov frowned, Elija noticed it also. "What is it?"

"That sounded like Elsir. One of the men under my command in Oakwall. He's the traitor who disappeared shortly after Oakwall was set ablaze." Irkov lifted his dagger, and he gripped it, his expression darkening. "Is that *you*, Elsir?" he called out.

A bickering laugh returned, but no other reply.

Irkov sighed. "No one laughs like that but him." He shook his head, irritated, and then he called out again. "You do know what this means, do you not?"

"Turn away, Irkov. Tell these merry fools to do the same. They won't want this blood on their hands."

"We're past that already. You and your hooded friends are in our way."

"You don't even know what *that* is, so there is no being past it. *Turn away.*"

There was a long silence. Arius nodded and waved for him to continue. "Keep them talking. The longer they're distracted, the better."

Irkov nodded. "Why did you leave when we needed you most, anyway?"

"I've a new purpose, Irkov. I'm not going home. I work for the King of Thieves now. I told you that when you threatened to gut me."

"Too much a coward to be a devout Man of the Forest, eh?" Irkov's grip on the knife tightened. "Couldn't face your biggest fear and overcome it like the rest of us, and earn your oaken grave? Your name will never be carved onto the forest's faceless watchers. Your family has been dishonored by your actions, Elsir. Your sins will one day devour you because of it."

The wind rustled the leaves. "You know . . . I always feared *leaving* the most. So I think I've honored our people by doing exactly that. Betraying everything we *Men of the Forest* were contracted to do. Abandoning Black Temple's brainwashed little coven of obedient wall guardians was my trial, Irkov. You know the truth of that more than anyone. What'd they ever really do for us there, anyway?"

"They gave us immunity. For our children, and for theirs, until the end," said Irkov. "Unless we betray them."

"How do you know? Immunity from what, really? Diseases that shook people so long ago that no one dies from them anymore? I was never happy to have such a weak rope chafing at my throat, Irkov."

John grew angry. "Saura's planning on Breaking the Vial, Elsir." Elija's head jerked. So did Irkov's. "She's given the order to prepare for it. That immunity will be for nothing if no one is there who can stand in the way of it even if it's unleashed. That immunity is the only reason Greenmen can fight against her without fear. You weren't just guarding Black Temple; you were commissioned to fight against the guild if the wearyworn ever needed you to do so. You're on the wrong side of this."

"Nah. No thanks. I've been more comfortable living this way. More fun. Better company — "

A gun blasting through the canopy cut short Elsir's boast, and it was followed by several curses and more gunfire. The shadows above darted away, though several fell from the branches. More gunshots echoed farther in the trees, and they were echoed by the mouth of the cave that none of them could yet see.

"After them!" shouted Arius, and the Enforcers who'd snuck away to shoot several of the monks above rose with the rest of them and charged forward.

As they rushed forward, a blade sliced through the leaves just to Irkov's right, and Irkov spun and grabbed it and turned it against the monk holding it. He froze as a wet gasp cut through the leaves. John slowed, surprised when Irkov knelt with the dying man. "You leafy, red-bearded *fool*," snarled Irkov.

"Well, that's a foul surprise," laughed Elsir, that bickering laugh of his breaking apart in the blood that gurgled past it. "At least I had some fun, you one-eyed honor-junkie," he said. He lifted a bloody hand and slapped Irkov's cheek, brother to brother. "He's a glorious liar, Irkov. I loved working for him, more than I ever . . ."

"What am I to tell your sister?" asked Irkov. "I cannot lie to her!"

"Tell that psychotic, rat-faced goat I went and got myself free from the contract. I overcame my worst nightmare, and it was the spitting, funniest thing I ever did," laughed Elsir. And as blood spilled from his lips, he stopped breathing.

Irkov's fingers stretched over Elsir's face, and then his fist closed and tightened. He shoved the dead man's body away and pulled the knife away as he stood. "I suppose he did die with *some* honor, after all. He'd always been more terrified of the forest than I. Would never brave it even to leave camp. Those dark ghosts." Irkov shook his head and slung the blood from his hand.

He and John hurried forward, and the light began to dim as the forest led into the huge cavern.

They fought until the walls began to quake. Debris fell from above, killing a few of the men nearby. Some of the rubble bruised John's shoulder and right arm. He and Irkov dove from a massive stone that crashed and shattered into thousands of slivers. Several men — monks and Enforcers alike — were killed by it. The dust that stirred up muffled the sounds of the fighting and made it almost impossible to see. Small rays of light pierced the thick curtain that choked them, and John retreated against the cave wall, holding his sleeve to his nose and his mouth as he coughed.

He felt along the stone, but he tripped over another bit of what he thought was debris. It wasn't. It was a small rail, torn from the wall and bent sideways. He fell forward, dropping his gun and his dagger, and then there was nothing on which to catch himself.

First, his shoulder struck the wall. Then his ribs struck the corner of another rock, this one much lower . . . and then his knee and his wrist cracked on another protrusion, even lower. And then he landed on his back so hard his head struck the ground and he saw white and could not take another breath. His lungs closed, and his body lost all feeling except the immense pain that clouded his awareness. Only a thread of air slipped into him with the greatest and most enduring effort, until dizziness stole him next.

Everything was so dark that he could not see the faintest silhouette of any shape or form where he'd landed.

He tried to move, but his hand only slid down the stone wall, leaving behind the smell of blood. Every tendon and bone felt shredded in his hand; from his knuckles to his elbow, the fire radiated viciously.

The thread of air grew fractionally wider as his lungs finally filled to capacity, but they still wouldn't work to pump the oxygen he needed so desperately. He couldn't breathe . . . couldn't . . .

His senses drifted away, and he lost all awareness of time.

When John came to, he ached substantially. Everywhere. His head spun when his eyelids fluttered open, and that same darkness was all that greeted him. But he tested his body regardless. His hand wasn't broken, it seemed. No splintered, unsupported bones seemed to hinder or cause pain in his shoulder or his leg, either. Possibly several fractures of various types, but he was able to breathe again, even though his ribs and his back were very sore. His lungs felt as though they'd been stretched and had torn, but he suspected he was mostly okay. He had feeling and movement.

John groaned when he tried to roll over. Everything hurt worse when he did so.

There were no other sounds but for those he caused, which echoed down what sounded like a very long corridor. He had no clue whether this corridor was natural or man-made — he couldn't see the cavernous thing. There was not even a *pinch* of light.

Head pounding, he took a deep breath, and then he pulled his hands under him, put his weight on them, and shifted. He hissed when a line of razored fire shot through his back, along his left scapula. When he rolled the muscles and bones carefully, assessing, he guessed it was deep bruising and brutally scraped skin. Small rocks that had imbedded in his flesh began to fall as he moved, and he dusted himself off. He felt something wet trickling from his nose, and he realized it was his own blood as he wiped it away.

He was lucky that fall hadn't broken or killed him.

John looked up, and still, he couldn't see any light. He had no idea how long he'd been unconscious, either. It could be simply that it was nighttime. He heard nothing above, so either everyone there was dead or they'd all moved on.

John checked himself. All he had left of his weaponry was his sword. And half the blade had broken off.

He whispered another quiet oath and then thought of what his brother would have to say about that. Armed with only a broken blade, and no idea where he was in enemy territory. "Reid'll have my hide," he chuckled, sheathing the broken weapon. He had no idea where the other half of his sword was. He also had no idea whether there were any other pits to fall into, so when he placed his hand on the wall again, he did not stray from it. And he stepped carefully.

Hours and hours later, John's fingertips were sore from scraping along the rough stone continuously. The corridor *felt* straight, although he had no way of really knowing whether that was the case.

Eventually, he knew he would find some kind of entrance or exit, or it would veer off another direction. It had to. He was sure he'd already walked ten or more miles of tunnel. He was tired and sore, even though he was still determined to find an exit. And he was growing desperate. If it was nighttime, he had only the rest of this night and then two more days before his brother's execution. And that was only if he'd been unconscious just a few hours rather than days.

John's steps quickened as his dread grew more intense.

Something hissed. The sound was long and piercing in the darkness. He could not tell whether it came from ahead or emanated from behind him. But the sound penetrated him viciously. He felt its cold touch drifting through him, like an ethereal hand, and he shivered, wrapping his arms about himself as his shoulder scraped the wall. His instincts whispered to turn around as the hairs on the back of his neck stood on end.

But he gritted his teeth and kept moving. It was a snake. It had to be a snake, nothing more. And it sounded too far from him to harm him.

Hunger began to claw at him a few hours after thirst had already made his throat raw. His canteen offered no water, as it had been destroyed when he'd fallen. He had no rations with him. And he did not trust the dripping sound coming from above, as he imagined that whatever was causing the sound was infused with whatever was making the tunnel smell so badly. The odor was reminiscent to that of the dead, but . . . worse. Not that there was much that *smelled* worse.

He couldn't identify this scent, though. It was unfamiliar. But it burned his nose and made his eyes sting.

Those hours of walking turned into more hours, and then more hours . . . until his knees buckled.

But he had to save his brother . . .

He could hardly think, and when he placed his hand on the ground to try to get up, his strength left him, and he fell forward instead. He was barely aware when the ground rushed upward to greet him, and he did not feel the cold surface strike him. He did not feel his own hot blood pooling about his face where his head continued to bleed . . .

He had to save his brother, a fleeting thought reminded him . . .

Then . . .

Nothingness.

An atrocious scream awakened John. He could hardly move his head when his eyelids fluttered open, and he grimaced from the faint ray of light that shone down from a grate far, far above him. He nearly lost consciousness again, but another scream erupted from another strangled throat.

His senses began to buzz, and adrenaline coursed through him as a sense of dread filled him. Something was wrong. But what was wrong? Why was that screaming inspiring such a feeling of fear in him . . . ?

He just wanted to . . . to sleep.

Movement ahead caught in his vision, and when he moved his head against the damp stone, everything blurred in and out of focus.

The sunlight was so very faint down here . . . His eyes began to close again.

Slowly, John became aware that he was hearing a man being *strangled*. But he couldn't see anyone.

Then the faintest gleaming golden color came into focus. *Pale hair . . .*

John heard a monstrous sound. A demonic, inhuman sound, and then he *felt* it — a sound so primal and hungry that it set his heart racing and flooded every vein with an intense fear he could not explain.

A body crashed to the floor just a few feet from him, and John's wide eyes followed the shadows upward, to a clawed hand that was covered in blood . . . and behind that bloody appendage were golden eyes that caught the faint sunlight and multiplied it and reflected it back eerily, as though the light came from within those eyes rather than from without.

Then John was staggering backward, away from the monstrous being, his mind confused and too filled with terror for him to realize what he had just witnessed, or what this being was. It felt ancient. Its eyes were filled with a gruesome knowing and a tainted power that he could not explain.

The instinct screaming inside him to *run* jerked him backward when the being turned his gaze upon him.

He felt something brush against his mind, and a cold sweat broke out across his flesh as he stumbled backward instinctively like a terrified animal. The being's face twisted as if to grimace.

The ancient being opened his mouth . . .

All John saw was blood, and then he was running for his life. He didn't know why, and he didn't care why. He'd *never* felt such fear in him. He only knew he was about to die.

The sound of the demon followed him, and the walls themselves began to crack, and rubble began to fall about him. John fled blindly, having no idea where the first turn he took would take him. The hallway began to wind upward, spiraling toward the grates above. The hairs on the back of his neck rose on end when he reached out, crashing into the wall in front of him, and he turned onto the next spiraling flight of stairs.

He felt the being's presence reaching out for him, and he fled from it as it grew closer and closer. Even as the distance between them closed inch by inch.

The grate moved much more easily than he'd anticipated when he threw his weight against it, and he crashed through it and fell onto a cobblestone alleyway, and he clawed at the stones to get back on his feet.

Something seized him, and he could not move another inch. His fingers wouldn't respond. His breath wouldn't come or go. His mouth had frozen open, though not a sound would leave him.

He couldn't look behind himself, not even when he heard the grate begin to scrape slowly across the ground. Sweat began to bead on his forehead, and his heart felt as if it were about to explode —

And then the presence was gone, and he was released from its grip. His breath rushed out in a distressed, desperate gasp, and when he got the nerve to look behind him, he saw that the grate was fastened in place as though it had never been moved at all.

John was alone.

His entire body shook as he stood and backed away. He didn't know why he felt that fear, or what it was, exactly, that he had seen. But he knew he wanted never to be near it again. He had *zero* curiosity for whatever was in the tunnels beneath this city. Even if Avery himself was down there, he wouldn't dare enter the tunnels alone again.

He left the alley, still shaking, and went into the street, where he saw smoke rising from the buildings. The wearyworn had gotten into the city while he'd been trapped in that tunnel.

John stared at the broken gate, which still sizzled and sparked violet where it had been turned to glass. It was the same strange glass that had been created in Black Temple and Five Tower. It had been made by the same mysterious bombs. Dread filled him at the sight of it, and he thought of his daughter and prayed she was safe and well.

He flinched away from the guards who ran past him, but they were uninterested in him. They were more concerned with keeping the Enforcers and the wearyworn out. Wounded citizens fled by him, and another explosion destroyed the building across the street.

John limped toward it, his instinct to help the wounded so strong for a moment that it nearly clouded his judgement and exposed him. He realized a monk had broken from among the guards' sortie against the intruders and had noticed him. The monk had paused, suspicious, and John hid his hand as he turned so that his ring would not be seen. He limped away.

Another of Aelynhold's guards stopped him abruptly, grabbing his shoulder and forcing him to turn. John winced. "The wounded were ordered to evacuate this part of the city hours ago. Why are you still here?"

John realized he must look a right mess if the guard was mistaking him for a wounded citizen. Normally, his attire would have given him away, but his clothes were so shredded and stained by his own blood that it was hardly recognizable to the guard as not being something worn in Aelynhold regularly. John opened his mouth, but he was unsure what to say.

"Get going!" snapped the guard.

John nodded, and he backed away. He wasn't sure where to go, but he knew it was going to be in the opposite direction of that gate. So he followed the main road, and in so doing, he passed probably two hundred or more of Aelynhold's monks. Many were on the rooftops, among the archers. Many waited in the shadows. All of them were armed.

They seemed to watch him. No matter where he turned, there were more of them. And scattered among them were a few of Aelynhold's guards . . . and a few Enforcers. John's heart began to race again. He knew what trouble looked like, and this was certainly it. He didn't know what they were waiting for, but whatever it was, it wasn't good.

Dizziness overtook him, and he leaned against the stone facade of a small shop, which was closed. The window remained cracked open, though the door was bolted shut. He moved toward the door and knocked. He simply knew he had to get out of sight, to cast off any suspicion before anyone realized he wasn't from Aelynhold. "Can you let me in, please?" he called. He wasn't even sure there was anyone inside. When he received no answer, he knocked again. "Please — "

The door opened, and an angry old woman smacked him in the face with a broom. "We're closed! Go away!" The door shut once more.

"Momma, he's hurt!" cried a young woman from inside. The door opened an inch, but the older woman slammed it again.

"We don't know him, Alita! Stay away from the door."

"Shame on you, Momma!"

The door opened again as John's calf seized. He grimaced, clutching at the open wound. "I don't need much help," he rasped. "I can pay for any you offer."

The older woman saw the ring upon his hand and blenched. "Throw him to the street, Alita! He's — "

"I'm a field doctor. I'm not from Aelynhold," he said. "I came to rescue my brother because your leader here is going to kill him. I want no other trouble. I did not come to murder anyone. *Please*."

When he looked up again, he saw Alita's chin trembling. She blinked back tears and then put her dark hair up. And then she stepped forward and slipped her arm under his and helped him inside.

"Alita! Alita, you'll get us exiled!" cried the older woman.

"Shush, Momma. Black Temple's guildsmen are honorable men. How dare you ask me to throw one to the streets? They'll kill him!"

"They'll kill *us* if they find out — "

"Then I suggest you shut your loud mouth, old woman, before the monks hear you, shouting it for all to hear. Goodness, Momma, be quiet!"

John nearly missed the chair Alita led him to, and a pale haze almost took everything from his sight as he wavered.

"That's an awful lot of blood," said Alita, and she darted behind the bar and retrieved a basket. "You're lucky we sell some things for those who know anything at all about medicine, sir. He's pale as a ghost — Momma, get him something to drink and eat, and then get me that bottle of *Rack* from the shelf. And the sewing kit! And be quick about it! He looks as if he got run over, stomped, and then crushed just after! I'm sorry, but I've not stitched anyone this seriously hurt before; it'll be terrible work. I'm not sure what other injuries you may have . . . I'm not trained for anything more than sprains and simple injuries. I've little experience with any serious stuff. I used to learn from the doctors who came through, years ago. But I was just a girl then. I'm afraid I may not be adequate if you require any sort of surgery."

"Just give the needle to me, I'll do the stitching," said John. "And something to wrap this leg with. At this point, it just looks worse than it is. I cannot stay long, so I'll leave once I've eaten and paid you for your trouble."

"Oh, no. No Black Temple doctor pays for food or care under this roof," Alita hissed. "Don't you even dare. It is our honor to serve you, sir. I would not dare turn away any proper guildsmen. Not me. I'm not like those monks, or my Momma here, scared out of her mind by all of this. Lord Drake did all the damage he could these last few years, since his cousin left everything to him. He was a *terrible* man, Drake was. But it'll be right as rain soon, I promise. The lord is dead, that's the rumor. And his wife is only hiding it because the King of Thieves wants it under wraps until . . ."

"Until what?"

"You said your brother? You're here to rescue your brother?"

"Yes."

She looked away. "There was a man executed three days ago. In the city square."

John shut his eyes as he felt a tremor run through him.

"An outsider. I hope it wasn't him. They displayed it. It was the most unusual, sickening thing, to display an execution. Drake was a bad man, but he never did that. He just let those wolfmen take people. But even then, they didn't stay in the city after sunset."

"Three days ago?" John's mouth felt as though it had filled with sand. He sucked in a deep breath. "Did you see the execution?" His heart was ready to burst with grief.

"Heavens, no. I never wanted any part of that horrible thing."

"Was there any detail about him that reached you?" It was difficult to form any words at all. When John looked up, her face blurred, and when it came back into focus, he felt his heart struggling to beat regularly. He took a deep breath, trying to calm himself, telling himself not to give up until he knew for *sure* that it was his brother who had been executed.

"Hair like yours. Blue eyes," said Alita's mother coldly. She uncorked the bottle and poured it on his wound before he had time to process what she'd said.

John's teeth nearly shattered as fire soared through his nerve endings. Alita opened his hand and placed a threaded needle in his palm. He gasped, leaned forward, and almost emptied what little was in his stomach. She caught him before he fell from the chair, and she pulled him back toward the counter.

"He was searching for a man who can cure my daughter," John struggled to say. "He can't be dead."

"Maybe it was another. Hair as light as yours isn't unheard of, and blue eyes aren't uncommon," she said. "You keep yourself together until you know for sure."

What if it *had* been Reid they'd executed?

"Pour the alcohol on the string and the needle," he said through clenched teeth. She did as he'd commanded, and then she continued to hold him upright as he lifted his leg, braced it on the stool next to him, and set to work on his opened wound.

"Was that an arrow or a knife that got you?"

"First the one, then the other," John hissed. "My family and I had just left Black Temple when we found Isold burning. Your city's monks were killing everyone there. That's how I found out my brother was being held here, accused of some crime — I don't even know what crime he's supposedly committed. They didn't say. But I know he is no criminal."

"He was framed?"

"Most assuredly. They wanted me to come here. They wanted me to bring my daughter, to trade her. She's special to them for some reason."

Alita's apprehension showed plainly on her face. "Lord Drake often sold anyone infected with the Violet to the wolfmen. He had those cannibals traipsing about the city during the day. It really wouldn't surprise me at this point. I am sorry my liege was such a terrible man, and I am sorry about your brother's predicament. If there is anything else we can do that wouldn't put our heads on a spike, ask, and we will do what we can."

"I just need to know where I am going. I don't know this city. I don't want to run into anyone that will draw a sword against me, because I am not here to fight. I just want my brother."

A stale loaf of bread slapped the counter before him, and a cup with some foul-smelling fluid slid next to it. Alita's mother stared at him. When John looked up, he noticed tears glittering in the old woman's lashes. She crossed her arms and shook her head. "I'm not completely in agreement with my daughter's kindness, but you *seem* honest, young man. And desperate enough to have risked your own neck to get here in these conditions, what with the wearyworn revolting and tearing down the gate, and the Enforcers outside, and you being in the condition you're in, yet still asking. I think *maybe* Alita's right about you."

Alita wrapped his leg as he grabbed the loaf of stale, tasteless bread and tore into it with startling hunger. The drink was bitter, but he gulped it fiendishly, and then he returned to the bread. Half of it was gone before Alita had fastened the wrapping. She poured some of the bottled alcohol onto another cloth and dabbed at the bloody mess on John's head. He hissed, cringing.

"Don't worry about the rest of me," he said. "Nothing else is quite as exposed for infection to take hold. I can take care of small injuries later." He reached into his tunic and drew from a pocket a small leather purse. He tossed it onto the table in front of him. "I said I would pay, and now I have. You've risked yourself to help me. How do I find where they would keep my brother, or where they would execute him?"

Alita's mother moved to the window and drew the curtain aside, briefly. "The road leads up to another curtain wall. Follow that wall to the north side, and you will find a stairway there. It's a small one. An old one. Never guarded. Mind your steps, some of them are unstable. You'll want to climb those steps until you reach the catwalk. Follow it up to the top, between the towers, and you'll find yourself staring down over the old highway bridges. They've reinforced them several times since they were built hundreds of years ago, but there are still some precarious sections you'll want to tread carefully. You'll see the temple at the square."

John nodded, but her instructions were not complete. She continued.

"To the east, the main road below splits off and begins to roll uphill. At the top of that hill is a small forest, where sits the lord's manor. You should see the rooftops among the trees. Keep following the catwalk until you find the last stairwell. That will take you to the main road, which leads directly to it. The eastern wing of the manor leads down into the dungeons. But you cannot get to that wing if you do not enter the main hall in the manor. The windows are barred, and there are no other entrances that I know of. Just the one behind the iron pillars therein."

Alita stared at her mother. "Maybe your soul can be saved, after all."

"Hmph. I'm sending him to get himself caught. I did my duty. I'll not get exiled for it, and he was already sewn up when he came into this city. Anyone who saw him come here asks, we only saw the ring on him and sent him to get caught. After taking his gold, of course." The old woman winked at John and then left the room. The gold purse left with her.

Alita shook her head. "Momma's a basket of wasps," she said. "She stings a lot but never worse, if you can handle it." Alita placed the cloth on the table. "The square where they executed that man is just out front, before the mansion. But there are a lot of guards and a lot of monks there. Lady Normane's daughter — if she is back — I would recommend you avoid her. They're good women, but they conceal themselves as otherwise. They wouldn't be above killing you, if it meant saving this city or pacifying the monks and the King of Thieves."

"Do you know anything about him?" asked John. "We've gotten relatively little information on him. But he's the reason my brother was arrested. And he intends to attack Black Temple."

He watched her react to that news. She didn't seem to like the idea at all. "If he wants to destroy or hurt your guild, then he can go to hell," she said. "I'll go with you. I have friends who can help bring that matter to the lady's attention. I doubt she would agree with such a thing."

John refused, however. "You go find your friends. I'll find my own way. I couldn't risk your life, having you accompany me." He finished the last of the bread, finished the foul drink, and stood carefully. She'd wrapped the injury tightly. He could stand on it well enough. "I thank you for your hospitality, Alita. I am indebted to you and to your mother for it."

Alita's head bowed. "Then go save your brother. Use the back door, just through there. That's the direction you'll be heading anyway."

John moved toward the door.

"Wait."

He turned.

"Hide your ring."

He looked at his hand. "Ah . . . Thanks." And he removed the ring.

CHAPTER FIFTY-FIVE

Broken Gate

NYMERIA HELD HER BREATH AS the wagon careened out of control. She'd lost the reins, and her eyes widened as the archers over the wall began to fire flaming arrows at the refugee camp outside Aelynhold's walls. The trees were on fire, and smoke poured from the tents, and there was screaming all around her.

The bright crimson color of blood drew her attention like brilliant flags waving across a field of gray and ashes, and the color stirred the cold feeling growing inside her. She felt it rippling under her skin. It coiled beneath the surface as though preparing to strike the world around her. The cold, evil thing could sense the deaths all around her, and it seemed to draw strength from them.

She told herself to fight it. She would never let it out again. *Never!*

Nymeria clenched her teeth and continued to try to reach for the reins as the horses screamed and raced from the gunshots and explosions around them. The rioting wearyworn kept them frightened and racing in a wild frenzy, and as they plowed through the fighting mob, the Enforcers took defensive stances and raised their weapons against the angry people. The horses veered from the aggressive clamor, and the wagon teetered dangerously, and the wearyworn converged.

The Enforcers there never stood a chance. There were too many wearyworn.

Her fingers grazed the tether briefly, and she thought she heard a whimper from under the canopy behind her. Then the wheels crashed over a series of ruts, and the rail came up and bruised her ribs. She recoiled with a cry as the first arrows struck the wagon.

"Stop that wagon!" came a scream from over the gates, and Nymeria looked up as a raven-haired woman waved her arms and pointed at her and the horses.

The Enforcers near the gate dodged the great, bouncing, wooden vessel as it headed toward them, and she saw how the horses struggled to turn, both pulling in opposite directions but bound together and fast coming upon the gate. She gripped the rail, grasping for that tether, and the wheels left the ground.

A scream from the back made her head jerk, and her heart rose into her throat. That was her brother's cry! *"Jamie?!"* She knew that voice better than any. As she recoiled from more arrows, her knees struck the bench, and then a thick coil of that black energy pulsed through her body. She looked up at the gate again, distressed. They were going to crash into it. Her chin trembled, and she reached for the rail again, desperately. "Stop!" she cried to the horses. "Stop running!"

Their wild panting parted the smoke.

The gate loomed overhead.

Nymeria shut her eyes tightly, and the breath left her as she realized the mistake she'd made. She shouldn't have thought she could make a difference.

And then the ringing in her ears ratcheted up in volume, and then she screamed as the Violet coursed through her and tore itself from her, ripping through her skin and burning every cell in its path as it went. Everything bathed in the white-hot light, and she felt the wagon dissolve from around her as she was thrown from it. The crash was terrible, and she rolled violently. She felt her bones crack and tasted the earth where her face planted. But then that darkness began to filter in behind the aching and the loathsome burns the light had left in her. At first, it was a trickle as she gasped, curling in on herself. But then she felt her bones mending, and it made her feel sick. She gulped the air as though it had been pulled from her lungs too long.

It was so cold, that shadow in her.

She could feel him, shivering and in chains, his mind filled with nothing but screams and agony. She could feel his skin, taught across his bruised ribs, his own blood all over the ground around him. The stranger's presence became so clear to her that she seemed almost to drift from her own body, to become part of him. She could feel his grim and harrowing hatred, his thirst for vengeance, the yawning ocean of sorrow and madness that *was him*. His throat seemed to have become fire. His tongue seemed coated in earth. His veins felt as though they were filled with lava and glass, and his fingers felt cold and meatless.

His blindness crawled over her, through her. She saw nothing but darkness. Felt it. Tasted it. Smelled it. It was like an oily substance she couldn't wash away, couldn't emerge from . . . and then, within it, she saw clearly a memory that she knew belonged to him. It drifted, fleetingly, through his fractured mind — like dust, expelled from the rafters of some skeletal ruin.

"You should have just let us execute you, Mihai," came the cold, angry voice of a man from the other side of a stone wall. *"Look at what you've done. What you've become. Are you even in there anymore? Or are you just this . . . creature now? A fiend, bent on some mad quest to destroy us all? Let us end your life. It would be kinder than this."*

The stranger's hatred scalded her, it was so icy, and Nymeria recoiled from it.

She could taste his words as they rolled across his tongue, *"Dae ziet'u eka . . ."*

We will kill you all . . .

The echo chasing after his voice penetrated the resilient silence that continued to choke and dim his consciousness. But rage rocked through him in tremors, until his entire body convulsed and tensed and drew strength from it. Until the fire scalding every cell in his body began to burn with agony again . . .

Nymeria fought against the memories that belonged to him. To the stranger named *Mihai*. She did not want to be swallowed by his shadow again. She had to save her uncle. Her father. *Her little brother.*

When she opened her eyes again, there was fire everywhere. The panicked wearyworn were running in every direction. The dead littered the ground in heaps of burnt and bloodied flesh, and the gate itself had been turned to glass — and it had shattered. Giant shards of glittering black sparked with bolts of violet as the shards crumbled and splintered.

The surviving archers who'd been atop the wall near the blast were screaming.

Below, the injured echoed the screams, and Nymeria saw shadows in the forms of men bleeding from the smoke billowing among them. The same marks that had crossed Mark's shoulder crawled across their flesh.

Nymeria's heart beat wildly with fear at the sight of those unholy creatures. They loomed overhead like vile demon trees, burning with black flame, and their broken horns glistened with cinders and rising smoke.

The dark things stood amidst the carnage, seeming unseen by the rest of the world. The people who were screaming leaned away from where the creatures touched them, and they clawed at their eyes, and their mouths began to bleed, and yet even *they* seemed unable to see the creatures. A man vomited blood before her, and his dark eyes met hers, briefly, before they rolled back in his head.

"*Save us . . .*" he rasped, and his hand stretched out for her. "*Save us, Bright One . . .*"

Nymeria cringed as the world began to change color, to bleed into reds and blacks as the other colors began to fade. The ground beneath her began to sizzle, and when she struggled to get up, to move away from the creatures and the death that was all around her, she saw the shadows curling under her skin.

The tall creatures shifted as one, and the shadows radiating from them moved as though a breeze had stirred them. And she heard them call out as one, "*Sssssiiiiiiiiisssssssssstttteeeeeeerrrrrrrrrr . . . Rrrreeeeettttuuuuuuuurn tooooo uuuuuussssssssssss . . .*"

She gulped when she heard her brother's hysterical crying, and she remembered him with sudden clarity. She clawed at the dirt, desperate to get back to the wagon.

"Myria!" cried Jamie. "NYMERIA!" He'd never wailed so loudly. She knew it meant he was hurt, and badly. The creatures would kill him, she knew, and terror seized her as she crawled toward him.

The wagon was aflame, and he couldn't get out from under it. But part of the side of it had turned to black glass and was cracking, much like the gate. It was the only way to get to him.

She knew she would have to risk the shards cutting her to save him.

The horses struggled against their tethers, screaming as the fire burned them, and she cringed when she sensed the pain they felt. She wanted to help them, too, but she had to get to her brother first. She wanted to help the other people who were being hurt by the creatures and the glass, too. But Jamie was screaming.

And then the archers surged over the bridge above the gate again, and the Enforcers regrouped, and the fighting intensified around them, like a great and savage sea of rage and death. And worst of all was the thing inside her, beating at her from the inside, devouring the chaos around her like a living entity all its own.

She could feel every death.

Every.

Single.

One.

She could feel every cry, as though every one of them were her own.

She wanted to scream at them all to stop, but she couldn't find her voice.

She was powerless to do anything but try and get to her little brother, to protect him from it all.

The archers atop the wall took aim again, and her heart seized as part of the wagon's frame collapsed and her brother screamed. Some of the glass fell away and reflected the flames brightly.

Her fingers curled into a fist as she found her way to her feet and raced back to him, and as she crashed into the burning bed and rolled out of sight of the archers, she heard the whistling of sailing arrows.

Her brother, she saw, was curled small against the sacks of wheat and the broken crate, and ashes drifted down over him as the smoke bellowed about them, and he was choking. He covered his eyes, his lashes clenched tight against the tears that flooded his cheeks, and he continued to scream in his fear. Nymeria shuddered and took a deep breath, and she looked over her shoulder.

She winced when another flame of that stranger's anger rolled through her, and she felt it pulling at her, drawing her in. It felt as though it was trying to drown her, to erase her. And that scared her. She felt that anger telling her to *make* them all stop. To make them all . . . *die*.

Nymeria nearly recoiled when Jamie threw himself at her and grabbed her and held on to her.

"Take me home! Please take me home, Sissy! I wanna go home! Where is Daddy?! I don't want to be here!"

Nymeria felt his whole body trembling, and she, too, shook as she wrapped her arms around him. "Why did you come with me?" she wept. "You weren't supposed to come, Jamie." Her stomach rolled at the sight of the blood on his cheek when he looked up at her. "Are you hurt?"

Instead of answering her, he continued to cry, and he laid his head against her again.

He seemed only bruised and scratched and afraid, though it was small comfort. They would soon burn alive if they didn't flee the relative safety of the wagon; yet the arrows would kill them if they left it.

Nymeria sniffled as the heat radiating from the burning wood grew more intense. "We can't stay here, Jamie. The wagon is on fire."

"I'm not going out there!" he cried. "You can't make me!"

"We can't stay here, we'll die," she said. She pulled him with her against the planks opposite the flames as the shadow rolled through her again, and she hugged him, gasping.

"You're hurt," he whimpered, and he looked up at her. Then he saw the shadows in her skin. "What is that, Myria?"

"I don't know," she choked.

She held out her hand, and the grass beneath it began to die. The decay spread under them.

Horrified, she pulled away from her brother. "*I'm a monster*," she said, and sorrow bubbled up from within her, until she couldn't breathe through the tears. It was just like the dark things. They made the plants wither and die.

Her brother reached out for her again, but she cringed from him, afraid she would harm him. She knew she shouldn't touch him again, not if everything was dying because of her.

She wanted it to stop. *She wanted all of it to stop.*

"Don't!" she shouted, and so Jamie began to cry again.

The horses had become silent by the time the first volley of arrows had ended, and the wearyworn who had been shot contorted on the ground, screaming. More ear-splitting screams erupted as oil poured from the wall when the wearyworn tried to ram the cracked gate. Then there was a great uproar at the gate, and when Nymeria peaked around the side of the wagon, she realized the entire gate had turned to glass — and so had some of the wall.

That crack grew wider, and the rest of it shattered and fell as the wearyworn threw projectiles at it and hacked at it. "Let us in!" shouted many of them. "Give us food and water!" shouted some.

But those who were near death near the wagon screamed nothing at all.

The decay kept spreading, until it reached the dying wearyworn, and Nymeria held her breath as she saw the black creeping through their veins, infecting them. The whites of their eyes began to bleed, like the others before.

But then the archers were taking aim again, and swords began to chime in battle again as the gate was breached.

Then a set of hands gripped her shoulders fiercely and unforgivingly, and Jamie screamed as Nymeria was dragged out from behind the wagon. The archers were knocking their arrows and leaning forward and taking aim, and the man who had grabbed her held her up as a shield against them, and Jamie ran after her and her abductor as she fought and clawed him. Her fingers raked across the man's jaw, and he hissed. Then his fingers were wrapping around her throat, and she was choking.

And then an arrow sliced her cheek, and another sliced across the side of her ribs.

She gasped, recoiling from the blood now trickling down her skin, from the knowledge that she was going to die.

The blood . . . The smell of so much blood . . .

Another of Mihai's memories bled into her mind as she shut her eyes and tried to draw a breath to scream again.

A forest, littered with hundreds of bodies. Blood on his hands. The smell of smoke and death curling through the trees as the breeze ruffled the branches. The feel of a cold, heavy blade gripped in his fingers, the way it sliced through flesh with ease and crunched against bone. The screaming inside his head as the creatures possessing him compelled him to take the throat of another. The feel of the victim's hands clutching at his own throat to try to pry him off, to try to kill him. A knife slicing through his wrist, and the screams . . . the never-ending screams . . .

She couldn't scream, not even when Mihai's wound traced her wrist as though the phantom knife had sliced her instead of him. But she was only barely aware that it had marked her, or that another arrow shot from above had driven clean through her shoulder and left a hole that then stitched itself together, and far faster than any other wound she'd ever healed from.

She couldn't breathe . . .

Nymeria's body jolted.

She forgot her vow never to try to use the Violet again, and she let go of her abductor's hands as he choked her. She grabbed his face as rage consumed her, and she commanded the Violet to burn him. It coursed brightly through her flesh, through the scars that remained. But then it blinked out, and instead, shadow took its place. The black shadow infected him instead of the Violet, and he dropped her and began to scream as it crept through his skin and his eyes.

The marks upon him began to draw the dark things, and as Nymeria clutched at her bruised throat, gasping for air, an Enforcer who was battling another of the wearyworn fell into the man who'd tried to use her as a shield from the arrows. The infected man fell into the fire consuming the wagon as Jamie raced to her side and cowered there with her.

The man kept screaming as the fire began to consume him, and he kept screaming as he crawled from the fire. But his voice began to change, to turn into something else. Nymeria and Jamie stared in horror as he clawed at the ground, moving toward her and her brother. His eyes began to turn red, and the screaming turned into a creature's guttural growling — like some diseased animal. And then he grabbed Jamie's foot as the blackened blisters on his face burst and wept.

Jamie screamed and kicked at him, and Nymeria tried to pull the man's hand off her brother's ankle. Another arrow pierced the man's forearm and pinned it to the ground, yet he kept growling, even as black blood began to ooze from his mouth and his eyes and his ears. Gray veins began to creep through his skin where the shadows had burned him, and he writhed and hissed as they spread.

Her brother's foot came free, and Jamie fled, screaming as the man reached for them with his other hand, pulling himself further from the flames.

Nymeria crawled to her feet and ran after her brother, never looking over her shoulder, not even when the wagon exploded. But she still heard that man growling and hissing until the sounds of the battle drowned him.

She heard shouting that came from over the gate. "Fall back! The gate is breached! Fall back!"

Her brother had run through the gate.

Nymeria was horrified. She pursued him, even as she saw the raven-haired lady overhead being dragged away by several of her men. The lady had been injured by that second blast. Nymeria saw the blood that dripped from the lady's temple, all down her jaw and her neck. She could hardly stand on her own, but she was fighting her men, screaming at them to block the gate.

The lady looked down, and their gazes met. And when the lady's mouth turned downward at the corners and then her teeth pulled back into a snarl, Nymeria knew she'd become a target. Something about the way the lady looked at her told Nymeria she'd seen *everything*. She'd seen what Nymeria had done to the man. She'd seen the decay spreading. She'd seen that Nymeria had turned the gate to glass. She'd seen her little brother.

Nymeria put the rest of those thoughts to the back of her mind as she searched for her brother, and the battle spread inside Aelynhold's walls. The Enforcers regrouped behind her. One of them tried to grab her, to pull her away from the fighting, but she darted from the man as she continued to scan the awful scene for her brother. Jamie was small, but *surely*, she could spot him.

Yet he was nowhere.

What little of the gate that hadn't become glass caught fire behind them all.

"Cut them off before more of these fools get in!" cried the Enforcer who'd tried to grab her. Nymeria saw that he had only one arm, but it didn't slow him. She'd only narrowly darted beyond his fingertips. "Get them under control before the city burns! They'll riot and kill everyone they can inside the walls. We cannot risk Avery's life! Regain the peace! Let Aelynhold's men deal with the ones who have gotten through already!" He looked at her again, worried. "And someone get this child out of here before she's killed!"

She looked about wildly when she heard her brother crying, and then she saw a messy-haired woman scoop up a little boy from a street corner two blocks up the hill. *Jamie!* she cried. "That's my brother!"

"Sissy!" shouted Jamie, and he held his hand out to her as the woman carried him away from the rioting wearyworn.

"I'll take you to my cousin's," Nymeria heard the lady tell her brother. The woman was afraid, and her voice was trembling as Nymeria raced after them. "We'll find your mother and father after this is over, if they're alive. It's too dangerous here, baby boy. I'll keep you safe. Nona!" She hollered to another woman across the street, a plump woman to whom clung many fearful young children about the same age as Nymeria and her brother. "Nona! We must leave now! We cannot stay any longer!"

"Hannah, be careful!" hollered Nona, and then Nymeria lost sight of her brother and Hannah.

"Jamie!" she shouted, and she pumped her legs harder than before, desperate to catch up to them. "*Jamie!*"

Nymeria gritted her teeth as more Enforcers tried to cut her off. She raced toward the fighting mob, and then she darted toward the alley between the buildings, and the mob, and the wall when her path was cut again and then again.

An Enforcer woman wielding an axe held out her hands, trying to offer peace. "*Stop*, girl! You'll get killed if you keep running toward them!"

"Get out of my way!" Nymeria shouted. She drew her ruined pen tool. "I have to find my brother!" She wiped the tears from her eyes and held up the tool as though it were a knife. "I will stab you if you don't leave me alone!"

The woman reached out to grab her, and Nymeria ducked. True to her word, she stabbed the woman in the leg, just behind the knee, and then she rolled to avoid getting caught by the Enforcer as the woman grunted in pain and staggered forward, no longer able to stand on her injured leg. And then Nymeria was running again, before another Enforcer could cut her off.

Her pen was broken. Only half the diamond tip remained. She clutched the stem anyway, and she slid it back into her boot. It could still serve as a weapon, though she doubted it would work any longer. She had to get to her brother, though, no matter what. She would never forgive herself if anything happened to him.

"What the hell happened?" asked one of the other Enforcers. Nymeria looked over her shoulder as she reached the alley between the buildings and the wall, and she lunged out of sight. She hid behind the columns there and let her head fall against the stone wall, heaving. She was near tears. She had no idea where Hannah and Nona would take her brother. She didn't know whether he would get hurt, or whether one of those angry people might kill him, but she did know he was probably still crying and terrified because she was not with him.

She began to cry silently and tried to shut it off, to shove it deep down. She knew crying would do no good, not now. But it was difficult to stay in control of her fear and her grief.

The one-armed Enforcer helped the woman Nymeria had stabbed after pulling the fractured diamond from her.

"That kid stabbed me. Moved as if she'd been training for years how to fight. I'm a liability now, Robin. I can't fight this mob like this. I can't bloody *walk*!"

"Which way did the girl go, Kesha?"

"That way. I don't think she's a refugee."

"What makes you say that?"

"Lady Normane just gave the order to capture her a few minutes ago when they were retreating. Andy and I both heard it. She had something to do with whatever in the *Seven Hells* just happened to the gate. That's what they were saying."

"Help the men to make sure this line holds," said Captain Robin. "Keep the rest of the wearyworn out, and calm them. Have them block the gates with the trucks. I'll take about a hundred of the men to start searching the city for Avery. We'll start at the main temple and the highborn family's mansion. Call the rest here, and advance when you're given the order to. Get that injury taken care of."

"Yes, sir."

The captain called to another of his Enforcers. "Erin! Search these alleys for that girl! If she's had something to do with the gate's destruction, she may be in danger! Be quick about finding her!"

Nymeria bit her lip, and she moved from the wall.

She crept through the narrow space as quietly as she could, trying not to draw attention. But it was littered with debris, and accidentally dislodging any of it would arouse attention.

Then she came out on another street, and she darted to another alley. The wearyworn had spread outward several blocks and were setting everything on fire and breaking into shops and houses. They threw bombs they'd stolen from the Enforcers they'd attacked, and they shot and stabbed many of the innocent people they crossed.

She wanted no part of it. She only wanted to find her brother.

As she climbed over a small retaining wall and crept under a canopy of thick vines and heavy foliage, Nymeria heard stone scraping against stone. She peered around the corner, and there she saw two hooded monks exit from a secret passage in the wall. One was injured and limping, and the other was helping him to walk.

Both said nothing as she hid there silently and watched them walk right by her. She could have reached out and touched their knees, yet they never saw her. So she waited for them to be gone so she could search for her brother.

"We should use the sewers, I told you," said one.

"We cannot do that, Morris," said the other — and she recognized Lukas's voice.

Nymeria gulped. *Lukas.* Lukas knew where her uncle was, surely. She knew he had a hand in everything. He was far too sly not to. She wouldn't be surprised if he turned out to be the King of Thieves, too. But what about her brother? Should she still search for Jamie? Jamie was being watched over by a kind lady right now, but her uncle was running out of time.

Nymeria looked back to the alleyway, torn, and then Lukas continued.

"What we need to do is get the hell back," said Lukas. "Carriah's done her job. John Ivan is here. That was him, that man who was shooting at us."

Nymeria's ears perked. Her father had seen them?

"He's probably dead," said Morris.

Nymeria sucked in her breath, fearful.

"That guildsman is too stubborn to die no matter the number of arrows shot from the wall. He took cover. And we need him, or this is far less likely to work. We need to hurry back to the Keep and reassess our options. Find out what else has happened. We might have to move his brother, and if things get worse — "

"If you keep trying to involve yourself directly, you're going to get caught again!" Morris hissed. The monk stumbled and nearly hit the ground, but Lukas helped him regain his balance.

"I'm not worried about getting caught."

"What if you're recognized?! Everything we've worked for — "

"Shut up, Morris. I'm not interested in your *what if.* We're getting results. The plan is working. John is so worried about his brother's death that he's come. And if he's come, that kid of his is likely somewhere nearby. That's the predictable thing about him. He'll be too afraid to keep them far away. Probably in Tarvet. That's where I'd leave my family, if I'd come, especially if Saura's finally shown her true colors. Griggori's failed to get the girl himself, and he said the Ivans fled. So Tarvet is the only place they can be, and with my cousin's filthy wolfmen friends camping there, I'll bet they won't stay long. They'll flee this way, probably aiming for a small town to the north. So we'll get them. The girl will be easily plucked from them."

Nymeria gritted her teeth. Her uncle was alive. That was good. But the things Lukas had set in motion and the predictions he'd made angered her. She hadn't even thought to plan against it. She should have seen it coming! She'd left her mother alone out there!

She wiped her face with her shoulder, trying not to move too much because she didn't want them to notice her.

Lukas huffed. "If anyone recognizes me, kill them and think not on it. The mission comes first. I am not going to get caught or let any of them figure out where we've hidden Avery Ramont."

"The bastard would roll over in his grave if he knew what you've done," grunted Morris.

"Oh, the dead bastard is rolling, all right. A dancing skeleton, Morris. Rolling over, and over. Next corner. Even if they find the body, they'll never find out what he knew. What we know. Why we killed him."

Nymeria followed quietly, swearing that she would go back for her brother. She had to stop Lukas and his friends from killing her uncle first. Then she would save Jamie and go back to find her mother.

They stopped.

She hid again.

"Lukas, there are Enforcers all up and down this street. They're blocking the whole damned road."

"I can see that," grunted Lukas.

"Use the sewers. You can't be that afraid of him, surely."

"You have no idea what he does down there, Morris. I do. I don't want anything to do with those sewers. That's his domain. I don't want it back."

"So the King of Thieves just gives up his crown, then? Gives away his prize den? Can you *hear* yourself? What happened to you?"

"More than you could ever know. My nerve is gone, Morris. I can barely hold a knife without feeling my hands tremble. I see things most others cannot. All he must do is read my mind, and then he'll know what happened to his brother. That it was my fault. I'll be a dead man if he finds out. I'll just be another body in the sewer, strewn among the mountains of dead down there. Neither my station nor my crown would ever protect me."

"You've turned into a coward."

"It is why I am still alive. Do you know how many of our men died, trying to be brave? Do you know what they *did* to us in the Gray Halls? His brother was part of it! Not that he wanted to be, but he still was. I saw enough in the Violet that I nearly ended my own life because of it. I damned near lost my mind like the rest of the men. Avery deserves what he got, Morris. Avery was brave. I'm not like him, which is *why I am still alive.*"

"Your daughter said it wasn't pleasant."

"Oh, I'm still furious about that business. But she's been helpful, and I'm grateful for it. When we get back, we need to get Reid Ivan out of that dungeon. Make sure he isn't dying — I already know my wife has been torturing him for her disturbed joy of it. She's become one twisted piece of work, and I keep underestimating her. She wants vengeance for every mark he's given me, and it's not even for my sake, or her love for me. Honestly, I've lost my trust in her. She'll probably try and kill me to take my place soon." Lukas sighed. "But by the *bluest seas*, I loved her. I never meant for any of this to change her."

"What do you want done with the doctor's brother?"

"Put him on display so John can see the state he's in. I want John Ivan driven to his knees. I want him to suffer. I want him to have to choose between his daughter and his brother, and I want it to hurt. And then he's going to lose them both anyway."

"You're the one who's a twisted piece of work, Lukas," laughed Morris.

"It isn't personal," said Lukas. "It's just what has to be done. He has to be taken out of the picture after we're finished. He's another pawn needing removed from the board. If you don't kill them, they come back for you."

Nymeria's teeth clenched. She wanted nothing more than to hurt Lukas right then. Instead, she continued to follow them, and she worried about her brother all the while. She continued to pray he was still okay.

A few blocks later, Lukas and Morris stopped again. "See?" said Morris. "We have to take the sewers."

Lukas swore an oath. "Wait here. Some of our men are hiding there." He let go of Morris, and the injured monk leaned against the wall near one of the grates. "I'll give the men a few new orders before you get your way." He darted away, and then, moments later, he returned with another monk, who helped Morris from the wall. "It's done," he said.

Morris looked at him, his brow high. "What's done?"

Lukas smirked. "We'll draw them close to the manor, and then we'll get rid of them. Word is, Saura's coming with her men. They've been spotted near Oakwall. This will be fun. I know what she's after. After all, why would she come to wonderful, quiet, little Aelynhold?" He laughed. "It wouldn't be for news of Avery's captivity here. She was already warned not to look for him once, years ago. She understood the danger then, although I do hope she hasn't changed her mind."

CHAPTER FIFTY-SIX

*P*URSUED

THEY HAD BEEN UNDERGROUND for two days. Lukas and Morris cleared the passageway without incident as noxious fumes rose to choke them. Occasional explosions rocked free small bits of rubble, which splashed about their feet, and Morris complained about his injury, worried about infection.

Morris's blood smeared the gray-green, moss-covered tunnel walls along which Lukas stumbled several times with his friend. Morris was quickly losing strength; he was pale from blood loss, and whatever he was trying to say now was somewhat incoherent.

Lukas gritted his teeth. He needed his friend to keep himself together and stay alive. The man had always been one of the few he felt he could trust with his life; he was one of the few men Lukas had never lied to. He owed Morris a lot. The man had not only risked everything to keep Avery's secret hidden, but he had helped to keep the late Drake Normane from the truth and also assisted Lukas's wife to survive Drake's schemes. Morris had also helped to create and disguise the reason for the creation of the Brotherhood. Simply put, the debt Lukas owed to Morris was one he could never repay, and letting such a loyal and effective friend and ally die in the sewers was an unforgivable idea.

"Starlight . . ." murmured Morris as he looked up, and his vacant gaze followed the drifting particles of dust where they fell through shafts of sharp sunlight filtering in from above. Morris stumbled again, and Lukas grunted under the weight of his friend.

"Stay with me, friend," said Lukas. He huffed as he gripped Morris's wrist and shoved his shoulder under Morris's arm again. "Lean on me, we're nearly there. Barely a quarter of a mile to go. And we'll be out of the sewers soon, too. Get that leg cleaned up."

"It was like starlight, Lukas . . . Do you remember? It was a beautiful night."

"I remember everyone screaming," said Lukas. "I remember you saving my life twice, and your vow to get back home to make sure my orders to the men were carried out. You've done well. All of you have kept Black Temple and Caol guessing, and for far longer than I had hoped. But we cannot stop here. We have to get moving."

But Morris stumbled again, his breath coming and going in sharp bursts. "Lukas . . . You must leave me behind. I'll get you killed. Or caught. They'll learn the truth. We cannot risk it."

"You never left *me*."

"Yes, I did. When Caol turned on you . . . But god, that light was . . . it was beautiful, wasn't it? She was so lovely."

"*She?*"

Lukas frowned, and he looked at his friend, worried.

"Eyes unlike any other . . . I remember the color. But they put her in that box and covered it, as if she was dead. But that light. We should have killed all of them and saved her that night. Nothing ever mattered but her. When they took her, they hurt her."

Lukas gritted his teeth against the memory of Caol's betrayal. "Nothing was in that box but glass. Caol did his share of harm, experimenting with it."

"There was a child, though. I saw her. I saw the explosion in that tomb where they found her. I saw the creatures. I saw everything . . . I felt . . ."

"You were on the surface with me. You saw nothing I didn't see. We all felt the rumbling beneath the earth, but you upheld my order to the men to stand back as the rest of Rhael's and Caol's men came fleeing the mine to the surface. Half of them were mad and killing one another, and the rest were terrified out of their minds by it all. And of that other group, we only ever saw a few of those foreign warriors who'd been mining. Don't you remember, Morris?"

"But . . ." Morris's knees gave as confusion drifted into his expression. "Why do I remember . . . ? I remember the water. I remember seeing her adrift in it. She'd been in a watery tomb, alone before all of that — in the blue light where the dark creatures couldn't get to her. Then that wall fell . . . I felt it — *She* felt it. That's what woke her . . . Her eyes were like starlight."

Lukas gripped Morris by the shoulders, his heart beating hard. "*Think*, Morris! How can you remember any of that? You weren't down there. The weapons. Remember the weapons? That's what we were all there for, to steal them from those foreigners. No one expected that catastrophe. No one knew what they were digging for, or what they would have found, or what it would lead to. You and I joked about Caol's madness, about his terror of every moving shadow thereafter. You have to *remember* — "

Then he saw the blood oozing from Morris's neck, where he'd been sliced. Imbedded in the wound was a small but brightly pulsing shard of violet glass. He reached to pull it from his friend's neck. But he paused, afraid to make even the merest contact with it. "You've been infected," he exhaled, aghast. "I didn't realize she was already in the city somewhere." He swore again. "Morris. Listen to me very carefully. These visions you are having, these fake memories — they will only worsen. They're not yours. And those demon creatures will be drawn to you because of it. Do not look at them. Do not listen to them, and do not speak to them. They'll try to offer peace during the worst of it. Do not accept it, do you hear me? Focus on what matters, and *only* on what matters. What we've spent years trying to accomplish. What we've risked and sacrificed *everything for.*"

"It . . . stings." Morris said, seeming to notice it only then, and his brow lowered as if he was only now processing the injury. He lifted his hand to his neck and touched the glass. It had fused to his skin already, and it had partly dissolved there, just as other shards had done with Lukas and the others before. When Morris looked up again, his eyes began to glow dimly with the curse's color. "But what I remember — "

"Those are not your own memories. None of those are ours. *None.* They belong to the *thing* they found in the mine. John's daughter was likely exposed to a mountain of it to become what she is, but even she isn't the true source of them. Those memories came from something ancient. It's spread through the glass. It's like a vicious, living curse. You must fight it."

"Can you remove it? Will it stop me from remembering — "

"It's too late to remove it."

"But how did you beat it?"

"Focus on our purpose. Tell yourself over and over, even when you can hardly think through it. You cannot give up. That's why I am still alive. It is the only thing that can save you from the madness it brings. Or from the death that comes soon after."

"There is so much starlight . . ." Morris said, and his head fell back against the wall as he slid to the ground. He could hardly catch his breath, and he blinked hard against the Violet infecting him. "The only thing, you say . . . Yet I feel I could simply drift away into it and be at peace with the rest of them. Whose memories are they?"

"No one knows. It's all nonsense, all of it. The mountains, the prisoner screaming for help and then becoming *something else*. The memories go on and on and on, and each one becomes more monstrous than the one before. No one knows what it means. Just that it's horrific. Those who want to find out always die when they try to touch the rest. Ignore it all. You cannot accept the beautiful ones without taking the rest, so push them all from your mind and focus on what we are fighting for."

"It's beautiful, though. I could look at them forever and feel I've stepped into a heaven I'd never imagined possible. The light is . . . surreal."

Another explosion caused more rubble to fall, and blood began to drip down into the sewers with them as bodies bled out over the grates overhead. The screams echoed, and Lukas heard the smallest splash of quiet footsteps behind them in the tunnels. He looked up as the hair upon the back of his neck stood on end. They were not alone.

He realized they hadn't been for quite a while. They were being hunted.

Lukas gritted his teeth. "I am aware of that. But the thing just behind that vision is blacker than any bottomless pit, and it will destroy you, because that's where the door for the shadow creatures awaits. Get up, Morris. We're being followed. If *he* finds us, we're dead men. We have to go!"

"She's here, Lukas," said Morris, who had become enthralled by whatever vision he was experiencing. "We have to help her. It is our purpose — "

"Get up!" Lukas hissed.

At this rate, his friend would soon be completely consumed by the Violet. He didn't know how to help Morris, except to keep pushing. For all the good *that* had done in the Gray Halls as he had watched friend after friend die under the torments Caol and Eiran had chosen for them.

"We shouldn't leave her alone, it isn't safe," said Morris. "The *Shadei Ra* are calling for her. We cannot let them have her — "

"How many times do I have to tell you to ignore it all? *Come on!*"

Lukas gripped his friend's forearm and pulled him from the wall, but Morris fell forward. He barely caught him.

Morris shook his head. "I can't — I can't . . ."

"The grate is just up there," said Lukas. He pointed behind himself, to a winding stairwell that spiraled upward, toward the piercing shafts of bright sunlight. They could see fragments of the towers above, which marked the beginning of the old highway, even as more debris fell about them and blocked some of the grates overhead. "Do you want to die down here? If you do, you won't be able to help anyone, let alone the bright creature you are sensing in the Violet. You have to fight it, or you will be of use to no one at all. *Get up.* The city is being torn apart by the wearyworn. Our *home* is being destroyed."

But Morris shut his eyes. "They'll kill her. We can't . . ." He took a deep breath, and then he let go of Lukas's arm, his fingers curling, and he pushed Lukas away. Morris's palms flew against his temples as he bowed, and his hair fell over his face and brushed the ground in front of him. He trembled tumultuously, rasping, and Lukas stared at him.

"Morris — "

"Shut up!" shouted Morris. "Shut up, damn it, I cannot *think!*" He gulped down another breath, the sound scraping his throat, and then another. "I cannot . . ."

Lukas bit his tongue against another comment. He understood what his friend was going through, but they could die many ways down here and then be utterly forgotten. Unimaginable things would happen to thousands of innocent men and women and children if that happened. Hundreds of thousands, if not *more*. "Our lives and hers are not the only ones in danger," he said quietly at last. "Please, marshal your strength and see this to the end with me."

He held out his hand, and he prayed Morris would take it. He looked at the blood still dripping from Morris's leg, and he held his breath.

Morris's trembling calmed a long moment later, and he let go of his temples.

"We're running out of time, Captain Bourgeois."

Morris nodded slowly and then finally allowed Lukas to help him to his feet again. But something caught the man's attention. "Forgive me," said Morris quietly. "But are the shadows over there moving . . . ?"

Lukas swore and grabbed Morris's shoulder, and he dragged his friend away from the point where Morris's gaze had turned. The creature's black tendrils stretched out, like smoke spilling over the floor and the walls, as if pushed by some ghostly breath. His skin prickled.

Morris lost his balance, and as the familiar coldness stretched out about them, he seemed to at last comprehend Lukas's fear, and he tried to get up. His injury prevented him, and a ribbon of shadow curled about Morris's leg and dragged him back. He kicked at it, gasping as though its touch burned him. "Get it off!" he cried.

As though drawn to another, stronger source of Violet, the being's grip loosened. Lukas managed to pull his friend free, and the two hobbled away from the odious cold pouring into the tunnels behind them. At last, Morris's mind began to clear, and he shook himself, rattled by the encounter. "What was that thing?" he gasped as they fled, and he continued to look over his shoulder. The violet light had faded from his eyes for the time being.

Morris gritted his teeth when he heard the creatures' voices. "And what unholy message was it *whispering*?"

"The only time I ever understood them, they were calling for the *Bright One*," Lukas admitted. "No one else knew what language it was, except Rhael."

Some of the color had returned to Morris's face, and the shaken man shuddered. "I couldn't — Is that what they *do*? That's how they get you?" He was mortified.

"Shut it out, I warned you. The next time you look at it, you may not survive."

Neither said another word about any of it as they trekked the stairs toward the shafts of light. The rails creaked and groaned, but the smell of death finally began to dissipate.

When at last they surfaced, the air was thick with smoke. The fire had spread up the hill, and they hurried toward the series of bridges. The catwalk swayed dangerously over the ruined roads.

"Why are we going this way?" asked Morris finally. "Are you *trying* to have us fall to our deaths? There are other ways to the temple, Lukas."

"Because we are still not alone. We've been followed the entire way." He looked about, but still he saw nothing. He only felt the presence of their assassin.

Below the catwalk, and below the bridges just under them, he saw the rioting wearyworn surrounded by over a hundred of Aelynhold's guards. They had reached the temple at the square, and as the clocktower below began to chime, Aelynhold's guards raised their weapons and advanced. The wearyworn began to stop fighting as they realized they were outnumbered, surrounded, and likely to die if their wild aggression continued.

But it was only a thin line of guards that separated Aelynhold's own displaced, panicked people from the combative, angered refugees.

A few blocks down, the Enforcers were closing in, and they moved as if they were already primed for another battle. He turned his head when he caught more movement in his peripherals, and he realized there were even more Enforcers advancing along another street. And another street.

Lukas swore.

"This is going to become a mess, isn't it?" sighed Morris. "They won't give up until they have their High Commander. You know that."

"All we can hope for at this point is just to keep him from them as long as possible," snarled Lukas. "I don't want to have to kill the lot of them, but it may be the only way."

"We knew it was a possibility years ago, Lukas. When we made our decision and did what we did."

"I never counted on Reid or his allies being so effective in their investigations. I wish I hadn't screwed up and gotten caught by him. The biggest mistake I've ever made on a mission, and it ends in catastrophe on this scale."

"Holy hell. The arrogant bastard isn't perfect. No one saw that coming," Morris snorted. "Yet we're still behind you."

Lukas grimaced.

"Until the end," added Morris.

"Even if the Leviathans kill us all to wipe the slate clean? Even if humanity is erased because we fail?" asked Lukas.

"Even so," nodded Morris. "Power like theirs should never be held by a man like Caol. *Never.*"

CHAPTER FIFTY-SEVEN

NYMERIA AVOIDED THE reaching shadow, still watching Lukas and Morris as she followed them. The small debris cascading down around her made the air smell more wretched, and she zeroed in on the droplets of blood that fell like rain from above. Like crimson rubies, flashing brightly in the darkness through stray shafts of angled sunlight.

She could still feel the injuries and the fear drifting outward from the rioting horde like a giant, poisonous miasma — a great black serpent swallowing the air and turning it into a blistering heat and a breaking cold. Waves of it cascaded against every building and pooled in every street. It seeped into every crevice, pouring down into the tunnels below like echoes that were felt rather than heard.

But she pushed on. Even the sight of the shadows could not deter her now. The two men were close, though they could not see her. She would wait to confront them once she knew they were near the surface again. That way she could run if she had to.

Her heart beat erratically, and she was beginning to hear the low rumbling of one of the creatures from the back of her mind. Its presence caused chills that radiated down her spine, and its existence tasted of hatred and longing, and of agony and thirst. It burned her within — her every vein, every cell, every fiber, and every bone felt the trace beginnings of Mihai's fiery hell. She fought his dark presence with every breath and ignored the pangs of hunger as she followed Lukas and Morris through the tunnels. But Mihai was reaching out as every particle of his soul and his being screamed . . . and screamed . . . and continued to scream.

And what Lukas had told his friend had left her breathless. Lukas had seen some of the visions. He knew about the man in the dungeon. He knew the dark things meant death.

She'd wished she could hear more of what Morris had said, because he'd told Lukas about the ocean of starlight. She'd *seen* that ocean. It had felt peaceful and beautiful, as though she'd been among a sea of angels. But he and Lukas had hurried ahead through the sewers, and she'd caught nothing else.

Then they were outside, and they were high above the streets below. The stairways they passed led down to different levels, but Lukas and his friend continued along the catwalk, seeming to know every precarious step to take. The bridge rumbled dangerously, vibrating with the explosions below, and small cracks formed.

Nymeria knew then that they'd come here for a reason. They knew she was following them, and they intended for her to fall to her death. She sensed Lukas's intention as clearly as she saw the open sky above them, now that the waves of fear and death had receded below them, where the violence continued to broil.

Nymeria pulled her broken pen tool from her boot and looked down at the mob. She saw the monks on the rooftops. They were gathering, drawing closer as though they'd been told to wait for him to emerge here. One by one, the stairwells were closed off, beginning on the far side of the catwalk. The temple's streets below were crowded and bloody.

She didn't want to fall.

She steeled herself and kept climbing after them.

Lukas was afraid of her. She would use that to force him to free her uncle, no matter how many monks or guards stepped in her way. And then she would save her brother, and then she would find her father.

A woman fled up the nearest stairwell — one of the monks drew his blade. Nymeria heard the scream cut short.

She gripped the pen tool in her hand.

"Nymeria!" screamed her brother.

Her head whipped about, and she searched for him as she halted.

Lukas froze. Morris leaned against the building, gasping when his knee buckled again. He clutched at his leg as Lukas let him go.

Lukas turned to face her, his mouth turned downward as though it upset him to realize who was pursuing him. "I didn't realize you were the one following me," he said, and his voice caught, as though it might break. As though he was afraid *for* her. "Be careful . . . I wouldn't have led you here, had I known who — "

"Lukas," rasped Morris. "We have to protect her."

"We have to follow through with the *plan*, Morris," snapped Lukas. "She's important because of that, and *only* because of that."

Her fingers were white on the weapon she gripped, and she held it up like a knife. "Give my uncle back," she said. "Or I will kill everyone in my way to get to him."

"You give the creatures what they want every time you let those dark impulses drive you, Nymeria," said Lukas gravely. "Surely, you know that. Murder marks us. It curls under our skin like ink."

"Everyone who is infected with the Violet can see them, can't they?" she asked, and she glanced at everyone below.

"Don't you dare!" Lukas took a step forward, but then he thought better of it and put his hands up. He had paled.

"I can fix both of you," she said. "But I will do it only if you release my uncle and let us leave."

"You cannot take it back from us. No one can." Lukas stood there, and she swore his chin trembled with the grief in his voice before he looked away. When he looked at her again, his black gaze was hard, and his jaw ticked aggressively. "And I cannot let you leave, either," he told her. "You have no idea what you mean or how important you are."

"If you want me to work with you, you will free him," she said. "Otherwise, instead of taking the Violet away, as I did when I first sensed you and pitied you for what it did to you, I will make your curse much, much worse. I will make sure you see *everything* in it."

That made him intensely uneasy.

The monks drew their weapons as they finally neared the bridge.

Her ears began to ring, and she blinked hard against the fire racing through her head. Nymeria gritted her teeth, intent on convincing Lukas that he should do as she asked.

Lukas stepped back as a threatening crack ripped through the catwalk. "You have to *stop*," he cried.

"Myria!" cried her brother again.

Nymeria wiped her eyes and searched again for her brother. Lukas remained very still. He took not a step closer.

"Don't provoke her!" he shouted to the monks. "Give her space!"

"Lukas," choked Morris. "She needs Gabriel's help. He is the only person alive who would know where her *other* is. He is the only one who can help them both."

"Gabriel will rip me apart when he finds out what happened to Rhael — I already told you that it is not an option!" Lukas swore. "Nymeria. Listen to me carefully. The only reason I imprisoned your uncle was to draw your father. To get to *you*. Everything is about *you*, child. All of it. If you come with us, we will free your uncle. The rest of your family will be left alone. No one else will be hurt."

The pen tool pulsed brightly with violet light, and the crack in the catwalk grew wider and began to turn to black glass. "You are the King of Thieves," she said, and Lukas's eyes narrowed. He seemed surprised that she'd figured that out. "You command the Brotherhood. You can order my uncle's release where you stand now. I'm not stupid enough to just take you at your word and go with you. Give the order," she demanded. Great pieces of the blackened catwalk began to splinter and fall.

Lukas stepped back again, and Morris reached out to steady him. "Get her, or I will," said Morris.

Lukas's gaze caught on something below, and Nymeria followed it, her eyes narrowing. The lady from the wall, injured but fighting. He shook his head when he noticed Nymeria had seen her, too. "Don't you dare, or I will just kill you and be done with it."

"That's who you've been protecting from your schemes for years, is it?" Nymeria said. "Your wife. And that evil woman in Isold was your daughter, wasn't she? The one with the violet eyes, who killed everyone and sent the message about my uncle."

He couldn't seem to fathom how she knew what she knew.

Mihai's anger rolled through Nymeria, and she shivered. The ringing in her ears worsened. She wished she could just rest her splitting skull against the cool stone wall in the shadow of the tower. But she couldn't give up on her uncle or her brother.

The woman below, as well as many others, had looked up. They saw the glass spreading. They saw the falling debris. They heard the rumbling danger overhead.

They were already beginning to move away.

"I told you twice already. This is your last chance," said Nymeria. "Release my uncle. You are the one in charge here. This mess is your responsibility. People are dying because of you. Your city is being torn apart because of you. Your daughter is infected because of you, and your wife is injured because of you. If you do not release my uncle and let my family leave freely, you will be responsible for a *lot* more than the things you've already done."

He opened his mouth as the truth of her words sank in, and then he closed it. Again, he started to speak, but the agonized look on his face told her he had no idea what to say to her. The emotion in his eyes was unusually honest; he was filled with too much sorrow and was unable to voice it.

Morris pushed himself from the wall, wincing. "I'll get her myself — "

"Morris, *don't!*" Lukas snapped, and he held out his hand to block Morris from passing him. "*Look* at her. She's extremely dangerous! The girl is no ordinary child. All of you, stay back!"

Nymeria snarled.

"Calm down, Nymeria," Lukas pleaded. "Before you lose yourself to your dark gift completely. Do not let Mihai's anger infect you. His anger is corrupting your gift, and it is killing you."

"*You* are the one making me angry," she hissed. "I already told you what I expect from you. My patience is running out. All you have to do is give an order, and you won't even do it! *Why?!*"

"What about your brother?" Lukas asked. He waved behind her, to one of the stairwells not yet occupied by monks or guards.

At the thought of her brother, the ringing in her head became a deafening sound, and she shuddered, almost brought to her knees. She held her head, fighting tears. She couldn't think. The anger was too much for her.

Nymeria stared at the stairwell, her jaw ticking, her fingers digging into her temples, and she saw her brother. He was running toward her, panic upon his face when he saw the men with swords all around them. Lukas held out his hand when one of his men moved forward to grab the boy.

"*Do not touch the boy!!!*" he shouted.

Nymeria blinked as Mihai's rage choked her — and then she had her brother safely behind her, and the monk was screaming and on the ground, holding his bloody hand.

The monks began to converge, and more of the rage inside her began to bubble to the surface. She closed her eyes.

Then she heard her brother's whimper.

Another wave of fire scalded her head, and she held up the pen tool like a knife and forced bright Spirit into it. The light was blinding, and the monks nearest them recoiled as one.

Nymeria screamed as black energy erupted behind it. The catwalk and bridge turned to glass and began to quake. Large sections began to break away as the structures continued to shake violently, and her brother sucked in his breath to call her name again.

She saw the horror on Lukas's face. He dodged a blast and threw himself at the wall. Morris caught him before he lost his balance and fell over the edge.

"Nymeria!" shouted Lukas, and he held out his hands as though praying she would stop.

But she couldn't.

CHAPTER FIFTY-EIGHT

BRIDGE

JOHN SAW THE MOVEMENT, all as one, as the monks began to shift their attention. Several disappeared from the nearest rooftops, each one turning toward the evening sun and the rising towers that supported the precarious bridges strung between them.

He clenched his teeth, grateful they were not interested in him. The rest were releasing weapons from their holsters and sheaths and were moving toward the Enforcers and the wearyworn far below. As he hurried past every building and every tower, he caught glimpses of the large militant movement — even *here,* he could hear the clamorous violence of it. The screams of the civilians and the roars of the fighters. It was a sound he knew would haunt him for the rest of his life, just like the flaming, bloody devastation outside the walls when he'd witnessed people burning alive in the oil that had been poured on them and ignited.

John gripped his broken sword handle and limped forward. He could see parts of a large temple the monks seemed to be protecting — probably their base. It seemed a religion here, to become one of the *Brothers of Mercy,* and it was fitting how the temple's face looked almost like a centuries-old church. But the rest of the temple protruding from the shadows of multiple bridges looked like some alien crown.

It was not the temple he was looking for, though.

John searched for the small forest that was within Aelynhold's walls, and as he passed the next tower, when the bridge he was on began to curve upward and to the right, he glimpsed it. Just a league from the temple itself, the sea of foliage upon the highest hill concealed part of the protruding, angular roofline. That building was the noble family's mansion, attached to which was the guard house, and the prison. That was where his brother was being kept. John moved more quickly as hope began to swell in him.

But the stonework underfoot ripped itself apart as a huge crack unzipped the surface, and John caught himself before his next step toppled him into the creaking ravine. The entire bridge rumbled, and bits of it gave way. Again, he clenched his teeth and steeled his nerve.

The old woman had told him about the state of the bridge. He'd known to expect danger, even if this was worse than he could have planned for.

At this rate, the explosions below were going to rip the structure apart before he ever crossed it.

John quickened his pace, his heart beating fiercely against his ribs, like a hammer forming a new blade. Adrenaline surged through him. He was not going to let this bridge's wobbling deterioration keep him from rescuing his brother —

A blinding light reflected off the buildings ahead, and John put up his hand to block the light.

When he looked up again, he saw blurry vestiges of what he thought was movement on some of the stairwells all around him. He lifted his makeshift dagger, blinking hard against the after blindness, and then he realized they were monks. There were about thirteen of them, but they all rushed past him. He was shoved out of the way by several of them as they struggled to regain their sight also.

None bothered with him, just like the others on the rooftops before.

He knew he should have slunk against the wall after that close encounter, before they realized who he was or what he was after. But something felt wrong about all of this. Something in him corded tight with anxiety and set his teeth on edge, just like when he'd been in the sewer tunnels with that . . . *thing*.

John tried to put it out of his mind, and when he heard Lukas shouting, he barreled forward.

Then he heard a child's scream.

The sound washed away rational thought and blinded him to the danger of the volatile explosion on the bridge, even as huge chunks turned to glass and began to fall.

The monks turned on him when they realized he was headed into the thick of them, and he was shoved back again. It was likely his last warning before they attacked him. He knew he should turn and try another way, but through the clouds of dust and debris, and through the violet arcs of lightning, he glimpsed his son's face. Horror drove through him like a sharp nail. He bit down on the ash that drifted into his mouth as another intense tremor shook the bridge. He was unable to fathom how his son had come to be in Aelynhold.

John saw Lukas nowhere, but his son was screaming and was curled up on the ground near a growing fissure, where bright red blood pooled under and around him.

The blood was also on his clothes . . .

John realized Jamie was injured, and badly. He could see the broken bone and the torn flesh, and his gut clenched. He sucked in a breath. *"Jamie!"* John breathed. He began to slash at the monks who guarded the site as he tried desperately to move toward his son.

A deafening crash came from below, and his son was swallowed up by the mountainous plumes of smoke and dust, and detritus. A blade bit his wrist, and John snatched his hand back and then lunged again. A monk cried out and fell, but others took his place.

Still, John fought to get to his son, choking on his panic and his tears, and on the taste of ash, and of grief.

He had to get to his *son*!

John was instead driven back, even as the staircases began to crumble behind him. The towers teetered dangerously. One began to collapse, kneeling over them as its great face cast a growing shadow upon them.

"JAMIE!!!" he shouted. Still, he could neither hear nor see his son. He could hardly even hear *himself*.

Another blade stole from the thickening haze and nicked his brow. And then he lost his senses as, in rage and panic, he threw his blade in a dizzying, broken series of slashing and stabbing arcs.

There were too many monks . . .

CHAPTER FIFTY-NINE

SACRIFICE

NYMERIA REACHED FOR HER brother on the ledge below her where the concrete had buckled. Jamie was screaming as though he was badly hurt. Tears caught in her lashes, and when she gripped his good hand, her belly digging into the large chunks of stone and old rebar, she saw all the blood dripping from his other arm. He screamed again as she pulled him up, using all her strength. He was smaller than her, but he was still heavy. Ash and dust clung to her cheeks, and the crack grew wider.

Nymeria finally pulled him onto the ledge with her, and she held him, crying against his shoulder as her hair trailed his ruined arm, and she scrambled back from the ledge with her little brother.

Another tremor shook the bridge as though an angered titan had risen from the ground, and the shaking began to pull every structure supporting the bridge from its foundation.

Lukas and Morris backed away as the fissure grew wider, and the bridge and catwalk twisted again as another crack circled Jamie and her. Nymeria bit her lip hard, her body quaking.

"Nymeria, you have to come with me!" Lukas shouted above the groaning. "Leave your brother, or bring him! It's too dangerous to stay! The bridges are coming apart!"

Her heart somersaulted when the stone began to blacken around her, and she kissed her brother on the cheek and held him tighter. "I'm sorry, Jamie," she whispered. "I'm sorry."

And then she shoved him away from the ledge as the concrete and glass shattered. Jamie cried out in pain and fear, his eyes wide. And as she began to fall, she saw her father's face emerge briefly from another group of monks. His expression turned to one of absolute horror when he saw her brother, and then she could see him no more as the great destruction cascading below collapsed upon the temple and smothered its standing spires, breaking them. A poisonous plume of smoldering debris rose like a maelstrom all around her, choking her, cutting her, burning her.

She clawed at the ruined, caving walls around her for any desperate purchase. The first one she found seemed to nearly rip her and her arm apart, and she cried out and then choked on the cloud that consumed everything in sight when she tried to gasp. She tried to grab again, but she couldn't find anything to hold on to as the stone slid beneath her, as she rolled and felt the skin torn from her hands and her knees, and from her cheek and her forehead. Shrapnel sliced her viciously as she was struck and bruised by the next protrusions that wedged between the two towers that had collided with one another overhead. Their bellies had burst open and now groaned where the stone buttoned against each of the towers' sagging sides.

When the thunderous noise began to settle, Nymeria heard a great wail rise across the city square. And then she realized she wasn't falling anymore. Her tunic was ripped and covered in blood along her ribs, but she neither felt nor saw any tragic wounds. And as she inhaled the fumes and coughed again, she looked up and saw the sharp gouges her fingers had left in the steeply slanted catwalk's splintered stonework. Her fingers ached, raw from the friction, and they threatened to give out.

She had only barely avoided death. Half her torso hung from the broken bridge; her feet and legs dangled over the destruction below. She couldn't get her feet over the edge, though she tried. And the large shelf of broken concrete that she clung to shifted threateningly.

She couldn't take the breath she needed to scream.

Nymeria shut her eyes again and laid her head against the stone, trembling. But she heard her brother crying from above.

She was grateful that he was alive, even if he was hurt. She knew her father should also be safe. He hadn't been very close when the center of the catwalk and the bridges had collapsed. And her father would soon tend to Jamie's arm. They would both be okay.

Again, her head thrummed, and Nymeria felt herself slipping as she felt the other thing in her stir. It reached out, calling to Mihai's shadow, and cold fear washed over her as her vision began to darken. She didn't want to see the bodies or the blood. She didn't want to hear him begging her to help him when she was about to die. She'd just wanted to save her uncle. She hadn't meant to hurt her brother. She hadn't meant to get anyone killed. She didn't want to die.

Her fingers slipped.

CHAPTER SIXTY

ℛ ETREAT

LUKAS AND MORRIS HACKED and coughed, and they covered their noses and their mouths as they retreated from the catastrophe. The dust and the smoke blasted away everything in sight, until it was like walking a bridge over an active volcano. Every sound reverberated through them, and Lukas's head was pounding from the ear-splitting volume.

He knew the child wasn't dead. He'd seen her clinging to the ledge. As long as she held on, he could get his men over there to help her. But he and Morris couldn't risk their own deaths to get to her. He prayed the brat would hold on.

"I saw her," said Morris. "She isn't dead yet."

"I know," coughed Lukas. He wiped the dust from his face, and they hurried as quickly as they could down the stairwell. "A lot of people saw us up there. Saw her. Even my wife saw what she did."

"She wasn't in danger of the — "

"No." He nearly lost his balance again when the stonework he reached out for crumbled away. Better not put his weight on any of the walls, then. Just do his best to help Morris down. "She was out of the way. But the bridge and the tower landed directly on the temple. That means our tunnels are gone."

"That's rotten fortune," huffed Morris.

Lukas agreed as he assisted his friend and kept from the walls.

Some of the smoke blew aside as the wind picked up, and Lukas's eyes strained as he looked through the haze. "My wife is there with the men. I'll have her send some men to get the girl. And there is Captain Robin."

"What if Anna's men don't get to the girl first?"

They stepped over more glass. Some of it crunched underfoot.

"Nothing changes," he said firmly. "We kill, lie, steal, or negotiate for her. Whatever it takes."

Morris's brow furrowed. "You should get out of the city while the possibility still exists. We can take care of the rest of this."

"Leaving is out of the question right now," said Lukas. Even though he wanted to do just that. "And it will remain so until we have the girl. That may take a few weeks, depending on the situation. If Anna's men don't get to her first, and if we can hold our ground at the temple. By then, some of those tunnels should be cleared."

"That's a lot of *ifs*."

"I know. I don't like it, either. I don't see things going well for us, though, and I'm grasping at our potential eventualities."

They watched the wearyworn and the citizenry try to flee the area. The Enforcers had gathered and blocked every exit, though. Worse, Aelynhold's monks and guards couldn't let the bystanders through. There was no place they could safely exit. It meant Aelynhold's protectors were surrounded — on one side, by terrified people who were willing to kill to get away, and on the other, by angered soldiers who were willing to kill to find what they were after.

"The wearyworn are in a panic again," said Morris. "I don't think Anna's men will get to the girl in time."

"I noticed. And everyone else on the bridge is dead, or very near. Or infected with the Violet now, like us. They won't get to her in time, either."

What a predicament. He tried not to dwell on the possibility that the girl might fall to her death. Might have already fallen.

"We're going to let Anna know the plan has changed," said Lukas. "We need a scapegoat."

"I'll do it."

"You aren't my first choice, you fool."

Morris made a noise in the back of his throat as they avoided more debris and navigated almost blindly the settling dust. "I know. But I have been helping to run this stupid farce in your absence. I am the wisest choice. Very nearly the only one. A lot of things point to me. My name is on a lot of paper between the Alliance's citadel and Aelynhold, Lukas. I have issued a lot of orders among both the Enforcers and the thieves in our Brotherhood. I practically took Avery's place when we made him disappear. I made sure his death was kept secret among even the Brotherhood when your cousin went digging for the truth so he could turn everything he found over to Caol. He even thought *you* were dead when you disappeared, just like Anna and the rest of us believed. I've done my duty — "

"And you will continue to do so, but not by letting them get their hands on you."

"Is this an order from the King of Thieves, or from the Lord of Aelynhold?" Morris asked bitterly.

Lukas shook his head. "Don't you dare put me in that position. Not after everything you and I have been through."

"Which is it?" demanded Morris.

"It's an order from your *friend*."

"Get rid of your conscience and let me do my part. This is not the time to be sentimental about how long we've known each other. If I die, I die. Same as the others. We all knew what we were getting ourselves into."

There was movement below. The one-armed captain was giving orders to his men, directing them to move forward despite the pandemonium. Ideas raced through Lukas's head, one by one, and each was determined as useless because of that captain's thoroughness. "They've already closed off the streets. Every house, every shop, searching as they go. Men are also on the rooftops, signaling the movement of ours." They were blocking the sewer grates also. "That captain is *very* thorough. In any other circumstance, I would be pleased that he'd been trained so well."

Morris snarled. "I suppose that was my fault. I can't blame him for it. At least he *means* well. Could have been another corrupt bastard. One of Drake's."

"Or Caol's." Lukas sucked on his tooth. "I would hate to kill him," said Lukas. After all, that captain was probably the one directing these Enforcers. "I would rather him turn that energy to rooting out Caol's and Drake's other plants at the Alliance instead of wasting it here on finding the High Commander."

They took the last set of stairs and struggled to fit under the small archway as more rubble fell from above. "Watch it," Lukas hissed. "You'll push me into the path of that crap, and I'll be dead for nothing."

"I've an idea."

Lukas frowned. But he was open. "Do tell."

"Everyone saw what the girl did, correct?"

Lukas blinked. The laugh that erupted from him was raw, and he licked the spit and the dust from his lips. "I wondered when you would catch up. As I said, all we need now is someone else to blame."

When they reached the throng of Aelynhold's guards who were protecting Lukas's wife, she was barking commands left and right. But she was in a lot of pain. Her shoulder appeared to have been broken, and her face was bleeding still, but she was as poisonous as ever. She was angry over the destruction of their tunnels, and she sent several men into the ruins to try to dig out at least *one* of them so that they could find a way through.

"So help me, I will claw your eyes out, you   scoundrel," she was saying to a cowering guard. "Get more men on it! Get that rubble out of the way of it, or your eyeless, disembodied head is going to adorn the table when I am forced to break bread with our enemies! I don't care how large you said that rock is. AND I WANT THAT GIRL CAPTURED!!!"

Lukas smirked. Such a beastly temper for such a beautiful woman. He'd once thought her too centered and calm to motivate the men so.

When his wife saw them, she smiled viciously. It was a promising smile, and it gave him chills.

He smiled back. "We've much to discuss, the three of us," he told her.

Her dark eyes glistened like ice, and she wiped the blood dripping down her cheek, smearing it. Her head dipped once in agreement. Her voice was velvet and poison when she spoke. "Of course, sweet Husband. I would love to listen to your next lies. Come with me. The only place we can talk will be inside what's left of the temple."

"Where are the rest of the men?" asked Morris.

"They've been captured," said Lukas's wife. "Or killed. Or cannot get to us yet."

Chapter Sixty-One

Hatred

JOHN FELT THE DISTURBANCE in the air over his throat where another blade sung. It *just* missed him, and the next blow he parried reverberated through his broken sword and up his arm. He almost dropped it as he staggered back and dodged another deadly blow.

A fist struck him in the jaw, and he staggered again and raised the ruined weapon to protect himself.f

A teetering wall came up against his back, and he looked up and saw the sun glint off the weapon of his enemy as it swung in a downward arc, toward him.

John's boot struck the man in the gut before the blade tasted of his flesh, but then he slipped because the wall gave way behind him. The monk's blade rang loudly when it struck the stone. John grabbed a handful of dust and flung it at the other monks around him.

He was losing.

His son was still injured, and too close to the deteriorating edge.

He gritted his teeth and got to his feet again, and he lunged at the nearest man, tackling him with a roar.

Several pairs of hands grabbed him. He fought them as the man beneath him kicked back at him. One boot struck him in the injured leg, and he groaned, dropping his weapon as his leg gave. He tried to grab it, but they pulled him back, and another fist struck him.

His son . . .

John spat the blood he tasted, and he bared his teeth, reaching out. He grabbed one of the hands and pulled it free, and he bit hard.

One of the hands retreated, and then a knife was at his throat. It began to bite back.

Jamie . . .

He was going to die. His son was going to die . . .

"*My son!*" he gasped. He tried to grab another hand and failed. His fingers wrapped around the knife. He felt it slicing into his fingers as the monk struggled to slit his throat.

Then the blade was gone, and there was a bark of pain in his ear. And then another monk fell to his left.

John staggered back, clutching at his throat, and then Irkov was in front of him, steadying him. He was saying something, but John couldn't focus on Irkov's voice. He pushed away from the group and moved toward Jamie. His son was crying, and he lay in a broken heap upon the precipice, which could crumble and lend to his death at any moment.

"Jamie — " he choked. The swords behind him clamored with other swords, and he hobbled toward his broken son.

His strength gave out as he reached him, when he saw how bad the injury was. Jamie was shivering, his head turned against the stone. He was pale.

"Jamie," John said, and when he reached out, he couldn't stop himself from shaking. He was afraid to cause that injury to hurt his son even more. He knew moving him would make the boy cry. But he had to. He had to —

"Daddy . . ." Jamie wept, and when he looked up, John felt his stomach twist into a knot.

"I'm here, Son. Listen to me, Jamie — I have to set your arm. It's going to hurt, but I have to do it. I have to."

And then Irkov was kneeling by him. "Where is Nymeria?" Irkov's voice was uneven. Raw with anguish. "I saw her up here with that murderer."

John could hardly touch his son's arm. He wiped his eyes when his vision blurred, and he placed his hands on Jamie's arm. His son whimpered.

"No," Jamie said, and he tried to pull away. "Daddy, please — "

Jamie's scream shredded John inside. His teeth ground against one another, and he bound his son's wound, ripping his own shirt to be able to do so. He was going to have a hell of a time trying to clean it later, to keep it from getting infected — to keep his son from losing that arm. He already knew it might be too badly ruined to ever use again.

Jamie's eyes rolled as he began to lose consciousness, and yet he grasped at the ledge as John pulled him away from it, trembling.

"Where is Nymeria . . . ?" Irkov asked, quieter, and he placed his hand on John's wrist.

John could hear his teeth cracking, he was clenching his jaws so tightly. His fingers closed into a fist, until the knuckles turned white. "She brought him here," he said. He sucked in a breath, and the next one that came out churned with even more hatred. "That little bitch almost killed my son. She brought him here — "

John felt Irkov's blade under his chin, and he saw the shock and the revulsion in the Greenman's gaze. "Say another ill word about that precious child, and I will end your life, you treacherously simple-sighted, *dim-minded* fool of a man!"

John felt the snarl engraved upon his face, and his anger boiled hotter inside, until he wanted to scream. He turned to glare at Irkov, to dare him to try to kill him.

Irkov snarled back with the same venom he'd always held for John, but it was now somehow more. "She was here. There is no way she can be dead . . ." Tears glistened in the Greenman's eyes, and the blade pressed deeper. "You had to have seen her. You were up here. Did he *take* her, or did she *fall*?"

Jamie began to cry again, and he reached out, as if trying to pull himself toward the plume of dust and still-crackling concrete and metal and glass. John grasped his shoulder to keep him from moving closer to the deadly, crumbling edge. "Remove your sword from my throat, or I will make sure you're the next one to go over the ledge," said John. "That evil, spiteful creature deserves what's happened for trying to kill my *son*!"

Irkov's blade hand shook at John's words.

Jamie's sobs tore at him. "Myria's down there, Daddy," Jamie wept, and Irkov's gaze snapped to the ledge, immediately searching. "She kept me from falling."

Irkov's fist struck John as Elija and the others finally reached them. "GET HIM AWAY FROM HERE BEFORE I KILL HIM!" shouted Irkov, and he moved toward the ledge, until the edge began to crumble beneath him. When he looked down, he gasped as though he was horrified at something he saw below. As though Nymeria was still there. "SOMEONE HELP ME GET TO HER! *GRAB ON TO ME SHE'S ABOUT TO FALL!!!*"

Jamie lost consciousness, and John struggled against them as he tried to hold on to his son. He didn't want her. He wanted them to let her fall —

And then his son's words began to sink in, and his heart shattered into thousands of little pieces. *Saved him.* Even though it had looked as though she'd tried to hurt him. John looked away from the edge, holding the pieces of his heart in place and refusing to let them cut him further. He was torn between heartbreak and anger and fear, and he couldn't decide which emotion was strongest or which one was right or wrong.

He was dragged away, toward one of the remaining stairwells, and he watched sullenly as the men struggled not to cause the ledge to crumble any further.

A long time later, Irkov emerged carrying John's daughter. She was bloody and bruised and torn, and she was barely conscious, and strands of tangled black hair lay across her pale face like thin spiderwebs. Irkov pulled the hair from her face gently, an expression of horror and sorrow etched into him deeply, and John felt the faintest trace of déjà vu — for he had himself done the same in the middle of a blizzard just a few years before. The Greenman cradled her as though she were precious and fragile. And John stood, wary of her, just like those people in Five Tower had. The reversal was bitter, like ash clogging his throat.

Her eyes were as black as obsidian, just like they'd been when she'd set her teeth to the throat of that monk in Isold. Just as they'd been on the bridge over Black Temple when she'd not been herself. Not a flicker of green to be seen.

She stopped breathing, and John's heart stopped for a long moment as fear and guilt trickled into him. John looked away, buried his face against his son's shoulder, and he rocked him. His eyes were burning, and his throat was closing.

"I think she's broken a rib," stammered Irkov, and his voice cracked with heartbreak and fear. "Her breathing is too shallow and uneven, and she's bleeding from the mouth. . ." The Greenman could not hide his tears as he cradled her, his hands shaking as violently as his voice. "Please do not die on me, my precious little grim spider. Stay alive for us. Stay alive, sweet child."

Elija rose from before Nymeria and Irkov, and he moved over to where John knelt. He stood there for a long moment, saying nothing at all. When John finally looked up, he saw Elija's disgust. The lieutenant nodded to the stairwell without saying anything directly to John. Elija shook his head and turned from him, and then he began to descend the stairs. To the men and Irkov, he said, "We'll meet with the captains near the square."

"I want to be the one who kills the thief," snarled Irkov. "I'll be a rotten *nothing* if I do not avenge this child's injuries. He led her here to kill her. I don't care if the Reformation wants him. I don't care if you want him alive, any of you! I've warned you. So stay out of my way. Especially *you*, Doctor. I should have known not to trust you to be so honorable. You're a damned snake. And a worthless, unworthy father."

"I have done all I could since the day we saved her," cursed John. "She's done *nothing* but bring trouble and ruin to my family! And grief! I should never have taken her in!"

Irkov said nothing for a long moment. When John looked at him, Irkov was staring at him strangely with that one good eye. "Are you saying the child isn't even your daughter . . . ?"

"She's an orphan that even Five Tower sought to be rid of. We should never have brought her home. We should have let them burn her alive under the shroud they gave her when they told us she was cursed."

"Does she even know?" Irkov's jaw ticked furiously.

"*No*," John spat. "We never told her. She doesn't even remember it."

Irkov snarled but restrained himself from attacking. "You don't deserve her. None of you."

"It's not as though you have any say in it. Once my son is fine, I'll address the issue with my wife. *She's* the one who wanted the accursed creature, and she only wanted that girl because we can't have any more children. We should have given her away to become someone else's nightmare. No one in my family would ever have died or been harmed if it wasn't for her. None of them!"

John rose with his son, and he followed Elija. He heard Irkov's various guttural curses behind him. He flinched when Irkov's blade struck the stone beside him, just as he turned.

But he continued down the stairwell without looking back. All he wanted to do was tend to his son's injuries properly, get his brother, and go back to his wife so they could go home. Or so they could make a home elsewhere, since Saura would likely try to hunt him down. The hell with that evil problem child, and with everything else tied to her.

He was too angry to feel guilty about his thoughts or his words. His son had almost just *died* because of her.

Once they'd reached the Enforcer's lines, it was already dark. Torches and bonfires marked the lines on both sides. John took his son as far from the city square as he could before he was stopped by another Enforcer. "You're the field doctor, aren't you? I saw you in Crow Post several months ago, helping to run the place. You did well with the crisis."

John tried to avoid the man, but the warrior placed his hand on his shoulder and held firm. He gave John a warning look, which told him he would be going nowhere. "I must tend to my son's injuries. Let me go."

"We have a lot of injured men and women who also need your help," said the Enforcer. "You can use our supplies to help your son first, but we need you. Do not set aside your duty."

"I have reasons for being here *other* than tending to the wounded," John warned. "Stay out of my way."

Two more Enforcers joined the first, moving from a doorway nearby. Each of them looked beaten and angry. "Help the wounded, Doctor. Or we'll destroy your hands so you can never help another person again. You are sworn in your duty to aid us, as we are sworn to aid your guild and bring justice and peace. Our men need your help, as he said."

John stared at them. They glared back. They weren't going to let him go anywhere.

He might as well use the connection. "I'll only help your people under one condition."

"And what is that?"

"Get me to Captain Robin. I want to speak with him."

They looked at one another. "Why?"

"That's none of your business. Get him, or I won't help you. You won't be able to stop me from walking out of here with my son."

The first glared at him, and then he finally nodded. "Tara. Go get him."

"Where are your wounded being kept?"

"This way. But be warned, some of them are wearyworn. They're still crazed, some of them. We've had to restrain a few. We've given them the food we've confiscated from the area, but they're still wild, and they're angry over not having been helped during the siege. Or for the months before it."

A few hours later, John's son was resting peacefully on a cot. John had already helped as many men as he could, and he'd gotten a short opportunity to slip away to see his son. Jamie had lost a lot of blood. His injury had been terrible, and John was sure he'd never be able to use that arm again. He pulled Jamie's sandy hair upward so that it stood on end. His son needed another haircut. It was getting too long to stand on its own.

He was so small, so fragile.

John began to doze, his heart aching. He hadn't seen his daughter since he'd left her with Irkov. But the guilt had come creeping in, and the words he'd said and the thoughts he'd had now burned a hole in his stomach. He didn't want to eat, even though the uncomfortable twisting in his stomach told him he needed to. He didn't even want to drink anything, though he knew he should. He felt as though he'd become just like *Griggori*. He'd said exactly the same sort of thing that bastard would have said. Cold, heartless, brutal things. Things he had at the time wished he could have said to her face to watch her heart break. Things she hadn't deserved.

Yet he couldn't get the bitter taste out of his mouth because of his anger at his daughter for having brought his son to Aelynhold. That she would defy him and come here *knowing* the city was a dangerous place for her to be.

He wasn't sure how he would feel the next time he looked at her. Or if, when his mind was right again, he would be able to forgive himself for what he'd said and felt.

That feeling of uncertainty ate at him as dreams began to burn behind his eyelids.

The Enforcer from before stepped into the doorway of the shop where John and his son were, and he held up a lantern to add some light to the dying one John had left alone. "Wake the hell up, and follow me. Captain Robin's just finished his briefing. He doesn't have much time for you, but he said he would let you speak with him."

John looked up groggily.

"Get *up*."

He nodded, and he got up and followed, taking one last mournful look at his son before he left him. "Have you seen — "

"If you're asking about Elija and the others you were with, they've instructed me not to say a word to you of their whereabouts."

"Even the little girl with them? She's my *daughter*. I want to know where she is."

"You can take that up with the captain. I'm sure they've already spoken with him on the matter, since he's issued an order to follow their wishes regarding her."

John bit back a curse.

Soon, they reached a large house that faced the city square. The monks had thrown wagons and all manner of detritus in the way of the street's entrance to form a blockade to keep the Enforcers and wearyworn out.

He could tell even now that it wouldn't hold for long when the battle began again.

They entered the house, and John searched the room, unsurprised to see how pinched and drained the men here were. What did surprise him was a one-armed man with black hair talking to Irkov in the corner. John had the urge to open his mouth and demand Irkov return his daughter, but then he thought better of it. Especially because that one-armed man was none other than Captain Robin himself, and he'd seen John enter and had scowled at him.

"The field doctor, John Ivan?" asked the captain, and he waved Irkov away. "Go on, Greenman. Get some rest. Leave Aelynhold while you're still able. The men will escort you."

"He's not leaving with my daughter," John said sourly.

Irkov snarled at him.

"Shut up, both of you, before my head explodes." Captain Robin drank deeply from his goblet and then set it down. He stood, wiping the dried blood and wet drink from his mouth. "You're Reid Ivan's brother, aren't you? You look a bit like him."

John nodded. "That's what I wanted to speak to you about."

Captain Robin's brows knitted together. "You've brought news from him? How's he doing?"

"How is he doing?" John couldn't believe it. "You mean to say that you don't know what's happened? My brother is being held hostage here in this city. I know where he is being held, which means Avery is probably close by as well."

The captain's hand retreated from the handshake he was about to offer. He stood back, his expression displeased. "Here, huh? That would explain *your* presence at a time like this. I've heard you're the wildcard and the coward of the two of you."

John bit his tongue against another angered retort. "They're up the hill. That's where the manor is. It's where their prison is. Eastern wing."

"Is that where you were headed?"

John frowned.

"The men reported your presence on the bridge just before it collapsed and killed half of the wearyworn and half of the citizenry here. Luckily, we've managed to get some semblance of an upper hand because of it."

"What are you saying?"

"I'm asking if you were responsible for the murder of innocent men and women and children, Dr. Ivan. Did you cause it?"

John's lips pulled back against his teeth. "*I did not.*"

"Well, you weren't the only one up there. Someone caused it. We're thankful, but it also puts the High Commander at greater risk. They'll kill him if they grow desperate." The captain's gaze darted to John's empty holsters and sheaths, and he seemed displeased that John was now without any weapons. "Wildcard or not, the men will see to it you're given arms from our fallen. We cannot spare a gun because they're limited, but you'll be supplied with whatever else you need so you aren't caught defenseless when the battle picks up again."

John was grateful, and he was about to say so when Captain Robin asked, "Do you have anything else, more useful, to offer?"

"Where is my daughter?"

"She is being looked after. Don't trouble yourself."

"Do not allow him to have her," warned Irkov.

Captain Robin raised his hand again. "I've got it from here, Irkov. I thank you for your assistance."

"I am not leaving the city," Irkov muttered. He stepped outside and disappeared among the other Enforcers who were still rushing to and fro, delivering supplies to the front lines and helping to fortify their position.

"Dr. Ivan, I would mention before we speak any further that I am a father." He looked up, and John met his gaze fiercely. Neither of them cared for the other. That much was certain. And John didn't appreciate the subtle, unspoken threat. "I would never leave my child to die. Now get out, unless you have something useful to me."

"The King of Thieves invited me here under the guise of demands of reparation from the Temple," John said boldly. Why else would the prisoner Arius had brought into Elija's tent have mentioned John's daughter, after all? Especially after what the woman in Isold had claimed? His brother was bait, and his daughter was the golden prize in whatever twisted endgame Lukas and his disturbed friends were playing at. "You'll need me to negotiate with him. He wanted to barter for my brother's life. You won't have a chance at finding Avery if we do not draw this *king* fellow out from hiding — and how better than to use me? My brother will know even more, if we can free him. He wouldn't have come to Aelynhold without several solid leads in his investigations. And he wouldn't have been framed and arrested if he hadn't gotten too close."

Captain Robin frowned again. Then he conceded, and he grabbed his chair and pushed it forward. "Sit. Tell me everything. I'll decide what to do after."

Chapter Sixty-Two

Negotiations

ARCHERS FROM EITHER SIDE flexed their bow strings cautiously, awaiting their orders as the sun rose. The number of Aelynhold's guardsmen and monks had nearly doubled overnight as the wearyworn elsewhere were subdued.

Lukas stood above on the roofline, dressed in the arrayment of Aelynhold's battle-exhausted guards, a sword that was covered in blood and gore at his hip, the blade scratched and chipped. He'd taken it from a dead soldier, and the familiar weight of the armor and weapon calmed his nerves and set his mind to thinking the way he used to, when he'd judged similar situations regularly. It was almost alien to him to do so again. He'd gotten so used to sneaking and thieving, to analyzing the moves of one man at a time and trying to outmaneuver him . . .

Large scale battle. Politics. It was almost another lifetime to him now. But this was home, and that life would probably again be if everything worked as he'd set it to.

Lukas remained mostly apart from the scene — just a ghost observing the negotiations from some dim, forgotten recess. His wife below wore gray plumage across her helm, but all else was black, even her nails. He could see the stitches upon the side of her face when she removed the helmet, for they, too, were black, and her raven hair was like bound snakes, the braids almost like black serpents' scales.

She was accompanied by several bodyguards as she strode to the front lines, and from Lukas's view, he could see the heated determination written thinly upon her face, as easily removed as any other mask she'd displayed before. He couldn't help but feel a small sting of pride. She'd learned to don the many masks he'd worn for a very long time now, and she sported them well.

Across from her, Captain Robin, with his own bodyguards, stood unimpressed. His face was less visible, as he never removed his helmet. But his hand rested against the pommel at his hip, and his missing arm sported an armored shoulder piece that extended farther than the armor on his other side to accompany his vulnerability.

Both armies stood in the smoke, covered in soot and dust, and in dried blood. Both sides were prepared for the negotiations to sour again.

"We want the ones responsible for this monstrous act, Captain. You are to leave our city immediately after."

Captain Robin didn't rock with anger, and his hand never tightened on the pommel. It rested easily, the sword and sheath perfectly still where they hung. He spoke calmly, but clearly. "I have already told you what we want. We know you were lying. Avery is here."

"He hasn't been in Aelynhold for over thirteen years. Need I remind you — "

"Cut the bullshit, good Lady. We'll start anew. Release Reid Ivan."

Lukas sucked on his tooth, and he looked down at his arm when something landed there, pattering quietly — almost too quiet to hear. A raindrop. The dimness of the sky above promised a heavy rain. It would put out some of the fires and wash some of the pollution from the air, and it would mean he would remain concealed more easily. But it also meant the next battle would be a difficult one to sludge through, and that escape could become even more of an impossibility.

Lukas's wife showed no provocation and smiled sweetly. But he sensed her hesitation. Weakness. "I am unfamiliar with the name. Why do you want him?"

Not for a second did Captain Robin believe her. "Reid Ivan is a retired range commander who was working as a consultant for both Black Temple and the Enforcers' Alliance. He is wanted for questioning over the murders of Cyan's sole survivors, the last of the noble house of the Taramine name, Mary and Ames Hullen, as well as the kidnapping of their son Michael Taramine. This is your last chance to cooperate with us, Lady Normane, before we tear this city apart and kill every man, woman, and child, along with the rest of your armed forces, with your own execution at the end of it. You can deny the presence and imprisonment of Avery Ramont all you like, but by your own hand, you have penned a confession of the arrest of the range commander. That confession is currently in our possession. Reid Ivan's crimes against Cyan take precedence over any petty crime he might have committed in your city, even if it includes the murder of your husband. We will give you fewer than six hours to hand him over."

Lukas's fingers cut into his palm. "The clever bastard," he said quietly, and he began to move, slowly, along the roofline.

But his wife was not so easily persuaded to step aside. "Find the girl responsible for destroying our sacred temple and bridges, who injured and killed a hundred innocent bystanders. Deliver her to us. *Then* we will give you Reid Ivan. We have witnesses who saw what happened on the bridge. We also have witnesses testifying she is the same girl who blew up the gate. I do not care that she is a child. She has blood on her hands. The death here today is because of her, just as much of it is because of you. Your Enforcers have set siege to an innocent city, and the rest of the world will know about it."

But Captain Robin was not deterred, either, and he undermined her claim. "Innocent city? You call yourselves innocent?" Captain Robin stepped forward and held out his hand, implicating all of them, and he did not flinch when her bodyguards pulled their weapons from their sheaths and raised them to warn him. She did not stop them, either. It was a poor decision. She should also have stepped forward and shown no fear and no weakness, and she should have kept her guards in line.

Captain Robin continued. "Your city, under your own orders, has breached our centuries-old contract, Lady Normane. You commanded your archers to maim, murder, and burn alive the desperate wearyworn outside your city's walls. You refused to offer sanctuary. And by every account — as well as the eyes of my men who have seen the monks here fighting alongside Aelynhold's guards — your city houses the religious sect responsible for the rampage and destruction of over thirty cities, holds, and posts, from Tulian to Five Tower, and from Aegis Port to Lorenton. We have evidence that your husband Drake Normane was directly involved. That makes you automatically responsible. You are his wife. And don't lie to me again, and tell me he is out of town on business. We know he is dead. His crimes fall upon your hands, and by denying us, you are both accepting responsibility and admitting complicity."

Lukas cursed under his breath when his wife said nothing, which allowed Captain Robin to talk even more. She should have already anted him. "Furthermore. We have no idea who the child is that you are requesting, or where she is. And we do not have to deliver her if we find her. We have the right to sentence her ourselves if she is found guilty of sacking your gates and endangering an entire city. I did not decide to join these negotiations to come to some trade agreement, good Lady. I told you what I expect of you. If you step down and concede, we may overlook *your* crimes, and your late husband's will not be held against you."

The Lady of Aelynhold huffed. "Then we are at an impasse, Captain. I have only defended my city, and I have the right to do so. The wearyworn lost *their* right to enter Aelynhold when they began rioting. We would never have barred them had they not become violent."

"You barred them weeks, if not *months*, before they became a mob," countered Captain Robin. He remained cool and level even as he flung her statement back at her.

She held up her hand to signal some of her men, and the Enforcers around Captain Robin grew tense.

Lukas smiled despite the way the negotiations were turning because he knew the Enforcers would soon be on the losing side of this. John would show himself in his desperation, and so would the girl. She hadn't been among the dead. He knew it. Morris had verified it, and none of the soldiers had found any evidence of her death among the rubble. So he moved to the next rooftop, careful to keep himself out of Captain Robin's line of sight.

One of the men on the eve turned, startled when Lukas slid behind him and placed his palm on the man's shoulder.

"Are the bombs in place?"

"Yes, sir."

"Good."

CHAPTER SIXTY-THREE

Wrath

IRKOV HADN'T LEFT NYMERIA unattended since she'd awakened after the bridge. Currently, he stood before the window, and in his hand was a small canister of dark green paint. Three fresh lines of dark pigment stretched from his forehead over his murky, ruined eye to his jaw, although the rest of his green had worn away. Beneath those fresh lines was an expression that was both pensive and guarded. His eyes were hard. He was worried about her and about a great many other things.

The bowl in front of her had grown cold as she picked at the splinters on the edges of the wooden table. One broke off. She picked at another, her chin trembling as her father's hatred-filled words played through her mind again and again. Her vision blurred.

She couldn't think of anything else. She felt hollow inside because of her father's words, as if the things he had said had stripped her entire life of meaning, crumpled it into one despised heap, and tossed it away. She hadn't even heard all of it, but she'd heard enough.

The splinter she pulled at turned to glass and snapped.

Nymeria withdrew her hands, put them together, and clenched them tightly.

Irkov still hadn't said a word, and he'd been staring out that window since the dark hours of the morning. By now, her father would have said so much her ears would have been begging for peace.

But then her father wasn't here. And he was angry at her. He hated her for her brother's injury.

Her fingers went to her necklace, and she traced the new hairline crack and then squeezed the crystalline heart.

They could hear Captain Robin outside bartering with Lady Normane. "Are they going to give me to them?" she asked quietly. Irkov did not reply. Neither did he move from his position by the window. "Is what he's saying about my uncle true?"

Still, he gave no reply.

Nymeria closed her eyes against a fresh set of tears and tried to push her emotions back, to subdue them. Surely, her father wouldn't stay angry with her forever. She hadn't meant to bring Jamie. She hadn't even known he was in the wagon. Surely, her father would realize it wasn't her fault . . . even though it was.

When she heard Irkov move at last, Nymeria looked up. He paused at the sight of her tears, and she wiped them away again, hastily.

"You've met my brother Griggori," he said finally, and the tin of paint disappeared into one of his hidden pockets.

Nymeria nodded, unsure what he intended to say.

He took a long moment to consider his words. "It's not up to me to forgive or rebuke your father for you. But you need to know that while some men are born broken, like my brother, others become that way when they face what is really inside them. When they see themselves losing what they want or care about most. They can become dreadful creatures."

His words stung.

"He loves my brother more than me," she surmised. But she understood why. Jamie wasn't difficult. He was a simple child with simple problems.

Maybe she was crazy. Maybe she was losing her mind. Maybe not all of what was happening to her was real. But enough of it was that it made no sense, and things that didn't make sense were difficult. And she was dangerous, and that was difficult. She didn't deserve to be the one who was loved most, especially not now.

But she *was* determined to try to do better.

Elija adjusted his elevated foot on the chair in front of him, listening to them as he tended to his broken toe. But he said nothing, offered no comfort, showed no obvious sympathy. Elija had said almost nothing since she'd awakened, either. But she had the feeling they'd talked plenty while she had been unconscious. That both men were vehemently opposed to each other's ideas.

"He cannot change that he loves your brother more. There would be no world where he could rightly choose to, either." Irkov watched her reaction, his gaze darting to Elija and then back.

"It was my fault," she said finally. "I deserve his anger."

"Did you do it on purpose?" asked Elija at last. "Whatever that was on the bridge?"

Nymeria shook her head, her eyes wide. "Never. I wouldn't."

He shook his head. "Irkov. Her power is demonic," he said slowly. "No normal human could do that to the bridge. Or the temple."

Irkov's jaw ticked, and he moved away from the window. "That doesn't matter, Elija. She's still just a child. And despite her being his daughter, you heard what he said about her."

"Yes. But I also know he was distraught, and that sometimes people say things they don't mean in similarly dire situations. He almost watched his son *die*. He angered even me when he said all of it, but he's still her father. And I don't think he really meant it. It's not our place to intervene. We cannot protect her. We're not her family, or even anything remotely close."

"I have as much right to claim her as my family as he does," snarled Irkov. He shook his head. "And he said what he felt. He meant it when he said it. If we give her back to him, is he going to abandon her somewhere? Or give her to these people here? She destroyed the bridge. What do you think they'll do to her for that? They'll think to kill her or to turn her into a tool to destroy other cities." He growled low in his throat at the thought. "I won't let them have her. I've seen that man scared out of his mind for her, and in situations nearly as dire to him as that bridge. He fought for her, but his heart has changed toward her. He hasn't even come to terms with it, but he's afraid of her. He blames her for things she never meant to cause, and for things she had nothing to do with. I cannot believe what he said was an opinion he would retract in any instance, not truly. He is a coward who is unable to face himself. And as you pointed out back there, a bad father. The only thing I won't say is that he doesn't love her. There is no doubt about that. But love and fear are like oil and water. They can never truly mix."

"What are you saying?"

"She is a threat to the rest of his family. That's what I saw him realize. That is the anger that seized him yesterday when he got to his son and saw those injuries, Elija. The boy will be disfigured for the rest of his life, it not crippled as well."

"But he is still her father. He'll get past the grief because his son is still alive. She is his daughter; he has raised her."

Irkov sighed. "Jeana will be heartbroken to find out how he left the girl and cursed her on that bridge. It'll destroy her." Then he approached the table Nymeria sat at and brushed back her hair so that he could see her face. "There you are, Little Creature." His smile was a sad one, and it didn't reach his eye.

Nymeria pulled away when she heard her father calling out to the Lady of Aelynhold. "My father is speaking to them?"

The chair under Elija's leg tipped back when he moved his foot to put on his boot. He shrugged again, and he tapped the sword and sheath upon the table. "At this rate, they're probably about to start fighting, or something sly. But the captain knows what he's doing. He knows they'll lie about everything they can, and that they'll try to cut us down the way a snake would. But he's demanded your uncle's release and made it clear they have no alternative. Letting your father speak may or may not help, but they did summon him here. It's likely they'll barter some deal."

"You should eat," said Irkov. "Unless you found some food you stole, I doubt you've had anything to eat for a couple of days, what with this madness going on."

Nymeria pushed the bowl away, even though her stomach hurt from emptiness. She didn't want to eat. She wasn't hungry.

Nymeria watched Elija lace his boot as he mumbled about the broken toe. "You want to see your father, don't you?" he asked. "I know that look. You want to *do* something, to help somehow."

Irkov stiffened but did not object. "Expect the worst, child. Be on guard. He may still be upset. And even if he seems to have realized what he said and did was wrong, he may be just as cruel in the future. Words like that repeat themselves in other ways over time."

"You won't stop me from going to him?" she asked.

Irkov's brow wrinkled. He pointed at his eye. "And lose the other one? I'll pass, sweet Demon Spider. Keep your fangs in."

* * * * * * *

They threaded through the lines of expectant soldiers. Occasionally, some of the Enforcers would turn to see who was coming upon them, and several of those frowned. Some started to open their mouths to tell her to leave the area for her own safety, but the presence of Elija and Irkov behind her seemed to make them change their minds. A few looked on curiously as she continued toward her father's voice.

"I was summoned by the King of Thieves," said Nymeria's father, "on account of my brother's crimes. He was to be executed three days ago. Tell me, is my brother dead?"

Nymeria bit her lip, the tears threatening to return at what her father had said. She hadn't realized the execution date had already passed, and she prayed that the riot had kept him alive on the merest chance because of the battle to control the wearyworn and to stop the Enforcers' advance.

Lady Normane replied tartly. "The King of Thieves?" she asked. "Has he no name, either? I am getting very tired of these names and titles I do not recognize."

"I am sure you know him, Lady Normane. Or *of* him, at least. His daughter burned Isold to the ground two weeks ago. She and her men killed everyone they could find, except the messenger they sent to Black Temple. She said her father, *the rightful Lord of Aelynhold, King of Thieves*, killed your husband. The demand was reparation for Reid's crimes, and the nature of those crimes was never mentioned. His arrest is a farce. What the King of Thieves wants is my daughter — "

"The girl on that bridge was your daughter?" Lady Normane's interruption was accusatory.

"She didn't blow it up," Nymeria's father said. "Or your gate. She does not know how to make a bomb, let alone have the courage to knowingly bring one and detonate it. The girl is only five years old."

Irkov's hand touched the top of Nymeria's head just as she stepped closer to an opening between some of the soldiers. "Don't get any closer, Little Creature. Don't let them see you."

Nymeria could only barely glimpse her father across the square. "I can't see."

"Be careful. We'll see your father after, if this doesn't sour. This is a dangerous place to be right now."

Her father continued. He was red-faced, and he looked utterly exhausted. "She is an innocent bystander who happened to be in the wrong place at the wrong time, Lady Normane. If you want the one responsible for that bomb, try going after a man named Lukas Maverick. He was near the scene at the gate, and also on that bridge — both places, just moments before the blast. He is a known murderer, and a thief. So whatever politics you are all playing at, I implore you. Leave my family out of it. Just give us my brother. *Please*."

"So you actually think this *King of Thieves* gentleman is the *rightful Lord of Aelynhold*?" she asked. Several of her men snickered at that. But her voice betrayed no such humor. "I don't know where you're getting your information, Dr. Ivan, but *I* am the rightful ruler of Aelynhold in my husband's absence. And he is no King of Thieves, either. As for this man you're claiming was atop the bridge when the bomb went off, no such reports were ever given to me. But now that we're on the topic, surely you have had a hand in this destruction as well, if the child is yours. I do not understand why you haven't already been arrested."

"Dr. Ivan entered Aelynhold with my men. His innocence is not in question, Lady Normane," said Captain Robin. Nymeria moved closer. This was the man who'd tried to keep her away from the rioting wearyworn when she'd tried to get to her brother just inside the city's gate. He'd meant to have her protected.

"Dr. Ivan. Captain Robin. We have witnesses. If you want Reid Ivan, turn over that child. I don't care how young she is, or to whom she belongs. She will be judged by Aelynhold's laws, and she will be punished for her crimes."

A commotion stirred among the wearyworn nearest the ruined temple, and two men were dragged from their midst.

Nymeria couldn't see them, but her father's horrified gasp set her teeth on edge. When he tried to move forward, he was stopped by several Enforcers, and a lot of the lady's monks and guards shuffled on their feet, instantly ready to cut him down.

Nymeria could hear the chains rattling as the men were dragged closer to the square, and the remainder of the lady's men drew their swords as apprehension swept through them. They expected this to provoke a fight.

Nymeria crept closer, keeping low to the ground, pushing the Enforcers' hands out of her way. She needed to see.

The two men hissed in pain when they were shoved to their knees, and her father's hands went to his hair and pulled tightly as his grief showed plainly upon his face. "*Reid*," he mouthed. His hand went to his hip where he kept his gun, but there was no gun there anymore, and he just grasped at empty air.

Captain Robin gritted his teeth and signaled for the men to keep her father from doing anything they might all regret.

And then Nymeria stood quietly between the Enforcers at the front.

Her uncle was there, and so was Taiir. They were both bruised and bloody, and they both appeared badly injured. Her uncle's clothes were torn and stained where a blade had gone into his shoulder, and he'd lost weight, and his hair was matted with dried blood. He was gaunt and pale, and he hardly reacted to her father's voice at all. He gasped with pain when the guards squeezed his shoulder unkindly, and when he opened his eyes again, they were vacant. Haunted. There was none of the warmth or the life in them that she remembered. No spark of recognition. It was as though these people had killed a piece of him in their prison. Taiir was in no better shape physically, though he seemed to have some sliver of resistance left in him.

Her uncle was shivering sickly, and the cuffs were digging at his wrists. Just like the visions and dreams of *Mihai*. She could only imagine what he'd gone through — and her imagination was gruesome because she'd seen hideous things done to Mihai. She'd *felt* them.

Nymeria clutched at her necklace. It was suddenly very hard to breathe. She shook her head in horror. She wanted to run to him, but she couldn't seem to move. She wanted to protect him . . .

Her ears began to ring, and she raised her shaking fingers to her temples as she bowed over, trying to calm herself and think of how she could rescue him. But she could hear the dark things whispering again, all at once. Her senses began to open, until she could very clearly smell the blood of every victim upon every blade and every hand. She felt the stains of murder upon every soul in Aelynhold's temple square . . .

And she felt her uncle's injuries. His hunger. His thirst. His bruises. The flame in his shoulder. She sensed the brutality they'd offered him and Taiir, and she knew it was because they had interrogated them mercilessly. They hadn't even done to Taiir nearly what they'd done to her uncle. As if the abuse had been both personal and to serve a point.

Anger began to broil in her, until her head hurt from the pressure. Until she was clawing at her temples, trying to restrain the black energy it gave life to. Black curled fiercely beneath her skin, until it felt like worms, eating at her flesh.

Her heart beat loudly, drowning out almost everything . . .

"*Nymeria* . . . ?"

It was her uncle's voice, drawing her from the depths she was teetering over. A cracked whisper. That was his plea. It was a broken sound, a wounded sound that stabbed at her heart and fed the cauldron of emotion within her.

Nymeria shut her eyes.

She wanted to be somewhere else. She didn't want any of this to be real.

But she heard Lady Normane speak again. She felt the sword touch her uncle's throat, smelled the fresh blood ooze from the small cut and drip onto the ground where they had him kneeling. "If you are unwilling to turn that child over, then you will watch the range commander's execution. I will not give *you* six hours, Captain Robin. You've got ten minutes. Then you will see the heads of these two criminals rolling at my feet. Their guilt-ridden blood will leech from their corpses in a pool, and then we will continue to discuss this situation about your trespassing in my city. Otherwise, we will kill all of you, and we will take no more prisoners."

"*Nymeria* . . ." her uncle breathed, trying again to call out to her, to have her hear him.

Nymeria opened her eyes, but she could barely see through her tears, or through the red bleeding across the world. He was looking at her.

Nymeria parted from the crowd as her uncle's lips moved; the urge to save him was too powerful for the grief and horror that had rooted her to the ground. He couldn't get his next words out, but he was shaking his head as if telling her to turn around and leave him. But she couldn't. And every step she seemed to take toward him seemed to break another piece of him.

Irkov realized too late that she'd revealed herself.

The sword left her uncle's throat. Lady Normane smiled.

She heard her father's intake of breath. "*No* . . ."

She tried to open her mouth, but she couldn't. She couldn't speak. Couldn't rebuke the woman for what she'd done to her uncle. Couldn't demand his release.

The anger boiled hotter.

She stared at Lady Normane, who smiled wickedly in triumph.

"Nymeria, get back!" cried Irkov. But he could not reach her. The archers on the rooves shot arrows to stop him. One pierced his foot, and he roared in pain and knelt to tear it out, and red ran down his foot in a bright stream when the shaft broke.

Her next deep heartbeat felt like fire, and it scalded her.

Three more arrows pierced Irkov when he rose to step forward again, and he broke the shafts, snarling —

Lieutenant Elija dragged him out of the line of fire.

"Stop! You'll get yourself killed!"

"Why are none of you trying to get her back from them?" shouted Irkov. "They cannot have her!" He snarled as Elija continued to keep him back, and he called out to Nymeria next in his rage. "Burn them, Little Creature! Burn them if they try to hurt you! Take their eyes and make them scream! Fight for what you love!"

The whispering sound was still so loud in her ears, and she was growing dizzy from the searing sounds that reverberated about her skull.

Lady Normane spoke again. "So. You're the one causing all the trouble. Come here. Let me have a look at you."

But Nymeria felt her teeth bare at the lady. The anger inside her became more poisonous with the lady's every word.

"Nym — "

Lady Normane snarled and gripped her sword, and she struck Nymeria's uncle with it. He cried out, and blood sprayed from his mouth. He collapsed. He was barely breathing. Barely conscious.

The pulsing enmity within her caught fire, and her head snapped up. She heard the ground hissing and cracking at her feet. Even as the Violet arced from it like lightning and sent Enforcers and monks and guards and wearyworn retreating in fear, Nymeria stood her ground, fighting it. But she was so angry. She wanted them to pay. She *hated* them for what they'd done to her uncle.

Taiir shook his head. *"Stop,"* he warned, and his lips pulled back until his snarl was all teeth and promise.

She couldn't restrain the anger any longer . . .

Nymeria's teeth clenched together, and her fingernails dug into her palms, and the blackness surged through her, and then she screamed as it raked through her flesh like blistering coals.

Blinding violet light exploded all around her. The ground erupted. Everything caught fire near her, and everyone touched by it screamed as though in mortal agony.

Lady Normane retreated as it spread, as the buildings exploded and debris sliced through the air like bullets. Glass shattered, and those fleeing the area were thrown from their feet . . . And then Nymeria couldn't breathe anymore as the black energy began to suck away her breath and burn her strength away. It then began devouring her . . .

Her body convulsed weakly, and then the world began tilting . . .

She was gasping for breath, trying not to scream again.

Her father caught her as she collapsed . . . He'd come from nowhere.

He was weeping as he held her against him.

"Get that child!" screamed Lady Normane. *"NOW!!!"*

"Fath . . . Father . . ." Nymeria gasped, and her eyes rolled as the dark things began to scream. She felt the burning, blackened hand stretching for her from the shadows that rolled toward her.

She needed to save her uncle . . .

Her uncle shuddered as the monks grabbed him and Taiir and dragged them away, and she reached out for him as grief burned another hole in her.

Swords began to clash as the Enforcers came under attack.

"Make it — *stop.*" She choked on the words. She couldn't breathe, couldn't . . . "Make it . . ." She didn't understand why he'd come to save her if he'd been so angry at her. She also didn't want him to cry. Nymeria squeezed his hand. "I didn't . . ." She could barely gather the breath to speak. "I didn't mean to hurt . . ."

"I know — I know, baby girl. I know." He kissed her forehead. "I'm so sorry that I said what I said," he told her.

The world was swaying.

"I didn't know . . . was in the wagon . . ."

CHAPTER SIXTY-FOUR

$\mathcal{M}$ISTAKE

LUKAS PULLED HIMSELF TO HIS FEET on the small catwalk, and his shoulder struck a cracked column and knocked pieces loose. The railing was now gone. He stared at the street beneath him. Something trickled down his face, and when he wiped it away, his hand was covered in his own blood.

That explained why he felt dazed and sluggish.

The Enforcers defended themselves and the Ivan family from Anna's men, and Nymeria was barely conscious, in the middle of a ring of them. He blinked, but the fog upon his mind didn't lift. Everything spun when he took another step, and he nearly slipped from the catwalk again. The detonator, he remembered. But he saw that the soldier who'd been assigned the task of pressing the button was dead. It lay there, in the dead man's fingers.

Red smeared the column as he let go. The rubble shifted, and the smashed, scorched helmet that had been atop his head fell from the catwalk with small bits of debris. He had to get to that detonator, to cut the Enforcers' troops in half. Otherwise, more would die than necessary, and they would not get the little girl.

Some of the dust cleared, and Lukas sucked in his breath, daunted. Black glass was *everywhere*. Nearly the entire city square had been turned to it, and it was an entirely alien sight to behold. It sparked dangerously with that accursed light. The screams he heard dragged him back to the Gray Halls, and his entire being quivered at remembered horror.

The catwalk ahead of him was littered with the glass. Some of the debris was of stone and wood and metal; the rest had turned color and caught the firelight and danced with the Violet . . . as though to draw its victims with its beauty, only to poison their minds with its madness-inducing prick.

He stepped carefully, his heart racing, and yet he still slipped. A sharp stone cut his hand, and he snatched it back. He'd almost touched the glass. Lukas stood, swaying, and he wiped the blood from his eye with the back of his bleeding hand, and he searched for the girl again and found her. Her father was holding her, shielding her from the fighting about them.

But he saw them get torn apart by the Enforcers as Aelynhold's men were driven back. He saw John fighting to get his daughter back. They tied her hands — they didn't seem to know what else to do with her. But they could no longer claim her innocence, or even claim ignorance of her presence.

His chance was slipping away.

Lukas grimaced and got to his feet again — and when he looked down, over the edge of the catwalk, he realized that Captain Robin had dodged the debris he'd knocked loose. Lukas's helmet was at the captain's feet, and the one-armed Enforcer was staring up at him.

The captain's eyes went wide with recognition, and Lukas swore, mortified that he'd been seen by him. He stumbled back from the edge of the catwalk as the captain looked at the stairwell against the building there.

"Lukas!" shouted one of his men from the other end of the catwalk. *"Sir!"*

"Lukas . . . ?" mouthed the captain. "The catwalk!" shouted Captain Robin as he charged for the stairs. "The catwalk above us!!!"

"Shut up, you fool!!!" cursed Lukas.

He prayed the bombs would still detonate as he raced across the rubble. He was furious. Desperate. He risked himself with every step, every stumble, and that black glass gleamed menacingly all around him, each twisted spire almost pointing, almost *reaching* for him.

Other Enforcers joined the captain, and Lukas began to taste his own, familiar fear. It was acrid. Bitter. He could feel his heartbeat ripping within him with every breath.

Then he was prying the dead soldier's fingers from the detonator and he was holding it in his hands delicately.

The captain halted, and he turned white when he realized what Lukas had picked up. He couldn't see the device for their distance from each other, but Lukas *knew* that he knew. It was written in the man's fear as he stumbled backward, into his companions. Just below the first of the bombs they'd placed.

Lukas knew he would be shielded by the rubble if he did it now. He held it up, heaving.

"Wait — "

He smiled wickedly and pressed the button. The explosion was deafening.

He fled the area.

The rest of the Enforcers would have to squeeze into the square some other way. The main road was closed off now by tons of detritus from the buildings above. Captain Robin and his men would have been crushed to death under it all, too.

When he saw the retreat of his wife's men, he smiled to himself, relieved. It was a wise decision on her part to have them retreat from that poisoned scene, to avoid being infected with the Violet. It would only become safe to remove when the light was gone from it.

But he sensed soon that something was amiss, and when he strolled into their perimeter, his hood drawn over him, Morris called out to him gravely. His apprehension grew infinitely more intense, until it felt like a rope had wrapped around his throat. "What is it?" he asked. "What's wrong?"

"Your wife, they caught her."

He rolled his shoulder and grimaced at the bruise there. "No matter. We've other cards to play, especially now that the main street has been blocked. She understood and agreed to the risk. We'll get her back, even if she's a bit bruised." She'd probably want to hand him over to them afterward, to teach him a lesson.

"You don't understand," said Morris.

Lukas looked at his friend, saw the grievous lines in his expression, the dangerous seriousness in his eyes. Something was acutely wrong. "What don't I understand? Are the Ivans gone? The child?"

"You killed her."

Lukas stared at his friend, suddenly wordless. "Wh . . ." The girl, or his wife? He tried again, but he found he couldn't say anything still.

"They had just caught her. They were taking her away from the fighting. You killed her."

He looked back to the square, which was blocks away now, down the hill.

"You're mistaken," he said. Morris meant his wife. He was talking about Anna. Lukas exhaled sharply and shook his head. "But I-I couldn't have — I never saw her . . . Where is she? She was supposed to retreat — "

"Your wife is dead, Lukas. She's gone."

His breath left him, and he knelt, feeling sick, and he stared at the ground as his men moved for him, to let him process what he'd just been told.

Morris knelt by him, grunting as he did so because of his injured leg. He put his hand on Lukas's shoulder. "The men are calling for a truce, sir. They're afraid. They are tired of killing their brothers for a lie."

"I had to do it," he whispered. "Their captain recognized me . . ."

"Did you hear me? We can't have a truce. They have to know that."

Lukas sucked in a breath — it rushed out of him as his lungs deflated against the air. It hurt to breathe. He couldn't have . . . He *couldn't* have killed his own wife! The entire reason he'd stayed away, for *years*, had been to protect her. To protect their daughter. To keep Caol from getting his hands on his family and doing to them what had been done to him in the Gray Halls.

"*But Anna* . . ." Another hollow, painful breath. His fingers clawed at the stone under him, and moisture dripped onto the gray surface, turning it almost black. "I couldn't have killed her . . ."

"Lukas, we need to retreat. They're winning. And if they get a hold of you, we'll lose a lot more than just your wife. Caol will win. He'll take back everything you stole from him. And our brothers will find out what you've done with Avery. It'll be all our heads. Please, get up! This is not the time to break!"

"She hated me because I never came home — "

Morris's fist found his jaw, and then Lukas's friend grabbed him by the collar and shook him. "Your men need you, you brilliant fool! Get up!"

Lukas's tongue throbbed where his teeth had cut down on the flesh.

The sharp pain did nothing to dull his raw sense of loss, but it did remind him of what he'd told Morris in the tunnels just days before. He gripped Morris's hand and nodded. He tried to speak again, but at first nothing came out.

Lukas cleared his throat and tried to focus, but his chest still felt like it was about to rip itself in half. He commanded himself to compartmentalize. To remember his many faces, to don the one he needed to continue. But it was nearly impossible to do so. He could taste his own heartbeat; it was a sickening feeling, almost like hands at his throat and copper in his mouth.

Morris struggled to get up, and he nodded for the men around them to help Lukas.

His throat closed once more, and his hand shook when he took the dagger handed to him. It was his wife's. She'd saved his life with it by poisoning him the night their daughter had killed his cousin Drake. It had been a wordless statement of her devotion to him, even if it had been a lie to a master liar.

He lifted the pommel to his lips and kissed it, wishing he'd not pressed the detonator. Wishing he'd still had to fear her betrayal. Wishing they'd gotten the chance to truly reconcile, to know one another again and work toward forgiveness and honesty the way she'd begged him to years ago, before Caol had betrayed him and made a murderous slave and coward of him.

"I want her body brought to the manor," he said at last. He could hardly recognize his own voice now. It was a raw, vulgar sounding thing, and it was filled with anger, and it barely held back a black tide of grief. "We will have only a temporary truce, so that I may grieve my mistake . . ."

He wanted to scream. He wanted to break his hands into useless, bleeding things against every man and woman before him — to kill everyone and everything. It wasn't fair that they were all alive and she was dead. The comfort of knowing she was alive and safe had sustained him for so long that now he could hardly see what his goals meant without her.

She was gone. And worse, it was by his own hand. Not by the hand of the enemy he'd feared would take her from him.

It was the cruelest, most detestable joke his sins could have spat back at him. And he had no man to turn his wrath upon, save for himself, because it was *his own doing*.

The circle of those he cared about was now smaller. His daughter. His nephews, both of whom he barely understood to care for. And his only real friend.

He had only them now, and his cause, and he was no closer to freedom, or to any kind of justice.

A day later, Lukas stood over his wife's body. The smell made him ill.

He never lifted the shroud to look upon her beautiful face. He didn't want to see what he'd done to her. It was enough for him to see her braids lying loose about her head. Some of them had been sheared. Some had been burned.

He had done this.

He lowered a torch, and her mattress of oil and kindling caught fire.

Lukas dropped the torch into the inferno, and he turned to his throne and sat upon it, and he stared at the burning corpse as the fire consumed it, chewing on his nails and unable to say another word about her.

"You will take my place as you requested," he told his friend after hours of silence. The fumes from the smoldering corpse were nauseating. "I'll not give them what they want. Neither will I sit upon this wretched chair when they enter my home and make their threats."

Morris nodded. "Of course. I already agreed. I'll do whatever it takes."

"Whatever. Just get that child. It doesn't matter if we're all Enforcers or not. It doesn't matter how many die on either side of this divide. Caol's son wants her. We will draw them out with her. I want him dead. I want all of their research burned to the ground. I want all their victims freed from the Gray Halls. No one will ever again use that power for the things he's already done, or for what his son intends. I want every shard of glass found after they're done, and destroyed. I want none of this to repeat itself ever again. That curse will be erased from existence."

"What about the girl?"

"She's dying. What about her? There is nothing we can do."

"But — "

"Morris, you're infected with her curse," Lukas snapped. "You cannot tell me that you do not sense what that unnatural power is doing to her. It is tearing apart her *soul*. No, it's tearing apart her *souls*, all of them. The ones in the glass, and the others within her body. Nothing can be done to help her — not even Gabriel can save her now. It is too late. She's let too much of it loose, and every time she gives in to that black thing inside her, it takes more of her life from her. She won't recover. All that is left to be done, after she has served our purpose, is to end her life quickly. It will be a mercy by then. It won't be the first time it's had to be done to one of the children like her, and it won't be the last. Some other child will bear the same strangely colored eyes and the curse after her, and we'll have to find them and kill them, too. Before those dark creatures take us all."

"I am not going to kill a child," Morris hissed. "Not even a demon child. Especially not when my instincts are warning me to *protect* her."

"That'll be your downfall, then. Remember I've warned you when you regret that decision."

"Sir — "

"Have a messenger figure out who is taking up the role of leadership among the Enforcers now that Captain Robin is dead. Send him my invitation. *Your* invitation, that is. The next man may be more willing to negotiate. And approach him differently with our demands. The situation is growing more delicate by the hour, and less fixable. This needs to end."

CHAPTER SIXTY-FIVE

CONFINED

JOHN ONLY REALIZED HOW WRONG he'd been toward his daughter when she had stepped apart from the crowd when his brother had been put on display before them all. He barely understood the emotion, but it rippled through his anger and his fear for his son. He realized his mistake for what it was. It was a hideous realization, a thing he could taste on the back of his tongue, like some putrid thing he wanted to cast from himself. He wanted to call out to her, because she'd put herself in serious danger when she'd moved toward Reid.

But everything that happened after she'd revealed herself was difficult to process. It happened too quickly.

The look of pain and anger adulterating her face. Nymeria collapsing just as he'd reached her . . . His daughter being taken from him as more fighting erupted.

He saw Lukas above them, holding a detonator as Captain Robin tried to corner him with several Enforcers. Another series of bombs destroying more of the square.

And then he was fighting for his life against the enemy — which seemed to be everyone — and with nothing but a borrowed blade and an aching heart, with terror caught between his teeth like nails and glass because he didn't know whether his daughter was alive or dead, or in whose hands. Because his brother was in such bad condition and had nearly been decapitated in front of them all.

He saw neither his brother nor his daughter through the billowing veils of dust and detritus, and he choked on the fumes and the dust and the ash as he fled the front lines in search of his daughter — he was torn by the decision to go after her, but part of him knew the monks and Lady Normane wouldn't murder his brother because he was their only bargaining chip. All they wanted was Nymeria.

And *Lukas* wanted Nymeria, which meant he would use the confusion to make his move.

The Enforcers had tied her up and taken her, and she was nowhere in sight.

John couldn't hear her at all. He couldn't see her. He clenched and unclenched his hands as he dodged weapons and threw men out of his way when they collided with him. His leg ached markedly as the stitches pulled, and he strained against every painful step. He had to find her.

"Nymeria!" he shouted. She didn't reply. "This can't be happening . . ." He choked again when he took another breath to shout, and he coughed against his fist until he was heaving and bowed over and dizzy from it. There was too much dust in the air, too much toxic smoke. "*Nymeria!*"

John then ran into one of the men who'd taken her from him. The man had tied her wrists while the others had blindfolded her and wrestled her away. John snatched him up by the collar, and his spit flew into the man's face as he roared, "*Where is my daughter?!*"

The man pointed at the rubble where Lukas had detonated his own set of bombs. The soldier was pale as a cloud. "We took her behind the blockade," the man said, but he was staring at the rubble behind them where Lukas had blown up the buildings and then vanished. "We put her in the truck — "

John gasped, sickened, and he staggered toward it all, searching for a vehicle he couldn't see. There was such a mountain of ruin spilled into the street that he couldn't tell whether the truck the Enforcer mentioned was buried beneath it, and his heart lodged in his throat. His feet quickened until he was upon it, but he still couldn't see the truck. He couldn't see her anywhere, either. There was no trace, not even a beam of light from headlights, or a horn blaring from the damage, or even the smell of engine fuel. He couldn't tell if she'd been crushed under the weight of those collapsed buildings, or if the truck hauling her had gotten through. "*Nymeria!*" he shouted.

Then he heard a brick shift. It rolled down the mounds of destruction, knocking a few others loose as it tumbled toward him. John looked up and saw Captain Robin and what was left of the men who'd followed him.

The captain was wheezing, his fingers gripping at the stones weakly as though to push them away. His fingers were dripping with blood, and the whole side of his face and neck were painted with its color.

John gritted his teeth as anger rolled through him, and he began to climb toward the injured captain. The climb was precarious, and twice, the rubble shifted and threatened to come crashing down, to bury him alive.

John wiped the blood from his own eye as he reached the captain. The one-armed man tried to sit up unsuccessfully, and he groaned. John pulled him upright. "Order your men to release my daughter," he cried.

The captain said nothing. He hardly seemed to hear John. His lips moved as he shut his clouded eyes, and he strained to say something.

John couldn't hear what he was trying to say.

"Where did your men take my *daughter*?" John cried, and he shook the man when he still did not answer.

The captain lost consciousness even as he continued to try to speak. All that he managed was the merest scraping sound against the back of his throat, and it hardly sounded like any word at all to John.

John's fist tightened, and when he looked over his shoulder, he saw that the monks and Aelynhold's guards were retreating. The exhausted Enforcers were regrouping.

More of the dust began to settle, and below, just on the other side of the street, he saw more bodies, crushed by the destruction. He swallowed against the knot in his throat as some of the Enforcers realized he wasn't alone on the stairwell.

"Are you injured?" one of them asked.

John looked down, and the Enforcer followed his gaze to the captain. She frowned and started to move closer, and when she realized who it was who was unconscious there beside him, she cursed and ordered several men to help.

"You! Gather some more men to help me get the captain down from that stairwell!" Of John she asked, "Are the others here dead?"

He nodded as she climbed quickly to join him, her men not far behind. "He has a concussion," said John. "He may have internal bleeding, too. I just reached him as he lost consciousness."

"You're Dr. Ivan," she said before John could say another word. "You look very much like your brother." She looked about them suspiciously. "Were you part of this? If you were, I'll slit your throat right here and orphan that girl of yours."

His mouth shut, and he shook his head, unexpectedly emotional at the thought of leaving behind his family with the world in such chaos about them. "No, but — "

"I'll let that be your answer for now, but if I find out you had a hand in blowing up the square, expect me to wield the sword that cuts off your head. I'll gladly do it if my captain dies and it is your fault." She signaled something to some of her men and returned her piercing attention. "Your daughter's been arrested, and Lieutenant Kesha's ordered that you will also remain under close observation until you are cleared, Dr. Ivan. You are a suspect in this bombing. And if Captain Robin dies, you'll be executed as if you killed him yourself. So keep the captain alive until we can sort out this mess."

"Where is my daughter?" he demanded.

"You don't get to ask any questions right now. So shut up and help us with him. Kesha will be debriefed on the situation here. She'll decide what to do with you and your terrifying little demon child."

His teeth snapped, and he glared at the Enforcer, itching to shove her from the side of the stairwell. "My daughter isn't a demon — "

"I saw dangerous, powerful witchcraft, Dr. Ivan, and nothing I say to my peers will change that they saw it, too. Many of them will react worse than those among us who know more about her condition. Your brother warned us about her power in Edantine, and now we've just seen how right he was. Look around you. Everything is coated in black glass! Whatever your daughter is — demon or not — she'll probably be executed for what she's done here, even as young as she is. Keep your mouth shut so the new target on your back doesn't get bigger, and we'll meet with Kesha to decide how to proceed. You just focus on doing your job, and we'll do ours."

He was roiling with anger by the time she finished telling him what to do, and neither of them said more than another word to each other afterward.

The urgent desire to get his family out of here increased exponentially. He couldn't let his brother or his children be killed, and he'd had it with the Alliance as much as he'd had it with Saura and her lies!

And yet, he was terrified he wouldn't succeed in saving even one among his family. How could he if his daughter was being treated as if she were a terrorist? All he knew was that the world was wrong if an entire city and army thought of her and treated her as if she were dangerous to them. She was a child!

The contemptuous female officer gave her orders to her subordinates to keep him under observation while he tended to Captain Robin and the wounded Enforcers and wearyworn. She stated that he was not to look for his daughter, and worse, that he was also to be denied visiting his son. His protest was quieted by the knife she patted at her hip, and by the equally repugnant treatment by the untrusting Enforcers he'd been given to.

"Count yourself lucky you're a doctor," snarled one of his guards. "You may be beyond our jurisdiction, but that is only for now."

Captain Robin's injuries consisted mostly of a few burns and some bruising, but the one to his head was bad enough that it worried him. John prayed the captain would wake up soon so that he could get his daughter back.

The captain had seen Lukas holding that detonator. Surely, those explosions — all of them — had been the murderous thief's dealings! He was certain Lukas was at fault for all of it. Or he was responsible for *part* of all of it. His daughter was innocent. She couldn't be responsible; it was impossible. There was no such thing as magic, no such thing as demons.

John impatiently tended to the wounded as they came, all the while contemplating how he might get his son and his daughter *and* his brother out of danger — and all the while frustrated because he could not see a solution. Worse, if he did anything, the Enforcers could do whatever they wanted to bend his will — it would also make things worse for his family.

He didn't know if Jeana was alive or dead, or why the kids were in Aelynhold.

The captain's condition never changed. He remained unconscious, and his bruises darkened and his blistered burns wept as time crept agonizingly onward.

When Irkov was assisted into the small makeshift surgery by Elija, John and the Greenman stared at one another, both as angered as the other.

"Boot off first," said John stiffly.

Irkov snarled. "Where is she?" demanded the Greenman.

A tremor ran through John's hands as he washed them. Irkov saw it, even as John tried to hide it by drying his hands on a yet-unsoiled cloth that had been taken from one of the houses nearby.

"You don't know where they've taken her, do you, you rotten coward?"

John sat on his small broken chair and stared at the Greenman's boot. He motioned at it. "Can you take it off or not?"

Irkov snarled and ripped the boot off, and the arrow cut him and sliced the leather in the same motion. He held up the bloody boot and tossed it behind him angrily, as if making a point, and then his fist curled up into a ball as if it took every ounce of control for him not to swing it. "If they hurt one hair on her head, I'm blaming *you*."

"They won't let me see her."

"You left her on that bridge, you son of a bitch! That precious child! She clung there, holding on for her life, and she heard nearly every rotten thing you said about her except the part of your not being her real father! How could you have wished her to fall to her death?! *How could you have dared to speak such words?!*"

John grabbed the remaining portion of the arrow's shaft and leaned forward to look under Irkov's foot. Just as he'd expected, it had bitten clean through. "The arrow's missed every bone in your foot." He shoved it through and yanked it out.

Irkov's fist struck his jaw, and the Greenman stood, heaving.

The arrow in John's hand found Irkov's throat as he lunged at him, but Elija had darted forward and now pulled him back before the head could slice. Elija pushed them both apart from one another.

"Stop it! Both of you! Do you think that trying to beat each other up, or that killing one another, will do Nymeria any good? As far as I can tell, you two are the only ones who can protect that little girl. You're the only ones here not bound by the commands of senior officers. You're the only ones here who won't be court-martialed for any actions you take to help her. So start working with one another so we can find out what's been done with her."

"I'm not working with this coward," snarled Irkov.

John shrugged. "You won't be doing much of anything with or for anyone soon if you don't get those wounds taken care of, Irkov. And you don't have any right to judge me."

"I already *have*, Doctor," snarled Irkov. "I have judged you as garbage. You turned your back on that little girl, and you wished her dead. I will never forget it, and I will never forgive it. You might as well have slit her throat just as my brother slit your wife's. That's all you're good for, getting your own family killed — "

Elija shoved John back again. "Irkov. John. *Stop*. You, *sit down*. You — "

"Stay out of this, Elija. This walking tree fungus wants me angry enough to cut out his tongue. I've put up with his shit for *years*. I'm through trying to make peace with him!"

Elija hissed and left, shaking his head. "Come and find me when or if you decide not to kill each other. I've better things to do. There are a lot of injured men who need our help, and a lot of innocent people who have been hurt in this disaster."

"I'm not allowed to leave," John snarled. "Your friends won't even let me see my son. I don't know if he's still unconscious. I don't know if he's developed a fever . . ." His voice shook as Irkov glared at him, and he turned and grabbed the towel again. He nodded to the chair. "The least I can do is repay you for saving Nymeria, and for helping with my injury on the way into this accursed city."

Irkov was still ready to fight him, still too furious to let him do his job.

"Sit down, Irkov."

"I think I'll find some lesser pig of a man to stitch me shut." The Greenman turned to leave.

"I shouldn't have said any of it," John hissed. He wrung the towel. "All right? It was wrong. I realized I blamed her for that collapse — she didn't even cause it. I was blindsided by the sight of my son's blood. I was angry because he follows her *everywhere*. What I said is going to echo in my head for a very long time, and I am going to have to live with knowing what I said and how I reacted, Irkov. She didn't deserve it. I don't even know why my children are here, or if my wife is alive or dead! Why else would they be here?"

"It's too late for your guilt," said Irkov gravely. "Your daughter came here knowing they would try to kidnap her, Jonathan. But she came anyway, because she feared you would get yourself killed because of your injury, because you could barely walk, and because she was terrified for her uncle. She's vowed she will fight to protect all of you, even if it costs her life. No child should ever have to make such a grim promise. She knew they would try to take her, and now you are letting it happen because you are a coward who cannot even face what you really think or what you really feel in order to overcome it and be the better of your rotten self. I am not giving up on her or letting some chickenshit guard hem me in to keep me from finding and rescuing her. I am going to find her, and I am going to take her back to Jeana. You can burn in the hottest of the Seven Hells."

With that, Irkov bent to pick up his boot, and he hobbled away. John tried to follow, but his guards barred the way. "Where do you think you're going? Step back inside."

John stared after Irkov silently, cursing him, even though he was glad the Greenman felt as he did about Nymeria. John returned to the tent as the next injured soldier was admitted behind him.

CHAPTER SIXTY-SIX

CLAIMS

LUKAS STOOD BEHIND THE THRONE with the other armed monks, his hood drawn low, and Morris sat upon the throne in his place. Their guests had arrived, seven of them. They had been stripped of their weapons on the terms of a peaceful attempt to negotiate anew.

A woman had stepped up as the new leader of these Enforcers. Her mask, as Lukas's wife's had been, was all strength and no vulnerability. Yet he clearly saw the blood and the bandages. She'd been run through during the battle.

He forced himself to focus, to put all else aside.

"Come in," said Morris. He was dressed in the fine armor of a lord, and he sat, relaxed, as if he feared no danger at all. As if he was slightly bored.

The woman strode forward cautiously with her fellow Enforcers, her suspicious gaze darting about the room. She nodded curtly, though the motion was stiff.

"I am told no one has truly taken Captain Robin's place after his death," said Morris.

"You mean until he *recovers*. Do not worry about our command right now. It is being sorted."

Lukas held his breath as anger threatened to consume him. He'd failed to kill his target when he had instead murdered his own wife?

He remained as still as he could, turning his head slightly as his teeth ground dangerously against one another.

"I heard he was dead," said Morris. The man leaned forward.

"You heard wrong." She looked at the smoldering body upon the floor. "You're not Drake Normane," she said. "Lady Normane kept claiming he was still alive, away on business. And I've met him. Who are you?"

"I am the King of Thieves," said Morris gravely. "I do not give my name." He waved at the corpse. "She was an ally, and a tragic loss. Killed in the square."

"What happened to her husband?"

Lukas could hear Morris's grim smile. "I murdered him. This throne belonged to me, and I did not like wolfmen in my city, or near my holy temple. She stepped aside to do my bidding. She was good at what she did. What do I call you?"

"I didn't give my name. I'm just another lieutenant. According to your dead Lady, Reid Ivan was the man who murdered her husband."

Morris held up his hand, and Lukas and the other monks sheathed their swords and moved away, to the gloomy corners of the room. They remained ready. Alert, should anything happen to put Morris in danger.

He saw Morris's cautious, admiring smile as the man studied the lieutenant carefully.

"I've a gentler way of words than my late ally," he said. "The girl. May I have her?"

"She's been arrested. Why do you want her?"

"You want the truth?"

"Yes," said the lieutenant. She practically snarled when she said it. "We're tired of the lies. I want the truth. The real truth."

"She is my daughter."

Lukas nearly swallowed his tongue. He'd never coached Morris to say such a thing. If Morris could convince them he was the child's real father, the ploy would be *brilliant*. Especially because it was such an obvious lie.

For just a moment, he felt a small ray of hope. But that hope was weak, and it was heavily burdened by his grief. It was hard to tell whether he should have any hope at all.

"Why else do you think I would have gone to the trouble of finding her? I don't care about your quarrel with Lady Normane, or her lies about Avery Ramont or Drake Normane. Give me my daughter, and you can have Reid Ivan and search the city freely for Avery, for as long as it takes until your captain is satisfied."

"She is Dr. Ivan's daughter." The lieutenant's eyes had turned to slits.

"Ask him where he found her. Two years ago, I lost her in Five Tower. On the Bright Night. It was during a bad winter, and I had to smuggle what I stole from the city. I went back for her, and Caol's nephew admitted that she had been taken from the city by a doctor named John Ivan and his mute wife. Ask him and see. Once you and your people are finished here, I'll appoint a new name to lead my city, and I'll disappear again. You'll have no more problems from me, or from Aelynhold."

"Lady Normane wanted the girl, to punish her for her crimes against Aelynhold — "

"The Lady is dead. She never would have gotten to lay a finger on the girl, even if she hadn't been killed. Stop kicking her carcass. I've already told you I don't care what she wanted. My reasons are my own. I just want my daughter to be returned to me."

The lieutenant studied him for a long time, and then she turned to her comrades. They spoke quietly with one another until she returned her attention. She hesitated. "We'll have to talk with the others. Until Captain Robin wakes, the final decision regarding the girl will rest with Lieutenant Kesha. How will we know you will not steal from us the same as you did Caol? We expect you to follow through on your word."

"You don't. I have nothing of value to any of you for trade. I cannot give you the range commander until I have my daughter. Once she is safely in my care, I will fulfill my word. He will be alive when I give him to you, and in no worse shape than what the Lady had already ordered done to him."

The lieutenant was still unsure.

"One more thing," said Morris. "She has a birthmark behind her right shoulder. Here, along the neck." Morris tilted his head and touched the spot with two fingers.

Lukas frowned. Birthmark?

"A silver feather." He smiled sadly. "As if from a small dove's wing. It does not fade the way her scars do."

"You do know she blew up the square, don't you? That girl has . . . *abilities*. Dark ones."

"It is because of what the Lord of Five Tower did to her. She is ill. I intend to leave Aelynhold with her, so that she may not hurt another. She will be able to recover, away from others, and live out a peaceful life."

Morris stood, then, and his eyes turned violet as he stepped forward. "The gift runs generously in our family. We know how to set it to rest so that no other will be harmed by it."

The lieutenant stepped away from him, shaken.

"Hurry and speak with your people," Morris said gently. He did, indeed, sound like a father who missed his daughter.

For a man who'd once not been able to lie with a straight face, he'd learned well.

CHAPTER SIXTY-SEVEN

Denial

WHEN JOHN WAS SUMMONED, he'd only just fallen asleep, his head aching from having been awake for so long. He was startled awake by loud footsteps and a brusque command outside his confines.

"Wake up, Dr. Ivan. Lieutenant Kesha's asked to see you."

They walked through streets filled with grumbling soldiers who were all still very alert, though every one he looked at had bloodshot eyes and down-turned mouths. The pungent food being eaten by a few had no recognizable smell.

It was still dark, and they could still hear screams elsewhere in the city, and gunfire. He saw the dull glow of fire on the horizon, reflecting off disbursing towers of smoke. He steeled his nerve, knowing the quiet in this part of the city could easily erupt again, just as it had before.

John followed his guide until they entered another of Aelynhold's angular-faced buildings. Candlelight spilled into the street where the door was left open. He prepared himself to be barraged with accusations and be questioned as a criminal, and he stepped inside.

Several lieutenants and a few sergeants were present, and all of them seemed to judge him the moment he stepped in.

A woman among them nodded for him to walk toward the center of the drab room. "Where did you find the girl?"

The question caught him by surprise. He immediately thought of Irkov and vowed cruel things silently. "I beg your pardon?"

"A blind fool would be able to tell she isn't your daughter. Tell us how you came by her."

"Five Tower. She was orphaned."

"During a blizzard, yes?"

John frowned. He opened his mouth, and then he closed it again.

"Answer the question, Dr. Ivan," she commanded.

"Yes — what does this have to do with anything?"

"So you took the child."

"Yes. She was abandoned, and she would have died from the cold. Why is this important — "

"Next question, Dr. Ivan. Did you ever bother trying to find any of her relatives?"

"We were told she had none."

"By whom?"

His heart sank. What if Taiir had been wrong? *Was* someone from her family looking for her at last? Or was it worse? Had Lukas and his men devised something else? Yet that didn't make sense, because Lukas couldn't have known about the blizzard . . . unless he had been there during the Bright Night . . . ? He opened his mouth, hesitant. "Taiir . . . He was part of Five Tower's guard at the time. He fled the city about a year later and aligned himself with Black Temple. With my brother, specifically — "

"Where he could remain close to watch the girl," she surmised. "You are aware Taiir was an executioner and a torturer, aren't you? For Five Tower."

"No, but Reid vouched for him. He helped us to save her life — "

"Are you aware that he has sworn an oath to kill the child if anything reminiscent of the Bright Night ever happened again?"

John sputtered. "What . . . ? How could you know that? How could you believe it as true, either? Taiir has been an *asset* — "

"Dr. Ivan, we've been given Taiir's signed confession along with this staff. You do know what that weapon represents, do you not? Look at the carvings and tell me what you see."

When he said nothing, she rolled it across the table. It fell to the floor and kept rolling, until it was at his feet. John picked it up, and he looked at the ornate black cats, confused. "It's just a — "

"Surely, you aren't so stupid," she said. "Did any other guard carry such a weapon when you 'found' her?"

"What are you saying?"

"I'm saying your brother's friend is still working for Five Tower. He was one among fifteen assigned to ensure her death. We've caught other men carrying the same exact weapon, each one loyal to Five Tower, each one hauling captives infected with that violet light. The truth was extracted from each one, and in every instance, the staff is upheld as the oath of an assassin. To find any and all with the potential to do what your daughter did, and to slaughter them in cold blood. The useless among the Violet-infected were to be rounded up and taken to some foreigners and sold on Caol's orders. His son Eiran wants some of them for his own agenda, likely to create more of them and try to turn them into what your daughter is capable of."

John said nothing, stunned, and she went on.

"Dr. Ivan. Only the most ruthless families in Five Tower assign weapons as ornate as these, and only for the most brutal intent. No guard takes them because they are ordered to. They do it voluntarily, requesting the right to carry it. Accepting the possibility of public torture and beheading if they fail to carry out the responsibility they sign for by taking that weapon. Why would your brother trust an executioner from that city even while knowing all of this? Is there anything you want to tell me about that?"

"I don't — "

"Then tell me this. How can we trust you or your brother when you admit enemy spies among your ranks? Around your children, even? We know about Five Tower's intent to destroy your guild, and ours. Are you a traitor?"

"I . . ." He gripped the staff. "Of course, I am not a traitor!"

"Honestly, you're in a position that makes your denial questionable. But there's been some disagreement about it in this room tonight. The Greenman, Irkov, defended you. He also defended Reid Ivan and Taiir Eskat. Adamantly, before we had him forcibly removed." Her lips pursed as she let that sink in.

"Dr. Ivan, I am only sure of one thing, and that, by your own confession, is that you are not that child's biological father; therefore, you have no right to decide what is done with her. She, by some inexplicable means, has injured a lot of people and lay waste to an important part of this city. They will never recover what she has destroyed."

"But — "

"She is to be taken to the manor in exchange for Reid Ivan and the executioner."

John felt sick. "You can't do this — "

"Has the captain awakened yet?" she asked coldly.

The Enforcer who'd brought him in shook his head.

"You can't do this! Nymeria is my daughter! We took her in. We've raised her — "

"Frankly, until the captain wakes and decides otherwise, then as the senior officer, I am the one in charge here. Which means *yes*, I can. And I *am*. Take him back to that nasty surgery room and guard him. Saura's men should arrive in a few days."

John was infuriated. "You can't — you don't understand! Lieutenant Kesha — "

He was thrown from the premises and dragged back to the shop. He tried to fight, but one of the Enforcers knocked his head against the bricks on the side of the building. He was hardly conscious when they dragged him inside, and when he tried to get up, he couldn't seem to gather the strength to do so. Everything spun mightily.

Chapter Sixty-Eight

Feared

NYMERIA FELT THE ROPES digging into her wrists, tasted the sweat and the tears that soaked the gag they'd put over her mouth to keep her from screaming and biting at them. They'd even tied a blindfold over her eyes to keep her from seeing where they were taking her.

They were afraid of her. They wouldn't let her father near her. They wouldn't let Irkov or Elija come see her, even though Elija was a lieutenant now. They themselves wouldn't even come near her after she'd been put in the lightless trailer of an armored Enforcer's truck.

All she could see was darkness. All she could hear were the whispering things. All she could feel were those ropes, and the gag, and the steel plates and frame under her turning to glass, and the fire raging in her body with every breath and every heartbeat. It hurt.

She felt a void around her as the soldiers kept a distance from the truck. She was guarded like a deadly creature that might escape this cage she'd been placed in, and she wanted to claw at the metal, to rend it, to . . .

But she sensed what echoed in these Enforcers' fearful minds. *Demon. Witch. Creature . . . Evil.*

Nymeria shivered, her side aching where they'd thrown her against the wall and shut the door. The dark thing hadn't been able to reach her before the Enforcers had taken her from her father, but it was still nearby, still searching.

"I didn't mean to . . ." she wept against the cloth that muffled her words. But no one could hear her.

Another wave of fire scorched her, and Nymeria felt her body convulse. She saw the violet light brighten the dark interior of the truck, even through her blindfold . . .

Nymeria sensed Mihai's tortured shadow, and she reached out to him. She knew it was a mistake, but she also knew instinctively that his presence made her invisible to the creatures.

And then she was separate from herself.

She felt every knife that stabbed Mihai, every bullet that ripped through him, every set of claws that slashed. The barbed arrows, the fiery bombs that tore at his flesh and scorched him . . . She tasted the blood upon his tongue, the hatred within his being, the madness within his mind. So many voices . . . Too many voices — until he couldn't understand their words anymore. It was garbled disorder, and they were trying desperately to kill him.

Every breath Mihai took gurgled with blood and malicious promise, and the dark things cringed from him as the blue light arced within him, craving release. She felt her lips part, heard the sound of agony leave her mouth . . . But it was Mihai's mouth that spoke, his voice she heard as he cursed his enemies. "Give her to us . . ."

She saw flashes of distorted memory. A man's head, rolling across the stones of some ancient courtyard. Rain. A man with red eyes and blond hair, teeth sharp enough to draw blood, holding his throat and choking as he staggered away from Mihai. And then a blinding white light, followed by Mihai's enraged, agonized screams.

A prison around him. Chains upon his wrists · · · His blood turning slowly to dust · · ·

The chains breaking · · ·

Taking one last breath to call out her name in one final, anguished plea · · ·

An ocean of violet stars · · ·

Then the vision was gone, and it was only Nymeria again. She was still in the truck.

The door opened.

She lay there, numb. She felt herself convulse weakly, just once.

And then a coarse set of hands were dragging her across the floor, toward the warm light outside. The breeze that blew in felt cool, and it smelled of rain. "Ranking officers said to take her to the manor, to Lieutenant Eska," said one.

"Zane, she's cold as ice," said the other. "She's shivering."

"Don't worry about that. She's not our problem anymore, or the doctor's. She belongs to that creepy guy who's calling himself a king. She's going back to him."

Nymeria whimpered when one of them grabbed the ropes around her wrists and hauled her up from the floor. Everything spun as she was thrown onto his shoulder.

"I still disagree with this whole thing," said the man holding her. "I think he's just figured out a better way to get this little girl. I don't believe he really could be — "

"He knew enough he wouldn't have known otherwise," said Zane. "The doctor couldn't deny how he found her. Hurry up. Go, already."

"But I really think we should have waited until the captain regained consciousness."

"They don't think he's going to wake up at all, Gabin. He's probably going to die. Bleeding on the brain, that's what they said."

"I don't believe that for a second. That old man's too tough for that sort of death. It'd take a lot more than a brick to the head. You heard about what happened in Edantine almost three months ago, didn't you? They cut off his arm, and he refused to lay down for the posted doctor to help him there. Got right up, him and the range commander — both of them wounded — and took out a huge force of armed monks. And they caught several traitors, to boot. While wounded. One missing an arm, the other barely able to walk for the sword he took to the leg. And then they went and hunted down the Cyan child's abductors and fought off a pack of wolves, and another squadron of Lord Crostor's men. There is no way a little rock could take him out! The captain is a walking legend!"

"Well, blame her. She did it. She took out a lot of men today. They're infected with that violet color in their eyes, the lot of them. It was bad enough to watch them go through that, Gabin. Let alone what she actually did to cause all of it."

"She wasn't the one who hurt him, though! I heard the thief from Dr. Ivan's escort took out the captain — "

Zane grew impatient. "Save it. Witchcraft or bombs, it doesn't matter. I don't want to hear anything else about it." Zane slammed the trailer's doors shut and slid the bolt. "To be safe, don't let her say a word, scream, or use her hands. We don't know how she did what she did, so don't give her the chance to do it again . . . Probably some kind of hell chant, or hand-waving thing, if it was witchcraft. Anyway, the sooner we get Mr. Ivan, the sooner we get some answers. Lieutenant Kesha and the others are waiting for you to get this kid to Eska. They've got horses ready. Follow Eska's orders when you get there, and do not ask questions. You don't have the rank to, anyhow. Make it quick."

Gabin muttered under his breath, adjusting Nymeria on his shoulder, and he cursed Zane's attitude. "I'm sorry about this whole thing, kid. I don't really think this is right. It feels like a cheap trade, and a lie. I'll try to carry you gently, at least. It's all I can do for you, aside from offering some prayers in your behalf."

She felt his hand squeeze her calf reassuringly.

She struggled against him. She didn't want to be taken away. She tried to ask where her father was, but the words were muffled. She grew dizzier, until her head fell. She still couldn't *breathe*.

Nymeria was barely conscious for hours as the dark shadow within her beat at her head and clawed at her veins. Her jaws hurt. Her fingers ached, even. Her wrists burned where the ropes had rubbed her flesh raw.

They rode on horseback, passing building after building, and she felt the sunlight soften to shade before it alternated to warm light again.

She could still smell the blood. Feel the death. Hear the screams. It wouldn't stop.

And then the swaying slowed, and the next thing she was aware of, she was being lowered gently to the floor in some echoing room. She didn't remember being brought into a building at all.

And then she heard a voice. A familiar one. "Why is she tied up?" The voice was shaken, angered. It belonged to the man who'd been with Lukas, the one she'd followed through the tunnels.

Her heart beat in her throat. They were giving her away. Where was her father? Why would he let them give her away?

Nymeria tried to pull away from them all, but Gabin held her shoulder firmly. The female lieutenant spoke as Nymeria began to cry.

"For everyone's safety, precautions were — "

"Untie her immediately."

"Where is Reid Ivan?"

"I said to untie her. She is not an *animal*."

He truly sounded angry at her mistreatment. It confused her.

The Enforcers remained silent and still for a moment.

Nymeria blinked against the bright torch light that lit the room when the blindfold was removed. She shut her eyes tightly as everything continued to spin. And then her ropes were cut and the gag was removed.

"Bring her to me."

"Where is the range commander?" demanded the lieutenant.

"You will get him soon, as promised. This is the last time I will tell you to bring the child forward, Lieutenant — "

The lieutenant drew her sword and put it to Nymeria's throat. She meant to say something angrily, but she choked on her words.

Nymeria flinched.

Gabin's hand fell from her shoulder, and his body hit the floor. She smelled the blood.

The lieutenant held her throat, still choking as her guards were cut down around her. Her sword clamored to the stone, echoing loudly, and then the lieutenant followed, though she struggled to remain conscious. She died choking on her own blood, her fingers clutching the air when they fell from her throat.

Nymeria's chin trembled.

Morris waved the assassins away. "The Lord was busy," he said to Nymeria. His violet eyes burned clearly in the darkness. "Honestly, he's afraid of you."

"Where is my uncle?" she whispered.

He stood from the throne and walked toward her, each step an echoing threat.

Nymeria brushed her tears away and looked up at him as he knelt before her and cupped her shoulder. "Do not fear me, Nymeria. We do not intend to hurt you." His grip was gentle.

"Your friend's name isn't really Lukas, is it?" she asked. "And you're not the King of Thieves. He is."

Morris let go. But he continued to stare into her eyes. There was no anger in him, though. No guile. Just sadness. She felt his sorrow.

"Do you want me to take the Violet from you?" she asked. "I can feel it hurting your soul the way the darkness is burning mine."

But he shook his head. "No. It is as Lukas said. If you do, it will kill you. I've seen enough of the memories now to know the only reason you are alive is that you have given us that light. We guard you against the *Shadei Ra*. It's why they haven't found you yet. They always get close, but they cannot find you. They take us first because we were meant to shield you from them."

"You don't know about Mihai, yet, do you?" she asked. "What they did to him. Why even the dark things are afraid of him."

Morris was quiet for a long time, and then his violet eyes turned away. "It'll destroy me to see more of it. I am already doing all that I can not to look into the Violet. I only know from the glimpses that what happened to him was a horror no human mind could withstand. That you have endured more of it than any other is almost impossible to understand."

"Where is my uncle?"

Morris held out his hand for her to take.

She stared at it.

"Come with me," he said. "I'll take you to him. You will stay with him, but we are releasing him in a few days. You will not be released with him."

"Where is the King of Thieves?"

"Avoiding you for now. He does not want you to try to use your power against him again. The idea unnerves him."

"He is a coward," said Nymeria. "He would never have been an honorable Greenman. Tell him I want to talk to him."

CHAPTER SIXTY-NINE

Old Promise

NYMERIA FOLLOWED MORRIS down the very dark corridor. Not all of the old windows had been boarded over, and pigeons fluttered in from the low-hanging eve outside. They flapped their wings a few more times as she stepped around their droppings. The birds stared dumbly at them as they went by, then flew back to their nests.

"Mind the glass," he said softly, and he held out his hand to allow her to descend the stairwell first. "No one else wants to contract the Violet."

Her eyes narrowed. Her fingers itched for her broken pen tool, but it was gone. It had been lost on the bridge. She was sure he remembered it anyway. She'd blinded his friends on the bridge with it, after all.

She had also lost the knife in her boot.

She stopped before the stairwell, peering doubtfully into the echoing darkness below. "What you did was wrong," she said. "Why did you have them killed?"

"They were instructed to come unarmed. They did not. And they raised those weapons to threaten you, and to threaten me. I am not like Lukas. I don't care to mince silver words when something important is on the line. He is much more subtle than I." He waved at the stairwell. "Despite how it looks, those stairs are still quite intact."

"They look wobbly. That is a lot of rust."

"If they cave in, I would be the one to fall to my death. I weigh more than you do."

"Who is Lukas really?"

"He used to be an Enforcer. Lukas was his brother's name, before he drowned. He's actually Drake Normane's cousin, Lady Normane's first husband. She remarried after he left a little over a decade ago."

"But Drake is dead, and now Lukas is back," she surmised. She looked up at him. "He killed my grandparents, you know."

"He's done worse things than kill old people. Such is his responsibility. He's accepted that, but he is not at peace with it, I assure you."

She began the precarious descent. Each step creaked and groaned, until the hairs rose along her arms. "If my uncle is not down there, I am going to make the Violet hurt you more," she said. "I'll make you see what I saw."

She heard him pause on the stairway, and when she looked back at him, he was looking at her strangely. Sadness darkened every shadow that clung to him. And those violet eyes of his pierced her, until it almost felt he was staring into her soul.

"Such a thing will kill me, surely, but I am not afraid of it. My death is already written," he said quietly. "I've felt it coming since the day I was infected with the Violet." He looked over his shoulder briefly. "And in your condition, you shouldn't be considering adding to the blood already on your hands."

At last, one final door lay at the bottom. He procured a key and unlocked the door, and when he held it open for her, she saw another set of stairs, and a vast hallway filled with cells. There were a few flickering torches, and the dungeon reeked of urine and sweat, and of feces and blood, and of death. Just like Mihai's prison.

The door shut behind her, and she flinched. He spoke through the door. "He wants you to stay here. Your uncle and his friend are along the left wall, nearly at the end."

Nymeria felt something crawl over her foot and told herself not to look down as she held her breath. She moved forward. The torches were too high for her to take one.

The smell of the dungeons was so very familiar. It clung to the back of her throat in a most gruesome and unpleasant manner.

Nymeria touched the wall to keep herself aligned straight, but she flinched away when she sensed the past of this place etched into the stone's surface. Instead, she hugged herself. She didn't like the lonely feel down here. She didn't like sensing the recent cruelty, or the older ones.

And to smell the old, dead blood . . .

A cockroach scurried across the floor in front of her, just as she was about to step into another dim circle of torchlight. Someone coughed. She heard a chain rattle, and her heart sped up. "Uncle Reid . . . ?" she whispered.

He groaned as she approached the cell the sound had come from. His silhouette began to take shape, and so did Taiir's. Taiir was asleep against the far corner. Her uncle lay on the floor against the wall itself, shivering occasionally.

"Uncle Reid . . . ?" Her fingers curled over the bars.

Taiir's eyes snapped open. They were black as shadow, and they were filled with anger. "Have I gone mad," he grated, nudging her uncle, "or is that your niece?"

Her uncle stirred. "I told you not to — " Reid hissed as he rolled over, and he held his side. "*Nymeria?*" He squinted against the torchlight behind her as he set the violet shard she'd given him months ago on the floor. The light in it dimmed, but even so, she saw his shirt there, cut to ribbons . . . Was he making a rope? What for? There were no windows from which to dangle it.

Then she saw his shoulder. It looked infected.

She gripped the bars as tears began to form suddenly, blurring his features.

"What are you *doing* here?" he asked

But then Taiir was at the gate, and his fingers were reaching for her throat.

"Taiir, stop!" her uncle cried.

She gripped Taiir's hands, her eyes wide as he grabbed her collar and tried to pull her closer. His eyes were filled with murderous intent, and his teeth flashed as he shouldered her uncle off.

"She didn't mean to hurt anyone!" Uncle Reid exclaimed, and he clawed at Taiir's hands, trying to make him let go.

"I told you I would kill her — "

Nymeria gripped at his wrists as the room started to darken, just as his fingers found and threaded her throat.

"It's not the same as Five Tower! *I said to let her go!*"

Taiir's head knocked into the bars, and his lip split. The smell of blood reached her even as everything else began to fade. His fingers tightened until her air was cut off.

She was barely aware of clawing him. Of his cry of pain as he let go. Of sinking her teeth into his wrist and tasting sweet blood that made her teeth clench tighter.

Part of the iron bar sparked with violet and turned glassy and black as she hit the floor, gasping. He'd tried to *hurt* her!

She began to cry.

Reid retrieved his torn shirt rope, staggering and weak as he was, and he wrapped it around his arm and his hand. He looked at the glass on the bar and told her to look away as she stared up at him.

It shattered.

"You are welcome," said Taiir, and he shrank back into the corner, his hand still bleeding.

"I swear to god, Taiir," snarled Reid. "If you ever threaten her like that again — "

"I did not harm her. I merely gave her a fright." He laughed from the shadows there, but it was a tired sound. "It would have taken years to weaken those bars, Commander. That rope would have broken long before you could have ever bent them with it." He raised his bleeding hand, yet he sounded amused. "Teeth like a tiger, that one. Claws, too."

"I hope you lose the use of your hand."

Her uncle reached out for her as the door swung open.

Nymeria leaned into her uncle's hug, grateful for the comfort he offered, and he picked her up and kissed the top of her head as he held her tightly against him. She felt him wince when she laid her head against his shoulder.

She'd missed him so very much.

Finally, her uncle set her down, and he smoothed back her hair. Then he noticed the blood, the filth, and the rope burns on her wrists. Her uncle's startled expression told her how it hurt him to see those marks upon her wrists, and his thumbs brushed the discoloration gently as he searched her face for answers. "What happened, Myria? Why are you here, in Aelynhold? Why did your father bring you?"

"He didn't," she said. The bruise on her uncle's jaw was very dark. She felt again, the sting of anger. Remembered how Lady Normane had hurt him.

"Then tell me what happened?"

She told him everything, and he offered not a single beratement. His eyes glimmered halfway through, so that she thought he might cry, when she told him about the black glass in Black Temple and the knife she took from her father to take down the monk at Isold. He grew very concerned when she told him about her brother, though. "I didn't know Jamie was with me, Uncle Reid. I didn't mean for him to get hurt. But I saw Lukas. He's — "

"I know. He's in charge of things here. Calls himself the King of Thieves," her uncle said.

"You already know?" she asked.

"I've learned enough about him that it makes my skin crawl when I so much as hear his name."

"That's not his real name, though," she said. "Lukas was his brother's name. He stole it."

"I know about his twisted family circle. About Drake and Anna Normane. Is your brother all right? What about your mother and father?"

Nymeria bit her lip. "I don't know. When the square blew up, everyone started fighting again. I got tied up and thrown in the back of a truck. I heard another explosion after that, and this morning I was brought here. Morris killed the guards who brought me, because they didn't trust him and came armed."

"Who is Morris?"

"The man who brought me down here. He's pretending to be the King of Thieves right now so Lukas doesn't have to face me. Because Lukas knows I am not afraid of him, and that I know *he's* afraid of *me*."

"Tha girl has been through hell, hasn't she?" muttered Taiir.

Nymeria glared at him. "Nobody's talking to you, you *jerk*." Then she remembered what her uncle said to him. "And what did you mean about telling him it wasn't like what happened in Five Tower? What happened in Five Tower?"

Both of them exchanged looks, and she sensed a lie coming. She held up her hand when her uncle started to open his mouth.

"Before you lie to me, remember who you are talking to, Uncle Reid. I'm not stupid. I can see the lie forming in your eyes."

Taiir shifted. He was the first to bare the truth. "I swore to end your life if another Bright Night ever occurred."

She glared at him again. "Why? How does the Bright Night have anything to do with me?"

He shrugged. "Your power caused it. Destroyed most of tha city and killed thousands. You infected countless more with tha Violet."

She frowned. "But I've never been to Five Tower." When she realized her uncle wasn't looking at her anymore, she grew less sure. "Have I . . . ?"

Neither answered the question. Her uncle rubbed at his temples. "Myria, I've told him about your gift. I told him you were learning to control it."

"Which is why you are safe from me, Little One," added Taiir. "But recent events have raised my concern. What happened on tha bridge? It is gone. Was that you, or some other device?"

"I think it was me," she said quietly. "You wouldn't really kill me, would you?"

"That depends on you."

"And it stops with my getting in your way and lopping off your head," said Reid. "Taiir, you might as well cut the bullshit. You're just as fond of her as the rest of us, and it would set you on a murderous rampage if anything happened to her."

Taiir hid his expression by keeping his face in the shadows, but his voice seemed humored. "I am a man of my word. Why would I ever betray my vow?"

"Then why'd you stick your neck out in Tallil to try and find a cure for her? You're as desperate as I am for answers. To help her."

"What are you thinking, Little One?" Taiir asked.

"That I want to wring your neck for scaring me," she said. "How do we get out of here? Have either of you made it farther than this door at all? Or do you actually *like* it down here and plan to stay?"

They looked at one another, and each bore guilty expressions. "We hadn't really, no. Except when we were brought out and . . . Yeah." Her uncle looked at the wall farthest from them, and he picked up the dim shard. As he and Taiir stepped out of their cell, her uncle drove his elbow into Taiir's side. Taiir gasped and gripped the bars, cradling the injury. He was bleeding from some other wound still, and reacting to the abuse of her uncle's elbow seemed to have opened the other wound. Fresh blood seeped through his filthy, stained shirt.

"Even *pretend* to hurt my niece again, and I'll break that rib."

Taiir raised a hand and waved Reid through. "Worry not, Commander, unless it is necessary. Her fright served its purpose, however, did it not?"

"I could have picked the lock," Nymeria said coldly to him. "All you had to do was ask."

"Then I fear my actions were not well-considered," Taiir grumbled as her uncle searched a pile of old chains and seemingly worthless refuse. "Lock picking is not a skill common among five-year-olds."

"This cell has stolen both intellect and patience from both of us, Taiir," her uncle admitted. "But the least you can do is remember how smart she is."

Her uncle seemed intent on finding something, and when his hand closed around it, he stopped searching and lifted it. "Damn," he said quietly, and he knelt, his head down. "They took everything except for this. We don't have our weapons, our gear, the evidence . . . Nothing. Just these. We could break the jar, but . . ."

"What is it?" Nymeria asked, and her uncle clutched the item and brought it close, as if to open something.

"Come here, kiddo," he said. He removed from a slender glass cylinder a small missive. "I'm not sure if they're going to let us live, so I think I should give these to you now." He handed her the jar, and a bitter but pleasant smell wafted from it when she took it and peered inside. "I'm sorry it isn't quite what I'd promised."

She sniffled. "Are . . . are these cacao beans . . . ?" He'd remembered his promise.

When she looked up, she realized her uncle was having trouble trying to say anything. He held out his hand, and she took it. "I'm sorry," he tried to say, but little sound came out. He pulled her closer and rested his chin on her head.

"I will search tha cells behind me," grated Taiir. The warrior gripped his side and stood tall, and he, too, went to work searching the place for anything they could use. His voice, too, was strained with exhaustion.

"Thank you, Uncle," she whispered, and she took the lid from him and replaced it. "Are those chains very long?"

"No," he replied. "Not even long enough to wrap about my wrist, and the iron is crumbling, it's so old."

Days passed, and neither food nor clean water was brought down to them. They never found an exit, never found anything to use as a weapon. It was cold, and the smell never faded. The roaches crawled over them when they tried to sleep, and the floor was hard, even though her uncle and Taiir had tried to make it more comfortable for her.

The torches winked out, and they were left in the radiance of only her uncle's shard and the occasional silver light that twisted through her remaining scars.

And then several of Lukas's men came into the dungeon and took Uncle Reid and Taiir. They threw her back down the stairs and locked the door between them. And then she was alone, crying because her uncle and Taiir were no longer with her. Their angry voices faded as they were taken through the halls across the premises, until she couldn't hear them anymore. Until she could not hear footsteps or curses, or anything. Just the occasional flutter of pigeons, very faintly, from beyond several flights of stairs in an echoing stairwell. She didn't know whether those people were going to kill her uncle and Taiir or release them.

Her fingers clutched the jar and both of the necklaces she wore, and she cried until her energy was gone. Until she was staring into the darkness, barely able to separate herself from Mihai's memories of his own dungeon. Until she was barely able to remember she was herself, or that her family was probably fighting to get her back.

CHAPTER SEVENTY

Debriefed

REID AND TAIIR DRANK and ate what they were given, neither in the mood to answer a bunch of questions about their true intentions or where their loyalties really were, or even what they had really been doing for months. "That's right," he said to Lieutenant Kesha. "I vouched for the man sitting next to me. I'll let him explain to you why he left Five Tower. Nothing I can say will satisfy you on the matter. Even I don't have the full story, as I didn't need it to make my decision about him. But neither of us are traitors. Nor is my brother. After everything is laid bare, I would voice some questions of my own and debrief you on some troubling information I've come across."

Lieutenant Kesha handed her crutch to an officer who laid it against the wall, out of the way. Reid leaned forward, and the chains on his wrists rattled and then scraped across the table as he lifted his hands and rested his eyes against his palms. The cuffs dug in, but he didn't care anymore. He'd nearly gotten used to the ache. Besides, these Enforcers would see soon enough that there was no use for the restraints.

"They gave you our things when they turned us over this morning," he then said against his knuckles. "Have you found my ledger? I told you where it was. Secured behind the seat in a false panel, in a metal case. After the incident in Edantine, I would not risk letting it be found or destroyed. Or the other contents of that box."

Lieutenant Kesha looked over her shoulder and held out her hand. Another officer gave her the box Reid had hidden. Both handled it very cautiously.

Reid groaned when he saw it. "You haven't even opened it? You could have broken it open. Haven't you even a lockpick among you?"

"We're not about to open a possible traitor's box, not when it belongs to a man who may not have any real fealty toward Black Temple or the Alliance," she said. "We're not fools, Range Commander."

He felt the side of his face pull. "Ah . . . You have a smart point there, my apologies. Hand it here, I'll open it — cautiously, so as not to spook any of you. I've no explosives in it, or vials in there containing anything infectious. I don't normally carry those. That is more a part of my brother's job."

He opened the box with the tiny key he removed from his ring. Carefully, so that they knew he was up to nothing, he opened the box. He reached in slowly, pulled the journal from it, and set it on the table. The cover had old blood-spatter, which cracked as he opened it to the back jacket. He removed the note hidden there, and he slid it toward her, along with the journal itself. Reid nodded to the box as well, to the papers that had been beneath the journal. "That letter along with a few others was in Avery Ramont's quarters at the citadel. It was hidden in the wall, behind loose stones. That one seems to have been a promise of a confession, written before he disappeared. He'd planned on returning, even though he never did. It mentions the nature of his investigation — not many details about *what* that was, but *why* and *who*. It states how urgent it was that he investigated it himself, in person rather than by sending men to do his bidding, as he should have as the leader of the Alliance. It mentions the entering of a covenant with Lukas Maverick, and it even mentions the King of Thieves as having had a part in keeping the investigation quiet. It doesn't explain their role or say how they were to aid him, though, or even whether he thought they might betray him. The letter does, however, give a clue to where the rest of the information was hidden. It's here. In Aelynhold. Likely with Avery himself, wherever he's being held — or wherever he's been buried."

The lieutenant's brows were drawn, as though she had no earthly idea how Reid could have gotten his hands on such an important piece of evidence. "I wasn't aware you had contacts at the Alliance headquarters. Why did one of my people give *you* such an important document?"

Reid grimaced. "If you haven't forgotten, the Alliance has been corrupted. Many of your comrades have become questionable, and both the captain and I have been very careful with whom we have spoken and how we have proceeded in the investigation on the Alliance's traitors. I have sent intel back to Black Temple with the instruction for their people to be especially careful in their dealings so that we may all avoid the provocation of a war between us. If you don't believe that letter is real, I'll name a few men who can verify it. Or you can find several yourself."

She looked at the seal upon it and studied the handwriting. "I have seen enough of his documents to know this is certainly Avery Ramont's penmanship, and the seal is authentic. But why you?"

"I have friends everywhere, Lieutenant. I was an Enforcer for fifteen years. I was promoted to range commander early in my service, and I served as such for over ten years." That statement seemed to surprise her, but she did not interrupt him. "I've seen more bloodshed than I would ever have cared to see in a lifetime. During my service, I traveled more of this continent than many Enforcers who serve their entire lives. I pursued quite a few cults, ended several rebellions, and helped to enforce peace among peoples who did not want it. I was good at it."

An Enforcer Reid knew not the name of spoke next. "He is held in high regard along the northern and eastern shores, Lieutenant Kesha. He's the one they called the White Dagger. I heard he was extremely successful there. An incredible strategist. Some said on par with Avery himself."

"The one who broke the ice," she said. The lieutenant frowned. "Why did you leave?"

"I retired two years ago because my family needed my help." He saw her look and then indulged her with a more detailed explanation. "The decision has served both Black Temple and the Alliance well in that I can act as a bridge between them. My wife had given birth to our child during my tour, and my daughter was already four when my brother brought Nymeria home and sent for me. At that time, my parents and my wife were ill, and the catastrophes in Wireshon and Hagath after the Five Tower incident meant my brother and his wife had their hands full. That is why I left. Afterward, I began to help train Black Temple's people and to reinforce what they lacked in security. I found I preferred it to being separated from my family for years at a time."

She unfolded the letter and began to read.

Taiir set his cup down after a slow drink. He pushed it away and stared at the door. "What little time we have is fading, Reid," he said quietly.

Reid nodded. "I know. But they must understand our motives are not corrupt before they will trust anything else we have to say." He then waved at the box. "Taiir has been a strong ally during the investigation, and he has also been helping me in my search of a cure for my niece," he said. "She isn't well, and I am certain it's because of what they did to her in Five Tower."

"Explain that," she said, looking up from the letter. "Why you have befriended an assassin sworn to murder your niece." She shifted forward as she stared hard at Taiir. "We received your confession and your confiscated staff from your accusers."

Taiir scowled. "I have nothing to defend," he said. "I do not care how you judge me."

"Taiir," said Reid. "Tell them everything."

The warrior grunted. "It is not their business to know my disloyalty and secret sabotage," he said. "I was never pledged to tha Alliance. I was pledged to service in Five Tower, and I betrayed everyone and everything there. Those crimes are my own, between Five Tower and me. I ask for no excuse from these Enforcers, Commander. Not pardon, not understanding."

"If you do not explain it to them, I will be forced to do so myself. I think you would prefer to tell it in your own words than have it be told in mine."

Taiir turned his head and held Reid's gaze with his own very icy one. He leaned back, and his boot scuffed the floor. His head shook side to side, displeasure written plainly in his posture and upon his face.

"I would recommend you explain it in full, Mr. Eskat," said Lieutenant Kesha. "We would not be beyond our rights to execute the two of you under the suspicions and accusations placed upon you. Especially since the evidence is not kind toward either of you."

Taiir said nothing for a long moment. Reid was about to prompt him again when the man's head fell, and Taiir's hands clenched and then unclenched several times. "So be it."

"Everything," she said again.

"I concede," he said. Then he began. "I knew little of what Caol actually did to tha people he had us take to tha Gray Halls, though I did often hear tha screaming. I would not claim to know tha politics behind what he did, but I was one of many who carted his victims. Lukas Maverick was one of tha men I took there. More than a thousand died in that place. It left a bad taste in my mouth, and a dark stain on my conscience. I did my job; I tortured and killed for Caol, drawing confessions and forcing political alliances for him. But none that I did was as vile as what he and his sons did in tha Gray Halls. I had enough after I witnessed tha children killing one another."

Taiir said nothing for a long moment, his hands wringing. "They gouged their eyes out, like most of tha others . . . Started eating one another. Their screams weren't human anymore, not after whatever Caol's son had done to them. After seeing that, I started saving tha ones I could. First, it was only a few to keep him from realizing my betrayal. Then Caol and his ally, a man named Rhael, parted ways and on ill terms. I set tha rest of Caol's survivors free. About three hundred of them. Before I could also leave tha city, tha Bright Night happened. Tha orphan who later became tha Commander's niece was left to die at tha Bright Night's epicenter as tha pinnacle of blame for tha event. It was Caol's orders. She'd been one of his victims. Tha subject of his final experiment, gone wrong. He also wanted all tha fugitives I had set free found, and he wanted all of them tortured to death alongside tha man he thought had freed them. Rhael. They never suspected my betrayal, not that I am aware. To keep it so, I requested tha right to tha black staff to ensure I could later leave tha city at will, and to return if it was ever a necessity. It kept suspicion from being painted upon me so I would not be delivered to tha Gray Halls myself. I helped tha Ivans save tha girl and burned tha body of another dead child in her place. A year later, when Eiran's inner circle shrank and I no longer had access to help any there, I left. I could do no more in Five Tower."

Lieutenant Kesha's lips pursed. "How did you come to be allied with Black Temple? To befriend the range commander? And why did you continue to carry that staff, knowing its symbolism and the oath it tied to you?"

Taiir shrugged. "Part of my oath was honest when I took tha weapon. I had no trust or love for tha child, and I did not want to see another Bright Night for as long as I lived. Even now, if tha child causes another, I will uphold that vow and hunt her down. And I will kill her."

Reid's teeth clenched, but he did not interrupt his friend.

"But tha girl is not of tha same evil Caol and Eiran drew from her. I will protect Reid and his family until my oath turns my hand."

"How did you come to be allied with the range commander?"

"I told him what I had sworn and why I had decided to find tha girl again, and I nearly lost my life for it. But he let me speak when I offered another oath in exchange."

"What was that oath?"

"I have a copy in that box" said Reid. "But I have others elsewhere, sitting in a few vaults. What he gave me was his signed confession, which will be forwarded to Five Tower, Black Temple, and the Alliance in the event of either my death or when certain other requirements we've set are met," said Reid. "He also confessed what he did for Caol and what he did to betray him. With other evidence to back it up, it would be enough to arrest the Lord of Five Tower and remove him from power. We've been very busy, he and I, and we've discovered that Caol's crimes were farther reaching than either of us had believed. Everything ties back to Avery, Lukas, the King of Thieves, and my niece."

Several of the Enforcers started speaking quietly with one another, but Lieutenant Kesha quieted them. She opened her mouth to say something else, but Reid wasn't through.

"Taiir has always honored his contract with me, Lieutenant, and so I have kept his company despite his intention to kill my niece if she ever causes another Bright Night — and she won't if we can stop it. Taiir is a man who lives by a strict code of honor. He swore to help me not just to protect my niece and my family but to turn assassin to Caol and his entire family if anything ever happened to her. I've known him and worked with him long enough to know Taiir is a man of his word. He did appalling things for his loyalty and in the name of his honor, until he could not stomach them. If I'd been in his shoes, I would have gutted Caol and his sons myself and set that city aflame instead of such subtle decisions. He is more graceful than I in the matter of Five Tower's evil."

"An Assassin's honor," said Taiir, "permits only one kind of betrayal. As long as I intend to honor tha pledge I took, then I have not fallen from tha Keeping and therefore have not fully committed a betrayal to tha city my allegiance was assigned and then sold to."

"Assigned and sold to — you're a contracted *Aseaian*? From across the sea? You are very far from home." Lieutenant Kesha considered their situation again.

Taiir nodded. "I am."

"Unexpected. But do continue."

"Taking that pledge meant I could stand between Caol and tha slaughter he wanted after tha Bright Night," Taiir reiterated. "I do not regret it. I still think tha child inhuman, and tha range commander has now accepted that. Only recently has he begun to realize and understand what I already knew about her."

"And what is that?"

"You have seen tha black glass across tha entire square."

"What is she?" asked the lieutenant directly.

Taiir shrugged. "Cursed. But what manner of creature, we do not know. We intend to break her curse so that she can live a normal life."

"I've heard enough," said another lieutenant. He'd already skimmed the contents of the box and the entirety of the ledger. "I don't like the range commander's brother, but I believe them. One of my cousins worked with the captain in Edantine when they discovered the rot in our own guild and started rooting it out. I've helped where I could, and I've never heard a single foul thing of this man or of his Assassin friend — as unlikely a friendship as they have. They've only done good for Black Temple and the Alliance. I'm sure once Captain Robin recovers, he will also be able to vouch for them, and that will quiet anyone else's suspicions."

"What questions did you have?" asked Lieutenant Kesha. "You said you had questions."

"First, I wanted to know if you'd made the connection between Lukas and the King of Thieves," said Reid.

"What connection?"

"The two are one and the same."

"Then that means this entire city is in his pocket," said Kesha. She was displeased. "Our two guilds will clash over his arrest . . . What is it, Andrew?"

The other lieutenant had a puzzled look on his face. "It also means it was Lukas's daughter whose men attacked Isold. Saura's not happy about it."

Reid felt his heart quicken. "Do you mean the Lady of the Temple has sent men to deal with this? I told her not to risk getting in the way or provoking — "

"Actually, the Holy Matron herself arrived just hours ago with her men, and she demanded your brother's arrest. She expressed her desire to leave you and your friend unharmed and made it clear that she wishes to work with us."

"Arrest?" stammered Reid. "What could John have done?"

"It must be serious, if Saura has come herself," said Taiir.

"She is angry," Kesha told them.

Taiir and Reid looked at one another, both knowing his brother's hot temper. "Would you permit me to leave, then? I would like to speak with my brother, and then to Saura herself. Where are they?"

"What other information do you have for us?"

"That is all I can give to you for now until I piece more together," said Reid. "I wish to speak with my brother."

"He is under supervision currently, but I'll have the sergeant take you to him. You'll both be needed soon anyway. Keep him under control. He and his daughter have caused enough harm."

CHAPTER SEVENTY-ONE

PALE SERPENT

JOHN LOOKED RAGGED, and he was injured, moving about with a mild limp. His hair was a mess, and his eyes were ringed with shadow and were half wild. He looked as if he'd been through worse hell than Reid had. "Get out of my way," he demanded. "I want to see my son!"

Reid rubbed his sore wrists, glad not to be wearing the cuffs anymore but knowing they might have become useful because he might have to restrain his brother. He knew that wild look, and he pitied the Enforcers who weren't familiar with his brother's polar shifts or how to avoid triggering them. John would not just harm them; he would dismember them in that state.

"LET ME SEE MY SON!!!"

Reid darted between his brother and the Enforcer at the doorway. Taiir took John's left arm, and Reid took his right just as his brother snatched the Enforcer's sword from its hilt at the man's side. Reid's brother was too upset to even notice he was being held by people he knew and should recognize. He turned to cursing as Reid and Taiir wrestled him away, and Reid forced the sword from his hand. It clamored to the stone, and the Enforcer behind them moved to pick it up. "Stay back, if you know what's good for you. This homicidal lunatic would slice his own brother right now — "

John's teeth sank into Reid's shoulder, and Reid bit his tongue, cursing. He thrust his brother against the door, which cracked. John staggered. Taiir kicked the sword away.

"John! Look at me — "

John inhaled to scream his curses, began coughing instead, and writhed against them. "My son — " he gasped. "I haven't seen my son . . ." John's voice trailed off as recognition seemed to filter in at last. His voice broke when he spoke again, and he seemed to lose his fight. "Reid . . . ?"

"That's right, it's me. I'm here. They released me."

John swallowed hard against the emotion that set him to quaking vehemently. His knees gave out, and he slid to the floor, heaving. "I thought they would kill you anyway. I thought . . ." He took another deep, shaking breath and clutched at Reid's arm. "Jamie's been injured. Badly. They won't let me see him, Reid. They gave my daughter to them. They gave her to them!" He shook his head, trembling. "It wasn't her fault — they knew that, and they gave her to them anyway . . . *I know Lukas is behind this!!!*"

Reid dried his face on his shoulder, and he and Taiir let their grips loosen.

"Please tell me you saw her, Reid — Please tell me she was okay." Another deep and trembling breath. John shook his head, his eyes rolling toward the sky and reflecting the empty blue before he shut them and again shook his head side to side. "I've not been permitted to leave this damned station, and they have threatened to execute me if Captain Robin doesn't wake. The injury he took has put him in a coma. I have done everything I can. These Enforcers have believed not a word of it, not even after all I have done, or after all that

I have sacrificed in order to help their guild and ours. Everything I have ever done, and I am treated like a criminal and a coward, and they won't let me see my own son. That injury could kill him. His arm was nearly ripped in half."

"John, you have got to calm down. Turning yourself over to a mad rage will only make this worse. And speaking of worse, Saura is here."

John's fingers tightened about Reid's arm, his grip suddenly stinging.

"What happened for you to have pissed her off?"

"Griggori," he gasped, shuddering with anger and fear.

Reid's blood ran cold when he heard the name come from his brother's lips. "Where is Jeana?"

"I left her in Tarvet," John shuddered. "But something may have happened to her."

Reid grimaced at the thought. If Jeana was killed or their son died, John would become but a ghost of a man. He lived for his family just as Reid did. "What does Jamie need?" asked Reid. "I'll make sure he's cared for properly until you can do so yourself. Can you trust me to do that?"

John looked up at Reid, his eyes searching Reid's, and he nodded, desperate. "Please. Until they let me see him. Tell me if he is awake. If they've been kind to him."

"He's the child of a respected field doctor. Despite your temperament, they'll be taking the best care of him as they know to give. They're used to field dressing wounds like his, they're soldiers. He won't die because they don't know what they're doing. But I'll ensure it is to your standards and mine. I'll tell them what you need them to know so they have the instructions you feel they should follow, and I'll report back to you on Jamie's condition for as long as I am capable."

John exhaled his pent-up anger and fear and nodded. "Thank you."

"I know it's a lot, but I need you to tell me everything that's happened, all right? Now that you can think semi-straight. I need to know why you came here, how you even knew where to find me."

The next day, Reid and John were instructed to follow an Enforcer to the same glass-covered building where John had said Lukas had detonated a bomb and injured Captain Robin. The rubble hadn't been cleared, and the sight was as alien as what John had described in Black Temple. Taiir was not with them, as he had expressed his desire to steal back his staff and head to the manor where they'd been held. He intended to locate Nymeria and to figure out a way to free her quietly while Reid and John and the Enforcers met with Saura and her men.

Lieutenant Kesha and Saura stood staring each other down, neither seeming patient as John and Reid made their way to the top of the rubble. "You'll remain here until we decide what is to be done," said an Enforcer quietly to them. Reid acknowledged the order with a brief nod, and he placed his hand on his brother's shoulder to remind him to remain calm and collected — ready to pull him back if need be.

"I finally figured out why Nymeria likes to bite," said Reid under his breath, and he rolled his aching shoulder. John looked sideways at him. "You're the bastard who taught her it was a defense."

"I took that lesson from her, actually," said John. "It was all I could think to do."

"Even knowing you could catch something if that was someone else you'd bitten?" Reid smirked as his brother turned from him angrily. "I'm not letting you do anything stupid, John. You're staying right here with me."

John snorted.

"As you see, they are in our care," said Lieutenant Kesha to the Lady of the Temple.

Saura's copper claws glinted in the sunlight as her fingers tapped a pattern along her arms where she crossed them. "Turn them over to us," she said in reply. "Where is his daughter?"

"She has already been given to Aelynhold in exchange for her uncle."

Saura's expression became cold. "Why? She does not belong to Aelynhold."

Lieutenant Kesha stated the reason clearly. "Because her father is the King of Thieves. Reid Ivan was our priority."

Saura became even more unhappy. "Then turn over Dr. Ivan and his brother."

"We cannot. Dr. Ivan is responsible for his daughter's destruction."

"We will handle his punishment," said Saura. "Let us deal with our own."

"Dr. Ivan is caring for a crucial member of the Alliance at this time."

John shifted uncomfortably. Reid's grip tightened on his brother's shoulder to remind him to attempt neither a regrettable nor an irresponsible act. "I'm not going anywhere with you," said John. "I am finished with your lies, Saura. I gave my life and my service to the Temple, and you housed my wife's would-be killer and protected him. How can I trust you after such a lie?"

"You, who would turn our people against me and commit high treason?" snapped Saura. Her eyes glittered with anger. "You, who would try to murder another in this guild and permit your wife to hold a knife to the throat of the one who commands you? Dr. Ivan, my patience with you has finished. You will be tried accordingly — "

"What trial did you give to Griggori!?" John demanded. He was shaking when he tried to step forward. "None. You hid him and kept his sins so quiet that only those closest to me ever knew what had happened. Now I know why you wanted it quiet. I should have known what a serpent you are. Griggori wanted to sell my daughter, and you wanted her dissected. Deny it. I dare you!"

"Range Commander, keep your brother quiet so that we may negotiate properly," clipped the lieutenant.

But Saura held up her hand. "No. I prefer that he speaks what he thinks. I've spent enough time trying to calm him. I'm curious how far he will dare to step. I am *very* tired of restraining him."

"How many have you sold to Five Tower?" asked John. "What could they possibly give you that you would want?" John demanded.

"Peace," she said without hesitation. "That is what they can give us. I would find and give to them every person infected with the Violet in order to achieve peace. And afterward, I would wipe Five Tower from the face of the earth for their crimes against the innocent with the blessing of our ally, the Alliance."

Reid studied Saura, appreciating for the first time how ruthless she was. He'd used the same tactic in the past, though on a greater scale. He liked her less now, even if he respected her more. She was certainly a serpent, and now he understood her whispered nickname.

"Even though Breaking the Vial would kill our allies and the wearyworn we are sworn to protect," hissed John. "That threat is worse than anything I have ever done or would ever dare to do. All I have ever done is attempt *and fail* to avenge my murdered parents, and try *and fail* to kill a man who raped my pregnant wife and murdered my first child! A man *you* allowed to live. I have the conscience not to let the rest of the world perish for either of those criminals' evils. What could have made *you* so heartless that you would order good men and women to murder the innocent and guilty alike?"

There was a very noticeable ripple of unease among the Enforcers when John's revelation struck them.

John spat upon the ground in her direction. "It is no wonder Ellie refused to call you *Mother*! Why she refused to talk about you. Why she did everything she could to separate herself from you her entire life!"

Saura opened her mouth, but Reid spoke first. "How would Gabriel react to the Breaking of the Vial?" Reid asked. She stumbled over what she would have said, and then her dark eyes burned into him hotly. It was too late to hide it. She'd already revealed her ties to the Dead One.

Lieutenant Kesha caught it, too, although she knew not what it meant. "Lady Saura, we cannot authorize the Breaking of the Vial," said the lieutenant.

Saura's jaw ticked, and those copper claws of hers moved fractionally where they rested on her arm. "I had intended to negotiate properly on that matter, Lieutenant. Where is your captain?"

"Incapacitated for now with other business. Until he is available, or another officer of a rank higher than mine reaches Aelynhold, I am in charge. We are willing to turn your doctor over to you, but there will be conditions."

"She will only try to silence me," snarled John. "To protect whatever other lies she is keeping quiet."

"You will want to return," said Saura. "I cannot promise Griggori will not retaliate because of your assault upon him."

John and Reid were both fuming over the threat. Then she held up her hand, and her men parted. Wylem was forced forward, along with the others who'd intended to help him. Reid's brother corded with tension, and then Griggori stepped into view alongside Jeana. She was gagged, and Griggori held a knife to her throat. Her own knife, the one she'd inherited from her family. The one she'd stabbed him with years ago. The one Griggori had cut her open with before John had tried to kill him.

Wylem struggled against his bonds.

"What is the meaning of this display?" asked Lieutenant Kesha.

"These are the men and women he's inspired to become traitors," said Saura coldly, and she raised her hand as Wylem struggled against his bonds. Several of her guards unsheathed their swords.

Reid's hand slipped from his brother's arm when the swords swung as one.

Their friends' heads lay separate from their bodies, and Jeana wept, screaming against her gag. Her own knife dug deeper against her throat where Griggori held it firmly. "Shhh," Griggori said against her ear, and he rested his head against hers, as though thrilling in her grief. He had that putrid look upon his face again, the same one he'd had years ago when Reid had first met him. "Just imagine what this next one would feel like," he said against her, intoxicated by the power he had over her.

Only Wylem remained alive, and his eyes were wide with rage and grief. Saura herself strode before him, and when Wylem looked up at her, defiance blazing in his eyes, her copper claws lashed out, and Wylem's throat was torn open. She slung the blood from her claws as Wylem bowed over, trembling as though in agony as his throat spread a very wet, very large red stain over his clothes and across the ground. The sound of him trying to take a breath was agonizing, and her guards shoved him forward. The rope upon his wrists snapped, and he clutched at his throat, blood seeping from his lips as he sputtered.

A long moment later, Wylem lost consciousness. And after that, he didn't seem to be breathing, and his face lay in the blood pooling from his mouth and throat.

John exhaled as he stepped forward, but he stopped, frozen, afraid that another step would cause his wife's demise next. "*What have you done . . . ?*"

The distress in John's voice echoed what Reid felt. Wylem had been one of Saura's most devout, admiring students. He'd never been a doctor, but he'd given his life and his passion to

Saura and the guild, such that he'd become a highly respected member of her High Council. One of the Thirteen. Yet she'd cut his throat as though he'd never meant anything to her at all. As though all of them were refuse. Worthless, expendable tools.

A cold chill ran down Reid's spine when Saura looked at him again, as if silently promising the same to him.

"Do not give my brother to her," Reid managed. Lieutenant Kesha sighed, knowing how complicated things had just gotten with Saura's brutal display.

"Dr. Ivan," said Saura. "Don't ask me to execute your wife as well. That is all I will offer in the way of encouragement for you to urge these Enforcers to return you. Do not worry about avenging your parents' deaths, either. I intend to deal with those who have dared to attack us directly."

"What about my niece?" said Reid. "What do you really intend to do with her?"

"I don't care what happens to her. Jonathan will receive a trial, however. As I have already stated."

His brother still hadn't moved, and he'd said nothing else. Reid knew John was aware that Griggori would kill Jeana just to spite him if he stepped forward. Saura had little control over the vile man.

"What about the doctor's brother?" asked Lieutenant Kesha. "What is your intent for him?"

"Nothing, since he has committed no crimes. I only want to speak with him directly."

"You can speak to me directly where I am," said Reid. She frowned. "You know I stand with my brother. I trust him before I trust you. I can sever my ties with Black Temple without fear of punishment; I've sworn no oath to you."

"I'd thought you were more intelligent than your brother," she said.

"Oh, I am," Reid said. "But you've lost my trust with this display, and if you cannot say what you wish to say before these Enforcers, then I've nothing more to discuss with you. You knew what you would look like when you made this move, so accept the consequences for it. And Saura. If any further harm comes to my sister-in-law, you will have more than just me turning against you. I will ensure you are removed from power and locked up for the rest of your life. Unlike my brother, I have the connections to make that happen. I might tell your master what you've been up to and let those consequences find you instead."

She bristled but denied it in the same moment. "I am the Lady of the Temple. I have no master but for the duty I must uphold."

"That's all you will say?" he asked. "Fine. My brother and I will focus on efforts to rescue his daughter. If you are unwilling to help us, or to help the Enforcers, we're finished here."

"Reid," said John quietly. Reid looked at his brother, and he started to shake his head when he saw the look on John's face.

"No. You can't — "

"I cannot leave Griggori alone with my wife. Ensure my son is safe. You promised me that you would."

"She may just execute you the first chance she gets."

"I risked that the first time I turned a blade to Griggori. I'll not have him kill my wife, or touch her again."

"What about your daughter?" demanded Reid.

"I'm not giving up on her," said John. But his voice was too quiet. John turned to the lieutenant. "Turn me over. If Saura doesn't execute me, then she may have other motives and may not be as irrational as she currently seems. If she does, kill the bitch the first chance you get. Otherwise, you won't survive her."

Lieutenant Kesha ruminated. "Will the captain die if you cannot care for him any longer?"

"The trauma was to his head. Continue the treatments I have already been giving. If he does not wake up in a few days, he won't ever do so. Either way, I'm finished. I want you to end this, Lieutenant. Arrest Lukas and send him to the Reformation. Rescue Avery, finish cutting the corruption from your guild, and take down the corrupt lord in Five Tower. And if my wife and I are dead by the time you find my daughter, give her to my brother. Don't hurt her. What happened isn't her fault."

Saura gleamed with triumph when the lieutenant reluctantly gave John the small mercy he asked for — not that it was much of a mercy. Griggori grew unhappy as John began to descend the rubble toward them, and a snarl etched itself across the vile doctor's face. He removed the knife from Jeana's throat and shoved her forward, where she fell on her side sobbing.

"Stay your hand, Griggori," said Saura. "The blood shed by us will cease until a decision is made. They're not your toys to torture as you have." She nodded to the lieutenant. "You've made a wise decision, thank you."

"Do not think for a moment that I trust you, Pale Serpent," said the lieutenant.

Saura's smile was serpentine. "I have sent a messenger to the King of Thieves," she said as John was taken by her guards and bound before he could even reach his wife. Reid's teeth creaked with the anger he felt as he ground them together, and he watched as his brother and his sister-in-law were taken out of sight. "He has agreed to meet with us," continued Saura. "His demand was for reparation for crimes against a city whose destruction the range commander has had nothing to do with. I have agreed to pay him fully."

Griggori laughed wickedly as he sheathed Jeana's knife.

"We'll be present for those negotiations," said the lieutenant.

"Do as you wish. I don't care in the slightest."

CHAPTER SEVENTY-TWO

$\mathcal{D}$ISASTER

LUKAS STOOD AMONG THE monks again, disguised. He recognized Reid, although Reid's brother was not present. He recognized Saura, though she had aged much since the last time he'd seen her just over two decades before. Captain Robin was still missing from the Enforcers, although there was no word whether the captain was dead or alive. He'd told Morris not to accept Saura's offer, that they should leave the city now that they had the girl. But Morris had been correct. They had nowhere else to go at the moment, not with the tunnels in the state they were in. The other passages were out of their reach currently as well, and he was still sure the sewers would mean his death even if he had the girl with him.

Morris believed they could find some way to outmaneuver the Lady of Black Temple and the Enforcers without giving Avery to them. Without getting themselves arrested.

But Lukas's gut feeling was that it was all wrong. He was anxious. Angry. Nervous. It wasn't like himself to be unable to focus on developing a clear strategy. He knew to trust his instinct and get out *now*, but he had little opportunity to escape with such a dangerous child in tow. She would use that black power of hers and ignite the Violet in him if she got close enough to touch him. She would call the dark creatures to devour him.

He surveyed the assembly, noting the number of Enforcers had increased. They'd subdued the rest of the wearyworn who'd rioted and regrouped. They were far too effective. And now their ally stood at the front of the company she'd brought with her.

Morris sat upon his throne, his violet eyes blazing, glowing eerily in the dark, and the color slithered under his skin. It made the Enforcers uneasy. It even rattled the Lady of the Temple when he looked upon her, his eyes like a haunting abyss of flaming glass. Lukas knew what it really meant. His friend was battling the Violet with all his will, and he was losing. He sat like a statue, cold and uninterested in what was before him, and annoyed.

He looked like an angry king.

"What may I call you aside from your title?" began Saura. "I am Saura Idathet, Lady of the Black Temple, Holy Matron of the Glass Chain."

"Call me whatever you wish," hissed Morris between his teeth. "I have little desire to be here, and little faith that you have anything that might repay the damage that has been done to my city or my family. I have already told the Enforcers that I will soon install the next regent so that I may leave with my daughter. I am awaiting my successor's return."

Lukas saw the angry promise upon Reid's countenance. Reid did not like it at all that Morris had claimed she was his daughter.

"Griggori," Saura said quietly, as though she'd sensed Reid's quiet hostility.

Lukas saw a man he didn't know remove a familiar dagger from his hip to threaten the range commander to remain silent . . . He'd seen the blade somewhere other before, but he shook it from his mind as he searched for other signs of danger or deceit they might encounter during this farce.

"Well, Thief," Saura continued. "I would like to know where you really are. This charade has gone on long enough."

Lukas felt his heart quicken. Morris did not blink, did not react. He just continued to gaze down upon her. "My stance has been made known already. You may search this city along with the Enforcers if you wish. Avery is not here. He never was."

"My apologies," said Saura. "I think I was unclear." She waved to her guards, who brought forward several heavy bags. "I did agree to and promise reparation. I may have been out of order."

The guards lowered the bags to the stone. The contents did not clink like metal or glass. Not even like the sound of golden liberties. What sort of payment was it? Lukas was unsure he wanted to know. Nervousness fluttered in his gut, but he contained it. There were over a hundred monks in the Great Room, and barely forty of his combined enemy in the small space. No guns or bows had been permitted, although both sides carried their swords and knives for insurance and kept their distance in the giant, echoing chamber.

But Saura smiled. Hers was a cold and unfeeling smile. An intelligent, serpentine, provocative one. "Your payment. The first half."

Then he smelled it. Death.

The guards opened the sacks, grabbed them by their ends, and turned them over. Severed heads rolled to the ground in various stages of rot. Wolfmen's heads, other men's heads, glass chains . . . There were over a hundred of them.

Reid grimaced at the stench, and the man named Griggori began to laugh under his breath.

Morris did not seem remotely interested. "Thank you," he said. Saura blinked. "That trouble has ended at last. You've piqued my interest. What other half could you have that would conclude such a bountiful gift?" He stood, and the monks moved aside for him. They knelt, Lukas included.

"You don't claim them?" asked Saura. Her temper remained in check, but she was still angered by his lack of reaction.

"I claim them," he said, however. "My prior regents have made trouble in my absence. They've mimicked my tricks and twisted them in the name of an enemy I did not want in my city. I've had them killed for it. The glass we wear does not represent the symbol they've tried to make of it." Morris knelt and picked up one of the heads, which belonged to one of the wolfmen. "You have my blessing to kill more of these unwanted beasts. Those in this hall today are the only men I trust, as they are the only men whose interests are the same as mine. Five Tower's corruption has not just filtered into the Alliance and upended cities and harmed the wearyworn, it has robbed my citizens of peace and of the honesty and kindness they once wore proudly. Even before my gates were destroyed, my city was suffering."

"*Honesty*, says the King of Thieves," clipped Saura.

"I am an honest thief and an honest king of them," replied Morris. He looked at her when Griggori sniggered again. The man dropped the wolfman's head.

"He is the King of Liars," said Griggori, and before Morris could say another word, the knife in Griggori's hand had sailed through the air and struck Morris in the throat.

Lukas flinched, overcome as his friend sputtered and laughed despite the tremendous pain such a wound would have caused. Morris seemed almost relieved by it. As if that end was better than the Violet coursing through him. Morris's shaking hand reached for the knife but did not touch it as he knelt slowly. Blood spilled from his lips as he bowed over, struggling for breath as the red pool below him grew in size. Griggori approached as the frozen monks did nothing, and he knelt by Morris, grabbed him by the hair, and leaned forward to meet the man's eyes with his own humored gaze. "King of Liars — that's what the King of Thieves really is. You're just a stand-in. A lousy one. A puppet. A fool who knew he was going to die. Why have you taken his place? You think he's your best friend? Is that it?" Morris only smiled.

The smile did not leave his lips when Griggori ripped loose the blade and then plunged it up and under Morris's ribs. He pulled it back out and then let him go.

The Enforcers were just as quiet as the monks. The shock was tangible. The audacity to turn a civil meeting into a bloodied scene . . .

Saura was much more dangerous than Lukas had ever thought. Far bolder than the intel his men had gleaned years before. Far less patient.

"I ask again," said Saura. "Where are you?" She turned her gaze to the rest of the shaded room about them. "I haven't finished repaying the damage. I want to speak to you in person, King of Thieves. Not to any of your proxies so that you may keep your face hidden from us."

Lukas had warned her before never to look for Avery. What could she possibly gain by deciding to seek the bastard after all this time?

She nodded to her guards as Griggori turned his back upon Morris's body. Lukas struggled not to react. He was trapped, he realized. His men knew it, he could tell, because they never moved, not even an inch. Neither did he. He knew the bloodshed that would soon follow. They would do whatever they could to protect him, but it wouldn't be enough if the manor was surrounded — and it likely was. He'd summoned the rest of his men, but they could not win a direct battle.

A captive was brought forward by Saura's men. He could not tell who it was for the cloak and the sackcloth over the captive's head. "I was told you were the rightful Lord of Aelynhold. Why don't you come out and speak with me as a proper lord would?" said Saura. "No need to play coy."

Another monk stepped forward, and Lukas tried to calm himself. He told himself to trust the man.

Saura motioned for her guards to remove the cloth before the man even had time to speak. "I would recommend not sending another puppet. I have your daughter."

And they did. They'd sliced her face, cut out an eye. Only one violet eye flared brightly.

"She's told us enough," Griggori grinned. He licked his lips. "Took a long while to get past the screaming." And then Griggori held his blade, still wet with Morris's blood, beneath Carriah's chin. "If that puppet there says a single word, or another one tries to pretend to be you, I'll just kill her."

Saura's cold smile held firm. They waited patiently.

"Tick tock," said Griggori. He sliced Carriah's cheek deeply. She bit her tongue to quiet herself, but the small whimper that escaped set Lukas's blood on fire. He'd already lost his wife and his friend to his cause. Was he strong enough to lose his daughter, too?

"Don't do it, Father," said Carriah. "Please — "

Griggori struck her, and the men holding her kept her from hitting the floor when her head snapped sideways.

He'd sacrificed years of his life for his family's sake . . . But he had a duty to fulfil, to call Caol from his fortress. But his *daughter*.

"Don't!" Carriah said, and she spat at Griggori. A strange look came over him, and his disgusting smile grew wider.

"I think I've found my new pet," he said, and he lifted a strand of her hair and brought it close to breathe in. "More of a fight in you than you pretended, woman. Seems you inherited a little of your father's gift for deception."

"Cut out my other eye if you like," she purred. "You wouldn't survive a woman like me either way."

"I know who you are," said Griggori to the room about them. A tremor went through Lukas. Surely, he didn't know what Lukas looked like. "Caol's most cunning lapdog," said

Griggori. The knife drew a whimper from Carriah. "I know your face, King of Thieves. I've seen you in Five Tower. Pale hair and black eyes, darker than the night itself. You once lied to Eiran's father when you told him you were merely a merchant from Tallil. It's Eiran's favorite lie. He's boasted how you'd used to be a proud, noble man. One of Caol's finest weapon's dealers, and the best thief he'd ever met. You were ruthless in your day. He boasted his father had broken the rightful *Lord of Aelynhold* to do his bidding. Now, you're more terrified of the night than Caol ever was. Not to worry, we've got a nice, dark cell waiting for you. Far from the sun as can be."

Lukas held up his hand when another was about to step forward. His fingers curled into a tight fist as he reached for his hood, and his friends drew their blades in response, ready to fight for him. "Not yet," he told them. Some of his hair came loose of its knot and fell forward as he moved into the light. "They will kill my daughter."

He looked at Reid, who glared back — Reid had known already, it seemed. He looked at Saura, whose smile tilted venomously. She'd won. She'd known she would. "Release my daughter. She's only done my bidding."

"I don't think I am willing to do that," said Saura. "Whether it was your bidding or not, this woman and her men attacked our sacred capital. I will give her back only if you turn yourself over. You will command the release of your prisoners by the time we are through with you."

They hadn't learned the truth, it seemed. He laughed quietly to himself, though his heart continued racing, and he looked at the Enforcers, one by one. He didn't recognize any of them from his previous years as an Enforcer. It didn't seem any of them recognized him, either. He swallowed against his dread. "I am willing to give up no one," he said. "You would have to take me by force even to have me. And you will have no success getting to my prisoners."

"You admit it. You do have Avery," said the female lieutenant.

"I do not have him." He looked at Saura, then. "Carriah is the daughter of a lord, I'll remind you. If you murder her, I will demand justice, and I will summon my allies. We will break from the treaty with Black Temple and the Enforcers' Alliance. You will find yourself at war with half the continent."

"Your successor led a raid against Black Temple, Lord Maverick," said Saura.

"You still do not have the right to end her life," said Lukas. "That right belongs to the Enforcers, and only after a trial. She would be imprisoned for a term at the Reformation before then, as the heir to Aelynhold. You are bound to those rules as much as I am, and as much as they are."

"Says a lord who also murdered Black Temple emissaries."

"Black Temple still has no right but to make a formal complaint and fill out some paperwork," Lukas sneered. "Any highborn you arrest under that cause is required to be turned over to the Enforcers for a proper investigation. Black Temple does not have the authority to do as it pleases to the ruling families of other cities and holds."

"Unfortunately, he is right," said Reid. "Only the Enforcers have the right to arrest him, Saura."

Saura's nostrils flared. "Stand down, Mr. Ivan. Those negotiations have yet to be discussed. Our current focus is in dealing with this criminal."

Weakness, Lukas saw. The only card he could play was against that, to stall for time until the rest of his men arrived.

"Where are you holding — "

He interrupted and spoke to Reid instead. "Your niece is no longer in the city, Range Commander. She is being taken to my client now." Reid's fist clenched violently, but the man controlled his temper.

"Who is your client?" asked Reid.

"Caol will be unhappy to realize one of his assassins helped to smuggle her out of the city," Lukas said cryptically. He knew it would provoke the man's ire.

"I should have let my brother murder you when he had the chance."

Griggori turned, amused. "What *is* it about this kid that's got everyone wound so tight?"

"Where is Avery Ramont?" demanded Lieutenant Andrew.

"He is not here," Lukas said.

"*Was* he here?"

Lukas did not deny it and remained neutral in his partial lies. "You will not find a trace of him here."

Griggori's grip closed on his knife, and he slashed Carriah. Her eyes went wide.

"NO!" cried Lukas as he dove toward his daughter. She clutched at her throat, and his men moved as one and kept him from descending the stairs.

"The only reason you're here still is that your client has not yet made himself available," said Griggori. "Why are you so desperate to get her to him?"

"That is none of your business!" Lukas heard himself say. He was staring at the blood streaming between his daughter's fingers where she clutched at her throat. The wound was shallow. A warning. But he was losing control of himself. "Reid, you understand what a man would do to save his family, do you not?" Why was he trying to reach that man, of all people?

"You murdered my parents and took my niece. You injured my nephew and threatened to kill me just to get Nymeria," said Reid. "Why would I care what happens to you or to your family? Why would you, in your rational mind, think I would *ever* help you?"

"I meant only . . . I . . ." He shook his head, distraught, and he looked at his daughter again. "I'm sorry, Carriah."

"Don't give them anything," she hissed. "The mission comes first. Keep your honor, or you never deserved to be my father!" She turned and bit the fingers upon her shoulder, wrenched free, and snatched Griggori's knife.

Lukas saw her hit the ground, the knife still in her fingers as Griggori tried to retrieve it . . . And then she wasn't moving anymore. She wasn't even breathing. The knife slipped to the stone, but he couldn't hear it hit the floor.

Lukas gritted his teeth as fighting erupted between his hooded friends and the others who'd come for Avery and himself. "Sir, you need to go," one of his subordinates said, and they pushed at him. "She's dead. There is no need to stay except to lose everything we've fought for. Honor Avery's wishes, remember? No man's family shall matter if Caol or his sons succeeded in their endeavors. We've all set family aside, and our sworn duty, in order to assist and protect what you know. You are too important! Go!"

Lukas stumbled, and then he swore he would avenge his daughter. "I want Griggori alive," he snarled. "When this is over, Saura will be strung up beside him. She swore that she would look the other way when Avery disappeared, that she would never look for him — she swore, the same as the rest of us."

"We need you safe first, sir."

"They've blocked every entrance and passage!"

"We've cleared one tunnel. We'll collapse it after you."

"Which one?" he demanded. "And what about the girl? This doesn't work without her."

"Already taken care of."

CHAPTER SEVENTY-THREE

Approaching Doom

TAERYN'S BLISTERED LIPS CRACKED when he opened his mouth again. The urge to give in to the fire burning inside his body threatened to overwhelm him. If he gave in, he would turn to ash, and the dark creatures would torture him for eternity. He must deliver Lukas . . .

He could not feel the ruined flesh upon him, or smell anything but the smoke and the blood that was beyond the Violet, in the red and the black abyss that was only a few short breaths away. He could feel the heat of the desolate place.

They wouldn't stop hissing. The screaming wouldn't stop.

The city was gray to him. Except where he saw the glass, which still coursed with the beautiful color of her soul.

He took another breath and another step as the city whorled about him.

Curled upon a filthy floor, shivering . . . Cannot remember where she is . . .

He couldn't think straight, couldn't focus. The Violet coursed through her, and so did the black, and she was screaming, and no one could hear it but him. Why could no one hear it . . . ?

Lukas, he tried to remember. The breath he exhaled wheezed sickly. He was going to kill him for what he'd done. This would end when Lukas was dead. Lukas had done this to him.

Taeryn felt the death of another who was cursed with the Violet, like himself. His body trembled in response, and he heard the low, maniacal sound that left him in response, rolling, like a wolf's warning. He kept moving toward the pale-haired man, following the sense of the shadow within him. But it had become difficult to sense it, or even see it, in this city. The glass about him. The child whose great suffering leached out into the glass and into him, and even into the other cursed — it was too much.

He could taste the ash upon his tongue. The blood.

The black flames licked at the edges of his vision.

Lukas.

He staggered toward the broken temple as that presence came closer. A person, a thing, tried to stop him, to speak — it was then dead, and he felt its blood dripping from his fingertips. He felt vaguely the bullets that sank into his flesh, and he kept moving forward, feeling none of it, fueled and kept alive by the agonizing river of the curse within him. He felt the blood seeping from his lips, and he killed another who dared to stop him. His eyes were riveted on the temple, where Lukas had fled. The shadow was there, and it was filled with fear, and it was weak. And it was desperate.

Taeryn's lungs expelled another gurgled sound that mixed humor and hunger and rage. "I'll kill him," he said again. "They shall have him before they take me . . ."

He killed the monks who tried to get at him, and Agarath fought alongside him, with Thretirak.

"Lukas!" shouted the monk Taeryn's claws sought next to kill. He crushed the man's wrist with his fingers, and the man screamed, and then Taeryn brought his teeth to the man's throat and tore it out.

Lukas turned in time to see it, and Taeryn reveled in the man's torment and bared his teeth in a deathly promise. "You cannot run," said Taeryn. "I said I would deliver you to the *Shadei Ra*."

Lukas saw Agarath and Thretirak behind him, and his movements began to jerk as he clawed at the entrance of the tunnel and forced his way through. "Close it behind me!" commanded the pale-haired, fearful man. "Close it behind me! Do not let them live!"

But they were too slow, and they were much too weak, and their blades could not kill him, not while the Violet coursed through him and burned him hotter than his approaching end. He looked down upon the startled monks who'd thought they'd dealt him his death, and he laughed at them. And he killed them, too.

"Our quarry," said Agarath triumphantly. "It has hunted well," the wolfman praised. "It has hunted better than any of Eiran's hunters. No wonder the Strange Ones appraised it so."

"I will deliver him unto the shadowed lands of the infernal end," rasped Taeryn, and the tunnel seemed to tilt. But then he was climbing through, after the pale-haired man whose sins called out for retribution like a shadowy flag. "We will devour him, and his soul will lose what hidden light it has not revealed to us . . ."

The wolfmen slowed, each looking at another, and then back at him. "Has it the yearning for our sacred right?" one asked. "It is not one of us. It has not the right to devour our prey."

Taeryn moved forward, hardly hearing them. "He is a dead light."

The tunnel opened ahead, and Taeryn heard his prey's bark of pain. As he emerged behind the wolfmen, he saw Lukas fighting off another man. He'd been stabbed in the gut but evaded another prick of the blade, and he held the wound as he continued to try to flee.

"GRIGGORI!" shouted another, a one-eyed Greenman who careened into the man who'd stabbed Taeryn's prey. Taeryn kept moving forward as those two fought to kill each other. The Greenman was the lesser of the men and fell back, gravely injured.

Meanwhile, the wolfmen engaged with another enemy, and Taeryn stumbled, pulled between the death the creatures demanded and the waves of confining agony and terror spilling into him from the river of Violet. From the child. His teeth drew blood from his own tongue as the taste of ash choked him, as confusion drifted in, briefly, before it was washed away by the corruption of the creatures' wrathful will again. The faint echo of her remained inside him, almost unrecognizable. *Save her* . . .

But the creatures were too powerful.

"*Kuuuuuuuveeeeeeeeeaaaaaaaaaaaahtttttttt* . . ." hissed the tall thing emerging from the darkness.

Taeryn shuddered, and he snarled. "He is *mine*," he hissed. "Get rid of them all, and I will sacrifice him."

The moment the one named Griggori killed Thretirak, the wraithlike creature's dark tendrils flared, and the cave began to rumble. The creature's screech startled all the men before Taeryn, and Lukas's back hit the wall, his mouth open to scream and his eyes as wide with fear as the others' eyes were, and the thing reached out for Griggori. Taeryn began to laugh as the creature wrapped around the man Griggori threw at it. The shadow thing's victim screamed and writhed as it drifted upward with him, and Taeryn locked eyes with Lukas.

Lukas and all the men here were ashen, and heaving, and clutching at whatever they could to get up, to flee the being's black hunger.

"What the *hell* is that thing?!" screeched Griggori, and then he shrank from his brother's frozen hand as the shadei ra dropped its writhing victim.

Taeryn licked his lips, craving the life they'd taken from the empty corpse as the body continued to scream. He heard the snapping of a chain, and the corpse arched, rigid, inhaling a backward shriek of agony.

Again, Taeryn's eyes locked with Lukas's, and Lukas saw his hungry, angry snarl. "Come here, coward," he said. "Face my wrath, and be given to them also, and we will devour you together."

The others looked at Taeryn, seeming to realize what kind of threat he was, and then all were scrambling away from him. Agarath tried to run, but the creature took him next because he was in Taeryn's way.

Lukas vanished into the dark hallway beyond, but Taeryn could still see his shadow. "You cannot run from us," he hissed. "We can see your shadow. We sense her within you. She is ours. Give her stain back to us."

"The dark ghosts from our forests," heaved the one-eyed Greenman as he shrank where he'd fallen, clutching at his own belly where Griggori's blade had bitten.

Griggori would be a fine meal for them, for the many murders staining his soul.

Taeryn forgot the fallen Greenman, the hunt overwhelming him again as the screams continued in his head.

CHAPTER SEVENTY-FOUR

*I*DENTITY

REID'S ENTIRE BODY ACHED from the battle they'd faced. When Taiir had appeared with a pair of horses, he'd abandoned the fight. His friend had a look upon his face that meant bad news. "You couldn't find her?" Reid asked, and he wiped the blood and sweat and dirt from his face.

Taiir shook his head. "They have moved her." He dropped the reins of the other horse for Reid as his own wheeled about nervously. "I bring other news also."

Reid looked at him. "What is it?"

"Captain Robin has awakened. He has not managed to speak more than a word yet. He is barely lucid. I did understand your name when he spoke it, however, so I came immediately for you."

"Does anyone else know yet that he's awake?"

"Everyone is fighting, from tha manor to tha gate. Tha Enforcers have left tha wearyworn to Aelynhold's care in order to reinforce their numbers here, and several have taken to rioting again. Now some of tha citizens have taken to tha streets to fight back. Tha situation has elevated, Commander."

Reid took the reins of the second horse and pulled himself into the saddle. "My nephew is still in this city, and very close to the captain. Are they fighting even there?"

"Yes. But do not worry about your nephew, for one of tha women living there took him to Saura's camp to get him to his parents. We should defend Captain Robin; there were only three men at his door when I left."

They rode hard for the square on the borrowed horses.

Only one guard stood at the door when Reid and Taiir dismounted and hurried toward it. "Halt — "

"Get out of the way. He's asked for me," Reid said, and he dodged the man's shaking weapon easily. The soldier paused when Reid knelt by the captain and took his raised hand in his own. "You're alive, you bastard," Reid said as the captain gripped his hand in a quiet, weak greeting. "I'm glad. But we need to get you out of here. The rioting has started again." He looked over his shoulder to the soldier. "Get as many of your friends as you can, and let them know Captain Robin is awake. We need more men to help guard him until he is out of danger here. We can't let him get killed in a riot; Lukas has already damned-near accomplished that end."

"Where is tha thief?" asked Taiir.

"Soured negotiations. They drew him out. Now everyone knows he's the Lord of Aelynhold."

"Reid . . ." groaned the captain. Reid steadied him, but the captain held firmly, his voice quiet but his gaze clear. "Reid, we were wrong, all of us."

Reid looked outside again as a bottle exploded and fire swept across the doorway. "Shut the door!" he commanded. The heavy door slammed against its frame, and Taiir barred it with the table and chairs he overturned. Taiir gripped his staff, ready for the door to be broken in by the mob they could hear just up the street.

"What do you mean, we were all wrong?" Reid steadied the captain, who shuddered, pale as a sheet.

"The man who blew up the square, I saw his face. I know him."

"That's very possible. He was an Enforcer," Reid nodded. "We've already learned that. He is the Lord of Aelynhold, *Lukas Holden Maverick.* The son of the late Edric Normane. And he is the King of Thieves — "

"He is Avery Ramont."

Reid's mouth moved. Nothing came out. The sword he held slipped from his hands when his sweaty fingers spasmed about the hilt, and he shook his head as though he could deny Captain Robin's words.

"He is Avery Ramont," Captain Robin repeated. "The name he gave you was a lie. I knew him. I knew his face. He hasn't aged a day since I last saw him fifteen to sixteen years ago — I don't understand how that is even possible, but I am telling you that young man is *Avery Ramont*, and he tried to kill me because I recognized him. He detonated that bomb to try and silence me." The captain let go of Reid's hand and grasped at his missing arm as he swayed.

Reid brought his hands up to clasp over his mouth as he rocked back onto his heels, his entire body shaking. "But he . . . Why would . . . Why would the . . . ?" He couldn't wrap his mind around Avery's motives, his lies, his crimes.

"The only personal thing I ever knew about him was that he once had a brother named Lukas," Captain Robin said. "That brother was dead. He'd drowned as a child, in or near Aelynhold. I don't know why Avery's done this," said the captain. "But everyone needs to be turned to the chase of this *Lukas Maverick* so that we can arrest him."

"But Avery was the *pinnacle* of justice," whispered Reid. "No one was more dedicated to peace and prosperity and justice. And yet the monks . . . Five Tower . . ." He realized something. "My god — Caol hadn't just . . . He was investigating Caol under that name. Caol didn't just kidnap a weapons dealer pretending to be a man named Lukas. He kidnapped and tortured and made a madman of the Alliance's *High Commander*." He wiped his brow, considering what kind of power Caol might actually have, to have achieved such a thing. That it wasn't just some crazed, murderous thief who had taken Reid's niece. It was the missing leader of the Enforcers' Alliance who had taken Nymeria. "*For what purpose* would the High Commander have betrayed everyone?" he cried. And not one other person had recognized him. "The Enforcers who've disguised themselves as part of the *Merciful* — that's why they parted from the Alliance," said Reid. "They followed him because they were loyal to him."

Captain Robin nodded. "Exactly. It explains everything except *why* all of this has transpired."

"I did not see this coming," said Taiir. "There is no mistake in your mind, Captain?"

Robin shook his head slowly. "You told me the negotiations soured. What happened? What else has occurred while I was incapacitated? How much time has passed?"

"You've been unconscious for about a week. We'll have to fill you in as we get you out of here."

"I'm not going anywhere except to call together another, more desperate search. I want the High Commander's identity to remain confidential until we get to the bottom of it all so that he is not killed for being who he truly is. I want everyone to focus their search for *Lukas Maverick*. Only the three of us, as well as my own closest and most trusted men, are to take him into custody or to be allowed direct contact with him. I do not want anyone else to recognize him until well after this is over and the nature of this investigation is declassified. Do you have any idea where he's gone?"

"I know exactly where he is heading," said Reid. "It will take him days to exit the city. If we rally quickly, we'll take him."

"*Alive*," hissed the captain. "He *cannot* die! It is of the utmost importance that he is apprehended in perfect health!"

Reid gathered himself, and he picked up his sword and stood. The captain moved slowly, reaching for his things. "Have they passed?" asked Reid of Taiir.

Taiir didn't back away from the small crack in the door. "There are only a few remaining on our street, and our Enforcer friends are about to put them aside. They are heading this way. We will be clear."

"I want to be there to look him in the eye when we take him down," Captain Robin said. "He has more to answer to than that corrupt Lord of Five Tower."

CHAPTER SEVENTY-FIVE

Water

AVERY GRIPPED AT HIS SIDE, heaving. Pain shot through him with every step. He knew he was done, but he couldn't stop. The cursed hunter following him wouldn't stop, either. They had that in common. The others he could outmaneuver, even injured. Not that hunter, not if he gave in to his wound.

He was lightheaded, and his grief threatened to rob him of what remained of his breath. But he kept moving. They didn't have the child. He did. They also didn't have Avery Ramont, and they wouldn't get him, either. He wouldn't tell them where he was or what had happened until this was over. And he wasn't going to let himself get murdered by his pursuers before he'd lured Caol with the message he'd sent. He might even be arrested as Lukas, but Caol would still come out of his fortress for the girl. Because the Leviathans would want her.

His groan echoed in the passageway, and he gripped at his side tighter, and his shoulder scraped the wall. He stumbled away from it when he thought he heard footsteps behind him.

Light. He saw light drifting into the treacherous shaft ahead. Dust, knocked loose by explosions in his city, drifted through the light in veils. He heard the hunter's deranged scream, heard the clinking of metal hitting stone. Like a blade breaking and then hitting the ground and skittering away.

"Save her . . ." he heard echoed from the passage far behind him. "I need to save her, not kill him . . . Please . . . stop the screams . . . in my head . . . I don't want to hear the Fallen's agony anymore . . . I don't want to help you anymore . . ." And then the snarling began again, as did the heavy breathing. The bastard's mind was almost completely gone. Worse than some of the others Avery had seen kill themselves. His desire for vengeance, like Avery's, seemed to be the only thing keeping him from ending what the Violet was doing to him. "Not to worry. She cannot keep the Violet from her thief anymore. He'll slow . . ."

Avery gasped when he felt that familiar pull within himself, and his knees gave. The Violet raced through his flesh. For a moment, he felt the little girl's screams rattling through him, and fear rose to choke him. He clawed at his side where he'd been stabbed. *"Gah . . ."* he gasped.

Taeryn screamed.

Avery clawed at the floor, desperate to continue seeing what was really in front of him. Every fiber of his being cried out, wanting him to retreat, to retrace his steps, to return so that she could give to him the fiery shadows that rolled through her being.

Morris had been right . . . They were supposed to protect her. He could feel it. Everything inside him screamed it. Demanded it. He couldn't block it out anymore.

Avery's fingers clawed deeper, and he gasped. The light burned brighter, bathing everything in his vision in pale light.

Snow . . .

He blinked hard against it, weeping. "Not again," he pleaded. "Take it back, Nymeria," he pleaded. "Stop giving away these memories, I don't want them! They kill everyone they touch!" He didn't know why he spoke. She was not there to hear him. He knew it, but it did not stop him. He'd had her taken as far from him as possible so this mind-destroying madness wouldn't return — yet it had anyway. It was supposed to be gone — he'd thought it was gone!

Then he realized what he'd heard the madman behind him say, and his heart fluttered with grief. He remembered her words to him when she'd told him she'd taken it from him. How long had she struggled to keep him free of it . . . ? How deeply had it marked her to do so?

The snow . . . His eyes followed the flakes . . .

The mountains.

Avery blinked against it, struggling for breath. Dust. Dust, not snow.

And then she was no longer pulling at the cord that connected him to her. He gasped, drawing in breath like a man who'd nearly suffocated. He clawed his way to his feet and staggered onward, heaving. He shouldn't have locked her in a cell. He should have realized it would have provoked her to remember . . .

And then he was outside, where the humid heat made his breath even thicker and more difficult. He staggered between the tall trees. Bark scraped his shoulder. Branches scraped his arms and his face. Roots tangled about his feet.

He dared to look over his shoulder, and he saw the snarling hunter, black leaking from his lips, his flesh sickly and weeping where he'd been burned. The hunter stumbled, his eyes glazed.

Avery kept going.

Where were his men . . . ? There were none here. Several should have been waiting.

Everything was spinning now. He looked down, and his hand shook when he realized how much blood he'd lost. His vision blurred.

"I'm not finished," he grated, determined. "I'm not . . ."

He felt a moment of relief when he saw his men ahead, and he moved toward them.

And then there was Reid Ivan, pointing a gun at him. Enforcers. He stared at them, and when he heard Taeryn's deranged, hissing promise, he staggered forward anyway. His men held their swords, determined to defend and protect him to their last.

"Avery, you're finished," said Reid. "Give up."

Avery, Reid had said.

Avery's knees gave. "*No* . . ." he cried, and he looked up, searching for the man who'd recognized him at the city square. It was the only way the range commander would have come to call him by his true name. Captain Robin stepped into view, his expression filled with an accusing anger. "I'm not finished . . . I'm not . . . not done . . ."

His men moved forward. Reid's gun cocked. "Tell your friends to stand down or they're all going to die, Avery."

"Remember that we cannot kill him," said Captain Robin.

"You cannot have him," said one of Avery's men. "Our mission is not complete."

"High Commander Avery Ramont!" shouted Captain Robin. "Order these traitors to stand down! We cannot risk your life!"

Avery's mouth opened and then closed several times as he looked about. His men did not want to abandon the mission, and he wasn't willing to, either. "I cannot," he said, and one of his men assisted him to his feet. "I — "

The man beside him staggered suddenly.

He flinched when he heard the ungodly scream that came from his subordinate, and he paled as he saw the black shadow bleeding around him. Then he heard Taeryn's deranged, gurgling laughter.

Avery turned his back to Reid, no longer concerned about the possibility of finding a blade or a bullet in his back. Their eyes were riveted on the creature, and on the screaming soldier.

"*Taeryn . . . ?*" Reid gasped.

"He is hardly Taeryn any longer," Avery stammered. "This is what Caol creates, Range Commander. I nearly became this." He shuddered, "I told you what he did! Do you believe me now?! This is what that glass does to us! These creatures come because of it!"

"Let me kill him," Taeryn hissed, his eyes still riveted on Avery. "Let us devour the creature who tried to kill us. The *Shadei Ra* deserve what is theirs, what is promised to them. Let me fulfill my contract so that I may descend into the Evernight."

Another monk began to scream as the first was discarded by the unholy shadow creature, and Avery could not tear his eyes from the arching corpse that was still twitching, still screaming where it lay. Its arms twisted until they broke, and still, the corpse shrieked. Its eyes began to bleed, and its mouth, and its ears.

"Nothing we can do will kill them," stammered Avery as the shadowy creature vanished.

Taeryn's eyes had glazed over again. Gray began to course through the madman's veins darkly and did not dissipate. Instead of moving toward Avery, Taeryn turned away as the shadow spread beneath his skin. "She weeps . . ." His steps carried him back the way he came. Something else within the Violet had overridden his desire for vengeance and drawn him away. Avery could feel it calling to him, too, and he tried desperately to block it out. His attempt to do so sent waves of agony through him and made his ears ring.

The monks had circled about Avery. He looked at the Enforcers again. The many guns, swords, and worse.

The pain that shot through his wound nearly dropped him again, and his bloody hand went to the shoulder of one of his men. "Lower your weapons, soldier. All of you as well. I can allow no more of you to die because of your loyalty to me . . ." He grimaced, swaying. "Take me to the range commander. I will not be turned over to our own until I know Caol's agents are gone from the Alliance."

"Commander — "

"Lower your weapons. Let me surrender. They do not have the girl. We are not through; as long as we still have her, there is hope. Eiran will never be able to take her."

The man gripped his sword as those near him hesitated. He lowered his blade fractionally.

"We are not going to surrender unless you are the one to take him into your custody," the man said to Reid. "That is his command."

Captain Robin became angry. "You would dare to try to wiggle your way out of justice? You've betrayed us all, High Commander Ramont!"

"You would not begin to understand what I've had to do," he struggled to say. "Let the range commander pass," he told his men, "but only him. He can place the cuffs upon me himself. Authorize it, Captain Robin. Let me be given to the retired range commander as his ward. Otherwise, we will fight you to our deaths. I will go to my grave willingly — this world, and all of you, be damned. None of you will ever learn the truth of what has been done."

A long moment passed, and Avery wavered where he stood. He wiped the blood from his eye.

"You are prepared to die, then?" asked Captain Robin. Avery remained resolute, and when his men shifted, ready to fight, the captain finally nodded, although he seemed loath to do so. "Fine. I'll authorize it. You will be the retired range commander's ward until you are released at the Reformation. That should appease Saura as well. Reid has proven reliable and honorable to both of our guilds, and his neutral position will keep the quarrelling to a minimum. I'll trust him with your life."

When Reid stood before him, Avery grasped the man's wrist with all his remaining strength. "As long as my men have her, no harm will come of your niece, I swear by my true name and by every vow I uttered in the Alliance." The Violet flared in him, and he cried out. Reid kept him from collapsing, even despite his intense anger. "I've sent for Gabriel," Avery gasped. The fire in his blood and his mind burned so badly he could barely speak. The child had let go of the Violet, and it now coursed through him so strongly he could barely talk, barely breathe. "He can cure her, Reid . . ." Avery's dizziness worsened, and he teetered, but he was desperate to finish what he had to say. "He'll come for her himself . . ."

Reid looked down when Avery's fingers dug at his arm, most assuredly bruising him. Avery's whole hand was covered in blood. Some of it had coagulated and thickened, until it looked like black leeches; the rest of it was bright and glistening. That much blood came from only the worst wounds. The kind men did not survive. Reid paled. "*Shit!*" he swore. "He needs a doctor! Send for my brother!!!"

Avery removed his bloody hand from his stomach and clutched at Reid. He knew Reid had been unprepared to deal with such a horrific wound. He knew he was likely going to die, even if they sewed him shut immediately. But *if* he survived, he needed Reid to promise him one thing.

"I must be taken to the Reformation. Away from Black Temple and the Alliance," gasped Avery. "My identity must remain a secret. Avery Ramont must remain dead to the world. It must be Lukas Maverick caught here today. The King of Thieves. The murderous Lord of Aelynhold, who is sent to the Reformation. *Not Avery*. Do not let anyone else know who I am, I beg you."

"Where is my niece?" asked Reid as he and Avery's men tried to stanch the bleeding. His voice shook badly.

"She's no longer here," Avery said, and the Violet robbed him of his next breath. Reid looked down at him, seeming for the first time to comprehend how grisly the curse must be. Avery's gaze followed the falling snow. He saw the ocean of stars. The beautiful ocean he'd tried for so long not to look at. It was breathtaking. Souls. Thousands of them now, when it used to be such an empty, watery horizon. Others, like him, who carried her memories.

"I sent her away from this city," he said. He could barely hear his own voice.

"*Where is my niece, damn you?*" Reid said again, his voice trembling.

"Lost in the Before. Her mind is gone." His hand fell from Reid's shoulder. "It's more peaceful than I thought. Like falling asleep on the water . . ."

Avery felt the water all around him, and the world drifted from him. What did it matter? His family was gone now anyway. There was nothing left to fight for. Nothing left for him to defend, to lie to protect, to betray in order to keep hidden. What did revenge mean anymore?

CHAPTER SEVENTY-SIX

*T*IES

JOHN'S HANDS SHOOK during the surgery. "He's lost a lot of blood," he said. "I don't know if he'll live."

Reid knew his brother wanted the man to die. He could tell John wanted to open the wound further and spill the rest of the blood in him. His anger was too raw. But Nymeria was still missing, and the murderer before them — *Avery Ramont* — had hidden her. Both of them knew that killing Avery would mean Nymeria would never be found.

Reid wished he could tell his brother the truth as he watched John struggle to process having to save the man's life, but the gag order Captain Robin had issued to protect Avery's identity was still active. *Very* few people knew the truth. John couldn't know the man was the missing High Commander of the Enforcers' Alliance. John could only know this man as the King of Thieves and the Lord of Aelynhold — a bastard, a murderer, a thief, and a child-abductor. Lukas Maverick.

Not even the Lady of the Temple was to be informed of the truth.

John pulled another stitch as Reid, Saura, and Captain Robin watched. No one else had been admitted. Captain Robin and Reid had both refused to allow any other doctor to tend to Avery, although Reid knew John had wished he'd chosen any other person. And Saura and Captain Robin were at odds with each other over who should escort Avery to the Reformation, so they'd decided both would send their men to perform the task when the time came.

One thing was clear among both parties, however; Reid was in charge of the escort. And until Avery was in any condition to be moved, both Reid and Avery would remain here, under heavy guard.

The tension in the atmosphere was suffocating.

Worse, Reid dreaded that his brother might be executed in a few weeks.

Griggori waited outside with Jeana as his ward. But something was different about the man. Something in him was broken. Spooked. He could hardly bring himself to be near or to look at John or Jeana. Didn't even threaten either of them, or look at Jeana the same as he'd done before. He wouldn't even touch a knife or a gun when Saura ordered him to arm himself. He refused, saying he would never kill another person for her or anyone else, that for as long as he lived, he would never let the creatures he'd seen devour him.

Irkov still hadn't shown up. They feared Griggori might have killed him in the temple. Even Taiir was missing, and it weighed heavily on Reid. He suspected both Irkov and his friend were still searching for Nymeria in Aelynhold, but he hadn't heard from Taiir, and no one had seen Irkov since he'd disappeared into the tunnel whose entrance the monks had cleared and then collapsed for Avery.

Everything they knew had become twisted. Broken. Wrong. Even now, Reid's brother was performing surgery on a man — saving his life — when that man had committed atrocities beyond what any of them had thought.

John's hand shook as he pulled the next stitch. Because, instead of being allowed to pray for the man's death, both were forced to pray for his life. For Nymeria's sake.

"He has to live," said Reid at last. "He's important."

"I know. I'm trying, Reid. I am. Whoever cut him open did a damned good job of it. I don't know how he wasn't already dead when you brought me to him. He's still exsanguinated. Cold to the touch. I don't know how he's still breathing."

A small sliver of violet light coursed beneath the High Commander's skin, and Reid bit his tongue, fighting his anxiety. It reminded him of his niece.

How much else had Avery lied about? Worse . . . how much had he *not* lied about?

Saura and Captain Robin came and went, but John and Reid remained under guard with Avery until John was finished and was dragged out roughly by Saura's soldiers. Reid had never been allowed the chance to talk to his brother alone, and neither had he been able to say goodbye.

Reid never left Avery's side, however. He slept lightly, alerted at the slightest noise and motion. He paced. He ate, watching the unconscious man's breathing carefully, looking for any minor twitch or sound that might let him know he would wake. It was nearly unbearable, yet he tolerated it.

Avery Ramont showed no signs of recovery until the fourth day, when some of the color had finally returned to him. But he still did not wake.

Captain Robin had visited and told Reid some of the things the Enforcers had found at the manor, along with some evidence they'd dug up at the temple. It wasn't much, but it seemed to paint Avery as having been an honorable man despite what he looked like. They'd found evidence of Drake Normane's deals with Caol, which had freed Avery of guilt and suspicion in that matter. It had been Drake himself who had recruited the wolfmen to his cause and created the vile stain on what the Brotherhood had become. Moreover, Anna Normane had for years sabotaged Drake's efforts behind his back. She had fed Drake's secret plans and deals to the original sect for years, and they had in turn waged a secret war on Caol's and Drake's wicked followers and infiltrators. Long before Reid or Captain Robin had ever found out about the corruption in the Alliance, Lady Normane's secret, uncorrupted sect of the Brotherhood had been fighting it. Even the attack on Raven Trail had been split to that end. Drake's men had been trying to kill him, while Anna's secret sect had been trying to rescue the King of Thieves so that his men would rally and overthrow Drake once and for all.

"I never expected he'd been so thorough," said Captain Robin. He nodded to the unconscious High Commander.

Reid massaged the backs of his eyelids. "He's lasted a long time without getting caught. Of course, he was thorough. What have you found out?"

"Lieutenant Elija found evidence that exonerates him completely. The original Brotherhood. Started by the King of Thieves, and then run in his absence by the late Lady Normane and Captain Bourgeois. They were following commands from Avery Ramont himself, which were written, signed, and sealed with his signet. Dated before his disappearance. Captain Bourgeois, Lady Normane, the King of Thieves, and many others thought to be traitors, had all been working to *protect* the Alliance. It was all in secret, every bit of it."

"Saura still doesn't know, does she?"

"No," said the captain. "Neither will she. This is an internal matter."

"Has anything else at all tied Lukas and Avery together in any other way, or hinted that the assumed identity and the High Commander are one and the same?"

"No. Lady Normane's marriage to Avery had been written only as a marriage to the son of Aelynhold's late Lord Edric Normane — who himself had raised two bastard sons and had never married. One had drowned when young, but his name had been scratched from Aelynhold's records."

"Lukas Maverick," said Reid.

The captain nodded. "The other had become an Enforcer, had inherited Aelynhold, and had married Lady Normane. Again, the name had been redacted. Yet Lukas Maverick's name was found in several documents, which showed Lukas had been Edric's younger son."

"Which is why Avery has managed to remain undetected for so long. What about Anna's previous married name, though? Wouldn't that have tied Avery to Edric, even in some small way?"

"Before Drake Normane married her, her last name was Ramont, yes. But it's been struck from the records as well. Anyone ignorant of the truth of Avery's identity would assume her last name was Maverick before her marriage to Drake."

Reid blinked, his eyes on fire. "I can't help but admire his meticulousness. The attention to detail is incredible. He was thorough in hiding his identity before he ever went undercover to investigate Caol. Not many men have such foresight, especially the kind that would protect them for years despite heavy investigations." He sucked on his tooth. "But why would he have gone through so much trouble? What could have scared the High Commander so badly that he would strike his own history and take such drastic precautions? He shouldn't have been afraid of Five Tower, not with the power behind him. Caol shouldn't ever have managed to have any kind of hold over him . . . It doesn't make sense."

"No, it doesn't. We don't know any of his reasons yet. Even the citadel has no information linking Avery to Aelynhold. He never talked about his family or his home but for the absolutely rarest occasion. The only instance I can think of is once, when he and I were drunk and in a bitter conversation over the Fuel War that Avery's father Lord Edric had caused and then won. All he said *then* was his brother had died in Aelynhold. Drowned. Nothing about his father, his lineage, or his home."

"King of Liars, huh?" said Reid, repeating Griggori's words from Aelynhold.

"Yeah. Would have been a better title. More accurate, anyway."

"I can imagine why he didn't share where he came from, though," snorted Reid. "Edric Normane caused a lot of deaths in the war thirty years ago, and bitterness over what he did is still spat in taverns with a lot of venom whenever the older Enforcers talk about their victories and losses. If they'd known who he was when he joined, he would have been killed in the middle of the night. He would never have climbed the ranks, let alone become the High Commander."

"Makes sense, the poor bastard. Still had it rough. He was young, like you. Pissed off a lot of captains and range commanders when he became our leader. He did right, and he did well, until he vanished." The captain laughed. "Hell, even after he vanished, I think. No one else could have run the Alliance while absent from it for twelve and a half years."

Reid found the truth of that quite humorous as well. "Twelve and a half years. Quite a feat. Didn't keep us from finding out, though, did it?"

Captain Robin shrugged as he stood to leave. "That's on you, Reid. You're the one who's made most of the connections and sent us what we needed to continue our work. The information you sent from Balthora and Tallil were extremely valuable. And you've been right about a *lot*. You're as effective at coordinating revolving components in your absence as he ever was. You really should consider coming out of retirement." The captain chuckled. "You're still doing the work."

Reid scowled and waved the captain away. "I'll let you know when he wakes. You've got work to do, so go and do it. And thanks for the intel."

"The pleasure is mine. The work you've done makes me look as though I'm good at my job."

CHAPTER SEVENTY-SEVEN

CONFESSION

"ANNA . . ."

Reid's eyes snapped open.

Avery's eyelids rolled back, and his black eyes glittered with grief. He shut them again when he saw Reid. "I was at peace with death, and you've had me robbed me of it," he said. "Are my wife's sons alive?"

"No," said Reid. "But your daughter survived."

Avery closed his mouth. "She wasn't breathing."

"Griggori paralyzed her with the same thing he'd given John's wife," said Reid. "A powerful sedative. Saura wouldn't let him kill her, just make you think it."

Avery's laugh was pained. "That snake," he whispered. "I thought I'd have to avenge Carriah. What happened to my nephews?"

"Part of the manor collapsed."

Avery became silent. Reid could tell the news upset him.

"How much did you lie about?" asked Reid.

"To you, very little, except by omission. To everyone else . . . so very much," Avery said quietly. "So, so very much."

"When are you going to tell everyone what really happened and why you did what you did?"

"When I feel the time and the people are right."

Reid withheld his irritation from his voice. "Who are the right people?"

"You are the right one for some of it," said Avery. "You and your brother are the only ones I think would go as far as I have to keep Caol and his sons from their goal. Because of your love for that girl. You would betray your family, your guilds, your duty, even yourselves and your love for her. That's the commitment it will take to keep her safe. To keep her alive, and to keep them from finding out about her."

"What did they do to you?" asked Reid. "You were all but a king for the power you had. You could have simply returned to the Alliance after your escape and then burned Five Tower to the ground. Why didn't you?"

"They did unimaginable things, Range Commander. You saw that thing. All of you did. What was put inside us was much worse than anything a torturer could have done. If my hands had been free, I would have clawed my own eyes out like the rest of them, chewed off my own arms — anything, to be rid of it."

"Taiir told me about the experiments," said Reid. "Are those wraithlike beings connected to you somehow?"

"Those creatures follow people infected with the Blood Light. We're usually the only ones who can see or sense them. If I'd ordered the burning of a city, I'd have been marked by it and devoured by them. Singular and small numbers of murders, like that of your parents, almost cost me my own life every time I committed them — and I committed a lot of them for Caol. I wouldn't have escaped murdering an entire city."

"That doesn't explain why you served him willingly."

"We were all half mad, and terrified enough not to defy him. I couldn't work against him. No one could. As Caol had proven ruthlessly with countless others, if he had suspected my betrayal after what he'd done to me, he would have given the word, and then his or Eiran's hunters would have set those creatures on me. If he was capable of doing that to all of those people and all of those children, what kind of horror do you think a man like that would have done if he'd realized he'd made a puppet of the High Commander of the Enforcers' Alliance? Tell me. What line do you think he would not have crossed? He would have used me to destroy both of our guilds, and then much worse."

Avery's fingers clenched into a fist. "I wouldn't be here now. You wouldn't be here now. No one would. This continent would have been slaves and embers a decade ago."

"Damn."

"Precisely." Avery nodded weakly. "I've plotted revenge since the day he betrayed my men and me. Now I am not even in a place of power. With all that I now know, I cannot do so much as issue a single order to have him assassinated without incredible fallout."

"Why did you decide you needed to deal with him in person in the first place? Why did you put yourself in the position where he was able to capture you and your men? You were a better strategist than that. Why that level of risk?"

"Caol is paranoid and suspicious, Reid. He would have never let even the *smell* of an Enforcer within a mile of him. I spent quite a while fabricating and building Lukas's reputation as the King of Thieves when I finally managed to gain access to him with that identity. It took my dead brother's name, and every other truth and lie I could spin together, and it took a lot of crimes to build that identity just to earn a meeting with him. And then it took months more to build his trust even after I met him. To get close enough to figure out what he was after and what, exactly, he was doing. We still didn't have anything more than rumors and occasional testimony, and the matter was too sensitive to use a heavy hand. He already had infiltrators in the Alliance. That's why I involved myself personally. And because what they're involved in endangers all of us. It's more than weapons. It's worse than that. He has very dangerous allies."

Before Reid opened his mouth to ask his next question, Avery continued.

"Even among *them*, Nymeria would be considered special."

Reid frowned. "Among whom?"

"The Leviathans. They're not like us. She needs to be protected from them, Reid. Every memory they gave her was worse than the one before."

"They're the reason my niece isn't well?"

"They're the reason she's *dying*, Range Commander."

Reid's heart skipped sickly. "How so?" he asked. Yet he recalled the contents of Rhael's letter.

"Even a few of those memories killed most of us," explained Avery. "That innocent girl has been exposed to all of them. Every. Last. One. When I first saw her, they had her in a cryotank that was filled completely with water. The Violet pierced her every time it arced from the glass they had in there with her. The night Caol and his sons first cursed me with it, they chained me to a table, slit open my left arm, and pulled one of those shards from her tank and put it in me. She was just feet away, a tiny creature locked in glass, with wires cutting into her wrists and ankles, and wrapped around her throat like . . ."

Avery shut his eyes and turned his head. His chest rose and fell at irregular intervals as he tried to hold his breath and failed, as he attempted to regain his composure. "What they did to us was bad on its own . . . But what they did to that child was monstrous."

Avery looked at him, his black gaze piercing. "Your niece isn't a normal human being." Reid's skin crawled. He started to object, but Avery shook his head, his expression grave. "Listen to me, Range Commander. Very carefully. There has only ever been one other like her. *One*. Caol and his sons used her for their wicked ends." Avery swallowed sickly as he recalled with morose detail what had happened. "Every time they took one of us down there and cut us open to curse us with the Blood Light, she started screaming. She wasn't even conscious, but every time, she screamed as if they'd set her on fire. I could hear her through the water and the glass. I could hear it every time after, all the way to the Bright Night, whether I was there or not. We all could. What they did to us, they did to Nymeria also. For twelve years, I have heard those screams, among many, many others, and it has been all I could do to shut them out. I cannot tell you how many children they tried to create like her, who died violent, horrendous deaths."

The image Avery painted was horrid.

"Nymeria should have been dead a long time ago," said Avery. "Even I had thought the Bright Night killed her. I don't understand how she survived, but she did. From what I've seen, she's suppressed the memories they gave her. Other memories, too, for her belief that you and your family are her own. But now she's losing touch the way the rest of us do before we're dead from it." His fingers clenched again. "If I could do to them what they did to us and to her, I would magnify it a thousandfold and extend it to eternity."

"What does the Violet do to those who are cursed with it? Besides driving them mad."

Avery grimaced and looked at him again. "Why is it that you seem to believe me? Everything I've said would not be believed by most, and I've also done very nearly nothing but lie. To your family. To everyone."

"Call it instinct, or extreme scrutiny, or whatever you want. Up until today, you've been a completely different person. This is the first time I've ever seen you behave as *yourself*. And honestly, at that."

"*Honest*." Avery shook his head weakly, the motion barely recognizable. "Being addressed in the same breath with that word doesn't even feel right anymore."

"What does the Violet do?"

What little color Avery had gained turned ashen. His left hand pulled at his restraints.

"Breathe easy," said Reid. "It's only been six days since my brother sewed you shut."

"Six days, you said," Avery winced. His breathing was labored, as though he was in a lot of pain.

"Yes. Captain Robin came to check on your status two days ago. We had a lengthy discussion about the forethought you had put into erasing your own identity. Answer my question."

Avery nodded, and his head fell back. "The first thing to go is the mind," he said after a difficult moment to gather himself. His discomfort slowly subsided. "Sometimes we see snow. Mountains. Beautiful, majestic scenery not from this continent. But there's a Bright Night there. After that, the memories are horrifying. Sometimes we see *him*. A shadow of a man. Never the face. Just the hands, covered in blood. Or the hair, black as night. Or, reflected back from water or glass, his eyes. Those are the brightest, most unnatural hue. Like Nymeria's. But the color is that of flaming blue ocean. There are visions of blue water, like the cryotank in which Nymeria was kept in the Gray Halls, but they are far older. More advanced. And then there are millennia of memories . . . all *his*, as if he is immortal. There is death, screams, bloodshed. Agony, unlike anything you could imagine or inflict upon another. Yet we know there is worse than what any of us have seen. There is always worse, and then we find those memories, too — and then there is worse again. It doesn't stop. It's nearly impossible to look away or even to exist separately from it once we've seen the first of it. Death is easier for most. His madness . . ."

Avery's breath wavered as the Violet coursed through his body, and he tensed, gasping. His knuckles turned white, and his eyes changed color as he pulled at the restraints. He became very pale as he struggled to rake air into his lungs.

Reid's own body had corded tight with tension at the sight, and his own heart continued to race with fear. Whatever was happening to Avery was nothing natural. And it was far from pleasant, from what Reid could see.

Avery convulsed, and the Violet within him brightened — and then it slowly dimmed, until it was barely visible beneath his flesh. But his eyes were still blazing with the curse inside him. The man shook violently, blinking away grief and pain, and gasping. He tried to talk, but his voice broke several times. His chest rose and fell, but the sound of his suffering barely escaped his throat as his hands clenched and then unclenched repeatedly over empty air. "I needed Rhael's help — " he managed, and moisture rolled from his eyes as he stared at the cloth ceiling overhead. Another, weaker convulsion cut his words.

The color in Avery's eyes finally began to dim again, but only a little.

"Caol wanted me to kill him, but I needed Rhael's help. Desperately. I didn't have much longer before the Violet took my mind from me and set the Shadei Ra upon me or turned me into another broken hunter. I was trying to find Rhael when I killed your parents. My first strike was unintentional. Fear-driven. But I couldn't leave the job unfinished. What I did and said to them was cruel, but their deaths were quick. Taeryn was the one I took the most time with. I thought I killed him."

"It seemed a job gone bad." Reid studied the unnatural light pulsing in the High Commander's gaze. "My parents were good people, though, Avery. It wasn't right that you killed them."

Avery shook his head. "I've done worse . . ." The High Commander clenched his jaws and said nothing for a long time. He seemed unable to bring himself to talk. They heard arguments from Enforcers outside, several meters from the tent. One of the men serving as their guard sneezed, and then the argument resumed. At last, Avery let out the breath he held. "I knew they'd had contact with Rhael," he said quietly. "But he was long gone before I reached them. With how fast they'd been traveling, I knew he had to have given them some kind of message. *Something*, anyway. He was not the kind of man to send messages, not unless it was dire and he had no other way. He wouldn't risk that kind of thing."

"So you knew him."

"Yes. But only barely. He is a powerful ally to have. He is the reason I didn't die in the Gray Halls before he and Caol had their disagreement. I returned that favor by making sure he escaped Caol's murderous, backstabbing scheme before the Bright Night. But Rhael and his brother Gabriel are both ghosts. You don't find them." Avery exhaled sickly. "They find you. Honestly, I think it's that way with all Leviathans."

Reid could tell the Violet still coursing through Avery's body was still hurting him. And blood now seeped through the bandages over Avery's side. The convulsion had torn some of the stitches beneath his dressings.

The High Commander seemed only able to control the side effects of his curse with the greatest effort. He shut his violet-colored eyes for a long moment. "The curse," he said, "causes us to fear *every* shadow after we draw those creatures for the first time. They're drawn to it. They swarm it, like moths to the flame. Those creatures manifest everywhere, any time they sense something bright enough or tainted enough they want to devour. And the Blood Light itself burns. From the inside, out. Sometimes like acid poured into us. Sometimes like dull fire. Sometimes a burning cold."

"You don't think it's the same for Nymeria . . . ?" Reid could barely even hear his own voice when he asked the question, for the blood racing in his ears. But he recalled the day she'd revealed her secret to him. It hadn't seemed to hurt her then. But John had described her nightmares and hallucinations — which Reid now no longer believed were simply hallucinations or nightmares. Not after having seen that dark shadow creature so clearly and having learned all that he had.

For another long moment, Avery seemed unable to speak or to breathe. His mouth opened and closed, but nothing came out until the Violet seemed to loosen its grip once more. "I shouldn't have put her in a cell," he said. "I didn't have anywhere else to safely hold her until I could get her out of Aelynhold. It's my fault it's gotten worse for her. That cell was too similar to what Mihai went through, and now she's lost her grip on the Violet altogether. It's my fault. I shouldn't have done it. She wouldn't be suffering now if I hadn't."

Reid was sickened when he realized what Avery really meant. "You're saying you can sense her, even now? As if you're tied to her? Just like the creatures?" He stood, no longer able to tolerate the chair.

"Everyone she infects with the Violet becomes *hers*. The more she suffers, the more *we* suffer. It's why she's still alive, I think. We're made to dim the onslaught of the horror coming from him. She's a demon, Range Commander . . . An angel. *Something*." Avery's eyes shut, and his jaw ticked violently. "Something *else*."

Reid grimaced at that, and he set his hands on the edge of the makeshift cot near Avery's left foot. Avery couldn't move for the ropes that bound him to the table. "What about the man? You said all of the memories are from him. Mihai was his name?"

"I don't know what that man really is, but it's evil and it's powerful. The *darkest pits of Hell, locked in chains and buried for eternity* kind of evil. They literally buried him in chains because they couldn't kill him. Even the shadow creatures are terrified of him. That's who your niece is connected to. That's what they did to her in Five Tower. That's what they did to all of us . . ." Another storm of light curled through Avery's flesh, ripping his words away. It lasted much longer than the previous waves, and the High Commander shuddered violently again when it ended. "It doesn't *stop*," he repeated, very clearly close to losing consciousness again. But Avery forced himself to take and then release a deep, even breath. Then another . . . Another.

Reid did not envy what the Blood Light was doing to the man at all. He finally fully understood Taiir's aversion to the shards. "Avery . . . This next question would sound strange to any other, but I am going to ask it anyway."

Avery laughed weakly. "Strange has long been normal to me, Range Commander. Ask. I will answer."

Reid considered how best to ask it. "Captain Robin . . . said something . . . *odd*. The day he woke, when he told me who you really are." He bit down on the flesh inside his cheek, considering it. But Avery wouldn't be the only one it applied to. It meant the same for Rhael and Gabriel. That meant it applied to unknown others. "How old were you when you left the Alliance under the guise of Lukas Maverick . . . ?"

Avery's brows drew together, and he appeared utterly confused by the question. "Pardon?"

"How old?"

Avery winced, and his fists tightened again. The Violet was brightening again in him. He tried to blink it away. His confusion only deepened alongside his suffering. That showed in the drawn expression on his face when he stared hard at Reid. "Explain why such a question is relevant to anything, will you? I was very nearly twenty-eight, I think."

Reid studied the man's deceptively young face. "It doesn't make sense that he seems to have been correct." He thought back to the night he'd caught Lukas. To the time since. "And despite what I've seen, you should have been as easily winded as — "

"Will you explain to me why that question is relevant?" asked Avery. "I . . ." Realization bloomed within his obsidian gaze, and he started to shake his head, as if denying to himself why Reid had asked the question. "But . . . *No*. No, no, no . . . You *cannot* mean — "

"He said you looked exactly the same fifteen or sixteen years ago. That was the last time he saw you. A couple of years before you vanished." Avery stared at him, his eyes wide as he became more horrified at Reid's every word. The High Commander began shaking his head side to side as if he could deny it, or as if he could stop Reid from saying it. "Avery, you haven't aged at all. Not even a day, he said. At your age, you should have just begun to slow. Yet you're still as sharp and quick as a younger man half your age. Quicker, even. Stronger than you should have been. It was a struggle to catch you near Crow Post, and it was harder still to bind you, or to keep you that way. Also . . . There was your wound. You should have died from it. My brother and I have seen many, many wounds lesser than that, each of which ended in death, and in a matter of hours, not days. You should have been dead."

"That's what Anna meant," he sighed bitterly. The High Commander's fingers curled, and he looked at them as he trembled with anger.

"It may be another effect of the curse," said Reid.

Avery shook his head slowly. "It's another thing entirely. It has nothing to do with the memories or the shards, or even that accursed light. His blood caused it."

Reid frowned, and his mouth opened. He shut it, unsure what to ask, or how. Again, he started to speak. "Whose blood?"

Avery swore. "They're going to find out eventually. This is not a thing one can hide indefinitely."

"Whose blood, Avery? What happened?"

Avery had grown even angrier, but he answered the question. "I screamed so much from the glass the night they cursed me with the Violet that none of them realized I was exposed to Rhael's blood also. I didn't know it, either. It means I'm not human anymore, Range Commander. I am going to live a very, very long time, just like Rhael and Gabriel. Upward of a thousand years, if I'm not caught and killed for it. I won't be able to hide that fact at the Reformation."

In any other circumstance, Reid would have thought Avery's claim was a joke or an outright lie. But despite how unreal it was, the information he'd learned about Gabriel and Rhael matched the statement. Gabriel was the singular being who had started Black Temple hundreds of years ago.

His blood ran cold again at the thought of what it insinuated. If Gabriel, who was a creature next to immortal, was a fugitive . . .

What could *that* sort of man fear? What had he been accused of, and who had framed him? And from whom was he running? Who could be more dangerous than a nearly immortal being?

Avery brought Reid's whirling thoughts back to the present when he swore. "On top of every goddamned thing else I've been through, and only *now* do I realize something so godforsaken important! I'll give it a decade before they find out I've become one of them!"

"Avery, calm down before you rip those stitches further."

Avery snarled. His hands trembled again as he pulled weakly at his restraints, and a fresh rivulet of blood oozed from the soaked cloth. Avery tried to suck in a breath and struggled to avert the fire he must have felt in his wound. "What good it'll do me," he managed to say. "It would be kinder to claw open my stitches and pour scalding embers into my belly, Range Commander. If the memories in the Violet are any indication, their people will execute me the same way they tried to execute Mihai, and it won't be a quick, clean death."

Avery was completely distraught. So very angry. His fists clenched again, and he struggled against his bonds and let loose several angry, quiet curses before he slumped back again, chest heaving. He was dangerously pale after the exertion. The man turned his head, and his grief scraped his throat raw. "I'm screwed . . ." The High Commander's head lolled when he tried to move again, and his words began to slur. "Everything I worked for will be undone as if it meant nothing. A decade cannot prepare you all for what is coming. And on top of that . . . having done to me what was done to *Mihalokh* . . ."

Avery's fingers curled when he tried to grip his side. A tremor ran through him as another dim wave of the Blood Light washed through him, and then the High Commander's body went slack. He had lost consciousness again. His breathing remained distressed for a few long minutes afterward, however, as if he would have been screaming if he'd been conscious to do so.

CHAPTER SEVENTY-EIGHT

QUESTIONS

A BREEZE FILTERED IN, cooling the uncomfortably humid tent, and Reid looked up. Saura had come to check on Avery's status. Her eyes glittered darkly as she looked at the man, and she stepped aside and motioned for two men to enter. One was from among her own Black Temple guards. The other was an Enforcer Reid recognized from Edantine. Captain Thames. He was a man Reid had a lot of respect for, one of several officers who'd helped with Reid's and Captain Robin's investigations.

"He's awake," she said as they entered. "One of you, help Mr. Ivan to move him. The other, drag Captain Robin and his officers back to the Command Center. Let them know the Lord of Aelynhold is awake."

"It's not yet a good idea to move him, Saura," said Reid as Saura's Black Temple guard left them. "His stitches tore open only this morning."

"The stitches will hold well enough," she said icily. "They'll just hurt and bleed a little." Then she was gone.

"You look like hell," said the captain to Reid. He nodded in reply.

"I'm glad to see you are in good health, Thames."

The captain waved off the sentiment and looked at Avery. Studied him long and hard. "I didn't believe it when Robin told me it was you, Avery. Yet, unless my own eyes deceive me, there you are. Exactly as he described."

"And here I am," said Avery. "Recovering, lest my guts spill from me unexpectedly. I may finally become a truly gutless man. Either that, or I'll be full of shit if my bowels weren't stitched to expel waste rather than retain it. His brother was none too happy to service me with my surgery, I'm sure."

"You were always full of shit," Captain Thames chuckled. "Gutted bowels or no. You haven't changed at all, have you?"

Avery went white when Reid and Captain Thames pulled him from the makeshift cot and haphazardly dragged him out of the tent where he'd been treated. Reid couldn't very well say why he felt a tinge of guilt or pity for the High Commander, but he did. He tried to be gentle. Captain Thames, who had, he'd heard, arrived only a day ago, seemed to be of the same mind. "We have many questions," said the captain to Avery. "Lean on us. We'll try to make this walk less painful, sir."

Avery laughed weakly. "*Sir,* is it? Don't tell me they've been digging through Aelynhold for even a ghost of what I was up to."

"They have," said Reid. "Among the few who know who you really are, you've ended up with a very mixed half-victim, half-criminal, almost-hero status. Your other identity, however . . . still a criminal. It may be your saving grace, considering your other issue, Avery. It's kept you alive this long. Very few men recognized you. And you're a very resourceful man. I'm sure you'll accomplish many foul things before they catch on. Knowing what I've learned of you, you'll probably escape long before they do."

494

Avery looked at him. He understood Reid had meant the other issue was his . . . unconventional, newly found *condition*, to put it mildly. The High Commander seemed to appreciate the encouragement, however. They'd spoken little about it since he'd awakened, but Avery had certainly made up his mind to fight through it, as he had with everything else. The man was nothing, if not consistent and stubborn. "That is appreciated, Reid . . . Thank you." The sentiment was genuine. "I'll focus on this traitor business of mine first. The rest, we'll handle after I've been delivered to the Reformation."

"You're no traitor, Avery," objected Captain Thames. "You shouldn't be locked away as one."

Avery laughed again, and then he groaned because it hurt him to do so. "When I surrendered, I never had any intention of being released, Captain. Even if our people were to find me fully innocent. Not until such time as Five Tower is no longer a threat. As it stands, any who know my identity should be sworn to silence. Avery Ramont needs to remain dead . . . Saura didn't seem to know. How many *do* know who I am?"

"Only the small contingent Captain Robin trusted," said Reid, "and Captain Thames, and Taiir and I. Robin had already issued a gag order regarding the nature of Lukas Maverick's arrest before we ever caught you, and Thames has since relayed it to his own men. For all intents and purposes, to everyone else, you are still Lukas. Not even my brother knows the truth. You will be questioned thoroughly, but Saura will be present for part of it, since Aelynhold's current heir committed crimes against Black Temple under Lukas's order."

Avery sucked in a sharp breath and cursed the moment he tried to stand fully on his own. He clutched at the side of his belly, suddenly almost as pale as he'd been several days before when John had sewn him shut. "How did you even find out that I'd gone to Aelynhold?" asked Avery. "You were over a hundred miles away. You shouldn't have been able to track me for months. I sent men out to several cities to find and capture you for what I had planned. But you were in my own city before I had even fully turned around, and you knew almost everything. You caught me by surprise and nearly ruined a huge part of the operation."

"Experience and luck," said Reid. "A man who has knowledge has power, and one who has luck has life."

"Despite how he just poetically and nonchalantly put that," laughed Captain Thames, "the retired range commander is being unduly modest. He's your equal, Avery. Better, maybe. A lot of Drake's corruption was easy to follow once we found out about it. But the bastard on the other side of you there? He went as far as Balthora and was prepared to go to Arsennia, too. Even I don't know how the hell he figured out where you were, or *who* you were. Or *when*. Or what *else*."

"If you don't . . ." Avery wheezed, "mind my asking. Where did you serve? How long ago?"

Reid grimaced. "Why does it matter?"

"Curiosity. You never recognized me, yet you've got the respect and complete trust of a lot of my men — what *were* my men, anyway. You're a strategist. A leader. You get your hands dirty the way I did, and you're terrifyingly effective, to have tracked me so quickly or to have learned whatever else you have yet to even mention you were after. It reminds me of one of my range commanders. I only ever promoted two of them I never met face to face."

"I was one of them," Reid acknowledged.

"Eastern coast? Or northern?"

"Northern and then eastern."

Avery faltered, and Reid heard his sharp intake of breath. "*That one.* Dear god, no wonder." Avery grinned, pale as they set him down before the Enforcers. The man seemed in shock when he craned his neck to look up at him. "The bastard who conquered the ice itself. Your men nicknamed you the White Dagger because you outfought, outsmarted, and outlasted, and even when your men were dead and captured and you were surrounded and disarmed, you took and broke the frozen ground itself and used a sliver of the ice to kill and maim and torture the enemies around you. The many heavy, blood-soaked rumors about you . . . Goddamned brilliant, brutal, vicious bastard. I never even realized you'd been *gentle* when you caught me in the woods near Crow Post. You're a much kinder, gentler man than what say the rumors about you."

Avery turned his head as he began to laugh quietly, and his mirth was long-winded. "If I'd had the thought to have put you on tour in the Midland instead of clear across the damned map cleaning up the dissent there, Caol never would have done what he's done. I'd have sent you to deal with him, the Others, and then still had missions to spare." His laughter continued. "I pissed off a lot of old blood when I spoke aloud the idea of making you the next High Commander. Jealous, ineffective bastards, the lot of them. Twice in a line, youngblood ruling the Alliance. Could you imagine? But you'd earned your rank, same as I. I should have recalled you to the citadel and put you in charge before I left."

"I wouldn't have accepted," said Reid, and he stepped aside. He grew concerned the laughing would tear those stitches, but Avery seemed not to give a damn at all despite the pain it caused him.

"*Modest*, vicious bastard!" Avery winced, struggling to sit comfortably, to remain upright. He continued laughing the way he had laughed in and near Crow Post when he had pretended to be his own dead brother. Reid didn't like it one bit. It meant Avery had something planned, or that he'd already done something unpleasant or dishonest.

The High Commander looked at Reid as if appreciating him fully for the first time, and he continued to laugh *still*. As if Reid was at the end of some loathsome joke only Avery knew about. "I'm sorry, but this may well end up the funniest day of my life. I never even realized it was *you* this whole time! *Truly*, as I breathe and curse . . . You have my utmost respect, Range Commander, and my deepest apology. What I've done cannot be made right, repaid, or otherwise forgiven. I am afraid we may even one day become good friends, you and I. Brothers, in a sense, despite my having been the fool who murdered your parents."

"High Commander," said Captain Robin.

Avery exhaled, his fists clenching and unclenching before him. He looked up, though he swayed dangerously. Still, he was laughing. He held up his hand, tears in his eyes. He couldn't speak, and his laughter continued for a very long time before it finally waned. Yet he did not share the cause for his humor, and he struggled to restrain it when at last Captain Robin opened his mouth to attempt to speak to him again.

"What were you investigating? What was Caol doing?" asked the captain.

"Weapons," Avery managed at last. He grunted when he tried to clear his throat and sit tall. It hurt him too much to do so. "Caol wanted weapons." Another, weaker fit of laughter shook Avery's frame, and his wrists were scraped raw by the ropes binding him tightly as he shifted painfully once more.

Reid and Captain Thames exchanged confused looks. "I don't like the sound of his laughing," said Thames uncomfortably, and Avery began laughing all over again, as if the acknowledgement had recharged his secret joke and renewed the strength of its humor for him. The laughter was worse when Avery tried to look at Reid and say something. He couldn't. "I remember the most wicked things he'd done having always accompanied that laugh," added Thames. "He reserved that for times when he'd outsmarted everyone in their fields, when he'd beaten them at their own games before they'd even known it. When he utterly devastated and humiliated them."

Captain Robin seemed equally uneasy, as if he remembered something similar.

Reid and the others looked up when Saura was allowed into the Command Center. She seated herself quietly and made no apology or excuse for her entrance. "I expect I'll be briefed afterward about any questions prior to my arrival," she said.

Captain Robin nodded curtly and returned to the questioning. However, there was one key difference. The captain changed his address of Avery, opting instead to call him by his late brother's name. *"Lord Maverick.* I shall repeat the question for the Lady of the Black Temple. What kind of weapons did Caol want?"

Avery sniggered. "That is classified, *Captain Morpheus.*"

Captain Robin's jaw ticked. "Why did you refuse to return to your station when you escaped Caol's grasp?"

"That is classified. Only the men I trust know that information, and they are not at liberty to tell you, either. It is an incredibly severe security risk."

Saura leaned forward with a question of her own. "Where is Gabriel?"

Reid's head snapped in her direction. *Now* she was open enough to acknowledge Gabriel's name? He noticed the faintest wicked twitch upon Avery's pale visage and knew immediately the man was about to tell her nothing she wanted to hear. He had returned himself wholeheartedly to the role of Lukas. "Pardon?"

"Where is he?"

"I don't know a man by that name. Only a thick-bearded woman I met years ago, who was unhappy she had three legs rather than two. You could try finding her in Wireshon. They've a circus there, and they love snakes. You would be quite charmed, I promise."

Saura did not bite. "You can lie all you want, Lord Maverick. I know that you are in contact with him."

"I think you're mistaken, Unholy Lady of the Temple."

"Why did you abduct the daughter of one of my doctors?"

"Classified." Avery laughed quietly to himself. "We can go round and round, ladies and gentlemen. This will not end as you want it to. Not even if you execute me, my daughter, my men, or my goat."

Reid felt a touch of humor at that. He wasn't the only one. There were a few inappropriate, quiet laughs.

It was odd to feel the need to contain a smile of his own when he was still angry at Avery and so very worried about his niece. But it was far stranger to feel as though Avery really meant to protect his niece rather than exploit or hurt her.

"Leave the goat's cousins out of it, they're innocent," Avery added, and he tilted forward as he struggled to remain upright.

"You're so willing to cast away your life?" asked the captain. Robin tossed a ledger to the ground, and it landed at Avery's feet.

"What's this?" asked Avery, unworried.

"That's what we wanted to know. It was in your late ex-wife's quarters at Aelynhold."

Reid heard Avery's pained exhalation. He saw the mask falter as Avery's procured sarcasm withered. His smile wavered and fell, and the amusement in his gaze turned to ash. Lady Normane's death had hit the man hard, if he was failing to keep up his ruse at the mere mention of her. It seemed to be the only thing to really get through to Avery. And Reid knew how stubborn Avery was. Even when he'd tortured the High Commander months before, he'd barely pried the man's well-practiced mask and glimpsed the truth of any of the stains beneath.

"Of course," Avery whispered seemingly to himself. Reid watched Avery's jaw tick. Saw his chin quiver as his head fell so that his blond hair curtained his face. The High Commander took a deep breath to compose himself, and he wiped his cheek with the back of his hand. But he didn't look up for a long time after.

The captain's voice remained hard, but Reid still read the man's sympathy. The captain had to ask difficult, unkind questions the same as he had to ask other, less painful ones. He could not be gentle. They needed answers.

"Lukas, the ledger contains your own orders. Instructions, left for your wife and your cousin. And for the Enforcers who followed you from the Alliance — "

"What can I say but that I was a fool?" said Avery. "Drake deceived me, and he also betrayed my commands. I was a *fool* to think him decent or trustworthy." Avery looked up at Captain Robin, his grief overcome by his anger. "You were going to ask about the nature of my contract with Avery Ramont thirteen years ago. Why I left the Alliance, started the thieves' guild, and then betrayed him to work with Caol. I never betrayed him. That was my cousin's doing when he turned the Brotherhood into a bloodthirsty lunatic's asylum. And my wife did what she had to do to survive. The rest is classified."

"Why did Avery Ramont trust you to investigate something he could have sent Enforcers to look into?"

"The Enforcers he first sent were killed. Thieves are more suited for those sorts of tasks."

"Why did you abandon the Alliance to become a thief?"

"Why fight a dragon for its treasure and light the whole damned forest on fire when you can send a thief instead? Thieves are better than Enforcers in those sorts of tasks."

Captain Robin's nostrils flared. He knew very well that Avery was not going to answer his questions, and Avery was getting under his skin despite that everyone present knew Avery could not answer half of it with Saura before them anyway. It was frustrating even to watch.

Saura asked the next question. "What did you do with Avery Ramont? You're his last known contact."

"Classified."

"Then what did they do to you in Five Tower? We know Caol betrayed your group. That the men with you were killed. Why were you the only one to survive? What deal did you strike?"

Avery blinked. "Classified. It pertains to the mission."

"Was it Avery who set the mission, or Gabriel?"

Yet another lie came from Avery. Reid could tell from the glittering blackness in his eyes. He'd returned to his Lukas persona again, more determined than before. "Thieves are absolutely famous for following orders from mythical men. We get paid in hair. The more we obey, the less bald we will become when old."

Captain Thames snorted and burst into laughter, and then he nearly had to excuse himself because of the glares he received from the others. "My deepest apologies. Continue," he said, and he cleared his throat and stared very hard at Avery's boots.

The questions went on and on. Hours and hours of it. And Avery countered, denied, or claimed "Classified" one sardonic way or another. What the High Commander had told Reid had been far more honest than nearly every small thing he gave to them.

At last, they got fed up with his games and his fiery wit, and they wanted nothing more to do with the obvious waste that the questioning had become.

Some of the humor had finally returned to Avery by the end of it, however. The hours and hours of questions had seemed a good way for him to vent. He'd been able to deny them again and again, until their tempers were broiling and only barely held in check. It had given the High Commander some small measure of joy and satisfaction, Reid could tell. And by Captain Thames's watering eyes and ticking jaw, as well as the hidden, barely contained laughter among a couple of the other Enforcers who were present, that vengeful humor had been deeply appreciated.

Reid helped Avery to his feet.

"Why doesn't Reid Ivan question him for us?" asked Saura tartly. "He's interrogated the man before and gotten much more out of him."

Reid very nearly wanted to say, "*He wasn't the leader of the Alliance then.*" Instead, he chose a different approach. "My methods are not appropriate for this situation, Saura," he said. "Neither do I have the authority to interfere in Alliance matters. He is only my temporary ward, not my prisoner. The questioning is the Alliance's right. Also, Lukas did nothing but lie to me when I interrogated him months ago."

"You give yourself too little credit," groaned Avery. "You're a scary bastard, and a rough one. My ear still stings at the memory, and that was the easiest of what you did to me."

"Get him out of here," said Captain Robin. "We're through with him. They'll get it out of him at the Reformation."

"No, they won't," said Avery.

Captain Robin eyed him. "You or one of your men will break eventually."

"You'd have them torture your own," smirked Avery. The unspoken words there would have been *your own High Commander*, Reid suspected. "What has this world come to?"

"Come on, *Lukas*," said Reid. He saw the slimy sneer on Avery's face just before the High Commander's painful struggle to get back up wiped part of his humor away again.

"Let me just say before I go," said Avery, "the only honest thing I am willing or able to share at this time."

The High Commander was looking at Captain Robin with a sleazy, underhanded grin that told Reid it was likely *none* of them would enjoy what Avery was about to say.

Captain Robin's gaze narrowed. "What is it?"

"Persuade Reid Ivan to rejoin the Alliance after I have been delivered to the Reformation. You will need him for what is coming."

Reid's jaw clenched. The idea was not appealing in the least, and he was unsure where Avery was leading with it. "I am not interested in rejoining the Alliance."

Captain Robin held up his hand. It was a quiet request for Reid to let him confront Avery's comment. "Why?"

"Because Reid Ivan is your missing High Commander. He has been for almost twelve years."

Reid bit his tongue, his fingers curling tightly over Avery's arm. Anger coursed through him, and he swore. "The hell I *am*, you asshole."

Avery struggled not to laugh again, but he very nearly failed in that endeavor. "The document attesting to the truth of what I have just told you is hidden in Balthora, signed by the High Commander Avery Ramont, and sealed with the High Commander's signet. Dated thirteen years ago last winter, and detailing the commitments of his resignation that he was to carry out as well as the time of his successor's appointment — "

"Of all the lies and round-abouts you have told us today," said a very enraged Saura as she stood. She was shaking, and her face had turned scarlet. "You would expect us to believe such a brazen — "

"*Be quiet!*" Captain Robin snapped. "*This* is an Alliance matter in which Black Temple has no right to speak or involve itself." The one-armed captain leaned forward, and Reid suddenly found all eyes upon himself.

Reid's skin crawled as he cut his angry gaze at Avery again.

The High Commander had been toying with him earlier. He'd already *done* what he'd said he'd only *considered* doing. Reid's vision was swimming in red, he was so angry.

"*Why?*" Reid demanded. "Why would you say something like that? Or *do* something like that?"

"Piss off the old blood," chuckled Avery wickedly. "Avery stepped down from his position thirteen years ago when he wrote that document. One other soul knew about it besides me, and that was my friend Captain Bourgeois. Who is now dead. As well as you have proven yourself, Avery's decision to name you his successor had been correct. You are the man for the job."

"I retired two years ago!"

"No High Commander can retire without selecting a successor. Avery Ramont named his when he resigned thirteen years ago. Your promotion went into effect when we made Avery disappear *twelve* years ago." Avery's black gaze glittered, and the amusement in his twisted expression made Reid want to deck him in the jaw. "You've just been on vacation. Welcome back, *sir*."

"You're — "

"An asshole. I know. But you're two of a kind, you and Avery." Avery winked.

Never had Reid felt a wink could be vicious until then, and yet it was a vicious, silently *boastful* one. Now Reid understood the reason for Avery's laughter before the questioning had begun.

"You, too, are a clever, effective asshole who will defy the odds and commit great atrocities to do what is right," said Avery. "Precisely what the Alliance needs at its head. His choice in his successor was a good one."

"I should rip your stitches and let you bleed out on the ground."

Avery laughed, though he wavered where he stood. Perspiration beaded on his forehead. "Yep."

"Where in Balthora is the document?" asked Captain Robin. The captain wasn't angry at all, Reid noticed. In fact, Reid saw amusement upon the man's face also.

"This is *funny* to you?" Reid demanded. "I cannot and *will not* accept such a responsibility."

"If the document exists," said Captain Robin, "I don't really think I would be opposed to it. It is a bit funny."

"It is," agreed Avery. "That was part of the reason Avery did it." He laughed again at the irony.

"*But why?*" Reid demanded. His grip on Avery's arm squeezed tighter, until Avery was cringing subtly from it.

"It was the Alliance's perfect defense from Caol's infiltrators. Even if those infiltrators had become captains or range commanders and then killed Avery, not one of them could have become High Commander and then handed Caol the keys to the Alliance," he explained delicately. "Captain Bourgeois's role was to reveal the document should such a situation arise. He is dead, so that responsibility fell on me. And I thought it was the perfect time to spoil your long drink of retirement."

Captain Robin repeated his question. "Where in Balthora is this document?"

"I will reveal that information when I am safely at the Reformation. I'll even tell you where Avery Ramont is buried and how he died. But only after the range commander assumes his proper place will I tell him everything that I know, everything I have done, and everything that is coming."

Reid's pulse beat furiously at his temple, but he restrained his anger.

Avery gripped Reid's wrist, and Reid looked at the slithery bastard again. He bit his tongue against worse retorts.

"You'll have better means to protect your family," said Avery flatly. "That includes your niece. But you'll soon be their next target. I would offer my apologies, but *congratulations* seems in better order . . . ?"

CHAPTER SEVENTY-NINE

*P*ENANCE

JAMIE'S ARM WAS SWOLLEN and bruised hideously, and Jeana cradled him as he wept, her lips brushing their son's forehead several times to soothe him as Griggori changed his bandages. Jeana's hands were bound, as were John's.

John stared Griggori down, his blood boiling the entire time Griggori was present. But Griggori said nothing, tried nothing. Something was wrong with the man — or right, finally. But John didn't want the man near his family, and yet Saura had the bastard guarding them day and night on the journey back to Black Temple.

The kindness in Griggori was unsettling. Weird. And the man's eyes were bloodshot from lack of sleep. He wouldn't leave the wagon, just shook madly, saying nothing, curling inward at every noise, every bump in the road — pale as could be for the entire journey.

"What changed you?" John said at last.

Griggori nearly came out of his skin but said nothing.

"You've not even looked at my wife since Aelynhold."

"The Dark Ones," Griggori stammered. "She warned me . . ." He shut down again, his face bloodless.

Jeana cringed from the sound of his voice and held her son, who screamed and wept because of his injury. Every jostle of the wagon set it off.

Griggori tried desperately to open the small bottle of medicine that would send Jamie to a numb sleep so that he wouldn't pass out screaming. But his hands shook furiously, and it took him forever to open it. He was uncharacteristically gentle, and then he retreated to his corner, where he stared past John, out the window. He was a ghost of his formerly vicious, vile self.

Isold rolled into view. The fire had been extensive, charring the mountainside. But the post was undergoing repairs. The bodies they'd seen were gone. The towers were manned.

Later, they saw similar repairs occurring when they rolled into Black Temple. Little of the black glass remained, even though it had been everywhere. Some of the towers and arches had been rebuilt already, and everyone seemed to be going about their business, busy as always. It was as if the bombs had been forgotten.

Jeana and John and their son were moved to a guarded room, deep within the recesses of the labyrinth, near the archives, where they had no chance of trying to escape. There, they waited for John's trial, with Griggori keeping watch and tending to their son.

When he was finally summoned, Griggori wouldn't leave Jamie or Jeana alone. John was forced out of the room despite shouting and struggling to stay with his family, while Griggori remained with them. But his trial did not begin the moment he was brought to the High Temple's guest hall. Saura and Black Temple's elite were along the long table. They spoke with a young man John had never met before, who was dressed unlike anyone from the Temple, and when John looked out the windows, he saw along the shores of the dam a fleet of fifteen ships with sails marked with Five Tower's gray and white emblem. A crystal suspended in water. He swallowed, his mouth dry against the gag his guards had placed over his mouth to shut him up.

"The gift is welcomed," Saura said politely. John recognized the subtle distrust in her voice.

"I assure you, my father and I would like nothing more than to repay the damage caused by the misunderstanding with the wolfmen," said the young man. "They have greatly exaggerated and defiled both our contract and our intentions."

"You can tell him that I will withdraw my command for the Breaking of the Vial by the month's end. Take the Violet Cursed with you and do whatever you want with them. I want no disease I cannot cure in my own city."

"How far has it spread?" asked the young man.

"Far enough the Enforcers got involved. We've eradicated what we could. The next time I see such a strange phenomenon, I will come after your father. Make sure he knows that. And you and your father will uphold your word to allow my people entry to your city to ensure this peace lasts."

"Doctors will be welcome, he has agreed," said the young man. "Enforcers will not."

John bit down on the cloth.

"In the name of peace," nodded Saura as the young man stood.

"Our humble agreement, for peace. Thank you for returning our fugitives. We have been looking for them for a long time."

Saura nodded, and the young man excused himself. John cringed when she looked at him, after their guest, Caol's son, was gone. "Black Temple will relocate its assets to Sacred Wake," she said to the others. "Bring him in and remove his gag. Keep him restrained, however."

John was urged forward after the gag was removed.

"That is how politics work, Jonathan. Civil. Underhanded. Sometimes bloody. And often by breaking bread with your enemy and discussing what each side desires as if you would really expend a moment's heartbeat caring at all for any of it. You've a lot to learn, and a lot of damage you cannot repair alone. We have, however, decided you are too valuable to execute, just as we decided with Griggori five years ago. You never meant absolute betrayal but to uphold your sworn duty. That alone is what reconciles your many transgressions."

"All Wylem and our friends did was help me and stand up to you when you were wrong," he said. "You *executed* them for it. The High Council will retaliate when they realize — "

"Wylem and his coconspirators wanted to help you. They were otherwise good men, and they were good at their jobs, but I had other reasons to execute them. They only made themselves easy prey when they left Black Temple in the dead of night. You simply trusted the wrong men. You need know nothing more. Their sentences were passed, and their chapters were closed. What is on the table now is what to do with you and your family. You've been stripped of your title and removed from your position as a field doctor. Your privileges have been revoked, and you are to be branded for your crimes — for the damages you and your daughter have caused. In two months, you will be reassigned to Five Tower in Griggori's place."

Horror washed over him in a cold flood. "I can't — my daughter can't return with me to Five Tower, Saura!"

"Be silent, or I will have that gag replaced," she hissed. Her voice continued to reverberate about the room as she spoke in a tone that warned against defiance. "You will exist as an escort and an advisor for the medical staff to serve there, and you will serve as a messenger between them and the Lord of Five Tower. Like Griggori, you know brutality, and you operate well despite it. The feud between you two will be set aside. Griggori will remain with you for the entirety of your penance as your overseer, to ensure you do as I have commanded. If you deviate from my commands, you will be executed as a traitor, with your family as witness. I don't care what you do with your daughter in the meantime. That she is so highly sought after and that you cannot handle the dangerous child means she is not only a threat and a liability to Black Temple but to your own family. When we are done here, you will be given the time you need to figure out how you will get your affairs in order."

John bit back a strangled cry.

Saura was not done, and her eyes pierced him angrily. Her claws caught the sunlight filtering in through the open window. "Once your brother assumes his long-abandoned duties as High Commander of the Enforcers' Alliance, your wife will be relocated to the Alliance citadel and serve as my informant."

"*High Commander . . . Have you gone mad?!*" John stammered. His shock choked him. "My brother isn't — "

Her anger was palpable. "It has been confirmed that he is, indeed, the Alliance's missing High Commander. Avery has been dead for years, murdered by Lukas Maverick and his thieves' guild. Avery's last act was to name your brother as his successor, and that document has surfaced intact, in Balthora. Your wife will tell me your brother's every move and every decision. Neither of you will even *think* about disobedience. She knows I will end your life if she steps out of line, and I will send assassins after your entire family if Griggori raises even my slightest suspicion of your defiance."

"You can't do this, Saura — "

"It is already done. This is the only way to tame the wildfires that you and your family are prone to set. Five Tower will be my best use for you, just as it was the best placement for Griggori. You will learn humility and self-control, and to direct your hostility at the correct opposition, and only at the correct time. Which is only when I command it." She waved to the guards. "I am done with him. I have other things to discuss with the members of the Council. Take him back to his family, and then escort them to Crow Post to get their affairs in order."

"What about my daughter?" John cried. "Has anyone found her? Please, Saura! Tell me!"

"No one has found her. The King of Thieves hid her well."

John was taken to his family, and though they seemed unharmed, there were now more men waiting for him. The fireplace crackled where Saura's men stood around it, and apprehension filled him as he was pushed into the room and then forced to his knees. His signet was pulled from his finger, though he struggled to keep it. Jeana tried to go to him. To step between them. But one of the men held her back.

Griggori still sat in the chair he'd been in when John had been taken from the room. The man kept his head bowed. Refused to watch, revel, or even react.

The men who turned from the fireplace held a red-hot iron. They held John as he struggled. They forced his head back when he tried to bite them, and they held the hot metal to his face and seared the skin. Dragged it from above his temple to just under his jaw. The white-hot pain blinded him, and he screamed as the hot blade marked him twice, vertically. Then they turned its sharp edge to carve upon him the mark Saura had promised.

He passed out as they took their time carving him.

CHAPTER EIGHTY

Broken Glass

THE END OF TAIIR'S STAFF prodded the corpse's face. The face lolled, and the sunlight filtering from above touched the bloody mess that had been the man's throat. The body was somewhat fresh; it hadn't even hit rigor yet. He'd heard the man scream . . . An unnatural scream, it had been.

Whatever had happened to this man, it wasn't caused by the creature that had taken the wolfmen who'd been after Lukas.

"What in the hells happened to him?" huffed Irkov.

Taiir looked at the Greenman. "Tha foreigners tha range commander and I saw at tha bell tower did this. No others are down here but for us and them. No animal's teeth make these marks."

"Are you saying those foreigners tore his throat out with their teeth?" gaped Irkov. The Greenman shuddered sickly. "What are they, rabid? Is it wise that we're following them, then?"

Taiir stood. "How is your wound? Can you yet move again?"

"Yes. I hope my brother is dead, the honorless bastard. Tried to gut me like a tree rat before that . . . that *creature* appeared. You were a sight for luck, finding me when you did, Taiir. I owe you my life."

"So you have said thrice now."

"Greenmen do not forget such things," said Irkov. "I am indebted to you."

"I am no doctor. What I have done is not enough. Your wound is not as clean as it should be."

"No matter. I'll make it. We have a little girl to find. I'll search until she's safe, or until my heart stops beating. Have you picked up Taeryn's tracks again? Or just those Strangers'?"

"I have," said Taiir. He pointed to some small, oily-black circles on the floor, at the edge of the dim shaft of light. The droplets would have been easy to miss. They blended with the stone and the moisture and growth that accumulated on the walls and floors of the passages. "His wounds are weeping still."

"How did you figure out he's tracking her? And how is he doing it?" Taiir held out his hand, and Irkov took it. The one-eyed Greenman staggered when he pulled himself to his feet, and he grabbed his stomach, groaning. "Gah . . . That smarts." He drew his cloak tighter, shivering. "Rotted fever. Miserable nuisance. Well?"

"Taeryn should be dead from his wounds. Everything about tha arrangement is unnatural. He hunted for Lukas until Nymeria's illness caused tha Violet Cursed across tha city to react. Tha rest have not moved a specific direction, yet Taeryn has. As if his tie to her is strongest. He is a hunter now, like Caol's victims, and Eiran's. They have a sense for vile things, and sometimes for one another. Tha *tainted*, I have heard it called. A shadow. It is like footsteps in tha mud to them. You and I heard his words before we could no longer get at him."

"What do we do if those foreigners get at him first? You think they'll kill him the way they did this fellow?"

"We will improvise responsibly," Taiir shrugged. He looked at the corpse one last time, and his hand clenched about the staff. "Let us move from here before we are blocked by tha Enforcers who are still scouring this city of its evil and its secrets."

Irkov nodded. "We've been down here how long? A week? Two? What if . . ." The Greenman rubbed his face, and then he cleared his throat. "What if little Nymeria is dead? Or what if her bright gift is out of control? What if we cannot save her?"

"Think not of that but what we can do," said Taiir. He stepped over the corpse, and Irkov followed. "Keep your words low, Greenman. Tha foreigners went left, though Taeryn went right. They must have found something they wanted. Following Taeryn will place us between both. We cannot afford to fight either."

Irkov stumbled clumsily and sucked in a breath. Taiir pitied his wound and the circumstance that had brought it.

The tunnel became much darker as the last of the sunlight faded, and the stench wafting from the sewer vents in the tunnel had him nearly gagging. Irkov was affected the same, for both men held their sleeves to their faces, and both squinted as their eyes burned.

"I hate sewers," hissed Irkov. "The forest is where I belong. Not here, in the literal *bowels* of a city. I'd rather dance with the bees and swell from my throat to my toes at their blasted pricks."

A few hours later, they heard Taeryn's wheezing. The man was weeping. His long, slow wails sounded filled with sorrow, pain, regret. "Stop . . ." wept Taeryn. But he kept moving forward, and so they did as well. They could see the faintest violet tendrils pulsing beneath the man's flesh when they got closer . . .

And then the tunnel before them opened into another deep cavern. The floor was covered in glass chains, and all of them were pulsing brightly with violet light. Some of them had shattered. Others were lying as if discarded. The scene nearly blinded them.

As Taiir's eyes adjusted, he felt Irkov's hand grab his shoulder and tighten. He held up his hand. Taeryn had trudged through the glass, crunching it. It sliced his feet, and he left a trail of blood toward the center, where there was a cage large enough to house a sizeable wildcat. It was surrounded by men and women in robes — all entranced, violet eyes blazing but empty. The bars had turned to black glass, though that glass, too, blazed with the Violet.

Nymeria lay there, chains wrapped around her in layers, as though they'd tried to bind her but had stopped halfway through. The door of the cage was ajar, and two of the Violet Cursed monks still held the chains loosely, their eyes bright but empty, their faces filled with grief and pain, their breathing difficult and restricted.

Taiir recalled his conversation with Reid weeks before, when they'd speculated why the chains had been created. Neither of them had considered that the chains could be used to curve the Violet and keep it from spreading, yet that was what the chains seemed to be doing, even if only haphazardly. Those chains hadn't merely been created as an adornment or symbol, or even as a tool to initiate new members, he realized. They'd been made for this very purpose from the start. The Violet seemed to be directed from link to link in an eerie, serpentine manner, almost like living flames, trapped in the glass.

Taiir stopped Irkov from moving forward. "Not yet," he said. "Do not draw them to see us, and do not step on that glass or you will become infected also."

"She's not — she's not moving, Taiir," whimpered an emotionally wrought Irkov. But Taiir wouldn't let him move forward. Not yet.

Taeryn stumbled into the cage and went to his knees, shivering. He took the chains from the others and began to remove them from her, his hands shaking violently. "Stop . . ." he gurgled. "Stop the circle . . . Break it from her, it hurts her . . ."

The chains slid from Nymeria, and they shattered when they hit the floor. They turned to dust and lost their light.

Taeryn drew her from the floor, and she convulsed, her brilliant eyes wide open but not seeming to see anything. They blazed like the violet eyes of the monks, like the glass around her. But instead of the purple, the color was like fire within an emerald. "Let us have the memories," said Taeryn, and he placed his cheek against her head, and he rocked as he held her. "Let them go," he wheezed. "It is our right to protect our queen," he said. "Remember who you have become. Remember *Now*, not *Before*."

"*Nai mierya . . .*" she whispered.

"You do have the memories of what *is*," he said. "Let go of the violet sky, it burns you to try to keep it from us all."

"*Krekorti Shadei Ra vigor eika-eh elisia ian*," she said. The language was the same the foreigners had spoken, an eerie, power-laced language that was both flawless velvet and soul-piercing threat. But when Nymeria spoke it, the words were woven with so much crackling energy that the ground itself seemed to be trembling. Taiir grew weak because of it, as though his consciousness was about to be pulled from him and flung into the abyss. Irkov appeared to be affected the same. "*Mihalokh i tir'hae ti koruat adreae, i kreika-eh'sae aniai.*"

"Mihalokh does not see you. You cannot break his chains. Let the sky alone, the Shadei Ra cannot sense you anymore."

"*Mihalokh i tir'hae . . .*"

"What is she saying?" Irkov wheezed. "What language is that?"

Taiir blinked dizzily and merely shook his head. "I do not know . . ." He clutched at his chest, tried to suck in a breath.

"It's woven through with that power of hers," Irkov grated. "You feel it, too? I can't — I feel I cannot breathe — "

Nymeria convulsed, and then she screamed, her tiny body arching as Taeryn held her gently. The light winked out within her, and then she was sobbing. Taeryn slumped against the bars. "Take . . ." he whispered. The echo carried, barely, over the girl's sobs. He looked up, over his shoulder at Taiir and Irkov, as though he'd known all along they'd been following him. "Take her . . . home . . . Keep her hidden from them."

Taeryn's hand slipped from her, and his head fell back against the glass bars. His chest rose and fell with every breath, but he seemed otherwise empty. No expression. Nothing but for the flaming eyes, staring into the distance — at nothing.

Taiir and Irkov had barely left the cavern with her when they heard the foreigners enter behind them. The men spoke her language, but with nowhere near the same power in it. As Taiir and Irkov shielded her and kept to the darkness as they quieted her, Taiir peered cautiously around the corner and saw them examining the glass. One of the foreigners knelt to look at Taeryn. Taiir knew they recognized the catatonic man. He'd been the one the wolfmen had given them. They'd thought him valuable, from what he'd been able to tell.

Taiir couldn't understand what they were saying, but neither he nor Irkov waited to find out. The two left just as the foreigners placed a strange bracelet on Taeryn's wrist.

The journey back to Crow Post was very difficult and took weeks. Nymeria was not the same child she'd been before. She barely spoke. She had the same vacant expression they'd last seen Taeryn with when she wasn't screaming or trying to claw out her eyes. Irkov had had to restrain her several times, and Taiir had several times watched Irkov break into tears when neither could calm or soothe her. When neither could find in her the smallest hint of recognition of them.

She did not heal the way Taiir had seen her heal before. The marks remained upon her, slowly fading, taking the entire journey to close even a little, and she barely ate. Barely drank. She bit both of them, drawing blood on more than one occasion, and then she became aroused to hysterics at the sight of the very blood she'd drawn. She seemed barely able to understand them when they spoke to her, trying to calm her.

The night was the worst for her.

She'd been broken. Her mind was gone.

Taiir could barely look at her, barely be around her without being affected by her in the worst of ways. It made him want to rage, to return to Five Tower and burn the entire city to the ground, to torture Caol and his entire family to death most gruesomely. What they'd done to the child, it was an evil blacker than the creatures that had become tied to Taeryn.

He did not let Irkov or the child see him when he could not breathe because of the storm raging inside of him anymore, when he could not think anymore for what emotions her tragedy stirred in him. He kept his face hidden or turned away when he himself had to hold her to keep her from harming herself, or when she wept like a tiny, frail creature, curled small in his arms.

The thunder became constant, and lightning flashed across the gray sky brilliantly as they approached Crow Post. Taiir did not look forward to the reunion. He was unsure whether John would be able to help the child. He also dreaded his oath. He dreaded the look upon his friend's face when the range commander saw her in the state she was in. They'd rescued her, but it seemed they'd only saved *part* of her. That was not enough. Reid would not forgive it. John would not forgive it.

Taiir couldn't forgive it.

The first soft mist began to moisten the air, cooling it rapidly, and then the wind became restless as they rode into Crow Post.

Nymeria held the necklace her cousin had made her as she continued shivering. When he looked down at her, she seemed barely to recognize the place that had been her home for years. She was barely present at all.

Irkov collapsed when he tried to get out of the wagon. He'd lost consciousness. Taiir let him alone as a woman exiting the post's medical guild house saw and rushed out to tend to the Greenman. Taiir couldn't hear what she was saying as he descended the wagon with Nymeria. He walked toward the guild house, and when he entered, Nails looked up. The fat man went pale as he dropped his tray and immediately began to shout. "Someone get John! Get John an' Jeana! NOW!!! Tell 'em Nymeria's been brought home!!!"

Taiir didn't know how much time passed after that — he could barely let the child go as Nails sought to take her from him. He didn't know how long it was until John came, like a ghost. His face was ashen — and it was *branded*. Taiir stared at the mark, but he could barely talk to any of them. "Her mind is gone," he told the field doctor. "We could do nothing." The words that finally left him felt numb. Hollow. Washed out.

John's steps were slow, as if he couldn't believe his daughter was home. "She's alive . . ." The man's expression was haunted, broken. And then he shook his head and began to cry, and he stepped backward, away from her. "I can't . . ." John took a breath. "Amos, do not bother. You won't be able to fix what is wrong with her. You'll just contract the Violet if you try to help her, and then Saura will give you to Five Tower, too, for them to experiment on further."

Taiir looked down when he felt his leg stinging, and he realized he'd clawed himself. His other hand was gripping his staff so tightly that it was shaking where he held it. "Why . . . ?" he breathed, not comprehending.

"You have to take her to the Reformation," John said to him. "You must. We cannot help her. If I'd never taken her home with us, my family wouldn't be in ruins."

"Father . . ." It was the first coherent word Nymeria had spoken since Aelynhold. It seemed the first time she'd had a glimmer of recognition of anything besides whatever had broken her.

John shook his head, his savaged face pulled by agony, and he wouldn't look at his daughter. "Promise me, Taiir. You have to take her. I've been reassigned to Five Tower, and she cannot come with me. Caol cannot ever know she is alive, and I cannot hide her from him if I am living in that city. I cannot have her *die* just because I cannot protect her properly. They will always come for her if they realize who she is." John's fist clenched over something he held, and he cast it to the floor. His father's ring. His own was gone. "That will get her entry," he choked.

Taiir could say nothing. He looked at Nymeria, empty of words . . . and he hated that he understood John's reasons. That he agreed with him. That . . . even as much as he cared for the child, there was nothing else that could be done any time soon. After a long moment, Taiir nodded.

Nails's torment was written all over his face. "Yeh'd give yer daughter away . . . ? Why, John? *Why?!* The girl needs yeh . . ."

"My daughter is the reason your son almost died. She is why he lost his mind," John said quietly, and he turned, grief etched deep into his face. Nails sniffled, delicately treading his own sorrow as John left them alone.

Jeana had never even come.

"*Nai* . . ." Nymeria said. Fear had filtered into her voice. She tried to get up, seeming to sense that her father was abandoning her. She tried to say more, but she couldn't through her tears.

"Where is tha range commander?" Taiir asked. He could hardly speak. Another crack of thunder deafened them.

"I don't know. John has said nothin' teh none'a us, an' Saura's guards are with him day an' night. There are rumors that a Bright Night happened in Aelynhold an' in Black Temple, but not a soul has confirmed or denied — he won't say a damned thing about why. No one will. What happened in Aelynhold? What happened to Nymeria? She was bright-eyed an' feisty a'fore they left. Why is this poor child's eyes glazed as if some foul, wicked being has taken her soul . . . ?"

"It was not a Bright Night," he said, and his voice shook as he picked up the ring and turned it over in his hand. "Where is tha range commander's family? His wife and daughter?"

"Still gone, in Lovael. The city suffered a bit, but they survived the attack upon them. Hordes of wolfmen."

Nymeria began to weep louder as she stared out the door. She pulled at her necklace, her hands trembling — the glass heart shattered, slicing her. She didn't even react except to continue to cry after her father.

"Yeh don't think teh actually take her teh the Reformation, Taiir?" stammered Nails.

Taiir looked up from the ring, and his fingers closed around it.

"She will remain endangered if I do not, and I cannot care for her by myself. It has been too much, tha trip from Aelynhold. John cannot take her to Five Tower with him, and if none other of her family are to be found, then until I locate them, I have no other choice. I will not leave her with another unsuspecting family."

Nails tried to have Nymeria uncurl her hand from the glass heart she'd broken as she wailed, but she would not let it go. Blood streamed through her fingers. "*Nai* . . ." she wept, and the sound of her tears raked at them both like a hot blade. Taiir wanted to flinch from the sound of her heartbreak and fear, for the rawness of it.

Taiir gathered her again, and he stood. "Do not tell tha Greenman where I have gone. I do not want tha man to die, trying to take her in as his own daughter. He would not survive her illness. Tell none, or Nymeria will no longer be safe. Evil men are after this child."

Taiir stepped out into the rain. Nymeria shivered, her arms wrapping around him, her face against his shoulder. "I am sorry," he said against her ear, and he let the side of his head rest against hers. He should never have allowed the Ivans to take her. He had judged wrong that wintry night. He should have taken the girl far from the city himself and spared that innocent family the irreconcilable damage that had been done to them by her. He shouldn't have believed their determination to help her had been a blessing upon his conscience. He had merely wanted to give her the chance to have a real family. One that obviously wanted to care for her. One that could erase some of the vile, supernatural devilry that she had been exposed to in the Gray Halls.

"I will not abandon you," he told her finally. "I will guard you fiercely until my end. And I do not have to be cursed to make that decision. I need only be a human being."

The glass slipped from her fingers and crunched under his boot, lightless, and a sheet of icy rain curtained the street, nearly blinding him as he carried her away, seeking her safety.

CHAPTER EIGHTY-ONE

Wretched Heart

REID IVAN WAS DRENCHED WHEN he made it back to Crow Post. He was anxious to hear news of his niece, and he was mentally and emotionally drained. Avery had told him a great deal on the trip to the Reformation. Nearly everything, save what he himself hadn't seemed to know.

He understood exactly why Avery had abandoned the Alliance and committed his many crimes. If Reid had been in his shoes, he would have done exactly what the man had done. He also understood why Avery had not been willing to be honest with anyone, why he'd refused to confess, and why the Reformation would never break the man. Reid was still chilled and badly shaken by what all Avery had told him. From what he'd learned, it meant he and Taiir had been *lucky* to have escaped the foreigners they'd seen months ago. Lucky that they'd not been noticed.

Reid prayed his niece would *never* be taken by those people. The hell with Caol. Caol was nothing. A puppet. A bystander. Reid now knew why Saura had asked about Gabriel, and he now understood never to trust her. He needed to get his brother out of Black Temple. If they had to travel to another *continent*, he would have his family do it. Not that it would matter, but at least to *try* to find some place they could hide for longer meant more time.

Reid spat the rain from his face as he lifted his hand and knocked urgently on his brother's door. "John!" He knocked harder. The wind ripped at his hair. He looked over his shoulder briefly. "John!" he shouted through the wild thunder and rain.

The door opened — Reid stared at his brother's marred face, his words suddenly gone from him. John's piercing, haunted gaze stared back at him, as if he was seeing a ghost. Jeana shot by her husband, a knife in her hand as she held her son close, and she put it to Reid's throat. "*Go*," she mouthed, and he realized her eyes were red from tears. "*Do not come to our house again.*" Reid caught her wrist and took the knife away, and she shoved him from their doorstep. He could barely hear her when she tried to speak. "I will not have you kill my husband in your anger. *Go!*"

John put his hand on his wife's shoulder and turned. "It doesn't matter," he said quietly, his voice haunted. John was drunk. Reid smelled the alcohol when the wind turned. "He will do what he will do. Let him do it anyway."

Reid caught the door before Jeana could slam it. "What happened?" he demanded, suddenly angry. But he tasted dread on the back of those words. "Has Nymeria been found?"

Jeana glared at Reid and said nothing else. John didn't answer him, either.

"What happened to his face? Who carved up my brother's face?!" He slammed the door behind him. "And where is Nymeria?!"

"Saura had it done," John said, his voice weak. Tired. "My penance. I'm no longer a field doctor."

Reid's words tripped over one another. "Wh . . . what?"

"She's taken everything," hissed Jeana, her voice breaking and hardly understandable.

The thunder outside raked at their ears and made the house shake.

"Sissy's *gone*," wept Jamie against Jeana's shoulder.

Gone. That word had so many meanings. Reid thought his heart was going to explode in his chest. "*Dead? Or gone, as in not here?*"

Jeana and John tensed, anger across both of their features. There was friction between them that had never been there before. Anger that was more akin to hatred when Jeana looked away. "She will never come back into my house and harm my son again."

"But Myria didn't hurt me," wept Jamie.

"Shush, Jamie. It is done." Jeana's anger was raw. "That nightmarish child is *gone*."

"Go away, Reid," John said as he laid his head on his desk, his elbows on his knees. John's voice raked with grief, and he shook quietly from it when he exhaled.

An odd mixture of anxiety and rage began to well in Reid when he saw Nymeria's glass heart necklace, broken, on John's desk. Covered in blood and mud. "Where is my niece?"

"Gone. I cannot take her with me to Five Tower."

Reid shook his head, trying to understand what his brother meant by it. Not wanting to. "Gone — " He looked at the glass heart again. "You mean they found her — " He gasped. "What do you mean *gone*?!"

John sat up, and Reid's gaze went to the hideous brand on his brother's face again. John wiped his eyes with the back of his hand and then clasped his hands, wringing them. "Gone . . ." His voice broke. "Removed forever. I sent her away. She is never coming home. I cannot help her because she will get us all killed . . . We cannot protect her as she needs."

It felt as though John had stabbed him. Each breath seemed to scald him as he tried to process John's impossible words, and his grief threatened to overtake him at each raking intake. Every word his brother said sliced him deeper.

"So she is out of our lives for good," said John. "I gave her to Taiir, and he has taken her somewhere not even you will be able to find her."

Before Reid even knew his anger had taken him entirely, he'd already thrown Jeana's dagger at his brother, and his knees struck the floor as he screamed. He screamed, and he screamed, until he couldn't breathe, until his head pounded and he saw red and it started to turn dark. Jeana backed away from him, afraid. He was barely aware of her movement, except for the urge to slap her for the cold words she'd uttered moments before John's explanation. *Both of them . . .*

Reid's fingers clawed the floor as he gasped for air. "I'll *never . . .*" he said, his entire body shaking. His fingernails had torn and were bleeding where they dug at the floor. "*NEVER forgive you.*"

Reid saw red when he stood. John held his shoulder where the knife had struck, his chin trembling. He didn't even care that Reid had stabbed him. "HOW COULD YOU SEND HER AWAY?!"

Jamie was crying, he thought. He could barely hear anything except his breath and the violent thrumming in his ears.

John pulled the knife from his shoulder and set it down on the table in front of him. His gaze just drifted to the floor, devoid of anything more than hollow, empty grief.

"*Where is she?*"

John didn't reply.

Reid recalled the image of his niece's smile, and it rolled into another memory, of the bruises on her wrists from having been tied up in Aelynhold. That image whirled into so many others that were happy, sad, fearful, grim . . . Everything hit him at once, and it was like a slap to the face, how cold he suddenly felt. *Removed*, John had said.

"WHERE IS SHE BEING TAKEN?!"

He could barely feel himself. Barely reconcile any of it.

Silence was his reply —

And then Reid had knocked over the desk, the oil lamp, and the chair, and John was bleeding beneath him, bruises forming where Reid's fists struck him. He barely registered Jeana trying to pull him off his brother.

Reid saw his niece's broken necklace and he stopped cold, withdrawing, his chest heaving. He looked at his knuckles. He couldn't see anything but the red on them because his vision was too blurred. He shut his eyes, clenching his fists.

John hadn't even *tried* to fight him. Not even to defend himself.

Reid rolled off his brother as Jeana wept over her battered husband, and he stared at the fire that was now spreading through their home. John sputtered, and he rolled over on his side and spat one of his bloody teeth to the floor as he sat up and let his back fall against the desk. John waved off his wife, still saying nothing, and just laid his head back dizzily. His blood curled across his face from his temple and dripped from his jaw, until it began to trail down his throat instead and wet his collar, and it also coursed from the wound upon his shoulder and crept down his arm where it draped over his lap.

John didn't even look at him.

"I'm done," Reid said. He could barely hear himself.

Tears fell fresh from his brother's eyes when he closed them. Still, John said nothing.

"I'm done. I don't want to see you ever again. I'm not coming back. I'm going to take my family when they return, and we're leaving. When I find Nymeria, she's going to stay with me. With Marissa and with Ralleigha. You will *never* be allowed to see her." He snarled again, gritting his teeth until they felt they might shatter. "You are no brother of mine, to abandon your daughter like this. You can rot in the Seven Fiery Hells. Once I'm gone, don't you *ever* try to contact me."

"Saura said you're High Commander now," John said at last.

"Go *fuck* yourself, John."

CHAPTER EIGHTY-TWO

ℛEFORMATION

NYMERIA LOOKED AT THE imposing fortress, a great black silhouette against the night sky. Her father didn't want her because she was unwell. Because of the things she saw, because she couldn't control any of it. She'd known when she'd seen his face. He didn't love her anymore.

Taiir brushed a long strand of her black hair from her face, and she squeezed his other hand with her own and looked up at him. "I'll get better," she told him. But she could tell by the sad look on his face that he didn't think it was possible. "I'll find a way," she told him. "I want to go home. My father will love me again if I am better."

Taiir didn't look away this time, and she saw how her words cut him. "He did not send you away because he does not love you, child." He studied her for a long moment. "How long do you think you have before those visions take your mind again? You are never out of them long anymore."

She wavered where she stood, and she could barely hear him as it was. The great tide of memories was about to come again. "Not long. They will not rule me for my entire life, Taiir. I will overcome this curse. I am going to go home."

"Those who are admitted to tha Reformation cannot leave of their own will," he said, however. "But I will stay with you. You will not be alone."

She looked at the fortress again. "Avery is here," she said. "Mark is, too." She felt the cold and saw the blinding white drifting across her vision. It was again a scene filled with death and great sorrow. She trembled, and her fingers curled about the Cyan ring her uncle had given her. At least he was alive. At least the rest of her family was safe.

"What do you see now?"

"Snow everywhere. Dead Leviathans littering the road. The Violet killed them. Mihai is in a cryotank, and his sister and his father are taking him somewhere. His mother is already dead. I've seen part of that one before. It's not the worst one."

Taiir said nothing, but Nymeria could tell that he was very upset. She could feel it, and she could see it on his face, even though he was still trying to hide it. He didn't want her to know that he wanted to cry because of what was happening to her. But she knew anyway.

"He used to know a girl who looked like me," she said. "She had the same eyes. They were friends. But he watched her die. And then he saw another one die who looked just like her . . . I think there were a lot more people like us, but I don't know what happened to them all."

"How long ago do you think tha one you are now seeing happened?"

"Thousands of years ago. It was a long time before the Modern Age."

Taiir sighed. "That is a very long time ago."

"He's still alive," she said. "He's still possessed by the dead the Leviathans put inside him."

"How do you know he is alive?" he asked her quietly.

"The same way I know that you're not really human, either."

Taiir looked at her again, and a sad smile stole across his face. "I have spent a very long time pretending. Shall we keep that a secret between us, Little One?"

"You're afraid of what others will do," she said slowly.

"It is not *others* I fear, child. I remain hidden from a cursed Leviathan king."

"What is his name?" she asked.

"Tacitus. Never a more wicked immortal man could you meet."

"He has red eyes, doesn't he?" she asked. "The color of blood."

She'd seen that man in the Violet.

GLOSSARY

alderoot — New species of plant found in Taiir's cold, snowy, mountainous homeland. It is very rare, but it has a great many uses, especially for blood flow and revitalization. Appears as a black liquid in medicinal form.

Aracanian — A people native to the Eastern Shore. Northern and southern accents vary slightly but are often strong and sometimes very difficult to understand.

Aseaian — Pronounced "ah-shy-an." They are a people native to a cold, mountainous land across the sea. They speak a language called Ashai. Many are highly skilled assassins, trained from early childhood. Some live in exile. Others were massacred. Some have come to the mainland and have sold their services in accordance with the Keeping. It is rare to befriend or earn the trust of an Aseaian.

Black Oath — The proper name of the Black Temple oath that is sworn by all doctors, regents, and leaders who serve within the Temple. The shortened motto "*Wrath and Mercy*" are painted upon every Black Temple wagon and serves as both a warning and a welcome. Capitalization of certain key words within written versions of the motto are retained for emphasis and notation of importance.

> "*Wrath and Mercy shall draw blood for both the Bloodied and the Bloodless. When the Wound festers, we cut the Rot. We bind the Bleeding at the Source. We Break from Death, and we Deliver unto Death. We see the First Breath, and we see the Last. In warning, our Banners fly, and upon retaliation, our Vials break. Until the Fever is gone. The Glass Chain will not shatter but by the Master's hand. Blood for the Bloodless. Shadows for the Living. Compassion for the Infirm. Knowledge from the Dead. We Men and Women of the Glass Chain shall serve, for Wrath and Mercy are One.*"

Blood Light — A symptom of those who are cursed with the Violet.

Break the Vial — A catastrophic Black Temple order that could murder millions.

Bright Demon, the — The one who caused the Bright Night.

Bright Night, the — The violent, possibly supernatural explosion that nearly destroyed Five Tower. The fire was not golden but violet.

Bright One — A term used by the Dark Ones as they call out, searching.

Brotherhood of Mercy — A corrupted thieves' guild that is now full of wicked men and women.

Dead One, the — The Dead One is an elusive man named Gabriel.

Defector, the — The Defector is an elusive man named Rhael. He once worked with Caol, the Lord of Five Tower.

dark things, the — (See *Dark Ones*.)

Dark Ones, the — Hell Cursed, or *the dark things*; the Shadei Ra; Hell Souls. Shadowy, terrifying creatures which are attracted to the Violet. Those who are not Violet Cursed cannot see them.

Descendants of the Moon — Cannibal Priests from the Wolfshadow clan. These are among the most vicious, dangerous, and dedicated of the wolf cut.

Enforcer — A soldier from the Enforcer's Alliance. Ranks include the following: Enforcer, Corporal, Sergeant, Lieutenant, Captain, Range Commander, High Commander.

Enforcers' Alliance — A military alliance which sends its soldiers (called Enforcers) out to ensure all cities, holds, and major guilds are working in accordance with a centuries-old treaty. The Alliance works closely with Black Temple, especially during the traveling season, when new apprentices are delivered to Black Temple. However, the Alliance is currently facing peril.

Fallen — A cursed being who is at the heart of the horrendous visions within the Violet. Once, his name was Mihalokh (Mihai). Also called *the stranger in the dungeon, the man in the dungeon, the tortured man, her Other*, etc. *Mihalokh* is pronounced "Mi-ha-lokh" (the *kh* is reminiscent of a mixing the sounds of *g*, *k*, and *h*. Often, the final consonant is all but dropped so that the name seems to end in a long *o*.)

False Brother — A term of respect but also of dislike, which is spoken by wolfmen. It describes those they have allied with and have allowed to dress or act as they do.

fire brandy — A family of spiced alcoholic beverages made in Edantine.

Five Tower — A corrupt city at the heart of many crimes.

Glass Chain, the — The Glass Chain is a strong symbol that has been spoken of by Black Temple's members for seven hundred years. It speaks of the delicate balance that should be struck by all major guilds, cities, and peoples. The men and women of the Glass Chain are the doctors, servants, attendants, regents, and other members of Black Temple. They are also called *Servants of the Glass Chain*.

Gray Halls — A very bad place beneath Five Tower.

Greenmen — A people who are the remnants of the tragedy of Tarvet. They live in Oakwall, dress in shades of the forest, and apply green paint to their skin and their faces. They are sworn to defend Black Temple, and they believe strongly in honor and duty. Greenmen cannot leave Oakwall without casting their honor aside unless their contracts have been paid, and only specific people can pay those contracts. The Greenmen often refer to themselves as *Men of the Forest*.

Goldenrod — An alcoholic beverage made by the Heinzrichs.

Hell Cursed — The Dark Ones, or *the dark things*; the Shadei Ra; Hell Souls. When both parts of the name are capitalized, it refers to either the race as a whole or to multiple entities. When both words are lowercase, the name refers to only one being among them. These beings are shadowy, terrifying creatures which are attracted to the Violet. Those who are not Violet Cursed cannot see them.

Hell Souls — (See *Hell Cursed* or *Shadei Ra*.)

hex lights — Lights which work from something other than the science we know and are familiar with.

High Commander — The High Commander is the leader of the Enforcers' Alliance, which is a military alliance. The current leader is a man named Avery Ramont.

High Council, the — Thirteen regents who travel to and from Black Temple and its major cities. During the apprentice season, they return to the Temple to carry out important duties.

Holy Matron — A respectful address for the Lady of the Temple.

hunters — Men and women who have survived being cursed by the Violet and can either sense others like themselves or set the Dark Ones upon others. Most have lost their minds, their speech, or even their sight. And most eventually lose their lives as madness claims them.

Keeper — Keepers are specialists who work with some of the last remaining Modern World machines. They also guard the last existing databases from our world.

Keeping, the — A belief and honor system abided by all Aseaians, which they are taught from childhood.

Keeps — The Keeps which are a part of Black Temple are located in large cities such as Arsennia. They hold vast archives filled with knowledge from the Modern World, and they also contain highly guarded databases and machines from that bygone era, many of which are the last of their kind. The Keeps which are part of the Enforcers' Alliance contain similar items and knowledge of interest, but one Keep is mentioned above all others by the Enforcers: *The Keep* — which is located within the Alliance's citadel.

King of Thieves — A devious man, who pulls many strings and knows many secrets.

Lady of the Temple — The current Black Temple leader is Saura Idathet, who is also known as the Pale Serpent. "Lady of the Temple" and "Lord of the Temple" are the titles given to the rulers of Black Temple.

Leviathans — A race of people one would not wish to anger.

Master of the Temple — A fictional man robed in white and silver who supposedly started Black Temple over seven hundred years ago after the Fall of the Modern World. His story is told to young Black Temple apprentices to inspire them to become good doctors instead of evil, scheming, murderous ones. His title is still used in both polite and respectful conversations, especially regarding great tragedies and blessings and wishes for safety and well-being.

Melancholy — A strong alcoholic beverage brewed by the Heinzrichs. Stronger than it tastes. Not as harsh as *Goldenrod.*

Men of the Forest — Another name for the Greenmen.

Modern Age — A term for our modern time, used by those who live seven hundred or more years in the future, after the apocalypse has come not by fire but by disease.

Modern Civilization — The nations and peoples of our modern time. This term is used to describe us by those who live seven hundred years or more in the future.

Modern World — (See ***Modern Civilization***.)

nai — A term Nymeria Ivan uses for the word "no." Her strong foreign accent has not faded, and on occasion, she still says things in her native language. That language is unknown.

Other, the/her — When Capitalized, "her Other" or "the Other" refers to the Fallen. (See **Fallen**.)

other, the — When lowercase, "*the other*" refers to a separate, dark entity within Nymeria. Also referred to as "*the other thing*."

Old Roman Brandy — An alcoholic beverage.

Pact, the — Refers to the Greenmen's sworn duty to serve and protect Black Temple. They are paid by Black Temple envoys that pass through Oakwall.

Pale Serpent, the — The whispered nickname of Saura Idathet, the Lady of the Temple.

Raise the Vial — A catastrophic Black Temple order that commands its regents and doctors to prepare themselves to murder millions. It is a dreaded order.

Rack — A potent and bitter, but also nutritious, alcoholic beverage made in Aelynhold.

Reformation, the — A giant prison for the insane, for political prisoners, for prisoners of war, and more. It is a separate and neutral entity that does not bend to the will of any other guild, city, or hold. The Reformation accepts various prisoners requiring different levels of security based on requests and contracts.

Scales — A deadly, unpleasant disease.

Seven Dead Men, the — Statues placed in the Flooded City, which serve as directional markers for the Greenmen.

Servants of the Glass Chain — A term for those who work for Black Temple, especially those who perform medical and leadership roles.

Shadei Ra — The Dark Ones; *the dark things*; the Hell Cursed. When both parts of the name are capitalized, it refers to either the race as a whole or to multiple entities. When both words are lowercase, the name refers to only one being among them. These beings are shadowy, terrifying creatures which are attracted to the Violet. Those who are not Violet Cursed cannot see them.

sojourne — A brief, common prayer for one who has died.

Soul Cursed — Leviathan dead who cannot pass on.

Spirit — Also called *Shadekur*. It refers to an energy that radiates from the soul. It is akin to magic.

Strangers, the — When capitalized, *Strangers* refers to the two foreigners who speak an ancient language, wear unusual armor, and wield strange weapons.

Summons, the — A Black Temple order that is sent out annually before the raining season begins. It details instructions on deliveries, apprentices, and other things.

Temple, the — When capitalized, it refers to Black Temple.

travel season — A seasonal trip referring to the massive haul of apprentices, supplies, news, and other items and details from posts, holds, and cities to Black Temple. It occurs before the heavy spring rains and subsequent flooding, often just after the last snows and freezes.

Vael, the — A term used by Rhael and certain others. It describes something between a supernatural gateway and a supernatural place or state of existence.

Violet, the — A curse involving violet light and horrific visions, madness, and even death. It is a shortened version of the term *Violet Curse*.

Violet Curse, the — A curse involving violet light and horrific visions, madness, and even death. It describes the ability of the Violet to infect people.

Violet Cursed — Those who are infected with the Violet.

wearyworn — A term used by both Black Temple and the Enforcers' Alliance describing the common people. The term is rarely capitalized in text except when elevating the group as a whole in certain contexts, as when comparing them as an entity to Black Temple or the Enforcers' Alliance as separate, equally powerful groups of people. The strength and power of the wearyworn are in their number.

White Dagger, the — A nickname for one of the deadliest, most violent Enforcers in Alliance history, whose tactical and investigative capability was on par with High Commander Avery Ramont's.

wolf cult — A cult of cannibals composed of several clans. They worship the violent, cunning kills of wild wolves, dress themselves in wolf skins and skulls, and refuse to carry metal weapons of any kind — preferring instead to fashion blades from the bones of the dead they have eaten.

wolfmen — Members of the wolf cult.

Wolfshadow — One of the clans of the wolf cult.

Wraithes — The dead Leviathan souls that possess the Fallen (Mihai).

LANGUAGE

TRANSLATIONS

"Aiya." — Please.

"Aiya tzedaket'hae ian." — Please help me.

"Inak muori nuot Vaelania. Neakh mekan'yath krethan." — The words are in ancient Vaelania. But they make little sense.

"Iyutha . . . ?" — Who is there . . . ?

"Khevakh neija?" — What is the result?

"Kae'da vos . . . Kae'da vos . . ." — Get it out . . . Get it out . . .

"Ki adeitus ris'viaht-eh tu, ir Kaniakat?" — Why have you hidden yourself for so many centuries, My Queen?

"Krekorti Shadei Ra vigor eika-eh elisia ian." — I don't want the Hell Cursed to hurt anyone else because of me.

"Mihalokh I tir'hae ti koruat adreae, I kreika-eh'sae aniai." — Mihalokh and I will die if I let the light go, and no one else will survive either.

"Nai." — No.

"Nai!!! NAI!!! Kretu henna ian avae'ue!!! AIYA!!!" — No!!! NO!!! Do not abandon me to them again!!! PLEASE!!!

"Neija." — What.

"Sojourne." — The open door.

"Shadekur." — Spirit, or soul magic. (Always capitalized because it is highly revered or considered of great import by those who call it by name.) *Ekur* translates literally to *reaching mind* but is often written as *magic* in text, since that is what the phrase *reaching mind* technically means. It is almost always combined with the prefix *shadei* (the **i** is cut) to form the word *Shadekur*.

"Shadei Ra." — Hell Souls. (Loosely, also "Hell Cursed." When both parts of the term are capitalized, it refers to multiple of the creatures, or to the race as a whole. If referring to only one among them, both words will be lowercase.)

"Tir'nieta." — I'm fine.

QUESTIONS FOR THE READER!

I would love to hear your thoughts about the book!
Tag me on Twitter under @SennaCrow or @7Bloodfire with your answers.

Favorite character, and why?
What do you think will happen in the next book?
Who or what is the Fallen?
What are Gabriel and Rhael hiding from, and what have they done?
What is the truth about Nymeria?

Which character is more badass? Reid, Taiir, Irkov, John, or Griggori?

(Or Nymeria?)

Who would you like to see return in the second book?

Leave a Review?

Reviews are extremely helpful for authors, so don't forget to leave one on Amazon, or wherever else you may have purchased my book.

Share your review on social media with the hashtag #TheVioletCurse to encourage others to read the story, too!

Thanks for taking the time to support my work!

7Bloodfire.com

And Other Media

For books, merch, art prints, giveaways, and other information about writing, editing, and illustrating, visit my website.

My YouTube channel is "7Bloodfire Art & Story," where I share about the writing, editing, illustrating, and other Indie Publishing processes. (And other things!)

Writing community at Facebook.com/7Bloodfire.writer

Leviathans series fan page at Facebook.com/LeviathansFans

Twitter, Wattpad, Instagram, Pinterest, and elsewhere: **@7Bloodfire**

My author profile on Twitter is: **@SennaCrow**

I would love to hear from you!

ABOUT THE AUTHOR

MY NAME IS CINTHIA MCCRACKEN, and I write paranormal dystopian fantasy under my pen name, Senna Crow.

I began writing seriously after I had a nightmare about vampires when I was fourteen, and I've dreamed of being an author / illustrator every since. This book is the result of many, many rewrites over a period of seventeen years as I attempted to find the right way to tell the story. (It just isn't the same as a completely unintentional teenage chick flick.)

The Violet Curse is my first officially published novel, and I have plans for many, many more *Leviathans* books. I'm just getting started!

I also love to draw, and I have an eclectic collection of experimental styles, media, and art studies.

For those who are interested in my processes, planners, tips, and behind-the-scenes, I'll be posting on Patreon, on my YouTube Channel *7Bloodfire Art & Story*, and on my website, listed below. Keep track of news, releases, and more by joining my mailing list at

7BLOODFIRE.COM

www.ingramcontent.com/pod-product-compliance
Lightning Source LLC
Chambersburg PA
CBHW020906110726
47900CB00001B/33